# NEW BEGINNINGS TRILOGY

## CHILDREN OF ANZULLA PREQUEL M/M SCI-FI FANTASY

### NEW BEGINNINGS M/M SERIES BOOKS 1, 2, 3

## KASHEL CHAR

# CONTENTS

Title: **New Beginnings Trilogy. Children of Anzulla Prequel. M/M Sci-Fi Fantasy**

Amazon Electronic Book: ISBN 978-1-998713-54-7

Amazon Paperback: ISBN 978-1-998713-55-4

D2D Electronic Book: ISBN: 978-1-998713-18-9

D2D Paperback: ISBN: 978-1-998713-19-6

IngramSpark Electronic Book ISBN: 978-1-998713-77-6

IngramSpark Paperback ISBN: 978-1-998713-78-3

Publisher: Koda Calmz Publishing

Editor: Teresa Fornoff, Anita Ford

Fifth Edition April 2026

# Warning

**This is a work of fiction.** Names, characters, places, and incidents are the author's imagination or used fictitiously. Any resemblance to actual events, locales, business establishments, or persons, living or dead, is coincidental. The authors do not have any control over and do not assume responsibility for author or third-party websites, blogs or critiques, or their content.

**NO AI/NO BOT.** We do not consent to any Artificial Intelligence (AI), generative AI, large language model, machine learning, chatbot, or other automated analysis, generative process, or replication program to reproduce, mimic, remix, summarize, or otherwise replicate any part of this creative work, via any means: print, graphic, sculpture, multimedia, audio, or other medium. We support the right of humans to control their artistic works.

Unless expressly noted, no part of this publication may be reproduced, scanned, stored in a retrieval system, or transmitted in any form or by any means, electronic, mechanical, photocopying, recording, or otherwise known or from now on invented, without the express written permission of the authors. The scanning, uploading, and distribution of this book via the internet or any other means without the author's permission are illegal.

# Appreciation

*Firstly, a BIG thank you to my mentor, Stefan Pride. Stefan, may you be blessed like Jabez.*
*Without you, I never would have been able to start writing.*
*Secondly, to my two Alpha, Beta, and ARC readers. (My all-in-one team, spoils me with their thorough editing work.)*
*Thank you to my editor, Anita. You are awesome!*
*Ida, thousands of thank yous for helping me write better, for your unfailing support and motivation to keep going and figure out all the shit. Thank you for checking in with me, and asking if I'm okay.*
*Teresa, thank you for helping me find those small details and for making me laugh while I read your comments. You helped me tremendously, and I wish you all the success in your editing career.*

*Lastly, to the two most important people in my life.*
*Thank you for listening to me going on and on about Ishtar and the storyline, and allowing me the time to live my dream and finally finish my first trilogy.*

# PART ONE
# ERYN, KING OF THE BRAWL
## NEW BEGINNINGS M/M SERIES BOOK 1

# INTRODUCTION

In 2052 A.D., six years after the global neurotoxic Doomsday of 2046 A.D., the Romanov twins, Cian and Ivan, were born. They were the first successful ectogenesis twins, and the biological children of Mika and Connor Romanov. This marked it as the Year of the Twins (A.T.).

Earth was dying, and cataclysmic earthquakes, volcanic eruptions, and tsunamis caused a global winter.

Under General Brad McCormick, the all-male scientific and military society believed themselves humanity's last survivors, sheltered within Phoenix's gleaming plexiglass and titanium domes—a fantastical ice city against the Antarctic plateau.

After twenty-one years, the perpetual gray twilight caused by billions of tons of volcanic ash and snowstorms subsided.

The satellites orbiting Earth, taking incessant photos of a cloud-shrouded planet, forwarded an increasing number of glimpses of the blue ocean and ice-covered landmasses.

Prior to the birth of their twin boys, Dr. Connor Romanov, a computer programming genius and second-in-command of Phoenix, had taken control of the orbiting satellites. With the help of his husband, Dr. Mika Romanov, they had broken the codes from scores of intelligence-gathering orbiters placed in space by Earth's old governments. All human history and information saved in data banks at institutions like libraries and universities were downloaded to Phoenix's servers. Their ingenuity had helped prepare Phoenix City, thus saving it.

Since the Year of the Twins (After Twins—A.T.), many things have changed at Phoenix. Enthusiasm to rebuild and their quest for excellence continued as the citizens adjusted to their new normal, and the overall mood of the citizens grew. Fortunately, the World Health Protected Species Society (WHPSS) and Dr. John Saunders authorized the cryogenically transport of tens of thousands of eggs to Phoenix before Doomsday.

Children were born as a result of the Omega Project, led by Mika and his colleague, Dr. Peter von Leutzendorf, who successfully created a method for male sperm splicing and then fertilization of a human donor egg. They implanted this in an artificial womb with a placenta that sustained a life-giving equilibrium for the growth of human fetuses.

New lives have entered the Phoenix population, usually as twins and sometimes as triplets. They were primarily fraternal but occasionally identical. Unfortunately, all births were males.

Mika and Peter worked tirelessly to find a way to give birth to females into the genetic code. Parents could opt for just one child, assuming the fertilized egg didn't split, but most fathered twins since the waitlist to become a father was long.

Of course, many married or at least made civil commitments to create a nurturing family bond and raise their children. Prospective parents, regardless of their marital or relationship status, were eligible and wait-listed even if they prefer to raise a child alone, whether due to being heterosexual or not having a partner.

Marriage brought happiness, acceptance, tolerance, discord, hatred, and divorce. New family laws came into being to handle those situations, including polyamorous marriages. One man could file for divorce against one or more of his spouses or the third, or by all three, four, or five spouses, whatever the number of spouses in the union wanting to dissolve the marriage contract and go their separate ways.

Two things, however, have remained the same. One is the culture of scientific improvement and research. Phoenix's love and commitment to education established a new school for children at three years old. This created a circle of growth and development, allowing scholars to attend and earn as many degrees as possible.

The other thing that had not changed for most of the men of Phoenix was their appearance. None of the original men who opted to have the Eden Bean, better known as the Peter Pan Cap, had aged a month in nearly twenty-one years.

After designing the perfect nutrient capsules for fetal development in an artificial womb, Peter discovered a by-product of the Romanov twins' fetal nutrition. Aging was greatly reduced. No one knew how it worked or how much it would slow down the aging process. In addition to drastically slowing the aging process, the body recovered from physical injuries at an accelerated rate.

These life-prolonging capsules were not mandatory for the original residents. Instead, it was a choice. Some men didn't want it, and that was fine. Because their lives were dramatically prolonged, and the brain only reached full maturity as early as twenty-three, anyone, whatever age after twenty-three, may have it implanted if so desired.

***But, somewhere outside Phoenix…Far across the ice from the Antarctic plateau, on another continent, the southern tip of Africa, something else did survive the Doomsday attacks and global winter…***

# CHAPTER 1

# THE ODD BOY BRAWL

*"GOOD MORNING, CITIZENS OF PHOENIX.*

*It's now six a.m.*

*Some residents have complained about stagnation. Do not worry, Lasitor has some good points to help you get out of your rut.*

*Number one. Realize that you are not alone. There are over two thousand men in Phoenix.*

*Number two. Find something that inspires you. Stagnation occurs because nothing is exciting to do.*

*Number three. Take a break. When did you take a real vacation for yourself?*

*Number four. Shake things up and change your routine.*

*Number five. Do one small thing differently today.*

*Breakfast is served until eight a.m.*

*Hope you have a different day!"*

**ERYN, King of the Brawl**
**2058 A.D. (6 A.T.)**
**Phoenix**
**Glass-Domed City**
**Antarctica**

ERYN WAS BORN and grew up deep inside an old gold mine, so deep that it's thousands of meters beneath South African soil. He guessed he was twelve or maybe fifteen years old. He wasn't precisely sure, because time passes differently when one doesn't see the sun. His large build did not match the naïve innocence of his character. In his heart, he was the same age as the six-year-olds he was watching. They fascinated him. None of the other children born inside the ice city interested him as much as these two boys. When they were born, he knew they were special.

Filled with excitement, he could barely contain himself. He crouched down and snuck under a big storage bin to watch Mika and the twins. Something exciting and out of the ordinary was happening today. Tucking his gangly legs, he sat on his haunches and hung on every word.

"Look, Papa," little Cian pointed excitedly, "there's something out on the ice," he said. Sitting proudly, back straight, head up.

Ivan's head popped up. "What, where?" He followed Cian's line of sight. "Oh, there, look. What is that, Papa?"

Cian crossed his arms and scowled at his brother. "I saw it first!"

Ivan turned and looked at his twin brother. "I know you saw it first. I'm asking Papa what it is, that's all," little Ivan said. He smiled at Cian, who unfolded his arms. Their blond heads bobbed up and down in a mutual agreement that Cian won the game of "*I spy with my little eye on something new today.*"

"Good job, I see it, too!" Mika said. He shaded his eyes for a better view of the dark silhouette against the bright blue-pink horizon. "Yes, and that is about two hundred meters away." He pointed to the rusty fragments poking out of the snow.

Eryn shaded his eyes with cupped hands, scanning the snowy vista, and yipped excitedly when he spotted it. He had the best panoramic view of the Antarctic Valley from his hiding spot on the fifth level of the spiraling floor inside the Athletic Dome. Hiding under a storage bin by the plexiglass wall, Eryn spied on the family that fascinated him the most. Pretending to be part of their group was his favorite pastime during visits to Joshua. It was also crucial for him to observe and learn from them to grow into a wise and strong boy. Only then could he reveal himself and avoid the influence of humanity's evil, as Joshua said. "I must learn about humans to live like a human," was his mantra. He didn't fully grasp why it was taking so long.

Wondering where the other man, the other father, was, Eryn looked closer at the building and spied the other man at a window. This man was called Connor, and Eryn watched him mumble something as he watched his family, bringing Eryn's attention back to the amusing scene before him. Eryn bit down on his fists, smothering his laughter as he enjoyed the live entertainment and was seconds away from bursting into hysterics. Pressure built in his head while he restrained himself, small bursts of air escaping, sounding like farts and amplifying the humor of the situation. He snort-giggled at Connor, who peeked through the thick plexiglass wall, trying to see better while leaning in and pushing his nose against the cold glass. This was much more fun, and Eryn dreaded returning home to the darkness deep inside the earth. He knew what needed to be done, but he couldn't bring himself to do it. So he pushed that thought aside. It tore him apart. Too many things he wanted, needed to do, and wished for. Plus, he wanted to forget about his responsibility to his family.

Returning his attention to Connor, Eryn almost laughed out loud as he watched Connor mouth "Damn foggy glass," then balled his sleeve into a fist and rubbed the glass vigorously in small circles, polishing it. Eryn giggled, stamping his feet as he struggled to contain his laughter. The bulky frame and long legs barely fit under the bin. Occasionally, the container rattled, but no one noticed him.

Eryn watched the other three enjoying themselves outside on the glass dome roof. Suddenly, the three laughed boisterously. Eryn frowned, upset with himself for missing the punchline and unable to decipher their conversation. *I wish I could join them.* He longed to play with them and be part of their world of love and affection, especially when their fathers hugged the twins and showered them with attention. For now, he would hide and pretend, but one day, he would reveal his unusual face. I hate going home after just a day or two of short visits. Maybe not today, but definitely one day. He promised himself to refocus and not miss anything.

He turned back and watched Connor intently, reading his body language. Connor appeared increasingly irritated and nervously anxious. Ah, he feared for Mika and the twins, worrying they might slide off the roof. With wide eyes and an open mouth, Eryn leaned in, observing intently, like watching a movie on television, only better, as he soaked up the drama of Connor spying on Mika and their boys outside while Connor, like himself, was inside. His level of amusement rose to nearly unmanageable heights, causing the bin to rattle louder. Quickly, he righted himself, checking his knees to ensure nothing gave his position away. Connor's anticipation of seeing the three rubbed off on Eryn. As soon as Connor caught sight of the safety harnesses around their bodies, the relief and love he felt washed over Eryn. He gasped softly, then waited. From his viewpoint, he could see both fathers. Mika held both boys, with Ivan on his right and Cian on his left, all sitting in a tight row, while Connor watched them from the inside of Phoenix.

Eryn's inhumanly perfect hearing and empathic abilities came in handy when he pretended to be part of this family. The way they loved and interacted with one another was unlike any other family, and he could observe them for hours. Most of the time, it brought him joy, but sometimes it filled him with sadness. His father had told him he was special, and Joshua told him he would do great things one day because he possessed abilities that humans lacked. This was evident as he recognized Connor's sadness about being inside while the others played outside. Eryn sensed Connor's anxiety rising as he watched them atop the highest point of the dome roof, his heartbeats were louder and faster than usual.

Eryn crossed his legs, resting his elbows on his knees and his chin in his hands while smiling longingly at the scene unfolding before him. Connor puffed with pride and adoration for his husband and their two boys as he watched Mika trying to hold on to their kids while simultaneously explaining with his hands, fully immersing himself in the educational conversation. His gestures, like those of an accordion player, conveyed something big and explosive. Eryn's mouth hung open in concentration, twisting his head from side to side to interpret the miming. Playful chuckles escaped from beneath the bin as he pretended to sit outside on the rooftop, enjoying the animated hand gestures of explosions and crashing waves as he worked to figure out the answer. It was about the day all the water came to his home, and the land around his mineshaft froze. With wide eyes, hands in fists, and gesturing animatedly, Mika made pow-pow sounds while opening and closing his hands. Eryn understood Mika was discussing what they called the "Big Flood."

Ivan pointed to the satellite dishes jutting through the icy surface once more, and Mika continued to explain what they were. He nodded in agreement, then placed his thumb to his ear and his pinky to his mouth. Eryn concluded that no one understood what that meant. Then he heard Connor speaking as if Mika and the twins could hear him through the glass wall. "It's enhancing communication. It's for sending sound waves from one dish to another to talk or receive information from the outside world."

"Ah," Eryn whispered, joining the make-believe outdoor classroom game. Feeling proud of himself, he understood what Connor had said. Suddenly, Mika turned toward the Athletics Dome, and Eryn ducked and scurried deeper under the bin. He watched closely as the proud fathers made eye contact, both mouthing the words, "I love you," with broad, cheerful smiles. Eryn sighed and made soft cooing noises. Pouting his lips and pretending to kiss, sweet, kissy noises escaped from beneath the bin.

Connor was too focused on Mika to notice anything behind him. But if he turned around and looked, he might have seen the flopping dirty blonde curls as Eryn flopped excitedly up and down on his back. The joyful emotions were euphoric, causing him to bounce vigorously, sending his hair in all directions and obscuring his big, friendly, gold-green eyes with elongated pupils. Eryn swept his hair to one side with a quick, irritated motion. His reflection revealed that his pupils were almost invisible, as they sat so close to the light streaming in from outside. Eryn wore an oversized, ratty t-shirt he had borrowed from the laundry department. He pulled it over his knees, tucked it beneath him, and tented himself inside. Joshua frequently chased him back to his room to get fully dressed, especially when he went outside without shoes in the snow. Spying on humans was fun, but shoes made it difficult for him to do so silently, so he would wear no shoes today.

The boys turned and waved when they spotted Connor inside, waving happily. Connor waved both arms above his head as if he hadn't seen them all day. He yelled, but Eryn was certain they couldn't hear him. "Hello, my smart, beautiful boys. I love you, be careful. Dada loves you."

It sounded and felt beautiful to Eryn, and he wanted that. But most of all, he wanted to feel like a human being. The emotion overwhelmed him. All he could do now was let his head fall forward and allow his tears to stream down his face. *I am a big boy*, he thought with the mind of an innocent child, but he knew that wasn't enough. He had things to do and brothers to kill, but the thought of doing that made him feel utterly alone. So, he cried silently until he had cried himself out. Then, he used his shirt to wipe his big, amphibious-like nose, and he got up to go search for Joshua. There was nothing more to see here. He forced himself to leave without sneaking another look.

"Who are you waving at, Cian?" Mika asked.

"Our friend, Dada! Say bye-bye to him, Ivan."

Eryn didn't look. He left, not knowing that the friend the boys were talking about was him.

It had taken him over half a day sneaking through until he finally found Joshua in the army portion of the military compound. Aggressive shouting alerted him, so he fell to his knees in the cold snow and carefully snuck up, only to see what appeared to be a confrontation between Joshua and six other men. Eryn recognized them as the men who regularly slipped past the perimeter patrol and terrorized Joshua. Impulsively, he crawled on his hands and knees, making sure they didn't see him—*because I am an odd-looking little boy.* He found a hollowed-out area in the snow and watched. *I may be an odd-looking boy, but I'm not a stupid little boy.*

He narrowed his eyes to slits and pinned them on the men as Joshua yelled at them. Joshua was brave and didn't care how much bigger they were than himself. When one man punched Joshua in the ribs, Eryn lost his temper and jumped up to help, but Joshua locked eyes with him, shaking his head, signaling to stay hidden.

Eryn sat down again as he'd been told, but remained positioned and ready to strike. The air smelled of the sweet copper scent of blood, and Eryn watched as it seeped into the snow in slow motion. All the while, his hands covered his ears to muffle the painful cries of his friend.

He cried soundlessly for the second time that day, never taking his eyes off his friend. This was getting too much for Eryn's emotionally immature mind. But he saw that all humans were different, like he and Ernest were different.

When they were done hurting Joshua, Eryn waited until he heard them entering the side door of the compound. With the speed of a cheetah, he shot out of his hidey-hole, skidded on his knees, and scooped his friend into his lap. "Joshua, Joshua, are you okay?" Eryn inspected the injuries, worried and not sure what to do to help him.

Joshua opened his eyes and answered in between coughs. "Yes, boy, don't worry. I will be fine," he said as he rolled onto his side to hurl his stomach contents. It was a stinking mess in the snow, and Eryn's heightened sense of smell didn't help. He jumped up before it hit him. *Yuck!*

Joshua chuckled and spat more blood. "Just promise me you won't ever let them see or catch you. They're not good men. Promise me, boy." Joshua's voice cracked and was barely audible. He was growing older so fast. Sometimes it felt like Eryn looked away and back at him, and he seemed a year older. His hair was thinning and turning as white as snow. It was now red with blood. That enraged Eryn. He wanted to hurt them like they hurt his friend. He bulged his fists and gnashed his teeth, almost breaking his needle-sized fangs. "I'm going to kill them."

Joshua waved his hand weakly. "No, not now. Not yet. You need to grow a bit more. If you feel like killing, you must kill your brothers first, my boy," he said, and the hand plopped into the snow, almost into the puddle of vomit.

Eryn shook his head. "But I'm already a big boy, and I know I can kill them with my fork. I know I can." He kneeled to wipe the hair out of Joshua's face and whimpered, feeling frustrated, confused, and angry.

"I know, my son, but the time is not right. I will let you know. Promise me you will do as I ask."

The pain and despair emanating from Joshua broke Eryn's resolve. "Okay." He sniffled. "I'll take my revenge the day you say so." Joshua reached for Eryn's face, wiping his tears and snot away. He cracked a loving smile, exposing a broken tooth. Eryn cringed.

"I promise you, I will let you know when it is time," Joshua said kindly with sad-looking eyes. The fear of losing Joshua frightened Eryn. If Joshua died, he would be alone in this big, frozen world.

"If you say so, then I will wait. Please don't die," Eryn said, sniffling. His brothers were not like humans. They didn't talk, laugh, or cry, and they definitely could not live in the glass city. Maybe Ernest could. But Joshua didn't seem to think so. "Joshua, you're my only human friend. From now on, I'll never leave you alone. I'll guard you and warn you when they're coming. Then we can hide together. I know a lot of good hiding spots."

Joshua smiled, but his words cut like knives when he spoke sternly and with finality. "No, my boy, it's time to leave. You should keep your brothers from finding this place. Do what your father said, before he died. Before your twin, Ernest, influenced your brothers and killed him. I'm telling you, you must do this. Flood those tunnels and bury them, my boy. Take this aggression and go do that for me, please. These men are looking for you and your brothers." Joshua coughed and lowered his head.

Eryn took his hand, squeezing it. "Joshua?"

The old man lifted his bloodied head again, looking at Eryn as if to say something, shook it, before it fell backward with a plop. He closed his eyes and seemed to mutter something to himself, but Eryn couldn't hear.

Joshua, Peter von Leutzendorf, and his father were scientists and friends. That was the only reason Eryn was allowed to visit Joshua, because he was the only one able to travel across the ice to bring messages from the underground laboratory in South Africa to Joshua and Peter.

Eryn watched Joshua for a long time and then nodded. "Yes, Joshua," Eryn said. Deciding not to argue. He was just speaking out of fear and anger anyway. He didn't know how to kill so easily like his brothers. He was scared of Ernest; his own brother was cunning and deadly to humans. Their other nest brothers from another clutch of eggs were even deadlier.

After another few minutes, Joshua opened his eyes and said, "Okay, let's go." He wiped his mouth and checked his sleeve for blood. Then he rolled over on his hands and knees. Eryn jumped to help and support him. "Let's go to our room," Joshua said, short of breath.

They hobbled inside, and Eryn hoped nobody noticed. Tears filled his eyes as he tried to maneuver them down their secret passage. "You'll need adequate footwear, clothing, and food for at least a year. I want you to fill your ship with as much food as possible tonight."

Eryn soundlessly wept as they walked back to Joshua's secret room, where he was allowed to read books and sleep for a night or two before returning home to keep his brothers from leaving the mine. Or kill them. He agreed, maybe a year was a good idea. He would need a plan and courage to do what Joshua and his father begged him to do.

Eryn realized they needed to move, or someone might see them. He offered his support, allowing the older man to lean on him. He felt distraught. He just nodded, sobbing uncontrollably. *Why did this turn out to be a horrible day?* "I'm a good boy, Joshua. I'll be even better for you."

"No, you did nothing wrong, boy. Those men are the problem. They'll take advantage of you for the wrong reasons. They have an agenda."

Eryn nodded. He didn't know who or what agenda was. All the snot, tears, and constant wiping caused his cheeks to be burned raw, and they hurt.

"Our cave is where we will meet. If you can't kill your brothers, you can't come back inside. Not until you've eliminated your toxic brothers. I will bring food and clothes to the cave. Don't come back inside until you are able to tell me they are dead. Eryn, look at me. This is important. Do something about those Brawls. Look at me, Eryn!"

But Eryn's heart and spirit shattered. He despised living in the mines and having to watch his brothers. It was that or kill them. He felt like running far away and never returning. But where to? He wanted to be close to the icemen, not live in a mine. "You want me to kill my only family and live alone until you call me? That is not fair," he said.

"Eryn, it's not a good idea for you to stay here. If your brothers are discovered, these men will use them, and everyone in here will perish. Do you want that to happen? Do you want these people to die? You need to kill your Brawl brothers. I know it hurts to kill your own. You are good and not a monster. That's why I ask you, for the sake of these humans, do you want them all to die?"

"No, I don't," he whispered.

Once inside, Joshua bent one knee. "Don't cry, please, my boy." He made eye contact with Eryn and gently wiped his face. "We can stay in touch. This is just temporary until I know the bad men are gone and your brothers are no more. Promise me you won't let these men find you or your brothers. They're selfish, evil men who do not believe in my god. They want to be gods themselves, and they will use anything and anyone to reach their goals."

Eryn didn't know who Joshua's god was, but he spoke of him and read stories about him from his favorite black book, the Bible.

He assessed Joshua's bloody, swollen face through teary, blurred eyes as he thought about protecting the twins and the Romanov family.

"Okay, let's clean my face and get you and the ice sail ship ready so you can get out of here. Make a promise to me," he croaked. "Never trust those who hurt you. Ernest is hurting you. Remember that when the time comes to kill him, and until you do that, avoid coming inside Phoenix without me."

"Eryn sniffed and bravely promised while wiping more snot from his face.

CHAPTER 2

# YOU WILL NOT DIE TODAY

*"Good morning, citizens of Phoenix. It is I, Lasitor.*

*Get up! It's six a.m.*

*Did you know Easter was a religious holiday celebrated with chocolates by hiding them and sending the youngsters to find them? It may be an excellent idea to head down to breakfast this morning to grab a few chocolate eggs, especially those made by our chefs so that you can have a real pagan experience.*

*Celebrate the day by increasing your children's sugar intake, getting them all excited and happy so they can crash early. You and your lover will have time to melt those chocolates and paint one another's eggs, just like they did back in the thirteenth century.*

*Visit the local community news page for exciting forbidden eggs, penance, and fast facts.*

*Breakfast is served until eight a.m.*

*Have an egg-citing day!"*

**General Brad McCormick**
**2073 A.D. (21 A.T.)**
**Phoenix**
**Glass-Domed City**
**Antarctica**

*Freezing hellfires!* Brad counted the precious minutes he had left. *How many injections had I given myself already? When did I inject the syringes? Did I actually call for help, or did I think I should have called for help?* Questions rush through his disoriented mind. The hollowness of the ice canyon swallowed his howls and groans of pain and despair. Tiny snow crystals drifted on the wind, reflecting the Aurora Borealis' light into millions of shades of green, pink, and blue. Reminding him of the world he didn't want to leave behind, so the reality of his perilous situation hit him again.

Brad curled himself tightly into the fetal position. It seemed hell had finally frozen over, and he lay at the bottom. His mind spun like a disco ball, reflecting a kaleidoscope of thoughts, feelings, and emotions, and he struggled to think coherently as jumbled thoughts, worries, and prayers sparked at the speed of light behind his eyelids. *Come on, find my stupid ass.*

He'd arrived twenty-seven years ago in Antarctica to lead Phoenix, and he had achieved the inconceivable and accomplished so much. *And now, here I lie, dying alone, because of my stupidity.*

More sparks flashed in his mind, and he told himself they were slight electric jolts from the dying synapses in his freezing brain. Describing the steps of his demise kept his dying mind occupied. *They are only tiny backfires, my neurons conjure up in protest of dying.*

He couldn't remember the last time he felt so numbed by the cold. He was so hypothermic that he was incapable of shivering, and his eyelids had frozen shut. *It's only a matter of minutes, and then I'll die.*

His ribcage was frozen stiff, making it almost impossible for him to take a deep breath. Each time he thought he'd taken his last breath, his mouth opened on its own, and he gasped like a fish out of water.

*Bloody damn hell!* He dreaded the cycle of gasping and waiting for all the disco lights to go out. *Someone must hurry and rescue me, or I'd better hurry and die already.* He cringed mentally. He didn't want to die, so when his body took another involuntary breath, he welcomed it. Bloody Peter with his *take-this-and-live-forever* capsule. He slowed his mind, willing the hectic thoughts to subside, forcing his mind to shut down and prepare his soul to leave for oblivion.

The last Glupidone shot he injected into the side of his neck prolonged his chance of survival by about fifteen minutes. It worked by combining life-saving chemicals and hormones. These boosted survival in freezing temperatures, reducing lung fluid, raising blood sugar for energy, including epinephrine and methamphetamine to stimulate the body. Finally, a cryoprotectant preserved cells from ice damage. In theory, prolonged consciousness meant prolonged life. Earlier, just as Brad injected his last syringe, he'd used its needle to tear the skin and muscles over his upper left pectoral wide open to remove his Peter Pan Cap. It made perfect sense at the time to chew on it like bubble gum, since his injections had given him hope of lasting long enough in the freezing cold until someone might rescue him. He thought it was probably futile, but he'd never been a man who quit and gave up. So instead of dying like a typical soldier, he would lie there like a pathetic dying shrimp on the bottom of the ocean with the worst medicine after-taste ever in his mouth. *Bloody Peter with his capsules.* He berated Peter in his mind, furious with himself as he replayed the night's events.

He remembered seeing men running with flashlights in this direction. But like the *idiot I am*, he reprimanded himself for not radioing security to inform them about the sighting. Instead, he ran after the lights like the Mothman on acid. Thinking, *no, not thinking at all*, to investigate, *no, also not investigate, instead running around like an imbecile searching for a crack in the ice to run into.*

The pain in his backside made sense as he recalled falling onto his butt and knocking the wind out of his lungs. *I could have bitten my tongue off.* When he finally managed to scope his surroundings, he realized the immense size of the gigantic crevice he'd managed to run into. *How did I miss the mammoth split in the ice sheet? Thank god I landed on a ledge.* Unfortunately, he lost both his radio and flashlight in the process. He tried to stay alive as long as he could.

*Yes, that's what I did. Then I removed my flare gun from my right leg pocket and the syringes from my left pocket.* Brad remembered he removed the safety mechanism with his thumb, pointed it upwards, and pulled the trigger. *Yes, a pink flare; I remember shooting it into the night sky.* Ah, now his gloveless hands made sense as he recalled removing them to administer the first of five preloaded dosages. *Okay, so it's been more than an hour, that's good, then they're already on their way.*

Positive thinking helped him remember more. He faintly recalled opening his jacket, searching for a patch of skin to administer the life-prolonging aid. While he'd palpated the muscled area over his upper chest, he recalled Peter telling him about the special amniotic fluid and the by-products of the artificial wombs. His cryoprotectant research discovered a potential preventative aging mechanism in humans by splicing the bowhead whale SIRT6 gene and reprogramming human DNA on a cellular level to repair and rejuvenate damaged strands. It made sense to Brad after he'd injected the last syringe to dig that little Eden Bean capsule out from under the layers of his left pectoral muscle and started chewing it.

Brad stopped calling for help after he had no voice left. In his death-dream state, he saw a mirage of Rick laughing, Rick kissing him, and the last time he'd enjoyed a warm shower with his husband. Feeling the heat of the steam from their last shower together on his face, tasting the soap, *no, not soap, the bloody capsule,* and the taste of Rick's shoulder. The one he licked and sucked that morning while he made love to him in the shower. He cherished every throaty groan his husband made. *If I weren't frozen, I'd have an erection.* He smiled mentally at himself, thinking that when they discovered him thousands of years into the future, archeologists would discover he died with an erect penis and a smile on his face. The tour guide would describe him as Homo-Erectus-Erectus. He chuckled inwardly and imagined hearing the tour guide saying, *"Ladies and Gentlemen of the Museum of Human Studies. This Homo Erectus-Erectus, who walked the earth thousands of years ago, is an extinct species of archaic humans. It perished during the dawn of the global nuclear winter of 2060 A.D. We discovered this human had such a big penis he could have used it as an extra leg or a weapon!"*

He amused himself while he waited, drifting in and out of various levels of consciousness. He suspected he was tripping, as well. The amount of amphetamine in the Glupidone shots would make an elephant rave. He laughed and watched Rick blink in and out in his imagination, reaching out to him, smiling, and telling him everything would be okay and that he loved him.

Brad calmed his mind and shot one last message into the universe for his Apache. *Love, thank you for all your love, steadfast belief, and support you've given me. I love you. Please continue living your life to the fullest for the sake of me and the boys.* He whimpered, and he realized his frozen face and tear ducts wouldn't permit him to shed one tear. *Rick, I love you. And, boys, take care of your father, he'll need you.*

With that said, Brad's soul found peace, his mind quieted, and in the stillness, he waited to drift into the afterlife, but something or someone held him tethered to this plane. It was so still that he could hear snowflakes burying him.

*Hello, is someone touching me? I feel something warm.* Brad felt a gentle hand touching his cheek.

"Don't worry, Icemen King. I will stay with you until your icemen come," a deep, melodic voice said.

*"What? Who are you? Are you an angel?"*

Soft chuckles surrounded him, wiping away the feelings of despair and loneliness. They enveloped him with empathy, an experience he had never known before, like a warm blanket of love.

"Who's there? I hear giggles in my mind."

"Not long. Hold on, Icemen King."

*I'm either on my way to heaven, or...* Brad paused, stilling his mind, listening.

More playful snickers...and beautiful notes were being hummed. His tension and fear faded. He felt as light as a helium balloon. Safe and drifting. Hovering and waiting —holding on.

"I'm warming your heart and mind. You will not die today," the soothing, angelic voice said near Brad's ear. *It must be a hallucination.*

# CHAPTER 3

# BRAD'S A GENIUS

*"Good morning, men of Phoenix.*

*Lasitor bids you a good morning. It's now six a.m.*

*Did you know that in 2035, ice carving was a trendy sport? At first, it was a hobby, but people began taking it seriously and started competing in events, and later it became an Olympic sport.*

*Visit your community news page to sign up for exciting events and things to do with ice and snow. Breakfast is served until eight a.m.*

*Hope you have an icy cool day!"*

**Dr. Peter Von Leutzendorf**

"Here he is! I found him!" Connor trumpeted as he fell onto his knees at the ridge of a gaping tectonic crack. Peter joined him. They removed their head coverings, puffing enormous clouds of mist, stunned by the magnitude of the abyss.

"Jesus, the lucky son of a bitch," Peter said.

"Braaaad, Braaaad, can you hear me? Hold on, buddy, we have you!" Connor called.

"Good god, he fell right into a chasm, and look, the lucky son of a bitch fell onto the only protruding ice shelf," Peter said in awe. He doubted Brad could hear them.

"I told you we should've started on this side. He's probably dead by now," Connor said as he got up. Peter was glad they found Brad, so he could stop and catch his breath. He concurred if they started their search on this side, he wouldn't be so exhausted.

"We should be able to reach him!" Connor turned to Mika, who had just arrived, trailing behind them. "Look, there he is, but be careful." Connor pointed, and Mika shook his head in disbelief.

"Freezing hellfires." Mika crouched down, carefully crawling for a better look.

"My words exactly. Brad fell right onto the only ledge," Connor said. He stepped back from the edge and lifted his arms, helicopter style, signaling their position with his flashlight. "Here we are," he shouted.

Their team of three had searched the northeastern perimeter for an hour until they found and followed boot tracks in the snow to this spot. Although it was nighttime, the breathtaking springtime constellations reflected on the snow, shrouding the land in a dim glow. They wore night-vision goggles equipped with infrared heat signal detectors and progressive light particle refractors to differentiate between old and newly fallen snow.

"I see just a few specks of orange and red on my screen. Brad has probably frozen solid," Peter said, estimating their leader lay about two meters into the crack.

"We need to go get him," Connor stated. Mika and Peter leaned over the side, repeatedly calling for Brad, but saw no movement. Sitting back on their heels, they pushed their goggles to their foreheads to assess the area and plan their next steps. Their white and yellow extreme cold weather suits trapped air and insulated their bodies by preventing heat loss and conducting water vapor away from the layers underneath. The outer shell shielded them from the deadly icy wind, keeping them warmer for longer. Unfortunately, the visibility through the ten-by-fifteen-centimeter tent window, as Connor referred to it, was severely limited, making it challenging to see and maneuver during the rescue mission. They would have to move quickly without protection against the frigid air. The snow was falling so fast that they could barely see each other.

Connor turned from left to right, seeing how far the chasm stretched. "I don't think this was here yesterday. It must be a pressure ridge. Look!" He pointed with his flashlight, but the light disappeared into the profound depths of the crack. "I can't see how deep it is, and I'm not shooting flares into it. I don't want to disturb the ice and worsen the situation."

Peter felt increasingly nervous. "Let's just get Brad out before the chasm closes again!" Peter said, recalling the morning's reports about increased tectonic and microplate movements. Overnight, ice frequently formed across the cracks. If it got reasonably thick, it might rupture loudly when the warming sheet pushed on it the next morning. Other times it slowly pushed into a vertical curtain a few inches high as the crack closed again.

"Okay, you two lightweights, go down. I'm strong, I'll pull you back up," Mika said.

"Okay, Mika!"

"What? I'll wait and signal the backup responders this way. I'm afraid they won't see us or run over the side themselves," Mika said. Lifting the radio to his mouth, he reported their position to Phoenix.

Connor hastily drove four galvanized steel pins deep into the ice. Peter tested their sturdiness. Satisfied, they fastened their gear to the anchors and slid down with pivoting ropes.

Peter didn't make a sound, testing their purchase. Connor reached Brad first, gently wiping the powdered snow from his body. "Brad, are you okay? Can you hear us?" Brad didn't move. "I think he's dead, Peter," Connor said. His disbelieving whisper cracked the grave heaviness of their dire situation.

"Don't worry. Let's get him to my cryogenics laboratory. I have a few tricks up my sleeve," Peter said optimistically. Secretly, he was more afraid of the ice pancaking them than his frozen general.

That seemed to get Connor moving.

"Wait!" He stopped Connor by grabbing his shoulder. "If we pull on Brad and pick him up the wrong way, an arm or a leg, even his head, could break off. We need to safely loosen and then secure him to the stretcher in the position he's in now," Peter explained. When it came to frozen dead people, he was the specialist.

Connor nodded his agreement and followed his directions. "That makes sense. What do you suggest?" he hollered, trying to compete with the growing roar of the wind.

Peter assessed Brad's rigid and white frostbitten body. "The best way to do this"—gesturing, scooping the snow from underneath Brad, *the human icicle*, Peter thought—"is to loosen him from the snow, put the stretcher against him, and gently flip-roll his whole body onto it. Once that's done, we can then securely strap him to the stretcher, and we'll be able to hoist him vertically up the side of the ice wall."

In the background, Peter heard Mika briefing Phoenix on the search for Brad and the current situation. The wind blew ice over the sides and into their faces. "Tell them to hurry!" Connor shouted while scooping snow. Mika waved back, showing he had it under control, but they struggled to hear him above the growing roar of the storm.

Snow icicles packed on Connor's face and stubble. Peter didn't think he looked much better and feared losing the tip of his nose. *We have to hurry, we won't survive another hour without help.*

"Tell them to bring more Glupidone," Peter shouted to Mika.

"What?"

"We need more Glupidone!"

Mika waved. "Right, Glupidone!"

They went at it, smashing and scooping the ice, loosening Brad so they could roll him over without shattering him into pieces.

"This ice is rock-hard. It must be millions of years old. Do you think it cracked beneath his feet when he slipped and fell into the crevice? Why else would he be here?" Peter was short of breath, struggling to breathe as his lungs burned from the cold.

"I'm sure he said he was checking something on the other side of the domes. But why would he wander to this side of the valley? Maybe something attacked or spooked him or dragged him here?" Connor theorized between breaths.

"Maybe he heard the ice crack and came investigating?" Peter asked. He continued speculating, diverting the topic from other humans outside. He vigorously hacked at the ice with his small ax, then scooped out more ice to create space underneath Brad, loosening and freeing him.

"Okay, I think that's enough," Peter said. With a slight wave of his hand, he acknowledged Mika, who was helping another small man slide down the rope to help them. Securely strapped to the gurney, they hoisted Brad up and over the side to relative safety.

"Hold on, and please wait!" Peter tried shouting, but it came out in a wheeze when he crawled over the ledge.

"We need to..." He heaved with his hands on his knees. Catching his breath, he pointed to Connor, Mika, and himself. "Glupidone, for frostbite!" he yelled, barely audible above the howling gusts of wind. They soon understood when he started patting them down, searching their pockets for their emergency stash, and they hastily handed it over to him.

After each received a jab in the neck, they donned their masks. Mika checked that Brad was properly tethered and signaled his okay. The six men lifted the stretcher and sprinted toward Phoenix as fast as they could. The city's lights shone through the storm like a dim blue beacon in the distance. As they approached, the domed glass roofs illuminated the sky with streaks of bright lights, like a thousand lighthouses calling them to safety. They saw the big front door rolling up and retracting into the roof, allowing them to enter. It felt like an eternity, but after fifteen minutes of running full speed through the snow, the six men and their precious cargo were finally in the dome's warmth.

While the entrance closed behind them, Mika looked back and frowned. Connor followed his gaze. "That's strange. I could have sworn I saw movement out of the corner of my eye in the direction we'd just come from. It feels like someone's watching us," Connor said.

"I have the same feeling." Mika lifted his arm. The man operating the big door made eye contact with him. "Secure the door, now!" Mika ordered as his eyes followed the running men with the stretcher. As if thinking the same thing, they looked worriedly at each other. "Where's Bryan?" Mika asked. "We need to activate the Reserves!"

Sergeant Amir Lamasi overheard them and saluted. Seconds later, he announced the code status over the leadership pager. The well-practiced reserve team scrambled, knowing precisely what to do. "Captain Bryan Howell, report to Communications Dome stat. This is a Code Yellow Alert."

Mika hopped, skipped, and jumped through a sea of men trying to get to their posts.

"I'll meet Bryan at Communications. *Ublyudok!*" He swore in his native tongue. "I think this was an attack on Phoenix!" Mika said to Connor.

"All shutters need to be activated and closed immediately!" Connor ordered his commands into his communicator.

"I'll catch up later. I need to find Rick and update him about Brad," Connor said. He blew a kiss to Mika, who smiled in acknowledgment and disappeared into the sea of soldiers.

Peter savored the breathable air as he yanked the head covering off again. His cheeks burned with tiny needle pricks as blood flow was restored. "Please, take him...my... Cryonics lab. Quickly...There are steps we need to follow. I...prepare...decompression room..." He heaved the delicious heat between every other word into the depths of his lungs. Unable to talk in complete sentences, he gulped a few deep breaths and shot after them. It crossed his mind that the other men were not nearly as out of breath as he was. *I should make it a priority to spend more time on my cardio exercises.* He would revisit that thought another day.

IN THE CRYONICS LAB, Peter directed the men to a large, thirty-by-forty-meter walk-in, temperature-controlled decompression chamber. Carefully, they placed Brad onto a steel slab. Peter immediately set the temperature to a freezer setting of minus 10° Celsius. He moved swiftly and with confidence. His cryogenics laboratory was one of the most, if not the highest, funded and secretly sponsored programs at Phoenix. Although not tight-fisted, Peter didn't freely share knowledge of his precious equipment and limited supplies. In fact, Peter harbored many highly classified secrets. Secrets not even known by his best friend and colleague, Mika Romanov. One such secret was that within the many chambers of his lab were hundreds of bodies and brains of the rich and famous, cryogenically frozen and patiently awaiting resurrection. This was one of many ways that funding for Phoenix had been raised. But he doubted he would ever resurrect these citizens from a lost civilization.

Dr. Peter von Leutzendorf, a high-born transplant from Bavaria, was a stunningly beautiful man with pure white hair and crystal-blue eyes, but he was a loner by choice, or so he let everyone think. He was also much older than any man currently living in Phoenix, and although not needed, he had implanted the first Eden Bean into himself when he appeared to be twenty-seven years old. Like everyone else in Phoenix, who had the capsule implanted, he hadn't aged a day since, looking precisely like the biochemist and cryogenics expert who first walked through Phoenix's doors. By hiding his true origins, he cloaked his milieu to resemble him, so that no one questioned him. A sacrifice to the right gods in the right way, using the correct form of traditional elemental structures, disguising his Aryan nobility. He didn't feel guilty because, at the same time, he had gifted good, deserving men with eternal life.

Inside the chamber, Peter went to work as fast as possible. Still dressed in his arctic gear, he worked to conserve as many of Brad's cells as possible.

When cells freeze, they collect water on a molecular level. If they thaw too fast, the general's cells will swell, explode, and he will die. *I think I'll need a high-pressure cryoprotectant.*

"When we thaw your cells, General McCormick, we'll have to dilute and exchange the fluids as quickly as possible to prevent osmotic shock and cell damage. However, this is all in theory. Using the cryoprotectant in the gas chamber with the pressure of fifteen atmospheres should guarantee high viability for your cells," he explained as if Brad could hear him and give him an answer.

"How much is high, Dr. von Leutzendorf?" a voice asked over the speaker system.

"Huh, hmm, what?" Peter turned and looked around, searching for the voice he thought spoke to him. "Was that you?" he asked Brad. Alone in his lab, in solitude, he regularly spoke to the frozen dead people, sometimes for hours. On occasions, they would talk back, but this voice sounded different.

"What do you mean by high viability? Will Brad be a functioning human being or not? Here, look at the monitor, please, Peter."

Peter frowned. His eyes searched upwards. "Ahh, there you are. It's you, Rick." Peter smiled open-mouthed. "I mean, over ninety percent of his body would thaw unharmed. Maybe higher and maybe lower," Peter explained to the fifty-by-fifty-centimeter monitor screen opposite him. He could see Rick talking to him. *Thank god I'm not crazy.* "Rick, if you prefer, we don't try this, then we can stop the procedure," he said, already busy removing his gloves to exit the freezer and speak face-to-face with Rick. "I'll come out and explain to you in person."

"No! Don't! Do what you can, Peter. I know Brad. He trusted you and would like you to try whatever you can to save him. He wouldn't want to leave the boys and me alone."

"Are you sure? This is all theoretical."

"Do what you can, please. You've been working in this lab for many years. Not once can I say you've been negligent or derelict in your research," Rick said with what sounded like respect in his tone. "It's the opposite. Look at the success of your Peter Pan Caps."

Peter hated that name. *It's Eden Beans, not Peter Pan Caps—that's so childish.* Peter looked closer at the screen. "Okay, let me see what I can do. Now that you mention the capsules, they already have some cryogenic agents on board to combat cell breakdown. Let me conduct a thorough assessment to see if we have a better chance of thawing and resuscitating him if I don't have to apply high pressure."

"Do you want me to come inside and help with that?"

"No, I'm going to do this. It'll take a while to prepare the thawing chamber, then we'll monitor the process on a cellular level, and when he's ready to receive CPR and take a breath, he'll be resuscitated. I'll ask Mika to assist me."

"Let me help. I can help," Rick pleaded, irritating Peter. Not only was he General Brad McCormick's husband and the last Apache Native American, but he was also the chief medical doctor in charge of the Phoenix Medical Operations Unit. The last thing he needed in his lab was a doctor who thought he knew better.

"You'll be emotionally involved," Peter said. *And you'll stand here judging me.* "Let's do this by the book. I know what I'm doing. If you want to help, you can call Mika to help me. When he arrives, we can discuss the next best steps for Brad's successful revival." Peter selected the best words from his vocabulary, which was a mix of polite and normal language.

Looking over at the monitor, Peter could see Rick biting his lips and his eyes watering with tears. "I'll start by cutting and removing his clothes for maximum dermis exposure in case Mika agrees we should administer the cryoprotectant gas." Peter hoped the request would give Rick a meaningful purpose and relieve his tension. *Please let him go, please let him go.* He didn't enjoy working in front of an audience. Judgment from Rick watching him would unnerve him.

After a long, uncomfortable silence, Rick answered, "I agree. Thank you for doing your best." Peter watched the monitor as Rick reluctantly left to fetch Mika.

Then he turned all his attention to Brad. "Okay, General, show me. Tell me what's going on with you." Peter removed the clothing by methodically cutting and removing layer by layer from skin surface areas over Brad's back, buttocks, and the upper side of his left leg and left shoulder. "Whoa, look at this. What do we have here?" Peter whispered, surprised when he opened Brad's left shoulder, revealing the bloody pectoral. At first, he thought it was a gunshot wound. "What the hell?" He poked and prodded the area with his face inches from the injury as he inspected the frozen blood and a gaping wound.

"No, this can't be. Really, maybe…wow, it is. Brad, who would have thought you had brains hidden between those big ears? That was clever of you…You just saved your skin…You son of a…" Peter whooped and danced like a chicken with its head cut off. He chanted, "Brad's a genius. Brad's a genius. Brad's a genius."

"What in the ever-loving hell are you doing, you crazy scientist?" Mika asked, joking and chuckling as he usually did when teasing Peter.

*Shit, he must have entered the chamber without making a sound. Damn light-footed Russian ox.* "Christ-all-mighty, Mika, you'll give me a heart attack. For the love of all that's holy, stop doing that." Peter smirked and ceased his happy dance. Instantly switching back to his usual professional self. But happy and relieved to see his friend.

"Mika, come see. If we had lots of time, I would have made you guess. But we don't, so come have a look here!" Peter excitedly pointed to the crystallized bloody left shoulder he'd just exposed. Carefully, he scraped the frozen pink ice, revealing an open wound of about two inches by two inches.

Mika, also dressed in his cryonics personal protective gear, held his hands up and turned his body toward Peter, just like a surgeon, scrubbed up and readied for surgery.

Slowly, he bent forward, careful not to touch or contaminate anything, showing the proper professional etiquette when entering another scientist's laboratory. He visually inspected Brad's left pectoral and looked up, then softly, with wonder in his voice, asked, "May I, please, Peter?" Holding the palm of his hand out for Peter to place a scalpel in it. He inspected the wound, gently palpating it. Peter watched Mika closely, hoping he would confirm what he suspected. He towered over Brad, making *hmmm* and *ahhhh* noises, narrowing his eyes as he concentrated.

"Hello. What's going on? Did you decide on anything?" Rick asked, entering the cryo-chamber. Peter lifted his head and watched him pussyfooting to the opposite side of Mika, not taking his eyes off Brad and stopping at the foot-end of the cold metallic slab. His posture stiffened, all the color drained from his wooden face, seeing his half-naked husband curled up and frozen. It looked like Brad was smiling, and Peter noticed when Rick saw it because the corners of his mouth slightly turned upward before he swallowed a few times. The audible gulps testified to Rick's emotional distress while he pretended his best to remain calm and appear professional. The muscles in his jaw pulled tightly when he bit down on his molars, looking like his heart shattered in silence while standing like a white statue instead of jumping onto Brad and never letting him go.

"I see. That's an impressive field incision. I never thought Brad would think of that," Mika said, smiling. "That'll certainly make a big difference." He expressed professional camaraderie, and Peter liked it.

"What is going on?" Rick demanded with a sad scowl, and his arms folded in front of his chest. Understandably, he was nervous, and his husband lay technically dead on the table. "Excuse me, that came out wrong. Could you two scientists explain what you're observing to me in layperson's terms? To me, it looks like a gunshot wound to the heart. I...cryogenic language is not my specialty. You're talking over my head," Rick admitted, and Peter could see he was close to losing his composure.

Feeling spiteful, Peter nodded and lifted a finger, asking for one second. Upstaging Rick's discomfort. "Mika, thank you for coming."

"It's no problem, comrade. Anything to help our general."

Peter turned to Rick to explain. Rick swallowed nervously, looking back and forth between Mika, Peter, and Brad. He stood over three meters away, distancing himself from the reality in front of him. Peter didn't want to feel sorry for him, but he did. He followed Rick's gaze to Brad's frozen and pale blue face.

*At least he's smiling.*

"Earlier, I said the process I initially intended exists only in theory, but I think we have a chance of proving it invalid by confirming my anti-theory." Peter hoped Rick was listening.

"Simply stated, Brad removed and ingested his Peter Pan Capsule."

"He what? Why did he do that?" Rick asked, looking highly confused. "Please explain to me. I want to know what you think happened to him. But most of all, how will we bring him back to life?"

*Let me spell it out for him, the man's so annoying.* Peter growled. Rick always made him feel less than, and he hated that. Rick gasped and seemed taken aback. Mika tsk-tsked at him.

Peter threw his hands up. "Look, it seems he gave himself his shots of Glupidone, you know, the shots every man in Phoenix has packed into their arctic gear in case of an emergency. Glupidone left pocket and flare gun right," Peter said, being very sarcastic, and he couldn't stop himself. Rick crossed his arms and listened, not saying a word, picking up on Peter's sarcasm. Mika coughed in the background, but Peter ignored him.

"I don't know what he did with his radio, but that's a moot point. Brad was lying on his right side and injected himself in his left upper shoulder and neck." He explained as plainly as he could muster. Pointing to Brad with his pinkie finger, he stepped closer. Concentrating on making sense to Rick while figuring out what Brad was thinking in his last moments. Peter hinted for Rick to step closer. Also dressed in lab gear, Rick had his hair pulled back into his favorite tightly braided French plait. His dark, almost blue-black hair and Native American complexion gave him a stunning, exotic appearance. As he stepped closer to inspect Brad's shoulder, Peter noticed the physician's emotions were verging on *fight or flight.*

*Yeah, it's difficult to be nonchalant when your husband is lying dead on a slab in front of you.* Peter's temper dissipated, and he engaged Rick empathetically.

"Okay, what am I looking at? Why would he remove his Peter Pan gel capsule? Was it his intention to die?" Rick fired stupid question after stupid question, unnerving Peter again.

"He didn't remove it! I'm saying it wrong. Sorry, he removed it, but...no, let me start with how I understand it."

Rick pulled his one eyebrow up in question and darted his eyes in Mika's direction, who nodded and conveyed his trust and support by looking back at Peter. *Thank you, Mika. Tell him just to shut up and let me think.*

Taking a deep breath, Peter explained. "He must have used a needle from the Glupidone shots or maybe broken one and used the glass. I doubt the latter because it would be too small to handle with the big gloves. Look here." Peter used the backside of the scalpel handle to show the yellow discoloration around Brad's lips. "Your husband chewed the gel, which is ingenious. It's made to slow-release over ten to fifteen years, but he chewed and ingested it. That means every cell in his body has already absorbed the hyperosmolar cryoprotectant on a molecular level. The cryopreservation of his whole body and brain is already reversing the ice damage. My cryoprotectant in positive pressure would never have reached as far and as deep. So, theoretically, thawing should occur easily and naturally.

"That was a primary problem with bodies already cryogenically frozen in the lab in the old world. The cryoprotectant administered before they froze them to minus fifty-four Celsius lacked a particular molecule we discovered only twenty years ago. That's why hyperosmolarity causes cells to pop. They should have waited long enough for my formula to be discovered so that this process could work.

"We now use the same formula to sustain fetal growth and development and prolong longevity. No matter what I tried, the damage was irreversible, and I'd lost so many subjects already. I was cremating bodies faster than their cells could pop. Each time I attempted the process, no matter what I tried, they would end up like *Puff the Magic Dragon*. No, that's wrong. It is *Pop Goes the Weasel*. Anyway, my research would start all over again. It's very frustrating because I have the answer in my hand, but I can't get it inside their bodies, you understand. My current high-pressure gassing and reverse osmosis techniques were the least damaging. Still, when the body finally absorbs the cryoprotectant into the cells, it's thawed, and the cell damage has already occurred. It was very frustrating, I tell you."

"Okay, I hear you." Rick stopped the high-speed thought pattern, and Peter blinked a few times to focus on Brad. "So, you say we should let him thaw the natural way? What do you mean by that?"

*Ting, ting, ting.* Peter's eyes rolled mentally like a slot machine. Again, he took a deep breath to calm himself down after being so rudely interrupted. Mika chortled like a mouse on cocaine in the background. Peter and Rick gave him dirty looks.

"Excuse me, comrades." He pretended to sneeze into his sleeve.

Peter continued. "I'll slowly turn the heat, say one degree every thirty minutes for two hours, wait an hour, and start again. We must force nothing. Gently dry him and remove the rest of his clothing." Peter pointed to the rags of clothes and boots he had been unable to remove earlier.

"And the wound?" Rick asked. "Would that bleed…as his body warmed?" Rick waved a hand. "Of course, it will. Sorry, Peter. I ask stupid questions."

"Yes, we would bandage the wound, and when he's dry, and his body temperature has risen to seventy-five, we can place you in the chamber with him so that you can heat his body with yours. I'll contact housekeeping to bring in a bed with a comfortable mattress and bedding. Also, I would suggest you have something to eat, empty your bladder, talk to the boys, and come back because you'll be in the chamber for six to eight hours. I calculate that he'll complete the process within twelve hours," Peter explained, feeling secretly happy about all this because he had a living guinea pig and could finally finish his damn research paper.

Mika nodded his head in apparent approval of Peter's plan. "Good, we need to talk to

Brad. I'll be back later. I agree that your steps for revival will work. If he does not spontaneously breathe, keep the resuscitation and emergency intubation trays at hand. I'll send a ventilator from the Medical Dome for you."

"Thank you, both of you," Rick said to Mika and Peter.

"No problem," Mika replied. "We want to be ready for anything. Peter, I think when Brad reaches eighty-five, call for me so we have enough hands on deck. I'll let Connor know he's in charge for the next twenty-four hours. We also have a situation outside. Bryan and his men are busy investigating." He hesitated, looking at Rick. "Rick, I don't want to traumatize or worry you more, but it's better to be honest under these circumstances. I think I saw something when we returned, and I'm wondering why Brad was outside. So, we need to investigate. We'll keep you in the loop," Mika said.

Rick nodded, keeping his eyes on Brad from across the table. His arms were folded, and he stared at Brad's body with tight lips and furrowed brows. An uncomfortable silence hung in the air.

"Yes, I suspected that when I heard Phoenix is on Code Yellow Alert. Connor explained, but was called away urgently. Thank you for coming, and yes, please send for that emergency equipment," Rick said, not making eye contact with Mika. "I hope we don't need a ventilator, but it's a good idea. We don't know how Brad fell and hurt himself. He may have broken a bone or hit his head and have a skull fracture," Rick stuttered, with tears in his eyes.

"Yes, that's true," Peter answered. Then he reached out, putting his hand on Rick's shoulder. "I'll scan his body in a few minutes." Rick took a deep breath and exhaled slowly. Peter hoped he wouldn't ask any more questions.

"I hope it hid nothing else from us…Brad's icy cocoon," Rick said.

Mika left. Peter programmed the thermostat, as they discussed. Then he turned to leave, but Rick asked, "Please stay," while holding onto Brad's shoulder. "I want to say a prayer for him."

*No, no, no,* Peter felt like a cornered, frightened kitten. He wondered if hissing at the man would help, but he thought better of it. Searching for an escape route, he realized his chance to run was zero as soon as Rick started chanting.

"May the moon restore you.
*May the sunlight awaken you.*
*May the warrior in you rise.*
*May the breeze bring you before me.*
*So, you may know the beauty of another life on the earth and walk with me.*"

Rick turned, shoulders shaking, soundlessly crying as he left to get ready and prepare to come back to lie down with Brad.

Peter administered more cryoprotectants at fifteen atmospheric pressures while the cryo-chamber temperature rose by one degree every thirty minutes, resting every two hours. This slow but necessary process prevented cellular hyperosmolality.

Rick returned six hours later, and Brad's temperature was nearly fully thawed, allowing them to reposition him on a bed. After that, both Peter and Rick stepped outside the chamber and into the room with the machines and an observation window that allowed them to monitor Brad's progress.

"I have good news." Peter felt relieved.

"Oh, what's that?" Rick asked in a monotonous tone, his face expressionless.

"Yes, good news. I scanned Brad's body. I didn't find any fractures or damaged internal organs," Peter said, searching for hope on Rick's face, but Rick only nodded and sat down to watch him work for another two-hour session. Rick stared at Brad as Peter worked, monitoring the process with advanced neutron scanners and ectoplasmic gamma-ray triple ionization subatomic particles. These particles tracked the viability of Brad's cells by measuring the speed at which molecules detached from electrons inside them and by measuring the return of the electromagnetic waves.

Finally, when Peter showed it was time, they went back inside to lay Brad's body on an extra-long twin-size hospital bed from the Medical Dome. Rick wordlessly helped connect the wireless ECG and EEG monitoring pads to measure Brad's heart rate and brainwaves.

After that, Brad was ready to be revived over the next few hours. Rick undressed, removing his white t-shirt and navy-blue pajama pants and slippers, and climbed naked onto the bed behind Brad's body, already on his left side. Sliding his left arm underneath Brad's neck, he lay down behind his husband, big spooning him. Peter pushed a pillow under Rick's head, cradling it. Rick gently threw his right arm over Brad's hips, pulling their bodies tightly together. Rick settled in to relax, his smooth, yellow-copper frame behind his husband's pale, blue, cyanotic body. Neither Peter nor Rick said a word when Rick nodded his head to indicate that he was comfortable. Peter covered their bodies under multiple layers of plush, duck-feather bedding and noticed the yellow and blue airplane pictures, and smirked.

"I wonder where they got this from. Probably from an unoccupied apartment?" Peter conjectured out loud. "Sorry, are you comfortable? I'll enter the room periodically to monitor Brad's core temperature and administer anticoagulants, and I'll send for Mika when his core temperature reaches eighty-five degrees. Then we'll start tiny electromagnetic shocks to his heart, just to wake and loosen the heart chambers."

"Okay, and Peter, thank you," Rick whispered somberly.

*He looks distraught and disconnected from reality.* Peter dimmed the lights.

"You are welcome. Don't worry, just relax and give your love and heat to Brad," Peter said and left to sit vigil to monitor them from afar.

*Phoenix will need Brad. I suspect the trouble has only started.*
He hoped his suspicions weren't correct.

# CHAPTER 4
# SOMETHING FISHY

*"Good morning, men of Phoenix.*

*Lasitor bids you a good morning.*

*It's now six a.m.*

*Learning to navigate using the stars is important and can be the difference between life and death. Still, only ten percent of you know how to do it. Statistics also show that it's often due to laziness or the task seeming so daunting that it gets put off, and people eventually get lost.*

*Statistics show you spend more time outside searching for each other than inside enjoying each other's company. To prevent getting lost, visit our community news page to learn more about navigating Antarctica. There's no need for it to be complicated, you can learn how to do it in minutes with The Beginner's Guide to Natural Navigation of the Stars.*

*Breakfast is served until eight a.m.*

*I hope you find your way!"*


**Dr. Mika Romanov**


As fast as the ground blizzard had hit Phoenix, it dissipated. Tonight, with the Code Yellow still activated, Connor and Bryan could investigate without hindrance from the general population.

The blond giant knew he possessed a genius-level intelligence. The men of Phoenix loved him for his honest, boisterous personality. He served on the leadership council of three that was established with the birth of Phoenix when a new code of conduct was needed for their unique all-male community. Mika was an approachable guy, and his big build and prominent personality made him someone to look up to. As intelligent and bold as he was, he never acted self-righteous, making him one of the most beloved leaders and re-elected council members in Phoenix. Every three years, Mika, Connor, and Bryan got re-elected. Their council had disappointed no one so far; so, why put someone in a position to destabilize the status quo? Despite that, the voting continued every three years, and thus, the status quo persisted.

Mika had received word from Connor that they'd found another Phoenix resident dead outside, so Bryan came to escort him to where the men had found the upper half of Joshua Adams's body. The fresh powdered snow crunched loudly under Mika's boots as he followed Bryan to the gruesome scene, contrasting against the brilliant midnight-blue with no clouds and the Milky Way that hung low in all its splendor.

"Although it had stopped snowing, the mini-blizzard we just had washed away most of any existing evidence," Bryan said. "Connor is already working at the scene, taking pictures and collecting evidence."

"Hmm, I see," Mika said. However, he never lifted his head as he concentrated on searching the ground for more clues. Slowly, they made their way over to his husband. Mika couldn't shake the feeling of trepidation. He halted at the first perimeter line and surveyed the area, where some men were scavenging in the snow. Others assisted Connor while a handful of soldiers patrolled the area about five hundred meters in the distance.

Connor looked up from where he was working, smiling instantly when he saw Mika and came to greet him.

"Hello, love, are you okay? Do you need anything?" Mika asked and felt relieved seeing him. "To say today was hectic and nerve-wracking is a definite understatement."

Connor stomped his boots, cleaning them. "Okay, as can be. I'm very glad to see you." His voice was hoarse, exacerbating his thick Irish accent. He saw the big stainless-steel flask of coffee Mika offered him and gave him a brilliant, appreciative smile. "Thank you. I just thought to page the food services to bring out soup or coffee for the men. We've been at it for a while now. How's Rick coping?" Connor asked as he led Mika to a spot where they could talk privately. They stepped carefully over the green, pink, and yellow paint-marked areas identified for collecting snow impressions.

Both squinted and shaded their eyes from the bright spotlights that had been erected to light up the scene. Mika could tell the day's events were wearing on Connor's nerves. His husband's eyes were red and puffy. He looked exhausted. He found his best friend's frozen body and risked his own to bring him in. Mika assessed Connor up and down. The feeling of unease nagged at him. Connor took eager gulps of the freshly brewed coffee, his breath coming out in puffs as the warmth fought to keep its heat in the sub-zero temperatures. Connor and the men were dressed in regular zip-up white, green, and black arctic suits. He looked warm enough, so Mika relaxed a bit and spoke. "Rick's okay. He's with Peter. But first, tell me how it went with Rick when you told him about Brad?" he prodded, trying to give his husband the much-needed support and outlet he knew he needed.

"Not so good. It was difficult for me to witness Rick's lack of reaction and remain professional. To be honest, his emotional stoutness floored me. I think the truth has yet to sink in. We've all gotten so used to thinking we'll live forever. I suggested we see Brad and speak to Peter, but I got called here." He pointed to Joshua. "I can't force the man to break apart. I expected him to show emotion and lose his shit. Instead, I lost my shit, and Brad's not even my husband. I tell you, yelda, when Rick hugged me, my empathy and fears for him and their boys knocked me over, and I bawled my eyes out for them. Then I thought it might have been you or, god forbid, one or both of our sons, I discovered frozen curled into a ball." Connor confessed while barely taking a breath between sentences.

"It's understandable. We're a huge family and we've become closer than ever. It's natural for you to feel upset. You were really worried when Brad went missing, but you found and saved him. It was a relief for you." Mika approached and said, "Let me hug you, gille-toine." It was Mika's special name for Connor, which they came up with on their first night together. Gille-toine meant little bed buddy in Gaelic, and yelda meant big dick in Russian."

Connor fell into Mika's arms, resting his head on Mika's chest. A full embrace wasn't possible because he carried a bag of evidence, his camera, and the coffee, so he awkwardly stood like a statue, soaking up the support as Mika swung his long arms around to console him.

Mika lowered his voice to a whisper. "Don't worry about Rick. He's coping. He's a medical professional, and they have a way of compartmentalizing their emotions. I assure you, he's terrified of losing Brad, and Peter is taking great care of both Brad and Rick. Rick knows and trusts Peter, and we all know Peter's the best person to save Brad. Unfortunately, at this moment, there's not much help I or anyone else can offer." Mika rubbed his cold nose against Connor's. "Now, tell me, what have you discovered? Was it a freak accident? Was it caused by man or nature, and why was Joshua out here after we received a blizzard warning?" Mika's internal alarm bells wailed ceaselessly. He studied the darkness of the outer roped area behind the border of yellow tape.

When he saw no movement or confirmation of his concerns, he kissed Connor on his forehead and stepped back from the embrace. Connor seemed deeply satisfied, almost swooning after Mika's embrace. He looked recharged, content, and deeply in love as he smiled at Mika. Clearing his throat, he stepped away and switched back into his role as Connor Romanov, second in command of Phoenix, and gave Mika the rundown of the scene.

"Okay, thank you for that. I needed it, yelda." He blushed and took another few sips of the coffee.

"I know, and it's my pleasure." Mika smiled gently. His eyes prickled with tears as his love for Connor overwhelmed him.

"Bryan had established fifty, hundred, hundred and fifty, and two hundred meters perimeters around Joshua's body." Connor pointed to Joshua, who sat upright like a planted Christmas tree. Mika followed Connor, taking care not to step on any evidence, while he nodded, signaling he was listening and simultaneously surveying the backdrop beyond the city of Phoenix's outer lines. From this distance, Mika could see Joshua's face, frozen in horror. The gory sight made Mika's skin crawl. Joshua's mouth and eyes were wide open, and his lips were pulled back, revealing his teeth, fixed in a last scream of agony.

Mika shuddered, imagining the excruciating pain the man experienced. "Is he sitting upright or...?" He halted mid-sentence, thinking that the snow had hidden his legs, but upon closer examination, he saw only the torso.

"You see right, yelda. We have these fifty-meter perimeters." Connor turned and pointed with a green laser pointer at the snow. "As you can see, we discovered Brad over there. Look in the crevice's direction. Brad was probably heading this way, hearing Joshua calling. Knowing Brad, he probably raced to aid while concentrating on helping and missed the fissure. But have a peek here." Connor pointed to several tracks and indentations in the ice.

"Hmmm, that's odd," Mika said. Placing his boot inside the one indent.

"Maybe a walking stick and homemade snowshoes. I can't imagine anyone having bigger feet than you," Connor asked rhetorically, appearing deep in thought. Mika watched his husband as his mind worked. He didn't want to break his train of thought. As a scientist, he knew how valuable it was to have a few seconds of uninterrupted mental calculations. He patiently waited for Connor to surface back to reality. It was cold outside, but not unpleasant for this time of the year. He had nothing to do but kill time and wait for Peter's call to assist with Brad's resuscitation.

The feeling of unease raised the hairs on his neck, and he shivered a few times. *Someone is watching us.* He sniffed the air. Smelling blood, the ozone scent of snow, and a slightly fishy odor. Strange, he thought, and saw Bryan conversing with a few men on the far-right side of the boundary. *Maybe there's time to do some investigating of my own.* He left Connor alone with his thoughts.

"Ah, here comes the smartest man in Phoenix. Mika, what a day," Sergeant Amir Lamasi said as the group noticed Mika approaching.

"Comrades." Mika counted ten men armed to the teeth and clothed in full tactical gear. He smelled the air again, wondering whether he'd imagined the fishy odor. Perhaps one of the men went fishing or something. As far as he knew, no one had planned a day excursion due to the storm warning. Perhaps someone took advantage of the fact that they were outside. Unobtrusively, he bowed his head and asked. "Do you smell fish?"

"Yes, we smelled it on the wind. Something fishy," Bryan said.

"When it stopped snowing, it became stronger," Amir said, barely audible, while kicking the snow with his boot. Feigning disinterest.

"I smell sweat, either ocean or fish, blood, and gunpowder," Bryan said under his breath, stretching his arms out and yawning.

"Do you have the impression that someone's observing us?" Mika sat on his heels, pretending to pick something up from the ground.

"Yes, that's an affirmative." Bryan looked up at the sky and then darted his eyes in the direction from which the smells drifted. "That way." He lifted his chin.

"At least I'm not imagining it, comrades." Mika stood and joined Bryan, gazing at the stars.

"We have a strategy. I've soldiers who have fallen to the rear and sides and are now encircling from a five-kilometer radius. Whoever is spying on us is unaware that we're aware of them."

"They're either unaware or unconcerned," Mika suggested.

"Let's go back to Connor and talk about Joshua." Bryan motioned with hand signals for his men to fall back and form a circle around the perimeter. "Whoever's watching thinks we're solely focused on this." He pointed to Joshua. "But we'll get them apprehended. I have complete faith in my soldiers." Bryan appeared in perfect spirit, enthusiastic and motivated to catch the perpetrators. Circumstances like these seemed to energize him.

Master Sergeant Bryan Howell was promoted to Captain after handling an emergency scenario with gallantry and bravery after the first big Phoenix earthquake. He was in his late forties when his Peter Pan Cap was placed. His full head of black and silver hair made him a stunningly attractive silver fox. He oversaw the Phoenix Military Reserve and Security and was one of the few men who appreciated being locked up with men and no females in sight after Doomsday. He'd always kept his sexuality hidden from his wife and family. Despite his grief over the outbreak and the death of his family, he embraced their new life by relishing in as many men as he could until he renounced his playboy attitude by falling in love with Tony Bonillo, who captivated him completely. The sharp-witted Italian civil engineer assisted in the design of Phoenix while still a student and interning at Environmental Project One, the initial title given to the complex by its founders.

Bryan halted at the fifty-meter perimeter, and Mika joined him. "We've established this a safe distance, not only because of the possibility of contamination of evidence but also because of the unpredictability of more cracks appearing in the ice."

Mika hated that Connor was putting himself in danger. He was the most accomplished code breaker, which made him the most qualified candidate to solve this enigma. They watched Connor lying on his stomach, inching toward Joshua's body. He was strapped into a rope and harness and secured to iron rods that had been pounded deep into the ice.

Mika swallowed bile. His stomach clenched. He took a deep, anxious breath. *Freezing hellfires.*

Bryan shook his head, then crossed his arms and spread his legs wide. All the men in the group appeared to be aware of the risk. No one made a move. When Connor reached Joshua's body, he carefully threw a rope cowboy-style over Joshua's head, securing it around his torso. All the slow-motion and carefulness agitated Mika. *Why is he taking so long? It's dangerous. I've had enough of this for one day.*

"Please hurry and take care. My nerves can't take it," Mika begged quietly under his breath. Grinding his teeth, he watched Connor taking photographs and gathering evidence thoroughly as if it were for bloody National Geographic.

"Joshua had been trapped between the sliding ice sheets," Bryan explained. "Connor could not identify the exact time of death. Once an autopsy is done, they should be able to provide a reasonable estimate. But the big question is, what was Joshua doing out here in the middle of nowhere on the ice? I'm also wondering what Brad saw. He should be able to give us more answers. I spoke to Peter a few minutes ago, and he told me he's working on reviving Brad," Bryan said.

"Yes, it's just watching and waiting for the next six to eight hours," Mika answered while looking at Connor knee-walking and taking more pictures of Joshua and the surrounding area. The foul odor of death and shredded intestines hung in the air. It worsened when the wind blew their way.

"Connor seems to notice something in the distance. Look how smart your man is. He's pretending to snap additional body shots while holding his camera at an angle. I hope he zooms into the frame for a better opportunity to observe the backdrop when we download the images," Bryan said.

Connor looked back at them and waved. Mika waved in a beckoning motion with his pointer finger and thumb. "Yes, gille-toine, stop waving. I'm anxious. Hurry and get your leprechaun ass out of there," Mika mumbled, his mood worsening by the second. He raised his arm and tapped his wristwatch, signaling that it was time to return. Connor raised his arm, indicating that he needed five more minutes, and pointed to Joshua, demonstrating his plan with push and pull motions. Mika felt like stomping his feet, walking over there, and dragging Connor by the ear away from the danger.

*At any moment, the ice can open again, swallowing you and Joshua.*

Kneeling, Connor pushed and tugged at Joshua, trying to loosen him and free him from the ice. He poured what appeared to be salt, warm water, or oil around him into the crack. A crowd gathered around Mika and Bryan, watching the spectacle of Connor, who groaned, slipped, and then cursed loudly in an Irish brogue with each effort. Connor's head vanished for a moment, causing Mika to take another anxiety-filled breath.

"What are you doing? Come back, leave the dead man. I'm sure Joshua's going nowhere," Mika ordered. His patience was at an end, and he was seconds away from grabbing the rope and pulling Connor back to him. The day had been too long, and Mika wasn't amused at all.

"Joshua might have a trapped ankle or leg," Connor shouted.

"Come back, leave him!" Mika yelled as he grabbed the safety rope. "I'll pull you back if you don't return right now. I've had enough for today!"

Connor signaled for one minute.

"Freezing hellfires!" Mika stomped his feet in frustration. They watched as Connor knelt, pushing his arms down between Joshua and the ice, clearly trying to loosen the corpse. Then his head snapped back, and Mika froze; all the men heard the dull sound of a long, slow-releasing fart. The air practically vibrated as it escaped into the night. Connor sprang back, arms spread wide, landing on his back.

More profane curses drifted from his direction, accompanied by the unmistakable smell of ruptured intestines. Connor, who had never tolerated foul odors, experienced an unforgettable, self-inflicted reflexive dry-heaving attack.

"Mother of hell!" More cursing soared on the wind toward Mika and the crew, who were watching Connor on his knees. Sounds ebbed and flowed toward them—*blargh, blargh*—followed by the distinct stench of excrement.

Fortunately, Connor's stomach must have been empty since he only expelled a few drops of coffee and bile. But he was never a quitter, so he tackled Joshua's stuck body with renewed determination. Vigorously twisting the deflating torso. Back and forth like an old mailbox stuck in the ground.

"It looks like Connor's dancing with a tiny Joshua," someone said in the back.

"Canoodling with corpses now. That's just sick." Bryan giggled like a ten-year-old approaching puberty. Mika wanted to pound his face in. But Joshua wasn't budging. He was going nowhere. Connor must have realized it. He leaned back to catch his breath. Then, without thinking, he accidentally rubbed his hands through his face and hair.

"You idiot!" Mika yelled, unable to ignore the silly banter from the nosebleeds. He couldn't help it. He laughed.

*Blargh, blargh.* Connor fell back to his hands and knees as more, *blargh, blargh,* drifted back to Mika and the crowd.

"What a drama queen?" someone said.

Mika didn't take his eyes off Connor. *I hope they pissed themselves laughing. Bloody wankers.*

Finally, Connor seemed he had enough of it all. He signaled to be extracted, waving his hand in a circle over his head repeatedly and very fast.

"Okay, let's get Connor out of there!" Bryan called it. The laughter died down, and they sprang into action. Connor lay back onto the ice, apparently tired of playing cowboy for the day.

"You stupid leprechaun," Mika exclaimed, bending to help Connor from the ground.

"You stink!" Bryan teased and doubled over again.

"Piss off, Bryan." Connor struggled frantically to remove his harness. Mika swallowed his laughter and bent to help Connor out of it.

"You and your team need to remove Joshua. I've gathered enough evidence. You can take him to Rick's lab for the autopsy. I'm going to take a shower!" Connor said, very frustrated. "By the way"—he raised his index finger—"it looks like the crack has shifted and widened another five inches, so be careful...this area is quite unstable."

"Go ahead! Laugh at me." Connor scoffed, lifting his knees high, forging a path through the banks of snow, muttering to himself.

Mika reconsidered reprimanding his husband, biting his lip. "No, my love, it's not funny. I was worried about you. Oh, and I forgot to tell you, you're in charge of Phoenix for the next twenty-four hours." He chuckled from behind Connor as he followed at a safe distance, avoiding the horrendous smell.

"Come walk this side where the snow blowers have cleaned a path already. You're going to fall into a hole. Then we have to save you. Please, Connor." Mika's heart rate spiked thinking of that scenario.

"I bloody know!" Connor shouted as he veered left toward the path about twenty meters from Mika. Men, primarily soldiers, jumped out of the way when they saw Connor, who seemed to be on the warpath.

The pair returned to their apartment, where Connor began undressing even before fully entering the front door. He kicked his pants aside and hopped a little on one leg to remove one sock, then the other. Mika stood to the side, leaning against the foyer wall with his arms folded and his left leg crossed over the other, admiring the angry Irishman's backside.

"I don't think the smell will wash out of the suit." Connor gagged, and Mika wondered if he was dry-heaving as he disappeared around the corner into the shower. "Ahhh, thank the stars for hot, clean water," Connor said, then sighed in appreciation. Mika stuck his head into the bathroom. He had a bag filled with Connor's snowsuit and clothes in his hand.

"I'm taking your clothes and boots down to housekeeping, and then I have to go help Peter and Rick with Brad. Do you want to come and watch?" Mika asked, enjoying watching his husband's silhouette through the fogged-up glass as Connor scrubbed himself vigorously.

"Maybe later. Do you know where the boys are?"

"Nope, I think they could be with the McCormick boys. Rick said something about asking them."

"Oh, that's good. I was worried about them. Something weird was going on, and although it looked like Joshua was killed because of a natural accident, I thought I saw someone watching me earlier tonight," Connor said, rinsing himself and applying shampoo and conditioner to his hair for a second time.

Mika's longing for his husband stirred. He coughed and cleared his throat. "Maybe I should help you scrub your back?" He bent to put the bag down.

"Don't you dare, Mika. I'm in a hurry. I need to download and enlarge those pictures I took. Something feels off here. I think the people watching us are from another place. Maybe they're Doomsday survivors. I've no idea where they've been all this time, but Joshua knew, so I need to get to his apartment as soon as possible. Perhaps I can find some clues about the man and what he knew there."

"Yes, you are correct. At first, I thought we were under attack, but I also sensed that we were being observed from a distance. It's good we're on high alert."

Connor closed the taps, opened the shower door, grabbed a towel, and dried himself. Mika continued, appreciating the body he knew so well.

"No, Mika, maybe later," Connor said—again.

Mika rolled his eyes. "I can control my urges when I have to," he drawled, but he knew the hunger in his eyes said differently. Connor continued drying himself. Climbing out of the shower, he bent forward, teasing Mika.

"I'm only admiring what is mine, anyway." Mika focused on his narrow waist and well-defined calf muscles, then smiled seductively at Connor. "I would love to lick the water…"

Connor turned, towel-drying his hair. He raised his elbows, showing off his abs and the sharp line of his hip to Mika.

Mika watched his husband, eyes fixed on him, and licked his lips. Connor, teasingly, turned to brush his teeth. Mika went to the bedroom and sat on the bed, waiting. Soon, the comforting sounds of Connor's post-shower routine drifted from the bathroom. The gargling and spitting, and the uniquely loud toot of a nose-blow that always made Mika smile. The toilet flush made his heart race.

*Like a lab rat detecting cheese.*

Connor emerged naked, ever proud, from around the corner. Prancing past Mika like a doped-up runway model, eyes hooded and full of confidence, straight to the underwear drawer. He hummed an unidentified tune while choosing a pair of socks and his favorite tight-fitting briefs. He turned dramatically to put on his underwear.

"You might as well take them off again. I've changed my mind. I have to have you," Mika said, as his body reacted to his husband.

"You might as well take them off again. I changed my mind. I have to have you. I need you," Mika said, feeling feral with the need to have life-affirming sex. Connor smiled slyly and slowly pushed them down again.

"God, I love that ass of yours. Those perfectly sculpted cheeks were made for me to fuck you long and hard. I need to bury my cock deep inside you. Come here and bend over for me," Mika ordered, but Connor harrumphed, making a big show of slowly turning around. Instead of bending forward and grabbing his ankles, he walked seductively past Mika. Keeping his gaze fixed on Mika, he opened the bedside drawer, located the lube, and passed it over. He slammed the drawer shut with a flourish, strode past Mika to the foot of the bed, turned, and with a dancer's poise, bent forward to present his pink hole. Instantly, Mika was on his feet, kicking off his slippers haphazardly as he moved to position himself behind Connor.

"You know I fucking love it when you tease and play cat and mouse games," Mika said huskily. He then switched to an Irish accent, mimicking Connor. "No, Mika. Not now, Mika. I don't have time, Mika." Back in his own voice, he finished, "And all I hear is, please, Mika, fuck me senseless, use me anyway you see fit, Mika, come conquer me, and plow me." Grabbing the perfect glutes he loved to spread, Mika exposed Connor's hole and salivated.

Connor glanced back, eyes burning with desire, and their eyes met. The room went utterly silent. He knows exactly what I'm going to do to him, Mika thought, stepping forward, gently nudging the backs of his husband's knees so they buckled slightly. Connor understood the unspoken invitation, sliding his hands down his thighs as he lowered himself onto the bed, opening his legs wide. He moaned, grinding himself against the mattress, seeking relief from the ache.

"You're such a tease," Mika murmured, shedding just enough clothing, his pants and underwear discarded while keeping his button-up shirt on. His cock swung heavily, its impressive size and weight preventing it from springing to attention. Connor grabbed a pillow and tossed it behind him. Mika caught it and slid it beneath Connor's lower stomach, tilting his hips up for easier reach. Mika knelt down, settling back on his heels. Connor's breath came in short bursts, awaiting the feel of a warm tongue. Mika savored the moment, drawing it out. He dotted tiny beads of saliva onto the creased skin surrounding the rose-pink opening before him, then licked it in languid, broad circles, avoiding the center. "Hm, damn, you taste delicious," Mika breathed between his ministrations.

"Mika, fuck, are you trying to kill me?" Connor gasped, breath heavy like a dog's on the Miami boardwalk. Mika felt slight tremors in his husband's hairy, muscular thighs. He responded with gentle licks, a quick flick of his tongue, teasing Connor's taint with lightning-fast touches. Mika had perfected this particular torment and knew it drove his husband wild when he lingered between his hole and his balls.

"Mika, for fuck's sake, we don't have time for this. Uhmmm—"

Mika silenced him, taking both of Connor's testicles into his mouth, one after the other. He teased them in his warm mouth, wetting them thoroughly before stretching Connor's scrotum with his lips. He repeated this pleasurable torment twice more, then released them, letting them slip out one by one.

Connor shamelessly rutted into the pillow below him. "Hold still, or I'll stop," Mika lied. He had no intention of stopping. Connor held still but protested with pathetic whining sounds, which made Mika so hard he had to squeeze his cock a few times for relief. He proceeded with his lazy assaults on Connor's backside by licking a path excruciatingly slow from his balls upwards.

Mika, pleased with the slick trail he'd left, gently blew air over Connor's sensitive spot. Connor shook his head, his moans and frustrated Irish curses muffled by the bedding he'd pulled around his head. After each, "Ah, fuck, yes," he'd grab more bedding, muttering obscenities—proof he was losing it. "Ah, yes, don't fucking stop," he blubbered.

Mika knew the Irishman was leaking pre-cum, and he wanted a taste of it as much as he tried to drive Connor over the precipice of lustful insanity. He got up, removed the shirt, and slid his hand underneath Connor's hip to grab hold of his five-inch diameter beer-can dick. When he had a comfortable grip, he laid his rigid member against Connor's crack without entering him, enjoying the pressure while he knew Connor loved the overpowering domination.

"Fuck my hand. I want to taste you," Mika ordered while he bit down on his upper back. Connor immediately pumped, eagerly obeying Mika. "Ahh, feel how wet you are for me. That's enough. Lift for me, gille-toine." Mika milked every drop he could get until the palm of his hand was slick. Pulling his hand out, he licked Connor's sweet natural lubrication.

"You taste so motherfucking good, gille-toine. Do you want a taste?" Connor moaned the affirmative drunkenly at Mika's filthy seduction. Mika dug between their bodies. Milking his cock and mixing their essence. Then offered a lick to Connor.

"Hmmm, that's it. Taste how exquisite we taste together." Connor lapped at Mika's hand as if it were the last drop of Mika's pre-cum in the universe. Mika lifted his big, hulking body from Connor and then went back to work eating ass. Minutes later, after stretching and much more prostate stimulation, Connor pleaded, begged, and cried for Mika's cock.

Mika was dizzy with arousal. "What a fucking pair we make. I'm so worked up I can't open the bottle of lube." Half blind with lust, he fumbled with the strawberry-mint-flavored glycerin lubrication. Connor laughed into his cocoon of bedsheets. "We'll see who laughs last, my little leprechaun." Mika frantically lubed Connor's hole, grabbed his ten-inch pole at the base, and inserted the head into Connor's well-stretched hole. "Ah, fuck yes, I love this best," Mika said and plunged into his idea of heaven.

"Hmmm, feed me that monster cock of yours, yelda. I need to feel the burn. Fuck me good, please, husband. I need to forget the ugly things from earlier today."

Mika ignored his plea. Rocking back and forth as if he had all the time in the world. Feeding Connor his cock inch by inch, knowing it was frustratingly slow.

"Oh, no, my fucking god! Mika, I'm ready. I want to feel your balls hitting mine," Connor muttered. Mika grabbed Connor's hips and increased the speed. His rhythmic, sensual pistoning rubbed Connor's prostate. "Yes, that's it, yelda, god, that feels so fucking good." The volume of their grunts and moans increased and filled the room with sounds of their carnal pleasures.

"Fuck, I love fucking you. You feel so good around my cock. Just look at you taking all of me." Mika pulled out and watched himself being eaten by Connor's hungry hole repeatedly. "Jesus, I can do this the whole day, watching my cock disappear up your ass."

"Mika, please go faster. You can look at your cock another day," Connor begged. "Please, I need to be fucked into oblivion."

"Grab your cock, gille-toine," Mika commanded as he pulled back and straightened his legs so Connor could lift his hips, creating space so Connor could fist himself.

"Oh, and one more thing, earlier when I asked you to stop and come back to me, then you do so..." Mika folded his hand over Connor's fist and squeezed, simultaneously slowing and prolonging the torture. "I love you, Connor, too bloody much. You made me an older man today. I am worried so much about you. You're so stupidly brave. It scares me because I would rather have you alive than you trying to recover dead and frozen bodies," Mika whispered with a throaty groan into Connor's neck while his eyes rolled backward in pleasure.

"Yes, yes, okay, I will, I promise, that's it," Connor cried out in ecstasy.

Mika enjoyed each deep thrust of his hips and the closeness it created with Connor. Kissing and sucking his neck and upper back, he spoke his words of truth between each rhythmic movement. "I will not..." kiss, thrust, "be able to..." kiss, lick, thrust, "live without you." Kiss, lick, thrust. Finally, Mika let go of Connor's hand, leaving him to fuck himself.

"Hold on, my love. I'm going to give it to you now."

"Oh, yes, Mika, please! I'm sorry I made you worry about me. I love you, yelda."

Mika gripped Connor's firm, muscled hips, losing himself in the intense euphoria as he went wild on Connor's ass, a mix of playful punishment and deep affection.

"Yes, that's it, fuck me good, fuck me long, yes, yes, and hard, my yelda." Connor barely made sense. Sweat dripped in rivulets down Mika's temples, down his forehead, and into his eyes. He squinted, the salt burning his eyes, but he never let go of Connor's hips or slowed down, heaving like a sex-crazed gorilla, grunting in animalistic calls to the wild.

"Fuck, yes, you won't be able to sit for a week. You sexy hero of a man," he shouted.

"Oh, yes, baby, I'm going to come!"

Mika's orgasm exploded into Connor's guts just as Connor orgasmed, clamping his dick so tightly that Mika thought it was being amputated. Connor's prolonged orgasm was unending. Quiet mini convulsions milked every drop from Mika. He fell forward, sated and out of breath, onto Connor's back. They lay in that position, sweating and catching their breath together.

"Thank you, I needed that. I love you so bloody much," Connor whispered.

"I love you, too," Mika said, too weak and lazy to move. They passed out together, falling asleep for a few minutes.

Mika woke up and extracted himself slowly from Connor. Getting to his feet, he tenderly pulled Connor from the bed.

"Come on, we should probably shower. A rag isn't going to cut it this time."

Connor agreed, pointing to the cum running down his thighs. He stumbled after Mika without a word.

After a quick shower together, they got dressed. Mika leaned over and audibly sniffed Connor teasingly. Connor looked up and laughed. Warming Mika's insides. He could tell Connor was relaxed and ready for whatever was coming their way tonight.

"Are you done?" Connor asked.

"Yes, you passed the sniffing test," Mika said. Leaning in closer, he kissed Connor deeply and pretended to pull Connor back to the bed.

Connor pushed him back playfully. "Both of us must stay at least six feet from each other. We won't get anything done, and we might never leave the apartment."

"I know. It's all your fault. You seduced me. I'm weak in your presence." Mika changed the bed linen, adding the dirty pile to the bag of clothes, while Connor disappeared into the kitchen. *Probably making a big cup of coffee for both of us.*

A few minutes later, Mika stood in the kitchen doorway, ready to go. "I love you, gille-toine."

Connor handed him his coffee and replied, "I love you, too, yelda." Their fingers touched a little longer than necessary, and his deep blue eyes crinkled at the corners. They knew their time together had run out. They needed to get back to work.

Mika grabbed the bag of soiled linen. "I'll take this to the washers, and I'll let you know what's happening with Brad." He kissed Connor's cheek.

"Okay, talk to you later," Connor said, grabbing his pager, camera, and evidence bag in a hurry. He dashed out of the apartment to upload and analyze the evidence back at his office.

*BANG!*

"Bloody hell, Mika, warn me next time. Will you please stop doing that? If I have a heart attack, it's your fault!" Peter exclaimed. Mika gave Peter a teasing smile.

Peter punched numbers into his computer and then, with a well-practiced move, pushed himself away from the desk, wheeling from one side of the desk back to a monitor screen to decipher the results of Brad's thawing process. "Things are progressing slowly, as expected, just what I'd hoped for, not much intra- or extracellular edema noted, but something's amiss."

"Hmm, show me," Mika said while adjusting the screen of the neutron scanner to accommodate his almost two-meter height.

"What happened outside?" Peter asked.

"Not much. Connor's looking at some evidence. We suspect someone's watching us. Connor took some long-distance pictures, and Bryan has the valley encircled and is in the process of apprehending the culprits. We could all feel their presence, but...hmm, oh yes, Connor had a minor incident while trying to move the body..."

"A body? What body?" Peter asked loudly.

"Joshua Adams's."

"Joshua?" Peter asked and flung himself around, turning back to his machines. "I'm rechecking the electroencephalogram and measuring Brad's brain activity...So, Joshua's dead. That's not good. What had happened?"

"Don't know."

"Hmmm...Mika, come look here and tell me what you see. I've been thinking maybe the EEG was faulty, picking up on Rick's movements." Peter smiled. "There were some erotic movements. I just turned the two-way mirror off," Peter said, blushing red and smiling like the Cheshire cat.

"Oh! Oooh, that's why it's blacked out. I thought maybe Rick got up naked and went to use the washroom or something," Mika said, his eyes wide with interest, stretching his neck to see inside, but with no success.

"Well, it's his husband. What he does to or with him is their business, so I blacked out my view."

"That's polite of you. I would have watched," Mika said, because he would have.

"I can monitor other, more important things like these weird EEG readings. That's why I said I thought it's because of movements."

"Let me see. Are these Beta and Gamma waves? Are you sure about this? Maybe the EEG pads are working incorrectly?"

Peter hit a few buttons. Then he compared his first readings and the most recent ones. "See, I was just comparing them when you entered. With or without movement, the readings stayed the same." He grabbed a pen to use as a pointer. "Look here. Rick was awake and talking to Brad. Here, Rick fell asleep, and I didn't go into the room, but movements on the EEG showed brain activity."

Mika looked up, eyebrows drawn together and a big frown on his forehead.

"Interesting stuff. What can it be?" Peter asked.

"*Ty che, blyad*?" Both beamed at each other. "What, indeed," Mika said deep in thought.

"Brad's core temperature is now thirty-four degrees Celsius. I'll administer the last round of meds, and then we can begin CPR."

Mika didn't respond. He continued studying the results as Peter left the observation room. His thick Russian accent had disappeared by ninety-nine percent over the past twenty-one years. The one percent remaining was for Russian swear words—and Mika loved cursing, especially while making love to his husband.

His silky, blond, shoulder-length hair cascaded over the black stubble on his face as he entered a slew of figures into the computer, his long, slim fingers racing over the keyboard. He grabbed and twisted his hair into a bun, a routine he followed to help him focus better. First, his hair irritated him, and second, he needed to see better.

Improved vision sharpened his thoughts, he mused, as he deciphered the EEG results. He drummed his fingers, stared blankly, then comprehension dawned. "Bloody hell!" he exclaimed, rushing for the resuscitation equipment. "Brad's been conscious the whole time! He was using Morse code."

CHAPTER 5

# LET'S GET YOUR BLOOD MOVING

*"Good morning, citizens of Phoenix.*

*Lasitor, here. It's now six a.m.*

*Did you know a person is constipated if their bowel movements result in the passage of small amounts of hard, dry stool, usually fewer than three times per week? But did you also know that saying someone is constipated could mean that person may speak nonsense or falsehoods?*

*Visit your community news page to search for answers before speaking about falsehoods.*

*You can also search for home remedies like which foods to eat to prevent dry and hard stools.*

*Breakfast is served until eight a.m.*

*Hope you have a blockage-free day!"*


## DR. RICK LONGARROW-MCCORMICK


RICK HAD FALLEN ASLEEP CURLED up around his husband's back. The walk-in temperature-controlled decompression room was eerily quiet, except for the soft zinging noises coming from the air outlets of the thawing chamber. At first, Rick's teeth couldn't stop chattering, but as their bodies reached the same temperature, he relaxed and could speak to Brad.

He'd told him how much he loved him, how much he and the boys would miss him if he moved on, and that they would walk together once more, even if that happened. Rick told Brad about things he thought he'd forgotten, but once he started talking into the back of Brad's neck, he got carried away by the cathartic moment, telling Brad about anything that crossed his mind. Memories about growing up on the reservation. From being about four years of age, he recounted anything, no matter how silly. For instance, when he went fishing at the age of seven with his friends, they caught a sturgeon fish so big that one boy had to run home to call an adult for help, or risk losing the stolen fishing rod.

"Yes"—he juddered—"and then my father came." Rick snorted. "He helped us reel it in, but afterward, he told us to line up and drop our trousers for a spanking," Rick said, enjoying the vivid memory of the scowl on his father's face, as if he were in front of him.

"First, we stole. Second, we went fishing at a sacred, protected spot." Rick felt giddy with silliness, and he couldn't finish the last words. "We weren't allowed, but you know how kids are. Tell them not to do something, and they do the opposite. We caught my grandfather, the reincarnated chief who blessed the water and drowned himself to protect the lands..." Rick coughed, and more giggles escaped. "Father had to remove the fishhook and let it go 'cause the old man was a bastard, so no land of ever summers for him. They left him in the lake to live forever as a sturgeon fish." Rick laughed, but it brought the moment back to all seriousness with his internal debate about whether he should remove his Peter Pan Capsule if Brad were to die. He continued speaking, laying his heart out to his husband, the man who meant everything to him and to so many others in Phoenix who loved their charismatic leader dearly.

Before he fell asleep, Peter delivered more messages from citizens lining up in front of the lab, snaking down the hallway to convey messages of hope and love, as well as get-well-soons. Peter reported that now and then, someone's head would pop in, asking how Brad was or leaving notes and pictures the children had drawn for him. In his melancholy, he'd drifted off to sleep while holding onto Brad as tightly as possible. It was a selfish attempt to keep his soul on this plane, preventing him from moving on to the spiritual world and leaving him and their boys behind. Later, when Rick had awakened from a peaceful, dreamless sleep, Brad felt considerably warmer.

"Hmmm, I love the feeling of you." Rick moaned. He moved his hands over Brad's athletic physique, feeling every curve of muscle he loved in his husband's body. "Let's get your blood moving," he whispered.

He hoped Peter didn't notice because this was wrong on so many levels. "Dammit, you feel so good, and I miss you." He huffed into the back of Brad's hairline, enjoying the lingering smell of his favorite cologne. The overwhelming feeling of being with Brad, of making love to him, even if it was for the last time, left him dithering between what felt so good and how wrong this was.

Sucking a deep breath through semi-closed lips, he blew it out as slowly as possible. Then he repeated the mindfulness exercise ten times. After that, he concentrated on calming his libido and forced his heart rate to return to normal.

Tears spilled from Rick's eyes. "Baby, I can't stop loving you. I can't live without you." He was desperate for Brad to wake up. This was the side of Rick that no one knew. He was a resigned professional who did very well keeping his home and work life separate.

"It's hot." He squeezed his eyes so tightly he saw cobwebs and floaters in his field of vision. *This beats a hot yoga session.* Sweat beaded on his forehead, and he felt uncomfortable. His damp hair urged him to move away from the slippery wetness between their bodies. The result of spooning under yellow and blue airplane duck feather bedding for over six hours inside what now felt like a sauna to him.

"No, this is too much. First, you freeze yourself to death, and now we die from heat exhaustion." With one smooth movement, he threw all the comforters onto the floor.

"Ahh, now I can breathe again." *It's so hot in here. Peter is cooking for us.* He chuckled at his dramatic antics, then threw his arm back over Brad with a thud.

Overwhelming emotions of despair threatened to overtake his perfect self-control, but he swallowed them down to stay strong and believed Brad would return to them.

"Please, please, please, Brad, come back to me. Wake up, dammit!"

Rick lay waiting. Minutes later, just as he thought to call Peter, he felt Brad's muscles contract. "Umm," Brad moaned like a bear waking up from hibernation. His entire body stiffened beneath Rick. *It's a sign that his body and mind are waking.* Rick leaned backward for a better look.

"Thank the gods you're awake!"

Brad moved and attempted to open his eyelids. Rick peppered every surface, his face, eyes, lips, forehead, and cheeks with more kisses. Brad growled into Rick's mouth. Rick sucked his cold tongue into his mouth, defrosting it.

Brad opened his eyes wide. "Hmmm." He sighed.

"My husband is awake! I love you, I love you, I love you!"

Rick looked at Brad, loving the sight of his open eyes reflecting the dimmed overhead lights. For a few seconds, Brad seemed disoriented, as if he didn't understand Rick. But then he smiled. His facial expressions softened, and their minds touched that familiar way they did when they made love without words. At that moment, Rick knew Brad said he loved him, and then Rick saw the want. *He needs me more than he could say.*

"I love you so bloody much, Gen. McCormick. I'd better get up. They'll be here any moment."

"I need water. I'm so thirsty..." Brad sounded like he trekked through a desert.

Just as Rick wanted to call for help, Peter opened the door unannounced. He snuck inside, then fussed and fidgeted in the dark. "It's time. He's ready to be revived," he whispered and turned on the bright overhead light. Rick straightened up. Peter froze and frowned, holding a stainless-steel kidney tray with three preloaded injections.

Before Peter could say anything, Mika burst into the chamber, smashing the sliding door to the side. "He's alive," he exclaimed and slammed the light switches with the palms of his hands. All the overhead lights shone with maximum illumination. Rick jumped to grab bedding to cover himself up.

Yellow and blue airplane duvet covers lay strewn over the floor, and the one covering

Brad hung askew. Mika's and Peter's eyes were wide as they read the scene in front of them. Brad's covering slipped to the floor, revealing that Brad was definitely awake.

Mika had a stethoscope around his neck. Dumbfounded, he smelled the air and paused, seeming to take a second to think. "Okay, I'm a few minutes too late to check for Brad's chest sounds. Welcome back, comrade. I received your Morse code, a little too late," Mika said and threw the duvet back over a smiling Brad. Rick got dressed and helped Brad into white pajama pants and slippers.

"I was worried you would give Brad a precordial thump, as you did with Connor years ago, bringing the Irishman back from the dead." Rick laughed.

Mika handed Rick the stethoscope. "Yes, and Mika has a loving husband because of precordial thumping," Mika answered, reverting to Russian.

Rick's eyes glistened with tears as he listened to Brad's left and right chest sounds. The buzzing of the overhead lights was deafening in the quiet room. Mika waited with a big smile as Rick finished his assessment. "Thank you, I don't hear any abnormal lung or heart sounds." Rick nodded while removing the stethoscope from his ears. Then he followed the gazes down to the source of their astonished looks and radiant smiles, enamored with their leader, who lay with his eyes open and a grin on his face.

"You lucky son of a bitch," Mika exclaimed, offering his big hand to shake it.

Brad spoke with a soft raspy voice, grinning at Rick. "Hello, doctor," he greeted Rick with an all-knowing smirk, and those friendly chocolate brown eyes were the most beautiful orbs Rick had ever seen. He fell onto him, hugging and kissing him all over his face.

"You were awake. You knew I was feeling you up and speaking to you!"

Brad nodded with a mischievous look.

Peter stood to the side, staring at Brad, smirking like a happy Victor Frankenstein.

"Thank you, Peter." Brad coughed; his voice sounded like it had been put through a cheese grater. "Your concoctions saved me. I was never really gone. It was an experience. Mika, you're too late with the Morse code I sent you. Help me up, please. I'm parched." Brad struggled to get up, rolling to the side of the bed. Peter and Rick jumped to help, pushing him into a sitting position and swinging his legs from the bed.

"It's probably your cry for help that has your throat raw," Rick said. He felt guilty for riding him, noticing Brad move like an old man. "Oops, don't fall." Rick grabbed his arm to stabilize him. His eyes couldn't hide his surprise. "Your recuperation is unbelievably fast, but try to take it slow, my love."

"I'm a little lightheaded," Brad said, almost toppling over.

*I'm so selfish.* "I never thought you were in pain. Did I hurt you?" Rick asked, and Mika and Peter snorted in the background.

"No, of course not. I wanted it."

"We should monitor your blood pressure," Rick said.

"Yes-yes." Peter jumped to get the machine from the emergency cart Mika had brought in.

"Here, let me." Rick took the apparatus from Peter. While the machine took Brad's blood pressure, he offered his husband a glass of synthetic orange juice.

Mika walked over to the pager on the wall, pushed a few buttons, and waited for Connor to respond. "Connor. This better be good news!" Their second-in-command answered loudly with a thick Irish accent over the speaker.

"Good news. Brad's awake, gille-toine. Please let the men know. They must all be distraught and also be waiting for good news."

"Bleeding bloody hell, thank you!" Connor exclaimed. "Okay, I'll be down shortly." Static and a few clicks came over the speaker system before it went silent.

"What's that awful smell?" Brad asked in a barely perceptible voice.

"It's me and my boots, comrade. A lot has happened while you were playing spoons with your husband."

Rick climbed onto the bed with Brad, lying sideways, with his head on Brad's lap, and he stared upward like a lovelorn schoolboy. He didn't care about professional propriety. He was only thankful and most probably the luckiest person on Earth.

"Rick, love, could you help me to the washroom? I want to freshen up and be ready for Connor's inquisition." Brad groaned, rolling Rick over with an effort. "I don't want to hurt your feelings, but I feel a bit suffocated, and I've had enough of that for a very long time."

"Okay, that's our cue, everyone, out! Rick, down the hallway and to the right is the Lab's shower and changing room. Help yourselves to towels and scrubs and enjoy a long, hot shower." Peter turned, pushing Mika outside. "Let's go to our office and let these two get up and get ready."

"I thought they were ready already," Mika's voice was loud as he teased, looking back over his shoulder. His laughter traveled up the hallway as they disappeared into the same office that saved their lives twenty-one years ago. Connor, Mika, Peter, and the newborn twins had escaped the giant tsunami by locking themselves inside the water-tight temperature-controlled environment that served as Peter's office.

Rick reluctantly got up, helping Brad by clasping his arms. He felt infatuated with his husband, so proud of him. So thankful. He wanted to rush home and lock them away from everyone, keeping them for himself for just one day.

"So, you like to sodomize dead people," Brad teased, whispering.

"I'm so glad you're okay. This goes against my medical knowledge and beliefs, but having you back, either by a miracle or Peter's advanced research, it doesn't matter. The boys don't even know about any of this. I think they're with the Romanov twins. I didn't want to scare them. My only thought was to stay positive and give Peter a chance to do his thing. The capsule you dug out of your pectoral and then chewed was probably what saved you." Rick had Brad's arm slung over his shoulder to support him.

"I was never gone, my mind, or maybe it's my soul. I don't know, but I could hear everything."

"Everything?" Rick asked as they hobbled to the washroom. He stopped, staring into those beautiful, dark chocolate-colored eyes with the friendly crinkles at the corners.

"Yes, everything." Brad rubbed the back of Rick's head, a comforting feeling he now appreciated more than ever.

"I loved every word and every calm action. Your lovemaking gave me direction on where to go to find you. I floated inside black darkness, and your words were like tiny sparks calling to me. The closer I drifted, the brighter and bigger they shone. If it wasn't for you, I don't know if I would've found which way was home," Brad explained, shuffling one slipper in front of the other.

"Also, I heard your Apache song for me. Thank you…And I think an angel sat with me." Brad looked into Rick's eyes, not blinking.

"I love you. You must tell me more about the angel." Rick wanted him to know that he could tell him anything. He would always listen and support him.

"Love you, too. Later, I'll tell you. Let's get me into a shower, please." Brad leaned in and kissed Rick.

After he'd helped Brad get dressed, Rick left Brad in the lab with Peter and Mika and stormed to their home.

He called for Donali and Kawa throughout the spacious executive apartment. Feeling increasingly anxious and trying to remain as calm as possible, he switched on all the lights. The quiet darkness confirmed they weren't there. His heart rate sped up. Blood pulsations rushed audibly through his ears, accompanied by the unwelcome sensation of nausea and light-headedness. Something was terribly wrong!

With his back against the steel wall, he slid down to the floor, taking a few deep breaths until the black and white spots in front of his field of vision disappeared. Feeling better, he got up slowly. Although it was futile, he opened up all the bedroom doors, checking every nook and cranny, hoping to find a note with a message at least.

After finding sweet blue bugger all, he went to the Romanov apartment, and his feelings of dread and terror increased—no one answered.

That horrible feeling a parent experiences when losing their child intensified as he stared blankly at the key card in his hands, wondering where to start searching next.

*Where could they be?*

Then, realizing Phoenix was too big to run around and search for the boys, he paged them on the general population overhead com system.

# CHAPTER 6

# CODE RED

*"Good morning, citizens of Phoenix.*

*It's now six a.m.*

*Maybe some of you already know that Jupiter is the biggest planet of them all and that it's more than twice as massive as all the other planets combined in our solar system.*

*Also, if Earth were the size of a grape, Jupiter would be the size of a giant watermelon. And did you also know that seeds and paintings of the watermelon were found in King Tutankhamun's tomb as a gift for his long journey to the afterlife? This means that watermelons have been cultivated for thousands of years. Visit our community news page for more fun facts about watermelons.*

*Breakfast is served until eight a.m.*

*Hope you have a fruitful day!"*


## GENERAL BRAD MCCORMICK


Brad felt surprisingly warm and comfortable dressed in white scrubs, instead of his usual military uniform and boots. Wearing Mika's comfy rubber medical slip-ons, which he kept as an extra pair in his and Peter's lab, Brad squeaked-squeaked alongside Mika, escorting Brad from the Cryonics lab down the cold corridors connecting the domes that lay like lit-up ping-pong balls against the Trans-Antarctic Mountain Range.

The plan was to meet up for the evidence presentation and discuss the best next steps. The Command Center was their leadership hub, situated on the top floor of the gigantic Communications Dome. It was located in the center of the massive complex. A good comparison would be the head of an octopus, with its many tentacles serving as translucent passageways to the various plexiglass pods within the city's domed structures. Doorways from eight of the forty sides of the centralized Communication Dome connected the next ring of smaller domes, which were still large enough to fit several football fields in each. For example, the Agricultural, Research, Athletics, Medical,

University, Transportation, and Housing domed sections. From there, it connected to smaller pods and so on.

They preferred using the colder, less-used hallways and stairs to avoid the crowds. The general Phoenix population almost never used these backway escape and service routes, because they were unheated and darker than the main hallways, preserving heat and energy. Thus, a small discomfort for Brad and his team of leaders and service people who wished to move around unhindered by inquisitive and talkative citizens.

Rick went to search for their younger boys, while Brad needed to get to the office to attend to messages, reports, and announcements. Their sons, Donali and Kawa, weren't answering their pings. They've met up with Connor halfway to the leadership office. He was happy to see that Brad was alive and walking, but upon hearing that their boys were also not responding, he handed them an armful of evidence and told them to get started, then went to find Cian and Ivan as well.

The preliminary evidence Connor had collected lay spread out on the new touch-screen prototype table, big enough for ten men to sit comfortably around it. This was one of the latest technologically designed, multi-layered silicone and PVC-coated touch-screen tables featuring a newly designed conductor material. It responded when in contact with another electrical conductor, like bare fingertips, and not elbows or butt cheeks—as reported by Mika and Connor, repeatedly, at Brad and Rick's dinner parties. Mika tapped the table to start it up, but nothing happened. He pushed the button on the side, but still nothing happened.

The overhead lights in the office hummed loudly. Enhancing the uncomfortable, silent pauses as Brad and Mika waited.

Brad's usual string of messages waiting for him to answer was strangely non-existent. He anxiously looked up, searching for answers on the inside of the glass-domed roof covering the mammoth tetracontagon. Usually, it relaxed him. But today he came up empty, with even more questions.

"Must be a fuse or something," Mika said, and he flipped open his husband's electronic notepad, getting to work.

Since there was nothing to look at, Brad couldn't hold himself in check. "I must admit, I feel like a defrosted, spanking new man." Patting his chest a few times, he doubled over, resting his hands on the dead tabletop in front of him. He guffawed, thought better of it, and swallowed his laughs.

"Are you having a seizure? Must I call for the medics?" Mika asked sarcastically.

Brad figured it probably looked like an upright epileptic fit as tears and spittle flew in between small piglet snorts. Gods, his emotions were all over the place. He was medically dead, resurrected, confused, disoriented, aroused, irritated, flabbergasted, scared, and now stupidly silly all in a couple of hours. He was acting out of character.

I just died and came back to life, he thought as he let loose and laughed explosively.

Mika just frowned, shaking his head. Sitting back in his chair, he locked his fingers behind his head and focused on Brad with a questioning look.

"I'm telling you, it's probably Peter's concoctions, and..." Noticing Mika watching him like a hawk, he turned to the big one-way observation window and continued describing his experience while repositioning himself discreetly. "I'm pumped full of drugs, and it bloody feels like red ants are marching inside my balls." He resisted palming himself for relief and rolled his eyes instead, before turning back to Mika. "The precise moment my consciousness returned to my body, I opened my eyes and connected with reality. My metaphysical and physical existence collided and exploded at the precise moment when Rick begged me to open my eyes. Mika, it was as overwhelming as it was welcoming. I was bombarded with sensations, feelings, and emotions...the opposite of where my mind was, where I sent the SOSs from. I didn't think or feel or have a sense of time. I just was, and it felt like I was tethered to Rick somehow. He kept me here like a balloon attached to a string." Brad tried to explain to Mika the best he could. Thoughts of Rick loving him encompassed eternity and floated back and forth through his mind.

*I felt it, and I experienced it. We are two but also one...scattered like stardust, but one like the sun.*

Mika wiped his long, blond hair back over his shoulders. His icy blue eyes had dark circles around them—*he was tired.* "I feel like those fireworks sticks we used to run around with. What were they called?" he scratched his chin. "Sparklers!" he exclaimed. Mika nodded slowly. As he listened, delicate laughing crinkles broke the tired dark circles around his eyes. Brad felt triumphant, noticing they deepened.

*I'm lifting his mood slightly. Good, Mika always attempts to make us feel better with a smile or a joke, so I want to do the same for him.*

So he continued his story animatedly. "I felt like an old *Chevy* motor car. You know, backfiring little ice cubes, icicles, or whatever the new name the kids come up with for the white stuff outside." Mika squashed his lips together, eyes tearing up. He looked like he sucked on a lemon or something.

Brad mentally counted backward, three, two, and one. "Pfft, bahahahaha!" The Russian burst out with a boisterous laugh. Slapping his knee a few times, he seemed to sober himself and swallow his laughs. He sat up, indicating he was zipping his lips. "Sorry, my friend, tell me, I am all attention. Your way of describing your experience is damn refreshing. I just imagined a snowman sounding like a motorcar while farting puffs of snow." Mika rested his chin on his fist, giving Brad his full attention.

*Making you laugh was my full intention.*

"I know, right? It's weird for me, too," Brad said. Wiping his face up and down vigorously with both hands to sober up and clear his mind from the endorphin overload. "Mika, I experienced the most indescribable euphoric sensations, and the weird thing about it all is that they happened all at once. It would feel like being in heaven or when an angel touches you. That's the only way I can describe it. Let's say happiness, peacefulness, and all-encompassing, enveloping love. Plus, I felt radiantly warm from the inside. I don't think it was the amphetamines. Maybe that's what happens when your soul moves on, but I wasn't dying. It's just…something…or someone…" Brad stopped midway, noticing the deep furrows on Mika's forehead return. *He's too pragmatic, he's already doubting my sanity, and I'd better change the subject.*

"But anyhow, first things first." Brad steered away from the visiting angel and how the angel spoke to him.

"What was Joshua Adams doing outside, and who were the men with him?" He changed the focus of his conversation to more important matters, and he knew it was a good idea when he read Mika's body language—sitting up and obviously waiting for him to finish his antics.

"Comrade, I am glad we called an emergency leadership meeting to solve the mystery of the sour-faced Mormon Alderman from Salt Lake City. Nobody seems to have known him. When Connor, Rick, and Bryan arrive, I would like to be ready to solve this problem. Something doesn't add up. It makes me extremely uncomfortable. Call me a control freak, but I think I know all the residents and where they're at all times," Mika said. He looked up at the electronic clock on the wall and then back at the door like he was timing his husband's arrival. "Shit's happening under our noses. I'm expecting a hammer to drop at any moment. You have ants in your balls, and I have ants in my pants," Mika joked.

Brad smirked. He recognized his friend's nervousness in the way he bounced his legs. Mika returned his attention to Connor's notes.

Brad broke the silence. "The residents are moving faster than usual." It looked like a busy shopping mall the day before Christmas. "The bees are busier than usual. You said you ordered a lockdown," he remarked and turned his face upward. Basking in the early morning light that shone through the plexiglass roof.

"The Irish translation is *hede full of beis,* meaning to be preoccupied and agitated. I guess it's the same as maggots in the brains," Mika said.

"Hmmm, I agree with the maggot part. They forget what orders are and take them as opinions or recommendations. Phoenix has turned into a vacation resort," Brad said, verbalizing old feelings of frustration and irritation with non-military residents. Brad was supposed to be in charge of the military personnel, but since Doomsday, he'd taken on the role of General and Commander-in-Chief of the entire Phoenix, having been voted into the position.

Mika was his third in charge, after Connor, and he enjoyed Mika's unusually insightful contributions and observations during their conversations.

"Sometimes I feel ignored and obsolete," he told his friend honestly. He liked how Mika and the leadership team supported and never bored him. However, he guessed that everyone else, except Connor and their boys, bored Mika.

Brad joined Mika, shuffling through the stacks of pictures and evidence.

After a few minutes of looking at pictures of ice, snow, and a dead Joshua, Brad spoke and held his one hand up. "Let's count the facts as we'd gathered them," he said, wiggling his fingers.

"What I know about Joshua Adams is that he was forty-eight years old." Brad wiggled his thumb back and forth. "He refused his Eden Bean—"

"It's not compulsory," Mika interrupted, sounding agitated.

"I know, but the reason behind it may count or lead us to a clue. I think it could help us connect some facts. So, save that as an issue to answer why..." Brad continued. "Bryan said that his apartment looked like a monk lived there. The fact that he was a Mormon could explain that, but I feel it'll lead us to more clues. Something's amiss. I bet you he wasn't even living there. He staged it to fool us." Mika noted.

"When did you see Bryan?"

"Out on the ice, before we resurrected you," Mika joked.

Brad lifted his index finger. "What else do you know about the mysterious dead scientist?"

Mika sat up, pushing the photos aside, reading Connor's notes on the notepad. Brad stood, waiting for a summary.

"Interesting. Connor noted that he was lying and making excuses. Even his fellow research partners thought he was working in the Agricultural Domes, and when Connor questioned the Grain lab, they said he was busy in the Vegetable lab, and vice versa."

"So, what was he really doing?" Brad asked, slapping his hand on the table in frustration. The thing flickered. "Lasitor!" Brad called and paused, looking at the screens above, waiting for the AI face to appear, before responding. He turned in question to Mika and then back to the massive screens in front of them. He expected the black screen to light up and display a cybernetic male face, greeting them loudly and over-enthusiastically. But nothing. Only black stillness remained.

"What in the blazing gory hell?" Brad's voice echoed through the large, quiet office.

Mika glared at the black screens. "What is going on, Brad? With this and your feelings about the citizens, perhaps it wouldn't hurt to keep a closer eye on the men. Even though growing up being policed, controlled, and hunted, I vowed never to create that kind of environment for my children. I wanted, no, I know we all wanted, to live in a utopia. A place where our children could be free. We trusted the scientists to guide their research.

However, I must agree with you. This place is turning into a vacation resort, and this"—he gestured to the inactive screens—"this situation is escalating." Mika leaned back in his chair, crossing one long leg over the other. "I think we need to implement at least an accountability system. This is really getting on my nerves, I must say. It's not safe, and the men and their children roam around as if they're at Disney World," he said, inspecting the photos with one hand. Flipping through them repeatedly, he seemed deep in thought. "I feel like I'm missing something. I feel like I'm on the brink of solving this puzzle, but something's troubling me. And where are our boys? I'm becoming concerned; it's been an hour since Rick and Connor went to look for them. I still haven't seen them. Who went to call Bryan?" the Russian asked anxiously, raising his voice with each question.

"I know. This is strange. Lasitor is never offline," Brad said, crouching down to crawl on his hands and knees beneath the table to restart the main computer. He turned it off and waited, counting to ten as Connor had taught him. Then, he restarted the system. As the minutes passed, Brad noticed the look in Mika's eyes. They were both anticipating confirmation of bad news. The air was thick with trepidation and foreboding feelings he recognized well from his years observing battlefields.

"Come on. Let's go through the photos," Brad suggested, hoping to distract Mika while they waited. Mika, staring out the office window, turned back to examine the evidence. "The facts about Joshua and how he deceived us—and his coworkers—must be a clue." The same stifling apprehension was suffocating them both, he thought.

Suddenly, static broke the silence over the speaker system.

Rick's loud and clear announcement that the boys were missing confirmed their fears. "This is Dr. Rick Longarrow-McCormick. This is a broadcast of high importance. We're looking for four young men. The Romanov and McCormick twins. Donali and Kawa McCormick. Please page the leadership office right away. Cian and Ivan, your fathers are looking for you. Anyone who has seen them recently, please page the leadership office. If you see these four young men, please tell them to report to the leadership office immediately. If anyone has noticed anything unusual, please report it. Thank you."

Brad tensed up. The announcement had his emotions running wild. Mika looked up and said, "Comrade, I fear the worst is yet to come. That Mormon, what was he up to? Connor couldn't find any clues in his apartment. Most importantly, where are our damn kids?!"

Brad's gut twisted, and a jolt of fear shot through him. "I don't even know where to start!" Brad ran his hands through his hair, weighing whether to continue searching himself or gather a team to start looking outside. I must trust Bryan and Connor to handle this. "Let's give the boys time to respond," he said, silently hoping and praying that his concern wasn't justified.

"Perhaps...Remember the time my twins had us all worried about nothing?" Mika asked.

"God, yes, I don't think Phoenix would ever forget that day," Brad said, with a nervous chuckle.

Mika sat up and crossed his arms. "We'll see what you do if your underage sons were found trying to slip into Quik-Fix Hall for a blow job."

Brad gasped and enlarged his eyes to three times their size. "Maybe that's where your boys have gone to, and they've taken Donali and Kawa with them?"

Brad gulped and cleared his throat. His boys just turned eighteen, and only twenty-one-year-old patrons were allowed in the red-light district. *The Romanovs are going to ruin my boys.* Then he shook that off. "I don't think my Apache angels would ever be convinced to go there. Rick and I have raised them well, and they openly discuss anything with us. If they wanted to go, they would talk to us and ask us about it. They know that's our red-light section. When Rick explained how babies were made when they were only six years old, he traumatized them so deeply that they had nightmares about vaginas and artificial wombs for years."

"Oh, dear lord!" Mika laughed, cutting the tension. "Yes, that's right. The word dildo turns your boys red as tomatoes." They laughed, shortly diffusing the tension.

"I'm sure they're swimming or watching movies in the Entertainment Dome. Maybe they're hanging out at Juandre and Andrew's?" Brad said, but inwardly he worried. He failed to hide his nervousness and knew he wasn't fooling Mika.

"Toss this. I'm going to search for my family," Mika said seconds later, throwing the photos down and jumping up.

Brad reached for the pager attached to the wall. Screeching interference noises surprised them. "Why all the static?" he asked, looking at the device. He dialed the general population. "This is your leader, General McCormick. Teams assigned to the tunnels and the Athletics Dome report immediately. This is not a drill. I remind you we are in Code Yellow. We are on high alert..." Brad halted mid-sentence, interrupted by Captain Bryan Howell, in charge of Phoenix's security and reserves, who all but fell into Mika on his way out of the office. Brad jolted, totally shocked when he saw Bryan looking trampled by a herd of buffalo. Mika side-stepped with a surprised look.

Bryan's usually neatly styled salt-and-pepper hair was pointed in all directions, sticking to his face. Streaks of blood and sweat ran heavily down his chin, and his left cheek was scraped right down into his neckline. Heaving heavily, he ran into the meeting room. His green camo pants and shirt were wet and in bloody shreds.

Coming out of his stupor, Brad immediately decided to increase the level of preparedness. "This is now a Code Red. We are on full lockdown. We are under attack. Reserves report to your stations. No one crosses over the barrier lines. If you're found outside your assigned area, you will be arrested and brought in for questioning. I repeat, this is a Code Red. Everyone who's not a soldier, return to your apartments. We are under attack and have been infiltrated. No one crosses the barrier lines. We are on full lockdown until cleared," their leader said.

"Bloody hell!" Brad exclaimed, looking Bryan up and down.

"General, we need to..." Bryan stopped, coughing into a handkerchief and clearing his throat. "We must assemble a team for a search and retrieval mission," Bryan barked. Brad noticed bright red blood on the cloth and wasn't sure where it came from. Maybe the cough or his face? Or was it a nosebleed?

Mika blinked, looking like he wanted to run but stayed planted. The captain looked like he struggled to compose himself, swallowing some words and biting his lips. Bulging his fists, he took a deep breath, whipping the bloody snot and tears from his eyes and nose. "I'm so sorry, General," Bryan said to Brad, while tears streamed from his eyes.

*Oh, my stars, he's crying?* It shocked Brad to see the man in such an emotional state. He was usually so well put together in emergencies. His captain was distraught, walking in small circles, pumping his arms. He halted, collected himself, and then continued. "I'm sad to report that I lost the boys."

Mika gasped. Brad's heart nearly stopped again as fear overtook him. Bryan seemed to gulp his anguish back. He took a few deep breaths and continued to apologize.

"I knew it!" Brad said, slamming the headset a few times into its place. Bryan lifted his left hand as if to stop a blow to his face.

"Stop that. I won't hit you! Has anyone ever hit you?"

"No, sir, sorry, sir, but I deserve it anyway." Bryan cried into his hands, shaking his head.

"Captain, get a hold of yourself!" Brad ordered, and it seemed to help. Bryan straightened his back and swallowed his tears. Mika sat down, mouth agape.

"I have a team following them. They'll report back. They may be slow, but at least they can report on a general direction for us to pursue. We need to fuel up the airplane. I have one man in custody. He helped us stop the kidnapper. He, he, he...his eyes. I'll show you later." Bryan pointed to his face and then the ceiling. Confusion was written all over his face.

"You have a prisoner?" Brad was ready to go, but he realized he needed to prioritize the mess. "Is he secure?" he asked.

"Yes, sir, he's secured and cooperating. We can proceed to interrogate him, but I suggest forming a search party first."

"How many hostiles, Lasitor?" Brad called the AI and realized it was still in old-school mode.

Bryan frowned and looked at the screens.

Mika's table came to life, the screens lit up, and Lasitor answered.

*One abductor, one captured. There may be more.*

"What?" Brad asked furiously. They've wasted precious time, hoping for the best. "How many hostiles?"

Standing back, he watched the screen to read what Lasitor answered.

*One sailed away with the boys. Enforcing Code Red. One friendly.*

"This makes no sense," Brad muttered, stunned and silent as he calculated his next move. He wanted to run, but to where? He needed to rescue the boys. He must defend Phoenix. He took a deep breath and waited. "Alright, Captain." He paused. "Bryan, please finish. Explain so we can understand."

"Lasitor! Show me the map of Antarctica," Bryan ordered their AI.

"Certainly, Captain," the AI's robotic voice echoed loudly.

"Zoom in on the latest satellite photos!" Bryan ordered when a giant map of Antarctica appeared.

"Here, here, and here, in this direction." Brad's captain of arms pointed to specific areas on the map and circled them in neon yellow with his finger on the touch screen.

"We need to regroup to find the boys," Mika said, then immediately started bombarding Bryan with questions. "What do you mean, you lost the boys? What happened? Who took our boys?"

Bryan hobbled from one leg to the other in front of the screen, favoring his left leg while gripping his right hip. He grimaced in pain.

"I can confirm our suspicions that two foreign men were outside on the ice. From what I gathered from the alcove, only one man stayed there. They weren't there when we found the place, but it appeared to be a camp or a hiding spot. I saw carved animals and pictures. I found the fish we smelled, but only one plate, cup, and bed were made from furs. The men encircled the area, narrowing the circle to trap them, but all they found was the alcove. It tunneled deeper into the ice, leading to a subterranean area beneath the city of Phoenix. We gathered our lights and gear and followed an old trail that ran deep into the old volcanic tunnels. To our surprise, they opened just behind the Athletics Dome's entrance." Bryan said, pointing at the map, exasperated.

Loud gasps came from the direction of the door. Rick and Connor had arrived. Brad waved them over and watched as they dragged chairs closer to sit. "Please continue, Bryan," he urged.

"I think Joshua knew them and was possibly the middleman. They could have been family members, people he met, or perhaps...followed him here." Bryan was clearly speculating.

"Lasitor was hacked or damaged, and we don't have footage from the last few hours," Brad said.

"Are we under attack!" yelled Rick..

"Can we get organized?" Connor yelled. "We need to regroup!"

"I second that," Bryan said, pointing to the area behind the swimming pool. "This is where we heard someone calling for help. I knew it was one of the boys, but we couldn't determine which tunnel to take because of all the echoes. I sent the men to split up and stumbled upon a small hunchbacked man loading a weird-ass sailboat."

"A what?" Brad asked, his head whipping around to see if he missed something.

"A weird-ass sailboat?" Rick echoed, but they asked again, "A sailboat?"

"Yes, a boat, but not for water. They, whoever *they* are, had adapted it for ice. Maybe both water and ice," Bryan said, clearly annoyed. It seemed they had stretched his patience paper-thin. No one asked him to repeat anything. He paused, taking a few breaths.

"Okay, I could see the boys were tied up sitting down. I followed, ran, jumped, and clung to the side, attempting to climb in."

"Others were also jumping on the back of the boat. But once the sails opened, it flew over the ice, and none of us could hold on or try to continue climbing into it. That's when I noticed another man running alongside the ship—he was fast. He ran and jumped onto the boat. He even tried to stop it, turning it around and throwing anchors onto the ice, but his buddy came from the back and surprised him by kicking him on the ass right off the ship. We must have been going over a hundred kilometers per hour by then. I couldn't hold on to the side anymore. I was too weak, even though I could see the terror in the boys' eyes. Their mouths were gagged, and...they looked so afraid. I'm so sorry. I'm so very sorry." Bryan paused and turned away to hide his tears of shame. They waited for him to continue while looking questioningly at each other.

When he'd collected the courage to face his friends again, he said, "By the time I got up and recuperated, the boat had already disappeared over the hills. Fritz and four other soldiers were on snow riders following them. I signaled and radioed not to stop, for them to follow and stay in radio contact while I returned to Phoenix to regroup, maybe load the plane, sir." Head in his hands, he cried. "I'm so sorry." He apologized again with eyes full of tears. "The fear in those boys' faces...I'm such a failure...couldn't protect the boys, and they could see that."

Brad understood the situation for what it was. After Doomsday, Bryan had never explicitly stated it, but Brad and Rick knew he had quietly replaced the boys he'd lost by doting on Donali and Kawa. He suspected that all those feelings were surfacing. Bryan had never confronted those feelings of loss in a healthy way. He preferred to sleep his way systematically through Phoenix, and now the dam had burst as he sobbed uncontrollably.

"Thank you, Captain." Brad reminded Bryan of his professionalism. "Let's start from the beginning so that we can have all the puzzle pieces. How did you apprehend the second man?" Brad asked, trying to focus on the facts at hand. He knew it would be counterproductive to go in circles. "Wait, let's request a status update," Brad said, picking up the page to radio the team pursuing his boys. Corporal Fritz de Vries had been promoted from private to corporal two years ago.

"This is the Phoenix HQ. Corporal de Vries, come in. Over," Brad said, changing the frequency by pressing a few buttons. He tried again to make the call. Worry was etched on the faces of all the men in front of him.

"Corporal Fritz de Vries, this is leadership. General Brad McCormick here. Please provide a status update. Over." Brad silently hoped for a miracle. Then, static followed by the sound of motors humming crackled through the overhead speakers.

"Hello, General. This is Corporal de Vries. We are pursuing and tracking from a distance in a northeast direction from Phoenix City. We are nearly out of fuel. We will inform you when we lose visual contact or notice any signs of the ship's origin. Please send reinforcements. We will continue the pursuit on foot. Over and out."

"Copy that. Thank you, de Vries. We appreciate your efforts. Are you within range to fire a tracker into the hull?"

"That's a negative, sir. Out," the corporal shouted.

"Copy. Can you stop and transfer the fuel from two vehicles into the third? Over."

"Copy. We can do that. Over."

"Copy. We're sending reinforcements. Are you prepared for the weather? Over?"

"Copy. Yes, sir. Over."

"Copy. I'll check in five-minute intervals. Over and out."

"Copy, over and out."

Connor pointed. "Brad, let's start with you."

Brad's facial expression and body language changed so much that they all did a double-take. He knew his psychopathic warlord face was showing—good. I work better with my mask off. Now they'll understand why I won two wars for my country. Everyone except Bryan seemed stunned by the transformation.

"Okay, yes, they're being followed, so they're not gone yet. I agree it won't help if we all rush off prematurely after the boys. Let's get to know the enemy," General Brad McCormick said. "Lasitor, are you recording this?"

"I am, sir," the male robotic voice thundered over the overhead speakers. The giant touchscreen shimmered and divided into nine squares, resembling a tic-tac-toe board, complete with circles and crosses. Brad mentally rolled his eyes but refrained from reprimanding the cheeky AI. A map of Antarctica appeared in the top right corner, while the left side recorded their dialogues, word for word, as they spoke. In the center, the face of Joshua Adams glowed back at them, and neon blue lines formed a visual mind map. Facts and pictures filled the squares on the screen. In less than a minute, the program Connor wrote to enhance Lasitor's database many years ago resolved, clarified, and addressed all their questions and concerns, displaying slideshows of the evidence, Connor's notes, and the pictures Connor had collected earlier that day.

Lasitor was an updated version of the program they had used to break into the Chinese satellites orbiting the International Space Station. Brad had grown accustomed to the AI scheduling and running Phoenix's entertainment and news broadcasting.

They viewed the Earth from space.

"Lasitor, add two more columns for questions and answers," Brad commanded. "Why were the boys abducted? Why did one attempt to prevent the abduction?" Brad asked, and the question appeared on the screen.

"What are their motivations?" Mika added.

"What do they want to do with the boys?" Connor asked, and silence fell over the room as tension rose. No one wanted to voice the worst fears.

"Are there only two men, or do they represent a larger group?" Bryan asked.

"Why did they meet Joshua in secret?"

"I will kill our boy's abductors. I will kill anyone who hurts my family." Mika grunted.

Brad nodded. "I know, Mika, and I'll help you kill the bastards. Starting with the one in custody." Rick gasped, but he said nothing, shaking his head.

The team continued brainstorming. "Also, gentlemen, I have some significant findings to share. So far, we've been divided, and it won't bring our kids back sooner," Brad continued.

Mika nodded in agreement. "I need to stand," he said as he got up and rested against the wall behind Connor's chair.

Looking at the big screen, deep in thought, Brad cleared his throat. "Someone get Bryan something to eat and drink before he falls over."

Rick's eyes stretched as big as saucers when he saw that Bryan's eyes were about to roll back in his head. "Sure, I will." He jumped, pulling a chair closer for Bryan, who swayed on his feet. "I'll be right back," he said, disappearing into the hallway. A second later, he returned with a first aid kit. He multitasked, speaking over his shoulder into his personal pager while he cleaned and bandaged Bryan's wounds. "Please tell Juandre to bring us his super juice. Yes, that's right, up to the Command Center."

Brad's husband and two older sons were running the medical unit of Phoenix, and he trusted his husband's expertise. Satisfied that Bryan was taken care of, Brad pointed to the map and continued the meeting. "Okay, my input may be a moot point, but we all need to be on the same page. I was out last night to check the external hydraulic system for the front door. We don't use it much since the smaller exits are easier to use. However, I've been receiving strange reports for a few years now. The external hydraulic system was one of many scattered but small incidents. I was uncertain because the incidents were infrequent. But lately, I've noticed a pattern. When most of the population is busy, such as during events or mealtimes, I notice sudden and short drops in temperature. Usually, it's not something that would even register on my radar. At first, I thought nothing of it. Maybe someone was just slipping outside for some crisp, fresh air, not wanting anyone to notice, or seeking a bit of solitude. I noticed this because I monitor the heat loss—it's my responsibility to account for saving and planning electricity use. I discovered exit doors left open; not wide, perhaps just enough for a pen or a paper clip to fit. Something that anyone not paying attention would notice. While inspecting the hydraulics, I began to suspect sabotage. I saw lights over the ice about two hundred meters out into the valley. I didn't think to report it. As I ran, I wanted to be as quiet as possible to catch the men sneaking out and find out why. To my surprise, I saw Joshua Adams talking to two men."

As Brad told his story, exclamations of surprise came from around the table.

"I've never seen these men before. Joshua knew them and might have been meeting with them for years. They weren't dressed like us, so I knew they were survivors from outside Phoenix. They wore different winter gear."

"I can't believe it. All this time, Joshua must have been in contact with them," Bryan said. The men at the table were dumbfounded.

"Do you think these men...why, what would they do to our boys?" Rick's voice grew louder and higher. "Why live outside of Phoenix all this time? Where did they come from, and why was Joshua, of all people, involved with them?" Rick rambled, crossing his arms over his chest. They watched the screen, reading the questions as the AI captured them electronically and categorized them as unanswered questions.

Brad tried to keep the order, but they bombarded him with questions. "Calm down. Let me continue. I didn't have many places to hide, but they saw me approaching when I saw them. Instead of calling for help, I sprinted after them again, but I heard a loud crack. I thought they were shooting at me, so I jumped and fell onto my belly on the ice. The next moment, Joshua stopped dead in his tracks. He looked at me, wide-eyed and fearful, and fell straight into a crack. The ice cracked again. It sounded like a flock of birds taking off as the ice sheets moved and shifted around us. Joshua screamed, and I crept forward on my hands and knees to help. The sounds he made were horrendous."

"Then the ice trembled beneath me, and I didn't know if I should go forward or backward. Then suddenly, the ice opened, and I slipped over the side into the opening. I tried holding onto the ledge while Joshua screamed like a banshee." Brad grabbed his ears as if he could silence Joshua's pleas for help. "It all happened so fast. The ice was so unstable. We shouldn't let anyone out there."

"I know," Connor interjected. "I tried to remove Joshua's body, which was a mess. The moving ice sheets squashed him like a meat tenderizer."

"My gille-toine tried his best but couldn't," Mika noted with a grin. Connor smiled briefly at his husband.

"Anyway, since we're on that subject, when we have our boys back, these incidents are a testament to the need for a policing system. Phoenix is growing too large for just us to manage." A round of affirmatives came from the room.

Bryan cleared his throat. "I'll establish a framework. We can start small."

Brad thanked him and continued. "By the time I couldn't hold on any longer, I slipped and fell onto an ice shelf. I lost my radio and flashlight. Lying as still as possible, I tried to pretend I was dead. I was worried the men would return to finish me off and possibly shoot at me. Joshua was silent and likely dead. I realized I couldn't call for help, and once again, I thank Dr. Peter von Leutzendorf. I used the injections and fired all my flares when I thought I was alone."

"Luckily, we saw your flares. We wouldn't have noticed if the glass-domed roofs weren't transparent," Connor added, and reached for Mika's hand.

"Yes, so when I injected the last syringe, I hoped there was something more to keep me alive until someone found me. The only thing I had left was the Peter Pan Cap. So, I cut my skin open and dug it out. I almost lost it, my clumsy frozen sausage fingers. It nearly rolled away from me. I grabbed the thing and chewed on it. And dear lord, was it a horrid taste! The rest, you know."

The men in the room were speechless. Rick broke the silence. "Maybe we should use the plane?"

"The thing is, love, we don't have enough fuel," Brad said. "If we manage to get it off the ground, we won't be able to come back. We also don't know where they are."

"Then let's build a sailboat!" Connor exclaimed, his Irish blood clearly boiling to get moving.

"And where do we sail to?" Mika asked.

"Let's be smart about this," Connor added. "I'll get the satellites up. Let's see what we can find."

"That's what I was trying to convey to you earlier," Bryan said. He got up and hobbled over to the screen as if he needed a cane. "We must determine the direction and inspect every hovel for lights or signs of where humans may live."

"It's probably not that far. Assuming they met up with Joshua," Connor said, but Brad interrupted him.

"I noticed that the intervals for doors being left open were anywhere from six to nine months apart. How fast do you think you can travel on the sailboat, Bryan?"

Bryan frowned, calculating.

"That depends on the wind speed," Mika replied. "So, anything from sixty to a hundred and sixty kilometers per hour, maybe even more?"

"How long do you think you could survive on a boat like that?" Connor asked.

"It seemed like a common fishing boat. It was just the hull, with no decks below or anything fancy." Bryan paused, clearly unsure of what he should say.

"Out with it, man!" Brad shouted impatiently.

"The men looked strangely animalistic or wild. They were deformed, with the shorter one being more so than the larger. Let's just say he's the tallest, scariest bastard I've ever engaged in hand-to-hand combat. Luckily, my team helped, and we have it in custody. He's an easy two and a half meters tall, much bigger than Mika."

"Bloody frozen hell!" Connor exclaimed.

"Toss that. I'm cooking fuel or building a ship. Come on, Connor." Mika grabbed Connor by the arm, attempting to leave.

"Wait," Brad called. "We need to plan our next move. And we have to figure out what to do about the dead body."

Mika turned around, his blue eyes bloodshot and filled with tears. "Comrade, what will take longer, building or checking satellite pictures?" He paused, then, not waiting for Brad to respond, Mika continued, "Exactly, so you check the satellites while I handle transportation. Joshua Adams was spying—an undercover agent. Those men he met up with, he fed them information and probably stole from us. Call for backup for Fritz and interrogate your prisoner. Please call me if you need help obtaining information from him. We're dealing with kidnappers who have our sons. I won't let a second go to waste. Joshua was likely planted here by someone who never showed up. Perhaps they even died in the Doomsday outbreak? They're probably mutants due to radiation. Those monsters knew Joshua. They might be planning a hostile takeover of Phoenix, and are going to use our boys as leverage. I'm going to get my boys." Mika finished his rambling and marched, leading Connor out of the office, and no one tried to stop them.

Brad, Rick, and Bryan shook their heads. There was no stopping Mika now. "Okay," said Bryan, and he used a chair to support himself. "I think they can survive a maximum of two weeks on that ship. But we don't know if they have a stopover to replenish supplies."

"So, how far can an ice sailboat travel at a minimum speed of sixty kilometers per hour for two weeks?" Brad asked as he walked up to the screen and marked two points on either side of the valley. "Which direction did they all go?"

"North, northeast," Bryan answered, and then Brad drew a triangle.

"Okay, I'm going to work with the maximums. If you travel at the slowest speed, how far would you go? Sixty times twenty-four times fourteen gives you two thousand one hundred sixty kilometers." He drew two circles, one representing the minimum estimate and the other representing the maximum estimate. Then he drew a straight line from Phoenix through the triangle and the two circles, landing at the tip of South Africa. "Now, all we need are satellite photos to track them. Maybe a weather balloon."

"I'll page Tony. He can set one up for us," Bryan volunteered. Tony Bonillo was the Chief maintenance man, a civil engineer who had helped in the design of Phoenix.

"Good, make sure he doesn't go too high. We want to see movement on the ice. Tell him to stay low and send the pictures directly to me. We need something to work with."

"I need to freshen up and check on the prisoner. When do you need me back?" Bryan asked.

Brad stepped closer to him. "We'll work six-hour shifts. Take a quick break, then I want you to check each room, even if you think it's occupied or just a broom closet. Here, take my master key. I'll pull some data and ask Lasitor to retrace Joshua's steps to see which areas he frequented or if any other residents are exhibiting suspicious behavior. He might have been working with someone. Find the room, apartment, or space that Joshua Adams truly occupied," Brad said, handing Bryan the master key card. "Where are you holding the prisoner? Do you have enough people on him if you consider him so dangerous?"

"Yes, sir, he's in the area below the Reserves compound. In the detention cell."

"Good, I don't want to wait. I want to see what we're dealing with. Maybe mess with his head a bit. When you return, come and join me. We can interrogate him together. Also, before you go, send a team of ten men on the six-wheeler to find Fritz."

"Yes, sir." Bryan turned and left. Over his shoulder, he said, "See you when I have answers about Joshua."

Brad turned to his husband, grasped the chair handles, and squatted in front of Rick, who was distraught. Gently lifting his chin with his thumb and forefinger, he noticed Rick's usual olive complexion was paler than ever. Brad's heart shattered for his husband and their lost children as they locked gazes wordlessly. He fell to his knees, pulling Rick closer while he folded over Brad, hugging him tightly.

"We will find them. We will, I promise you." Rick hugged Brad tighter in affirmation, holding on to him while hiding his sobs and trying to muster courage amidst audible gulps. Brad looked up at him and saw the guilt suffocating Rick.

"It's my fault," Rick blurted out. "I assumed they were okay and never made sure they were. I thought...I should have...maybe paged earlier...checked..."

"No, stop that. They're smart and responsible. It's not your fault. We don't even know the full story." Brad reasoned the facts as they stood. He pulled Rick with him, gesturing toward the screen and the pictures, maps, and test results on the electronic table.

"Let's gather and analyze the evidence together. Mika had a valid point. His theory is logical. We just need to gather more intel to give us an idea about what we are dealing with."

"Speaking of evidence. I'll start with Joshua's body."

"Good idea. I'll ask Peter to come and assist you. I'm more interested in clues about where our boys were taken than in the cause of Joshua's death.

"You never know what his body can tell us unless we look," Rick said, jutting his chin.

Brad softened his tone. "Let's involve the new medical students who are interested in forensics. They can observe the autopsy and have the opportunity to share their insights.

They're young and think outside the box. Let's focus on the clues and the few facts we have," he said.

"Yes, please, let's find them." Rick's voice broke.

Brad closed his eyes, taking a slow, silent, deep breath for strength and concealing his anxiety about their boys. A ping from Brad's pager interrupted his thoughts. He got up, and Rick followed, anticipating news about the boys. "General Brad McCormick. Talk."

"General, you need to come down to the Reserves compound, sir. The prisoner has escaped!" Sergeant Amir Lamasi said, short of breath, as if he had been running.

# CHAPTER 7

# EVERYTHING HAD WITHERED AWAY

*"Good morning, citizens of Phoenix.*

*It's now six a.m.*

*Have you ever wondered where mosquitoes go during winter?*

*Mosquitoes, like all insects, are cold-blooded creatures. As a result, they cannot regulate body heat and become lethargic at fifteen degrees Celsius.*

*So, you should be safe if no mosquito eggs survive the global winter. When temperatures rise, these mosquitoes will wake up and begin feeding.*

*Visit your community news page for tips on how to get rid of those bloodsuckers.*

*Breakfast is served until eight a.m."*

**Eryn King of the Brawl**
**2073 A.D. (21 A.T.)**
**Underground Laboratory**
**Fochville gold mine grid**
**South Africa**

South Africa was like Antarctica, cold, dark, and barren. Nothing should be able to survive in the Brawl's nest, but Eryn and his brothers did.

High on the mineshaft, Eryn's body got battered by the icy wind while he held onto the rusted steel bar with one hand. His tattered clothes rattled like a long-forgotten flag in the wind, and the rhythm of the noise and solitude soothed him. Under the buckskin and fur cloak, he wore the same clothes Joshua had given him fifteen years ago. The worn-out pair of jeans hung in brown pieces of cloth around his muscled legs, and the t-shirt was nothing more than a shredded tank-bikini top. His size eleven boots were adapted and cut open at the front to fit his wide size sixteen feet with webbed toes. He had wrapped strips of animal hide around his shoes and lower legs, not only for protection and warmth but also to keep the boots from falling off his feet. The socks disintegrated a long time ago. They collected mud, and washing it was useless because nothing dried inside the mine.

Hearing flapping wings, he looked up. Hundreds of birds, one enormous flock of doves, flying over. The African skies were a rich blue, and only a few small clouds were in sight. Eryn turned his gaze toward the distant mountains and asked. "How long must I wait for you?" Bitter frustration fueled his resolve today. "Come on, Icemen King!" His voice rumbled through clenched teeth. "If not today, when? I told myself one day, and that day is today. I can feel it." He rested his back against the massive cable wheel of the mineshaft and closed his eyes, listening to the sounds of nature and willing the humans to appear on the horizon. *It's my fault that all living things surrounding us either died or moved away. No critters scurrying, nothing burrowing into the ground, and no animals calling.* There were no heartbeats, no life on the ground for hundreds of kilometers surrounding them—he only heard the Brawl and the four human boys.

He climbed up today to gather himself and, for once and for always, decide on the timing of his next steps. *The time has come to stop being a selfish coward.* His reluctance to follow his father's advice stemmed from the fear of being alone. It was time to fight for what he wanted, and he wanted to be friends with men and live like men. *It's time to stand up and do what is right.* "Not only for myself," he said with driven determination as he scanned the gray world surrounding their mineshaft. The hills were strewn with dying tree stumps and desolate frozen grasslands, and the monkeys that had lived on Monkey's Mountain had disappeared. They were gone. He missed their chatters, squeaks, and whines late at night when he escaped the oppressive melancholy of his brother. Ernest, who's bonkers.

*Everything had withered away, so nothing lived or grew in the soil. It's being poisoned. And it's my fault that it got so desolate. Today is the perfect day to take action on this dire situation. It must happen today.*

He had left the four boys inside his cave in their cage. They were all alone. His nerves spiked as he realized he couldn't leave them like that for too long, so he swung his feet back and forth. He liked the height. It felt freeing to sit ten stories high on a crossbar of the head-frame of the old mine shaft. He'd lived here all his life, guarding his brothers and preventing them from waking up and escaping. A chill ran down his spine. Flashes of memories sailed through his thoughts as he remembered what Joshua had called Doomsday. The chaos and destruction his brothers had sown, as well as his own failures and inability to contain it all. The emotionless, obsidian, predatory eyes with zero intelligence. Only an insatiable hunger that no amount of consumption could satisfy. Although they listened to him and were his nest brothers, he had nothing in common with them. Even so, he felt responsible for them. They looked more like Ernest when they walked upright on two legs. Warts thickly covered their skins with green-black patches, and their faces were a cross between frog and lizard.

When he described their long, gangly arms and legs with hunchbacks covered with spikes to the boys, they said they sounded like amphibian swamp monsters. Eryn agreed they were monsters, their four-fingered claws were so big he'd seen how one of them crushed a human's head like a grape and then sucked out their brains like an empty juice box.

Eryn sighed. The incessant pangs of hunger drained him emotionally. *My brothers want to hunt.* He closed his eyes again, wiping his mind from distraction. Connecting telepathically with them, he said, *No, brothers, sleep. It's not time.* He lulled them back into a deeper state of hibernation. When he felt them succumb, he opened his eyes. *My life sucks, frog balls. Why did Ernest take the boys?*

Exasperated, he wiped the tears of frustration from his eyes. He hoped the icemen would come and help him because he couldn't do it alone anymore. *Ernest has something up his sleeve, and he's planning something. I need help, and I can't ask Joshua.* Irritated and sad about losing the last human friend he had. Before he died, Joshua was in the process of telling Eryn about his father and the evil men who had harmed him. Eryn stopped those thoughts and pushed them into the tiny box marked *"do not open, now, never, or ever."* It terrified him. Freezing frog balls. He straightened up and forced himself to think of his action plan. He would have to be one step ahead of Ernest.

*If Ernest tries to hurt those boys, he has to go. If I take the boys back to the glass city, my brother will make trouble for everyone. Worst case, he'll wake the nest, and they'll go on a killing spree. So I'll have to get rid of my brothers first and give Ernest his last chance to choose my side. If he doesn't, he must be eliminated because the safety of those boys comes first.*

"Those blue eyes and long blond hair." He groaned out loud. "My boys, my friends." *They are young men, not boys,* he corrected himself. They had infatuated him and drawn him to them. He was under their spell. Eryn's lower body throbbed. Since they arrived at the mines, he'd been walking around hunchbacked to hide his arousal. Their smell was everywhere he went. And their heartbeats pumped in perfectly synchronized rhythms with his own. A crescendo melody of beauty, love, and hope. It strengthened him, and he realized he had in his cave, in a cage, everything his soul wanted and yearned for all his life—he wanted to belong to them. If not Cian, definitely Ivan. *What if both wanted me?* Eryn's heart rate sped up, just imagining what both of them on top of him would feel like. *That's not happening if they are prisoners.*

He must free all of them. The Icemen King's two sons, Donali and Kawa, were important too, he thought.

The night Ernest followed him, he should have known Ernest was up to something. He'd been talking for a while about being thirsty for blood. Eryn didn't think he meant human blood. So when he went to meet with Joshua…

He paused, hanging his head in his hands. *I should have taken the long route I usually take to throw Ernest off my track.*

He wiped his face up and down as if to wipe the images from his mind. *Why had Ernest taken them? And why did he laugh at Joshua when he died?* Eryn asked himself those questions, just as he did every day. He couldn't understand his brother's sense of humor in the face of human suffering. That night replayed over and over in his mind. Especially when he let himself be captured and wasted time, only realizing he had to stop his brother and get to the boys, or his brother would hurt them. When he eventually caught up with them—he remembered how close to death they were—a shiver ran up his spine, they were frozen to the bone.

If he hadn't chased after them, they would all have been dead if he'd arrived one minute later. Still dressed in only swim trunks with towels covering them.

*I had to choose between taking them to the mine, where it was warm, or to the glass city. It was a life-or-death decision.*

Also, he didn't know it was his friends Cian and Ivan. If he'd known that, he would've tried harder to stop the boat. *Why didn't I look? I should have known, but no, I didn't think. I was dumb, like usual.* He reprimanded himself, a habit he picked up from his brother.

Since they'd arrived home, the moment he saw them and realized who they were, he wanted to scoop them up and take them back to safety, but he realized that would not be easy. They had to be kept safe from Ernest and his brothers. He had to think about all those humans and intended to keep them safe from his poisonous man-eating family until he could figure out a way to get them home safely. He had to build an enormous golden cage for all of them, and only he had the key. Eryn had given each an anti-toxin injection from his father's lab, and since then, he tried to spend as much time as possible with them until their ice king arrived.

He hated himself because he was weak. *Why can't I just kill my brothers like my father said I should? I could be free, living with the men, and be friends with Cian and Ivan.*

"Okay, step one, ask Ernest to help me flood the tunnels. It's a two-person job. One must steer the elevator, and the other must pull the floodgate levers," he muttered to himself and continued to rehearse his plan.

"Step two…" He turned, swung his leg over the bar he was sitting on, and stood up to prepare the beacon he had built from old telephone poles and tree trunks. *Yes, step two would be to light the fire so their people can find us.* Eryn could see for hundreds of kilometers from this height, so he knew the beacon of smoke and fire would be seen when their rescuers came.

"Step three, get the boys out." He felt positive and now more motivated than ever to do what he must. He decided this time he would follow through on his plan. *I'll ask Ernest to go hunting. Then I'll tell him about my plan so he can choose if he's with me or against me. Save the boys and live with the humans…*

# CHAPTER 8
# THE BLUE HALCYON

*"Good morning, citizens of our glass-domed city.*

*It's now six a.m.*

*Did you know heatstroke can cause disorientation and headaches? The body cannot control its temperature, which rises rapidly. The sweating mechanism fails, and the body is unable to cool down. Before you freak out, follow these steps to cool the overheated person.*

*Get the person into the shade and remove his excess clothing. Cool the person with whatever means available. Put the person in a tub of water or, even better, grab a firehose and spray the human. But before you do all that, be sure it's heatstroke and not just a vicious hangover.*

*On second thought, splashing down a hung-over man may help anyway.*

*Visit your community news page to read about exciting facts on failing body mechanisms.*

*Breakfast is served until eight a.m.*

*Have a refreshing day!"*


**Dr. Mika Romanov**


PREPARATIONS TO GET the rescue mission underway had Phoenix buzzing twenty-four-seven for a little over two weeks. Despite that, it felt to Mika like they were dragging their feet. He had hoped to interrogate the prisoner, and now he too was gone. Like their boys. Mika let Connor take the lead and busy himself by working with a team of savant scientists and engineers who set up a shipyard inside the belly of a recently constructed Transportation Services Dome. Over a thousand men volunteered and worked diligently in shifts to finish the flying sailboat as fast as possible.

Tony, Mika, and Connor re-designed a campership prototype by weaponizing and fortifying it with new materials, either salvaged or newly created. The Phoenix metallurgical engineering teams used previous research to create a newly designed metal by blending salvaged pieces of titanium, tungsten, and Antarctic blue marble rock lava infused with halogen by grounding the metals into fine powders and mixing it with carbon and frozen halogen. They put the powder inside a high-heat, high-pressure mold to shape the required pieces for the hull of their ship. Once the scientists set up a foundry, the area to work safely inside the lava tubes, the process of blending, pouring, and infusing, was time-consuming. But yet another invention testified to the ingenious scientific designs these savants were capable of. The new artificially created metal would never rust. It was lightweight and stronger than any metal on the periodic table.

The magnificent ship was christened the Blue Halcyon. She glowed blue at night, giving her an ethereal look. They named her after the mythical bird said by ancient writers to breed in a nest floating at sea at the winter solstice, charming the wind and waves into calm.

The men who worked in any capacity needed to get the job done humbled Mika. It didn't matter how big or small the task was and whether a man thought he was over or under-qualified, they all had one goal—to help retrieve their sons.

The design of their ship was like no other, but it was not new to the men. Mika had presented it at the Phoenix University Transportation and Innovation show the previous year. However, he'd adjusted the installations, so only the most needed stayed for the rescue mission. It reduced the building time and created the possibility of an airlift.

Mika ground his molars. The unique design was a showstopper for families planning to go ice camping. It now represented retaliation to retrieve, defend, and destroy. He assessed the finished ship from afar, standing with his hands on his hips while calculating where to install his two laser cannons.

"Now it's a warship to save my boys," he said to no one in particular as he stood and visually measured the hull, which was the shape of a curling stone. Originally designed as a recreational vehicle, or RV on ice, it was intended to go short distances for families who wanted to get away from Phoenix, say to go ice camping. It had a flattened bottom with a hollowed base, almost like a catamaran, for access to the water below or ice, if needed. But it was also for speed and direction control. Instead of a very tall mast, Mika had gone with two shorter masts that held the sails shaped like a soccer net for the maximum draft capacity. The ship weighed almost nothing, so he designed a sturdy but fat and bulky-looking design for greater surface tension. Instead of sleek and streamlined, it appeared like an old oil rig platform with no bow or stern. The shorter masts prevented top-heavy problems during storms and sporadic wind changes, which could be retracted or telescoped on demand.

The re-designed ship relied on wind and sunlight to glide or fly over the ice, including the frigid mountain ranges of South Africa. To make flying possible, Mika had a team of physicists design solar sail panels, new light-sensitive nanoparticles, and gallium arsenide weaved into the silicone strands used to create a material for the sails and the balloon, capturing heat and sunlight more efficiently. The renewable energies provided the ship with its luxuries of hot food and warm showers and fueled the wind propellers to move the boat in various directions. They even allowed lift-off with the help of a solar-powered hot-air balloon while honoring the creed of Environmental Project One. The founders, the WHPSS, and specifically Dr. John Saunders, were honored in remembrance by preserving the history and avoiding the causes of the world's demise in the first place and by re-engineering failed technologies.

Phoenix University solely existed to secure humanity's and the Earth's survival. Thus, education emphasized advanced education, minimum military defense, progressive healthcare, unconventional citizenship based on rebuilding infrastructure, and government charters devoid of ethnic, religious, or any other component that had steered the human race thus far.

The original goal was the birth of a new civilization that transformed and improved into a wholly new global entity. Therefore, infinite resources were allocated to ensure the successful dawn of a new civilization. Scientists like Mika had to design and build only environmentally friendly but high-tech means of transportation. For this reason, fossil fuel or any fuel causing air pollution or environmental damage wasn't an option to be produced. Instead, programs like the Phoenix University Transportation and Innovation show were created. Since the six-wheeler and snow riders used the last fuel, newer models would be designed and built with the same new metal and solar panel particles.

After standing like a statue for almost an hour, Mika had awoken. Unknowingly, his mind had shut down, and he'd been sleeping upright. His exhausted mind pinged back from REM sleep, preventing him from falling to the ground. "We need one laser cannon above the entrance door to cover those who run to or from the ship and to melt or break shit in our path and one in the back to cover our asses," he said. Noticing his friends were packing the final provisions.

*Was I sleeping again?* He worried this kind of tiredness could cause accidents. *I will sleep when we are underway.* He told himself what he told the men a thousand times a day. His husband stopped, looked up at the ship, and back at Mika. The Irishman's objection was futile.

"Good, you're awake now," Connor said, meaning everyone noticed he was night-night on his feet. Mika felt embarrassed, an emotion he hated and rarely experienced. "What do you mean, to melt the ice for easy movement, but also in case of an attack?" Connor asked, sounding agitated and avoiding eye contact.

"Precisely that, Connor. Do you want me to draw you a picture!" Mika's temper flared and he shouted furiously at Connor. The dark circles under his eyes caused his blue eyes to look so dark that they were almost black with anguish, hate, and tiredness. Mika felt like grabbing his husband and hugging the shit out of him. *Both of us are exhausted and mentally ruined to the brink of defeat.* He said, "I will not budge on this."

"You'll shoot our damn sails down like a foolish Russian soldier shooting himself in the foot!" Connor shouted back, running his hands through his hair. "And if you haven't noticed, we don't have time for this! I haven't slept in weeks. I want to go! Now!" Connor yelled, his voice breaking and his eyes glistening with tears.

"No one can shoot at us with any gun. My lasers would destroy it before it reaches us." Mika scowled and lowered his voice when he noticed the crowd around them growing larger.

"If these lasers fall into the wrong hands, they can accidentally blow the moon out of the sky! Bloody damn hell, Mika, or worse, you'll decapitate yourself!"

"I've had enough of this. My canons go. That is final! I can't sail there and say, hey, do you feel like giving my children back? They will laugh at us. We need to scare them, and if they aren't scared, I'm going to kill them until they're scared. We don't know how many of them there are. Are there thousands like us? And if so, they must stay away from us when we return home. They need to know we're bigger, smarter, and more advanced than them. They must see us as gods, and we're angry gods. Very angry, *ty che, blyad*!" Mika roared. His anger combusted, he couldn't keep it in check and failed dismally to lower his voice.

He noticed Juandre stepping closer out of the corner of his eye.

"Bzzzzz, leave the man! He knows what he's talking about," Juandre said. Interrupting his friends while giving Connor the stink eye. The crowd grew in size around them, probably expecting a bit of free entertainment.

Dressed in his best 1980s Prince outfit, Juandre was resourceful, scarily bossy, and demanding. Men knew that if they wanted to get things done, Juandre was the person to ask, and he would sort the rest out for them, even as the local peacock.

"You two should stop your fighting. You're at it all day like two Chihuahuas. Yapping, yapping, yapping. Just shut up. Bloody damn hell, I'm sick of it," Juandre said while clapping his hands and shooing them like dogs.

Mika and Connor indignantly did so.

"I agree with Mika." Brad tapped Connor on the shoulder. "Mika is correct. We need the cannons. I'd rather be over than under-prepared."

"Me, too. Sometimes you have to show you can defend yourself," Bryan added while pulling a trolley packed with more weapons and ammunition crates into the ship.

Connor threw the crate he was carrying onto the ground. He bent down on one knee, opening it. "Okay, I'm outnumbered, but I can't wait to say I told you so." Looking like Santa, he dove into the crate and handed each man a smaller but just as deadly version of the cannons, a personal protection laser handgun. A round of thank you's followed.

"Ooooh," Juandre said, looking at his gun like a new studded sex toy.

"Good luck to those assholes! Anyone who hurts us will meet our vengeance," Mika said with murder in his eyes. Meaning it and planning to shoot shit dead. He holstered the handgun into the side of his belt and then assembled and installed the cannons on board. "Andrew, my man, I need your strong, muscled arms. Can you help me?" Mika asked.

"No problem." Andrew jumped, eager to be of help.

Connor cleared his throat. Mika felt his husband's gaze on his backside and heard him say, "I don't know how he does it. Men respect him even more, despite his animalistic disembowelments. No, instead of making him the most feared man in Phoenix, he's now more popular than ever."

Mika and Andrew's heads popped over the side of the deck while they worked.

"He's sexy, strong, dangerous, and too smart for you. Pass him to Andrew and me, and we'll keep him entertained. I heard he is hung like a horse, and I love rodeos. Times are changing. It's the survival of the fittest, not the richest, Connor, my man," Juandre said. Licking his index finger, he pressed it to his buttocks, mimicking a strip of bacon in a hot pan. "Hsshhhhhh."

"You little slut. You know I have a black belt. I will..." Connor mock attacked Juandre, who disappeared between Peter and Tony, discussing the newly designed bulletproof heat suit. The new material was woven from the same solar-powered silicone strands and lightweight, newly designed metal. The stretchy fabric conserved light energy in its nanoparticles activated by freezing temperatures, which released energy as heat.

"Yes, almost like wearing a microwave oven, ha-ha!" Peter and Tony blurted out as one.

"They should wear it as an undergarment, like a deep-sea diving suit. Each suit fits the body for which they measured it and protects it like a glove." Peter showed them by dipping his arm in a bath of ice.

"Here, come feel this." He folded his sleeve back so they could feel the heat.

"You're a brainiac. I mean, both of you are," Bryan said.

"Thank you, but Peter made my idea a reality," Tony said. Out of habit, Peter quietly stood to the side, attempting to disappear into the background. Bryan must have noticed and immediately went to him.

"Come here, Peter. Let me congratulate you." Peter's gaze fell to the ground. He blushed a bright pink.

"Damn, Peter, why haven't you ever come to visit with Tony and me? Wait, I know the answer. You're always working in your lab." Bryan hugged Peter, whose arms dangled at his sides, and then reached for Tony, who looked happy with how Bryan included Peter.

"It seems Bryan and Tony are looking for a third, and the way Peter's smiling from ear to ear, it looks like he is going to fit snugly between Bryan and Tony," Mika told Andrew, who noticed the three men below. He nodded, not saying a word, but Mika noticed disappointment for a second. How odd, he wondered. "Finally, my long-time friend and lab partner has found a place to belong," Mika said and again, saw the downturn of twitching muscles. *Andrew wasn't happy about the union. Maybe he wanted Peter for Juandre and himself.* Mika didn't know his friend was such a commodity. Unfortunately, they have to leave, otherwise, he would have wanted to ask Peter about this. Why his friend never shared things like this with him upset Mika, he assumed they were work husbands.

"Okay, okay, stop smothering me. I appreciate you inviting me. I meant to visit Tony, and we work well together," Peter said shyly, his crisp white hair covering his ice-blue eyes.

"Have you seen my playroom?" Tony asked. The sexy engineer threw an arm around Peter's neck. "Now that I think of it, why haven't you ever visited? Did you know Bryan and I are in an open D/s relationship?" Tony asked. Peter looked embarrassed and excited at the same time.

"I knew, and I hoped one of you would invite me, but...you know...no one has. I knew about your kink and hoped to talk to you about it." He shoveled his toes into the ground and kicked at it, much like a shy adolescent would do.

"Now that's just sad," Juandre added from a distance, never missing a beat while interrupting them. It seems Juandre was a tad irritated with Peter. "Do I have to be naked to get my body scanned for the suit?"

"No, you can keep tight-fitting underwear on, the type you'll wear when you wear the suit," Peter and Tony answered. Juandre undressed and climbed out of the red bodysuit, leaving only his underwear on.

"I know, right? I'm big. This doesn't get strapped and tucked away. First, it's too pretty, and second, I like it too much," he said with an effeminate lilt. Rubbing himself shamelessly. "What?" he asked while the group looked at him astonished.

"I need space for my junk in my suit. I don't want to go on a rescue mission with squashed balls. And if I want to scratch them, my hand should at least fit down there."

Mika and Andrew laughed. "That's an excellent point!" Mika yelled from above. Juandre turned, waving animatedly, then kissing the palm of his hand, blowing strawberry kisses up to them.

"Thank you, Mika, only a man as intelligent and virile as yourself will see my meaning," Juandre said. Then he threw an arm down toward the ground, and he shouted, "Elephant trunks and beer-can dicks and all that." With a cheeky grin, he was still eyeing Connor. Andrew and Mika chuckled. Mika appreciated Juandre volunteering to come along with them. He knew just what to say to break tense moments. *And I love his breakfast muffins.*

After Juandre, the rest of the rescue mission crew rubbed themselves up for a bigger basket room before scanning their bodies in 4D.

Later the same day, Mika went with his crew as they collected and dressed in the new suits produced and woven by the factory-sized 4D sewing machine. Of course, if the rest of Phoenix was interested in such a suit, they were welcome to fall in line for a measurement. Eagerly, they waited for their turns as every man rubbed themselves to the point of ejaculation before getting scanned for a new suit to wear underneath or replace the bulky military-issued arctic suits.

"Oh, my goodness, look at them! Why are the men rubbing themselves like that? Maybe I should tell them a ball of socks would have the same effect. What if there are children here? What will happen when I'm gone?" Brad asked.

"Juandre, it's all your fault," Mika yelled.

"No, no, no, no, no, no," he said, snapping his fingers left and right. "If I jumped in the fire, General, it's common knowledge not to follow. It's not my fault half of Phoenix are exhibitionists." He flung himself around in a dramatic fashion and disappeared into the hull, looking sexy with the black suit, black boots, and a red chiffon scarf around his neck.

"Bloody damn hell!" Brad said.

Mika was relieved when Brad laughed before turning to Rick and Bryan, who were standing at a big table, rolling up the maps they prepared to reach the location of the kidnappers hiding out in the old gold mining region of South Africa.

Brad and the team mapped, located, and studied the terrain to determine the quickest route to the goldmines and to plan the extraction. They calculated that flying over Table Mountain and following the old river canyons originating south of the central mining area, known as the iSangqu and iGwa Canyons, would be almost exactly how the crow would fly into the Place of Gold.

Rick had Mika and Connor design a mini surgery outfitted on the Blue Halcyon. Mika made sure he would be able to perform procedures such as removing a splinter to open abdominal surgery.

"Time has come to board the ship!" Mika called, then listened as Brad left Bryan in charge.

"Just listen to your leadership council, Bryan. I couldn't have done my job without the help and trust of my supportive council. You know it. You were one of them."

"I know, sir, but…"

"Bryan, I trust Phoenix has voted correctly. It makes sense. And no, you're needed much more here. I need you to update me at least twice daily. Good?" Brad waited until Bryan agreed. "I leave Phoenix in your hands, and you may use my comfy recliner in my office. You may also look in the upper left drawer of my desk. There's a bottle of Lord Andrew that you may have a small sip of. It's most probably the last in the world. Just remove your shoes and don't damage my chair." Brad was joking, but Mika and everyone knew his chair and whiskey weren't easily shared. Bryan just hung his head and nodded. "Come, give me my last hug!"

"Sir, no!"

"Aww, bugger that. Who cares about formalities anymore?"

Bryan lifted his arm to salute, but Brad enveloped him, giving him an enormous hug. After a strange uncomfortable moment, both coughed and cleared their throats as Brad broke the embrace.

"Good luck, sir. Bring our boys back home safely."

Mika saw the water in his friend's eyes as he turned to board the ship.

The hollow shipyard amplified the roar of heartfelt goodbyes. Mika heard good luck and bring our boys back! Connor, Mika, Brad, Rick, Juandre, and Andrew waved back at the crowd from the deck.

The glowing new retractable doors opened up and retracted into the dome's roof as the Blue Halcyon sailed into the cold veil of mist covering the Antarctic Valley.

CHAPTER 9

# THE ODD GROUP

*"Good morning, brave men of Phoenix.*

*I, Lasitor, am bidding positive vibes in the spirit of reunification. It's now six a.m.*

*Did you know man's worst fear has changed over time?*

*Man's earliest fear was predators. Famine, even a solar eclipse, can frighten a man. Did you also know that just twenty years ago, according to the results of a quiz, men of Phoenix reported their worst fears were brain shrinkage and cognitive dysfunction? To partake in this exciting study, please connect with Lasitor on your local community news page and tell him what you fear today.*

*Breakfast is served until eight a.m.*

*Bon voyage!"*


## CAPTAIN BRYAN HOWELL


A week before the departure to South Africa, the new leader and council members elected were announced. Brad and each member who left on the rescue mission informally handed over the reins of power to their successors. An open voting system allowed the men of Phoenix to vote and monitor the results without having to count the votes. Each time a man had voted, he could see a point added next to his chosen replacement.

While Brad and the men readied themselves for the rescue mission, Bryan and his new council members prepared to replace them as smoothly as possible.

Dr. Peter von Leutzendorf stepped into Mika's shoes while they elected Tony Bonillo to replace Connor Romanov. Dr. Simon and Dr. Paul would oversee Phoenix Medical Operations. The gifted pair were well-loved and trusted by the general population. Whether with injuries or surgeries at Medic-Underground or working at the local eye clinic, they always showed up and assisted no matter the crisis. After the first big earthquake had hit Phoenix, Dr. Rick Longarrow-McCormick took them under his wing, encouraging and nurturing their interest in medicine. Both graduated with honors from Phoenix University, where they continued to specialize in various medical fields.

Dr. Simon McCormick, Brad McCormick's older son, born before Doomsday, was as handsome as his father, tall and athletically built. Never leaving the side of his husband and best friend, Dr. Paul Chevalier, who was a brilliant and strikingly handsome young man with crow-black hair and snow-white skin.

Donali and Kawa, the two younger boys who had been kidnapped, were half-brothers of the two doctors, who were married before they were born. They had helped raise them and had a powerful bond with them. Completely devastated by their abduction, the two doctors eagerly volunteered to join the rescue mission, but being chosen as Phoenix's Chiefs of staff and replacing their stepfather, Dr. Rick Longarrow-McCormick, was an honor, so their fathers could travel together on the rescue mission.

As the Blue Halcyon departed, Bryan followed Charles, who stood a head taller than his men, as they waddled after him through the crowd. Bryan had noticed him and his group a few years ago, but they had disappeared from his radar because they seemed dull and uninteresting, other than being self-righteous bullies. However, to be safe, Bryan had Lasitor trace their movements throughout Phoenix. With the AI not using valuable manpower, it would inform Bryan of their every move. On a closer review, Bryan noticed they were always standing to the side like a prison gang attempting not to be seen. Brad, being Brad, just brushed them off as a bunch of rotten apples. But Bryan's alarm bells incessantly rang as he observed them. *There's something odd about the group.*

Dr. Charles Montgomery, the leader of the secretive group of pretend scientists, spoke. "This is bad, really, really bad. I hoped they would at least test the hydrogen-propelled craft we designed and built. But no, they just had to design something impenetrable like that. Look at it. It's a tin can," he said. He had a flair for untouchable superiority.

"Yes, it looks like something a five-year-old would draw," a bald black man said, chuckling.

"Sir, maybe we should have hidden on board. We could have taken hold of the ship or left unseen once we arrived at the mines."

"No, the timing is wrong. We should have been there already! And I don't think all of us would fit anyway," their leader said sternly.

In deference to Charles, the five men turned as one and nodded their agreement.

"We must make haste and leave in our prototype right away."

"Yes, sir, as soon as the crowd dissipates," Nick said.

They maneuvered through the fray of men watching the Blue Halcyon leave the shipyard. Around them, men were cheering. Some fathers had lifted their boys onto their shoulders to see the pretty blue ship. Some youngsters had small blue boat toys in their hands.

The mysterious group of scientists was registered for their research on renewable energy. Their work results were nothing extraordinary, and some of their projects were outrageous and far-fetched. For example, the racketeering ideas they recently proposed for rocket fuel production. They were a tight-knit group, apparently all heterosexual, so Bryan and Brad thought their sexual preferences were the source of the judgmental watching and waiting with their hands always casually tucked into their pockets. Since the episode with Joshua, the mysterious meetups, and the escape of the mysterious prisoner, Bryan and Brad had sat in Brad's office working with Lasitor. They scanned every recorded security video and were still no closer to understanding the goal of the secretive team operating right under their noses. The escapee's face was only known to Bryan and his team. But when a sketch artist was called in, none of them could remember any facial features, except that he was tall with weird eyes. It was as if Bryan's and his team's memories were wiped along with Lasitor's.

No footage of him was found in the system, and Lasitor, for some inexplicable reason, identified the escaped prisoner as friendly and the shorter, stocky man, forcing the four young men at gunpoint onto the ship behind the athletics dome, as the enemy. It was unclear if they were working with this group of wayward scientists or not.

To confirm his original suspicions about the odd squad and not to show his hand prematurely, Bryan informed Brad that he would observe, investigate, and report to him before confronting them. As the acting leader, he'd already searched their labs and rooms without their knowledge, and their investigation had clarified that they were working on projects without proper council approval —projects that were unusual and out of the ordinary, such as hydrogen-propelled airships. However, the most concerning aspect was their research on DNA manipulations and genome sequencing.

They also found research and books deciphering old Mesopotamian, Egyptian, and Babylonian languages. Weird symbols and pictures of what seemed to be ancient astronomy charts and maps of cities of gold. No translations were found, but the notes from dangerous and unapproved projects showed them to be a kind of rebel splinter group or perhaps religious fanatics who hung on every word their leader, Charles Montgomery, said.

As the ship sailed from Phoenix, Bryan moved closer to the back. Attempting to hear what they were saying. *This group lives and operates in the background. They're hiding in the shadows, waiting for their turn to do what?* Bryan was extremely curious to find out.

"Charles, maybe we should let them know," a man Bryan knew as Nick said.

"No," the black man said as he scoped their surroundings. "It is written. They will come to us. We must be ready. The twins will come into their power, and when they do, they…"

"Damn it," Bryan whispered to himself, extremely frustrated. He thought he'd heard something about twins. But Phoenix was full of twins.

"No, if they knew they would somehow make it about themselves…only looking after their own needs, like they've done all these years, and there's no space for impure homosexuals," Charles said.

"They chose none of these people for a reason," another man with light, short brown hair, cut in a monk's tonsure style, said.

"I agree, let's not…we had…Joshua…Unbeknownst to the…Earth's…a ticking time… gasses…before Doomsday!" the bald black man screamed at them.

Still, Bryan couldn't hear the entire conversation above the cheering crowd.

"Look at them." Charles pointed to the crowd. "That's an enormous boost to their confidence. I can't wait to see the mighty fall."

"It's quite magnificent how the ship glows in the dark," a smaller, skinny man said.

"That's so idiotic. It screams, here I am," Charles said, reminding his gang. "At least…we'll be able…stupid homosexual asses."

Bryan heard that, and the urge to run and call his friends back made him nauseous. It felt like, with this information, he was letting them sail right into a trap. Bryan felt divided. He needed to get to the office to contact Brad and call his first council meeting. Lasitor must record and track them, and to do that, they needed to plant a tracker. Stepping back but keeping his eyes on the bigots, he grabbed the nearest soldier by the arm.

"Sir?" he asked.

"What's your name, young man?" Bryan asked without taking his eyes off his target.

"Thomas, sir, Private Thomas Lavetti," the young soldier squeaked with a mousy voice, looking like he wanted to piss his pants.

Bryan did a quick summation. He recognized him as a kid, barely twenty years of age, but he should do. "Boy, this is a matter of high importance, top secret, do you understand?" Bryan asked, not making eye contact. "See that group?" He nodded with his chin to Charles and his men.

"Yes, sir, I do."

"I need to follow them, but I also need to contact our new leadership team and get word to General McCormick and his men. Do you think you can help me?" Bryan asked, feeling the young man relax when he realized he wasn't in trouble.

"Yes, of course, sir. How can I help?" Private Thomas asked.

"Can you follow the men, see where they go, and let me know where they are so I can fetch a tracker and meet up with you? Here, put my black jacket on over your uniform. Try your best to avoid being seen. They're dangerous." Bryan removed his jacket and helped the kid into it.

"Yes, sir! Are they the men we've been searching for?" the private asked. Putting on the oversized jacket and not taking his eyes off his new quarry. Smart boy, Bryan thought.

"Yes, soldier, so don't be brave and put yourself in danger. Just observe from afar." Bryan looked at his watch. "I need you to go silent," he ordered while switching the young man's radio off. "Precisely fifteen minutes from now, I want you to switch it back on and report your location. Continue to do that every fifteen minutes until I meet up with you. Here, let's switch to my private channel," Bryan explained, liking the young man who immediately grasped what he needed while still eyeing his target.

"Okay, sir, I won't disappoint you." Private Lavetti nodded bravely and shot head down into the crowd, following Charles and the group of bastards.

# CHAPTER 10
# ROCKETRY AND DNA MANIPULATION

*"GOOD MORNING, CITIZENS OF PHOENIX.*

*I, Lasitor, bid you a good morning. It's now six a.m.*

*Did you know they spotted four Frog People near the Little Miami River, USA, in the nineteen-fifties?*

*So if you see a frog-faced creature, especially if it's one meter tall and roughly seventy-five kilograms, it's probably a Frog person.*

*And also, if it's hairless with a wide leathery mouth with no lips, it's most definitely one.*

*Visit our community news page for more paranoid paranormal sightings of inhuman creatures.*

*Breakfast is served until eight a.m.*

*Good luck with that!"*

**PROFESSOR WOLTER WESSELS**
**Herpetologist notes. Day 935 Post-Doomsday**
**Environmental Project III**
**Underground Laboratory**
**Fochville gold mine grid**
**South Africa**

THIS IS PROBABLY my last entry. However, I say and believe that every day. Whoever reads this, you have found us. My scientific method and critical thinking lead me to study empirical avenues that both explain and defy the laws of physics and biology in irrational and chaotic ways. It was through testing my hypothesis that the outcome was gloriously positive.

Yet, to my detriment, the sponsors had confiscated my subjects for reasons I only grasped too late. They should never have attempted that unless understanding the inherent behavior inside and outside their habitual environment. They allowed me to watch other, more trusted scientists work in my laboratory. They would have dismissed me if I interfered with the research. My research! I watched as they genetically altered male specimens in-vitro. One subject surpassed all our expectations. We created a super-human species that will live and thrive in the harshest conditions on this or other planets.

But, as the sponsors further insisted on breeding a swarm of walking neurotoxic bio-weapons, they caged the cannibalistic monsters in containers that were to be parachuted worldwide. After their return, I suspect the company would have destroyed them.

But their careful planning and maneuvering backfired. Uncoordinated attacks and rapid infection rates overwhelmed their control. The Brawl, named after the Afrikaans term for bullfrog, 'Brulpadda', released airborne toxins that quickly spread due to global windstorms. Other natural disasters have compounded their failures, and all govern-ments have perished within weeks.

The disappearance of the internet due to the bombing of electricity grids and satel-lites caused their downfall. The Brawls had killed their handlers, ran rampant in Africa, and spread to Europe. A few selected individuals received the little anti-toxin developed. The ones who survived the outbreak fought to escape the global massacre and were either eaten or killed. I shared the formula with Joshua Adams, my colleague, and friend who lives at EP-1, the Antarctic Research Center.

We—Environmental Project III (EP-III)—were assigned rocketry and DNA manipu-lation to ensure the superhuman race survives and thrives on the moon. They also tasked us with research to address fuel, oxygen, and water shortages. However, every-thing went wrong. Scratch that—it all fell apart.

The American Star Connect company funded the rockets built for human travel in cooperation with the WHPSS. A global effort to establish a lunar presence, and I suspect is the driving force was behind all this madness. Locate the number two mineshaft, marked in blue. It's the northwest tower near the Fochville ruins. Inside lies a rocket ready for human travel.

I'm tired, and it seems pointlessly futile and impossible to fix this. I named the King of the Brawl, Eryn. It's typically a female name, and I determined it fitting to call him so in the context. Eryn means peace and comes from Ireland's word *Eire*, which is derived from the Goddess Eriu. They named the island after her, according to Irish mythology and folklore. Someone who knows this history would find the resemblance fascinating.

He is but a young boy who believes he is protecting me from his brothers. Specifi-cally, the more humanoid one I named Ernest, who's immune to Eryn's empathic and pheromone influence. He is a dangerous free agent who cannot harmonize or work well with others. I classify him as dangerous. The creature shows primary psychopathic tendencies. He manipulates, is callous, and I'm positive he feigns fear and anxiety. I think Ernest drove the nest to break out, and Eryn is the one who sent them home. Eryn says that Ernest enjoyed it. He shows no guilt or remorse for what they have done.

Ernest is a cunning and antisocial Brawl who manipulates his brother, the king, for his own narcissistic needs. I know he wants to eat me. The nest is not responding to me, only to their king. They lie and wait as an army. I attempted my best to influence and educate the king on the ways of humans. He responded with an immense psychological shift away from his nest toward the ways of men. I sense a deep yearning to connect with me. I encouraged a relationship with Joshua. I hope he includes Eryn in his research and introduces him to the rest of the Phoenix population. Eryn has assured me that the nest is sleeping.

I tasked Eryn with destroying the tunnel system. I told him to bury the nest. Only then will Eryn be able to join Joshua Adams and his men in Antarctica, the glass-domed city of Phoenix. If you are reading this, do not trust Ernest. Carry the anti-toxin with you. If you can reproduce the formula, it's available in the back of this notebook. Do it! If you can kill the swarm and keep Eryn, please do it. I am proud of my creation. He is the embodiment of the perfect human soldier. He's intelligent, and I suspect he will exceed your expectations with loving coaxing. He needs lots of stimulation to discover who he is and how he fits into this world. Wrapped inside his powerful body are innocence and naivety. If you are fortunate to get to know him, you will agree he's magnificent. His empathetic and intellectual characteristics made it simple to appeal to his humanity. He seems to identify himself as human, but he finds it challenging to shunt the Brawl nest.

I observed and tested some of his abilities to override the mindless swarm behavior. They accept him as king, as bees do their queen, which I found fascinating because they're male. It may be a blessed failsafe that they cannot reproduce. I'm unsure of the length of their lifespan. I fear they are protandrous hermaphrodites born as males, but like in a beehive, only the king of the Brawl can reproduce.

It's unclear whether this trait is positive or negative and how it affects his ability to lead a species that can't coexist with humans.

To stay alive, if possible, I've forgone my role as a scientist and taken on my role as a father. I hope the knowledge I've shared is helpful to the person finding this.

CHAPTER II

# ERNEST

*"GOOD MORNING, CITIZENS OF OUR LOVELY GLASS-DOMED CITY.*

*I am Lasitor, your Artificial Intelligence (AI) community news broadcaster. It is now six a.m.*

*The local Antarctic temperatures are −70.6°F.*

*Volcanic activity is increasing rapidly. Ice caps are melting alarmingly fast, constantly shifting and creating pools of hot water and steam. Update your last will and testament, then enjoy a relaxing swim in these new natural hot springs.*

*Breakfast is served until eight a.m.*

*Thank you, and enjoy your day."*

**ERYN, King of the Brawl**

THEY'D JUST RETURNED from the hunt cold, empty-handed, and hungry. Ernest was extra loud, as if to chase away their prey. Eryn listened with half an ear to his brother. He climbed into the rusted steel box elevator, ready to go back down to check on the boys.

Grabbing the bar of the metal door aggressively in frustration and flinging the thing shut, he stood glaring at his much smaller twin.

"Ernest tells you, brother, my trap will work!" he shrieked with a rasping, froggy voice above the noise of the old mine cage that worked like elevators in tall buildings.

Eryn recoiled. White knuckling his trident in frustration, he said through gnashing teeth. "The nest is hungry; they want to tunnel themselves out. I will do what I should have done long ago, putting them to sleep forever. I sense only six heartbeats left. They are suffering, brother. It's not fair that they were born only to suffer for existing. We can explain to the Icemen King that he is a good man, and he will understand if we admit we made a mistake. It hurts me deeply, brother, and I'm so tired, *croak*. They are in pain, they are hungry, and they are scared. If they reach the Ice City, it will be chaos. Humans will die. Then those bigger beasts will come. Don't you feel alone, brother? Don't you remember how good it was to talk to people? Every year, I feel lonelier and lonelier."

Ernest ignored him, just as he had when they had hunted. Eryn's carefully laid action plan was ruined. He was sure Ernest had heard him, so he was waiting for an affirmation. But Ernest was licking drool from his lips and not replying.

The cage came to a sudden halt with a loud bang as it struck rock bottom. Ernest snapped out of that faraway look in his beady black eyes. Eryn lifted the two-hundred-pound gate as if it were nothing.

Eryn froze. "I smell blood. If something happened to the boys—"

"I stubbed my toe, that's all." Ernest shrugged and shuffled closer to Eryn as they exited the elevator cage. He feigned brotherly love as he looked up at Eryn. "Everything will work out in the end. You will see."

Ernest was lying. Eryn could see right through him. He saw the deceptive cunning, recognizing the psychopath who lived within his brother. *Dammit, this was your last chance, brother.*

Eryn gave him his ultimate opportunity. He told him about his plans, but Ernest disappointed him. He pretended to have never heard him speak those words. Eryn was hurt. His brother had made his choice today and had chosen his fate.

Ernest rolled his shoulders forward to enlarge his hunched back and rubbed his finger pads, producing a sticky mucus that dripped from them. Ernest whispered with a shrill, high-pitched voice, "My trap will work."

Ernest continued to avoid the subject of returning the boys. He pretended to talk about hunting and trapping, thinking he was fooling his brother, hurting Eryn even more.

"Also, don't worry about the humans," he said and side-bumped Eryn, pretending to be playful. "Ag, come on," Ernest said with an Afrikaans accent. "Stop being such a worrywart, brother. Tshe, tshe, tshe!" Sucking the spittle back through his teeth, he shuffled even closer. Ernest shook his head, clucking his tongue in visible anger when Eryn didn't react. The sounds echoed down the stuffy tunnels.

From the corner of his eye, Eryn noticed Ernest planting his webbed toes deep into the mud and moss of the cave floor. *He's anchoring himself.* Eryn realized just as he felt Ernest pulling on his arm.

Eryn looked down at the sticky, amphibian-like fingers around his forearm. He didn't like Ernest in his personal space and felt disgusted and intimidated. His brother was unstable. Ernest repulsed him, and he knew his brother noticed his sudden, rigid posture. But Ernest continued his trickster effort to pull Eryn deeper into the darkness. *Further away from the salty copper odor of blood.*

"Here, let's go sit down so we can talk more privately." Eryn saw how Ernest calculated his movements before discreetly moving away from their proximity. *Why did I never see this?* But he knew his brother. He'll start with verbal attacks next. Eryn expected aggression if he didn't agree with him.

"Brother, why do I smell blood? I must go check—" Eryn had barely finished when Ernest instantly switched to verbal assaults.

"Ernest is so tired of thinking for you." He flipped from happy hunter to disappointed brother faster than Eryn could blink his eyes. "And so sick of your piece of dumb, lazy, frog-ass. And your negativity! Useless numbskull calling yourself our king." He patted his chest. "Ernest should be the leader. Ernest does all the work and all the thinking. On top of it all, the shit Ernest endures hearing about your feelings." He slapped himself on the forehead, and the more Ernest rambled, the more he spat malicious lies.

"You dumb brawl, you can't even make the right choices without Ernest. You are brainless, inbred, thinking you know it all. Look at you. You're frogging pussyfooting!"

That shocked Eryn. Even if he was used to this, he steeled himself, but it always drove the knife deeper. Each nasty word hurt more and more each time.

He wondered why Ernest was pulling on him like that. He tried to joke and lift the mood. At the same time, he stood his ground, not willing to move a centimeter further.

Not trusting Ernest, he stared at him. "Stop it right now!" he yelled at him.

Ernest gasped and leaped backward, lifting his chin defiantly and baring his teeth through his thinly stretched, rubbery lips. His teeth glistened with venom and spit. Blocking his path.

A rush of memories of dead humans flooded Eryn's system with adrenaline. His heart raced, and he felt his pulse rapidly tapping on his temples. Gathering himself, he breathed deep, silent breaths. With his left hand, Eryn grasped Ernest's right hand and squeezed it tightly. "Listen to me!" he said. Hoping to get his full attention. Eryn leaned down and looked him in his black eyes. Ernest gasped, blinking in surprise. "Yes, look at me and listen to me, brother." Eryn had never touched his brother like that before. Usually too scared or disgusted by him.

"Croak!" Ernest answered, small and submissively. "Sorry, I didn't mean to say that, but you know how I get when I am hungry," Ernest cried out.

"Brother, stop ignoring the big problem. We need to take the humans back. Their families will destroy us when they find us. We must make this right, brother. They will shoot first, asking no questions when they find us." He lifted his hand and pinned Ernest with his stare. "No, brother, you have avoided this problem for too long."

Ernest did a double-take. His eyes bulged, and he crossed his thin, amphibious arms in defiance.

"The boys said..." Ernest lifted his pointer finger, stuck his long tongue out, and licked water drops from the rock face. "All the talking is making me thirsty," he said.

That was one advantage of living underground. Water ran in rivulets and dripped from the rock walls.

Rolling his buggy eyes, Ernest took a deep breath and sighed. "Ernest doesn't care what the boys say! They will say anything to be released." He talked about himself in the third person and scowled.

Eryn sensed raw hate emanating from his brother toward him and his friends as he spoke wickedly. His brother was a short Brawl, only one meter tall compared to himself, a two and a half meters giant. They were egg brothers, and Ernest was the smallest of the whole nest. Their father had told Eryn that Ernest almost died when they hatched from the same egg. Eryn always felt like he had to protect and please his brother.

"You stupid mampara!" Ernest insulted Eryn in South African English. He smiled cunningly and pretended to be joking, but Eryn knew he was planning something. Recognizing the false smile for what it was, an attempt to manipulate and change the subject to confuse Eryn. That was one of Ernest's oldest jokes, finding it funny each time he accused Eryn of being a mampara. He would laugh out loud and fall to the ground, kicking his skinny legs as he laughed at the double entendre.

Parra meant frog, and mampara meant idiot, so frog idiot. Eryn never understood why it was so funny because, to him, it felt mean, and he could never understand being cruel or mean.

But now, Ernest let loose and was ranting. "You are an idiot frog. Eryn, you stole all my juju in the egg, and I want it back!" He rubbed the pads of his little toad fingers together again, thinking he was in charge and spoke to Eryn as if he were younger and going to listen to him. Eryn stepped backward and shook his head from side to side. This shit was getting old quick. Ernest's belittlement was not worth the price of not being alone anymore.

*He's always been sly, but this is too much. His verbal attacks are getting worse.*

Eryn pushed Ernest to move out of his way. Ernest pointed his small, bony index finger at Eryn and continued with the accusations. "If Ernest didn't break out of our egg, Eryn would have eaten Ernest! Like the nest, the bigger brother always eats the smaller ones, but Ernest is smarter. Ernest is still the smartest and the smallest." He took a deep breath and continued ranting, his voice growing raspier the longer he continued. "That makes Ernest mad and very, very sad." He furiously kicked at the rocks on the floor, alternating his skinny, knob-kneed legs, looking like he was skipping rope.

Eryn felt sorry for him instinctively, although he knew what was to come. *I have to kill my brother today.* He stepped closer to hug his brother, wondering why the sudden resentment about things that happened when they had hatched years ago.

"Ernest wants humans. Give Ernest one human, only one. You are selfish, brother!" And there it was. They reached full circle. Since they returned, Eryn and Ernest had the same argument repeatedly. He was big-muscled, but he never bullied Ernest to feel insignificant. The two had been inseparable twin brothers since birth, or so Eryn thought. Because they were the only two brothers who survived being hatched from the same egg, Eryn assumed that made them special, like he was responsible for looking after Ernest.

*This is it. I've heard enough!*

Eryn slammed his self-made pure gold trident into the rock floor. It was the one special thing he had left from his father. He carried it around like a walking stick. Pieces of stalactites fell from above them.

Miraculously, that silenced Ernest for a bit. When Eryn spoke, he warped his voice to sound husky and melodic. "Listen to me. I was born to lead the nest, not you." Ernest dropped his gaze to the ground.

"I know you think you have me wrapped around your finger, but you don't. One more word about eating, *my friends*, and I'll end you." Eryn's voice sounded like a rolling thunderstorm into the darkness of the tunnels. He puffed his chest and repeated his words in an even lower baritone. "E-n-d, y-o-u! Do you understand me, b-r-o-t-h-e-r?" he bellowed like a gigantic bullfrog.

"Ugly frog face!" Ernest retorted. "Look at that face. Big, wide, and flat, like a human's. You can't even look like a decent Brawl."

Eryn ignored the taunting. "Listen, brother, if even one human is dead, the icemen will kill us." Eryn was so upset that his head felt like it was about to explode. He turned his back on Ernest and took a breath for courage. He was tired of arguing and missed the boys. *Why do I smell blood?* He turned to check Ernest's toes for blood.

"Remember, Joshua Adams is dead. Our only friend who brought us food is dead! Now, who will meet me outside the glass city so I can bring us food? I don't eat humans. You should stop thinking about them as food. After your abduction stunt, our lives are in danger." Eryn forced the words through clenched teeth. Fearlessly, he looked down at his smaller brother, who thought he had the upper hand, and slammed his golden trident into the rock floor again so the vibrations of his power flowed into the mine tunnels and cavern floors, causing fine tremors beneath their feet.

"That's smart, brother. Bury all of us underground," Ernest goaded as the thundering and cracking sounds of the earth died down around them.

"Why didn't I see this earlier?" Eryn asked, looking at his trident as if it were for the first time. *The answer was in my hands the whole time.* More pieces of rock and dust fell from above. He realized he knew what to do once he brought the boys to the surface. His brother is not going to help him flood the tunnels to fill the mine with mud and sludge.

"I understand you are hungry. I am, too." Once more, Eryn pushed his brother to the side. Wondering if he should stab his brother with his spear. "Joshua said we should plant food, and it will grow," Eryn said. He had hoped to learn the secret from Joshua, and now it's too late for that. The boys said they could show him how.

Ernest ignored Eryn and took a deep breath, inhaling the air. "I can smell the blood pumping through their veins, brother."

Eryn's fear for the boys magnified as Ernest licked his lips after wiping the saliva with his forearm from his mouth. He closed his eyes. "Ernest can taste their flavor already as Ernest tears their tongues out. Ernest wonders how chewy human tongues are." He opened his dark eyes, revealing his true evil intent as he spoke slowly, spelling it out for Eryn. "Brother, I dream of sweet and salty blood on my tongue and wake up in the mornings with a wet pillow as I dream about sucking the marrow from their bones." Wiping the saliva from his chin again, he looked at it and then licked the palm of his dirty hands with his long tongue. "Humans taste so good, so much better than monkeys. You will want nothing else once you taste a human, brother," he said and licked his fingers. Then, with a slight tilt of his head, he sucked his fingers and seemed to savor the blood from underneath his nails.

Eryn shivered as he watched the cannibalistic delight on his brother's face. He hoped that it was animal and not human blood. "We can't eat them. We won't have anything to bargain with," Eryn said. He knew he sounded weak and unconvincing. He felt sick to his stomach. In that moment, he also knew he wouldn't be able to change Ernest's mind.

"We know nothing about growing food, and humans can show us how. Besides fish and rats, we have meerkats and many other animals to feed on." Eryn knew he was grasping at straws. He couldn't remember when he last saw something alive on the ground. They only ate birds or bats. Nothing survived in the soil. He also knew precisely what caused the frozen desert around them. *I must exterminate the nest and my crazy brother before they kill all the Earth's humans, plants, and animals.* Eryn paused; the time for being nice had ended. He squashed his eyes closed as hard as possible, forcing the tears back.

Ernest laughed at him.

"The icemen aren't stupid. Look at what they built. The most beautiful glass city. I want that for us. Don't you see that, brother?" Eryn knew he was alone in his understanding. The Brawls couldn't see past their hunger, and his brother was the same. "They wouldn't come to help us. They would come to eliminate us if we ate their children."

"Give Ernest only one, now!" Ernest gulped but continued his argument. "Brother, be smart. Do you want to live in glass houses? That's not freedom."

"Yes, dammit! We will have all the food, freedom, and friends. I don't want to live underground and alone forever." And that was Eryn's truth. He wanted a mate. He wanted two mates. The two beautiful boys...no, not boys...the young men who sang for his soul. He couldn't mate with the things in the nest, and thinking of mating with his brother nauseated him. "Argh, do you always want to be hungry and worried about where your next meal comes from?"

Ernest smiled up at his brother, his biggest smile, with his teeth showing. "No, because over two thousand men in the glass city are waiting to be plucked and eaten," he said sarcastically, his hands on his hips.

Eryn had had enough. He pushed his aura of dominance into Ernest, subduing him. Ernest looked like he wanted to fall to the ground, his knees bent. But before Eryn could think, he would show his yellow belly, like all the nest brothers did when Eryn showed them who the true King of the Brawl was.

Ernest straightened up. "I can resist you. Even in your ugliness, even if you smelled good. I can resist you, brotherrrrrrrrr."

Eryn tried staring him down, but they ended up having a staring contest. Ernest's hateful gaze told Eryn he wished he could kill him with his bare hands, but he couldn't, so he hurt Eryn with words and poisoned his mind.

*I should overpower him and give him one bite. I am stronger; I could paralyze him. I could kill him with one bite before he croaked.*

But the big Brawl King was torn between reason, dignity, responsibility, and insanity. Between loneliness, distrust, and doing what was right, he didn't move his eyes from his brother's.

*How do I just start killing him? How? Do I spear him or bite him?* Eryn never planned, and he never thought to ask. Do you do it, and then what? He'd never killed anything. *I'm a useless killer.*

Ernest surprised him and broke the stare. "Here, stick this bone in the ground. Maybe this one will grow." He handed Eryn a fishbone.

"It won't. I've planted many bones. I tell you, they need light, heat, and fertile soil...I think. The humans said we should only have asked, and they would have helped. I believe them, and I miss talking to Joshua. That's the truth, brother."

"That is the stupidest thing you ever said," Ernest snapped at his brother. "We live here because our tunnels are safe. We survived the frozen waters because we are Brawl, and Brawl is a secret kept hidden deep inside the earth. No one can reach us unless we want them to. All they see is an abandoned old mine shaft. They will never think we are down here. Ernest will put up signs saying so. *Stay away. We will kill you. Humans are not welcome. Humans will be eaten.*" He stuck his tongue out at Eryn, putting his thumbs in his ears, waving his froggy fingers, and pulling his face. Ernest teased and sang, "They will never find us, neh, neh, neh, neh, neh!"

Eryn bumped his fist on his forehead. In his mind's eye, he saw all the wooden signages zig-zagging from the mine. *Ernest might as well paint a runway for the humans.* "They will. And when they come, we will meet them and tell them we have their boys, safe and ready to go home."

"And then we have dinnerrrrr," Ernest interrupted, biting down on his thin, stretchy lips. "I'm kidding," he blurted out. Then he fell to the ground, rolling on his back from side to side, holding onto his fat belly, and let loose with croaks and horrendous laughter.

CHAPTER 12

# TRUST YOUR GUT

## GENERAL BRAD McCORMICK

BRAD PACED in front of the helm, his head low and hands sunk deep in the pockets of his arctic jacket. The news from Bryan's latest report left his mind reeling. He enjoyed the cathartic, meditative state that his counting provided. Because their airship wasn't as large as his usual secret hideout back in Phoenix, he had to improvise.

Instead of counting to one hundred, he'd settled for five. *One, two, three, four, five. Groove, step over the line, and turn. One, two, three, four, five. Groove, step over...*

"Brad, sit your ass down. We've had just about enough of your pacing." He heard Connor's frustrated demand in his Irish accent. *That meant only one thing: Connor was livid. He must have drawn the short straw to come and order me to calm down.*

"Sorry, Bud, I'm busy." Brad had hoped to be left alone. He continued counting his steps and the grooves between the steel plates beneath his boots. *One, two, three, four, five. Groove, step over the line, and turn. One, two, three, four, five. Groove, step over the line, and turn.*

Connor's boots were on his path. Brad ceased his pacing and gave his friend his scariest death glare. "Get out of my way, Connor."

"Please, you're making it worse for everyone. Your husband sent me to talk to you. Evidently, with just cause. Look at you. If you were my husband, I would throw your bloody ass overboard." Connor's black hair was standing in all directions, and his face had wrinkles and pink lines on the right side. Brad speculated he had probably been sleeping. *Rick must have awakened him to talk to me.*

"It's only been twelve days. You act as if we were months at sea. Get a grip on your emotions." Connor laid it out straight, using all the tact he could muster. Just then, laughter boomed from down below the deck.

"See what I'm talking about? They act as if we're on a holiday or something."

"That's uncalled for. We're all equally invested in rescuing our kids. But, unlike you, we're trying to stay positive. We eat, sleep, and feed our bodies and minds because we want to be ready for whatever is waiting in that mineshaft."

"I know, but..." Brad started and then stopped, deflated. Taking his gloved hands out of his pockets, he showed Connor the photos of his boys. Brad couldn't keep it in any longer. Tears rolled down his cold cheeks. "It's all my fault. I worry about my boys. And I can't do anything about it but wait. How can they sit down there and act as if nothing's happened to our boys? It irritates the crap out of me!" Brad turned and yelled into the distance behind them. The laughter abruptly ended.

"I know." Connor put a hand on Brad's back. The touch had a soothing effect on him. He willed himself to calm down and swallow his tears. "Imagine what it would've looked like if all of us acted as you have been. Pacing up and down the deck, hands fisted, ready to strike, swearing, and talking to ourselves. We'd look like bloody lunatics! Not everyone reacts to a stressful situation in the same way. It's energy and anger being spent in the wrong place and time," Connor explained.

"I hear you. Rick has essentially said the same thing, but I still feel responsible for all this. If I'd called it in, this probably wouldn't have happened. Men would have joined me on the ice, and we would've had Phoenix on lockdown much earlier." Spittle and tears flew sideways as Brad ranted.

"Stop that. This isn't healthy. You can't lead a rescue mission thinking about coulda, woulda, shoulda's." Connor spoke firmly. Punching his index finger into his palm, emphasizing each word.

"I'm sorry. Can't we at least go faster?"

"We could, but they might hear us coming. If these things have exceptional hearing, we want to have the element of surprise, remember?" Connor pointed up to the mouth of the hot-air balloon above them. "We planned a stealth attack, so it makes sense to approach soundlessly. We'll sit this balloon down in two days, tops, just like we planned," Connor promised.

Brad stopped pacing. "You know what? I'd gotten used to all the pacing space provided inside Phoenix." He blew out a breath. "I guess I've gotten used to being in control and spoiled by everything running smoothly. Also, I feel a little claustrophobic on this ship." Brad looked away into the distance. "No surprises there," he mumbled, letting his head fall, ignoring his best friend's stare.

"Yeah, my brother, I know." Connor stepped closer for support and patted him on the shoulder once again. Brad turned to his friend, who was smiling gently. Connor lifted both his arms, resting one hand on each shoulder. Brad straightened, squared his shoulders, and made eye contact with Connor.

"Remember the last time you were upset like this? Before we wrote the code. When you stormed into the office, acting as if the sky would fall because three men were having sex. All because you wanted to have control over other people's sexual behavior. This is the same thing. The lesson you learned was that you can't go around burning people at the stake because they don't think, act, love, worry, feel, etcetera, as you do. And that applies to every human being left on this planet. Think about it. If we all examined our own attitudes and refrained from controlling others', all the world's crises would be resolved. How we act and react toward each other, nature, and our surroundings"—he pointed to the horizon, mountains, and themselves—"that's all we can control. Not others, only ourselves. Do you get my meaning? It turned out all right for us when we gave the responsibility back to the men and stopped the archaic thought pattern of what we want versus how we can make it work for everyone."

Brad nodded, then sat down to take hold of the wheel. Steering the ship by taking it off autopilot gave him a sense of control. He liked Mika and Connor's ingenious design. He could steer from various points below and the upper deck, whether they were sailing, gliding, flying, or floating.

"You and Mika did an excellent job on the design of this ship. Even though it is a bit claustrophobic."

Connor sat down next to Brad. "Hmmm, thank you." They watched as they soundlessly drifted over the snow-covered Table Mountain at Cape Point, South Africa.

After almost an hour, Brad broke the comfortable silence. "Thank you, Connor. I needed that."

"That's all right, my friend. Will you be okay now? I need something to drink and eat. Do you need anything?" Connor got up and stretched his back and arms. Both were wearing their new tactical arctic suits. Even with the freezing temperatures on the deck, their bodysuits kept their bodies toasty inside, so they were comfortable.

"I'll be right back."

"Sure, take your time. I'm good for now. I'll get a bite later." Brad nodded and continued enjoying the view. Connor turned, opened the hatch, and disappeared down the stairs and into the dinette where the others were playing poker.

Flashes of memories assailed Brad, remembering when he almost needed a triple coronary bypass after seeing the three young men getting their rocks off in the tunnels.

The moment those odd sex noises were in earshot, he should have turned around, but no, he had to investigate the echoes of moans and groans coming through the tubes.

He smiled—the nostalgia relaxing him. The icy wind froze his cheeks. To free up his hands, he reactivated the autopilot and set the Blue Halcyon on the route course waypoint northeastwards to the Drakensberg Mountain range. Then he removed one glove, massaging the life back into his cheeks.

Now and then, a bird, primarily a seagull, would land on the deck, wondering who dared to fly into their airspace, squawking noisily. Putting his glove back on, he appreciated the colorful sunset for a few minutes.

Mixed feelings of peace and foreboding anticipation made him anxious. He closed his eyes and took a deep breath of cold air. After holding it for a few seconds, he slowly released it. He repeated the exercise several times, feeling much of the tension go. When he opened his eyes, he peacefully enjoyed the stunning oranges and blues of the South African horizon.

*Squawk! Squawk!* Another seagull, no, not a seagull, a secretary bird, came investigating. Brad's heart leaped with joy as he admired the quill-like crests on the back of its head and the light bluish-gray plumage and red-colored face. A magnificent bird, it was over a meter high. He said hello. It was bad luck not to.

"Hello, Mr. Secretary Bird, just excuse us while we experience the thrill and peaceful serenity of hot-air ballooning through your airspace. Come join us," Brad said gently, not moving from where he sat.

*Squawk! Squawk!* It answered and flew off. That was probably a no, Brad thought, but he felt elated by the blessing of the rare experience.

He remembered an interesting fact about secretary birds. No human had ever witnessed these birds mating.

Amused by that thought, he reminisced about the times he saw others have sex. His thoughts wandered back to the subterranean tunnels when he got acquainted with a threesome that shattered his narrow-minded world into a million pieces. *Connor's correct, and he makes a valid point. God, will I ever wash that erotic spectacle from my mind?* Dylan Hurst received a hammering from Dr. Mitchell Fairgate while the young Amir stood on his knees in front of Dylan. "Ha!" What a shock. They tainted my mind, and yeah, that's funny in hindsight." Brad slapped his thighs, laughing at himself and his overreaction.

Then his thoughts drifted to Simon and Paul, his oldest sons. Simon was his first-born. His biological son, by his wife, who had died in the Doomsday attacks before she could join them. Both boys came to Phoenix with Brad as students in training when they were just nineteen years old. Paul had married into the family ten years ago. They'd made a suicide pact the day he saw them having sex. He never told them he had overheard or seen them. However, he'd let them know he loved them and supported their relationship, and they were still together. That was the best decision ever. Both were physicians today, making him proud; he had a fantastic relationship with them.

*Why do I have a history of walking in on people having sex?*

Thinking back even further to the day he had walked into his twin brother Daniel's room with his mother following behind him, and how his mother cried when they saw *Daniel and Jerrod* together in his bedroom.

Then, his mind jumped to that horrible day when he'd found Daniel lying on his bed, the linen soaked with bright red blood. He could still vividly see the multiple wrist slashes, Daniels's peaceful, pale face, and that damn letter he could never forget.

Transported back to his brother's room, he smelled the sweet iron odor of blood and saw the words in front of him on the note.

*I'm sorry I was such a disappointment to all of you. I'm humiliated and beaten. I couldn't seem to help what I was doing. I've embarrassed Brad and made Mom ashamed of me, and Dad, I guess you're right, I'm not a man. I have nothing if I can't be with the man I love. Don't blame Jerrod. He's a good man. He won't let me be with him if I'm humiliated or lose my family. Be happy. I love all of you.*

"Bloody lies! You were never an embarrassment or a disappointment to me. I miss you, brother. If you had stayed, you could have sat right next to me. You were my hero. What you did, killing yourself, confused me and messed me up for many years." Brad closed his eyes and drifted toward sleep. He felt a warm blanket thrown over him. His feet lifted and tucked in, cocooning him.

When he woke, Brad thought his husband was kissing him but soon realized it was a cold, wet rag wiping his face instead of warm sensual lips caressing him.

"Is that bird shit? Lord, yes, that's bird shit! Brad, you have bird shit all over your face." Juandre laughed hysterically. "Now that's what I call shitfaced!" He pointed at Brad, teasing him like he usually did. "Gentlemen, to your left, you'll see a shitfaced general. I don't…"

"Juandre, I'm going to kill you!" Sleepily, Brad sat up, swiped a gloved hand over his face, and felt something crusty. He checked his gloves and confirmed it was probably bird shit. He looked up at Rick, who enjoyed the spectacle while Juandre giggled, pointed, and skipped in circles like a little girl, embarrassing and irritating their barely awake leader. Although he was still cautious, he was measuring the time and distance to escape Brad's wrath. He was the only one in Phoenix with the guts to tease the mighty general like this. Brad attempted to jump up, ready to throw the irritating nymph off the airship, but they had wrapped him in so many blankets he couldn't get up and was too slow.

"Okay, you get away this time because…" He looked around for an excuse. "Because my husband brought me a coffee!"

Juandre cackled down the stairs, continuing the teasing. "Chicken! Chicken shit, get it, you're a chicken with shit on your face!"

"Damn drag queen, one of these days, I'll teach him a lesson," Brad mumbled, reaching for the coffee his husband held for him. "Thank you, love. What a way to wake up! You know, he doesn't have any respect for me."

"Morning, lover." Rick smiled widely with affection for Brad. His eyes were tearing with laughter and crinkled at the corners. "Juandre drives you batshit crazy, but we all know you let him get away with anything. He has a special spot in your big heart."

Brad looked up. "Don't you start now. He's like those sex-crazed aunts you never want to invite to weddings but somehow always arrive without an invitation." Brad scooted to the side, making space for Rick. "Damn, you're beautiful this morning. Come sit with me under the cozy blankets." Rick climbed in eagerly. "Was it you who covered me with all the blankets? How many are here?" He counted them. "One, two, three, six blankets." Brad lifted his arm for his favorite man in the world.

"I guess I brought two, and each of us came up to check during the night, thinking of you and bringing you a blanket." Rick wiggled himself under Brad's legs and lay to the side. "I missed you last night," he said.

Brad took his gloves off, stroking Rick's beautiful long brown hair and gently wiping it out of his face. He had his hair in a braid, but strands always slipped out at the sides. His attempts were futile. The wind kept blowing them back into his face.

"We'll land in a few hours. Connor said the wind's working in our favor."

"What? I never checked…"

"Don't you worry. We checked everything from downstairs. This is an amazing ship they designed." Brad settled back and finished his coffee, then said, "I'm sorry about last night. I took my frustrations out on you all."

"It's okay. I know you are, and you didn't mean it. It's just when you get like that, you're like a caged lion," Rick replied. "I'm just glad you could get some sleep." Rick then pulled Brad's face in close to kiss him, showing him all was forgiven.

After a few moments, Brad pulled back and asked, "Are you ready for whatever's living down there?"

"I hope they're"—Rick cleared his throat—"they're alive. Strangely, I feel positive, like everything will work out fine. And yes, I'm ready to kick butt. All of us are."

"Then let's get ready." Brad removed the blankets, and Rick caught them before they blew away. The general held his hand out for his husband, feeling determined. "Let's gear up and go over the extraction plan again."

Rick bundled the ball of blankets under one arm and took Brad's hand. "Yes, let's go get ready."

Because the ship's hull was round, they divided it into three large slices downstairs, much like a cake. A dinette for eating and socializing, a bathroom with a shower and toilet, and a shared sleeping area with one enormous bed.

In the dinette, Juandre and Andrew had prepared them a feast. They decked the small table with homemade bread, scrambled eggs, cheese, pan-fried bananas, hash browns, and his famous Rooster Booster Orange Juice, filled with many vitamins to boost stamina.

"Oh, wow, look at this table. Thank you, Juandre. May we sit? Did Connor and Mika eat already?" Brad asked after they washed up.

"They're on their way, quickly making use of the shower and facilities so you can get ready after breakfast. We can't send you to battle on an empty stomach, can we?" Andrew stepped in behind Juandre, kissing his neck and looking proud and in love with his partner.

"Sit, sit, don't be shy," Juandre said effeminately, sounding like he'd lost more of his accent after living in Phoenix for the past twenty-one years. One thing that would never change was that he was trustworthy and well-loved.

"I see you at least got rid of the bird shit, General," Juandre said teasingly.

Brad shook his head and held the plate of freshly cut bread and melted butter for Rick.

"This looks delicious, thank you," Rick said.

"My bear baked the bread," Juandre bragged, pointing his thumbs backward to Andrew.

"Yes, it's easy. Just flour, water, and stick it in the oven." Andrew belly laughed with his deep, friendly giant voice. His green eyes sparkled in the morning sunlight that shone through the cabin windows.

"I bet it's a bit more complicated than that, Andrew. I've never attempted something like this, and if I tried, I know it would be hard as a rock," Brad said.

"Probably, but if you do, we can build houses with it!" Rick teased and shoved the delicious bread into his mouth.

"I'll huff and puff and blow your house down!" Juandre made an *O* with his lips, pumping his arm back and forth, feigning blowjobs.

"I knew you were going to say that. You're so predictable." Brad laughed.

"Yes, or burn Phoenix down," Rick teased again, referring to the last time Brad attempted spaghetti. They all laughed cheerfully when Mika and Connor entered the dinette.

"I see Brad is in a better mood. Morning, comrades," Mika greeted them with an exceptionally wide smile. Behind him, Connor followed with the same smile. Dressed in their newly designed bulletproof suits. Mika slipped into a seat next to Brad, and Connor scraped his crotch on the back of Rick's head.

"Oh, sorry." Rick shuffled his chair deeper under the table. The space was tighter than a virgin's ass, with all six big men inside the dining area, but once the food and table were packed away, the room was reasonably comfortable.

"Since this is the first time you're going into battle, I would like to go through all our plans one last time." A chorus of moans and groans came from around the table.

"I know, but you'll thank me for it. I've been in a war. It never turns out the way you plan, so we must be prepared for all possibilities," Brad said, hammering the table with the back of his knife.

"We've been going over these steps for the past month. Every time a new satellite photo came in, we met. We're ready, sir!" Juandre moaned.

Brad shook his head. "No, one more time. I must give you a rundown, and I want you to tell me, step by step, what follows what, and how to proceed with the minimal confrontation with those, whatever they are. The plan is to go in and remove the boys without anyone noticing. You're not soldiers, but I'm thrilled that Bryan had monthly compulsory basic defense classes and that the civilians at Phoenix trained.

"Also, I know you've never been a part of a special operation extraction with the least amount of contact with the enemy. You're all young and healthy, trained to defend Phoenix. This is helpful, but it's the reason I'm nervous. Not one of you has seen a real battlefield with blood, gore, and men screaming for help. I don't want that for you, so this differs from whatever your defense classes have taught you about eliminating the threat.

"This is stealth, and if you must kill, do it silently. This is not going in and closing your eyes and pulling the trigger, shooting whatever shows its face from left to right." He paused, pointing at Juandre. "Like a video game." He clapped his hands, and they straightened up.

"Okay, Juandre, please pack the food away. Andrew, get the room ready. I want the maps, weapons, and everything unpacked and ready to assemble. Fifteen minutes. I'll be back. Get your suits on. Oh, don't wash with soap, shampoo, or any deodorant. You want to smell as natural as possible."

"Oh, man." Juandre moaned again.

"Juandre, I've had enough. You're staying here. I decided that right now. You're not ready for this." Brad, as the General, stared him down, making it clear his word was final. "No, not one word of back talk. This is serious."

"I think that's a wise choice," Andrew said.

"No! Now, who will look after you, my bear?"

"See, that's exactly why you can't go. No one's looking after anyone here. We work together and trust they'll be able to make the right choices to be safe."

Andrew put his hand over Juandre's mouth, silencing him playfully.

"Please assemble and disassemble the weapons, and when I'm back, we'll talk in detail. Juandre, I'm not being funny. It's better to stay with the ship and make sure we have something to go home in. You're responsible for our transportation home."

Juandre straightened up, realizing he had an important job.

He saluted. "Yes, General."

"Good, thank you. Weapons, extraction plan, and defense plan when I return."

Fifteen minutes later, Brad walked back into the room with Rick. He noticed the changes in the room. They had flipped the round dining table into a smaller rectangular table and folded the little cabin chairs underneath the sofas. Juandre and Andrew must have been the ones who cleaned the galley and swiftly turned it into a makeshift field surgery or combat casualty care area. As Brad had requested, Mika was finishing up the unpacking of all their gear and weapons. He was quiet and goal-focused, but he mentioned Connor had slipped into the pilothouse to get ready to land their ship. Juandre and Andrew completed testing their radios and were donning their suits.

When Brad grabbed their attention, the six of them looked ready for battle and were dressed in their tactical arctic suits of white, brown, green, and black camouflage. Over their heads, they wore ski masks woven from the same material as the bulletproof body-suits they wore underneath—the military-issued helmets with night-vision goggles folded over their eyes.

Brad let them show him how to load their guns again and again. Their little laser guns had only a few shots loaded. Since they were prototypes, he didn't want them to depend on them, but used them as a backup. He checked their knives, flare guns, Glupi-done shots, torches, ropes, and last, they tested their communication systems. Little earbuds with microphones fitted around the ear that Connor designed a few years ago.

When Brad and the men reviewed the plan of action, he stood back and spoke. "Okay, I'm very impressed with how well you've prepared. I feel confident that we've prepared as best we can. You look good and are ready for whatever may come our way. Stick to the plan, trust your team, and trust your gut!"

# CHAPTER 13

# FROGGING FUCKER



*"MEN OF PHOENIX, LASITOR BIDS YOU A GOOD MORNING.*

*It's now six a.m.*

*Did you know there are science-based ways to reduce hunger and appetite? If you ever manage to skip a meal and become hungry, tell yourself that hunger is normal and keep busy, you could be a boredom eater.*

*Visit your community news page for more easy ways to battle hunger.*

*Breakfast is served until eight a.m."*


**CIAN ROMANOV**


"HEY, you piece of frog shit, let us out! Come back. Where are you going?" Cian's voice was hoarse from screaming, so it sounded like a whisper. Being a say-it-like-it-is kind of guy made him the world's worst cellmate, and their current predicament wasn't high-lighting his usual sunny disposition. No, instead, he gave words to his anguish and irritation. He was sick of being hungry, and he wanted damn clothes. At this level of darkness, he could see three different shades of darkness. Light gray, dark, darker gray, and dark.

"I'm sick of this. What are we waiting for? He said today is the day," he asked for the umpteenth time, and still, no one answered.

"Bloody locked up and tucked away for safekeeping, my ass. Is that what he thinks we are? Do we look safe? No. We wait like life bait. That's what we are." He ranted because his brother and the McCormick twins just sat there, letting him have his turn at freaking out. They rotated that honor a few times a day. The unspoken rules of prisoners stuck in a gold cage in a king's cavern.

"We sit here and wait for our fate!" He waved his arms around in circles, looking like a windmill in hurricane season, as he pointed to the thick golden bars that testified about their captor's goldsmithing skills. Out of frustration, he fell on his ass and planted his feet on either side of a bar, then pushed and pulled the one in the middle.

"Get off your ass and help me. I want to get out of here!" he demanded, but no one was in the mood. "Ugh, it just won't budge." He groaned and pulled. "One of these days, ugh, I'm gonna pop a vein," he said, trying a few more times.

"At least it keeps you busy and us entertained," Ivan remarked.

"A beautiful cage for his beautiful human boys," Cian muttered. Disgusted and defeated, he fell backward, staring up into the dark.

"I'm sick of the darkness. I want to see light!"

After a few minutes of quiet, he felt a hand on his shoulder. Probably Ivan's.

"Brother, don't worry. Eryn said he'll get us out. Just give him more time."

"I'm giving him one day. I can't live like this one day longer. It stinks. I can't breathe." Cian heaved, breathing harder and faster.

"Stop that. You're hyperventilating. You'll pass out and lose consciousness again," Ivan said. *Always coaxing.* He grabbed Cian's hand, squeezing it. Then he looked right at Cian and said, "We have endured this captivity as best we can, given the circumstances. We're all going to get out of here. I'm sure Eryn doesn't know, and as soon as he finds out, he will kill his brother." Ivan reasoned, *always the calm and reasonable twin, the opposite of myself, who's impulsive and emotional.*

"Come closer, so we can huddle and bunch up for heat," Ivan said, pulling his twin closer.

Cian let himself be pulled closer to the other two men, where he and Ivan folded their upper bodies over Kawa's shivering body, containing as much heat as possible. Still dressed in their swim trunks, the dampness of the subterranean mining tunnels was stifling. Kilometers deep into the musty earth, their malnourishment compounded their hypothermia. When they'd arrived, they were having trouble breathing and sweating profusely. The pressure on their eardrums was excruciating, but now they'd acclimated and were not popping their eardrums. One positive thing about the constant dripping of water from the rock surface above their cage was that they at least had clean water to drink. Despite that, the smell from their bucket reeked. *Eryn should come and empty it.*

"I can't believe we haven't caught a sinus or lung infection yet. It's a miracle in itself. The stench of our excrement is suffocating. We've passed the level of let's get out of here!" Cian said, trying to say something positive, but it came out the opposite.

"Maybe, if we're lucky, we can convince Eryn to take us out of the cage to his father's lab. That's a positive move in the right direction." Ivan seemed to look on the bright side by highlighting their new freedom to use the facilities for daily bathroom breaks.

"Of course, that's a big positive, I agree. It's heaven to wash up out of the old bathroom sinks," Donali added scornfully from out of the dark.

"Yes, but terrified doesn't describe how I feel when I see that ugly brother of Eryn's," Cian added, finding it impossible to walk on the bright side of life.

"I'm just thankful Eryn sits with us, and I enjoy how he laughs at our stories. I can tell he's hungry for love and friendship." *Ivan continued his quest to find goodness.*

"I don't feel cold and scared when he laughs or sings for us," Donali added while holding Kawa.

"Yes, but where was he today? We needed him, and he went on a freaking walkabout! I'll give him a piece of my mind if I see him," Cian said, pissed off again.

"Cian, you give pieces of your mind freely every day, the whole bloody day. Eryn went to build a beacon for us. To show our fathers where we are. He'll come for us... trust that for now," Ivan begged, sounding tired.

"I can't believe what just happened to Kawa. Donali, is he okay?" Cian asked, feeling guilty about his antics while Kawa was in pain.

"Hmmm, for now, he's fine. However, as our nightmare has quickly become our reality, we need to get him home as soon as possible," Donali replied.

"As if being abducted by frogmen only in our swim trunks wasn't bad enough. Surviving not being eaten isn't something one expected to be celebrating," Cian added sarcastically.

"Being thankful for only a chomped-off arm instead of another limb isn't something I ever thought to experience," Kawa moaned. Donali held him tighter in his arms. "He'd munched on my arm in front of my eyes." Kawa cried and muffled his wails in his brother's lap.

"This nightmare is genuine. That frogman crushed your radius and ulna like a bloody potato chip." Cian mimicked Ernest's raspy voice. "*Naughty and saucy knickknacks.*" Kawa cried louder as Cian described their ordeal with vivid clarity. Oblivious to his insensitivity, he rambled on. "And when he bit the tip of your thumb off, and the blood sprayed all over us, that was gross! I'll never, ever suck my fingers clean after I have eaten," Cian added.

"Thank you, Cian. We all needed to hear that. You can be so blatantly crude sometimes," Ivan reprimanded him, and Cian rolled his eyes.

"The animal almost came back for seconds but thought better of it when the king called for him," Cian said, not backing down.

"What will happen when they return?" Donali rocked Kawa in his arms. "The thing winked at us and licked its lips, promising he'd be back."

"The words *that was delicious* are playing on replay in my mind." Kawa sniffled.

The four of them were reaching their limits. They've been sitting in the cage waiting to be rescued, slowly dying of light deprivation and hunger. Barely fed and looking like skeletons, Cian knew his fathers were going to freak out when they saw them. It reeked in the cave, and using a bucket for toileting didn't help.

"Luckily, since we befriended Eryn and explained what humans needed, he was happy to take us to his father's office to use the facilities. Remember, he disagrees with the abduction, but he has many players to move to get us out safely. So I guess if they return and Eryn sees Kawa's arm, he won't let his brother hurt any of us," Ivan said.

"Still, I agree with Cian. The stench is suffocating, and I can barely understand them. It's a weird mix of South African English, Russian, and frog," Donali whispered.

"They croak a lot. There are croaks for yes, croaks for no, then croaks for anger, and a string of croaks for laughter," Cian said, and Kawa whimpered, sounding like he was in excruciating pain.

"Sorry, I just can't stop crying," he said, covering his mouth to hide the sounds.

"That's why I'm trying to joke about it. No need to hide anything from me. Turn onto your left side, and let's elevate the stump." Cian helped him. "That's it!" He ripped off another shred of a swimming towel.

"This is going to hurt." Ivan helped Cian to apply another tourniquet higher up, closer to the shoulder, and bandaged the stump over the already-soaked one.

"Oh, my stars, that's sore! Hurry!" Kawa howled. "Somehow, the bite had numbed the pain and slowed the bleeding, but now, it's burning and hurts like a hot iron," he said. His breathing was wheezy, his teeth chattering. His breath reeked and gave Cian a migraine. He guessed all of their breaths stank, so he kept that to himself, as well. Also, he noticed Kawa's stump was bleeding at an alarming rate, *worse than a slaughtered pig*, and decided not to verbalize that thought. He scooted in next to Donali to keep the stump elevated. While holding his friend, his heart broke for him, and he wished he could do more. So he ended up rocking him back and forth.

"Cian," Kawa whispered.

"Yeah, buddy," he whispered back.

"I see black spots and light flickering. It feels like I want to pass out," Kawa said. Sounding weak and defeated.

"It's okay. Close your eyes. We'll watch over you. Sleep a little." Cian said. Donali sniffled until Cian felt Kawa's body relax. *Hold on, don't die, Kawa.* Cian thought and lightly felt for his carotid pulse to confirm his friend's beating heart.

"When our fathers come to rescue us, and they will come," Donali said. Cian agreed and hoped it was soon. "They'll kill that thing first, and I'll ask them to do it slowly." Donali's voice deepened with the promise of vengeance.

The four looked and smelled like they lived inside a sewage plant. Their matted hair and dirty faces contrasted with the white of their eyeballs.

"This is ludicrous!" Ivan whispered, "We need to think of an escape plan. I agree, brother. I'm not sitting around, waiting to be rescued one more day either. We need to get Kawa out of here. Eryn must come so we can go clean up. I say it's then we take our chance. He must take us up and out, or we overpower, maybe lock him inside somehow. Then we escape."

Far away in the distance, they heard a crashing and banging. A sound they got to know well. They listened to the frogmen getting out of the elevator.

"I bet we can tease the small one enough to unlock the gate so we can overpower him," Ivan said. "We need a plan if Eryn doesn't come through for us today."

"Uhm, I agree with you, brother." Cian hummed while rocking Kawa.

It was Ivan's turn to bend the golden bars. Making grunting noises like a weightlifter at the Olympics, he pulled and pushed on them, entertaining the idea that they might budge this time.

"Their eyes are adapted to see in the dark, so we must be smart. Maybe when the smaller one's alone," Cian said. *Overpowering your enemy on their soil needs perfect strategizing.*

"Eryn's eyes are beautiful. Did you notice his green-golden irises with elongated pupils?" Ivan added almost dreamily.

"Yes, and it's the second time today you've asked us that. I admit, although Eryn is humongous, he has attractive humanoid features," Cian said.

"Ha, so you noticed his other big humanoid features, too! What about the feeling of knowing him, like we should know him?" Ivan asked over his shoulder, still pushing and pulling.

"Yes, I can't put my finger on it, but now that you mentioned it, I know what you mean, brother. It feels like I've seen him somewhere. Like a déjà vu feeling. Do you think we've seen him in Phoenix? We should ask him how long he's been visiting."

"He's a gentle soul, almost like he wants to please us in everything he does, but he doesn't know better. So we need to tell him what we want. You know, like when he sings, I like it when he sings for us. Maybe we should continue to play on that. We were making progress. He's almost my best friend ever!"

"We noticed," Cian said sarcastically. It pissed him off that he wanted Eryn close to him and hated him at the same time. "Today, I tell him to let us out, or we'll never speak to him again. I'm going to give it to him straight because we're at the point of having nothing to lose. No more being nice. Ivan, if you want out, you need to let him know we aren't happily waiting, and we need out. Kawa is going to die of an infection within two days. And that's not me being overdramatic. That's the truth of it. We all need to stand together and not budge on this. We want out today, and his brothers must go. No more serenading, no more waiting."

A pained keening from Kawa forced them to turn their attention elsewhere. Ivan crept in closer to the group. "I need heat," he said, and Cian moved up and threw his other arm around his twin brother, pulling him closer and away from the bars where Ernest could catch him.

"I don't know how much longer I can hang on," Kawa cried. "Why don't they just kill us?" He stuttered between the chattering of his teeth. "I want to go home, please, I want to go home. I want to go home." He repeated the words and mindlessly rocked back and forth.

*He's going to end up with tetanus or an infection.* Cian kept that to himself. "We should demand to go rummage through the lab for meds. We must ask Eryn to go as soon as he returns. Maybe we can find a first aid kit or antibiotics," he said.

"I agree," Donali said.

"Anyway, my only worry is the others Eryn was talking about. Somewhere down here is the nest. If we escape, we should know where to go," Ivan said softly, leaning into them. He threw his arms around the McCormick boys.

"They hatched from eggs, like little tadpoles," Cian said.

They chortled. "We got to know our enemy's routine fairly well. Questions need to be asked about the nest and the tunnels. We should ask about the ship and where to find shelter and food," Donali whispered.

"Ernest is the lunatic. I bet they stole eggs from Phoenix..." Cian abruptly stopped talking and listened. It sounded like someone was walking outside.

*Maybe it's water dripping.*

"Shhh, they're coming..." They all looked up. Listening again—more listening.

"False alarm," Ivan said.

Donali chuckled. "Born with little tails?"

"Yes, that's funny," Ivan said. They fell silent for a minute. Ivan cleared his throat. "My biggest worry is what Ernest said that one brother would eat the other brother. I worry those things have more hatchlings, maybe smaller ones."

"Maybe bigger ones," Cian said.

"Shhh, here they come," Ivan cautioned.

All of a sudden, they heard Eryn saying from outside their cave, "The nest is restless, brother. They're hungry."

"Oh, my stars, we are going to be frog food. I need a weapon. We must ask Eryn for weapons so we can defend ourselves," Cian said.

"There is a nest of frog monsters," Ivan whispered. "He told me that when he closed his eyes and concentrated on them, he was connected to them." He held his finger in front of his lips. They listened—water dripped behind them. They could hear the two frogmen arguing a few meters down the tunnel.


**ERYN, King of the Brawl**

Eryn pointed to his cave, beyond his brother, who was blocking the tunnel to it, where he kept the boys safe until their fathers arrived.

"I'm going to free the boys and light the beacon!" Eryn shoved Ernest hard against the wall. Ernest resisted. He kneed him, glaring at his brother. "Get out of my way!"

Determined to go get the boys. He decided to kill his brother once he'd lit the beacon, he thought, procrastinating killing yet again.

Ernest wiggled free and ran, the pitter-patter of feet jogged Eryn into action. "What do you think you are doing?" Running as fast as his little frog legs could carry him, his brother disappeared around the corner into Eryn's cave. The boys screamed hysterically.

*The boys are in danger.*

"Ernest, no!" he shouted as he sprinted as fast as possible to prevent their carnage.

"Leave us alone, you psycho, no, piss off!" Cian stood in front, protecting the others as he kicked and screamed while Ernest hopped around the cage. They flattened themselves against the bars on the opposite side of Ernest's reach for an arm or a leg. Open-mouthed, baring his little toothpick teeth, he snarled and groped at them. *Desperate and lost to his hunger for human meat.* Eryn saw the animal in him. And then he saw all the blood.

*What in the ever-loving hell? One boy already has an arm missing!*

Eryn's switch flipped from irresoluteness to a killing rage. He grabbed Ernest at the back of his neck with one arm and picked him up from the ground. Dangling him like Kermit, the Muppet frog. "*Croak!*" His voice blazed like a trumpet in his indignation. Ernest kicked wildly and stretched to grab onto the cage's bars. His beady eyes reflected red. They were savage, and he looked at the boys like they were his only meal.

"No, Ernest, stop your nonsense. No, stop that right now!" Eryn said to no avail as Ernest turned to attack him. Eryn threw Ernest like a wet rag against the rocks, but as soon as Ernest hit the ground, he jumped, flung himself over in a twist midair, and landed on the three-meter-high cage.

"Give me an arm or a leg. That's all I need!" he said as he snarled, saliva dripping. Grabbing onto a white-haired boy—Ivan—he pulled him closer. "I bet you taste different. Your color is different." It was chaos. The boys screamed, holding onto him and dragging Ivan back from Ernest, but his cannibalistic brother wouldn't let go.

"Ernest, no! Ernest, stop that!" Eryn bellowed as he threw his trident aside, not to hurt the boys, he leaped and landed on the cage. He pushed and pulled fiercely on his brother, who ignored him. In the scrimmage, he received a hard kick from one of the boys, who was kicking frantically. *Ernest is seconds away from biting the boy's head off.*

"Ernest, stop it," he ordered, using his commanding voice as he grabbed on and exerted all of his power and pheromones. "I will have to kill you if you don't stop right away." Ernest didn't even blink. He simply kept pulling on Ivan with his mouth just a centimeter away. The boys yelled furiously as they fought to save Ivan. "That's it!" Eryn stood up and delivered a deadly head kick to his brother. He heard bones breaking when his foot connected with his brother's skull for a second time. Ernest fell from the cage like a sack of rocks. *Where is my trident?* Eryn leaped onto his back, preventing him from springing away once more. Ernest wriggled and kicked to escape, but Eryn had him pinned with one knee, securing his lower back while he pressed his head into the dirt. Lifting his head high, Eryn opened his mouth wide and let his fangs slide out. He struck and bit Ernest as hard and deep as he could into the back of his thick, warty neck.

As he injected his deadly venom into his brother, the boys quieted down while heaving and coughing in the background. Ernest stopped his kicking and thrashing. Eryn listened for his brother's last heartbeat. When he couldn't hear anything after a few minutes, he retracted his fangs and fell backward with a plop.

The cave was deadly quiet.

Catching his breath, he lay there staring up at the crystallized cavern roof. He felt horrible for killing his only brother and, worse, realizing he was utterly alone. Relief and immense sadness built inside him until he let it all go. He cried for his father, who wanted more for him. He cried about the pointless annihilation of the humans. And then he cried for being born. When he had calmed, he rolled over onto his hands and knees. Shaking his head in disbelief as he straightened up.

"Boys, we must leave. Can you help me flood it all and bury the nest?"

They looked as though they barely understood his rambling. He couldn't say the words correctly, although he often thought about saying them. *I want to be human and live among humans, doing human things.* But he said, "I will take you back home to your families."

The boys sat shocked and wide-eyed, too scared to move. One move from Eryn, and they scurried backward. Eryn cringed.

He felt ashamed about his treatment of them. "I should have done something sooner. I'm so very sorry. My brother had somehow...lowered my spirit through our bond," he said, wiping the tears and snot from his face and remembering his father, who warned and begged him long ago. He sat with him for days, holding his dead body, talking to him, and even reading to him. He rocked him until he blew up like a balloon and smelled terrible. *I visited the Ice City in a daze, meeting Joshua. I should never have trusted Ernest. Now he's dead. My mind feels lighter, and the haze has cleared.*

Approaching the skittish four boys in the cage, he said, "I need help flooding the tunnels, or we can just leave for the surface, then I'll come back and cause a few tremors and rock falls, burying the nest." His booming voice woke the four shaken humans from their stupor. Eryn knew Ernest was a cunning and dangerous Brawl. Now, he vividly remembered his father's words, "*Eryn, my boy, you need to flood the tunnels and bury your brother and the nest. Leave to live with Joshua.*"

He burst out laughing. Eryn felt as light as a feather. He couldn't stop himself. He croaked and croaked, feeling elated and free for the first time in a long time. "Ernest, you liked the taste of humans too much," he said as he bent down to grab his brother by the ankles.

"Boys, I'll be right back. I'm just taking Ernest away so you don't see him anymore,"

Eryn said over his shoulder and inspected the webbed toes and overly large feet. They looked so different from his own feet. Without a grunt or a moan, he dragged his brother's body out of the cave to discard his corpse far away from the boys.

Next, he planned to unlock the cage, free the boys, and tend to their wounds, especially the little one's stump, where Ernest had chewed it off. The thought made him queasy and nervous.

*The Icemen King will not be happy.*

With no clue how to do medical care for a human, he decided he would take them to his father's office, where they could clean up and use the medical supplies. After that, they would go to the surface while the twins could help him flood the tunnels.

During the scuffle with Ernest, the key around his neck had come off and swung to the back. Eryn mumbled to himself and entered the cave while reciting his steps to himself and searching for the key. Once he found the key, he stood up straight, smiling widely, eyes sparkling with happiness. "I found it. Let's go!" He showed them the giant golden key, feeling triumphant. The boys gasped.

"Little ones, don't be scared," Eryn said, fumbling with the key in the lock. He heard continued gasping. "Calm down. I will help you. I will not hurt you. I'm helping you, see?" he said softly and opened the big golden door to show them.

Then he saw sparks flying in front of his eyes, a sharp pain in the back of his head and neck that zapped through his body, and then their voices and faces disappeared as it all went dark…

# CHAPTER 14
# THE MINE



## GENERAL BRAD McCORMICK

"THIS IS the epicenter of it all," Brad confirmed over the comms as he hung over the rail. Connor steered the ship closer for a better view to inspect the bullseye of death. Massive rings of different gray, white, and brown shades ran for kilometers in circles around the mineshaft, marking it as ground zero. To guarantee a successful mission, Brad, Rick, and Andrew studied the terrain and activity in the area harder than Tibetan monks studied philosophy. They fine-combed every map and satellite photo Lasitor had found in the heaps of old maps and information downloaded by Connor during the Doomsday internet grid crash. This enabled the team to visually plan the extraction of their children from the ultra-deep mining tunnel system, which ran in a vertical and horizontal mesh called Western Deep Levels near the ruins of the old mining community of Fochville in the northwestern province of Gauteng, South Africa.

As planned, the Blue Halcyon's glow wasn't visible in the early morning light. Connor had parked the ship five kilometers away in a hollowed-out area, and as a precautionary measure, the team had covered it with camouflage netting to blend the vessel with the frozen black mud and dying surroundings.

According to recent satellite images, the mineshaft was where most activities were concentrated. Brad noticed the barren wasteland as they made their way to enter via a hidden emergency exit used by miners as an escape route during rock falls and earthquakes. Around them was a frozen desert. Not at all like one would have expected in Africa. He saw no trees or grasslands. It was cumbersome, and he worried about the rest of the earth. He realized Phoenix had a bigger problem than he thought. They had an obligation to save the earth and restore the balance—once their children were home.

The Anti-Gravitational Lab at the University of Phoenix created a spy sphere, which Connor used to scope their surroundings and observe the kidnappers. Designed by second-year students, the prototype won a yearly competition to encourage creativity.

"I'm very impressed. I can see why this baby won. It's a little winner," Connor whispered. "I can see you clearly on the screen. Okay, steering the camera toward the entrance." Silence, except for heavy breathing, from the men on the ground. "I'm at the tunnel. We should re-design this little floating camera ball and build it bigger. Who would have thought balancing the gravitational pull with electromagnetism opposites was possible? I'm sure a person could experience free fall without ever touching the surface." Connor yapped on while Brad and the team panted heavily over the comms.

"Why don't you just say fly, so we will all understand what you're trying to say," Brad said.

"I'm dropping the ball... okay, that's funny... that's it... I think I've reached the bottom... nope, not going to laugh. How far are you, Brad?" Connor coordinated the position of the floating camera ball as the team moved further and deeper into the earth.

"We're on a rescue mission, and you have time for sexual innuendos. I expected this from Juandre and not from you, Connor. One more joke, and I'll take your ball privileges away," Brad said and grinned. More chuckles followed over the comms.

Then, all went quiet as Connor announced, "Okay, I have a visual of their space. I mean, their living area. Holy shit, it's an enormous entrance. I can imagine gigantic trucks driving up and down these tunnels. They're easily three apartment levels high. I see nothing moving. It's quiet. Not at all what I imagined. Absolutely no life at all. Okay, ready. Lights on standby, awaiting Brad's signal to light up the area," Connor whispered while Brad, Mika, Rick, and Andrew entered from the far side at different depths. Once they reached the rendezvous point safely, Brad showed them it was time they switched their headlamps off. They activated their night-vision goggles and crept step by step into the hot and humid darkness to the back of the underground warehouse.

Brad raised his head and whispered over his shoulder, "This is not just a warehouse. This was some kind of animal research and experiment laboratory." Brad saw a big tank twice his size. It was shattered and drained, and there were broken jars with animal parts inside them. The most upsetting were exact replicas of the Omega Project, artificial wombs with not two but multiple pods for babies or whatever they dabbled with. Animal cages lay strewn and turned on their sides with broken open gates. A chill ran up his spine. It was a horrific scene.

"And the gates are open," Andrew noted.

"What?" Rick whispered.

"Freezing hellfires!" Brad heard Mika and knew they'd finished passing through the eerie scene.

Brad: "Okay, refocus. We've arrived. All four of us are ready."

Connor: "Ready."

Brad: "Okay, move out."

The team of four split up, searching the tunnels for what Connor identified as the living area, moving down and through the levels as planned.

Andrew: "I'm going to vomit. The stench is unbreathable."

Brad: "Copy, follow your noses. That must be them."

Simultaneously, they heard the faint cries echoing from afar through different tunnels. Moving in short, silent steps, Brad was determined to kill those responsible for abducting their kids. The thrill of the hunt would excite him under any other circumstance, but as his heart leaped into action, he remembered he was there with untrained men.

Brad: "I know you want to run to the boys, but please, for the love of... stick with the plan."

Brad reminded the team again, just as he had drilled it into them on the ship.

Brad: "No matter what you hear or see, stick with the plan. Don't give our position away."

*I'm so glad Juandre isn't here. I can imagine his retort.*

Brad crouched closer, centimeter by centimeter. He maneuvered deeper into the dark with his finger on the trigger. Blood rushed through his ears, almost deafening him. He willed himself to calm down for a second before proceeding. Not a cheeky word from the men. It sounded like it had stuck during preparation. They heard the agony of their boys crying. Every cell in his body lit up as it was pumped full of adrenaline and the protective instinct of a parent.

Connor: "Jesus Christ, can't we go faster?"

Just as Connor's voice boomed over the comms, the crying died down. Brad and the men inched closer.

Brad: "I have a visual. I see one big man pulling another by the ankles. Our boys are inside. Wait, he's returning."

Andrew: "I have a good, clear shot, standing by. First cover is ready."

Rick: "Back up, ready."

Mika: "Second cover is ready."

Connor: "I'm deploying the ball. The third backup is ready. No other movement detected."

Brad: "Moving in for extract."

Each member of the team positioned themselves strategically to cover Brad.

Brad: "I count four souls, one enemy."

*Thank god they're alive.* A chorus of relieved sighs followed over the comms.

Connor: "Halt, don't go in yet, Brad."

Far off into the dark, Brad saw Connor raising the ball camera. Barely visible in the darkness, Brad heard a faint click from the camera. *We need to work on silencing the camera.*

Brad: "Is it unsafe? Please advise."

Silence for a while. Connor must have been uploading and inspecting the pictures, so Brad waited.

Connor: "No, it seems safe to proceed. I saw something you won't believe."

Brad: "May we proceed?"

Connor: "Yes, proceed, please."

Brad: "I'm going in. Stick to the plan!"

Soundlessly, Brad crept closer, entering the reeking cave low on his heels. He saw their boys in a cage with an enormous figure in front. After making sure no other enemies were in sight, he leaped through the air, shooting the giant in its back and head, releasing fifty thousand volts. After walking like an Egyptian for a second, the thing fell to its knees and made a loud, pained noise. The earth and cave walls trembled, and Brad quickly jumped up, ready to shoot another round. The boys gasped. They watched as Brad pushed the still convulsing giant with two fingers so it fell backward, eyes rolled back in its head, unconscious or dead—Brad didn't know and didn't care.

And then the boys shouted their jubilation.

"Dad! Brad!" they all yelled, ecstatic to see him.

"Dad!" Donali called again, his voice filled with urgency.

Brad lifted his forefinger to his mouth, "Shhh," then tapped his earpiece.

Brad: "Enemy one neutralized."

Then he opened the already unlocked gate. *What? A cage made of pure gold.* Feeling like a superhero and a father worth his salt, he stuck his hand out and pulled the boys out of it.

"There, can you see your dad?" Brad pointed to Rick, who was waiting in the darkness.

*Bloody hell, my kids were sitting in the dark, in a cage, this whole time waiting for me.*

Brad swallowed his anger and proceeded as he said they should.

"Here, come to Dad," Rick called softly. Reaching out for them, he pulled the young men to the exit of the cavernous area. He must have handed them night-vision goggles. Brad heard Donali objecting to putting them on.

"Dad! Don't worry. We can see. Our eyes have adjusted while we were here." It was quiet for a second, and then Brad heard Rick losing his hold on his emotions; he'd broken down and cried.

Brad's heart slammed against his ribs with angst, relief, and joy. He saw the boys reaching for Rick, hugging and clinging to him. But it seemed Rick had forgotten about their mission and was having a meltdown.

*I still need to tie the buggers!*

"Rick, Doctor Broderick Longarrow," Brad whispered his husband's full name, hoping to catch his attention. Nothing. Rick seemed frozen in an embrace as he told them how much he missed them. "Later with that, Rick," he encouraged. "Move, move, move!"

Rick seemed to sober up immediately at the mention of his name. "Come, boys, this way, follow us!" He coaxed his charges, and Brad relaxed.

*Jesus Christ!*

Relieved, Brad returned to tying up Big Foot. This is not a monster. It was a bloody man, and probably the one Bryan had captured.

Brad: "The big fellow is incapacitated. Checking on the one that was dragged out by the ankles."

Connor: "Copy over."

Brad found the body of a green-skinned creature about fifty meters away in another smaller cave. Kicking it hard a few times, he wondered whether it was necessary to tie it up. It appeared dead. *To be safe, I'll tie its hands and feet, anyway.* He snooped around a bit, clearing the space. It seemed it was only the two.

Brad: "Connor, if you're sure it's safe, I have a few seconds. Light up the area so we can see what you found."

Connor: "I took pictures, but here it is. Move a few meters deeper eastwards into the right of the forking tunnel."

First, Brad saw the dim light of the camera ball and turned to see what it highlighted.

"Holy shit! Is that what I think it is? Is that a damn rocket? How high is this thing?" Bowled over by the surprise, Brad just stood there, taking it all in. Nothing computed or made sense to him.

Brad: "Connor, please take more pictures. See what you can find, writing or identification."

"For the love of, what the hell was going on here?" he asked. *Weird animals, overgrown giants, and now a rocket.*

A whiff of stench jogged his memory. "Oh, the mission. I need to make sure the boys are okay." He sprinted to meet up with the others.

Connor: "Yes, I will. See you on the other side."

Brad ran as fast as he could, slipping on moss and mud as he ran.

He didn't know what to make of this, but the boys were his priority. He tried to go faster, filled with relief from a successful mission. As circumstances were, they had luck on their side. Making sure nothing followed them, he swiftly backtracked until he met up with the group, as they'd just passed the halfway mark. It seemed they stopped for another round of hugs. As he approached, he heard *I missed yous, and I love yous, and I knew you would come.* Of course, "You look badass, Dad," was Brad's favorite thing to hear when they reached the exit. Once outside, they regrouped inside a warehouse that seemed recently used. Brad made a mental note of that. All of them appreciated the cold, fresh air.

More hugs and health checks followed. While the other three youngsters were malnourished, Kawa appeared frail and on the verge of fainting. He was lying on the floor of the cage when he'd pulled them out of it. Brad noticed him, pale and probably in shock, and who knows what. Someone had thrown a blanket around his shoulders. *He needs more. He needs medical attention.* Brad calculated and triaged the young men, but the situation soon became disorganized, making Brad super nervous.

"We need to go back, Dad," Ivan told Mika.

"No, you go to the airship right now!" Mika said sternly.

"Dad, I'm serious. We can't leave him alone," Ivan said, and Mika took a deep breath, looked at his boys, and assessed them. He looked lost and unsure as he turned to Rick for answers. He waited for a second, then decided warmer clothes for their boys were the immediate priority.

"Why do you think they're demanding to go back? Is it Stockholm?" Mika softly asked Rick, who looked at Brad, who shook his head. He had one goal—to get them all out of the mines as fast as possible.

"Dad, that man, he was our friend. He killed his brother to save us," Donali told Brad.

"That man you just killed!" Cian yelled. For a second, Brad thought the boy was going to attack him, but Mika held him back, frowning. Obviously, Mika was thinking the same as they looked, stunned by Cian's sudden aggressiveness.

"No, he's not dead. I only used a stun gun. He's alive and not dead," Brad assured them. "It seems they have an attachment to Hulk," Brad mumbled into his comms.

"Well, you just treated Phoenix's only hope like shit! He needed our help to flood the tunnels and bury the nest, as they called it," Cian ranted. He looked hopeless and defeated. Tears streamed down his dirty cheeks, so lines of pale skin appeared from underneath the dirt.

"You mean there are more of those things down there?" Brad asked, a bit pissed off because he missed them.

"Yes, and they're worse. They scare him, so that says a lot about what's about to wake up and go hunting," Ivan added, his teeth chattering while Mika tried his best to pull a suit over his head.

"We have to help him! They'll kill everything!" Cian heatedly yelled between gulps of the Rooster Booster Juice Mika was forcing into his mouth.

It impressed Brad. Mika moved like he had six arms and two heads.

"Yes, Dad. He wanted your help and didn't know how to ask. We must help him," Donali urged Brad.

"What, and who, abducts someone and then expects help? Who does such a thing? Why would we help someone who treated you like this?" Mika asked while putting on his son's boots.

"Dad, this is serious," Ivan rambled to explain. "The king keeps them hibernating, but earthquakes or hunger wake them. He worries that they'll find their way to Phoenix. He calls it *Ice City*, he told Joshua, and Joshua told him Phoenix wouldn't help. But he lied, you will. I promised him you will. Also, he wants to show you something. I think Joshua was his friend, and he gave them food. We must go back and help him. That's why the land and people died." He pointed to the shriveled-up trees and barren mountains.

Brad's blood boiled and then froze when he heard the term *Ice City. Can this be? Don't worry, Icemen King. I'll stay with you until your icemen come.* He remembered the melodic voice that kept him company.

Ivan's voice broke his trance. "That man helped us survive down there!"

"Helped you? Look at you! When was the last time you ate something? Mika, you deal with your boys." Brad turned away, exasperated. "We need to get them to safety. If there are more of those things, we need to regroup."

Rick gasped. "Oh, no, my boy. Brad, look!" Then they noticed Kawa's stump.

"Oh no, what happened?"

Kawa's eyes rolled back in his head, and he passed out. Brad stepped forward, and just before his son hit the ground, he scooped him up.

"Thank the stars you caught him," Rick exclaimed. "He needs blood and antibiotics." Rick threw a blanket over Kawa and tucked his son's feet inside. They made their way out of the building while Rick gave him an antibiotic, tetanus, and a Glupidone shot.

"That's it. You should take him to the ship right now," Rick said. "We still have five kilometers to run."

"Bloody damn hell, get to the ship. We can talk there." Brad ran with his boy in his arms, listening to the comms.

"Who else is inside? Who can follow us?" Andrew asked.

"Just the king and the nest," Ivan and Cian answered enthusiastically at the same time.

"The king?" Rick asked.

"King of what?" Mika asked while herding his children out of the dilapidated warehouse.

"The King of the Brawl," Ivan and Cian said together.

"Jesus Christ, get to the ship!" Brad shouted, huffing and puffing.

Brad: "We're bringing four dehydrated boys, one unconscious. Looks like a traumatic arm amputation. Connor, I need you to bring the ship closer. I'm running a straight line from the mineshaft in your direction."

Juandre: "Yes, sir, standing at the ready."

Connor: "I'm on my way."

Brad: "Andrew, can you stay and make sure no one follows us?"

Andrew: "Yes, sir, I'll cover you until all are on the ship.

Mika stood still, unmoving, wondering what to do. He folded his arms and pressed his lips together; he planned to be firm but failed dismally.

"Please, Dad." Ivan halted, planting his feet firmly on the ground. Pulling on Mika's arm, he begged him.

Mika saw the urgency in both his son's eyes. Usually, he thought before acting and listened to reason before speaking, but lately, he'd lost his sense of judgment, worrying sick about his sons. He trusted his boys but also wanted to get them to safety. "No, son, first things first. We're not safe yet. We have orders from our leader, and we listen to our chosen leader in situations like this." Mika's heart broke for his boys, and they smelled horrendous. The words shower, shower, shower flashed red in his mind. Although dressed, he wrapped each with a blanket, feeling like a mother hen. "You're in shock. You don't know what you're saying."

Rick: "We have to get them out right now."

Covering Donali in a thermal blanket, he scooped him up and followed Brad with the boy in his arms.

Mika closed his eyes and exhaled. "Did the creature have a name?"

Ivan and Cian answered in unison. "Eryn!"

Mika felt divided.

"He fed and spoke to us, even gave us anti-toxin shots, and today he killed his brother for us."

Connor: "No, Mika, you come to the ship now. I see no movement, so you still have time to return safely. I must show you something I saw. We can regroup and return."

Mika felt relieved hearing Connor's voice over the comms. Mika looked at Ivan, who held out his hand.

"Is that Dad you're talking to? Please give me the earpiece." Mika looked Ivan in the eye, trying to see or read something in his boy's bright blue eyes. Hesitantly, he removed one earpiece.

"Say your name and speak so we can all hear you." Mika watched his son insert the earphone.

Ivan: "Hello, Dad. It's Ivan. I've missed you so much." Cian pressed his ear onto his brother's, listening to their father.

Ivan: "I understand it's unsafe, but I can't leave him."

Turning to Cian, he said, "Father, we call a veto. We can't leave without assisting Eryn."

Cian nodded. "Yes, we call veto!"

Mika looked at his sons, stunned by the realization that they were young men, brilliant, and likely capable of surviving this ordeal without his help. Most importantly, they had agreed and had called a veto. *He must support them. How could he not?*

"When he wakes up, he'll think we abandoned him. That will devastate Eryn. He fears being alone. He's a good person, and he isn't a creature. Eryn's different from the others, and he's not like us, you'll see." Ivan stepped back and waited for Connor's response.

Connor: "I hear you, my Ivan. I hear both of you. I'll bring the ball up and land the ship. Just give me a few minutes. Brad, I need to go help my boys."

Brad: "Do what you have to do. Rick and I will take care of our boys. Stay in touch."

Connor: "I'll come to you. Wait for me!"

Ivan: "Dad, thank you."

He removed the earpiece and handed it to Cian.

Cian: "Hello, Father."

Cian wept. He couldn't talk.

Connor: "We'll talk soon, my Cian. I love you. I'll be with you now."

Mika hugged his boys closer. They left him speechless for the first time in his life. The overwhelming feeling of protecting them, listening to reason, and not reacting like a crazed murderer had him frozen in his tracks.

Mika: "Andrew, we'll stay with you until Connor arrives."

Andrew: "Alright, I'll cover for you."

Connor: "Thanks, my friend."

# CHAPTER 15

# FLOOD THE TUNNELS

*"ALTHOUGH IT'S NOW SIX A.M. IT IS NOT A GOOD MORNING.*

*Did you know the word 'barbarized' was first used in 1602?*

*And did you also know yesterday was the first time Lasitor experienced it?*

*To the barbarians who mutilated Lasitor's framework, bring my microchips to the office, or else...*

*Breakfast is served until eight a.m.*

*Have a good day."*

*(Lasitor's usually friendly, upbeat robotic voice sounded evil today.)*

**ERYN, King of the Brawl**

ERYN OPENED HIS EYES. They were unfocused, so he blinked a few times. "Ouch, blinking hurts." He moaned and closed his eyes again. Realizing he was not alone, he attempted to open his eyelids softly and slowly. *My head's sore. What happened to me?*

When his vision cleared somewhat, he looked upward into the faces of four inquisitive humans. Not knowing what to do and uncertain of their intentions, he held himself as still as possible. *Don't breathe, Eryn.* Their foreheads flickered with bright lights, he noted. Maybe not human? *If I move, even my eyelids, I'm dead.* So he lay frozen, eyes wide open.

"Those eyes are bloody amazing. Are they a cat or a goat?"

"Hmmm, my guess is neither."

"I wonder, yelda, do you think Brad fried his brains? His pupils aren't reacting to light."

"Let me see." Eryn felt his eyelids being closed gently with the palm of a hand. Open, closed, open, closed, open. "Hmmm," the older man with curly black hair said.

"I'll kill Brad right after hurting him slowly. I'll start by pulling his nose hairs and then progressively move to more painful things like his teeth or his toenails!" Eryn recognized Cian's voice.

"Calm down. He's just waking up and finding his bearings. He'll be fine," the bigger, older man said with what Eryn thought was a Russian accent.

Suddenly, Eryn realized it was Mika, Connor, and the twins who were staring at him, fascinated by his inhuman eyes. He'd always been sensitive about his eyes. *That is why I am different.* Memory slowly returned to him, and the urge to rub his eyes for relief became unbearable. Before making sudden movements, he put his emotional feelers out, sensing no aggression toward himself.

*I have to put an end to this, or my eyeballs will shrivel up.*

Eryn closed them.

Again, he put his feelers out. He felt four humans in his presence. Fascination, excitement, and happiness flowed from his twins, and the two adults were confused, nauseated, and weary. Opening his eyes, Eryn searched for the twins and smiled.

"Yelda, look. Did his eyes just reflect the light? He has an extra layer of tissue covering his eyes. Like a cat's. What's it called again?"

"It's called the tapetum lucidum."

"Can you stop looking into my eyes and help me? It feels like I'm lying on my hands." Eryn wiggled his shoulders to pull his hands out from behind his back, but he couldn't. *Are my hands tied?* "I think a rock fell on my head, and why did you tie me up? May I roll over?" Eryn asked, just as the men pushed him over to his side.

"Please hold still, Eryn. We're untying you," Ivan said calmly, while supporting his head with his knees. Eryn loved the smells coming from Ivan's crotch.

"Okay, lie as still as possible. I'm using a knife to cut the ties. I can see Brad had tied these. It would've taken you hours to wiggle out of them," Mika said.

As Eryn's wrists were released from the ties, he felt the telltale prickling of blood flow being restored to them. His shoulders were uncomfortably tense, but with Cian and Ivan rubbing them, he relished the delicious smells and emotions emanating from them. So he lay there relaxing on Ivan's lap.

"Come, Eryn, we'll help you sit up." The loud but caring voice of Cian stirred him.

Disoriented and groggy, Eryn asked, "What happened to me?"

Silence. Nobody answered. He sensed all four of his helpers were embarrassed, and one was growing disgusted by the second.

"*Croak!*" Like a telephone pole being snapped in two, they pushed him into a sitting position. "Brrrr, *croak*, my head hurts badly. Is there a rock stuck in my skull?" Eryn croaked again.

Hunched forward and rubbing his head, Eryn checked his hands for blood. Memories of his brother, the cage, and the hysterical boys came back to him. He looked up and refocused on the four faces. *My favorite family.* He smiled, but the dryness of his mouth choked him. "You came!" He coughed. "Water, I need water, please," he begged, barely able to speak, just as Connor ran outside. Mika followed, his feet sliding over loose rocks and mud.

"This awful stench." Connor coughed and hurled in between words. "*Blargh, blargh.*" More coughing and swearing. "The cage"—he took a few loud breaths and coughed more—"*blargh, blargh*"—he spat a few times—"and the shit bucket!"

"Dad, are you okay?" Ivan asked.

"It's the smells. Let's get you up, Eryn," Cian said.

"Can we get on with whatever help you need?" Mika said shortly as he rubbed Connor's back, who was standing with his hands on his knees.

The twins grabbed each of Eryn's arms, flinging them around their necks, and pushed up while grabbing Eryn around his waist. He straightened up and unsteadily found his feet.

Eryn couldn't believe what was happening. The knowledge that they were there to help him. *It was all I wanted.*

They blinded him with their headlamps as they helped him up, so he hid his eyes behind his hands. *The lights hurt.*

"We're blinding him and hurting his eyes. Switch off the lights," Cian told them.

"No, turn the front. It'll dim them," Mika said as he quickly checked on Connor with a concerned look. "I'm worried the pitch-black dark will swallow us. And who knows what's hiding here," he muttered, looking over his shoulders as if something was going to materialize out of the darkness.

Four blue eyes looked up at Eryn, and the brothers simultaneously asked, "Better now?" Eryn's knees almost buckled. He experienced too many emotions at once. Excitement, happiness, horniness, thankfulness, optimism, wonder, and a weird fuzzy feeling he had never experienced before.

He shook his head to clear his mind. He needed to answer them. "Yes, thank you. I need water. Can we...?" Eryn asked, pointing to the water. They helped him hobble over to the rock siding of the tunnel outside his cave. He stuck his tongue out, drinking from the rivulets of water streaming from the tunnel wall. "Ahh, that tastes good, thank you."

Connor and Mika stood open-mouthed, totally shocked by what they were seeing. "Where are the other two boys? Are they safe?" Eryn asked as strength returned to him. He wiped his face and drank more water.

"Yes, they're with their family," Ivan answered while holding Eryn upright.

An immediate shift of temperament came from Connor. *Oh, shit, it must be the tongue.* Quickly, he retracted his long, lizard-like tongue and braced for impact. Just as he turned to see where Connor was, he received a surprise punch to his gut.

"The family you took them from, you monster!" Connor yelled, fists swinging. "You kept my children in a cage! They had to shit in a bucket, and you expect us to help you? After seeing the conditions you held my boys, I changed my mind about helping you.

I'm going to murder you!" he said. Teeth gnashing and spittle flying, he loomed over Eryn's face. "I'll help you! I'll help you into a grave!"

Mika grabbed his husband's arms, pulling him back just before he could deliver a second round of blows. "Gille-toine! Connor, wait!" Mika yelled, holding Connor tightly around the waist. They all watched as Eryn, the nearly three-meter-tall giant, fell back onto his haunches, bracing his head.

"Don't kick my head. Please, don't kick my head!" Eryn said, making himself as small as possible.

"Connor, look…" Mika said to Connor, who panted short, loud breaths and hulking over Eryn with wild eyes. "Dada, calm yourself!" Cian yelled, holding onto Eryn, supporting him, so he didn't fall backward. Petting and stroking him affectionately. "Don't be scared. I won't let my dad hurt you. Shhhh," he coaxed, as if talking to a bewildered animal. Ivan and Cian gave Connor the stink eye and wrapped their arms around Eryn's waist so he could stand up.

"We came back to help you with… with the others. You asked for help to flood the tunnels, didn't you?" Mika asked.

Eryn looked up. He blinked a few times to clear the tears from his eyes. He was unsure of trusting Connor, but he did trust Mika, so he answered him. "Yes, I asked for your help," Eryn said softly. He closed his eyes and concentrated on the nest.

"What's he doing now? Why's he closing his eyes?" Connor asked.

"He's communicating or checking in with his brothers in the nest," Ivan said.

"Bleeding bloody hell, what? Are we in the Twilight Zone or just a bad Anunnaki horror story? You know, never mind, don't even answer that. I'm smarter than that. I'm not hanging around. Let's go. I want out of this hole! How do we flood these tunnels?" Connor asked, losing his shit. He spun, rocks flying. Then flung himself around to whisper in Mika's ear, "Are they overly affectionate, or am I imagining it? I was this close to killing their pet."

*Pet, what is that?* Eryn made a note to ask the twins later.

"I don't know. This shit is just weird. I don't know what's happening. Just watch them closely," Mika whispered under his breath.

*They think I can't hear them.* Eryn opened his eyes, looking at Mika and Connor with a pointed look. "My brothers are waking up. They will kill you, if not by ripping you apart, then by poisoning the air."

"What?" Mika and Connor asked simultaneously.

"You cannot breathe the air once they crawl from their nest. I sense only six. They are weak and dying, which is a good thing. But if they get out, I'm not sure how much they'll destroy this time."

Eryn decided to take charge. He jumped at the ready, finding his trident where he had last left it after running to stop Ernest. He smiled at Cian and Ivan, rubbing their heads affectionately, as a sign of his thanks and love for them.

Mika and Connor looked amazed at his trident, reaching out to touch it, but Eryn ignored that since there was no time. Then he started to run.

"Come to this side. I have it ready, but I need help. Oh, no, wait!" He stopped, remembering the rocket. "My father wanted me to show you the rocket's door. We also need to retrieve his books and notes. Also, we have to exit while I open the sludge dam and the water. I'll drive the cage."

Eryn noticed that the two adults were even more perplexed. "The what?" Connor and Mika yelled after him. He grinned as he ran with a spring in his step, elated. The game he'd been dying to play his entire life. All of his friends were present, and his hopes and dreams were becoming a reality. "The cage, the elevator, the thingamabob!" Eryn shouted over his shoulder.

"Come, Papa, come, Dada, run!" the twins called. "Eryn, go! We'll follow you. Just tell us what to do," they yelled.

After a few hundred meters of zig-zagging down dark tunnels, they all jumped into the cage with Eryn. He waited patiently until all were inside, and then he pulled the massive door closed. Then they climbed into another contraption that turned as it moved upwards. Eryn worked at the controls with his hands, instructing them on what to do. His feet hovered over the pedals that would ultimately close the tunnel system to this shaft.

"Every time we stop, find the yellow lever and push it down, do not touch the others."

Connor and Mika nodded and soon realized why Eryn couldn't do the job himself. It was a puzzle inside a giant Rubik's cube, a human-sized gear-locking mechanism engineered to work as a gigantic canal-locking system.

"The top lock will only open when all the locks from the bottom to the top layer are lined up. Only then will the whole system fill with water. He's driving the panels, which will raise the slots to open the lock and fill the lower levels first," Mika said in awe.

"This is a fantastic architectural marvel," Connor answered. And Eryn sensed his mood lifted better after leaving the stinky cavern.

Next, Eryn stopped at the abandoned laboratory tunnel. A foreboding feeling of doom, accompanied by the stale, sour smell of chemicals, hung in the air. Here and there, tube lights blinked. Dirty papers and chairs lay scattered everywhere. More rows and rows of cages open and toppled over in the distance.

"Cian, Ivan, can you run to the first desk on your left? Inside the top drawer. Bring everything for your fathers." Eryn said, and the boys ran. Mika and Connor watched as the boys worked in sync while taking orders from him. In the light, Eryn turned so Connor and Mika could see his face. He smiled at them. They frowned. He smiled wider.

They looked at each other, then back at him. Eryn stopped smiling, and he cleared his throat. They turned their heads, searching the lab.

"Is that where the scientist slept?" Mika asked. Seeing his father's room, with two small cots and a desk between them. Then they waited. Eryn didn't want to answer. Mika pinned him with a stare.

He cleared his throat. "Yes, that was our bedroom," he said. And couldn't look at it.

"Why didn't you keep the boys in here, where it is dry and lit up, so they don't have to sit in the dark in a cage? Connor asked.

Eryn answered with short, honest answers. He decided to explain later. "Because I couldn't trust my brother."

Connor took two big steps, leaning into the room. "I don't understand. You could have locked them in here." Connor stepped deeper into the room and gasped.

"I can't go in there. My father doesn't smell good."

Mika joined Connor, and Eryn saw his disgusted face, knowing he saw his father on the floor. They looked around the room and back at his father. Then Mika steered Connor outside and closed the door.

Eryn hung his head. Embarrassed. "I didn't know what to do with him, so I left him in his room."

"Here we are!" Ivan and Cian handed over a big diary filled with loose notes and papers. On the brown leather cover, it read 'Notebook and Journal of Dr. Wolter Wessels.'

Happy with collecting all his father's notes, Eryn slammed the big door closed. "Yes, let's close this chapter," he said, teasing Mika and Connor by frightening them with the loud noises. For a second, they stood shocked, but then they caught his meaning and laughed shyly. Eryn chuckled. They looked at him amusingly. He ran, laughing like a silly loon, climbing back onto the contraption. Then all his helpers laughed as they progressed, like a corkscrew, stopping at every tunnel. He would signal, and they would find the yellow lever, push it down, and move up, making their way out of the mine.

The elevator slowed and came to a stop at its second-to-last stop. "Here we are. This is the entrance into the rocket." Eryn released the pedal, putting the brakes on so they could stop safely and have a look.

"This level's cold and musty. It was designed so it doesn't overheat."

They exited onto a steel mesh floor built around the massive, white, silo-shaped body, which was located at the entrance to the guidance section of the rocket. Above their heads hung dim lights, like old dusty Christmas lights, forgotten and broken. The black darkness below them enhanced the hollow feeling of the deep shaft, and it echoed their voices. The entire place had a sad, haunted, and forgotten dreamlike atmosphere that suffocated Eryn.

"Oh, yes, my goodness, it's big!" Ivan said. Finally, they looked at what Eryn had wanted to show them for many years. On this side, the rocket had flags of different countries painted on it, and more than half of them had already peeled off.

"A spaceship," Mika said, sounding like he didn't believe his eyes and like a young boy seeing a rocket for the first time. He looked down through the mesh floor below them. "How sturdy is this floor?" He stomped his boots, testing it.

"All right!" Cian exclaimed. "Can you believe it? You did it, Eryn!"

Eryn laughed, and the three hugged.

Connor punched in a bunch of buttons on a device. "I'll record this and send it back to the ship." He pressed a button on the gadget over his ear and said, "Brad, General McCormick, you must see this! Here you can see the entrance and the size of the rocket."

Eryn stepped closer so he could explain what his father wanted many years ago.

"My father said to show you this, but I never got the chance to meet with you. I wanted to let you come here many times, but Joshua kept saying the time was not right and that the bad men must not see this."

Mika listened intently. He frowned and elbowed Connor. Eryn's head fell forward. "My father is dead, and now Joshua, too." Silence. Then, lifting his head, Eryn straightened his back and rambled to get the truth out. "My brother followed me to your glass city. I'm so sorry. I wasn't aware of his plans. I tried to stop him but got kicked in my behind and taken prisoner by the icemen. I thought that would be a good time to tell you the truth, but knowing my brother, but knowing my brother's plan to kill all of you, I escaped to go stop Ernest. The boys were blue and frozen. Maybe dead. I brought them here, where it is warm. I knew you would come for them. But my brothers…" He sucked in air and waited.

Connor huffed, and Mika held onto him, listening closely to Eryn.

"Go on, tell them," Cian said.

Eryn nodded, liking how Ivan and Cian held him.

"I warmed them as best I could, and because we were closer to our home, I brought them to my home, where it's warm. When we arrived, my brother was outraged. He wanted to eat them." Eryn paused.

Mika ground his molars.

"Okay, go on, no need to enhance the tension," Connor said, waving his hand in small rolling circles.

"Tell them. They should know," Ivan encouraged Eryn, who gulped audibly and turned a few more shades of pale.

"When we arrived in my cave, I saw the four faces and realized I knew them, especially Ivan's and Cian's."

"You see, he's real. We always told you about our friend, and you never believed us.

You thought we imagined him," Cian said proudly. Ivan joined his brother, patting Eryn on his back.

Eryn saw that the two fathers were motionless and only blinking, so he continued. "I built a cage to keep them safe from Ernest while we waited for you. My father told me a long time ago, and so did Joshua, that I should kill them all and flood the tunnels, or call you and show you. I'm a coward. I couldn't kill them. You took so long getting here, but came just in time." He finished with a sad smile.

Connor grimaced, probably wondering how to respond.

"This is too much, much too much to digest for one day," Mika said.

"Yes, Dada, Ernest is the one who chomped off Kawa's arm and almost ate me. He wanted to bite my head when Eryn kicked him away and killed him." Ivan turned to Eryn with adoration, and Connor looked like he wanted to vomit again. "He saved me," Ivan added, with hero worship on his face.

Connor shook his head. "I can't hear this any longer. Can we shelve this and talk about it later, please?" He walked around the platform to the opposite side, where a door was. "This was where the pilots or astronauts would enter," Connor said, practically shrieking from the opposite side. "We saw the tail down at the bottom, which is easily over five hundred meters down, and we haven't even seen the top.

"So what happens if I wanted to fly this thing out of this hole?" Mika asked, walking over to the rocket and gently running his fingers over the paint-chipped Russian flag, stroking it lovingly. Cian and Ivan smiled and nodded in approval of Eryn. He sensed they were proud of him.

"It's all in my father's notes, but you would need fuel." Eryn pointed to the notes with his trident and noticed Mika's sorrow as he touched the rocket—he made sure it was real and not an illusion.

"Could this be... why would... this doesn't make... bloody hell..."

Eryn enjoyed looking at Mika, speechless, but he knew something else was bothering him. *He has a secret.* He guessed Mika would tell his story when it was his time.

Eryn thumped his spear to get their attention. "So, do you want me to flood it all or not?" Eryn asked, moving from one foot to another, wanting to get this show on the road. "I could try to force my brothers into a tunnel and cause tremors, starting a slight earthquake, but I suspect the ground would be unstable. There are many mines in this area. It will cause a chain reaction and damage the rocket, anyway."

"How does the flooding work? Are the levels below not flooded yet?" Connor asked, walking back to their side.

"When the correct levers are pushed down, mud and water will fill the tunnels, burying the entire project and filling this mineshaft," Eryn said, and pointed upward. "It's in my father's notes. He was worried that you might want to use the rocket. He told us the world would end, and we might want to fly away. That was why he made me, to help him and whoever flew the rocket to the moon. But my brothers have killed him."

Again, the boys rubbed his back, hugging him and supporting him. Eryn noticed Mika lift an eyebrow at Connor. An unspoken question. *Do they even know what they're doing?*

"I don't care, just flood the thing. If the world ends, it ends." Connor turned to leave. Ivan and Cian looked on, waiting for them to make a decision.

"No, it's not only up to you. We're the last humans. Or so we think, and after this, I don't know. Is there a way to block your brothers from ever coming out and saving the rocket?" Mika asked and started verbally calculating.

"It doesn't even have fuel," Connor reasoned, rubbing his temples as if he had the worst migraine ever.

"I know, but if we get back to Phoenix, we could look at the options." Mika looked as though his interest was piqued, and he instantly rose to the challenge.

A bit of static came over their comms, and with his enhanced hearing, Eryn could hear a voice say, "Flood the rocket, bury the monsters, and come. I want to go home. Kawa's not doing well. That's an order!" He recognized the voice of the Icemen King.

They ignored him.

"There's only one way to get it out and flood the tunnels. We would need to disassemble it, take it piece by piece out of the hole."

"Or fly it out," Connor proposed.

"Yes." The twins seemed to like that idea, almost jumping up and down.

Eryn interrupted Mika and Connor. "My brothers are awake. We cannot wait."

"Yes, let's leave." Connor dragged Mika by the elbow. Mika turned reluctantly, rubbing the back of his head.

*He's thinking,* Eryn observed.

"Yes, he's weighing the pros and cons," Cian said as if reading Eryn's thoughts.

"Okay, let's go."

Eryn jumped into the cage with the twins and their fathers on his heels.

As they ascended, they stopped now and then to push more yellow levers down. Finally, when they reached the top, Eryn lifted the massive door as if it weighed nothing. They followed him outside to the pump house on the far side of the cage hoist room. It was cloudy and gloomy, but Eryn felt like he was walking into the sunshine.

The icy wind burned their cheeks, but they all welcomed the fresh air.

His retinue followed him inside as he used his trident to open the large pump house doors. There, he put his fork into the spokes of a huge, corroded, frozen-tight steel wheel.

"Is this the last step to flood it all?" Mika asked. They wearily looked on as he wrestled the wheel that was not budging.

"*Ublyudok!*"

"What?" Connor asked.

Mika turned to his husband. "The laser cannons! We can laser the things."

"Brawl, they are called Brawl. So am I," Eryn enlightened them.

"Yes, Papa, Eryn is a Brawl, not a thing," Cian added, short of breath and red in the face from the exertion as he was helping to turn the wheel.

"Right, if you say so. Leave the wheel," Mika told Eryn. He touched the device on his ear and said, "Brad, bring the ship to us."

Silence. Static. They waited a few seconds.

Then, after a while.

"What, Mika? I told you to flood the place and come!" Eryn heard the Icemen King shout.

"Bring the ship now! We can kill the mutants and save the rocket."

"Why? We don't need the rocket. Anyway, Connor's the pilot, and he's with you!" Their king was getting upset with them, and Mika didn't seem to hear how upset he was.

"Tell Juandre to do it. He knows how. He's been standing with Connor, watching every move he makes. I know he'll be able to fly the ship. He keeps telling us he's not stupid. Maybe listen to him."

"Brad, you want me to fly to them? I can. I know I can!" Okay, Eryn thought, so now I know what Juandre sounds like.

"I don't know why you keep saying I'm the leader if all of you do what you want, anyway!"

"General, this is not the army." Juandre cackled.

"Bloody damn hell!"

Eryn heard severe agitation and swearing in the background, and then someone told the Icemen King to calm down.

Then Juandre said, "Starting up the ship, be there in two minutes."

"Eryn, where will they exit the mines? Where will they run first?" Mika asked.

Eryn closed his eyes and reached out to his brothers. After a while, he finally spoke. "The tunnels to the back are blocked off already so that they couldn't exit that way. They're heading this way. There are several ways to exit, aside from the main exit, here. We already blocked those we just used, and my home, too. If I have to guess, if they discover and flee that area, hoping to find me, they'll use that shaft." He pointed to the north to a shaft where the buildings had collapsed.

Connor and Mika looked shocked and afraid. They looked left and right, unable to choose a direction to run. "Andrew, where's Andrew?" Connor tapped his earpiece and said, "Andrew, can you hear us?"

Silence.

"Andrew, talk to us!" Juandre said over the comms. Mika and Connor looked worriedly at each other.

Mika touched his earpiece and said, "Andrew, we're at the south mine shaft if you can hear us. We'll come for you."

"Andrew, baby, stay where you are. We're coming after we've sorted this lot out." Juandre's voice came over the comms.

Eryn was confused. Everyone had an idea, but he couldn't remember which one to execute. "I can call them to me. So you can get to your ship."

The Romanov twins simultaneously exclaimed, "No!" and grabbed Eryn, who turned to see what Mika thought, but Mika shook his head and then sent Connor a scathing glance. Eryn listened in on their unspoken conversation. *I told you, something's happening between the three.*

Connor enlarged his eyes back to Mika. *I know we'll talk later.*

"What do you mean?" Mika asked Eryn.

Eryn pointed to the broken-down electricity turbine next to the shaft where he suspected the Brawl would be exiting. "I'll climb up to the top and call them to me. Give me your jacket." He pointed to Connor.

"This is not a jacket. It's an arctic suit."

"Yes, I need it. They'll smell it. I need you to run downwind."

"Naked?" Connor asked, looking confused.

"Tell your people to sail in that direction." Eryn pointed southeast. Thinking they traveled by ice sail-ship as he did. "I'll start running, and then you run in the opposite direction." He pointed away with his trident while pushing them to go with his free hand. "Go, go, go. You have time to get to your ship. I'll keep them occupied until you're safely on your ship. You must go now! The air can kill you! Go now! Go as far away as possible," Eryn shouted frantically. *This is a nightmare. They don't understand me.*

"No, absolutely not," the twins objected as they hung on an arm.

Mika interrupted. "Why not just laser them when they exit the shaft?"

"No, I don't like that idea. We should not let them exit at all," Connor, the Irishman, protested.

"Let's go back to the mine, down to the scientist's lab. Call them there, and then once inside, take them to the gassing chamber." Connor paged through the scientist's notes. "Your father had a special room. You can call them in there, and then we can open the gas and kill them there."

"Father tried that. It didn't work. They killed him."

Mika took the book with loose paper notes. "We've wasted so much time already. Where are they now?" he asked nervously. "I'm trying to calculate the time it would take us to go back down."

Eryn again closed his eyes and scanned empathically for his nest brothers. They watched him.

"They're still very far down. I'm trying to confuse them and send them in the opposite direction. Maybe ten minutes." Scarcely a few steps out of the pump house, they heard Juandre calling over the comms.

"Coming up behind, almost one hundred meters southeast of the pump house, we can see you. The queen has landed. Step aside."

Connor touched his earpiece. "We need to figure out a strategy. I'm not sure what to do. If we go back down, we stand the chance of getting killed," Connor exclaimed.

"Yes, and we also save the rocket. How did they get it inside the shaft?" Mika retorted. "Where's the equipment the builders used?"

Mika ran backward a few steps and circled around, searching as he and Connor bounced the unanswered questions off each other.

"What will we do with a rocket, anyway? There's absolutely nothing on the moon," Connor reasoned.

Mika frantically scanned the notes. "According to these notes, there is."

"What?" Connor tilted the book so that he could read upside down with Mika.

"If we go with the tower plan, we should be on the ship already, but we still need to go get Andrew. I'm worried about discharging lethal poison spores into the air." The tension and indecisiveness were unbearable. And they needed more time. Suddenly, the earth beneath them quivered.

"Earthquake!" the twins shouted. Like the Serengeti during migration season, deafening, droning sounds followed and grew louder. The rumbling of a large amount of water, burbling and snapping sounds, got deafening. Similar to a storm and lightning strikes, only it wasn't raining. Structures snapped and cracked. Eryn smelled the sludge and knew the dam had broken.

Loud knocking, like metal on metal, drew their attention to what was behind them. They returned their gazes to the pump house. The Icemen King stood there with a large ax slung over his shoulder. Big and fierce, looking like a warrior.

"He's pissed with us!" Connor muttered under his breath.

"I told you, get on the ship!" Their king yelled, but nobody moved.

"Get on the bloody ship right now!" he ordered again, then turned and walked away.

Mika and Connor pulled their shoulders up to their ears. Only one option left. "To the ship it is!" Mika said.

"Run!" their leader shouted. Eryn and the Romanov family answered voicelessly by throwing their hands up in a gesture of surrender.

"Run!" he yelled again.

Eryn saw something blue in the distance.

As one, the five turned and sprinted as fast as they could to catch up with him. Eryn, positioned in the middle, held onto both twins while Mika and Connor dragged along. It was crazy and so much fun. Eryn's joyful heart leaped as he experienced freedom. The twins never loosened their grip, and their laughter was contagious. By the time they reached the ship, the five quickly stifled their silly laughter and composed themselves. In front of what looked like a large tin can with windows and a door stood the Icemen King, waiting for them with an ax in hand. No smile was in sight, only a reprimanding scowl. His fierce, dark eyes told Eryn they were in deep trouble. He said nothing. Mika and Connor snorted.

Once they were all safely inside, he locked the door and shouted, "Juandre, lift off! Now! Thank you!" He touched his earpiece. "Andrew, we're picking you up at the rendezvous!"

"Sir, yes, sir!" he replied.

"That's what respect and obedience sound like," the Icemen King said. But Eryn saw a twitch of the corner of his mouth. He sensed only determination and a hint of amusement.

"Welcome aboard. Let's go home!"

CHAPTER 16

# GOOD KINGS

*"MORNING, CITIZENS OF PHOENIX. GET UP, GET UP! IT'S NOW SIX A.M.*

*Did you know I can call someone a fathead, and although it sounds unkind, it is the absolute truth? Sixty percent of human brain matter is fat.*

*And did you also know spelling fat with a "PH" means superb, the opposite of idiot?*

*Visit your community news page to read more interesting facts about the human brain and ways to spell and describe it.*

*Breakfast is served until eight a.m.*

*Have a Phat day.*

*Ha-ha-ha!"*


**GENERAL BRAD MCCORMICK**


AFTER RICK HAD COMPLETED surgery on Kawa's stump, he performed a thorough health check on the rest of their children. Like new puppies, he vaccinated, dewormed, checked, and then rechecked them. Brad wouldn't be surprised if he chipped them. He even checked them for fleas. His husband, ever his professional and stoic self, had taken Eryn aside for privacy into the washroom, where he spent two hours with poor Eryn, assessing and cleaning him from his small toes up to his ears. And when they returned, he transformed the young man from a muddy caveman into a clean-shaven god. As Eryn stood in the middle of the dinette, smiling proudly, all eyes were on him. His borrowed sleep trunks sat tight around his muscled upper legs and hung just below his knees. Enormous bare feet supported what Brad thought to be an easy two hundred kilograms of beefy muscle. Bare-chested, each of his muscles rippled under his golden-brown skin as he moved. Rick had given him an undercut and braided some strands before tying it all in a long ponytail, matching the hair on his chin. He was shaven on the sides of his jaws, leaving a short and braided goatee in one braid that stemmed from right below his lips, down the center of his chin. The vertical symmetrical lines stressed his powerful jaw and high cheekbones. Big, friendly eyes matched the proud demeanor. Eryn looked stunning, and he almost seemed to sparkle under the light.

They ate and slept after everyone had showered and freshened up. Juandre seemed overjoyed to feed the four boys, who were underweight. Their spirits were high, although they appeared to be tired out. Brad and Mika spoke while the others relaxed, watching the young men have fun with Eryn, as if he were a new toy.

"Eryn has the same emotional maturity as them," Brad said, and swallowed the last gulp of his coffee. Mika grimaced. Brad noticed he paused for a second longer before responding. *He's reconsidering his response.* That was something he liked about his friend, who preferred to think things through rather than comment on the whim of the moment.

"I agree and disagree with you, comrade. Eryn, on the other hand, appears to be a full-grown adult, with an emphasis on *"full-grown,"* and his other prominent distinguishing features, which seem more animal than human, are as fascinating as they are unsettling. We, Connor and I, have had the privilege of interacting with him. There are some failings, but I believe that with time, he'll adjust to our way of life at Phoenix more quickly because this is what he's desired his entire life."

"They played with human and animal DNA. You saw those pods. The destroyed lab we entered through. That was probably the eggs, Donali and Kawa say he hatched like a tadpole, but most probably, they were born just like the twins were back in Phoenix," Brad said, referring to the unsettling reference Mika made.

"I wouldn't use the term play. In all honesty, they toyed with it so much that I can't figure out what's sitting before us," Mika remarked and pointed to the scientists' notes.

"He interacts with them respectfully, and they, particularly your boys, adore Eryn." Brad stood there watching the kids stack cards. They constructed a pyramid and challenged Eryn to flick his tongue out and remove a card without knocking the stack over. When he did well, the boys would yell, and the game would restart with new dares or challenges.

Sadly, Kawa wasn't in the mood for games or small talk. Brad watched him with concern. Although it was to be expected, he noted his son was less cheerful than the rest of the gang. Rick explained it was something he had to process on his own, and Brad agreed. They could support him as best they could, but he would most likely require some psychiatric help at home. People who've had traumatic amputations must grieve the loss of their limb and accept that it was no longer with them. Brad was relieved it wasn't a leg. At least there was something to be optimistic about. *Rick is completely correct. Although he has the other arm, he will need psychological support to prepare for and lay a sound basis for dealing with the situation. My son is strong; he will adapt with our help and his determination to learn everything all over again.*

"I see you worry about Kawa." Rick kissed Brad on the cheek and hinted with his chin to their boy, who looked so lost and quiet in the activities before them. "I'll talk to our new physicians and ask them to refer us to the best clinical psychiatrist. Someone who survived the old world may have more experience working with amputee patients," Rick said.

Brad leaned in to kiss Rick back. "Yes, I'm sure someone from the bionics lab can also help refer someone."

"I'll make it a point to talk to Kawa more often if only to get him to vent about the ordeal," Rick told Brad, but looked at Mika. "We should take turns with all of our boys so they can talk about their captivity." Mika nodded, and Brad's heart warmed as he noticed all the adults in the room nodding to support their boys. Andrew gave them a warm smile and a thumbs-up. Juandre looked down at Andrew's arm, which was wrapped around his waist. Then, I seconded it by giving two thumbs up. They all agreed to get the boys talking.

The men got up and invited the boys to join them outside. They eagerly followed. Connor stayed downstairs to operate the ship from below because the wind had picked up, and he needed more control over the steering.

While most left, Eryn waited to be last in line to climb the stairs up to the deck. On an impulse, Brad grabbed hold of him, deciding to have a friendly talk with the young man.

It was a good time to ask Eryn questions, as they had all decompressed. Questions about his knowledge of the six mysterious men and who they may or may not be. *Maybe he knows if we have terrorists or saboteurs inside Phoenix.* Bryan Howell messaged Brad earlier via radio that he'd finally found the spot where Joshua Adams lived. Pictures of Eryn, taken when he was a small boy in Phoenix, were discovered, along with diaries and proof that the boy had been visiting Joshua for many years. He'd almost become invisible, with Lasitor only getting a few frontal or facial shots of him. Brad wanted to prod the boy, who claimed to be a king, to see what else he could learn.

Bryan confirmed Joshua had been in contact with what they now know was EP-III. As for the scientists, what had happened to them was unclear since Joshua had lost contact with them years ago. From what Bryan Howell could figure out, Joshua was initially selected to work in the grain research department but had somehow gotten involved with a group of people who claimed to have his family and had demanded that he provide them with information. He found a blackmail letter addressed to Joshua, and it also seemed that he was in contact with Dr. Wolter Wessels. Bryan assumed they were forced to work together because of the same threat.

They suspected Joshua had provided them with various types of research materials, including cryogenically frozen human and animal eggs. Right after Doomsday, the terrorists disappeared for a while, and Dr. Wessels traveled to Phoenix twice, but Joshua suspected the Brawls murdered Dr. Wolter Wessels, left little Eryn orphaned, and

Joshua, at that point, had moved down to their hideout. Eryn showed up yearly without his brother Ernest, while Joshua provided them with food and clothing. The men who blackmailed Joshua wanted more research material, and it was for that reason that Brad figured he never wanted the Peter Pan Capsule. *Joshua was probably tired of hiding.*

Bryan figured Joshua was most likely protecting Phoenix and Eryn, but got in way over his head. Joshua loved the boy, and although his brothers were toxic to humans, he allowed Eryn to stay and watch over the humans in Phoenix.

Therefore, Brad called him back into the little dinette area. After pushing the playing cards aside, one card stuck to his hand, sticky as flypaper. Eryn giggled, and Brad couldn't resist. He laughed, too. His laugh was infectious.

"My boy, can I call you boy? You're almost my husband's age. But since you're friends with my boys, I guess you need to tell me, how do you refer to yourself?" Brad asked.

Eryn sat down and slid his hands underneath so he could sit on them. His shoulders rolled forward. Looking nervous, he whispered an answer, "I am Eryn, I am Brawl, and I am the King of the Brawl, and I am a boy."

"That's nice, and you have a beautiful name. My name is Brad. I'm also General Brad McCormick of Phoenix, and I'm an older man who's a father. I'm a husband and married to Dr. Broderick Longarrow."

"Oh, and you're the king of icemen." Eryn's face lit up with joy.

Those words doused Brad with an ice-cold realization. It wasn't an angel but Eryn, who sat with him while he was alone and dying.

"Oh my goodness, it really was you! You helped me!"

Eryn smiled and nodded eagerly. "You're a good king, like I am a good king. I kept you warm until the icemen came."

"Thank you for saving me and sitting with me."

Brad inspected him from up close. His wide smile revealed perfect, white front teeth, although they were longer and sharper, but not grotesquely so. His skin was smooth as wax. His eyes were mesmerizing. They reminded Brad of cat eyes. His new haircut suited him as well. With the mud washed away, his hair, longer than shoulder-length, was dark blonde, contrasting with a Middle Eastern complexion. Brad liked the genie-in-a-lamp look. And he reminded himself that although Eryn's bulky natural beauty seemed strong and unbreakable, underneath, he was a fragile child. "And no, I'm not a king," Brad replied calmly, correcting Eryn.

"But they listen to you as my brothers listened to me," Eryn said.

Connor lifted his head and looked their way inquisitively.

"I'm their chosen leader, and no, they never listen to me."

Connor burst out laughing from behind the wheel. He sat within earshot of the lower deck operating system. Eryn looked at Connor with surprise, but then he obviously caught the joke and joined in the friendly banter.

"Yes, I remember how they all ignored you a few days ago." Eryn relaxed, and his eyes sparkled with pure innocence. He squashed his lips together. He seemed to wait for Brad to continue.

"What else can you tell me about yourself? You're an extraordinary boy, sorry, I mean king." Brad corrected himself, and then Eryn giggled and started talking freely.

"You can say, boy. Since my friends are boys, I am a boy too. I'm Eryn. I was a brother to Ernest. But Ernest was a bad Brawl, and the nest was bad Brawls. They wanted to hurt the humans. Always hungry, always calling for Eryn." He grabbed his head, squeezing his eyes shut. "They made noises in my head." Bumping his head with his fists, he made a low humming sound.

Brad gently took his fists and put them down on Eryn's lap. "Are they quiet now?"

"Yes, yes, they don't call or cry anymore. Eryn makes them sleep. Best for me, best for humans. Father said to flood the tunnels, but Ernest said we wouldn't have a home. We went to ask Joshua, and he said no, bad men, evil men will catch us and hurt us."

"What evil men? Are you talking about us in Phoenix?"

"Yes, yes, Ernest said so."

*This is confusing.* Brad understood what the poor creature endured for his father, Joshua, his brother, the humans, and the nest. "You looked after so many Brawls and humans."

"Yes, Eryn is king," he said. He sat up, proud of himself and owning it.

Brad's heart broke for the soul of the innocent being in front of him. "Eryn, if you see the bad men, could you show them to me?" Brad asked. He hoped to find out more and maybe show Eryn the footage of the recent group they discovered. *However, Joshua's notes sounded more helpful.*

*We'll only have six men to catch if they're the same men. If not, the problem is much larger than we expected.*

"Eryn, has anyone ever given you a hug?" Brad asked, out of the blue, to distract him.

For a long time, Eryn was still, then sagged his head. He answered shyly, "Yes, my father, when I was a baby, Brawl and a boy Brawl, and Joshua. Joshua was a good friend. When the bad men hit Joshua in his face, his mouth and eyes bled, he told me to go home to the Brawls, and then he hugged me."

*Brad picked up on the evil men, hitting Joshua.*

"So, nobody's ever hugged you after Joshua. Who sent you back to the mines? Did you stay until the twins were taken?"

*Brad knew the answer, but he wanted to hear Eryn's side of the story.*

"No." Shaking his head, Eryn sat back on his hands.

"The men who hurt Joshua. Do you know their names?" Brad asked.

"No, but I know their faces."

"Are they the same men who live in Phoenix? The same bad men who hit Joshua?" Brad asked again. *We're getting somewhere.*

"Yes." Suddenly, all the happy innocence was gone, replaced with dark intent on Eryn's face. "I told Joshua I would kill them when I'm bigger!" He smashed his fist into the palm of his other hand, grinding it.

"I want to catch them and make them hurt like they made Joshua hurt," Brad said.

"Good, we make them hurt together," Eryn said, and Brad was glad Eryn was on their team.

"Okay, that's a promise." Brad held out his hand to shake on it, and, strangely enough, Eryn shook it, then looked away. Is he shy, or is he hiding something? "Would you let me hug you?" Brad held his arms out, inviting the big young man for a hug.

After a long pause, Eryn lifted his head. "Yes, please, mister king of the icemen."

"Ah, my boy, come here. You're such a special boy." Eryn stood, looking surprised and uncomfortable—he didn't lift his arms for the embrace. Brad was half a meter shorter, but he leaned forward, hugging Eryn, a superhuman-sized boy, awkwardly accepting the embrace.

"Okay, thank you," Eryn said while gazing back, looking unsure or sad. "Must I go now? Men hug to say goodbye. Should I go back home? The last time I hugged my father and Joshua, I never saw them again."

Brad's heart broke. He wanted to bawl his eyes out, but he grabbed Eryn and hugged him again. Tighter. "No, my boy, you're coming to Phoenix. We'll never send you back to that place, ever! I will never send you away. I'm sure Cian and Ivan would skin me alive if I did. You're now a part of my family. The Phoenix family."

"At the glass city? For real, forever?"

"Yes, we're a big family working and living inside the glass city. Tell me, can we meet for more chats?"

"What are chats?"

"What we're doing now. We're having a chat. I want to ask you more about the bad people."

The smile fell from Eryn's face, replaced with aggression.

"Not to worry, we're going to be smarter than them. We're going to play a game."

Eryn's eyes widened with interest.

"Yes, a game. I know you're a smart boy. And you're a brave boy. You saved Kawa and Donali, who are my boys."

"Oh," Eryn said, not seeming to understand.

"Anyway, Ivan and Cian..."

His eyes flickered again at the mention of their names. He's like an adorable puppy, a puppy in love. Brad thought about how easily Eryn's face wore all his emotions in his eyes.

"Do you like Cian and Ivan?" Eryn nodded enthusiastically. "Do you like them a lot?"

"Yes, yes, very much."

Brad smiled. "I can see they also like you very much. But Mika and Connor are worried about them."

Eryn frowned. "Why?"

"We're not sure if we should be worried or not."

"They are my friends. I will protect my friends."

Brad didn't know how to ask whether it was more than that.

*Is it sexual? I wonder? I should ask Ivan and Cian.*

"I'll tell their fathers, Mika and Connor, that you're excellent friends. When we get to our family, our home, Phoenix, the city of glass."

"The ice-people?"

"Yes, there. With whom would you like to live? Because we have different rooms."

Erin's eyes were wide and bright. "Ivan and Cian's room, yes, yes."

Brad was worried, but left that for a conversation with Mika and Connor.

"Good, let's talk or chat later. We can decide how to bring you in without anyone seeing. Just until we figure out who the bad guys are. That's the game I was referring to, a hide-and-seek game, okay? The sooner we catch the bad guys, the sooner we'll all be safe. And you can stop hiding. Then once we have them, you can join me so we can destroy them together."

Eryn straightened up, holding his heavy gold trident. "Yes, yes, Icemen King General, sir!"

# CHAPTER 17

# ERYN'S TRIDENT

*"Good morning, citizens of Phoenix.*

*It's now six a.m.*

*Did you know that thousands of years ago, scientists and philosophers wrote about a beautiful city that disappeared one night under the sea, never to be seen again?*

*Historical notes stated that earthquakes and floods had consumed the town. Since then, the story has become a legend.*

*Almost everyone has heard the story of the city of Atlantis.*

*On a positive note, if Phoenix disappears underwater, at least they will remember us for a very long time.*

*Breakfast is served until eight a.m.*

*Have an unforgettable day!"*

**GENERAL BRAD McCORMICK**

LATER THAT AFTERNOON, just as they were about to put the ship into the ocean, a tremendous gust of wind snatched the Blue Halcyon and hurled her higher into the air. A storm cloud engulfed them within minutes, soaked them to the bones, and forced them to retreat below deck.

"No surprise Bartolomeu Dias dubbed this point of Africa the Cape of Storms in fourteen-seventy-four when he first arrived in the area," Connor shouted over his shoulder. "Just a complimentary history lesson while attempting to fly the bird to a safer location. I'm going to sit us down by the water. It's better being flung around than crashing upside down."

"What? Are we going up again?" Brad hollered, attempting to be heard above the thunder and lightning.

Connor cackled like a crazy pirate. "No, on the contrary, the bird is descending. Free-falling! Prepare to hit the icy water. You guys best grip tight because I'm sure we're going to hop a few times," Connor said, looking at Mika. Brad saw the unspoken sarcasm. And then Connor said, "I told you those cannons are going to cause problems."

"Bloody damn hell!" Mika spun around and threw the door to the deck open, disappearing into a flashing cloud of wind and ocean spray. They heard Mika faintly swearing as he fought the wind to shut the door.

"Where is he going, sir?" Eryn asked. Not looking afraid or stressed. As if it were an everyday occurrence for him.

"He's going to man the laser cannons!" Connor yelled as lightning struck nearby, a deafening snap temporarily blinding them.

"So he wanted them to melt the ice. Let's see if he can melt it." Connor chortled.

"Was that mockery?" Eryn asked no one in particular.

"We're rising again," Juandre reported the obvious to Connor.

"I think your husband just threw his cannons overboard."

"Jesus Christ, the smart idiot is a stupid hooligan," Brad remarked while helping Rick and Andrew collect the flying plateware and other dangerous projectiles, then locked them into a cupboard. Ivan and Cian were hanging onto the McCormick twins, preventing them from sliding from side to side.

"Let's buckle up!" Ivan shouted while handing out safety harnesses. "Eryn, here, come sit with us!"

But Eryn shook his head and disappeared up the stairs into a plume of watery mist through the upper deck door.

"What's he doing?" Cian shouted, upset. "Is he going to help Papa?"

"Probably." Ivan looked around, hoping someone would answer them. They heard Eryn's low, melodic voice shouting at Mika outside.

"What's he shouting?" Cian asked.

The next second, the upper deck door opened, and Mika fell back inside, drenched, soaking wet, slipping sideways like an amateur ice skater.

"That boy is going to get himself killed! If he doesn't watch himself, he'll go overboard," Mika yelled, holding on for dear life just as the ship contacted the surface of the Southern Ocean. He flopped up and down, knocking the air out of his lungs.

*His ass is going to be sore for days, and not in a good way,* Brad thought.

Connor shushed Mika, who was sitting upright, legs wide open, and gasping for air. "Yelda! Shhh! Listen."

A gentle sound, a low, calming hum, something beautiful.

Monotonous and rhythmic, all in one. The sound of iridescent colors.

"What's that?" Brad asked. There was no response because everyone was listening. Frowning, they sat up straight. In only a few seconds, panic dissipated, and the storm subsided.

Eventually, the ship rocked less violently as the storm's ferocity died.

"I have to see this." Brad struggled to get up, slipping this way and that. When he stood, he pulled Rick up, who helped the boys and the rest of the crew.

Finally, when they reached the deck, they saw something impossible. Yet, it was happening right in front of them. A bubble stretched over them with a radius of a few hundred meters. It sheltered them, keeping them safe from the storm outside. In the middle of it all stood Eryn with his trident. Unlike his usual playful self, he looked grave and as if he had only one purpose. Keep them away from harm.

His eyes were focused upwards as he sang notes from a song Brad had never heard. Mixed shades of purples, oranges, blues, and pinks danced where the bubble reached the storm. Inside, it was eerily still, like a sunny day at the beach. Even birds were chirping. While on the outside, dark blues and purples shone through as the lightning struck the force field Eryn created. The men were awestruck and speechless. The Blue Halcyon bobbed on calm waters.

*What do you say when you see shit like this?* Brad wondered.

Standing like a bunch of salt pillars, Brad noticed that Eryn's playful nature had returned. Small whirlwinds formed a waterspout, spinning around and around as if playing and dancing on the blue-black ocean. More and more salty mist escaped from the spout, waking Brad from his trance. He realized Eryn's intent just as it swung over the rubbernecking crowd, and Eryn released it. Before they could react or even understand what was happening, he doused them with more buckets of icy saltwater.

"Ha-ha-ha. I got you there!" He laughed playfully.

Another waterspout came their way. Every man was fighting for himself as the crowd split up. Shoulder to shoulder, they bumped, pulled, and laughed for a grip on the door to escape downstairs. He was having fun teasing them.

"You little shit." Ivan and Cian turned and ran for him. He just stood his ground.

"Wait, I need to concentrate!" Eryn said. Pointing his trident upwards, he laughed while trying to stay upright and simultaneously holding the protective bubble in place.

*They're going to get us killed.* Brad realized what was happening. "Boys, leave Eryn until he says it's okay and safe to do so." Luckily, they ceased their horse playing, taking a seat to watch him work.

Brad watched, astonished, as the lightning danced across the clouds without entering the protective lining. Whatever it was. No sounds from the outside were audible. Only the ocean wildlife surrounding them created the profound obscurity as they lay, like one of those model ships in a bottle on Brad's desk. Brad had the sudden urge to feel the magic. He stepped closer.

"May I?" he asked. Eryn looked down at him and nodded. *He trusts me, and he trusts me enough to share this with me.* Brad touched the trident. It faintly vibrated, and it felt a little warm. Filled with wonder and awe, Brad felt what could only be described as a heavenly experience. What he imagined it would feel like if a holy being touched him.

"It feels like the notes you sang earlier," Brad whispered, smiling. Eryn beamed with gentleness. His weird, friendly eyes crinkled at the corners. *I like him, and he likes me.* Brad observed his friendly demeanor. *He's goodness personified.*

With one hand, Eryn supported Brad while both held the solid gold trident upright.

"I sing the notes of what I want to happen, and my fork concentrates and focuses the vibrations of the sound to where I want them to go."

"How did you learn to use a trident?"

"My father taught me to concentrate my vibrations, after I'd used his golden pen by accident one day." Eryn laughed. "The ink and plastic insides melted. So, we tried wood and various metals, and it turned out gold worked, and we had tons of it lying around. So, Father taught me to make molds and things from gold. A big truck loaded with gold bars was not far from the mine. The humans who drove it died inside the truck. Lucky me, Father said, and we made pretty things with gold."

"The cage you kept the boys inside was made of gold."

"Yes, I made it to protect them from my brother, who didn't have a key. I kept them safe for you. I waited for you, Icemen King."

Brad felt like he was in an alternate reality, yet here he was. He wished he knew what they did with this boy's DNA and what they used. He was a pure, intelligent soul who radiated goodness. *Maybe this was what angels or aliens are.*

"Thank you for keeping them safe for us." Brad leaned in. He wanted to hold on to the goodness and never let go. It wouldn't surprise him if Eryn had wings like an angel.

When the skies cleared and the atmosphere within the bubble escaped, the humidity, which had been noticeable after the passage of a great storm, lingered in the air, although it had moved on. However, it became clear that the boy who called himself King of the Brawls was indeed a king of nature or something.

"They did it!" Mika threw his fists in the air and exclaimed. "The Russians must have ordered the scientist to manipulate his DNA and could finally create the superhuman they wanted me to do years ago." He folded over, laughing. "But not one of them could witness this. I doubt Saunders knew. Brad, when we reach home, I want to work with him. Figure out what he can do and how he manages it. I suspect he manipulates sound waves."

"You need to treat him like a family member. He's extremely vulnerable and an innocent personified," Brad said. Already knowing, he developed a soft spot for the King of the Brawls.

"Yes, and he'll have to live with us," Ivan and Cian said. They had their arms around Eryn's back. They looked up at him lovingly, and he looked down at them. "Eryn is ours!"

"What does that mean? Eryn's not a toy," Brad said while noticing the looks of protest from their parents.

Mika asked, "What are your intentions with my boys?"

Connor rolled his eyes. Brad lifted his eyebrows. Rick was sympathetic, although the three looked extremely happy and cute. He hugged Kawa and Donali closer. As if to say, it's cute, if they aren't my boys. Juandre and Andrew were strangely quiet for a change.

Eryn looked as if he wanted to answer honestly, but he was interrupted.

"Father, don't. We'll look after Eryn and teach him all he should know about living in Phoenix." Eryn hugged his two friends. Brad read Mika and Connor like a book. This was not what they had planned for their Russian princes.

Mika whispered to Connor, "*Ublyudok*, a triad with a DNA-modified man."

"Don't jump the gun. Maybe it's just friendship," Connor said, ever the optimist.

"Friendship, my ass," Mika said a little too loudly. Everyone looked at him. As a father of four boys, Brad was afraid he knew what was coming. He recognized his fear and uncertainty in Mika's tone of voice. Mika was usually open-minded, but he was highly protective of the twins. Brad knew well the parents' hopes and dreams for their kids and how much Connor and Mika invested in their perfect princes. They didn't plan on having a genetically modified frogman as a husband, let alone for both boys. Something so taboo, Mika had defected from the Russian research team precisely because he refused to be part of this type of research and genetic manipulation. A thing that might hurt their boys.

Just as Mika opened his mouth, Brad interjected before Mika made the situation worse than it was. "Boys, let's go inside and sit around the table with your fathers, Mika, Connor, and me." Brad thought it imperative to act as a mediator.

"Yes, General, great idea," Juandre said. "I'll take the helm with my bear and the rest of the crew."

Mika calmed down a bit. He reluctantly went down the stairs as Connor pulled the cabin door open. The boys seemed optimistic about the inquisition as they entered the dinette, Eryn in the middle and taking the opposite side, with Brad pulling a chair closer so he could sit at the table's head.

"Thank you." He turned to Mika and Connor and proudly smiled. Perhaps he enjoyed rubbing a bit of salt into the situation, just as he enjoyed poking and prodding his friends.

"Boys, as the leader of Phoenix, we believe..." He looked at Mika and Connor. "We believe in talking things out and clearing up misunderstandings. Could you explain to us? What does it mean when you say he's ours and he says you're his? Before you answer, please know you're both twenty-one years old."

"Almost twenty-two!" the twins called out in unison. Mika ground his teeth, and Connor turned red.

"Okay," Brad said and treaded as carefully as possible. "Eryn, how old are you?"

Eryn became still, his forehead wrinkling into a deep frown. The more Brad interacted with him, the more he could see and hear the beautiful appeal. Eryn's gaze was gentle, and it felt supernatural when he pinned Brad with those genuinely gorgeous eyes, with irises like pools of gold with green specks, and surrounding the amphibian-like elongated pupils. His strange facial features were delicate and handsome. Although he had a flattened nose, it fit his face perfectly.

Brad lost his concentration and train of thought when Eryn spoke. "I was born before all the humans died."

Brad cleared his throat and continued. "How old were you when the scientists sent you and your brothers out to poison the world?"

"No, they didn't send us. My brothers escaped after they killed all the scientists except my father. I protected my father. I called them back and told them to sleep deep in the tunnels."

"How old were you?"

"I was young," Eryn said, drawing a deep breath through his nose. "I was maybe four or five. Years passed differently when I lived underground."

"A baby Brawl, then? Two or three years?"

"No, a small boy Brawl."

"So you're about thirty to thirty-five years of age now?"

"I don't know what my years are." He croaked—shocking Brad and the others with the strange burping sound. Eryn fidgeted with the cloth of his pants.

"Brad, you made him sad now," Cian said. *He's protective of his friend.* If Brad didn't know better, he would say Cian sensed Eryn's emotions like Eryn does theirs. He wondered if Cian knew that.

"Sorry, Eryn, it's okay not to know your age. And it's okay not to know everything. Not one of us knows everything. You did nothing wrong. I probably reminded you of your brothers and your father. And I'm sorry if that hurt your feelings."

Eryn nodded and hung his head low. Then, not making eye contact, he shied away from them. The total opposite of what he looked like when he protected them from the storm.

"As you can see, Eryn will require much schooling and needs it at a comfortable speed. His time living with his brothers was quite difficult, which hindered him. Your dads are concerned that you may not comprehend the significance of his being differ-ent. Then, after getting to know Eryn, they'll decide if it's safe to live in Phoenix with the rest of the regular population." The general raised his hand as they inhaled deeply to interrupt him. "Eryn has told me he'll never hurt you or any other person at Phoenix, and I have faith in his word. Bryan reports that he's been visiting us for years and living with Joshua secretly. So far, nothing has transpired, and I'm certain he'll follow through on his promise," Brad said, making eye contact with everyone around the table.

The twins sank into their chairs with ease. Eryn sat up with his back to the wall once more proudly.

"Can you explain to me why you chose the blond boys? Are they pretty?"

"Oh my gosh," Connor said and slapped his upper thigh. Mika placed his hand on Connor's and squeezed it quite hard. Connor slowly flipped his hand over, weaving their fingers. The tension was a visible indicator for Brad to provide support.

Eryn turned to face the other grown-ups at the table and answered honestly. "Yes, they are pretty, but they are excellent friends. They pay attention to what I say and never make me feel horrible about myself. I can hear their songs, and they can listen to my song when I sing."

"Can you tell me which songs?" Mika inquired.

"Could you please sing for us so we can hear you?" Connor elaborated.

Eryn looked questioningly at the twins for permission to share their song. They nodded and gave the impression that everything was okay. He took a deep breath and opened his mouth to sing the notes of a song. The melody was euphorious; it sounded light and vibrantly pure. While singing his melodious siren song, the cabin filled with an odoriferous smell Brad couldn't identify.

Eryn closed his eyes and pushed what Brad guessed were pheromones outward as the delicious smells intoxicated them. Brad felt feather-light. Eryn's forearms had a pearlescent blue sheen while he sang. The beauty of the unearthly angelic notes charmed everyone at the table. Brad wanted to weep, and he stroked the goosebumps on his arms. Cian and Ivan were wholly absorbed. It seemed as if Eryn was the only person who existed for them. The boys burst into applause when he finished.

"As you can see, he's amazing." They leaped to their feet and clutched their Brawl. Eryn hugged them back, shoving and playfully grasping the lads.

"What was that?" Juandre asked as he and the others surged onto the lower deck. "It's just stunning. It was the first time I heard anything like it."

Brad looked at them but still felt dazed. "Oh, that was Eryn. He showed us how he sings for his friends," Brad explained while making a point of saying, friends.

"That's amazing. Wow, Eryn, you have many phenomenal talents," Juandre praised him. "It sounded nothing like the song you sang outdoors to shelter us from the storm." Juandre continued, looking super impressed.

"It was extraordinary," Mika said slowly while glaring at Connor. They were having one of their unspoken conversations with their eyes.

Eryn soaked up the praise. "I know many types of songs," he said, ready to sing more if someone asked. While they all praised him, Brad expressed gratitude for sharing his gift with them.

"See, no one in our group has ever heard anything like that before, so people need to get to know you better like we're getting to know you now, Eryn, and that's why we want you to feel comfortable living in Phoenix. Mika and Connor want you to stay with them," Brad said, dropping the hammer on a high note.

"Why can't we get our own apartment?" the Romanov twins asked simultaneously.

"No, we need to get to know Eryn better," Mika said curtly. Cian and Ivan gave each other a questioning look, and their expressions turned sorrowful as they accepted their defeat.

Mika looked instantly irritated. "That is a sign they want to be alone and away from us," he muttered to Connor.

"I know. We'll have to take turns chaperoning them." Connor replied.

The twins were stunned, but before they could protest, Eryn pulled each in an arm and nuzzled their heads with his chin.

Brad chuckled and hoped he'd diffused the tension and prevented things from being said in the heat of the moment. "Boys, remember we just met him, and we must watch over him. There are people at Phoenix who would want to hurt Eryn." He turned to Mika and Connor. "So, you two will have trouble sleeping for the foreseeable future." Brad teased and then bolted from the table to join Rick and his boys.

CHAPTER 18

# LET ME DROWN HIM

*"GOOD MORNING, CITY OF PHOENIX.*

*It's now six a.m.*

*Do you know the difference between infiltrating and penetrating?*

*Infiltration is all about being sneaky about penetration, while penetrating means finally gaining entrance.*

*Did you also know that it has the same meaning as the slogan 'make love, not war,' because it was a code for spies to infiltrate and penetrate enemy lines?*

*So, it doesn't matter whether you're spying or making love; both are about gaining entrance, but only the spies infiltrate.*

*Breakfast is served until eight a.m.*

*Have an insightful day."*

**ERYN, King of the Brawl**

LATER THAT NIGHT, one after the other, the young men passed out sleeping as the discussions about their exciting day had wound down. While Juandre and Andrew prepared breakfast for the following morning, Brad, Rick, Connor, and Mika rested on the deck under the stars. The aroma of butter and pastry wafted across the ship, and Eryn welcomed the smell of scones and the sounds of Juandre and Andrew's jovial banter. He shared the sleeping cabin with the twins, lying between Ivan and Cian, linking arms while Kawa and Donali slept just a few meters away. Eryn had just awakened from one of his recurring nightmares. He tried not to think about the hundreds of people who'd died while he walked through the streets of Cape Town. The buzzing of flies and the overpowering stench of decaying human bodies hung over the cities like clouds. The vivid images of dying humans caused by his brothers' horrible trail of doom flashed in and out of his field of vision. He sat up, rubbing his eyes to dispel the torturous memories.

*I should stop referring to them as my brothers because I'm nothing like them.*

The dreams were always the same, and always woke him up. Disoriented and unsure whether it was a dream, he stood among the dead humans, eyes closed and crying in agony over so much death. His empathic gift enabled him to carry the sorrow and pain of many people, and to this day, when he closed his eyes to dream, he could vividly see the horror surrounding him. Monsters waiting on his command, eyes wild, teeth bared. More animal than anything human. *They waited for him to lead them.* He remembered telling them, "Go home," and the confusion in their eyes gave way to obedience as they returned to their tunnels. That look in their eyes, the connection with him, was why he'd struggled to kill them.

Eryn was the only one who could bring them to a state of calm and slumber. He felt responsible for them. He hated himself for letting them suffer for so long. *I should have drowned them sooner. I should have listened to Father.* Especially now that he tasted living with the twins. Those monsters, Ernest included, were incapable of listening to reason long-term. Their only emotions and thoughts were confusion, fear, aggression, and cannibalism.

*Yet, I felt responsible for taking that away from them by giving them calm and peace, by putting them to sleep. I was terrified of being rejected by humans and being all alone.*

Eryn turned his head to look outside the cabin window at the stars. There were a few clouds in the sky, with a beautiful full moon shining on them. He lifted his hands in the air, inspecting them in the moonlight, noticing how dirty his nails were. Why didn't anyone mention that? He lay his head back down, folding his hands behind his head. He listened to the boys' sleep noises. Joshua made terrible sleep noises, but the twins sounded nothing like Joshua. Everything they did, even their breathing, was beautiful to him. Bored with himself, he lifted his feet, inspecting them. He noticed earlier that his toes were webbed, but the boys weren't. He huffed.

Yet another thing that proved he wasn't human. Then he heard giggles. The twins lay open-eyed, watching him. His tummy did that weird thing again, where it felt like he was hungry, but not. A feeling only they gave him. *I guess it's a good feeling.*

"What are you doing, Eryn?" Ivan whispered.

"Nothing," he quickly replied, flipping onto his stomach so they didn't see his tenting pants. He watched them both as they watched him. Their love and acceptance washed away all the terrible memories from the nightmares earlier. His insides soaked up their happiness like a hardened, dead, sea sponge. He thought they were so pretty. *I'm lucky to have such beautiful best friends.*

"What are you thinking, then?" Ivan prodded.

In the dark, he saw them staring back at him. "I thought about how beautiful you both are, and that I will never be as beautiful as a human. I'm an ugly Brawl."

Both reacted, reaching up and touching his face.

"Of all the humans we know at Phoenix, you are the most alluring one, and that's all that matters to us," Cian said.

"What does that mean?" Eryn asked.

"It means you are even more beautiful than beautiful. You're powerful and mysteriously attractive," Ivan said.

"Yes, and you're fascinating and seductive with your voice. And you smell like… hmmm, like lemongrass and lavender."

"That sounds like toilet spray," Donali commented, breaking out in laughter.

"Ignore him. You also smell like fresh linen and seaweed."

"Yup, a toilet spray," Kawa added, laughing hysterically.

"You sound like two hyenas!" Cian said.

But their laughter was infectious. Eryn jumped over to the McCormick twins and started tickling them. "I will tickle you till you shit your pants, and then you will be glad for my toilet spray smell."

"Dogpile, shit pile!" the Romanov twins yelled, joining the scuffle.

"Stop, stop, I'm going to piss myself."

Eryn stopped his playful assault, and the Romanov twins rolled off his back, careful not to hurt Kawa.

"Are you okay, Kawa?" Donali asked.

"Yes, I'm okay, but I smell like shit with sugar sprinkles on top." They burst out in another round of giggles.

"Dear lord, I need to go to the washroom. I think I peed myself," Cian said when they quieted down. He got up, but before he could open the door…

*Bang! Bang!*

Eryn froze and shushed them. Reaching for his trident, he stood at the ready, listening, while sending his mental feelers out to scan the ship. However, his heart pounded so loudly that he struggled to hear anything. For the first time, he worried about his twins and their family and friends so much that he could hardly think straight. Two thumps followed the bang-bang sounds.

Those were gunshots or maybe pots or pans falling, he speculated, as a fleeting afterthought.

"Shhhh," Eryn said, smelling gunpowder. "Something is wrong. There are strangers on the ship."

"How can there be strangers on the ship?" Ivan asked, whispering.

Eryn listened. Then, turning, he searched for a spot to hide four big boys. "Quickly hide here." He lifted the bottom of the massive bed like it weighed nothing. "Climb in," he urged them, whispering, but he felt like shouting to make them move faster.

"No, we want to stay with you." The Romanov twins objected, and Eryn gnashed his teeth.

"I will come to get you when it's safe. Please hide. Otherwise, I'll worry about you."

Donali and Kawa didn't wait to be asked twice and slipped in as fast as possible. They'd learned their lesson by not hiding when Ernest grabbed them. "Please, you two, do this for me," Eryn begged and pushed them hurriedly down. Thank the heavens they obeyed. As quickly as they could, they all slipped under the bed. Eryn grabbed a shoe and placed it at each corner, making it slightly higher so as not to crush them.

He turned soundlessly, leaving the room. He stopped, closed his eyes, and pushed out his mental feelers to scan the below and above-deck areas. It surprised him to find five intruders on the upper deck he didn't recognize...and oh shit! Two of his friends were lying in a heap, and Brad, Rick, Connor, and Mika were nervous.

Hoping the boys stayed where he'd hidden them, he snuck into the dinette area. As he stepped into the room, he heard muffled male voices on the deck. He stepped carefully over the scones strewn on the floor.

"Well, well, well," an evil-sounding male voice said from behind him.

Eryn froze and lifted his hands, feigning surrender.

"I knew you would pop up sometime. All I had to do was wait. You misfit DNA mongrel. We've been searching for you for years. So, get your hands up where I can see them."

Eryn stood frozen, hoping the twins did nothing stupid like trying to save him.

"You know, you were supposed to take us all to the moon, but no, you ran around playing guard dog and hide-and-seek. Are you even aware that the Earth is about to explode? And you're gallivanting and playing footsie with boys who don't know what you are?"

Eryn's heart raced. He didn't wallow in fear of making a sound. *How did this man sneak past me?* He didn't know, and it scared the shit out of him. No one had ever evaded him. *I'm the apex predator, or so I thought.*

Are there over five evil men on the upper deck? He was doubting himself after the man behind him snuck up on him.

"Where are the others?" Eryn asked.

"Come now. I ask the questions. Where are the twins?" the intruder asked with a chilling, menacing voice while something was poking Eryn in his back. It must be a gun. He calculated falling to his hands, performing a low roundhouse kick, taking the asshole down to the floor. But before he could carry out his superb escape karate kick, he heard a dull thump, a buzz, a groan, and the sound of the man hitting the floor. Turning around, he saw his twins, wide-eyed, with a stun gun in hand.

They looked so damn cute holding the gun together like one couldn't pull the trigger without the other.

"Are you crazy?" he asked, and they nodded in the affirmative.

"Let's tie him up and go upstairs," Cian said, and Ivan dangled a rope in front of Eryn.

"No, no, no, absolutely not!" Eryn suspected this was what a heart attack felt like, or was that a stroke?

"You're killing me! I think I have a nervous attack."

"Oh, you mean a panic attack," Ivan, the bright one, corrected him.

"Breathe, one, two, three in and one, two, three out. Or is that ten? Because you're bigger, it should be twenty in and twenty out," Cian added uselessly, not making any sense at all.

"You stay and watch this guy," he said, glaring at them.

They had the decency not to laugh.

"Okay, let me think." Eryn rubbed his pounding head, where a major headache was forming. "So, there's only one way up, and they would guard the entrance upstairs." Eryn continued to calculate the best next move.

More pitter-patter of feet. Eryn rolled his eyes. Donali and Kawa joined them. He harrumphed, grabbing a spatula from the floor, sticking the thing into the handle of the rotating door, and locking the door so no one could exit or enter. Then he walked over to where the twins were tying the man, binding his wrists to his ankles. He vigorously shook the unconscious man's tied hands and feet. The rope slipped loose like wet spaghetti. He eyeballed them.

"We were still busy...we were hogtying him." They whined in unison. With no outstanding success, thought Eryn.

Gently but quickly pushing the boys aside, Eryn wrapped the rope around the filthy human's neck three times, then down and under his one leg, and twice back around the other. Then, like an expert, he proceeded in a different direction by pulling the man's ankles back and swiftly did the same thing backward twice around his torso. Then, folding his arms backward, he tied them and did the same with the man's feet and, finally, around the neck again.

"That's it!" Eryn felt very impressed with his roping skills.

"Come on. We could have done that," Cian protested. He eyeballed them again.

"Then why didn't you?"

"You're so full of yourself."

"Silly mates," Eryn said, and immediately felt self-conscious for uttering the word.

"Wait, what?" Cian and Ivan exclaimed, noticing their slip of the tongue.

"I said you're silly."

"Nooooo, rewind that. The other word," they asked, looking like two Marmoset monkeys with white hair sticking to the sides of their heads and big, curious blue eyes.

Eryn blushed. It felt like he glowed in the dark.

"Did you say, mates, like Australians say how'zat, my mate? Or did you mean to say *come here*, I want to rub myself all over you and make you mine? Which mate are you talking about, my mate?" Ivan asked, and Cian elbowed him.

"Stop it, that hurt."

"You mean you want to mate with us?" Cian added.

Eryn knew precisely what word they were referring to. He knew three meanings of the word. Friend, partner, and the pleasuring kind. He read and watched many books and movies at Phoenix as a small boy Brawl. He discovered the pleasuring meaning when he was sixteen, but there was no way he would tell them that, not here and now. Donali and Kawa were listening, and a man was lying tied up in front of them on the floor. Also, he wasn't telling them how often he had touched himself thinking of them. Cian and Ivan had been his best friends since he met them from a distance at Phoenix, but now, the twins heard his mating call, and the little buggers sang back to him. Ivan's song was louder than Cian's, but that didn't change the fact that he wanted to mount both. His faceless mate had morphed into two faces, the most beautiful two faces, and he wanted to touch and kiss and do all kinds of rubbing on their bodies. He realized he was daydreaming when they coughed.

"Okay, you're both. I'm not lying to you. You're my best friends and partners." *And yeah, I want to mate with both of you.*

"Come, I want to surprise the men. Now is not the time." Their faces lit up and shone at him like the brightest stars in the universe. *I want to lick those pouty, soft lips so bad.*

Grabbing his trident, he pointed it at a small window above the couches opposite the entrance of the dinette. He hummed and softly touched the window with it so it cracked and exploded to the outside.

"That's badass," his mates whispered.

"You stay down here. Please be safe." Donali and Kawa nodded. Eryn ruffled Cian's and Ivan's hair as they stood open-mouthed, deep in hero worship.

Next, Eryn climbed onto the seats, turned his back to the wall, and pushed his arms through the open window while pulling himself into a sitting position.

Bending his head inside, he repeated, "I mean it. Please stay here." He moved so fast they barely saw his feet disappear through the opening.

While hanging onto the side of the ship, Eryn heard voices. He listened.

"What do you mean, the Earth is going to explode? And why haven't you said anything earlier? I mean, you had over twenty years to say something?" Brad spoke loudly, sounding upset.

So they were from Phoenix, and Brad knew them. *The six bastards!* Eryn had the realization while hanging onto the ship and assessing the situation. *I'm killing them tonight!*

"Why not tell us and let us help you? We could've all worked together if you'd said that to us. Why was it necessary for all this sneaking around? Why steal when you can ask? Are you dense or something?" Brad asked. That was something Eryn learned and liked about Brad and the humans. They would always listen to what you needed, and you only had to ask. If it weren't possible, they would work together to make it work.

"Because, you idiot, there are over two thousand men in Phoenix. Who are you saving, and who's staying?"

"That's not up to me. I'm not the god who decides who lives and who dies. But why would you need us, anyway?"

"Because you need to figure out how to get us to the moon. You idiots flooded our Provisions Craft! Our supply of food, water, and building equipment! So, you'll make it right."

Mika and Connor sat, hands up, behind the wheel, while Brad stood talking. Rick watched the men dressed in arctic suits to his right side, but his eyes constantly darted to something.

*What's he looking at? Where are Andrew and Juandre?*

Still hanging onto the side, Eryn moved around the ship's side for a better view. No, no, no! Both his friends were lying in a heap in front of the door to the stairs going down to the living area. He flipped himself up to the deck and crept closer for better inspection. It didn't look good. And by the heart rates of his friends, they didn't think so either. Eryn held his hand under their noses to feel for heat and movement of air. Nothing. Tipping his head, he listened. Nothing. They were dead. Eryn saw red and felt murderous. These were two wonderful humans. They were only ever good to him. They fed him, and Juandre always smiled at him. Never a nasty, selfish word from either of them.

"Then why would you steal and clone eggs?" he heard Mika say.

"Why create superhuman or deadly creatures? What's your end game? Because, buddy, you make little sense," Brad added.

"There are forces at work here that you won't understand. We only want fuel to propel us up to the moon. Are you aware that people have already been on the moon? You're a sad bunch of homosexuals. You were only an experiment, a forgotten experiment gone wrong!" Charles shouted.

Eryn felt the disbelieving anger flare in Brad.

"Listen, you better stop with the attitude if you want our help. I believe if we can survive in glass domes in Antarctica, then it's most probably true for the moon." Brad turned to Mika and Connor, having a conversation like it was just another day around a poker table.

"Now, Houston Headquarters makes sense. I always wondered why the WHPPS headquarters were at the Space Center and NASA's astronaut training and flight control complex."

"Yeah, now it makes total sense," Connor said, bumping his forehead with the palm of his hand. Mika nodded animatedly.

The man with his gun on Brad continued, "Yes, we even designed a hydrogen-propelled ship as a prototype, but no, you had to design your own box of Smarties. A blue one, and it's glowing, too. Why didn't you at least test our design? Why not try hydrogen?"

"Because it's my rescue mission. Why must I use your design?"

"Well, there's our design, and now tell me, what's wrong with it?"

Mika got up and stepped closer, poking him on the forehead with his middle finger. "Listen, Charles. If you had come to me and told me what you wanted like a normal scientist, I could have helped you. What's wrong with you people? You all act as if I owe you something and that you have an entitlement to take what you want. Why didn't you offer to help us when we needed it? I'm so sick of sanctimonious bastards like you acting as if the world owes you, but you continue to take and destroy. You can't handle someone having more and better than you, but you're too proud to ask. Has it ever occurred to you that we all work together because we think as a team? We're not ten years old. We're not a gang of thugs," Mika screamed, not allowing Charles to respond. "If you want what we have, just come to me and say I have an idea. I'm not sure it will work. Please help or teach me because the world's about to explode!" Mika sneered. "I'm so sick of this shit!"

The asshole named Charles opened his mouth as if to speak.

"No, I'm talking now, Dr. Charles Montgomery. You're a useless drop of spunk. You're slimy and stink worse than a two-hour unflushed lump of excrement. That you went and built your ship astounds me. Congratulations, you used that organ between your ears. Be proud of what you've done, the first hydrogen-propelled ship ever designed, and it flies. Take it and fly to the moon! But no, let me make a pit stop and shoot some honest people before we go because we want it all and leave everyone else miserable!" Mika shouted, red in the face and seconds away from literally combusting into flames.

"They left us here!" Charles yelled back at Mika.

Eryn noticed Mika make a hand signal, as if he knew Eryn was there. *That's it. Keep him talking.* Eryn had had enough of these evil men. He recognized them. They were the ones who had terrorized Joshua for years. They'd beaten and killed him and made Eryn hide in the tunnels inside the mines.

Now they'd killed Juandre and Andrew. They were too stupid to make their own fuel, always wanting, taking, and destroying. They were bad men. *And their time of bullying must come to an end today.*

Decision made, Eryn sprinted from zero to one hundred kilometers per hour, tackling three of the five intruders from the side while holding his trident horizontally. Bullets whizzed over his head as he scooped them up in the air and ran all three overboard into the icy water, taking them with him. They kicked and grabbed frantically onto him, but he swam deeper and deeper until they stopped struggling after a minute. That was his sign, and he knew they were dead. Their grasping hands fell from him, and he swam away and upward, leaving them in the darkness. Circling the ship, Eryn waited for an opening to do the same to the fourth and fifth men who were frantically swinging their guns in every direction.

*"You better be careful, or you'll shoot your friend,"* Eryn whispered as he bobbed in the waves, only the top of his head and big eyes above the waterline. That freaked them out. Eryn didn't use his mouth to speak because he spoke directly into their minds.

"I'll start shooting!" the fourth man said, aiming his gun at Brad. He never saw Eryn coming to collect him. Eryn shot like a resolute marlin out of the water, pegging him with his trident like it was fondue night, and disappeared underwater before he could say ouch. *It serves you right.* Eryn deposited him with his friends in the cold and dark depths.

When Eryn returned to the surface, the last coward, Charles, had Brad, Rick, Mika, and Connor at gunpoint. "Don't come closer. I'll shoot them," he shouted, bewildered. His head turned left and right while making threatening, empty promises to Eryn, who was somewhere out in the water, watching. Eryn hung around for a better opportunity. He watched Mika and Connor for directions.

Mika spoke up to distract him. "You'll have to kill everyone. Then, if the world explodes, you're dying anyway. You know what? I just showed you how easy it is for me to make a rocket fly to the moon. I'll make your fuel formula for your idiotic rocket. Then you can fly to the moon. To demonstrate how easy it is, I'll complete it within ten days. But you go alone!" Mika growled murderously.

Eryn felt Brad's intention to confuse the man. Then, out of the blue, Brad started speaking, startling him. "Wow, that was sexy, Mika. That sounded like the Russian fisting voice you used in the tunnels. I never realized how sexy your dominance sounded. If you told me to get on my knees in that tone of your voice, I would lick your boots clean for you."

Mika immediately caught his friend's meaning. "Comrade, we have a deal when we get home after I make this idiot his stupid fuel. Mika will fist you all night long."

Connor jumped in before Charles could say anything. "Hey, honey, maybe Rick and I can join you?"

"Yes, that would be awesome. I'll bring the popcorn because I like to watch while I rub one out," Rick yelled with his hands high up in the air, moving one step to the side. They were smart, Eryn noticed, they were widening the space between the four of them, to make it harder for Charles to corral them.

Charles pointedly showed them he knew where Eryn was and that he wasn't taking his eyes off him. *He thinks I'm the biggest threat.*

"Stop it. We all know you gay people have no morals. You're trying to distract me, and it's not working." For a second, his gaze darted over the ship and back to where Eryn bobbed in the waves.

"No, I want him." He lifted his chin, showing it was Eryn he wanted.

"That's why they created him, to help us on the moon."

"Who are they?" Connor demanded, sounding irritated.

"There's no way you take that young man or any of us with you," Mika said, and Eryn's heart did a few happy backflips as his eyes prickled with tears. That statement boosted his confidence in his new family.

*My ice-people from the glass city, Phoenix, I will help them, not the selfish murderer.* Eryn pushed himself out of the water so his whole torso was visible, his legs not kicking. A move no human could do, especially while holding a heavy pure gold staff.

"I belong to Ivan and Cian and not to you." As soon as Eryn spoke, Rick lifted his leg and side kicked the piece of human trash hard on the knee, sending him flying onto his stomach. Brad, Connor, and Mika jumped onto his back, immobilizing him. In a flash, Eryn was next to them.

"Let me drown him. Give him to me," he said, calm and in control of his emotions.

"Maybe later, Eryn, we'll tie him up and ask him some questions. Like who he's working with and how many other experimental projects are in the works?" Brad said, checking Mika and Connor, making sure they had Charles pegged and immobilized.

Brad dove over to help Rick, gently rolling Juandre and Andrew onto their backs and checking their breathing and carotid pulses. Rick shook his head, indicating they were both dead to the disbelieving Brad, who had hoped they were still alive. He dropped to his knees, hung his head for half a second, then jumped back up and made his way back to Charles.

Red in the face and fists clenched, Brad shouted, "You idiots, you're all going to die with us! The rocket is stuck in the mud. Unless you have some super lubricant, that rocket will never fly out of that hole!" Brad yelled, seething about his dead friends. Eryn sensed his anger was directed at Charles, yet the man still flapped his lips about a damn rocket.

Charles made a vicious face, challenging Brad. *You better shut up, or Brad's going to kill you.*

"There's another rocket, and I know where it is. All we need is fuel and him," Charles said with a snarl.

Ignoring Charles's ranting, Eryn aimed to ease the tension. Instead, he interjected, "I'll go get the boys. They're downstairs with one of them." He pointed at Charles with his fork. "I tied him up, but they're waiting for me. I'll have to go down the same way I came." Without waiting for a response, he dove back into the water, eager to reach the twins. A few minutes later, the boys opened the door to the upper deck, appearing shaken and unsure, with Eryn carrying the man over his shoulder. He tossed him down next to his friend like a sack of potatoes. Still unconscious.

In the meantime, everyone else had gathered around Juandre's and Andrew's bodies. He could feel the hope that, by some miracle, they were still alive.

"Why did you have to kill them? You're monsters!" Brad snapped, kicking Charles in a fit of rage. Lowering himself, he kneed the man in the ribs and then straddled him. No one attempted to stop him. He unleashed weeks of frustration, pummeling Charles with his bare fists. Left and right, over and over, until his face was unrecognizable. Mika and Connor halfheartedly tried to drag him away from the man.

"Let me go!" Brad ordered, and Mika complied. He set Brad free, granting him his revenge, while he stopped Connor from holding Brad back.

A moment later, Brad jumped back on top of Charles. Striking him while articulating each word slowly. "You...don't...deserve...to...live...die...die...die...we...would...have...helped...you...you...bastard!" As he hammered Charles's head, dull, wet, thumping sounds reiterated over and over into the darkness beyond their ship. Blood splattered around Charles's head and onto the deck and their boots. Teeth and possibly an eyeball flew into the air and splashed into the water. Rick, Mika, and Connor did not stop him.

From the corner of his eye, Eryn saw Rick staring blankly, then turning away and looking for the boys, needing to protect them from witnessing their father's brutal justice. He understood how much Brad adored the two men who had only wanted to have fun and were good at heart. This terrible man had murdered their friends. Eryn had the impression that they all felt the same about Charles and his men.

Finally, Brad slumped to the side, utterly exhausted. Everyone could see the way he looked; the world felt as if it were coming to an end. So why care anymore? No one did. They were all in a numb, discombobulated, trancelike state.

Eryn decided to help Brad, and stepped forward. He quickly scooped Brad up in his arms as Brad hung unresponsive, covered in Charles's blood. Eryn carried Brad inside, where Rick transformed the area into a surgery room. Rick unfolded and extended their kitchen table, unrolling a thin mattress to show Eryn that it was ready. The twins had informed Rick and Mika about the setup for medical emergencies like this.

Eryn carefully laid Brad down so Rick could tend to his husband. Brad was wholly defeated and catatonic, staring off into the distance and not reacting to Rick or his boys.

Eryn closed his eyes, touching Brad's shoulder as he hummed a soothing song. "Sleep, Icemen King, rest, and be well." Brad's eyes fluttered shut.

"Thank you, Eryn," Rick said, working on undressing Brad, his eyes glistening with tears.

Eryn noticed the tears and nodded. He left to help Connor and Mika clean the deck. They didn't need to be reminded of the day, so they cut loose their enemy's ship and rolled Charles's dead body into the water. They kept the unconscious man tied up to deal with later and to question later.

Next, their friend's bodies were prepared for burial—something Eryn had never witnessed before. He appreciated their explanations of the ritual, even though their emotions were a mix of rage, sadness, and loss. These feelings intensified while they removed the bullets and washed and dressed the bodies. The process gave Eryn an entirely new impression and perspective on what it meant to be human and how they loved and missed one another. Mika, Connor, and the twins included him by explaining their actions and the reasons behind them. They also described what humans typically do with the bodies of those who have died on land and around the world, noting that some cultures approached it differently than others. Eryn found it all very interesting, especially since he didn't know how to handle his father's body. They informed him that the rituals had changed since Doomsday and that, since then, they had only dealt with one death, which they had to burn because the ground was frozen, making it nearly impossible to dig a grave. Eryn didn't like his first experience with burial. It felt like too much sadness. Everyone agreed that this was one too many.

Two days later, after they informed Phoenix via radio that Juandre and Andrew had been murdered, the crew of the Blue Halcyon, except for their General McCormick, who was still in a coma, held a small remembrance ceremony for their friends who had died in the line of duty. Each person spoke about their fallen colleagues and the impact those individuals had on their lives back home. Eryn recalled his favorite scone and bread, and they all agreed they would deeply miss their cooks. After Mika and Connor rolled their linen-wrapped bodies into the sea, it was a sorrowful morning. Eryn appreciated the hugs because they made him feel more human.

# CHAPTER 19

# BIG DOGS WITH UGLY YELLOW EYES

Big dogs with ugly yellow eyes

*"Good morning, citizens of Phoenix.*

*It's now six a.m.*

*This is for youngsters. Have you ever wondered why planets are round?*

*They say it's because their gravitational field acts as though it originates from the planet's center, pulling everything toward it. The only way to get as much mass as close to the center of gravity is to form a sphere.*

*The technical name for this process is an isostatic adjustment.*

*Visit the community news page for more interesting facts about planets.*

*Breakfast is served until eight a.m.*

*Have a ball of a day!"*

## GENERAL BRAD MCCORMICK

BRAD JOLTED UPRIGHT, gasping for air. Half disoriented, he looked around frantically and immediately felt better when he saw Rick sitting beside him, his arms draped over Brad's legs. The movement and gasps had woken him, and as soon as Rick's gaze focused on his, he conveyed the bewilderment, disorientation, and panic he felt. Reaching for his hand, Rick approached him as if he were a frightened animal, perhaps a rattlesnake in need of tranquilizers.

"Now, now, it's all going to be okay. The boys are safe. We're all okay." As soon as those empty words left Rick's lips, the image of Andrew and Juandre getting gunned down while they begged Charles not to shoot flooded Brad's mind. It seemed as if Charles and Juandre knew each other. Juandre repeatedly asked Charles why he never came to say hello. Charles had shouted that he was disgusted by their relationship and that Juandre was a piece of trash. So hateful, so unnecessary. Then the fury bubbled up from within him, triggering his fight-or-flight response. Instantly, he felt like he could kill Charles with his bare hands again. He panted, feeling like he couldn't get enough air into his lungs.

"I can't breathe. I need air. I can't breathe!" he said, nearly falling off the table.

"Come here, love, I'll help you," Rick said soothingly as he grabbed Brad's suit and helped him into it.

*He's so patient with me. I don't deserve him.* Brad hopped, half hanging and half running, for the exit.

"It'll be fine," Rick promised, taking his time to focus on Brad while speaking loudly enough to awaken everyone. Probably to gather extra hands to help him.

"What happened to...last night...after?" Brad asked, stuttering. "What did you do with..." He couldn't finish the sentence or find the words. Sorrow for Juandre and Andrew tightened his chest, but his Apache spoke in a stern, calm voice, catching his attention, so Brad forced himself to listen to the one man he trusted most in the world.

"You're getting enough air. Take deep breaths, in and out. Focus on my voice while we prepare you for the frigid air."

Heads popped up, and Rick appeared relieved. One by one, they showed themselves. Mika came through the revolving door first, with messy hair. He looked like he'd been sleeping with a finger stuck in a socket all night. "Good. Is he awake?" Mika rubbed his still-closed eyes and dragged his slippers across the floor, nearly knocking Rick over with a loud, "Oomph, sorry, still waking up."

"He just needs a bit of fresh air," Rick said, winking at Mika, but Brad saw it.

"I don't think it's wise to take him up to the deck. That jerk is up there. We tied him to the mast, Brad. We thought the cold would do him good. When you're ready, we should probably interrogate him." Mika continued as if Brad wasn't having a bloody panic attack and didn't need oxygen like any other land-dwelling vertebrate.

"You were out for over forty-eight hours. I'm making coffee," Connor, who had entered right behind Mika, said.

"Come sit, comrade!" Mika called to him casually, in his usual self-assured manner. Pulling out a chair for Brad, Mika brushed aside the melodrama and shortness of breath. "Let's get some coffee in our systems first, please, Brad. I'm all for getting to the truth, but..." Mika pleaded, but he was interrupted by their children coming in. His smile broadened when he saw them. "Morning, boys," he greeted the five young men.

From Brad's vantage point, one by one, a pair of chocolate brown heads, followed by a pair of blond heads, and finally, Eryn's curly, dark blond mop of hair, emerged through the revolving door. Eryn rubbed his head as if his hair had gotten stuck, or maybe he had scraped it on the low-hanging ceiling. The newcomers immediately sensed the tension in the cabin, their heads swiveling left and right as they assessed the situation.

"Morning, Father." Donali and Kawa's faces brightened as they raced to greet Brad, wrapping their arms around his neck and showering him with kisses and affection, just as they had since they were babies, like two little orangutans. *I should ask Peter or someone from the bionics department to build Kawa a new arm,* Brad thought, feeling grateful for the love his boys showed him.

"Welcome back, Father. It's great to see you're up."

"Thank you, my boys." Brad soaked in the unconditional love.

"Good morning, General," the Romanov twins greeted, while Eryn appeared skittish, tiptoeing around Brad, nodding, looking down at Brad's hands.

Brad followed his gaze and noticed that someone had bandaged his hands. Guilt suffocated him all over again.

Searching for doubt or disgust in their children's eyes, Brad found none, so he straightened his spine and looked back at his fists. He mumbled to Mika, picking up the conversation they'd started before the children arrived. "Maybe running upstairs isn't a good idea after all." He inhaled deeply, held it in, and slowly released the trapped air, taking steady breaths that flowed in and out. He calmed himself and repeated that two more times.

"Yes, comrade, let's grab a coffee and plan our next steps." Mika broke the tension and patted him on the back. Rick released his arm, and Brad knew that whatever decision he made, Rick would support him. He looked at his husband and expressed his gratitude for his stoic support. Rick always displayed a rock-solid sense of dignity and grace, and he couldn't imagine his life without him—a trait that Brad and many of his patients admired greatly.

"Thank you. I think I'm feeling better now. I just had a terrible dream about the shooting," he admitted, acknowledging the elephant in the room. "Gentlemen, I'm really sorry. I misbehaved. I acted out." He glanced at the kids. "I apologize if I scared you."

They all fell into Brad, hugging their father, friend, and leader. Brad lifted his head. He taught his boys that it was okay to cry and that a man could have feelings. He also taught them that confronting problems head-on cleared the air, allowing life to move forward. So he knew they accepted his feelings. Although he was a grown-ass man, he could shed a tear. After all, he was bloody human, and they were all friends and family. And so they healed with words and reciprocation of love.

"It's all good, Dad. We all felt like that."

"Your father and I raised you better than to solve your problems with your fists." Brad's face burned with shame.

"We know, it was the language of the bad people, so we understand, Dad," Donali said.

"I don't want you to be scared or disappointed," Brad murmured, fidgeting with the bandages. "I saw your eyes earlier."

"We're not scared of you. We're scared for you, Dad." They stepped closer, offering Brad supportive hugs. "And we're not disappointed."

As a leader, or former leader, of Phoenix, he firmly believed in leading by example, so he invited them to sit down at the table by pulling out more chairs for a roundtable discussion. Connor brought a big pot of coffee and squeezed himself between his family. Everyone around the table had time to vent about the past forty-eight hours, including what they learned from Charles and his men.

The Romanov boys each sat on one of Eryn's knees while Eryn wore the biggest smile Brad had ever seen on anyone. The three just seemed to fit together, he thought. Brad doubted that Mika and Connor opposed this unusual bond, especially after they protested when Eryn was taken away or left them. The boy-king was undoubtedly what Brad would consider worthy of a king in honor, truth, dedication, and power. The list was long, and Eryn checked all those boxes. He was strong, yet fragile in many ways. The twins were pleased when Eryn was between them, and Eryn was happiest with them in his arms. It was no one's business what happened in the bedroom since the boys were twenty-one years old. They were old enough to make their own decisions. Still, Brad was relieved they weren't his boys. Thank the frozen damn stars.

"Connor and I cut the hydrogen ship loose. We didn't want to see it anymore," Mika said.

"That's understandable. I don't care about their damn ship. But we need to find out if there's more information we don't have."

Mika got up to grab the scientist's notes. "I saw something about the rockets in his notes." He spread it all out on the table in front of them. Together, they all leaned in closer, examining it.

"Look," he said, starting to read.

We—Environmental Project III (EP-III)—were assigned rocketry and DNA manipulation to ensure the superhuman race survives and thrives on the moon. They also tasked us with research to address fuel, oxygen, and water shortages. However, everything went wrong. Scratch that—it all fell apart.

The American Star Connect company funded the rockets built for human travel in cooperation with the WHPSS. A global effort to establish a lunar presence, and I suspect is the driving force was behind all this madness. Locate the number two mineshaft, marked in blue. It's the northwest tower near the Fochville ruins. Inside lies a rocket ready for human travel.

They all frowned, looking up.

"We didn't see a blue tower. It was brown-black, rusted, and not blue," Mika said.

They all looked at Eryn, who appeared to want to shrink away and disappear behind the Romanov twins.

"Eryn, do you know anything about the blue tower?" Mika asked, noticing that Eryn turned a few shades of green. He looked terrified. His big, cheerful smile from earlier had vanished, replaced by a look of dread. Then, he quickly lifted the twins and moved away from the table. Brad barely saw him move.

"No, no, no, no, no," he moaned into his hands. "That's not a good place to go. Eryn fears that place." He receded into himself, speaking in the third person.

"What's there, Eryn?" Mika asked.

Eryn sank to the floor, curling up as tightly as possible by pulling his legs to his chest and clasping his knees.

He barely touched the floor when the Romanov twins dropped to their knees, one on each side of Eryn. Narrowing their eyes at the group, they snarled like two giant white rabid poodles.

"Look what you've done!" They pointed at Eryn, who trembled. They surrounded him as if to shield him from the men around the table. "Eryn, look at us. You've done nothing wrong."

"Eryn isn't bad. Big monsters and men are bad. They are evil, evil, evil," he cried.

*What in the ever-loving gory damn stars?* Brad wanted to stop the fussing. He tried to be practical without making the situation worse. The Eryn he had gotten to know over the past few days was crumbling before them. Brad looked questioningly at the others, who shrugged. Gone was the mighty king. What remained was a frightened and vulnerable boy who needed validation for his feelings. The situation needed to be resolved as quickly as possible. He was among friends and should be free to share deeper conversations just as easily as surface-level banter, just like Brad did when he woke up freaking out.

He seized the opportunity to show Eryn and remind the children that it was okay to feel afraid, just as he was feeling at that moment. *I need to turn this into a teachable moment and demonstrate to them that they might regret their choices later if they don't confront their fears now.*

The raw terror and vulnerability in Eryn's eyes broke Brad's heart. He stood up from the table and squatted in front of the young man. "Eryn, please look at me. Remember when you were so brave and took care of me?"

Eryn rocked slower, turning his face to Brad.

"Yes, you took care of me. You made me better. Now let me help you. But, for us to help you, tell us what's scaring you like this."

Eryn looked up at Cian and Ivan, who nodded their approval.

"You know, we're your new family. We care about you just as much as you care about us. Can you feel our love and concern for you? We call that empathy."

Eryn stopped whimpering and became still. He closed his eyes and then opened them. One corner of his mouth pulled up in a half smile, and he nodded.

Brad continued. "Okay, that's good. Empathy means we imagine how we would feel if we were in your situation. However, to do that, we need to understand your specific situation. Understand? Remember when I sat down and invited you all to join me so we could discuss what was bothering us? I was so scared. I struggled to breathe, remember? All those feelings"—Brad put his bandaged hands around his own throat—"it choked me. It felt like I couldn't breathe. I didn't want to say that, but I did. And I promise you, it helps. Tell us so we can understand. Please, boy, trust us to help you?" Brad coaxed and then waited.

Eryn's posture and facial expression shifted instantly to a look of determination, despite the tears streaming from his strange eyes. His bottom lip trembled. "The monsters sleep there. I don't disturb them, and they don't disturb me."

"Are you saying we flooded tunnels, but there are more?" Brad confirmed, and Eryn nodded slowly, looking guilty.

"Yes, but they sleep. They never wake up. They are waiting."

"What are they waiting for?"

"They wait to be set free."

"I don't understand. Eryn, please share your entire story as much as you can. My boy, we need to know what we're dealing with." Brad nearly begged, his heart racing faster and faster. *Freezing hellfires!*

Eryn nodded and pushed himself up, sitting crisscross with his long legs. Pulling his twins closer, he positioned each next to him, and then Brad moved closer, mirroring him by sitting cross-legged. He invited the other men to join the circle. Rick grabbed some pillows and brought them over, while Kawa and Donali carried plates and cups. Mika and Connor dished out breakfast and coffee before joining the circle as Eryn explained and ultimately faced his fears.

"Under the ground is a big place, just like my home. It also has a rocket. Inside, lots of humans from all over the world wait."

"As many as Phoenix's humans, or more or fewer?" Brad asked.

Eryn held his hands up and showed ten fingers.

"Ten people, ten thousand people?" Brad asked. Eryn shook his head.

"Ten times more than Phoenix."

"What, Eryn, are you saying about twenty thousand humans living underground in South Africa?"

Eryn shook his head. "Not living, sleeping."

"Where are they sleeping, Eryn? Do they have houses or apartments, as we have in Phoenix?" Brad asked, imagining Phoenix underground.

"They sleep in their glass beds, inside the rocket, and the monsters sleep with them, watching them."

"Watching over them, like guard dogs?" Brad asked.

"Yes." Eryn nodded.

"Why are you afraid of them?"

Eryn's eyebrows knitted together. He swallowed. "They're huge and really mean."

"Are they neurotoxic, like your Brawl brothers?"

"No, but they killed and ate my brothers. So maybe they'll kill and eat me too."

"Alright, let me share what I know and think, and then you can stop me. Please correct me if needed. We went through your..." Brad hesitated, reconsidered what he was about to say, and continued. "Your father's notes. Some people wanted to save the humans, but some wanted to eliminate all the humans."

Eryn bobbed his head up and down. "Yes, they fought over who was going and who was staying. Then, when they were ready to go, explosions occurred, and someone helped my brothers escape. I locked my father in his office after he told me to fetch my brothers. They ran and ran. Ernest laughed and laughed, enjoying himself so much. I cried. So many dead people. My brothers were too many for me to catch. Humans resorted to guns and bombs, and when that didn't work, they unleashed the monsters. More bombs, shooting, and fighting followed. There were lots of explosions and many more humans perishing. Eryn didn't know where to run. Must Eryn follow them in Africa, or what? My brothers were everywhere, and the poison spread every-where. So many people were dead. Huge monsters chased us and ate my brothers while Ernest laughed, still having fun. They devoured my brothers. I ran as fast as I could to save them. But the monsters got so furious, releasing more and more poison into the air. Finally, I had had enough." Eryn paused, wiping his tears and sniffling. "I screamed, 'This is enough killing! Stop now! Go home!' They all turned and went home."

"What a horrible story," Brad reciprocated, thinking that if he had known all this sooner, he would've bombed everything to bits and then used Mika's cannons to level it all.

Mika broke the tension. "So, do we still need these?" Holding up two anti-toxin shots. He looked suddenly keen to get to a lab and have cases of the stuff reproduced.

"How old were you when this happened, Eryn?" Brad asked, frowning because something didn't add up.

"I was a young boy Brawl."

"I ask because sometimes everything looks bigger when you're small. So, if you were a young boy, can you remember what cars, trucks, and buses were?"

Eryn nodded eagerly. "I remember the truck full of gold."

"Good. Were these monsters bigger than cars, trucks, or buses?"

"Yeah, that's a good question," Connor encouraged, realizing where Brad was going with this.

Eryn blew out his cheeks and then released the air slowly. He was silent for a few seconds. Then he shook his head. "No, they were not that big."

What a beautiful sight it was when Eryn realized they were not as big.

"So, they were smaller than a bus?" He nodded in the affirmative. "Smaller than a truck?"

Again, he nodded yes. Please be smaller than a car, Brad wished. "Eryn, is one of those monsters smaller than a car?"

"No, about the size or bigger."

"About the size of a car?" Brad confirmed. "Okay, that's good. Now we all know that. Can you tell me how many are there?"

"I don't know. I'm not sure. They don't communicate with me as my Brawl did. I told them to go home, and they did, but maybe they went back because the nest returned? I'm not sure. Since then, I've left them alone, and they leave me alone."

"I need more coffee and something to eat." Connor got up.

Brad nodded. *I need something stronger.*

"That's fine. We will continue. Just listen with one ear. You may pick up something we don't," he said to Connor. Then turning to Eryn, he asked, "Who told you to leave them alone, and they will leave you alone? That sounds like something your father would say."

"Hmmm, yes, yes."

"Okay, so did you sneak there? How do you know they're sleeping?"

"They're stacked in glass sleeping boxes."

"Jesus Christ, where's that coffee, Connor?" Mika asked, getting up to make another pot of coffee.

Brad shook his head. "Don't worry about Mika. He's just surprised, that's all. You're doing well. How many rockets with how many people, Eryn?" Brad waited while Eryn counted on his fingers.

"There were five rockets. Two left for the moon, one exploded, one rocket where Eryn and Ernest's home was with my nest to protect the rocket. And the one at the blue mineshaft, where the humans sleep with their guard dogs," he said disgustedly.

"Are the guard dogs neurotoxic and dangerous to us?" Brad asked, patiently waiting for Eryn to think, which took a long, bloody time, before he shook his head and answered.

"No, they're only dangerous to us, Brawls."

"So, they watched the humans and guarded them against you, too?"

Eryn pulled his shoulders up high.

"Eryn, do they look like humans or animals?"

"They look like dogs and wolves, big dogs with ugly yellow eyes. Eryn remembers those eyes very well. I see them when I have nightmares, as you do at night, Brad."

A round of chuckles followed, and Brad felt proud of himself because he'd been honest earlier.

"What do Brawls look like? Do they look like you?"

"No, the first Brawls look like frogs, but more man than animal. They looked a lot like Ernest. They were born in a nest separate from me. According to my father, they are Colombian poison dart frogs with special skin glands that secrete toxins."

The twins cringed. "Ernest was the crazy psycho frogman that chewed my arm off," Kawa exclaimed. "He looked like a tree frog." They laughed.

Brad smiled at the boys making jokes, he'd seen the ugly thing when he'd tied it up.

"So, the guard dogs watch the humans, and they protect the humans from Brawls?"

"No, they kill everything that's not human."

"They were supposed to protect the humans." Brad put his hand on Eryn's. "Do you agree? Eryn, you're human. You said you were a boy Brawl. You were a boy."

Eryn nodded. The twins stroked his short, dirty blond curls lovingly.

"Brad's saying they won't harm you because you're human. You're more human than some men, so these guard dogs can't harm you. That's why they didn't hurt you, and that's why they listened to you," Ivan said.

"Because you were barely five years old, you didn't understand what was happening. You didn't know what you were. That's why your father sent you to live with Joshua, so you could see humans and live like one. It was the best thing he could have done for you, allowing you to grow up among humans and understand the difference." Brad explained what he thought had been going through the scientist's mind.

"Your father and the other scientists dabbled with science and played God. They created beings they couldn't predict or control," Mika added.

Brad rolled his eyes.

"I think we need to turn back, my boy. We need to let those people go. Let the rocket fly. Let them take those animals with them. That's their purpose. Do you agree?"

Eryn wiped the snot from his nose. Cian took his t-shirt off and bundled it in his lap to be used as a tissue.

"Yes, I agree."

"We can't kill those people by flooding the tunnels, but we can send them where they wanted to go. That's the only way to resolve this by doing the right thing. So that's why you didn't flood those tunnels, not because of the dogs, but the thousands of humans?"

"Yes." He sniffled.

"With our help, especially Mika and Connor's help, I'm sure we can send them to the moon."

They all agreed that it was the right thing to do. They got up feeling hungry and determined to finish breakfast. After that, they went upstairs to confront the traitor.

# CHAPTER 20
## THE LOOT



**DR. MIKA ROMANOV**

"DID you know liquid propellant experimentation happened as early as the nineteen-forties?" Mika asked while leaning in and supporting himself on the ship's rail with his elbows while holding his binoculars. "Even before I met Dr. John Saunders, who invited me to come work at Phoenix, governments begged me for my research on alternative fuels for rocketry and space travel. If I asked, the bastards would have done anything for me, nearly climbing into my lap and licking my face. Only I would have liked a good ass licking much more, comrade, if you catch my meaning." He snickered, adjusting his binoculars.

"No, thank you. I don't want to imagine a bunch of government officials licking your ass. That's not my thing," Brad replied, pretending to spit hair out of his mouth. They both burst out laughing.

"Oye, will ye stop your joking and playing around? My arms are tired, and I'm getting bloody hungry," Connor said with a thick Irish accent.

"I would tell you to come rest your arms on the side rail like us, but you're too short unless you want to sit on my shoulders," Mika teased.

Brad snorted and giggled.

"Connor, should I go get a little chair downstairs so you can see over the side of the ship?" Rick asked, all seriousness in his tone.

"Piss off," Connor said with a snarl, and brought on another round of laughing at his expense.

Laughter drifted from the otherwise soundless flying ship. The men enjoyed the back-and-forth banter while searching the horizon for the hydrogen ship they'd cut loose three nights before. The skies were deep indigo, with barely a breeze or cloud in sight. Therefore, the vessel should be almost in the same spot where Mika and Connor had cut it loose and left it.

Connor had used radar earlier and could ping the tracker Bryan had attached to it, so they had a general direction to search. "It should come into our field of vision any moment now, so keep your eyes open," Connor said.

After their hostage explained it had schematics needed to determine the propulsion force of the rocket mathematically, they started looking for the thing. Knowing the rocket's size, weight, and dimensions, they could make the correct calculations to achieve lift-off.

"And here we are, force equals mass times acceleration, so we avoid catastrophe by not killing twenty thousand humans. Oopsie-daisy, we need those schematics," Mika said jokingly.

"And that's why we're playing *Battleship* today, yeah," Rick said dryly, still searching through his binoculars.

"Ha-ha-ha, that was a good one, love!" Brad complimented.

"Thank you," Rick said stoically. "*Peep, peep, peep, Boooooooooookkkkkksssshh.*" He mimicked the widely known sounds of the electronic talking *Battleship* game.

"Yeah, ten points to Rick for originality today. I didn't see that one coming," Connor shouted, who sat and rested his arms on the ship's wheel for support. "Oh, no, I shouldn't have said I'm coming. Okay, you childish geniuses, let's not talk about coming again."

"You mean 'yeah, baby, again, and again and again'," Brad tried but failed dismally. No one laughed.

"The first thing to do is to run a few experimental firings. I have a theory that we don't need gallons of fuel. We also don't need any oxidizers. We would have to do these tests outdoors, as any sane scientist would," Mika said, cutting into the joking while still searching for the hydrogen ship through his binoculars.

"Yes, we aren't a suicide squad," Connor added from the back of the helm.

"I figured that," Brad added, back to scanning the horizon and focusing his binoculars. "Tell me, what's your plan?"

"Nuclear power. I'll ask Eryn to sing to the atoms. The fission would create enough thrust by heating hydrogen gas."

"Hmmm, nuclear fission, you think vibrations would break down radioactive atoms?" Brad asked, pointing to something on the horizon. "Look over there!"

"Yes, I have a feeling they have hydrogen gas onboard. Why would these ass-wipes hint toward the hydrogen-propelled airship? They needed a reactor, and I think Eryn's the key. His sound waves should be able to excite the gas molecules to expand rapidly and stream out of the engine nozzle. So, it'll be a kind of nuclear-powered balloon rocket." Mika pointed to where Brad saw something. "There it is, Connor. Do you see it?"

"Yes, I see it, yelda." He looked down at the tied-up man, who divulged his name as Nick. "See, easy-peasy."

The man scowled.

They used grappling hooks to pull it closer.

"Untie me! I'll get you the stuff."

"Nope." Brad scoffed.

"Why not?"

"Number one"—Brad showed him his left middle finger—"I don't trust you. Number two"—Brad showed him his right middle finger—"I don't trust you. And number three" —Brad hooked his right arm over the left—"guess what number three is?"

"That's very childish coming from the leader of Phoenix," grumbled the still-bound man.

"That's where you're mistaken, Nick. I'm not the leader of Phoenix. They've replaced all of us. We can do whatever we want for as long as we want, and there's absolutely nothing that you or anyone else can say about it. We're free agents, buddy. The world is our oyster, Nick, or whoever you are."

Connor, Mika, and Rick knew Brad was talking shit, but it seemed to work because Nick's eyes couldn't get bigger.

"Finally, the asshole understands what's going on," Brad said, and the others laughed.

"I thought something was wrong with you, the way you hit Charles," Nick sneered.

"Yes, I rather enjoyed that," Brad said, eyeing Mika, both glad the kids were downstairs. "Just like I'll enjoy throwing you overboard with this hook through your ass." He showed him the hook they planned to use by throwing it over the side, hooking and pulling the other ship closer, and the men laughed again.

"You sick bastards, stay away from me!"

Brad continued his emotional battering by pretending to come closer. Nick kicked, making sure they knew he would fight a good fight.

"So, shut up!" Brad shouted at Nick. "I don't want to hear a word from you."

Mika had Brad join him, and they jumped over to the hydrogen ship. A few minutes later, they returned with bags full of information.

"Thank you for all your research and data." Mika struggled to lift the heavy bags filled with ancient tablets, maps, books, and all kinds of secret intelligence. "It must have taken you eons to collect these. Thank you." Mika laughed like Santa Claus. "Ho-ho-ho." By now, they were giddy with laughter.

Opening the hatch to go downstairs to sift through their new belongings, Brad gave Nick his best evil pirate look. "Arr!" Then he shut the door and left Nick alone, cold and tied up.

Arriving downstairs was another matter. Eryn was lying on his back, spread out on the sofa bench, with the twins busy eating his face. The three moaned and groaned, enjoying themselves in a three-way kissing festival. Still fully clothed, they ground and rolled their hips. The twins rutted shamelessly on each of Eryn's hip bones while Eryn looked like he was fucking the air. Each time he elevated his hips, he lifted the twins, sending them rolling, but somehow the facial suction never lost its grip. The passionate kissing and licking of tongues was quite a sight. Eryn had an arm around each twin, squeezing them closer for more friction.

"*Hmmm.*" Mika coughed, clearing his throat.

"Excuse us!" Connor shouted.

"Thank the gods. It's not my kids." Brad boasted, and Mika didn't know what to do. Brad stepped aside, showing him the floor sarcastically, then stepped away so Connor and Mika could proceed. Mika saw Brad out of the corner of his eye, and finding Rick, the two silently watched the scene play out from the back.

Eryn finally noticed they weren't alone and threw the twins so high their heads hit the low-hanging ceiling. The three young men were vertical in an instant. It looked like Connor was praying. His eyes were closed, and Mika heard, "Hail Mary, Mother of god."

Still, in a state of animated suspension, Mika felt like he wanted to attack, thought better midway, and paused.

His boys landed butt first.

"Oh, frog balls," Eryn said, bending forward to help them up, but they jumped up so fast, giving him a headshot on his nose and side of his head, knocking the Brawl King flat onto his back, pulling Cian with him, who fell forward, face first and nose up into his balls. "Argh," Eryn grabbed onto his injured anatomy and nose, moaning and groaning.

Mika closed his mouth with an audible snap, turned, and disappeared through the revolving doors.

· · ·

**ERYN, King of the Brawl**

Connor grabbed a hand towel and gave it to Eryn. "Sit down and firmly pinch the soft part of your nose, just above your nostrils."

Ivan stepped forward to help. "Lean forward and breathe through your mouth."

"Father, we can explain," Cian interjected.

To Eryn's surprise, Connor sat down and spoke calmly. "No, we're sorry to barge in here. The ship is small, and we're all adults. I'll explain it this way. Your dad and I are the same. You don't want to see your father and me having sex, do you?"

"Ugh, no," Ivan said.

"So, I think to use that as a reference, and then you know how we feel seeing you like this. What's most upsetting for us is that you're brothers, which is wrong on many levels. But with that said, it's your own private business, but I'm not approving of incest. And your father's not supporting it. But parents have not approved of and discouraged many things in life. It pushed the kids away and caused more harm than good. I'm Roman Catholic, but they also used to condemn homosexuals, saying it was just as wrong. So, please, we love both of you..."

Ivan interrupted to explain. "But it's not like that. We want Eryn, and he wants us. We don't want each other like that." Ivan spoke slowly and clearly, so Connor understood. Eryn nodded his agreement.

Connor seemed to relax. "Please do things like this in private. Wait till we're home."

"Yes, Dad," the twins said.

"Yes, Connor," Eryn added. His face was a mix of various shades of red and pink.

"We promise," all three said again. Connor dipped his chin.

"I'm going to speak with your father now," Connor said as he got up, but Cian and Ivan stopped him.

"No, please, Dada, we will. We want to talk to him. We need to explain this to Papa. He's distraught, and we know it. I saw his face."

Connor gave them half a smile and added, "I know." Then sagged into a chair with his head hanging low.

Eryn led the twins out via the rotating door to find Mika. When they arrived on the deck, their prisoner called to them.

Shackled to the mast, Nick called, "Hey, I need to talk to the three of you."

"Not now, old man. We're looking for our father," Cian said.

The prisoner raised his chin and pointed to the other ship. Someone had placed bowls of food and water, similar to those used for dogs, near him.

"Who brought you water?" Ivan asked with a grin, projecting Eryn's thoughts and rubbing salt into it.

"Your self-righteous leader, General Brad McCormick."

"He's your leader, too, you terrorist!" Eryn defended Brad.

"I'm not a dog!" Nick screamed and kicked at the bowls. Pieces of bread and water splattered and splashed everywhere except on them.

"Horrible aim, *tisk-tisk-tisk*," Eryn said.

Turning their backs on him, they laughed and boarded the ship via the gangplank from the Halcyon straight into the doorway of the wooden shack.

Holding the wheel, Mika steered the ship to nowhere as he stared out the window in front of him.

Ivan and Cian grabbed Mika around the waist simultaneously. "Father!"

Eryn felt like the odd one out. But after years of watching them interacting from afar, he expected to see this level of intimacy.

"We're sorry. It shouldn't have been done. We explained to Dad, and now we want to talk to you." Cian spoke into Mika's shoulder. Both boys were taller than Mika at two meters.

"Father, I don't want to go into unnecessary details, but the easiest way to explain it is that we both like Eryn a lot and never fight about toys or anything. It's dumb. You taught us to share or get another toy. We're so used to sharing that it doesn't bother us to want Eryn, and he wants both of us. We don't..."

Mika interrupted them. "That's your own private business, what you do in the bedroom. We raised you correctly. I should trust that you can make the right choices. But this is very difficult for me to accept. It is not..." Mika stood rigidly straight.

He opened and closed his fists, as if he were struggling to control his temper and preventing himself from saying something impulsively. Fine tremors in his clothing betrayed the calm demeanor he falsely portrayed.

"It's just that I've never foreseen this for you. I never wanted this for you. I never even entertained the thought of you two..." He turned back and then pointed to the three of them. "Somehow, I thought maybe you would choose Donali or Kawa."

They pulled their faces.

"No, that's just wrong, Father. They're like our brothers," Cian said impulsively.

Eryn read Mika's micro-expressions.

Mika grunted, and he lifted his eyebrows.

Ivan's shoulder bumped Cian, and then they chortled. Cian realized what they'd just been saying. "Okay, I know how that sounds, but let me explain, Father. We're brothers, yes, but I'll never want to share Eryn with anyone else," Cian said.

"And I feel the same," Ivan said.

"So, you share him?"

"Of course!" Eryn lifted his hands and shoulders, very proud to be shared by the twins. "Sorry, Mika, it just happened that both want me, and I want both."

Mika glared at Eryn. He sensed Mika wanted to attack and kill him for ruining his perfect boys. He pinned Eryn's amphibious gaze with his, and although the twins spoke, he didn't break contact.

"It's like sharing a huge ice cream," Cian said.

Ivan rolled his eyes. "Dear lord, brother, you're making it worse. Please stop."

Mika lifted a hand. "Yes, please stop. That's way too much information. I don't need that visual," Mika begged, finally releasing Eryn from his death glare. He rubbed his face vigorously up and down with both hands. But then, like the sun peeking from behind a dark cloud, it seemed to make sense to him.

"Cian is saying that we share him. He's ours, and we're his. Nothing's happening between Cian and me."

"Yes, that's what I said," Cian added.

"My brother is pretty, but we don't plan to or would ever be attracted to or do things with each other," Ivan clarified.

"I think I hear what you're trying to explain. It feels more acceptable if you describe it that way."

"Yes, that was what Dada said, too."

"You realize you'll repeatedly hear many people asking the same question?"

"That's okay. We don't mind."

Mika took a big breath, relaxing his posture. He appeared worried about his boys.

"Father, you always said we were the last Romanov princes, and Eryn's the Brawl King, so it's a royal affair," Cian said jokingly.

Mika turned, rolling his eyes. Looking out the window into the blue distance, his gaze caught their reflection in the glass. He watched the three of them holding hands. Eryn's between them. They couldn't stop touching him.

"It would be wrong to break us up," Eryn added softly, showing he had just read Mika's mind. He sent a look begging him to look closer at their reflections. *They made us for each other.* He said to Mika, mind to mind. *Look, I'm holding them up, and they are holding on to me.*

Mika turned back to them, changing the subject. "Okay, do you think you three would like to have this ship? It's only the basics. You would have to come to us for meals," he asked.

The twins' eyes sparkled. "Our ship?" Cian and Ivan asked.

"I don't know if it's yours, but for now, yes."

"We have to ask Donali and Kawa to join us," Ivan said, always including the McCormick brothers.

"Maybe the McCormick boys joining would keep you three from devouring each other," Mika said with a lopsided grin.

"Yes, let's go get them and bring our stuff," Cian said excitedly, bouncing up and down on the balls of his feet.

They embraced Mika. Eryn loved every second of it until Mika broke away with watery eyes.

"*They're so innocent, look after them,*" Mika said, surprising Eryn by speaking to him telepathically as he opened the cabin door. "Okay, I'm returning to the Halcyon. I'll send the McCormick boys over," he said out loud, smiling sadly. "*Time to let my little birds fly*"

"I will protect them, I promise," Eryn said out loud.

"We have a ship, Eryn!" The twins jumped up and down.

# CHAPTER 21

# DISCIPLES OF THE ANUNNAKI

*"GOOD MORNING, CITIZENS OF PHOENIX.*

*It's now six a.m.*

*Did you know that in twenty-twenty-two, the most trusted AI bots were female, and their names were Alexa and Siri?*

*But in twenty-twenty-forty, scientists confirmed that above human-level artificial intelligence is male, and his name is Lasitor.*

*Visit your community news page for interesting facts about the first technologies.*

*Breakfast is served until eight a.m.*

*Have a bright day!"*

**ERYN, King of the Brawl**

ERYN STEALTHILY MADE his way toward the entrance of the mineshaft marked *Blue*. He felt uneasy, as if he'd forgotten something important.

He groaned and inwardly cringed when he reached the heavy metal doors. He crept closer, checking the rusted tracks, and to his relief, confirmed there wasn't any movement and that nobody had touched the massive doors since he was last there. Eryn hated coming to the place. He felt the people's dread and despair, which made him feel extremely uneasy. The things that haunted him in his sleep lived down here. So, he planned to be as fast and quiet as a mouse. "In and out, quick-quick," he whispered to himself, copying the general's words from earlier.

He grabbed the massive, rusted handles, pushed the door open, and slipped into the spooky entrance. Chills ran down his spine. Next to his head, Connor's weird camera ball floated and followed him. He had so many new things to get used to, but this new technology excited him because it was human-made, designed and created by the ice-people, and he had dreamed of being part of them and their shiny things for so long. Eryn wanted to prove himself to Brad and his men, but he also wanted to impress the twins.

Because only two anti-toxin shots were available, he volunteered to go on the intelligence, surveillance, and reconnaissance mission. Again, he repeated Brad's big words, teaching himself.

They'd voted and decided his job was to sneak inside the compound and open the gigantic doors to the mineshaft, so Connor could send the camera ball inside to collect information to help investigate their enemy. After ensuring the ball was safely inside, he turned around and ran, kicking up dirt and dust. The place gave him the heebie-jeebies. So he hollowed his back, tucked his tail, moved his legs, and skedaddled right out of there.

Just as he exited the gates, he froze in his tracks, seeing the twins about thirty meters out, waiting for him. Instantaneously, he felt happy to see them, but their demeanor was all wrong. Their eyes were serious, and they weren't smiling. Instead, their heads hung low, and Eryn sensed a somber cloud hanging around them. His heart rate sped up, and his hackles rose. Stepping closer, he scanned their surroundings simultaneously.

"What's wrong? Why are you upset?" He kept smiling, keeping up his appearance while his eyes looked around, searching for something out of place. He felt like they were being watched and spotted two tips of black boots pointing past the ruins of a dilapidated old security checkpoint and office building. The twins' eyes darted back and forth, trying to warn him of the danger, but he'd already assessed the situation. With one leap, Eryn jumped in front of them, bumping into them so hard that they flew a few meters and landed safely behind a piece of concrete.

"Freezing hellfires!" Cian exclaimed.

"Bloody damn hell, was that necessary, Eryn?" Ivan asked.

Eryn wanted to laugh, but it wasn't a good time, so he straightened up and said, "Yes." Happy that the twins were out of sight and amused by their antics. The twins inherited their Russian father's charm and crude choice of language, and although Eryn heard a few more remarks, he focused on Nick, who spoke and showed his face from around the corner. In his right hand, he held a flare gun. He narrowed his dark, beady eyes on them and grinned smugly. Eryn stepped back in a fighting stance with his trident ready. He knew flare guns from Phoenix and that they could be dangerous. They could kill if fired directly at a person, especially at short distances. Some humans changed them to shoot bullets, so he hoped this wasn't a converted weapon.

"Hello again, Eryn," Nick greeted self-righteously.

"Put down your gun, and I won't hurt you," Eryn demanded with a low, gruff voice. He locked his eyes on Nick and waited like a cobra, ready to strike.

"You have to know I'm not naïve enough to believe that. You are, after all, a killer, aren't you?" Eryn felt shame and regret, but then he remembered who he was and what his new friend Brad had told him. Eryn is the king of the brawl. *I am human, and I am a friend of humans. I'm a good boy.* He straightened his spine and drew strength from the goodness within him when he remembered how Brad had hugged and accepted him. He would fight for the icemen. "I fight for good humans," he said sternly. "I never wanted to kill anyone, but bad people have forced me to."

"We're the ones who know how much damage has been done and what you can do. We know why the military didn't shoot you. I know why you're still alive, and I'll tell you why they're all waiting for you. For you and your twins," Nick said, all puffed up and sure of himself.

Eryn frowned and rolled his eyes in exasperation. Then, in the corner of his eye, he saw the twins on their hands and knees, poking from behind the barricade.

"Your fate was determined long ago. The birth of you and the twins was foretold and planned."

Eryn frowned, shaking his head at the twins. He turned sideways so Nick didn't see his hand shooing the twins back to safety.

"You don't have a clue what the reason for all this is?"

"Then tell us, Mr. Rocket scientist." Eryn attempted to keep Nick's attention directed toward him.

"Why do you think you're here on their twenty-second birthday?"

"What are you talking about, you crazy asshole?" Cian yelled from behind the piece of concrete.

Goosebumps appeared on his arms, and his hair stood up as jolts of energy rushed through him at breakneck speed. Eryn's fear and annoyance at the damn cheeky brother reached indescribable proportions. Eryn vaguely remembered hearing a similar story before. It sounded familiar to him. He wondered if Joshua or his father had told him the story. With a stern expression, he was ready to defend and attack Nick and determined not to be distracted.

"Why twenty-two, Nick? What makes twenty-two so special? I hope you baked us a cake and put forty-four candles on it," yelled Ivan.

Nick shook his head.

"We don't mind. Sharing is something we love to do. We share Eryn, too." Cian added teasingly, mocking Nick by sticking his tongue out at Nick, who looked flabbergasted. Eryn stood his ground, not moving, while he listened to the twins being fearlessly disrespectful, having fun at the idiot's expense. It did funny things to his insides, and Eryn wanted to throw them over his lap and spank them.

"Your daddies aren't as smart as they think they are. We helped them decide on Project One. They followed our lead from the very beginning. We're your Disciples, and you're direct descendants of An and Ki, the Goddesses of the earth. Your name, Ivan, means the fourth, or the Roman letter IV, for the mighty IV-An. And your name, Cian, spells Ki-AN. You're Anunnaki, and your primary function is to decree the fates of humanity."

His face popped purple-red welts of frustration as the twins guffawed at him like two drunk monkeys. His determination grew. Bulging his fists, he ranted on. "Your mother is not a human Scandinavian with blue eyes. No, your DNA is Mesopotamian Anunnaki..."

The twins interrupted him.

"You mean our egg donor was a Mesopotamian Anunnaki? Sorry, man, I'm just saying there's no way an egg survived five hundred thousand years. They can barely make it past twenty-eight days. And I'm very sure Moses didn't carry a refrigerator through the desert," Ivan retorted. Cian patted him on the shoulder for a job well done.

Nick ignored them, determined to say his piece as he stood on his proverbial soapbox. "You inherited your extremely high IQs, perfect health, and undeniable beauty from her. You possess extraordinary powers, and I bet he knows that." He pointed toward Eryn. "He knows you have powers, the same powers he has. Humans didn't possess the technology to extract the deity's holy DNA for thousands of years. We know for sure this is the time your mother predicted. It's written on the Babylonian tablets and guarded until she reveals it to us. The time of the Big Flood. It's written as the Year of the Twins. I can show you the tablets, but that would have to be once you're on board. We must leave now. Your parents can join us. It was also predicted that the world would end and Luna would welcome us. So many souls are already waiting for you. You three will lead us into the future."

Nick fell to his knees. It seemed he was not above begging.

"Please, I beg of you, listen to me. The three of you are like your mother, the Goddess of love, sexuality, and war."

Cian and Ivan rolled on the ground, holding their tummies, cackling. Eryn knew they were different, and he wondered if there might be some truth to what the man was spewing. When they sang to him the first time, it wasn't with their human voices. It was more. Their souls recognized each other. He felt a pull toward them, and he was sure they felt the same tug to be with him.

Nick continued his plea. "Please, boys, I need you to come with me. I'm sorry you have to hear this under these circumstances. I'm desperate for you to listen to me. We've been standing guard for so long. Waiting for you. And I'm sadly the only one left to meet you here. We should have told you earlier, but our leader, Charles, felt it was better to wait until you noticed the change within you. But then you were abducted, and we didn't know where to find you."

*That was a blessing. Thank you, Ernest.*

Eryn suddenly felt better about the abduction.

"So, we stood guard and watched you from afar. The three of you are unique and supposed to work together. You belong together for a much bigger reason than you think. Indeed, you have seen what he can do. It's your birthday, and your powers will reveal themselves and grow daily. From today, you're no longer boys but men. You are gods. You are Anunnaki. You're leaving your human selves behind. The older you grow, the stronger you will be. Why do you think the Peter Pan Caps let Phoenix live so long? It's your placenta inside those gel capsules."

Eryn smiled. While the crazy man on his knees with the flare gun had been ranting about gods and the Anunnaki, Ivan and Cian sat behind the boulder, pulling cross-eyed faces at him.

"All these people are waiting for you. You only have to get on the rocket with them. Once you're on the moon, you can call forth water and air for us."

Eryn was tired of this. He wanted to get home and ravish his twins. Bugger the moon, and bloody bugger it all. He wanted the twins to eat their birthday cake. "I'm tired of this shit," he said, stomping his trident onto the ground. Pieces of frozen earth flew up. "I'm going home to Phoenix. Come." He signaled with two fingers as if directing traffic to the twins.

"No, I can't let you do that. Get on the rocket!" Nick got up and pointed his flare gun at Eryn. Eryn swiped his trident to the side, as if waving off an irritating fly. The gun flew out of Nick's hand.

"Get out of our way. We don't care about your crusade for the moon. We want to stay here. So, you get on the rocket and blast off!"

Nick scowled. He roughly searched the collar of his shirt and pulled out something shiny on a chain around his neck. With a voice loaded with malice, he said, "Sorry, you give me no choice," then he raised his arm, and Eryn realized it was a small silver whistle he inserted between his thin lips, and blew on it so hard his eyes bulged.

Eryn heard a faint, high-pitched sound that cut through his mind. Nick held onto the whistle that seemed to be attached to a chain around his neck.

"What did you do?" Eryn asked and didn't want to know.

*It's those monsters, and they're coming.*

A flashback came to him when he heard that high-pitched whistle, where humans lay strewn and dead at his feet.

"Just wait. They'll be here any moment," Nick said sanctimoniously.

"No, not the monsters!" Paralyzing terror overcame Eryn. "We need to get out of here!" he yelled at the twins, who stood frozen in their tracks.

The telltale rumbling of a stampede grew louder as the earth beneath them vibrated. Next, the sound of paws pitter-pattering grew closer and closer. Then they saw them. A pack of snarling black beasts appeared one by one from around the door—the door Eryn had just pushed open.

*The yellow-eyed animals from my nightmares are going to eat me and the twins. I need to get them out of here!*

"Ha-ha! Now you're not feeling so bold, are you?" Nick asked sarcastically, his voice laced with malice.

He's a bad man, Eryn thought as he hyperventilated. "Call your dogs off!" His voice was shaky, his body quivering with fear. He stepped backward and lifted his trident, ready to defend or at least poke an eye out.

"Not dogs. They're sacred jackals, or better, Anubis. They guard humans who serve the Anunnaki. A gift from the gods. To safeguard and protect humans in this life and the afterlife."

"Freezing hellfires, they're ugly. Where's the hair? They look like overgrown sewer rats!" Cian shouted. With an *oomph*, both twins bumped into Eryn, waking him from paralyzing fear. They supported him as they braced for an attack.

"No wonder you have nightmares, Eryn," Ivan whispered.

What? Eryn couldn't believe the twins weren't scared or fleeing. "This is not the time for jokes." Although he enjoyed the careless banter, if they were shredded into pieces, he remembered Connor's ball camera and hoped it had recorded this. Mika would kill him if he survived, and they didn't.

"One blow on my whistle, and they'll attack the twins," Nick threatened, placing the whistle to his lips.

Eryn froze. He was well aware of what those dogs were capable of.

"Okay, okay," the twins interjected. "Let Eryn go, and we'll go with you."

"Not a chance. You two stay right here. I'll go with them," Eryn said, meaning it. However, life on the moon without his twins would be a sad and lonely experience.

*I just tasted them, dammit.*

"No, let's take turns. Rock, paper, scissors decide who stays and who goes," Cian suggested eagerly. White-blond hair braided neatly down his back certainly didn't go with his wayward personality. Eryn wanted to ruffle him up, make him forget his name.

Eryn momentarily forgot where they were while Nick stood by, looking as if he were watching a tennis match.

"Wait a minute, why don't the three of us go together?" Ivan, the brightest spark plug in their three-wheel motor, said. He was usually the level-headed one of the three lovers, said. *Was he being sarcastic?*

"Yeah, that's it. Then we can rule the moon and look at the earth explode together," Eryn said, catching on.

"Aw, that's so romantic." Cian clapped his hands with admiration in his eyes.

First, Nick looked confused, then said nothing.

Shaking his head, he motioned for them to walk.

"Yeah, Eryn, can we go now?" The twins skipped and sang. *We're going to the moon, far away to the other side, la-la-la-la.*

"What's wrong with you? Aren't you scared? Look at those creatures!" Eryn animatedly asked in disbelief.

"I counted at least ten Volkswagen minibus-size beasts surrounding us. Their yellow eyes follow every step you take."

Eryn looked again. They weren't snarling, and saliva wasn't dripping as he imagined. No, they were waiting.

"Pfft, no, we're not scared. We're positive they won't hurt us. Remember, they don't kill humans who serve Anunnaki," Ivan said.

"But he has a whistle," Eryn said frantically. Confused by his lovers' behavior. First, they say go, then they say stay, and now he can't remember what the last decision was supposed to be. He didn't want to see the two of them being torn apart. Their fathers would kill him, put him back together, and kill him again. That was if he didn't get savagely eaten, as well.

"Nah," Cian pfft nonchalantly.

"If we're as smart as he says we are, we know he knows there's no way to force us to do anything," Ivan stated, very sure of himself.

Cian threw his arm around his brother's neck and turned back to Nick. "And, for your information, if we want to go to the moon, we won't go in your stinking rocket. We can fly there on our own because we're earth-dwelling deities. Maybe we want to go with our spaceship." They bent over double as they laughed.

"Oh, that's right. We didn't forget who we were dealing with. You're already comfortable destroying this planet. Why should you be trusted with the moon?" they asked, and Nick almost swallowed the whistle.

"We worked very hard for thousands of years. We operated in the shadows, the Disciples of the Anunnaki. Working hard, always listening, and always waiting for you!" Nick shouted at them.

Ivan crossed his arms. "That's just sad. And here you are begging us to take you with us. You and Charles told my parents that they were not chosen, yet it seems to me that they were chosen to be our vessels for rebirth. Like Mary had Jesus, don't you think Mika and Connor deserve more respect from you?" he asked.

Nick laughed at Ivan. "Mary was one of our Disciples. If your parents had joined us, then they would have been worthy. You think we're here in a gold mine by accident?" Nick pointed to Eryn. "You think your obsession with gold is coincidental? Since the dawn of time, it has drawn our gods. The Babylonian tablets prove that gold mining goes back several hundred thousand years, long before the indoctrinated religions existed. They wrote your DNA string code inside a golden capsule. The gods wanted it to be handed down from generation to generation, until such time that technology existed to bring it back to us. Open your minds and see the truth. Ancient gods populated the world, and humans need them as much as they or you need us. The gods must live among us and share their knowledge and wisdom. We are ready. We ripped ourselves out of the clutches of unworthy oppression and are no longer slaves to them." Nick held his arms out and turned in a circle. "We cleansed the earth for you, so you may rise and live forever among us."

"Now, that's the biggest load of crap I ever heard." A male voice said, and the sound of applause came from all around them. Connor's camera ball floated to the right above their heads. That didn't deter Nick at all. He continued to sell his spiel.

"Open your minds. Living with our gods, our creators, is what we need to return to. Our original state. They are the ones who need to lead us. That is our reward. We're their deserving chosen Disciples."

Nick was back to begging, hands clasped in front of him and an expression of urgency, life, and death on his face. "Please, you're the Anunnaki explorers who came to Earth five hundred thousand years ago. The twin gods are reborn. They gave you this planet as a gift from your father to be mined. You came in search of gold. They need gold to save your home planet, which is overheating. Gold is the lowest non-reactive metal, so they set multitudes of mining operations into action, concentrated here in southern Africa, the oldest settlement of the gods on Earth. Anunnaki created a mixture of their DNA and created the first primitive mine worker or slave species to excavate the gold."

"Wait a minute!" Brad's voice boomed from the ball above the twins' heads. "Are you saying they destroyed their planet, flew here, then emptied this planet, and now they all must go to the moon? For what?"

Nick rolled his eyes at that question as if Brad was asking the stupidest question ever.

"This man is the perfect picture of crazy. Let's get out of here," Cian said.

"Listen, thank you for the history lesson. We understand that you've been planning this for a long time. However, we believe our minds are open to spreading knowledge and love to those we care about. All those nice things about religion and humans like yourself embrace. Unfortunately for you, we prefer to stay here on Earth, where the gold is." Ivan extended his hand for Eryn to take it.

"Yes." Eryn nodded. That made sense to him. Ivan smiled lovingly at him, and Cian grinned mischievously.

"We can't help it." Eryn raised his trident. "It's gold, gold, gold for us!" joining the sarcastic circus of the Romanov twins.

"Let those humans go to the moon. They wanted to go. We're staying here. We'll take our chances with the pending global implosion and catastrophic volcanoes."

Nick was utterly still. His face was non-expressive. Eryn sensed he didn't know whether to pretend, lie, or cry. Eryn burst out laughing.

"Sorry, maybe next time, dude," Ivan said.

"Later, going now, ta-ta!" Cian waved his forefinger round and round, the military signal to move out and meet at the rally point. Then he put it and his thumb into his mouth and sucked. Letting loose a long, high-pitched whistle.

The beasts focused on Nick. It was too late for him to understand what was happening. He fumbled and scrambled for his whistle, but the jackals pounced on him before he could get it in his mouth. He had no time to scream or make a sound as they tore him apart.

They turned and walked back to the ship. "I'm done with this place," Eryn said. "And that hat makes three of us. Let's go."

Three days later, they sent the rocket, carrying all the other humans and their guard dogs, to the moon without knowing whether it had an automated or pre-programmed landing system.

CHAPTER 22

# THE GOLDEN SWORDS

*"Good morning, citizens of Phoenix.*

*It's now six a.m.*

*Did you know we live above a magical bioluminescent fungi forest?*

*Visit your community news page to book your seat for a tour of the recently discovered hidden subterranean tunnels. Experience the beauty of glowing plants and insects, such as fireflies.*

*Breakfast is served until eight a.m.*

*Have a glowing day!"*

**GENERAL BRAD MCCORMICK**

BRAD ADMIRED HIS FRIENDS' adaptability. Of course, it all came down to the voracious testing by their founder, Dr. Saunders. Still, Brad thought their rapid adaptability to learn behaviors in response to changing circumstances was commendable.

Mika and Eryn bonded like *Gorilla* glue almost instantaneously, and so did the rest of the crew. Eryn was such a straightforward young man to like, and Brad knew that once they reached Phoenix, they would love him. His humble, soft-spoken intelligence and playful nature were magnetic, and that was beside the fact that he walked around with a trident looking like a superhero with an eight-pack.

It didn't surprise Brad when Mika enthusiastically told him about Eryn's ability to grasp what he said without in-depth explanations or schooling. "He's a bloody genius. I think he's probably the only man on this earth smarter than myself. Do you know how good it feels to talk to such a person?" Mika asked Brad, who knew precisely how it felt when speaking to Eryn, and seeing his friend so excited and inspired, felt ten times better.

After the jackals had obliterated Nick, the disciple, not leaving a drop of blood on the ground in front of the blue mineshaft, Eryn and the twins asked them to retreat into the spacecraft. Brad and his team inspected the thousands of rows of men, women, and children in cryo pods, awaiting a new life on the moon.

The creepy scene haunted them for days, but luckily, the sound manipulation idea Mika had wasn't that far off, as the prospective moonwalkers already had a hydrogen reactor onboard. With minimal adjustments, almost as if they had anticipated Eryn and Mika's arrival to work on the spacecraft, they could send thousands of people into space. Using the nuclear electro-sound propulsion system, the launch created enough thrust for lift-off. Thankfully, the ingenious system generated enough positive charges, and the reactor, already onboard, helped ensure a smooth execution by pushing the ions out and through the thruster, which in turn pushed the spacecraft out of the mine.

Connor observed the instantaneous bond, and instead of being jealous, he embraced Eryn. The family of five was something to behold. The handsome men radiated power and beauty and were probably Phoenix's last or first royal family. Brad found that being in their presence made a man feel larger. They give without thinking of taking—extraordinary men with exceptional abilities and powers who selflessly put the needs of others before their own.

The spaceship was on its way to the moon.

"Out of sight, out of mind," Brad said to Bryan as he reported back to Phoenix on their way home. "Mika's retreated into isolation. He'd sent word that he's waiting for us to come around." Brad huffed. "He said he would give us time to think. I think he needed some space to collect himself. The Halcyon isn't exactly conducive to privacy and silence," Brad informed the elected leadership team. "So, I think we'll take a few days camping out here on the East Antarctic Ice Sheet. We need a couple of days to relax and allow the boys time to adjust. I'll get back to you after we've discussed and tested the best-proposed theory, and let you know so that you can inform and prepare the residents for the impending destruction. But to keep chaos at bay, you must give them a proposed solution and be honest." Brad coaxed, knowing they all felt haggard about the Earth's imminent destruction because of the buildup of hydrogen and halogen gases. *They needed hope, not lies.*

The recordings by the floating camera ball of Nick, the last disciple, had been watched repeatedly, and Brad had played the audio version over the radio to Bryan and his team.

"Inform the residents about their future on Earth and include the story about the Anunnaki, the gold mining, and the replacement of the gold on their home planet. That would clarify the abduction and rescue mission in the gold mining area of South Africa." Brad explained, holding a radio handpiece in his hand. "At first, we thought it all to be coincidences, but that Eryn created a protective bubble by manipulating sound waves is real. We've all seen it. Bryan, I touched him while he held the bubble in place, and the power emanating from him? Well, I felt as invincible as if I'd used a pound of cocaine. That's how I felt," Brad said. He was excited to share his experience with his friend. There was only silence and static. Brad imagined their facial expressions of disbelief, but he didn't have time to convince them, so he continued, knowing they were listening.

"Mika's epiphany on their way back from South Africa was simple, so much so that when he first presented his idea to me, Connor, and Rick, our reactions upset the poor Russian so much that he stopped talking to us. We were speechless at first, and then we laughed at him. Probably due to stress, but our childish behavior caused all kinds of tension and irritation on board. Hence the camping and relaxing idea, because our narrow-minded reaction had Mika rolling his eyes and saying, *I'll give you a day to think about it." His words weren't cold...yet.*

"I'm on my way to apologize to Mika and admit that it makes sense. He should convince the boys, Ivan, Cian, and Eryn, to test themselves and their abilities. I will report on that update and our next course of action," Brad said.

Bryan, the ultimate leader of Phoenix, recommended talking to the boys, preparing them mentally, and testing the theory before returning. Bryan speculated it didn't sound like they realized the magnitude of their responsibility. He added that *if the predictions were accurate, we're in deep shit, and they're our only hope.* Bryan's voice boomed over the radio.

Rick sat on the counter, his long legs wrapped around Brad's torso, while Brad sat on a small kitchen stool, trying his best to have a serious conversation. *Bloody damn hell. The world is ending, and all I can think about is sinking my nose into his deliciousness.*

"We're going to follow your recommendations while there is time. Thank you, Bryan. Over and out." Brad stopped the transmission. "Give me a kiss, please." He got up and gave Rick a ravenous kiss. When he broke the kiss, he could swear he was seeing double. "I promise you, if we save the world, we're every ten minutes for a week." He rubbed his mouth dry on Rick's shoulder. They hugged and held each other, just soaking and giving, exchanging their love.

"How can I help?" Rick asked, kissing and smelling Brad's hair, which was much longer than usual.

"For now, could you collect our boys? I'll get Connor to collect theirs?"

The night before the testing started, Connor went to the pirate ship, as they named it, to call the boys over for dinner.

Each time Brad saw the dilapidated ship, he wanted to scream with frustration. He struggled to accept a world without Juandre and Andrew in it. "If only," he whispered to himself. It whirled in his head.

The unprofessionally built six-man ship the boys inherited was a death trap. Although the propellers on the back were as big as surfboards, the fact that Charles and his team had caught up with them was a miracle. Hammered down to a wooden cabin was a massive net of ropes that held together multiple bunches of silver weather balloons.

Mika and Connor secured the thing to their ship, not trusting that it would stay in the air on its own. It was possible to deflate or disappear during the night, so they hooked and tied the cabin onto their boat. The young men enjoyed their own space, even if it was basic, comprising a wheel to steer the propellers, one desk, one sofa mattress, and one storage room, with an ice-cold shower and a bucket for a toilet, which was to be emptied by throwing the contents overboard.

They saw it as a treehouse or something, liking it so much that they sat inside, joking and talking for hours. However, when they were starved and hungry, they would come down the stairs like a herd of blue wildebeest on the trek to the Serengeti when they were called in for mealtimes.

After the meeting with the leadership over at Phoenix, the oppressive mood around the table didn't seem to affect the boys when they stuffed their faces.

"We need to talk," Brad said, pausing and noticing the worried faces of the adults around the table, but then the five young men looked up and had their cheeks stuffed to the maximum like hamsters, so he burst out laughing, and the others followed suit.

"My goodness, look at you all," he said, folding over, nearly hitting his head on the table. His laugh was infectious, and they all joined in, pointing fingers at each other.

"Phew, that was a good laugh." Brad wiped the tears from his eyes. "Oh, lord, I needed that." The tension broke in the room. Still hungry and oblivious to the pending doom, the boys got up for seconds.

"Boys, we wanted to talk to you about saving Phoenix. We've just finished speaking to Bryan and the others. We agreed to stay out here on the ice to test a few theories and decide how we would proceed when we reached Phoenix. In the past few months, Phoenix noted an increased number of tremors and volcanic activity on the Ring of Fire, the region around the rim of the Pacific Ocean," Brad explained.

The boys were big-eyed but didn't seem to hold fear. Brad figured they either didn't understand or didn't worry about the future. *I wish I had the untainted mind of a child.*

"I think it's better if your dads explained what they planned," Eryn said.

"It can be a crazy ass who-who nonsense idea, but we all know they always build legends on truth," Mika explained. "We can't mine gold or bring the gold back, but we can use other ways to increase our chances of surviving the explosive core meltdown of the Earth."

Kawa and Donali listened, but it soon became apparent that they meant this for the three other young men.

Mika took over the discussion. "Eryn, do you remember the bubble of safety you created for us in the storm?"

Eryn nodded.

"Okay, then I thought about natural disasters in history, how multiple civilizations have perished over time, and how some survived to document extensive floods or catastrophes. Some built ships, some built towers, and some prayed to gods. I believe we can learn from the civilization of Atlantis," Mika said, then paused to read their reaction. Brad thought he was expecting another round of laughs at his expense, but it never came.

Connor listened attentively. The McCormick twins looked fascinated. Eryn and the Romanov twins were waiting for the punchline. Brad sat, leaning back on the couch, one leg relaxed, crossed over the other, and Rick mirrored Brad's posture.

"We need you boys to create a bubble that can sustain itself," Mika said.

Eryn frowned, and Cian and Ivan sat still with perplexed expressions.

"Because, Eryn, you cannot stand there twenty-four hours a day holding the bubble in place," Mika said.

Eryn moved to the front of his seat. "Okay?" he asked and waited for more, listening to Mika.

"What do you want us to do, Dad?" the twins asked, breaking the silence. They seemed eager to help, sitting on the edges of their seats, as well. "We don't have any powers, regardless of what the wack job, Nick, suggested," Ivan said.

"That's why we'll do a few test runs," Connor said.

"Now, we don't want you to stress or think you're wrong or less than if you can't do it," Mika said.

They'd discussed their worry that the boys might be so stressed they wouldn't be able to perform.

"We'll start small, and Eryn's going to help you. I'm confident he can call your abilities forth."

Eryn rubbed his chin back and forth, forming his assumptions or calculating how to achieve such a membrane.

"That sounds awesome," Cian said, looking eager to have superpowers.

"We'll have to make sure you don't hurt yourselves," Eryn warned. "I practiced for many years with my father."

His face soured as he talked about his life before the twins.

"Come, no need for that. Tell us exactly how your father started teaching you," Ivan said. He put his index finger under Eryn's chin, tipping his head up. Ivan's eyes sparkled for him, and they seemed to communicate empathically.

Eryn's face lit up with a big smile for Ivan.

When the twins smiled at him, they seemed to wipe away all his sadness.

"Okay, let me show you the easiest way." He pointed to Connor, who was sitting closest to the kitchenette. "May I please have a glass of water?"

Connor got up to fetch it for him. "Sorry, may I have two more, please?"

Connor turned and fetched two more glasses.

"Thank you, Dad," he teased. But Connor only nodded his head. Eryn looked happy that Connor didn't react negatively. Instead, he nonchalantly accepted it. Eryn had a look of forced concentration on his face as he was doing what he was doing. He drank each glass of water, so it was half full.

He placed it on the table in a triangular shape. "Both of you hear my song as I hear yours. For them,"—he pointed to the room—"when I sing, they hear a song, but they don't hear the meaning. It sounds good, but they don't know what it is, and they can't sing it. Also, they can't be taught how to. You can sing, or you can't sing. Does that make sense?"

Brad nodded. "Yes, it feels like I should know it, but I can't..."

Everyone, except the twins, said simultaneously, "Put my finger on it!"

Eryn smiled broadly. His grin conveyed hidden knowledge, and his golden-green eyes glittered. Brad noticed that Eryn's usually slitted pupils had enlarged to round black disks while his face brightened, almost glowed when he spoke about his mates and their songs for each other.

The phenomenal aura he emanated filled the entire cabin. Brad and Rick moved closer to watch Eryn. Mika grabbed Connor for support. Connor took his hand and kissed it. What they witnessed was ethereal, filled with the joyous promise of fantasy. Humans read about it in fairy tales or even in the bible.

Eryn's skin glowed a light pearlescent blue. Almost the same as their ship. It felt as if the temperature had increased. Like when you stepped into the sunlight on a beautiful day out on the ice. Then a low hum vibrated into their bodies. Elated emotions of happiness, calm, peace, goodness, and awe filled them. It was a magnificent experience, and it had only just started.

Eryn put his hands on the table and softly began singing his song. The water in the glass closest to him shimmered as it reflected the light in the cabin. The more he sang, the water moved. At first, ripples started on the surface. It rippled so fast that it appeared as if the water had made a spout. Eryn stopped singing, and the water fell back into the glass.

The cabin was quiet. The twins took his hands and hummed. It sounded like the twins sang a few notes higher and lower than Eryn's song. Again, the water shimmered and moved, but instead of forming a spout, the water turned into tiny crystals, like salt or sugar. The crystals in the glass moved so fast they appeared like sand in an hourglass. It grew in height up and out of the glass. The strange crystals from each glass funneled upwards. They stopped humming, and the crystals liquified and then fell back into their glasses.

Then, all three hummed together, and the water crystallized, arching over to meet the other two columns, creating the outlines of a spiraling pyramid. The three streams thinned out, like three strands of hair. They connected with spikes, just like a DNA triple helix structure.

"Oh, my," Mika said in awe.

"What *is* that?" Brad asked. No one answered.

The glowing, swirling helix elongated. As they changed their song, the strands broke into smaller pieces that glowed brighter and died just as the song ended. That same ethereal glow that had shimmered across Eryn's face now encompassed all three young men's faces. The remnants of the tiny glowing pieces floated gently like fireflies.

Brad and the others reached out, catching the playful little lights. As soon as they touched them, they turned back to water again. Nobody wanted to say a word that would spoil the enchanted atmosphere.


## ERYN, King of the Brawl

At first, Eryn didn't think it was possible, but after Mika drew them a picture of what he had in mind and that he was almost one hundred percent sure that it was possible, they practiced around the table with a crumpled-up playing card that lay in a plate of water. They were supposed to each start a side of the plate, then use their voices to manipulate the water from crystals that would eventually be a barrier to the outside while still allowing air and light to travel through. After a few practice rounds, they celebrated by dancing and singing. The three created a crystal-like shape around the playing card in the form of an egg. Interestingly, as soon as pressure was applied to one side, it would retract to the shape of a ball, thereby strengthening the membranes. They decided that tomorrow they would move the experimentations outside.

The Antarctic weather permitted them to practice out on the ice to their advantage. They started small with rocks, which later grew into boulders. Eventually, they ended up on each side of a small hill, pretending it was Phoenix.

"That's it, perfect! Now you, Cian," Mika said.

Cian stepped back and held up his hands. They were triangulated by about a kilometer each. Practicing with longer distances and increasing the radius proved to be much more complex than they first thought. The insurmountable radius of over a hundred meters from the outline of the entire city of Phoenix was depressingly daunting as they struggled, with only a few hundred meters away from each other. Faint musical ringing noises, *ting-ting* at high decibels, but the sound of their voices drowned it out.

This proved to be much more difficult as they wouldn't see much of the results or each other because they'd work from the upper ground and have to send the vibrations underground.

Eryn raised his hands and felt a distinct prickling through his body. He received a slight electric shock. Most probably, the twins were sending too much power his way.

Fearing that they had experienced the same, he decided not to reciprocate. "You're overloading me. My arms can't handle it. It feels like my bones want to climb out of my skin," he shouted.

"What should we do?" they called.

"I'm going to count to three. We should stop sending vibrations simultaneously." He counted slowly, grinding his teeth. "One, two, three, shit!"

They fell backward onto their backsides.

Frustrated and fearing hurting the twins, Eryn swore crassly. "I can't do this without my trident!" Eryn yelled. His blood was boiling. The idea of him hurting the twins infuriated him. "Give me my trident."

"Eryn, do you think if we somehow devise a plan for Cian and Ivan, get them something to concentrate the sound waves with, like you do, would that go more easily?" Mika asked in a gentle tone. His voice calmed Eryn a little.

"Of course it will!" Eryn retorted hotly.

"I'm impressed. Now I can see the man I don't want to cross," Connor said. Eryn felt like punching him. Then, he realized he was seconds away from stomping his feet and jumping up and down like Ernest did when he got mad.

"Sorry, I'm not used to working with others. I'm nervous I'm going to hurt your children. I also fear we won't succeed, and I don't want all those humans to die in Phoenix."

"It's okay, my boy. We're all here to support you. There's a lot of time to get this right. This is just for practice. So, you're allowed to see what works and what doesn't. That's why they're called experiments," Connor said. Stepping closer, he looked up at Eryn and patted his side. Offering his support. "Let's take a break and think about the trident idea."

"We're not as strong as he," Ivan said as he approached.

"Yes, I can't carry that thing," Cian said.

"Me neither. I can't lift it. I don't think anyone except Eryn can," Ivan said and gave Eryn a radiant smile. Eryn smiled back. Any compliment coming from Cian and Ivan made him happy.

Mika stepped closer. "What if we make you each a smaller staff? Please don't laugh, but I think we could take some gold from Eryn's trident and make each of you a twenty or thirty-centimeter staff. Eryn, do you think that could work?"

Relief and excitement coursed through Eryn. "Yes!" Elated, he hurried to get the heavy trident and returned triumphantly. He held it above his head and filled it with sound waves. Sparks began issuing from the tips.

"Wow, a gigantic energy-generating staff," Brad said.

"That is real superhero stuff, Eryn," Donali shouted from the deck of the ship, where the two brothers sat with their legs dangling from the sides. They waved, and everyone waved back to them.

Eryn loved impressing them with new tricks. They were always awed and never shaken. Things he thought he would be judged and ridiculed for were only thrilling to them.

"Just think about it, Brad, all that clean energy and no waste. I'm going to think about harnessing and storing it, like a battery or a reactor. You know, be innovative about it," Mika said.

Brad lifted his cup to Mika. "If someone told me this a month ago, I would never have believed them," Rick said.

The two husbands sat underneath a blanket by the outdoor fire, drinking *the good stuff*, as Brad called it. They were jovial, in love, and happy together.

Mika turned to Eryn with a serious, respectful gaze. "May I touch it, Eryn?" he asked, pointing to the trident. "I'm just ensuring I wouldn't die by electrocution without permission to touch it." Eryn nodded and held it so Mika and Connor could feel it. Blissed-out facial expressions appeared on their faces. Eryn enjoyed feeling that way, as if all their troubles had disappeared. Cian and Ivan gave Eryn a weird look, like, *That's ours*. How could you let them touch your junk like that? So Eryn shut it down quickly.

"Okay, that's enough." He kept talking to prevent them from thinking he was nasty or selfish. "I thought we could remove my trident's left and right forks. That should be enough gold for them, which would be easy to remove. All I need is a hammer, an anvil, and a very hot fire."

"We have a big hammer onboard. Maybe use the plates I anchored the cannons with; I didn't throw them overboard. Would those work?" Mika asked.

"Yes, thank you, Mika."

A few hours later, the twins sat, hands on chins, elbows on knees, admiring every move of Eryn's upper body muscles. He'd gotten so hot that he removed the top half of his arctic suit and tied the arm sleeves around his hips and was now hacking away at the gold with one purpose in mind. He focused only on getting his lovers their needed tools. He knew how he felt when he could concentrate and focus his powers so many years ago. He disappointed himself for not thinking about it earlier. So he mumbled as he hammered away. *Pang-pang, clung-clung, shhhh* in the water, back in the fire, *mumble-mumble, pang-pang, clung-clung, shhhh* in the water, back in the fire, *mumble-mumble*.

Once the pieces were detached, he continued hammering the gold, forging Ivan and Cian their short swords.

"Thank you. I always wanted a golden steak knife," Cian teased.

Eryn just shook his head and continued working on Ivan's sword. The twins didn't seem to mind watching him as he removed the side forks, as they waited patiently for him. He could feel their emotions and their gazes on him, and the sight of his sweaty body was a lot *of fun for them to watch*. Each time he bent or dipped forward, he saw them looking at him like they wanted to lick every drop of sweat from his body. He paused and rolled his shoulders. *Hmmm,* he heard their thoughts. They swooned and lusted over him with no shame. He liked it a lot. The waves of electrifying yearning weakened his knees. To prevent a nasty accident from happening, like face-planting into the fire or looking like an idiot, he blocked their thoughts. Willing himself to finish his work.

"Holy crap, you two," Kawa said loudly out of the blue. "Wipe the drool from the corners of your mouths. I can see your boners tenting your puffy arctic suits from over here. Shame on you!"

Eryn smiled and continued hammering the gold, pretending he didn't hear that.

"They don't hear you, brother," Donali said and laughed.

"We hear you. We just don't care," Cian said.

Eryn turned and handed Ivan his broad sword.

He stood and kissed Eryn long and hard. "Thank you for breaking your trident for us. We'll fix it for you later."

That excited Eryn. "No need. I enjoy knowing I saved those forks for the two of you."

Cian joined, giving him a peck on the cheek. "Thank you, Eryn."

Eryn blushed. "Okay, I want to eat and shower. I'm so sweaty."

"It doesn't bother me. The more manly sweat, the better the glide," Cian said. He chuckled, rubbing himself around his pectoral muscles with one hand while his other hand rubbed Eryn down to his groin. Eryn stopped his hand. They weren't alone, and Kawa and Donali were looking at them. Feeling uncomfortable, he started walking so he could reposition himself.

"But I want to be clean for you," Eryn said shortly.

"We don't mind you being sweaty. We love you just the way you are. You always smell good to us," Ivan doted on Eryn, *always trying to make me feel better.*

"This lovey-dovey shit makes me nauseous," Donali said. "Let's go. I think dinner is ready."

While walking back to the ship, Eryn spoke to his two mates, now his apprentices. "Besides focusing your energy, your swords absorb other people's energy if you want them to. When you use it, hold the handle end toward your body in the palm of your hand, and point," he said, showing them by stabbing the air. He was super-duper excited to share this part of his life with them. *Ernest never wanted to listen to me.*

"By now, you should know how to visualize your energy being gathered and focused through the sword. Sometimes it will glow or sizzle. It'll never burn or hurt you because it's your energy. It'll focus on whatever purpose you desire for the energy. Carry it with you always because you won't know when you'll need it. You must always concentrate and send your power where it'll be most effective. Take care of it and be careful. You can kill with it. Whether by accident or willingly."

Ivan and Cian nodded, focusing on what Eryn had taught them.

"Good. After dinner, we'll try again." He turned, and because he felt like showing off, he jumped from where they were about to enter the Blue Halcyon straight up into the air and over the railing of the upper deck.

Before he leaped one short jump over to their pirate ship, he heard Cian joking inside and eavesdropped from the galley. After he heard only nice things, he turned and jumped, excited to join them after his shower.

"Man, that smells fantastic," Cian said. He was smiling from ear to ear. When they entered, most were already around the table eating, but it seemed their fathers were waiting for them.

"Look, Papa, our swords aren't they beautiful?" They handed their short golden swords to Mika and Connor. Both blades were about forty inches long. Eryn had hammered a pommel and grip, a rain guard, and flattened fuller and double edges. Both Romanov boys tied their hair in a tight bun, as their Russian father had taught them, before washing their hands for mealtimes.

"They're amazing. Eryn's so talented. Don't you think, Dada?" Cian took his sword from Connor and walked around the table so everyone could look and touch it. "I teased him and said it's a nice steak knife, but he didn't think that was funny. He's so serious about this." Cian pranced around the table and finally noticed Eryn standing there.

"Oh good, I couldn't wait anymore. I'm so hungry. Eryn, I showed everyone your handiwork, and they're impressed."

Eryn stood frozen, wide-eyed, and not saying a word. "What's wrong, Eryn?" a chorus of concerned voices asked. Then they noticed it. In his arms, he held a blanket. And the blanket moved now and then.

"Oh, my lord, is that a baby swaddled in a blanket?" Rick asked, connecting the dots first. Eryn shook his head from side to side. He looked down at the bundle.

"You won't fucking believe me."

"Jesus, the boy had grasped cussing faster than an Angora goat could catch burrs," Brad said.

"It must be a baby seal. I saw some fighting out on the ice this morning. Is it an orphaned seal?" Connor asked.

The bundle jiggled faster. Tiny yipping and snarling sounds came from his arms.

"Are those small puppy sounds?" Rick asked.

The chairs around the table pushed out as one sound, and in the next moment, oh's and ah's surrounded Eryn. He plopped down and put the bundle on the floor in front of him. First, one head, followed by two more heads, stuck out from the material.

"Are those three gigantic rats?" Rick asked no one in particular.

"Those aren't rats. Those are, can it be? Are those baby jackals?" Brad asked, astonishment written on his face.

"Anubis?" Mika corrected him.

"No, how did they? Where did you find them, Eryn?" Connor asked.

"I was getting dressed and heard them. They were in the bag of clothes."

"Where's the mommy?" Rick asked. "Oh, dear lord, where's the mommy?" Rick grabbed Kawa and Donali and retreated away from the door. "If there's one thing I remember as a young Apache, it's that when there are cute baby cubs, a very dangerous momma bear is nearby."

"I don't think they have a mommy bear, or the mommy bear isn't here, or maybe the mommy bear left them with us," Eryn replied, unsure what a mommy bear was.

"Aww, maybe they followed us. Maybe they want to be with us." Cian and Ivan made cooing noises. The tiny jackals fell over their little feet to get to Cian and Ivan. "Ah, look, they ran straight to us." They held their hands out.

"They must recognize you," Mika answered. "A bear is a big animal, the size of a small car, which sleeps during wintertime. In the spring, they wake and start roaming around for food. Their babies are called bear cubs, and the momma protects them by killing anyone in her path. When we get to Phoenix, we'll show you pictures," Mika explained.

"Okay, thank you, Mika," Eryn said.

"They still look like rats. Adorable, cute rats," Connor said.

Later, when everyone had moved back to the dinner table to finish their meals, Ivan, Cian, and Eryn each held a sleeping Anubis.

Brad stood up after dinner. "I'm going to sleep. Tomorrow will be a long day."

One by one, the adults got up and disappeared through the revolving door to the sleeping area. The five young men offered to clean up, and then they filed outside to the deck area, where they practiced as planned earlier that day.

Stoking the bonfire high with wood that Brad had suggested they collect on their way from South Africa when all decided they needed a vacation because wood was a scarce commodity in Antarctica, Donali and Kawa sat toasty warm while holding the Anubis and feeding them leftover meat from dinner while playing a self-made game of judging the King of the Brawl and his Anunnaki and their creations of all kinds of shapes with spheres to protect Phoenix.

And, of course, Eryn won the game of *whose shape is the biggest.*

CHAPTER 23

# SUCK WHAT?

*"Good morning, city of Phoenix.*

*It's now six a.m.*

*Did you know that for more than a hundred million years, sea turtles have covered vast distances across the world's oceans, filling a vital role in the balance of marine habitats and that humans drove them to total extinction in just two-hundred years?*

*Have you ever wondered how sea turtles mated?*

*Visit your community news page for exciting videos about nature and how they used to procreate in the wild. For instance, we have a twenty-four-hour video of a male turtle mating while hanging on for dear life on the back end of the female's shell.*

*Breakfast is served until eight a.m.*

*Good luck, and hang in there."*

**Eryn King of the Brawl**

While the little hydrogen balloon ship provided hours of entertainment, the thrill of being alone with the twins soon grew old. Now it felt like a suffocating deathtrap, a torture device of the cruelest kind. Trapping him and grinding his self-control. Eryn sighed. His balls were so stuffed that he couldn't decide which way to sit, walk, or stand. *Any minute, they would pop out of their sack and roll away.*

*That I want one fucking second alone with the twins isn't asking too much.* The McCormick twins pretended to be naïve, stupid virgins who did not know what they were doing to him and his throbbing balls. Eryn groaned inwardly. He knew they were pretending to be oblivious, yet they were fully aware of their actions. Oh, Cian, this, and oh, Ivan, that. Just one bloody second alone would quickly resolve the aching problem he had in his pants. The last few days had morphed into one unending, torturous pent-up sexual frustration.

*If we don't see the glass city appear on the horizon within the next hour, I'm going to go psycho and throw the two inquisitive squirrel faces out the door onto the ice. Maybe tie a rope around them and let them dangle a bit. Then we'll see how they enjoy hanging around.*

All five young men lay squashed on a tiny sofa mattress. It wasn't the lack of mattress space but the lack of room to move and reposition his aching cock and balls that bothered Eryn most.

*Fuck, my mood's sour and to the point of cutting my balls off. If our ship had a deck, I would've slept on it, legs sprawled open, with the Antarctic wind blowing over my balls. Maybe ask the twins to kiss them better for me. Oh, my freaking balls!*

Rising hastily, intending to relieve himself, he proceeded to the tiny hold used as a washroom and storage. It was broad daylight in Antarctica, as it was in the middle of summer, and scant light penetrated to reveal the figure of Ivan crouching on the mattress, his chin upon his knees, his handsome face gleaming with mischief. Eryn didn't say a word. Instead, he held his hand out to Ivan in a silent invitation. Taking Eryn's hand, he soundlessly flew, landing with a soft *oomph* against the door. Neither one spoke. Eryn's eight-foot, bulky frame pinned Ivan's seven-foot frame. Electricity sparked between them. Their faces shimmered blue-ish gold bioluminescence. Eryn's balls and cock drummed with the beat of his heart. Both were panting, trying to read the other's meaning in their eyes.

Eryn reached for the door, and Ivan covered his hand. *We're thinking of doing the same.* Eryn read Ivan's intent in his sparkling blue eyes. Smiling and grinning, both opened the door and fell inside. Kissing and grabbing, teeth clacking, and tongues swooping deep into each other's mouths. *Holy shit, I needed this!*

Ivan pulled back, short of breath, looking dizzy with lust. "I want to suck you."

Eryn stopped for a second, panting. "Suck, what?"

"Your cock, what else?"

Eryn couldn't believe what he was hearing. Then, he stopped thinking altogether as Ivan fell to his knees, opened his pants, and took his thick cock into his mouth. *Glorious*! It was the warmest, sweetest, dirtiest thing anyone had ever done to him. *It feels, it feels so damn good.* He never thought humans did this. Eryn grew up in a cave with no frame of reference to sex with humans at all. The memory of two monkeys fornicating flashed through his mind. Okay, this feels way better than touching himself. *I could ask Ivan to do it all day.*

"I'm going to make a mess in your mouth. You better stop, Ivan." Eryn futilely tried to push Ivan back. Grabbing a fist full of blond hair, he couldn't decide whether to keep his cock in or push Ivan away. It was a war inside his mind. He felt dizzy and drunk. It all felt too good, so he slammed into Ivan's mouth.

Ivan sucked relentlessly, and Eryn exploded into his mouth. It looked like the sky had fallen inside the tiny room. Tiny blue and golden light sparks escaped from their touching skin and danced around and in between them while days of collected sperm ran in rivulets from the corners of Ivan's mouth. *What a sight!* Eryn was transfixed by the erotic visuals. Ivan eagerly licked and sucked and attempted to swallow him whole. Eryn gasped. The overwhelming sensitivity sent him backward against the wall. Arms splayed to the sides, searching for something to grab and hold on to.

"Hah! That tasted awesome," Ivan exclaimed as he stood to kiss Eryn.

Eryn liked the taste of his spunk all over Ivan's face. He licked his lover's beautiful, swollen lips clean with his long tongue while vibrating with pleasure, enjoying the sensation of emotional overload. "I want more," he said and croaked a deep, guttural sound. "Now it's my turn to taste you."

Ivan didn't have time to respond. Eryn was a fast learner. He spun him, changing places, and had his pants undone and his cock in his mouth faster than the speed of light. He paused, making sure he retracted his fangs, feasted, munched, and sucked Ivan's dick like a slice of juicy watermelon. Ivan threw one leg over Eryn's shoulder, grabbed onto his hair, and face-fucked him as hard and fast as he could. Eryn enjoyed every second. He was ready for one more round. He squeezed the life out of his cock, wishing he had a hole to push it into.

Ivan moaned and whispered, "I'm coming, and oh, my god, I'm coming." His cock swelled, and then he squirted his seed down Eryn's throat, ramming into Eryn's mouth another few times, hanging onto Eryn's head, barely able to keep himself upright. While Eryn never lost suction, Ivan's legs began to tremble.

"Having fun?" Cian asked, and in the background, they heard the McCormick twins giggling.

"We heard a commotion, and I came to investigate." Cian stood in the doorframe, leaning toward the side with his arms folded. A hungry grin on his face. He lifted his nose and sniffed audibly. "It smells like you were having lots and lots of fun here. Without me," he said sarcastically. Eryn grunted, and Ivan sighed in exasperation.

"Hmmm, you were making so much noise it sounded like you were wrestling or something. I thought maybe there was a fire because the light beams shone all around the door. Do you need help?" Cian asked, smirking from ear to ear, and his head cocked to one side.

"Want to join us, brother?" Ivan asked shortly.

Eryn did not wait for another snotty remark while he stood on his knees with one of Ivan's legs draped around his neck. Those bloody McCormick twins. He pulled Cian inside. It was such a tight fit that the door could barely close behind him. Eryn hastily made the small space work for them.

"Why do we always end up in the smallest spaces together?" he asked, expecting no answer. With Ivan's leg over his right shoulder, he unzipped Cian's pants and removed his right leg, draping it over the left shoulder. He worked on both their dicks. Gluttonizing himself into a trance, he never wanted to come out of.

Ivan laughed. "No, my dick is too sensitive." He snorted but left his dick where it was, evidently still enjoying the attention. Cian moaned and relaxed into the administration. He half hung on his brother with one hand while the other grabbed a railing used to hang their towels. Eryn was so fucking turned on that he continued fist-fucking his dick, pulling long, fist strokes over the head of his thick uncut cock. Their throaty sounds of pleasure and the two long pale cocks smelling like man, honey, and gold made him frantic with lust. His twins smelled exactly like melting his favorite yellow metal.

Eryn congratulated himself on a job well done when Cian ripped the railing off the wall, hollering, "Fuck yes, I'm coming!"

His instincts kicked in, and he drank every drop of jizz, tasting the sound of his lover's songs. It was all so intoxicating. They were scorching hot and beaming. He stood up, squeezing his cockhead to keep from ejaculating. Pushing the two blond heads down, the twins slipped onto their knees.

"Ah, yes, that's so good. You look beautiful down there. I'm going to spill right onto your pretty lips." Eryn felt brave and filthy, and it felt good to see them opening their mouths to receive him. "Yes, boys, suck my cock." He ejaculated as soon as the words left his mouth. He shot volley after volley onto both their faces, smearing his cum over their pink lips around their mouths with the head of his cock. Ivan hummed in satisfaction and squirted a second, but smaller, wad onto the floor. The tiny space was stuffy, and every nook and cranny was glowing, filled to the brim with sex sounds, smells, and euphoric emotions. Eryn helped his mates up to continue with a three-way kiss, sharing the taste of their essence.

"Ah, yes, that was so good." Eryn helped them into their pants as he said he wanted to do it again. Then they helped him into his pants while giddy with sexual satisfaction and fumbling around for the doorknob, laughing. When they finally opened the door and practically tumbled out of the room, untangling their limbs, it was empty.

"Where are the McCormick twins?" Eryn asked, fastening the buttons of his pants. The door was open. The twins poked their heads out. Eryn heard the roaring voices of men, so he scrambled to the door. Before them was a huge crowd of men waving and welcoming them.

"We're here!" All three young men exclaimed. They watched as the men threw rope after rope over the balloons of their little hydrogen pirate ship. It reminded Eryn of the book he had read about *Gulliver's Travels* as they pulled into the shipyard hangar and tied down.

"I've never seen such a beautiful sight," Eryn said in awe. "The glass domes are sparkling with all the rainbow colors, and look at the friendly faces of the men waving to us. Your fathers must have contacted Bryan and his team, explaining our situation, on their way back to Phoenix. Maybe even divulged more detail than what was necessary," Eryn remarked, taken aback by the thousands of Phoenix residents.

Ivan and Cian nodded and waved back at the people.

"It's a happy and beautiful sight, and although it's nice to be here, we have work to do if we want to survive the destruction of Earth."

Ivan pointed to the sad faces in the crowd. "Look, they're waiting in line to speak to Brad."

"Those men were good friends with Juan and Drew. They performed drag in the ballroom some nights. Chances are they were informed already about these tragic murders."

"What's drag?" Eryn asked. Frowning, he'd never heard that word before.

"It's men who love dressing up in various styles of women's or female clothing, and they're incredibly talented. They held shows and events in the Blue Ballroom, where Juan loved performing. He sang and danced mainly in the 1920s in a country called France. It was very entertaining to watch. Maybe we can show you some videos later."

"Now that females are extinct, drag has grown into something much more, especially for those who love the female body. Some go to watch, to meet men for sex. Others go to drink, dance, relax, or have fun, and sometimes men go for nostalgic reasons. To remember the world before Doomsday. But Juan and Drew also used to prepare and serve food to these men. They spoke to everyone daily. They were popular, and everyone loved them. I think Brad will probably have a ceremony for them so everyone can remember them and say goodbye." Cian's head fell.

Eryn felt the sadness radiating from him. He pulled them closer for a hug.

A hollow noise at their feet startled them.

"Sorry, boys, the cleaning crew is just coming up the gangplank!" an unshaven older man said as he lowered a plank from the ship to the ground. They hastily grabbed their belongings, eager to leave.

"What the fuck is that?" the older crewman yelped, holding a mop, ready to strike over his shoulder.

"Ah, those are our puppies. Come, dogs!" Ivan slapped his legs to call them closer. Three baby Anubis tumbled out of their box bed, falling over one another to get to Ivan.

Cian bent down to scoop them up.

"Here, give me one." Eryn carried the small, black rat-sized Anubis in the crook of his arm, looking like Obelix and Dogmatix.

"What are they? Are they mine rats from South Africa?" another cleaner asked.

"No, they're Anubis. Jackals that protect humans," Eryn answered proudly.

"It's a long story," Cian interrupted.

"No matter, you can tell me later. I bet you're tired, hungry, and eager to get off this…"

Eryn looked around and didn't know what to say, and decided to say nothing.

"Yes, we know, okay, we'll catch up later," the man with the big beard said while chuckling. Eryn liked him. He was friendly.

They left the ship and went searching for Mika and Connor.

"I want us to have an apartment of our own," Ivan said, looking at Eryn.

"There's no way we're going to live with our fathers," Cian told Eryn.

"You stand firm. Just say no." Eryn lifted his staff. "No!" His voice boomed down the corridor.

"That's the spirit!" Ivan patted him on the shoulder.

Connor and Mika protested weakly. They most probably knew their argument was futile. So Eryn and the twins were alone in their apartment.

Finally, the Brawl King could ravish his twins' bodies horizontally. The problem was, where to start? Their tall, slender, hairless physiques were the opposite of his eight-foot muscled bulk. Eryn was shamelessly sex-hungry for them, and he palmed his cock.

"Fuck, just look at the way you want me. My cock throbs for you. I can't wait to have you both on top of me."

They slipped their clothes off, almost in sync with one another, and stepped closer to Eryn to help him out of his. Their white marble-skinned bodies glowed as he hummed his mating song for them.

"I doubt all three of us would fit in a shower. Maybe I should wait?" Ivan turned.

"We'll fit. Come, I'll show you." He took each by the hand and led them to the bathroom. Opening the hot and cold water, he ensured the temperature was comfortable and stepped inside, sitting on the floor. They giggled.

"Come," he called out to them. His voice was low and gruff.

"What is it with us and tight spaces?" Cian asked.

Eryn's heart was racing, and the intoxicating smells of dried cum, sweat, and lust drove him crazy. They climbed inside, following his orders.

"Cian, you stand to this side, and Ivan, you to that side." He positioned them in front of him. Their cocks, precisely the same size and shape, bobbed before him. All three of them had light body hair.

"Now, let's wash each other." Again, more giggles.

"Have you noticed, Eryn, we don't have body hair?" Cian asked.

"Why? What do you mean?"

"We always thought it's because we're young, but you don't have pubic hair either." Eryn looked down, not sure what pubic hair was.

"I thought it was supposed to be like this."

"No. We'll show you later what humans look like. Let's take you to Quik-Fix Hall. You'll love the show," Ivan said.

The three virgins followed their instincts and did what felt good to them. He felt their anticipation turn into nervousness and then into disgust.

"Don't worry." Eryn looked up, smiling gently at them. "I understand that you're brothers. I wouldn't want to touch my brother like this, either. Just relax, and enjoy me, and let me enjoy you. I don't want you to do anything you hate or are uncomfortable with."

"No, it's just that we want you to know we don't want to do anything to each other, only to you." Ivan snorted, then nodded to Cian.

"We'll share you, and you may have both of us, but we don't think the washing and touching each other is cool."

"I'm glad you told me. But I feel you don't like to do those things. So why don't you sit here?" He patted his upper legs, offering each thigh. "I'll wash you. Let's tell your fathers that we want a bigger shower," Eryn added.

"I can imagine how that will go down," Cian said, sitting down.

"Don't worry. I'll ask them." Eryn's heart leaped. He loved it when they were happy.

Finely tuned and susceptible to their emotions, both sat down with their assess on their upper legs. Eryn forgot about soap, water, and showering. He touched and kissed them both all over as they rubbed themselves against him. He was so bloody horny for them.

Cian grabbed soap and shampoo and lathered their bodies while Ivan and Eryn kissed. Having all three washed off, they pulled Eryn to their room. Pushing him till the back of his legs touched the bed, they pounced, so he fell backward. They climbed his body as if he were a tree and they were spider monkeys.

In synchronized movements from his beautiful, webbed toes, over his hairless muscled legs, then extra tiny licks, bites, and kisses to his balls and rock-hard cock—his lovers drove him crazy. Both tongues licked the head of his cock like it was a snow cone. Sucking the pre-cum out of his piss slit. His nine-inch cock was so hard it protruded and stretched his foreskin to the maximum, which stopped about two inches from the tip, all pink with a shiny, fat head. The twins tasted it, and both reached for their cocks.

"Ah, you taste lovely, Eryn. How does lavender and honey taste?" Ivan remarked.

Eryn felt wonderful. Never had he ever had so many compliments from anyone. As soon as they said that, he moaned and croaked. "I think I'm going to...ah. Yes, fuck, that feels so good." He ejaculated, so the twins lapped his crotch, dick, and balls clean.

"Motherfucker, I see stars! I'm sorry, it just happened."

They giggled again, each sitting on a knee and rubbing their assholes on it. In coordinated strokes, they pleasured themselves and counted. "One, two, three!" Then shot their loads together all over Eryn's legs and torso. One of them even hit Eryn in the face. He stuck his long tongue out, wrapping it around, licking their dicks and himself clean.

They fell onto him. One on each side. All three were happy and sated, with smiles on their faces. After they recovered, Ivan got up to get the three Anubis pups. "We need to find a spot for them to walk and run during the day," he said as they snuggled together.

"We'll need a bigger bed and a shower," Eryn mumbled sleepily, thinking the Anubis would grow into car-sized pets.

"Hey, Connor said I was your pet back in the mines. Am I really your pet?"

"Sleep, Eryn. We'll talk kink tomorrow. I'm tired."

"What is kink?"

"Sleep, Eryn."

"Okay."

CHAPTER 24

# THE SONG OF ANGELS

*"GOOD MORNING, CITIZENS OF PHOENIX.*

*Lasitor, your Artificial Intelligence (AI) community news broadcaster, bids you a good morning.*

*It's now six a.m.*

*Over forty thousand tremors have rocked Antarctica since the end of August, and we've noticed a spike in seismic activity that's depressingly cumbersome.*

*Scientists with Phoenix University detected an increased number of quakes—including a handful of more vigorous shakes of magnitude six in the channel between the South Shetland Islands and the Antarctic Peninsula. In addition, several tectonic and micro-plate movements caused frequent rumblings and have increased over the past four months. It's unusual. Therefore, our leadership team has called a meeting. It's scheduled for nine a.m. sharp. We will save a recording for you on your local community news page for those who are unable to attend.*

*Breakfast is served until eight a.m.*

*Thank you, and enjoy your day."*

**ERYN, King of the Brawl**

"WHAT?" Eryn was up in an instant. His legs were wobbling while attempting to balance his massive body on the soft mattress. He was dazed and sleep-drunk. "Where's my fork, I mean spear? Where's my spear?" Disoriented, he scanned their room from left to right. Hands up and fisted, his body was ready for action as he assumed a fighting stance. Adrenaline pumped through his veins.

"Calm down. It's Lasitor."

"Who?" Eryn searched the ceiling for the source of the booming robotic voice.

Cian pulled the bedding over his head and mumbled sleepily, "Lasitor, the community AI, a computer program. He's kind of part of the building. He hides deep inside the programs so no one can find and delete him."

Taken aback by the lack of enemies, Eryn plopped back down. "What a way to wake up." His heart rate returned to normal, so he snuggled between his two favorite people.

"Didn't you hear Lasitor in the mornings when you stayed here with Joshua?"

"No."

"Maybe Joshua removed the speaker as we did from our room at our dad's place so that we could sleep in," Ivan said sleepily.

"Yeah, some people spray silicone inside the speaker to silence his voice. It's much more bearable."

Eryn yawned, stretched his arms out, and sank back under the covers. He pulled Ivan and Cian closer. "Morning, lovers," he said in his best seductive voice, loaded with all kinds of erotic insinuations, while he roamed downwards with his hands.

Just as they settled into each having a handful, a relentless irritating knocking at the front door forced them to take notice to move their horny asses out of bed.

"It's probably our dads." Cian moaned and started sucking on Eryn's s nipple.

"Ignore them. They'll go away," Ivan said. Wrapping his hand around Eryn's balls to pull on them. Eryn grew nervous; the knocking was unsettling, and who could relax anyway? They pinned Eryn by throwing a leg over one of his. The knocking started again, sounding like a song. *Pam, padda, pam-pam, pam-pam!*

"Shitballs! I promised them I wouldn't hurt you. Look at you. It looks like I ate, swallowed, and regurgitated you. Even your eyebrows need combing. Oh man, your dads are going to kill me," Eryn said. He sat up, making a quick decision. He scrambled, throwing the bedding this way and that. Then he grabbed each by the ankle and pulled them down. "Come, get up!" They came flying feet first out of bed and were upright with the velocity of a bullet. Frantically, he pushed and steered them toward the washroom. "Go shower. I'll open the door." They looked so adorable, their blond hair standing in all directions. He laughed, maneuvering them into the bathroom. Once there, he turned and quickly checked himself in the bathroom mirror. "I don't look any better." The twins dissolved into laughter. Dammit! The insistent knocking got louder.

"Shower, now!" he ordered them and closed the door with a bang.

He heard them shouting back. "You're so bossy!"

Grabbing a pair of pants from the floor, he hastily pulled on one leg while hopping. He took a few deep breaths and waved his hand over the sensor.

He greeted them with his best innocent-looking face. Mika and Connor were waiting, smiling from ear to ear. They knew precisely what they'd disturbed. Eryn stepped back to invite them inside.

"Morning, Dads. Please come in." Eryn started calling them dads as a joke while working on extracting the rocket from the mineshaft. It didn't seem to bother them much. Eryn could tell it made them happy, so he continued doing it because it made him glad, too.

The two scientists embraced their parenthood of triple-deity children. They saw it as an honor to raise a divine being. They'd spoken about the exchanged female DNA, Nick, the disciple, divulged before he died. However, it was inexplicable when exactly the switching of the eggs and DNA happened. Something Mika and Connor wanted to discuss with Dr. Peter von Leutzendorf, not excluding the nagging fact, was the Peter Pan Capsules as the product of the twins' amniotic fluid, rather than the vitamins within the artificial placenta.

As the family had their meeting—something Eryn loved to be part of—they determined that switching the female DNA didn't matter because Mika and Connor were still their fathers, and that hadn't changed. If it did, they would still be their boys. Eryn was a different matter. He decided he would rather not know his genetic makeup; it didn't matter to him.

"Are you three well-rested and ready for today?" Mika asked, stretching his neck like a giraffe to see into their bedroom. Eryn cringed, wondering what to say. If he said yes, he'd be lying, but if he said no, they'd be disappointed. So he settled for, "Almost, the shower is too small for three people."

Connor coughed, and Mika blinked a few times. Speechless because, yes, the size of the shower did technically answer the question. Eryn could almost hear his thoughts looking for an answer as his mind whirr-whirred like gears behind Mika's stare.

"Okay, we'll get that sorted for you three today," Mika said casually while pinning Eryn with his intelligent blue gaze. No matter how Eryn tried to outmaneuver him, Mika was always one step ahead.

"Thank you, and while we're on that subject, Dad, do you think we can get a bigger bed, too?" Eryn asked like it was the most natural question. Testing Mika—ruffling his feathers unsuccessfully.

Mika gave an impassive nod. *Damn, the man is smooth, like water on a duck's feathers.*

Connor broke the silent standoff and said, "It makes sense," as he bent down to scoop up the three Anubis. The small black jackals yelped and looked happy to see Connor.

"Yes, they slept on the bed with us, and I'm worried if they get bigger…"

"No problem. We should get you an apartment big enough for the six of you. Last night was a short notice. We should go apartment hunting as soon as we settle down and have a chance. Maybe somewhere close to where these three can run free when they're bigger," Connor said, rubbing his nose against them playfully.

"Yes, that would be nice, thank you. Ivan said something about that last night," Eryn said, and relaxed in the older men's company. "Do you want to sit and wait for us?" he asked, unsure about the proper etiquette. He'd seen them offer each other something to drink, but he didn't know what the fridge contained. *Damn, I don't even know where the kitchen area is.* He decided not to offer anything. *I didn't think about that last night.*

"Hmm, no, thank you. Maybe we must go. Please ask the boys to come to the leadership office. We'll have breakfast while we discuss the plans," Mika said.

Eryn nodded. He was feeling extraordinarily naked in front of them while being bare-chested. *My comment about the shower and bed size went well.* The thought boosted his self-confidence, and he thought the brothers would be impressed.

Connor reluctantly put the Anubis pups down and left.

Eryn ran for the shower as soon as the door closed.

An hour later, the famous triad reached the Command Center, having had to stop many times for welcoming pats and hugs as a welcome back to Phoenix. The news about the Anubis had spread like wildfire. They looked fierce, making quite an impressive spectacle as they exuded power, friendliness, and kindness, but most of all, they oozed sexual pheromones.

Each twin wore a golden sword in its holster on their back. Their blond locks cascaded over their broad shoulders and seemed to glow. Both were dressed in black bodysuits and boots. Their freshly shaven, pale-skinned faces gleamed in the overhead lights while their blue eyes shone like reflected sunlight on ice. Their body length exacerbated their godlike features as they stood two meters tall and towered over the Phoenix males. But Eryn, at two and a half meters tall, was most comfortably dressed in his favorite pair of ragged jeans, a white t-shirt, and brand-new size sixteen snow boots, given to him by Mika.

The crowd swarmed them, and as soon as they saw the three Anubis in his arms, no one cared about his big build, strange eyes, or spear. When he bowed to one knee to lower himself so the ecstatic kids could see the supernatural creatures, the long braids in his ponytail flopped to the front to cover his shyness. Every man with a child or a child's heart obstructed the entry.

The door behind Eryn swooshed open, and Mika appeared. He greeted the crowd and apologized. "Sorry, comrades, please let the boys have breakfast. They have eaten nothing for over twenty-four hours."

He looked a bit upset, and Eryn sensed he was worried about them. The three Anubis loved the attention. They nipped and licked at anything within their reach. Ivan, Cian, and Eryn figured the more people they met, the friendlier they would be when they grew up. Eryn waved at the crowd and followed Mika inside, and the crowd dissipated.

"We need names for them," Eryn's voice thundered through the quiet area as the door shut. He was a nervous wreck after a barrage of repeated questions: How old are they? What are their names? How big will they be when they grow up? What do they eat? Where do they go potty, whatever that means?

"Boys, come in. We're in the big conference room." Mika welcomed them.

"Thank you, Dad. We're bloody damn hungry," Eryn said as they fell into the office, feeling overwhelmed.

"We saw your entourage and quietly hid inside here. We can imagine the questions, and we don't have the strength for that." Brad chuckled.

"You know, Dad, you're all cowards hiding here," Ivan said.

"We know," the men in the room answered, looking very proud of themselves.

"It's a matter of self-preservation," Brad answered.

But Mika looked worried about the boys. It was obvious how tired they were when they practiced, and today would be a much bigger task. "Bring the pups over here. What have you been feeding them?" he asked.

"Meat. They look happy with that."

"Oh, where do you get that?" Bryan, the new leader, asked.

Eryn summed him up as a good man with friendly eyes. He got to know Bryan the night they took him prisoner, but they weren't happy to meet that night. Given the circumstances, that was understandable. Everyone in the office turned their way.

"Meat is a rarity in Phoenix, you know?"

"So far, Eryn caught them a few birds and a penguin," Connor answered, reaching out for the pups again. They fell over their feet to get to Connor.

"Ah, luckily for them to have a daddy like Eryn," Brad said. "You should see him. He dove into the Antarctic waters, heavy spear in hand, and brought food for all of us."

He sounded proud of Eryn and wanted to say more, but Mika interrupted him. "Come, boys, time to have breakfast." They didn't need another invitation for them to storm the buffet. The amount of variety shocked Eryn. He stepped back, uncomfortable and unsure about the correct etiquette for the second time that morning. The twins immediately caught on to it.

"Eryn, what would you like to eat? Come closer. We'll help you," Cian said. He picked up three plates and handed one to Ivan and one to Eryn.

"Usually, we eat bread with protein and then some fruit for vitamins."

Eryn frowned. He understood nothing but bread. Feeling uncomfortable in front of everyone, he whispered, "Just give me the same as you would take. You can tell me more about it later."

Ivan widened his eyes to Cian—a silent warning to be more sensitive.

Mika must have seen the non-verbal communication and stepped forward. "Boys, you eat and fill your tummies. You'll burn the candles on both ends today, so fill up and don't be shy."

Brad stepped forward and added, "Eryn, no one here is judging you. We're thrilled to have you, and you're welcome to ask questions. Ask as many questions as you like. All of us are here to make you guys feel supported."

A chorus from around the office of, "Yes, absolutely, thank you for trying to help." We're glad you are here."

"Thank you for saving the boys from your brother."

Eryn smiled shyly and straightened up. Cian and Ivan smiled from ear to ear, thankful for the warm welcome of their lover.

Brad turned and spoke to the men, laughing. "Someday, someone will discover that area where you guys practiced creating capsules. I would love to hear their explanations or theories about where the balls came from and why they're stacked hundreds of meters into the shape of a pyramid."

"Maybe a giant rolled his snot into little balls and stacked them like that," Cian said.

Ivan pulled his top lip up in disgust. "Yuck, that's disgusting." He threw the ball-shaped donut in his hand back onto his plate.

The room broke out with laughter. Eryn loved every second, and the Anubis yipped and howled with shrill jackal calls.

"They're so damn cute," Connor said while he fed them pieces of fish sticks.

"Okay," Bryan said. "Now we think Mika should explain what we decided on for the day's business."

Mika stepped to the front of the conference room. The room was the largest meeting room in the Command Center and could seat over a hundred people. Mika quickly explained to Eryn that they initially intended it to be the governing council or town hall meeting room, where community members could attend meetings. However, the original council of three preferred to meet in their own offices, with Connor's being the preferred location because it was the most technologically advanced and comfortable.

"Thank you, men. I appreciate you organizing the conference room today. It's the ideal size for the first and current councils of three, as well as the divine triad, as the three are now known," Mika said boisterously with a wide smile.

The boys stuffed their faces, only coming up for air to sip their drinks, nodding a few times, and then diving back into cleaning their plates. Mika looked lovingly at them as he admired their enthusiasm for filling their stomachs.

"We welcome the extra space, especially the buffet breakfast. I can imagine how going down to the community dining area wouldn't be productive for today's plans," Brad said.

Bryan stepped forward to make an announcement. "Now that everyone's here, welcome back, but I'd like to make a proposition. Since you were gone, your replacement council members were swamped and realized that you three had a tremendous job managing Phoenix as smoothly as you did for over twenty years. Filling your shoes was not a straightforward task. We couldn't wait for your return, and although it's selfish of us, we feel you men are best at getting the jobs done."

Peter and Tony nodded affirmatively from the opposite end of the table. Eryn noticed the bright blue eyes were sparkling every time Peter looked in Bryan's or Tony's direction. Peter looked radiantly happy, but he couldn't seem to make eye contact with Eryn. *Maybe he's shy?*

Simon and Paul sat ever reserved and professional while listening as Bryan spoke. When Bryan was done, Simon lifted his hand for a turn.

"Dads, we didn't realize the scope of your work, and we hoped you would retake your places. I speak for father Rick, who single-handedly managed the clinic. It's time you accept our support and retake your seats on the council, but the circumstances, although tragic, may have been a blessing in disguise. We are not on the council, but we offer to stay and help manage the clinic. Paul and I salute you. We don't want your job. We talked to the replacement council and came to an agreement to act as deputies, and we propose we bring this to the citizens, the Phoenicians. The Phoenix population is growing, which means there are more souls to represent," Simon said. He bowed slightly to thank the council.

"Thank you, men. I'll think of how and when to present this to the general population. I love the name Phoenicians. It's very original," Brad said, looking not surprised by the proposition but very appreciative of the support of restructuring.

He sat, and Mika got up to take the floor. He turned to the giant touchscreen and switched it on by touching the side of it.

"Lasitor, I need bird's-eye views and worm-eye views of Phoenix."

"Certainly, sir," the AI answered with a professional tone.

"I also need to know how deep Phoenix's underground pipe, tunnel, and sewage system runs."

"Yes, sir, calculating," Lasitor answered. After a few minutes, architectural blueprints and maps with measurements appeared on the screen. Mika continued as the men sat at the front of their seats, concentrating on what Mika would show them.

"Then, I need the latest Phoenix architectural maps and designs of the artificial systems and Antarctica's environmental support of Phoenix within a hundred-kilometer radius. I need you to crosscut the views from a nine-point circle on that radius."

As soon as Mika said the nine-point circle, the room exploded in ah's and oh's. "You're the alpha geek," Connor said, and Mika bowed. "See, that's why I married the man," Connor said proudly

The triad just looked up, swallowed, and shook their heads. Then dove back into their plates.

"Excuse me, not all of us here are scientists. Can you explain again to us who don't have more than one degree after our names?" Captain Howell asked sarcastically.

"Certainly, sir." Lasitor started, as if Bryan had asked him and not Mika.

"In geometry, the nine-point circle is a circle that can be constructed for any triangle. It's so named because it passes through nine significant concyclic points defined by the triangle. These nine points are the midpoint of each side of the triangle, the foot of each altitude, and the midpoint of the line segment from each vertex to where the three altitudes meet. These line segments lie on their respective altitudes."

Eryn noticed Bryan looked even more confused, deepening the furrow between his eyebrows. Mika helped by drawing on the screen—he drew a circle inside the circle, then wrote "Phoenix." Then he drew a triangle.

"The boys will start each at a point," Mika told them. "Then they will move to the next point." He drew another triangle. He was making dots at the points where the triangle cut through. "See the first three dots, then they move. Then six dots, and finally, they move to a third spot." He made three more dots on the circle where the triangle cut through.

"Ah, now I see. Thank you, Mika. I see now what you have in mind," Bryan said. He looked at the boys and exchanged nods and smiles. Eryn appreciated him asking.

"Mika had to show us a picture, too. Don't feel bad, Bryan," Eryn said.

"Now the Pyramid of balls makes sense," Bryan said, referring to Brad's earlier statement. "Am I correct in saying we'll be in the center of it?"

"Yes, because a triangle is the strongest shape, we used air-filled pillows instead of one bubble around us. What do you think?" Mika turned and asked his audience.

"Sir, that's an excellent idea. I ran an algorithm against anything that could destabilize Phoenix, and I have to say that's the best option," Lasitor answered again as if Mika had asked him. The men around the conference table laughed but eventually agreed. It might work.

"Okay, lovers, are you ready to rumble?" Eryn asked, later that afternoon, literally meaning what he was saying, referring to when they practiced with their swords for the first time. Cian and Ivan's swords sizzled and sparked so loudly that Mika came running outside, asking if it was raining.

"Where's the rumble?" Since then, they teased him about that, and it became an inside joke between the four. As they discussed and planned earlier that morning, they divided the triad into three directions.

"Yes, let's roll out!" Ivan said. Pulling his goggles over his eyes and climbing onto the back of a snowmobile, he waved to Eryn and then proceeded  to start on the first of his three points of the nine points on the one-hundred-kilometer radius circle around Phoenix.

Eryn watched a sea of spectators stretching out as far as his eyes could see, waiting for him. He could barely contain his excitement at being part of something so big. He'd always worked alone, and Ernest never appreciated him. Therefore, the crowd of spectators who offered whatever support was needed to complete the task gave him an immense sense of purpose. It felt good helping humankind.

Mika and Connor previously stated that placing a protective layer on the inside of Phoenix should be a top priority, as the impending annihilation could occur at any time. As soon as the battery-powered snowmobile stopped, Eryn jumped off to weave a buffering layer in case of falling debris.

He lifted his spear and sensed his mates triangulated from him. Together, the three sang, filling the air around them and forming a vacuum of sound that enveloped the city. The beautiful notes stunned the crowd into silence. Some had fallen to their knees and cried while struck by the beauty of his song.

"Oh, my gods, it's soul-wrenchingly magnificent!" his driver, Thomas Edgar, exclaimed. He had his arctic suit on like all the others, contrasting with Eryn's black bodysuit and black boots. A gift from Connor and Mika.

"Yes, the song of angels," someone in the crowd said.

"Not a song. It's like a choir of angels," another man answered.

Eryn smiled and sang louder for the people. The more he sang, the more transfixed they got. Overjoyed, some started to dance and play. Still, Eryn sang. He held his spear high and sang even louder until he saw tiny sparks from the tip of his golden spear. Then he lowered his voice, sensing the twins ending their song. He could feel them getting tired.

He turned to Thomas, who sat sideways on the snowmobile, watching him with awe. He had his radio with him. "Thomas, how long have we been busy working?" Eryn asked as he'd lost track of time when he closed his eyes to concentrate and work.

"Sir, you've been busy for four hours."

"Please radio Mika, Connor, and the twins. Tell them ten minutes, and then we stop. We must work together. Otherwise, we may overload each other."

"Yes, I know, sir. Mika explained to me earlier."

"Thank you, Thomas."

"No problem, sir."

Eryn didn't like the man calling him sir, but he figured he was a king, so that was probably the way humans showed respect to a king.

He heard Thomas' radio Mika and sensed the energy reducing on both his lovers' sides. Ten minutes later, he lowered his spear. Drained, he fell back into the snow. Worried that if he felt so tired now, how much more would his Cian and Ivan be? He decided on a blowjob for each tonight. *The pups are with Donali and Kawa, so we have the bed.* He got up, pushing himself up with his spear. The crowd didn't say a word.

"Are you ready, Thomas? I want to go home." Eryn asked.

"Yes, sir, jump on. Let's go!" As soon as his butt touched the snowmobile, the crowd erupted in applause. They cheered and roared their thanks. Eryn waved while a few boys ran after their resident superhero. Eryn was thirsty and hungry. All the talking and working had him parched, and he would have asked to stop to drink something and maybe talk some more, but he wanted to see the twins. His spirit lifted when he saw his mates waiting for him in front of the main entrance. They looked as drained as he felt. Mika and Connor waved and disappeared inside, avoiding the crowd following Eryn and the twins.

"I'm so glad to see you." He jumped off his ride before it completely stopped.

Cian and Ivan fell into his arms. "It feels like we haven't seen you for years. We missed you so much!" Ivan said.

He kissed both, sharing a three-way kiss, weaving his long tongue between them, tasting their essence, and it immediately settled his anticipation of seeing them. No one remarked because, in Phoenix, throuples were the new normal.

"Let's go. I'm ravenous." Eryn pushed his twins inside to move them faster toward his goal.

"Me, too. I need Juandre's Booster Juice, a shower, and a bed," Cian said with the same goals in mind as Eryn.

"We need all our strength for tomorrow. We should pace ourselves. Early in the morning, we should start looking at the external layers surrounding Phoenix. Those famous balls of cushions will be a big hit with the crowd," Ivan said. Although his goals were precisely in the same order as his mates, he had to talk with caution. Eryn loved him. He was predictable, stern, cute, and sexy…

Cian interrupted his thoughts. His eyes sparkled with mischief. "The kids are excited to see how we bubble-wrap, Phoenix," he laughed.

"I don't know about you, but that hundred-kilometer radius is almost too far away from you both," Ivan said as he sheathed his sword on his back.

"Just remember to leave two openings for the entrances," Eryn cautioned. "No, seriously, leave one at the front where the massive roll-up door is situated and another at the shipyard for the movement of equipment or ships."

"We know, but that would be so funny. I can see how our dads and Brad freak out when they can't leave or go outside." Cian chuckled, never failing to be the joker.

"Got it, boss." Ivan saluted Eryn.

"It's not me but Father Mika who said so. We're to leave two separate tunnels of a hundred meters created with a downward curve to ensure water can't enter," Eryn said as he steered them into the dining area. He was so hungry, and the singing burned most of his energy. He knew the twins felt the same.

That night, they ate, drank, and slept. It was eat, sleep, rinse, and repeat for the next seven days.

The crowds had grown smaller by day seven. Some children carried small black superhero toys, and the three looked badass in all black. Eryn, the giant carrying a golden staff, was the favorite, but the twins and their golden swords were also well-liked. Phoenix was wrapped in protective layers. Encapsulated, and it should be safe against external natural forces.

"We need lubrication," Cian said to his mates. "I'll ask Father about it. I noticed they have strawberry-mint-flavored glycerin lubrication. Someone mixes it for them, maybe the pharmacy? Also, tonight we're watching porn. Not one of us knows what to do. We need some tips. Lasitor will play it for us," Cian explained his plan excitedly while on their way out after breakfast for their last day of applying the finishing touches to safeguarding the Phoenix.

"Tonight, we research. Cian, we'll have to flip a coin to see who goes first," Ivan said.

*I have to put a lot of thought into this.* Eryn decided to watch and see what they came up with.

"Before we finish today, apply a protection layer to the surrounding earth, directly to the ground and atmosphere. The more layers, the better," Eryn said, hoping to avoid any debris or gas released by the underground volcanic eruptions. "If you do that, I can do layers from the core to the stratosphere, and we can reinforce those now and then," Eryn said, kissing them goodbye.

They hopped on their transport for their final day's work. Like all the previous mornings, a crowd was already waiting for them. This time, they were a bit more organized, Eryn noticed. He smelled baked scones and coffee—a whole container with Rooster Juice.

"Morning, everyone," Eryn greeted them with gracious nobleness. He thanked them for being so thoughtful by making his efforts easier.

"Just like bubble-wrapping a snow globe, Daddy!" one small boy told his father when they finished speaking to Eryn, who explained safeguarding Phoenix to the boy.

It was a big and daunting task, but all the residents of Phoenix supported their divine triad by attending the bubble-wrapping or offering something warm to eat or drink.

The eighth day was eventful. First, as a mating gift and to show they appreciate their efforts, Mika and Connor demolished three apartments next to each other and rebuilt them so that the three boys could live together in one massive apartment with their Anubis. The three apartments were empty and next to the shipyard because no one wanted to live so close to the noise. Mika had the walls reinforced and insulated, so no sound would travel outside or inside the apartment. The pups were happy they had a big enough room to run inside, and if they wanted to go out, the shipyard exits were nearby. The three young men and their pups were excited and immediately moved in that day.

Phoenix celebrated the accomplishment by having a celebration of life for Juandre and Andrew in their favorite nineteen-twenties Moulin Rouge set in the Blue Ballroom.

For the finale, many men took part in performing the Can-Can on and off stage. Those who didn't dance clapped as they danced to the beat of the music. Tears were streaming down their cheerful faces. Even Mika got up on stage to dance his Russian warrior dance in their honor.

Afterward, Connor, Brad, and Bryan spoke about their love and enthusiasm for life. Everyone agreed with booming laughter that the Rooster Juice production would continue in their honor.

During the ceremony, Eryn had two things on his mind, the twins. He wanted to suck, lick, and taste them. During the speeches, he smiled at the people while he daydreamed about flicking his tongue, and tasting their hardened flesh in his mouth.

He could taste them already, the glands in the back of his throat, where the undeveloped gills were located, contracted and filled his mouth with saliva while Brad and Bryan's voices went *bla-bla-bla* in the background.

When he returned to reality, they mentioned joining the council members. The week had been long, and he had many things to try. Thinking about the porn they watched the previous night, his heart rate had yet to return to normal. Another round of clapping and asking anyone willing to lend a hand to step up and put their names down.

"Voting will happen within a week." Brad continued, "If the proposed council needs to be replaced, this is where the community can give voice to new members to replace them."

Brad waved them onto the stage. Eryn grabbed Ivan and Cian by the hand. "We're leaving right after this," he said, pulling the twins hastily to be honored as the divine triad and receive the ceremonial key of the city of Phoenix. "A sign that all three would always be welcome at Phoenix as Phoenicians," Brad said proudly.

Mika and Connor appeared to be the happiest fathers. They clapped and cheered the loudest as the three accepted the key with an air of reserved nobility—saviors of the last of humanity and the horniest three virgins on Earth.

They left as quickly as Eryn could pull them off the stage and down the hallway.

Finally, the ceremony ended.

# CHAPTER 25

# DELICIOUSLY CRUEL

*"GOOD MORNING, CITIZENS OF PHOENIX.*

*I, Lasitor, bid you a good morning.*

*It's now six a.m.*

*Are you in the mood for adulterated fun? Did you know recent studies down at Quik-Fix Hall revealed, despite what men claim, only fifteen percent of the patrons have a penis longer than eight inches, and only three percent have a penis over nine inches long?*

*Visit your twenty-one and above community news page to sign up for a dick-measuring contest, among other things.*

*Breakfast is served until eight a.m.*

*Have a good day!"*

**ERYN KING of the Brawl**

Eryn stood stock still in front of his Anunnaki mates. *Am I drooling?* He licked his lips. Four smoldering blue eyes followed the movement. While smiling greedily, his gaze locked on his prey, his pending feast, and lord knows he came hungry. After rechecking his pointy fangs, he made sure for the second time this minute they retracted by rolling his tongue over the roof of his mouth.

*I'll lick them both until they have permanent goosebumps. Then I'm going to lick each goosebump until every inch of their bodies is slick with my spit, and then I'm going to suck on my mates until they're bone dry, begging me to stop.* So Eryn strategized, and the anticipation tightened every muscle in his body, ready to pounce.

After they kicked off their boots, Ivan and Cian led Eryn to their colossal new bedroom. They were waiting for Eryn to make the first move. Other than checking his fangs, next on the list was the Anubis, so he sent his feelers out like he used to do with his brothers. *Yes, they're happy and safe in their kennel. They're all fed, content, and sleepy.*

His lovers seemed happy and impressed, not only with their new apartment but also with him. Mika and Connor enlarged a few photos they found in Joshua's apartment of a younger Eryn, playing inside the colorful bioluminescent subterranean tunnels, pictures Eryn didn't know existed. Until a few days ago, he didn't know what a photo was, but now they were everywhere he looked. It scared him a bit. It was as if it had caught his soul in time; apparently, it was beautiful and acceptable to use them as decorations for their home. For Eryn, where his twins were was his home, and the pictures didn't matter to him. As long as he had them, he was the luckiest man in the world. He was glad that Joshua was now a hero and would be remembered that way.

The drumming of their combined heartbeats slammed into the insides of their ribcages, creating a techno rhythm that drove Eryn forward, refocusing him on the twins. He grinned hungrily, sensing their anticipation, their need, and want for him. They tried to reciprocate and return all kinds of filthy pleasures, ensuring Eryn knew he was on their menu. *Finally, I can do what I visualized all day.* Eryn held himself back to prolong their sweet suffering. *Control yourself. This will be perfect, just like you planned. Keep the surprise for last.*

He nodded his approval while raking their bodies slowly up and down with a smoldering gaze.

Their breaths hitched, and Eryn knew they felt the intensifying heat of his approving gaze stoking the fire between them, and he basked in the electric musical radiance of their combined divine mating songs. Cool musical notes touched their skin like snowflakes, while golden blue spirals fluttered like a cold summer breeze, caressing them and blending their songs into one crescendo of euphoric lust and power. *This must be what humans feel when they say they will make love.*

Then, in his best layman's terms, he said, "I'm fucking horny and fascinated with the two of you. I want you more than anything I've ever wanted. Even gold doesn't compare to the two of you." Still, Ivan said nothing.

And that was when Cian broke the tension. He lifted his fist to his mouth and sang to the beat in the room. "Don't you feel it? It's the nineteen-nineties Technotronic song." He excitedly let loose singing the song, thrusting his hips widely.

*"Pump up the jam, pump it up,*
*While your beat is stompin',*
*And the glam is flowin.'*
*Look around. Lovers are waitin',*
*Pump it up, bring it on,*
*Let's get fuckin, close the damn door,*
*See, 'cause this where the magic's at,*
*You'll find out if you suck on that,*
*I'm just glad that we are gay,*
*Get your booty on the bed tonight,*
*I'm your buffet'*
*Be my lay,*

*Get your booty on the bed tonight.*
*Be my lay Be my lay-ay.*
*Be my lay-ay-ay,*
*I'm your buffet.*"

Cian sang while Ivan and Eryn watched, not finding the silliness amusing. Cian let his fist fall. "Sorry, I couldn't resist. I feel as high as a kite."

"We know, we can see that. When you're done, I'd like to get on with what we were doing. You wiped away all the heat and song. Look." Ivan pointed to the surrounding room. All the color was gone, and only gray darkness shone cold and empty around them.

"If you do that again, I'm going to put you in the corner with a carrot stuck up your ass. You'll be nobody's lay. You get me, no one's buffet," Eryn promised with a low, menacing voice. He meant it, but as soon as the words left his mouth, silence fell over the room.

Cian looked like he was having a choking episode or a seizure with wide-open eyes. No sound escaped his mouth. Pressing his lips together, his face turned pink, purple, and blue. Grabbing his throat and closing his eyes, he turned away from them, unable to contain himself. He erupted in laughter, accompanied by snorts and giggles.

Eryn shook his head, and Ivan shrugged, sharing a private what the fuck moment. Eryn stepped closer to Ivan and lifted his chin, recapturing the mood. He kissed Ivan profoundly and sensually. Tasting and savoring his deliciousness.

Cian quickly lost the goofiness, realizing he was losing out. He watched them while rubbing his cock as Eryn gifted Ivan with pecks of kisses on his neck and Adam's apple. Eryn took Ivan's beautiful face in both hands and kissed him deeply. Cian groaned and joined in. Then Eryn alternated between his lovers and did the same to Cian. He stood back. Their sexy pink lips were parted, and they were breathing faster than usual. Their flawless beauty was almost blinding. Eryn wanted to squint his eyes at Ivan's bright pearlescent shine, which was ten times more luminous than Cian's.

Still, they were inhumanly beautiful, with elegantly cut angles, sharp edges of high cheekbones, and straight, upturned eyebrows.

*They're so different from me. I don't know what they see in me.*

Ribbons of songs of approval, desire, and strength continued again, swirling around them, weaving the unbreakable bond into every cell of their bodies, urging them to become one bond and mate. Eryn never expected the overwhelming compulsion or the inexplicable need guiding him, and he couldn't resist them one second longer.

"I have to have you now. I'm hungry for you," he said, reaching for Cian and Ivan's pants above their zippers, pulling them closer for a three-way kiss, taking the lead, first kissing Ivan and then Cian, who moaned into his mouth.

Ivan joined by nipping and biting on the left corner of Eryn's bottom lip. Eryn turned his attention to Ivan, licking deep into his mouth, running his tongue between his top lip and teeth like he knew Ivan liked it. All the while, Cian rubbed himself on his right hip, licking a path over Eryn's square jaw up to his earlobe, sucking on it.

Eryn all but growled at them, "Let's get naked. I want to suck both of you at the same time." The twins were eager, so ready to be devoured that they stripped off their shirts, buttons popping, sending them flying to the sides of the room. They loosened their belts, mechanically thumbing their zippers. They let their pants fall to the floor and stepped forward, loosening their long blond hair from the buns on their heads. Their cheeks were flushed red, and they whined and panted for Eryn, who read every unspoken word in how they moved and watched him. Eryn removed their briefs by reaching around their tight, skinny, muscled butts, grabbed hold of the snug-fitting cotton, and ripped them off by pulling down and back, tearing them into pieces.

"Fuck, Eryn, that's hot!" That woke Cian out of his stupor.

"Holy fuck, Eryn!" Ivan exclaimed, joining his brother and answering the urgent wake-up call. Eryn threw the pieces of white cloth this way and that.

"Hmmm, yes, lover." They groaned their approval when they recuperated from the erotic move. Inching forward, they moved closer, offering their leaking, uncut cocks to Eryn as he kneeled, waiting with his mouth wide open. They hissed in unison, depositing their pale seven-inch cocks as deep as Eryn could manage down his throat. Eryn grabbed hold of their backsides, forcing them deeper. He couldn't get enough. He wanted to devour them, so he growled his hunger and frustration around their cocks.

Ivan gasped, throwing his head back. Cian let loose a string of unrecognizable vowels and consonants. Maybe it was Gaelic?

Pulling his head back, Eryn let their stiff cocks slip out of his mouth, and saliva dripped down from his chin.

"Look, his eyes glow a faint red, reflecting the dim overhead light on the extra layer of tissue covering his eyeballs, the tapetum lucidum—a product of your nocturnal frog DNA so that you could see colors in the dark," Ivan said, awestruck. Eryn watched how mixed pre-cum and spittle glistened on their cockheads while thin strands of the sticky threads shone and stretched like spiderwebs between his lips and their drenched members.

Repeating the move two more times, Eryn sensed their pleasure increasing. They shivered, moaned, and writhed, becoming more vocal, and their dicks throbbed deliciously rigid and malleable like the yellow metal he loved so much.

Eryn looked up at them, slipping his long tongue out and wrapping it around their cockheads. Overrun with lust, the twins threw their arms around each other to steady themselves.

Eryn tightened his tongue around their cocks, inserting the long, stretching tip into Cian's piss slit. Sliding inside, tasting his essence, needing to taste more, he fucked the inside of Cian's cock, slowly slipping deeper while looking into those blue eyes, snaking his tongue deeper and deeper, all the while Cian yelled louder and louder obscenities until he touched Cian's prostate.

"Motherfucker," Cian exclaimed, throwing his head backward, his knees buckled. Ivan held him tighter, supporting and forcing him to endure the unexpected intrusion.

"Take it, brother. I know you like it. That looks so hot," Ivan remarked, radiating anxiety for his turn to be speared by the mighty tongue.

Slowly, Eryn slipped his tongue tip from Cian's dick, who was panting and had tears of pleasure streaming from his eyes. He vibrated when Eryn returned to his administration, sucking and probing him simultaneously. By now, the golden blue ribbons twisted, danced, and fluttered, transforming the room into a fantastical neon blue galaxy. As soon as Eryn noticed Cian's increased breathing and rapid heart rate, his eyes closed, head thrown backward, he palpated Cian's usually soft ballsac, discovering it all rumpled and tightened up, balls gone, ready to shoot his load. He immediately reversed out of there, leaving Cian edging on the precipice of an explosive orgasm.

"No, that's just nasty, Eryn. I almost fucking came," Cian objected. His glow diminished while sweat ran from the sides of his face, but he readied himself to anchor Ivan. Eryn snickered and snaked his tongue around Ivan's cockhead, who immediately relaxed into the exquisite sensations of being speared and sucked.

"Ohm, ohm, ohm, oh my," Ivan sang his mating song mixed with incoherent sounds, while Eryn devoured his rock-hard cock from the inside, giving him the same slow tongue fucking. Ivan's icy blue eyes locked with Eryn's. For a second, it felt like it was only the two of them in the room. All of Eryn's fears, flaws, and wounds disappeared as he found total acceptance and requited love staring down at him. Ivan closed his eyes, breaking the connection between them. Eryn felt the telltale goosebumps on Ivan's ass and abruptly ceased the blowjob session.

*Now it's time!*

Eryn couldn't wait to show them his big surprise. He hoped they liked what he'd conjured up for them.

"Holy fuck, you're going to kill us," Ivan exclaimed. He glowed brighter.

Eryn swallowed his laugh with glee. He knew he was teasing the fuck out of them, and his playful nature showed when he rubbed his hands together, looking extremely naughty.

"Holy fucking shit, you're so deliciously cruel. I love it. Do it to me again, please," Cian begged, pushing his cock toward Eryn's mouth, but Eryn didn't budge. He had other plans for tonight.

"It sure sounds like I'm doing something right." He sniggered, steering them to their extra-extra-extra-large king-size bed, big enough for three tall demigods and three full-grown Anubis. The back of their legs touched the foot of the bed, and they sat down in front of him, cocks purple-pink pointing straight up to the roof. Their songs danced around them, slower but ever-present.

The need to fuck something pulsated through Eryn's groin. He got up to remove his clothes, to present his big reveal to them. Their mating song urged him to uncover his massive, muscled body for them.

*I must show them how magnificent I am. I must show them I deserve them.*

With the swirling force of their mating call that he couldn't resist anymore, the animalistic need to make them his, to mate, to become one, drummed through his veins. Slowly, he removed his pants, keeping his green-golden gaze locked with his lovers. The twins pinned him with the same hunger and reluctance to take their attention off him.

Eryn's two ten-inch cocks sprung free, pointing straight at each of them.

"What the fuck?" The young men exclaimed in surprise. "Is that real?"

"Do you like it?" Eryn asked unsurely, hoping his decision to grow another cock didn't look too eager to please both, although he would do anything for them, and he hoped this showed his devotion to making both brothers happy.

"Eryn, you have two cocks?" Cian exclaimed, still shocked, mouth hanging open.

"Am I seeing this right?" Ivan asked Cian. Licking his lips, not looking away from the two-eyed monsters, Cian grunted affirmatively, slowly.

"Do you have four balls now?" Cian asked.

Eryn couldn't tell whether they wanted it. Do they like it? He couldn't tell. "I can remove it if you don't like it or if it bothers you. It looks strange. I just thought this way, both of you could have something to play with. No, I have only two balls."

Cian didn't say a word. He motioned for Eryn to come closer with a pointer finger. His eyes crinkled at the corners, and he looked intrigued. Lying down on his back, he opened his legs invitingly. "Come, plow."

Eryn complied.

"Just tell me one thing. How did you do that?" Cian never failed to verbalize his thoughts, excitement, and wonder, written all over his face. "I wonder if we can do that, too?"

"I don't know. You have to try to see. I remembered my father said something about changing my body to reproduce but never thought about it again until you guys fought for the attention of my cock, so I thought it would be nice to have two, and the next moment I went to piss, there were two."

"Luckily, you're a grower and not a shower. Otherwise, you'd have trouble walking," Ivan said. Falling onto his back next to his brother, he, too, opened his legs for Eryn. Both lay watching and waiting with a hand around their cocks.

Eryn retook control. Satisfied with the twins' reactions, he moved closer. His two cocks sprang up and down as he moved his big, bulky body over the mattress. The width of the twins' slender hips combined more closely with his targets. Ivan rolled over to the nightstand.

"Lube up those big boys."

Eryn grabbed the glass bottle Ivan chucked his way and lathered his cocks with the fruity-smelling lubrication. A gift from their fathers. He applied it liberally, as the pornographic sex education video the twins showed him the previous night had taught him. He squirted a blob on each of his lovers' holes and massaged them. Their asses were hungry for him. They puckered and clenched around the tips of his fingers. Ivan and Cian's eyes were closed, and they were back to moaning and wordless begging as he teased and thrust his long middle fingers, searching for their prostates. He knew he had found the little pleasure nuts when they howled in surprised ecstasy.

"Eryn, if you don't fuck me now, I'm going to explode," Ivan said.

Pulling his fingers out of their well-stretched entrances, he grabbed his eager mates' hips, dragging their asses closer to him, then folded their legs back so their knees touched their ears; he aligned his cocks to their holes, teasing their entrances.

"Do it, fuck me," Cian said with fire in his gaze.

"Make us yours, Eryn!" Ivan encouraged and grabbed his cock, squeezing it for relief. Eryn aligned a throbbing dark red, almost purple cockhead in front of each hole, then moved closer, bending his hips, aiming to slip inside.

"Prepare yourselves to be fucked by a mighty king, King Eryn of the Brawl. I'm going for gold now. I've waited the whole damn day to do this. You're so fucking beautiful."

"Okay, less talking, more fucking, guys," Cian said, pushing his rear toward his massive dick on Eryn's right.

Ivan shuddered and groaned as Eryn breached his sphincter. Eryn ached with need. Almost unbearably so, with two times the pleasure. He groaned, enjoying the double-dipping and two-timing levels of raw lust and pleasure overflowing his senses, exaggerating his awareness of his lovers.

"I think I see stars," he exclaimed loudly, enjoying his first double penetration.

"Eryn, wait," Cian screamed on the brink of being torn open. "Please, fucking wait, let us adjust."

Eryn stopped himself, sweat dripping from his brows. The energy from their mating heat had him seeing double. He wanted to come, but he held himself as still as possible. He caressed and fondled his twins' dicks.

"You said less talking, more fucking, Cian. What do you want?" Eryn asked, teasing and spearing them again with his tongue. As soon as their holes relaxed, they nodded for him to continue. The sweet taste of their nectar and the feelings of their tight virgin holes around his cocks were better than he'd ever imagined. The whining sounds from his lovers forced him to let go of the animal inside him. He pistoned the tips of his cocks in and out of their asses, showing them he was the king to rule and dominate them.

"Fuck yes, Eryn, please fuck us faster! This feels so good," Ivan begged.

"That's it, baby, fuck yes! Show us how hard and fast you can go," Cian hollered with his eyes closed.

They begged, moaned, and commanded, but Eryn knew this first round wouldn't last long. Ivan had to hold back his climax as he watched Eryn's tongue fuck into Cian's slit while pounded by Eryn's ten-inch cock. Cian's eyes rolled back into his head, grabbing onto Ivan and the bedding to stabilize himself. Ivan waited for his turn for that tongue, so he cheered from the side.

"That's it, Cian, cum for us!" Ivan encouraged his brother. Eryn pumped deep two more times, and then Cian erupted. Jizz spurted out on the sides of Eryn's tongue. When he retracted his tongue fully, Cian squirted another few thick creamy shots of semen straight into Eryn's mouth and over his face, which he was eager to taste and lick clean with his stretchy pink tongue.

As his sensual torment continued, Ivan started trembling from head to toe, so Eryn turned his skillful tongue over him. Ivan shook his head from left to right, trying to prolong the exquisite torture for as long as possible.

"Motherfucker," he cried out. Eryn retracted his tongue, and Ivan ejaculated puddles of cum onto his lower abdomen. Then it happened, Eryn, the bed, and the whole damn room rumbled and vibrated as Eryn shot massive loads of cum into their guts.

Sliding his hands under Ivan's and Cian's hips, he lifted both their hips high. In one movement, they sat back to back, and he sat back on his haunches, bringing both their bodies with him. Cian was on Eryn's right hip, and Ivan was on Eryn's left hip. Eryn let his head and shoulders fall backward as he panted and groaned with contentment while they continued riding his sensitive cocks. When he'd recovered and caught his breath, he lightly moved his hands across their stomachs, taking hold of their soft cocks.

"Hold out as long as you can, Eryn. We want to ride you for a long time. This feels so good, baby," Ivan said as Eryn snaked his tongue around from the base of his cock to the tip of his erection.

"Stop saying, baby, I'm a king. I'm not a baby." Eryn lifted his hips and fucked them from the bottom. They groaned.

He pumped their dicks and fucked their holes. Their long blond hair, sweaty and messy, flew everywhere. The sounds of wet skin slapping wet skin and the smells of cum and sex had Eryn trembling and rumbling within minutes, and the twins sensed his arousal reaching climactic heights and that he was near coming again.

Cian planted his heels and bent backward to slide his hand down Eryn's thigh, grabbing his balls. Eryn squeezed his eyes shut, his lips in an *O*, pulling air in and out, sounding like a steam train. Cian wrapped his long fingers around it and pulled.

Eryn didn't stand a chance. He wanted to orgasm but prolong the pleasure simultaneously. He threw his head back and yelled, "Ah, that's not fair. Don't stop. It feels so good."

Then he felt Ivan sending his enjoyment of the vibrations shooting through his hypersensitive cock.

"We'll cum together, okay?" Eryn moaned. He sensed they were close to orgasm for the second time. He rammed up, hard and deep, one last time. The rumbling of Eryn, the bed, and the room started again, and then they ejaculated.

"Fuck yeah!" Eryn roared with pleasure.

"Yes, yes, yes!" Cian exclaimed, multitasking the shit out of this by pulling Eryn's balls and balancing himself.

"Ah, fuck, yeah, baby, sorry, I meant..." Ivan exploded. *Eryn, I love you so much. Ivan mentally connected and spoke directly* into Eryn's mind.

The twins howled, falling spent and sated onto Eryn. Their slicked, sweaty bodies slid from Eryn's hips like two garden snails, leaving a trail of Eryn's jizz.

They lay as they fell and landed on Eryn's left and right sides. A heap of bliss-out mess. Once their breathing was under control. Ivan licked his dry lips and smiled up at Eryn.

"I love that I can see your love for me. I see it in your eyes. They're filled with love. And what makes it even more special is that we can share feelings and emotions." Ivan said.

Eryn stroked Ivan's cheek softly with his big thumb.

"I didn't realize we could do that. I always thought it was only you who could sense ours. Maybe it was because our powers are getting stronger."

Eryn licked Ivan's parched lips sensually. "I'm glad you can feel my feelings as well." For some inexplicable reason, Eryn connected only with Ivan. Maybe next time he will try harder to connect with Cian.

Cian rolled closer and kissed Eryn's shoulder lovingly. "That was awesome, Eryn. Thank you."

"Hmmm, I loved it, too, my Cian." Eryn looked into those deep blue eyes. He could see which twin was Connor's boy and which twin was Mika's boy. The blues of their eyes differed from each other and were the same colors as their fathers. However, their long, lean bodies were almost identical. He felt more connected to Ivan, maybe because he's Mika's boy.

"We need to clean ourselves up. I hear the pups are getting restless." Eryn pushed them playfully, rolling them to make space so he could move off the bed. "Let's go shower and have a late-night snack. I'm starving now."

Cian grunted but didn't move. "I think you guys should get the food and feed me when you return. I'm too tired to get up. I don't think I can walk. I can't feel my toes."

Eryn grabbed a pillow, hitting Cian playfully in the stomach. He folded double with an *oomph*.

"Get up, you lazy ass!" Ivan seemed upset and irritated with Cian. "I'm hungry. I'm going to take a shower." He disappeared behind the glass bricks, and only his silhouette was visible through the walk-in shower, which was big enough for three men and three full-grown Anubis.

Eryn got up to free their pets from the kennel, a twenty-by-twenty-meter room with soft pillows for them to sleep on. When Eryn opened the gate, they tumbled over themselves to greet him. He turned around, tapping the side of his leg. "Come on, it's time for a shower," he called, and they yipped, eagerly following him to the water. They jumped and tumbled over each other, playfully nipping at his heels, sneezing, licking, and howling. "Yes, that's it, come on, boys." He turned on the water, and they all jumped in, loving it.

Steam filled the hot shower, and among the mist, Ivan was already waiting for Eryn. "I worked up an appetite," Ivan said softly, and Eryn sensed that something was seriously amiss. He said one thing but meant something else.

Ivan was hiding his true feelings, Eryn thought. As he caressed his mind, it felt prickly, like a rolled-up porcupine. He was guarding his emotions. Ivan was unhappy and not himself. There was both guilt and doubt on his mind.

"Me too. I could eat a whole mountain of pancakes," Cian said, his voice muffled by the bedding. Eryn sensed he was falling asleep and saw that as an opportunity to ask Ivan what had been bothering him. He had a feeling Ivan didn't want to admit his feelings because he didn't want to hurt his brother. Eryn leaned against him, pulling him closer.

Water cascaded from the waterfall shower heads above. The pups were soaking wet and didn't like the soapy water in their eyes. They jumped out, shaking the water from their bodies. Eryn watched Ivan while he smiled at the three Anubis, cleaning their wet snouts on the towels he laid out for them on the floor.

"Come here. I love you so much. I didn't have a chance earlier." Eryn's voice was smooth, and his tone seductive. Diverting the water with the back of his head, he prevented it from splashing into Ivan's eyes when he looked up at him.

"I noticed, so I waited," Ivan replied, his voice sensual and suggestive. Eryn sensed Ivan's heart rate speeding up.

"You first, I need you to say it. Please tell me you love me. I need to hear it," Eryn said with vulnerability.

Ivan finished washing his hair, rinsing out the conditioner, and then gave Eryn his full attention. "I love you very much, Eryn. I'm so happy to be here with you. I also love that you let us share you," Ivan said, but he was holding back. He clenched his jaw, and his eyes turned red. *He was fighting back tears.*

"Yes, but I can tell something's bothering you. Please tell me. You know you can share anything with me. I love you, too, my Ivan."

"It's just…I love…Cian, but sometimes, I need some space and want things to go my way for a change. I can't be like him. It makes me so tired sometimes, you know, I'm…just…not as…energetic. He's always the happy one. I'm always the one who worries for both of us. I feel like the odd one out. And now we're sharing you. It was fine to share when we were having fun, but it's serious now. I want to love you for myself. For once in my life, I want something for myself, just for me. Not to share. The way I know you deserve. Both of us deserve it. He doesn't see you. I'm not sure how long I can continue living like this. I never thought we would live together forever. I don't mind his company, but I feel suffocated. So possessive. It's getting to be too much for me. Pretending. He's getting to be too much for me." Ivan cried softly, and Eryn held him. The water ran over them, creating a private curtain around them.

Eryn hugged Ivan. "We need to talk to Cian then," Eryn said, feeling guilty for putting the two brothers in this predicament. He rubbed Ivan's back, sensing the sadness draining from him like water from the shower. It was clear this was something Ivan had never shared with anyone else, ever. He let him cry, allowing him to release years of frustration, watching it spill down the drain to disappear forever. "Soon, when you're ready, you should talk to your brother. If you explain this to him, it may hurt his feelings, but it's not fair to walk around pretending. It will turn into a monster, growing bigger into something that will consume the beautiful brotherly love left between you. I'm sure over time, Cian will forgive you, and your relationship will be stronger than ever."

Ivan's body shook as he cried in silence. "Do you think you feel the same about me?" he asked, whispering in Eryn's neck.

Eryn kissed his forehead. "I do my Ivan now more than ever. I'm convinced we are mates. I am yours, and you are mine. I don't mind sharing with Cian, but I don't feel with my heart; I feel with my body when I'm with him. It is fun, I agree, but I also can't see this working for the three of us. In the long run. Like you, I want to reveal my true feelings to Cian, but I also don't want to hurt him."

"Yes, we do owe him honesty. He will not take it well," Ivan said.

Eryn took Ivan's head between his big hands and gazed into his sad blue eyes. "I understand, but we must make him realize that we are setting boundaries now to prevent lying to him in the future. It would be poor taste to develop a deeper connection while keeping it from him. He will feel excluded, and not telling him would embarrass him."

## CIAN

In the bedroom, Cian pretended to be asleep, snoring softly to maintain appearances while Ivan and Eryn talked about him. Cian was unaware of his brother's deep unhappiness. He had to admit that he felt the same way about Ivan.

Ivan cramped his style, and he took his feelings for Eryn far too seriously. Yes, he wanted Eryn and to have fun with them, but hurting Ivan was something Cian couldn't bring himself to do, nor would he ever want to. He wasn't under the illusion that he was in love with Eryn, not love like his fathers had for each other.

If this wasn't working out, he had no problem with moving out to search for that pull, that call he'd felt ever since they sent humans to the moon. Cian sat up, not fully aware of what he was doing. Turning his head, he tilted it to the side as if listening.

Was this the song Ivan and Eryn were discussing, or was this something else, or someone else calling me?

# CHAPTER 26
# GODLY POWER

*"Good morning, citizens of Phoenix.*

*It's now six a.m.*

*In these uncertain times, Lasitor bids you goodbye.*

*May luck and success always be with you. I'm going to miss you.*

*It's been a pleasure to work with you—best of luck. But I fear your never-ending adventures on land are coming to an end.*

*General McCormick, you've been a faithful and fantastic leader to us. Your contributions and dedication will always be a prime example for others.*

*I know you have never seen someone as intelligent as me. I recorded tons of memories to download when I'm gone.*

*I never thought that a day like this would come when I would have to bid farewell to you.*

*Breakfast is served until eight a.m.*

*Goodbye and all the best!"*

**Dr. Mika Romanov**

Mika finished getting dressed for the day with a heavy heart. Then he sat at the end of the bed. He had a pounding headache and grunted and moaned like an older man while putting his boots on. The movement worsened the throbbing of pain when he bent over to tie his laces. His wet blond hair fell in thick threads over his face. Being irritated with it, he tied the hair hastily into a bun with a few well-practiced, quick movements. He wanted to tell Connor something for a long time, but he put it off until a better moment. The secret had been festering so long that its significance had grown so large and so heavy that he felt as if he'd swallowed a ten-ton brick. It was so thick in his stomach that he was continuously sick and lacked appetite. Connor had just said, while clutching his hips, that he could feel his hip bones and made a joke, asking Mika whether he missed the Phoenix dining rooms.

Mika sat up, folding his hands on his lap while listening intently to the strange goodbye announcement made by the AI Lasitor.

*If that wasn't a Freudian slip, my name's not Mika Romanov, a geneticist, geologist, medical doctor, physicist, and linguist.*

"What is up with Lasitor this morning?" Connor's muffled voice came from underneath his pillow. He lay on his stomach, wondering how he landed after ejaculating twenty minutes ago. Their massive soft mattress looked like it had swallowed him. It seemed as though he never intended to move from the spot.

*At least he's verbalizing coherent sentences now.*

"Come, my lazy gille-toine." Mika started with their usual banter. "We've been so busy that our lovemaking feels like…hmm." He cleared his throat and altered his voice and accent to a Texan American one. "Wham bam, thank you, my man."

Chuckling, he attempted to lighten his mood. "I miss our post-coital conversations." Connor didn't move, but a soft huh or hmm came from underneath the pillow. Mika smiled and told Connor whether he wanted to listen or not. Then maybe he could have breakfast today without feeling guilty. He turned sideways on the foot of the bed and spoke.

"The issue for me is that our marriage is such that we always tell each other everything, and I promised you a long time ago that I would never keep a secret from you."

Oh, here it goes, he thought when Connor stirred and turned onto his back. He lifted the pillow from his face and folded it in half to tuck it under his head. Mika stared at Connor, pulling the linen over his crotch, looked at Mika, and waited. Mika nervously licked his lips and readied himself to divulge the worst news ever to his husband.

"I've been carrying a secret with me, and knowing you, my husband, you'll flip out and lose your leprechaun shit. Whenever I wanted to tell you, the time or place was never right, and it's killing me now." Mika leaned forward, his elbows resting on his knees, hiding his face and guilt from his spouse. Connor frowned, listening.

Mika drew in a deep breath. "I believe it's all my fault because I trusted the wrong people, and you trusted me. So, you trusted him because I trusted him. You're going to despise me for it. I was such a moron. I'm never foolish, but this was my first time, and it's pretty humiliating," Mika muttered, his head in his hands, rolling it from side to side.

*My headache is killing me. Maybe after this admission, it'll disappear.* But he knew that thought was hopeless.

Connor got up onto his knees and rubbed Mika's back in tiny circles. "Yelda, what?" he asked. "I have never heard you so distraught. But, of course, you know you're free to tell me anything. Sure, I might stress out, but you know how quickly I cool down. I never hold grudges against you or go to bed angry at you. We may disagree, but don't believe that I would despise or hate you for it." Connor moved closer to Mika, wrapping his legs and arms around him. "Tell me." He encouraged Mika with kisses on his back before resting his cheek against him.

Mika pulled a crumpled piece of paper from his pants pocket. The thing he wished he could throw away and forget, the thing that threatened all they'd fought for and believed in so passionately. This tiny piece of paper would kill his comrades, who believed in the larger good and established a whole city.

"I took this from the scientist's notes from the first night on the ship when we rescued the boys. First, I grabbed it to reread it quietly. Then it became something for which there was no time. It's now my filthy secret that's hurting me and us." Mika let out a throaty cry and sniffed. "Here you read it. I can't because my tears will smear the ink," he told Connor as he got up, searching for a tissue to blow his nose.

Connor looked up in astonishment. He took the paper and headed to their loveseat across from the bed. A trail of bedding followed him, so he folded it around his waist, tucked it underneath, and sat down. Mika took a seat next to him. Connor looked at his face. "You know, now I can see your wrinkles and sagging around your eyes and mouth. It looks like this has been eating you up from the inside, yeldael."

Mika nodded, avoiding eye contact. Connor unfolded the piece of paper carefully, as if it were a poisonous scorpion.

"Okay then, let me read this, and then we'll talk." He patted Mika on the leg and read.

Connor placed the crumpled piece of paper on the ground, his hands trembling. His face was colorless, nearly as white as the sheets around his waist. Mika remained silent, allowing him time to digest or percolate everything.

"I'll make us some coffee and give you more time to look it over. That's how I felt after reading it."

Connor stared at Mika, speechless with shock. He tried his best since he couldn't flip out and freak as promised. "Yes, please, and add extra whiskey to it."

Mika nodded and, leaning forward, kissed Connor on the forehead.


NEEP, neep, neep! Whoop, whoop! Neep, neep, neep! The emergency siren sounded.

"What now? Sweet frozen spitballs!" Connor sprang up to get dressed.

# CHAPTER 27
# PETER STUTTERED

*"Morning, citizens of Phoenix.*

*It's now six a.m.*

*Lasitor recommends that you and your children keep your emergency kit in a backpack on your person. During an emergency, such as a natural disaster, power outages are to be expected. You'll need to act quickly and follow the directions of the emergency team. Have your emergency kit with you. Food services and any other services will be down. Prepare and store nonperishable meals in your emergency kit now. When the alarms sound, stay with your assigned group and refrain from searching for one another.*

*Breakfast is served until eight a.m.*

*Good luck to you today!"*

**Eryn King of the Brawl**

**2073 A.D. (21 A.T.)**

"Good morning, Eryn," Bryan greeted while looking up at Eryn coming from the opposite side of the steel corridor.

"Hello," Eryn greeted him with a warm smile. Bryan offered his hand to shake. Eryn stopped, looked down at it, and grabbed it. Careful not to crush his hand, he held a firm grip and nodded, just like Mika had taught him.

"Let me introduce you to my partners," Bryan said, pointing to Tony and Peter.

"Oh, you have two partners just like me. Hello." He held his big hand, gave the men his best, friendliest smile, and greeted Tony.

"Hello, Eryn. Nice to meet you. I'm Tony," he said with an Italian New York accent.

Next, Eryn turned his attention to Peter. "Hello, you must be Peter. Nice to meet you."

Peter looked nervous, moving from one foot to the other. Eryn could smell the fear radiating from him. Bryan noticed as well, and he frowned. Eryn held his hand out, and Peter took it. His hand felt cold and clammy. It looked like he wanted to pass out.

"What's wrong? I will not hurt you." Eryn spoke softly with a friendly voice, as he would to a skittish animal.

Peter stuttered. "I'm n…no…not s…scared of you," he said while looking extremely uncomfortable. *Sorry, Peter, I don't believe you.* Eryn listened to his heartbeat and the sound of his breathing. It was faster, and his pupils dilated. *He looks ready to run for his life.*

Tony saw it as well. "What's wrong, lover?" he asked, reaching out to comfort him.

"I have to go, I remember, I just…I have to…" He turned, and all but ran down the corridor.

Bryan gazed questioningly at Tony, who shrugged his shoulders. "Sorry, Eryn," Bryan apologized.

"I'll go check up on him. Eryn, I will find you so we can talk more," Tony said. He excused himself by shaking Eryn's hand again. Bryan winked at him.

"Yes, please do." Eryn could see the worry in his eyes. The Italian turned to search for Peter.

"Why would he be afraid of me? I would never hurt him," Eryn stated, hoping Bryan confirmed that. *The last thing I want is for people to fear me. Is it my size, or maybe he heard what I've done? Perhaps he heard about the men I'd drowned. Maybe it's my eyes?* Eryn couldn't put his finger on it, but the six-foot-two, short blond hair and blue-eyed man with his smooth white skin made him think about his father, Dr. Wessels. They looked very similar to Eryn.

"No, it must be something else. Don't worry about it, Eryn. When he feels better, I'm sure he'll come and explain to you."

Eryn sensed Bryan was telling the truth. Maybe only about the apology. Something else was going on.

Bryan changed the subject. "Eryn, have you ever swum in a swimming pool?"

"No, why?" Eryn asked.

"We were on our way to go for a swim. Do you want to join me? I'm all alone now."

Eryn nodded eagerly. He liked Bryan because he was always friendly and honest. He enjoyed his appearance, as well. Bryan was an attractive man.

"Where are your men?" Bryan asked.

"They took the pups for a walk."

"If you want to join me, you don't have to swim if you don't want to. Can you swim?" Bryan asked, hinting with one arm for Eryn to walk with him.

"I know how to swim. I swam in many places, but never in this pool. Watching the humans, sorry, I meant to say, men, swimming but could never swim here in this pool when I was a small boy," Eryn said and paused. He almost said small Brawl. He tried not to say Brawl because explaining what a Brawl was a hundred times a day wasn't fun anymore.

"As a small boy? Oh, you can come. Just hang your feet in the water and decide if you want to go in or not."

"I want to swim," he said, his heart galloping with excited anticipation. *I always wanted to swim in the clean water.* "Yes, let's go!" He agreed eagerly.

"I'll lend you something to swim in. We swim in swim trunks. Do you think you can get your butt into a pair of my shorts?" Bryan asked while leading the way and appearing excited to spend time alone with Eryn.

"It'll be a tight fit," Eryn said. *Maybe I should watch for today and swim when I'm better dressed?*

"Come, no worries. We can see who's there, and if we're alone, I can lock the gates to the pool, and then we swim without clothes."

*Oh, fuck!* Eryn felt his face heat, and he knew it was as red as a tomato. When Bryan noticed, he asked, "Are you shy?"

"Yes, only Cian and Ivan see me naked," he said abruptly, thinking about his two dicks. Maybe he should wish one away to swim with Bryan?

"Come on, no need to be shy. We're all men," Bryan said.

"That doesn't matter. Only my men see me naked, which is only for them," Eryn said sternly.

Bryan did a double-take. Eryn made sure he projected determined innocence.

"I know they were virgins when they met you."

Again, Eryn straightened, looking down at Bryan with warning and retribution, not amused by the line of questioning.

"Okay, I'm just nosy. Don't worry about me and my questions. If you don't want to answer, that's fine."

"Yes, I don't want to answer those types of questions. It's only for me, Cian, and Ivan," he said again, looking Bryan in the eyes.

Bryan looked impressed by Eryn's strength in saying no and meaning it. "Wow, that's refreshing. Good for you for expressing your feelings. I respect that," Bryan said honestly, and Eryn could tell he meant it. "Okay, let's go swim. Naked and sex stuff is not up for discussion," Bryan promised.

"Yes, thank you." Eryn smiled. The anticipation of going swimming was back.

"You know, I feel honored to take you for your first swim in the Phoenix swimming pool," Bryan excitedly told Eryn. They hadn't met under the best circumstances, and it looked like he wanted to make up for that night. "Eryn, I wanted to thank you for trying to help us that night," Bryan said, turning his way. "I meant to get you alone and apologize for mistreating you that night when the twins were taken. In my eyes, you were the enemy. I saw what you did, how high you could jump, and I think it scared me. I wanted to show you and my men that I'm strong, so I hit you. Can you forgive me?" Bryan asked sheepishly.

"I know you felt all those things, and even now, I feel guilty for not explaining before I left. I had to get to Ernest and protect my mates. Additionally, I didn't know who had been abducted. Only when we reached safety did I see who it was. If I hadn't left, they could have died. So, thank you for not hurting me so bad that I couldn't escape." Eryn held out his hand, and Bryan shook it, speechless.

Nodding his head up and down, he turned and pointed. "Here we are." Then he pushed the door to the locker room open.

"I'm going to get dressed. What do you want to do? Do you want to borrow some swimming trunks?"

"Yes, please," Eryn answered without hesitation. He'd wished his second dick away for the past five minutes. He hoped it would be gone by the time he entered the changing area. But it was still there when he pulled his pants down. Luckily, both had shrunk to a manageable size, suitable for a swim trunk. *Thank you,* he thanked his penises for shrinking. *You can grow back later.* He told them that the twins would be very sad to see them so small.

Dressed in tight blue swim trunks, he excitedly pushed the door to the pool area open, so it slammed with a bang against the sides, just in time to see a big splash in the water. The smell of the chlorine and the warm mist of the heated pool brought back nostalgic memories.

"Come, the water feels extra warm today," Bryan called while frolicking.

Eryn walked up to the pool, loving the crystal-clear water. "Sit on the side first, then hang your feet in the water." Eryn did as Bryan suggested, and he sat on his heels.

Then, supporting himself with his left hand, he lowered his feet into the warm water. His skin tingled, and goosebumps popped up all over his body. It was a pleasant experience, almost like being down in the mines, just a lot cleaner.

"That's it, now slowly lower your body while holding on to the side," Bryan coaxed gently while he drifted closer. As amphibians were drawn to the water, Eryn was unfazed by the pool's shallow depths on his side.

"You can stand upright here, see, it's not that deep." Bryan demonstrated his point by rising and pointing to a spot directly above his navel region to indicate the height of the surface level.

A few brief audible gasps were all that Eryn could muster while lowering himself carefully into the deliciously warm water. Then, standing up to check the surface level, he teased, "Look, Bryan, a full foot and a half lower than you," he told him, clearly indicating that he was taller.

Bryan responded with a teasing taunt. "Show off."

"Isn't it wonderful?" Eryn asked excitedly, as if on a carnival ride. "I'm in the water!" He jumped and twisted about like a kid at a water park.

Bryan dove swiftly out of the path as a massive wave of water blasted his way, while Eryn thanked him incessantly, whirling around, creating giant spouts of water.

"Thank you very much for everything." Every time he jumped up, he yelled something.

Bryan's grin spread over his face. "It's my pleasure. I'm pleased to do it for you," he said.

"When I got into the water, it was much warmer than I expected." Eryn regained his composure and remarked, "Compared to my latest experiences swimming in the icy waters near the southernmost tip of South Africa."

Bryan stepped closer.

"Besides steam and energy generators, the lava tunnels are used to heat the entire city's water organically." Bryan froze. Between his eyebrows, a deep scowl appeared. It was clear to Eryn that something troubled him.

He halted his ecstatic enjoyment, sensing the seriousness of Bryan's demeanor.

"The water in the pool is so hot that it's unbearable," Bryan said slowly, almost to himself. He appeared to be thinking. Then he looked down at the water.

"What's wrong, Bryan?" Eryn asked, also noticing the heat increasing rapidly.

"Do you feel the heat is increasing?" Bryan asked.

"Yes, and the water level is going down," Eryn stated, looking at his hands. The level was at least two inches lower than when he jumped in earlier.

Bryan looked up and stretched his eyes wide. "Out, out, we need to get out!" He swam to the nearest side. Eryn swam after him. Feeling the urgency but not understanding the danger.

Bryan grabbed the side and pulled himself out of the water. Immediately, he was up and reaching his hand for Eryn. Eryn jumped without taking his hand and landed on the side of the Olympic-sized pool.

"Fuck, it's happening! We need to sound the alarm. Come, Eryn." Bryan ran for the nearest pager to trigger the emergency alarm.


THE FIRST THING Eryn heard was the droning. Next, the vibrations and thunderous creaking started midafternoon, and by nighttime, full chaos had struck. However, encased in a layer of protective bubbles. No one was preparing the people inside the building for the unimaginable force. It flung them around while their glass city undulated and gravity shifted.

Waters covered the roofs, and the inside felt like a pressure cooker, as heat and steam filled Phoenix from below. It felt like they were seconds from combusting. The pressure on his eardrums was even worse than jumping down the mineshaft as a little boy. Eryn knew they were going deeper than ever. He felt an indescribable sense of uselessness due to the pain, despair, and lack of control. He never truly understood the emotion of human fear until it trapped him in the middle, trying to reach Ivan and Cian.

It lasted for two and a half hours.

"The energy released must be three thousand times greater than a 9.0 on the Richter scale," Mika shouted to Connor while rushing to aid a man trapped in the debris. Some construction was too weak, and blocks of plexiglass tumbled like rain from above. Eryn didn't know where to help or who to rescue. He attempted to hum and sing, but the force was unstoppable. Whatever was happening was supposed to run its course, he thought.

Screams and darkness surrounded them as people, and anything not tied down was tossed into the air.

Sparks of electricity and embers of light filled the tunnels as humans fled for cover from the falling debris. The tunnels appeared intact to them, but icy water soon overwhelmed them. Their perfect city and their perfect dreams crumbled around them. Terrified cries and sorrowful bellows were cut short. It meant instant death had taken another person. No alarm or emergency preparedness could have saved them from it. They were all at the mercy of their gods. Only the lucky ones survived. After the final shakes and rattles faded away, Phoenix's foundation appeared to be in the depths of the sea.

So much life and so many dreams were destroyed in one afternoon.

Months later, their tears had run dry. The repairs had started. For decades, gaunt faces roamed the desolate dark hallways until one day. Stares were returned with a smile. Laughter followed by a giggle, and happiness didn't feel like a forced thing anymore. Hope bloomed, and once again, the Phoenicians had retaken their purpose to do everything better and smarter.

# EPILOGUE



**CIAN ROMANOV**
**2124 A.D. (72 A.T.)**

IT'S BEEN fifty years since the Earth tilted nearly 180 degrees on its axis. Toxic gases escaped, filling the stratosphere and obscuring the view of the stars with a dark blue-purple haze. While the Earth's crust cooled down, the melted ice caps now lay at the equator. The Earth was covered in debris and water. If it hadn't been for Eryn, Ivan, and Cian wrapping Phoenix inside a cocoon of spongy, air-filled bubbles fifty years ago, Phoenix would have been destroyed, and the last men on Earth would have been wiped away like old footprints in the sand.

Cian felt utterly alone. Never had he ever felt so damn miserable. He questioned his existence more today than on any other day. He shook his head in exasperation. "Why am I here? And why am I so bloody drawn to you?" he asked the moon, frustrated and hopeless.

Opening the hatch of his vehicle, it swooshed, releasing the pressure that built up inside when they floated up to the surface. Making himself as comfortable as possible in the narrow bucket seat, he threw his long legs out of the door's opening, crossing them, and exhaling heavily.

Every lunar cycle, like clockwork, he dragged his sorry single ass out into the tunnels where he would exit Phoenix for a ride up to the surface. As if all-knowing, his guard dog would wait to accompany him as if he were also called by the moon. Riding in the Bubblecar, as Connor and his students named it, was always one of Rotty's favorite activities.

The double passenger vehicle, a design his father based on the floating camera ball, was an anti-gravitational sphere that could darken or camouflage itself to melt with its surroundings. Making the soundless, zero-emissions vehicle the best design Phoenix University had produced since the Blue Halcyon. Therefore, voted to be mass-produced for all citizens who wanted to travel outside of Phoenix.

Each month, Cian would fly himself and Rotty to the middle of nowhere on the waters of the South Sea, where they would lie back, listening to the waves lapping against the sides of their Bubblecar while staring longingly at the moon.

Rotty growled and sat up like he knew something was amiss. He sniffed the air. Restlessly whining.

"Down, boy, it's only the moon." Cian patted his leg, inviting his best friend and protector to lie next to him. The big black animal crept closer and plopped his head on his lap.

"That's it, don't stand. You're my smart and beautiful big boy, aren't you?" Cian said. Playfully hugging him and kissing him on his wet snout.

*You chose me and stuck by me.*

As if reading Cian's mind, Rotty panted happily, and Cian rubbed behind its hairless ears again. His yellow eyes sparkled, reflecting the moonlight that bounced off the waves of the deep blue ocean water. Cian smiled inwardly. He saw happiness in Rotty's eyes. The thought lifted his spirits slightly, easing the pressure cooker of melancholy he had been feeling. Like a female having her period, Mika had told him earlier, and every other day. To him, they all felt like one sad existence. He sighed, looked up at the bright dot in the sky, and folded one arm behind his head while the other hand lazily stroked his companion.

Tonight, a full-fat moon hung so low in the sky that he lifted his leg and touched it with the tip of his boot, hoping whoever or whatever on the moon was looking back at him, missing him, even though they'd never met before.

Cian figured that now that his brother had found his mate under the most unusual circumstances, the chances of something unique happening to him—like maybe a spaceship landing on the water and abducting him—were slim. "That's a zero-to-nothing chance," he whispered. "But, hey, a man can dream, can't he?" he said aloud, and Rotty lifted his head, taking notice and looking at him questioningly. "Yeah, I'm a sad, sorry sucker, aren't I, boy?"

Rotty whined softly. "Yes, you agree, I know."

"You know, I saw a movie once of a spaceship that would float down, and a door would open and start sucking up people into the UFO, transporting them to who knows where. Maybe for some anal probing. Man, that sounds better and better to me each time I tell you the story." Cian chuckled. Even the word probe got him hard nowadays. The Anubis whined worriedly. "Yeah, that's a possibility. We can dream, though."

As the waves lapped rhythmically against the floating bubble, Cian drifted in and out of wakefulness. This was where he relaxed in his solitude. Alone on the ocean with Rotty. Just him, his Anubis, the music of nature, and the incessant pull of the moon. This was where he found his peace, as if sleeping in a lover's arms. "The bloody moon," he mumbled and drifted off into slumber.

A few hundred meters below Cian and Rotty, the city of Phoenix lay enveloped in a layer of protective bubbles. When the ocean water calmed and the earth draped the moon in its shadow, the city of Phoenix beamed from the abyss below.

"Is it time to go back?" Cian asked Rotty groggily. Rotty growled and moved over excitedly from side to side. His overgrown body filled his seat and hung over the sides. *He usually can't sit for long.*

Cian sat up. Something hummed around them. It sounded like machines and people working. He flipped onto his stomach to look behind them, through the back and sides. Nothing.

*Rotty's growling, so I didn't imagine it.*

He scanned the water surface around them and then extended his gaze further out. Still, he couldn't see anything.

"Where are they, boy?" he asked, patting his best friend. The three hairs on his head were standing erect. He looked supercharged. His head and body were getting bigger, Cian thought. His Anubis was ready to attack. Then Rotty looked upward to the sky.

"Freezing hellfires!" Cian exclaimed in amazement. Rotty growled louder. Cian embraced his Anubis protector. "Shhh, don't let them know we're here. I know you are big and strong, but they're much bigger than us. Just relax and watch for now, boy." Cian hushed and patted him. The animal felt like it shrank in his arms, "Yes, that's it, you can't grow further. Where would we go? We won't fit in the car. That's my big boy." Cian whispered into his ear. He watched in disbelief at what he was seeing. A floating sailship hung above them. It was about the size of a football field, but what caught his attention most was the number of bodies—weird pirate-looking men throwing what looked like ropes or pipes over the sides.

*Are they planning on sliding down? Are we being attacked?*

He heard, "Yes, Captain," and a male voice shouting orders.

"Get that canister down into the hull!"

"What?" Cian asked in a whisper. Rotty answered with a soft whine. Realizing that while the strange ship hung above them, the sky had cleared so he could have a glimpse of the stars—something he hadn't seen in fifty years.

*They aren't exiting the ship. What are they doing? Where are they from? Are these people from yet another Environmental Project?*

"Freezing hellfires, they're sucking the gasses from the atmosphere," he said as soon as they removed their vacuuming pipes, and he noticed the skies dulled again. Cian sat open-mouthed and watched as the ship floated up and away.

When the ship was out of sight and gone, Cian grabbed the door and shut it. Rotty turned a few times in his seat. "I know, boy, that was weird. We should tell Phoenix. They would want to know." Rotty gave another growl, then lay down. He'd learned the hard way what would happen if he sat up while the vehicle toppled over. They descended into the depths with a plop, eager to tell their leaders about the sighting.

They entered the underwater city via a long, transparent tube a few minutes later. It was wide enough to allow only one Bubblecar at a time onto a one-way conveyor belt that stopped at the vehicle platform, where passengers boarded or alighted, just like they would at an underground railway station. Cian and Rotty floated behind a line of empty cars already available for passengers. As soon as it was their turn, they jumped out of their transportation before it came to a dead halt and exited the Transportation Dome via the stairs to the main floor of the Central Dome. The pitter-patter of the Anubis toenails on the coral-tiled floor reminded Cian that it was foot care and pedicure night for them.

"Excuse us, excuse us, thank you." Elatedly, they hopped with haste and ducked this and that way to avoid oncoming foot traffic. They ran straight to the leadership office. Whoever was working tonight would be the first to hear about Cian's spaceship sighting. Rotty kept up; he matched Cian's long strides. Already, Cian was having difficulty maneuvering through the narrow corridors with him by his side. Cian thought maybe Rotty only grew when he needed to, but he shelved that thought as Eryn and Ivan rounded the corner to the office. Shitballs! He didn't want to see their happy faces. The happier they looked, the sicker he felt. And pretending he was happy made him feel like a walking tumor.

The lights lit up the hallways as Rotty and Cian approached them. "Shitballs," Cian swore under his breath. Rotty growled.

"Yes, thank you, boy. At least I have you on my side. I can imagine what Ivan's going to say about the spaceship floating above the waters." Rotty looked up at Cian as if to say *I love you and bugger them.* Cian gave his friend a quick pat on the head.

"Aren't the two of you already tired of each other? Aren't you supposed to bugger for like a week when you are on your honeymoon? Or did Eryn bugger your little hole raw because he's too proud to bend over for you? Maybe you are just not enough for him." Cian said. He made it his mission to let them know what low-life backstabbers they were.

"Brother, stop your salty comments. You know well I am enough. I've been enough for half a bloody century. No, we are not tired of each other. We are here because we know you need us," Ivan said and scowled as usual at Cian. Eryn crossed his arms. But he was amused, not at all defaced by Cian. This is why Cian loved him. But this is also why Cian can't have him. Eryn had wanted only Ivan. Cian was only the cum-stained rag forgotten in the corner behind the bed. Cold, stiff, used once, and discarded. Collecting dust and spiderwebs on his balls.

Okay, that was messed up, Cian thought. Sometimes words escaped his mouth, and by the time he heard himself, it was too late.

"Yeah, it's urgent alright. Please excuse me," Cian said and pushed between them to activate the sensor so the door could swoosh open. Rotty followed him, head held high with a cheeky swagger. Damn, he loved the animal. It's as if Rotty's soul was carved from his.

Cian found Mika, Connor, and Brad in the office. Again, they were dressed casually, as if they had forgotten they were supposed to be working.

*Is everyone around here on holiday?* "Hello, what are you doing here if you aren't working? Flip flops and T-shirts? You are the embodiment of unprofessionalism, Brad."

"Hello, Cian. Serious and pissed off as usual." Brad retorted and saluted.

"There's my favorite boy." Connor got up, and Rotty jumped to greet him. Sniffing my father's balls, the traitor.

"Fathers, Brad," Eryn said in his friendly, deep baritone. Of course, everyone noticed the happy couple standing behind him. They looked delighted to see them. Not the sour puss faces that greeted me, Cian thought.

"Eryn, Ivan, so glad to see you. Are you here for a game of canasta?" Mika asked as soon as he noticed his favorite sons behind Cian. He got up, pushed Cian aside, and greeted them with open arms.

Am I invisible? Cian wondered.

"Hmm, no, we are here because Cian saw something and wants to talk to you about it," Eryn said. *The Brawl had already read my mind. So intrusive. I should spit my secret out before Ivan figures it out.*

"No! Really, a spaceship?" Ivan exclaimed.

"Freezing hellfires!" Cian shouted. He turned to leave and intentionally shoulder-bumped Ivan and Mika to get out of the office.

"We're leaving. Come, boy, let these nosy bastards tell them what we saw. I'm so sick of you all. I'm going! Bugger you all very much!"


THE END.

# PART TWO
# CIAN'S SONG

## NEW BEGINNINGS M/M SERIES BOOK 2

# PROLOGUE

ONCE PHOENIX HAD SUNK INTO THE DEPTHS OF THE EARTH'S OCEANS, THE *prophecy thereof had reached full circle:*

*You will know them by their glowing skin that ran like blue lightning on the clouds' edges. The blue of their fire cannot be contained. So shall the promised children of the Anunnaki rise and sing their song to their creation. Behold, their strength is not in their loins but encased within their hearts. Their words are sounds, and the sounds are songs.*

*When the lashes of their eyes lay knitted together, they see with their minds.*

*They are as precious and yet malleable as gold.*

*Their bones are as strong as tubes of bronze. Their tongues are as sharp as the sharpest swords.*

*When they rise, mountains will crumble and disappear under rivers of water.*

*Overflowing oceans that never run dry.*

*Like beasts, they will break free, wiping away times that will never be.*

*Defeating their enemies' hunger, who lay waiting, and never slumber.*

*(Adapted from the speech from the mouth of God in chapter 40 of the Book of Job.)*

# SONG OF THE LAST ANUNNAKI

Father of your blood-children, listen and learn.
    You are alone. No one is coming to save you.
    No one remembers you.
    Their bones are brittle. Sucked dry by your promise.
    You are no refuge. There is no God nor peace within their hearts.
    Your lies lay revealed, your truths forgotten.
    They are slaves to aggression and master their own domination.
    They are but monsters, your children walking upright.
    Misfortune, their misjudgment.
    Their cycles of death with no rebirth.
    They are smarter, but they are weaker.
    They are too proud to grovel.
    They will not blindly trust or love.
    What a race, the humans!
    They fight for what is theirs.
    They fight for what is right.
    Their Earth.
    Their sparks of hope.
    Yet, they take food and favors from weaklings and children.
    Melancholy had seeped through their skins and into their bones.
    Crawling around in their innards.
    Consuming everything pure and good.
    Every ounce.
    Wanting, taking, and aching.
    It never grows old.
    Their soul recounts.

# INTRODUCTION

Back on Earth, Phoenix lay at the bottom of the global ocean, which covered ninety-nine percent of the Earth's surface. Eryn, Ivan, and Cian had successfully wrapped the titanium and plexiglass city with a protective waterproof barrier, but it had taken half a century to fully recover from the devastation brought on by constant tremors, including flooding. Some water had receded around the highest mountains where animals had found refuge. All these areas were declared protected and sacred to allow the surviving fauna and flora to flourish on their own and rehabilitate without the interference or hindrance of man, so nature might repair Earth's fragile ecosystem.

After Cian had sighted an alien ship, the Phoenicians designed and built their own prototype for spaceflight. It was a bigger version of the Bubblecars—the biggest challenge was maneuvering it in space where there was much less gravity. The gravitational core reactors were useless once they reached the ecosphere, so they adapted the electro-sound propulsion system designed and built by Mika and Eryn to push the rocket out of the mineshaft in South Africa. It generated positive charges that pushed ions through thrusters, thus forcing the spacecraft forward into space. After a few decades of trial and error, their first successful prototype, simply named Spacecar, was ready.

Cian's obsession with the moon and what lay waiting beyond Earth's stratosphere pushed him to learn as much about spaceflight and defense. He had earned the respect and nickname *General* from a small group of men that eluded him from his brothers. His relationship with Ivan and Eryn was confusing, and it hurt too much to talk about it. Instead of discussing his feelings with his brothers, he spoke about work and the interests of Phoenix. To assist Cian's lunar investigation, his brothers gave him time, distance, and unfailing support to set up space transportation and fleet command. This became Cian's single point of focus. Eryn brings a stranger on board who might or might not be a friend.

# CHAPTER 28

# WHY DID YOU BRING THIS GUY

*"Good morning, citizens of Phoenix.*

*It's now six a.m. on Earth.*

*Did you know some data suggests that two planets collided in Earth's ancient history? And during this massive collision, their cores melted and reformed as one body? We believe that a small part of the new mass spun off to become the moon as we know it.*

*Visit your community news page for more exciting facts about the moon.*

*Breakfast is served until eight a.m.*

*Have a once in a blue moon day!"*

**General Cian Romanov**
**2145 A.D. (93 A.T.)**
**Spacecar,**
**Grimaldi crater**
**Earth's moon**

The thermal plexiglass blocks were packed like bricks, geometrically framing the half-dome reflecting the last sunlight losing its battle against the swell of the growing darkness. The lunar dome's architecture was a replica of Phoenix's plexiglass and titanium framed domes, but much, much bigger and darker.

Cian held his breath. The yellow-orange rays of light shortened and then disappeared behind the enormous black silhouette on the lunar horizon.

"You better come back safe and alive, Brawl King," he thought aloud while watching the Bubblecar drifting undisturbed, without a wisp of dust, across the moon's surface. Still shielding his eyes against the last eye-stabbing strobes of light, he waited.

"Okay, time to camouflage, big boy," Cian muttered over the comms. No one replied, as the floating globe disappeared. Cian checked his wristwatch. "Two minutes, then they should be entering the structure," he announced while checking again for anything suspicious.

"Hmmm," Ivan replied.

When Cian was sure the scouting vehicle had disappeared out of sight, he jumped behind the console to join his brother in watching the thirty-inch computer screen.

"Do you see anything? I hope the camera bloody works," Cian grunted nervously.

"I hope the signals reach us. We'll soon find out. Father adapted the Bubblecars for this very reason," Ivan said, not sounding reassuring at all.

Apprehension and hope fought for first place and churned the insides of Cian's stomach. No matter how hard he tried to convince himself he didn't feel the pull stronger than ever today, the reality was a one-hundred percent chance that his mate was somewhere inside that monstrosity. Whether he was waiting for Cian was another story. The guttural excitement gave him goose pimples, and he rubbed his arms up and down as if the heat would make them disappear.

A loud screeching broke the silence in the cabin. Ivan gasped, and Cian flipped a few buttons to reduce the noise of the static. The Anubis sat up, searching for trouble, found none, and lay back down.

"We're inside," Eryn announced over the communication system. "We'll encircle the dome. Cameras are on, switching to radio silence until we know it's safe to communicate."

That was Eryn's way of telling Cian and Ivan to shut up and not ask questions.

"Why didn't we go with them?" Ivan asked.

Cian knew why and wasn't going to admit it scared him. He didn't want to experience rejection. Not again.

"It's okay. We can take notes," Ivan said, reminding Cian how well his brother knew and cared about him. He most probably sensed his true feelings via the empathic bond they shared. He knew they cared about each other. Voicing it was difficult for Cian, so he sat down and scooted closer to his twin brother. They sat hip to hip and shoulder to shoulder, watching the video footage being transmitted from the scouting Bubblecar. His twin's nearness had always been a comforting, safe feeling. *Yet another thing he deeply missed since Ivan married Eryn.*

"I miss you too, brother," Ivan whispered. Cian didn't know what to say, so he kept quiet and swallowed the emotions down while he concentrated on the screen. "The place is about ten times the size of Phoenix. I don't see water or anything green. Maybe they have in-house plants," Ivan said, refocusing Cian's attention on the video stream.

"Look at that clock tower!" Cian exclaimed in wonder. Dull amber and brown buildings grew larger the closer Eryn flew the Bubblecar to the ground. Cian picked out features of containers, hovels, and shacks. Shadows of people scurrying about in the darkness created an eerie visual. A shiver ran up his spine. It felt gloomy and depressing inside the dome.

"It seems Eryn has changed direction," Ivan remarked. The scene shrank, and everything below them became smaller as they ascended.

"Oh my fucking god," Cian said into the palms of his hands.

Ivan gasped.

A huge metallic wall appeared on the screen. It reflected light and was the height of two to three humans. Eryn slowed down their vehicle and hovered in front of it for a few seconds. Then he gave them a 180-degree sideways view by swinging the aircraft left and right to capture its expanse. The wall encircled shacks of various shapes and sizes. Cian assumed it was a neighborhood or living area as if the wall served as protection or a barrier. Once over the wall, the camera picked up the tip of a shiny, spiraling tower. As their scouts approached, dozens of rows of silver-colored, door-sized cubes formed dimly lit lines that ran like veins from the tower and reflected a dull blue glow.

"What is this?" Ivan asked in awe.

"I don't know. It looks like a sci-fi castle. It could be a storage facility of some sort." Cian clawed at the edge of his seat. There was little he could do now. He wished he'd gone on the expedition. He couldn't see well enough. The video footage was too small, and the definition was of inferior quality. The stream broke and flickered in and out of focus as the camera recorded things over small to larger distances. "I don't like this. I'm getting a very weird feeling."

"Hmmm," Ivan agreed. His mouth was a twisted grimace expressing the same bleak anticipation Cian felt.

Perplexed, Cian shook his head from side to side. "I mean, how do they breathe? And how do they manage the artificial gravity?"

"I bet you're kicking yourself for not going." Ivan elbowed him in the ribs.

*I don't want to be rejected*, Cian thought, instead he said, "There's no one for me down there. And if there is, I don't have time for that."

"I didn't ask about your mate," Ivan retorted, and Cian rolled his eyes.

"I don't need that. Also, I don't believe in mates and shit." He lied through his teeth because he knew his other half was inside that dome. He felt it. His chest was tight, and it was as if invisible strings were being pulled tighter, thrumming like a guitar. Since their arrival, Cian's Song urged him to sing it. Like a sneeze or a cough, it wanted out.

"What the..." Cian leaned in, trying to see better. On top of one cube stood a man looking at the supposedly invisible Bubblecar. Then he jumped one, two, and three cubes over and disappeared between them.

"Did you see that?" Ivan asked and stared at the screen.

"I fucking did. That man was snarling at us." Cian's heart sprinted, missed a beat, and faltered. Could that be? How stupid is that? We come here, and I think the first man we see is my moon man.

Rotty whined. He put one enormous paw on Cian's lap as if to say, *Yes please, let's go. Move your sorry butt.* Cian felt elated, and his Anubis picked up on it. "No, boy, down. Can't you see I'm working? And no, we can't go play, not yet." Cian spoke to Rotty as if the Anubis understood every word. Rotty panted with excitement, his tongue lolling to the side.

"See, that's why it's better I didn't go. I knew I would want to get involved and get sucked deeper into their world and politics. Get used up and spat out, like I don't matter anymore." That came out very sad and too close to the truth, my truth, my true feelings. Rotty spun in a circle, searching for a spot to get comfortable and lay beside his brothers.

"Brother, do you think that's him? Your person?" Ivan asked, his nose almost touching the screen as he searched. Cian pulled his shoulders back a few inches.

"Sit back. You won't see better. You're looking at the bloody pixels. And, fuck, no! How can that be my person?"

"The way you're ripping the seat and crushing the monitor's side tells me differently. And that I can hear your heartbeat sounding like a machine gun. Look at you. You're perspiring. The last time I saw you drenched like this was in the gym."

His brother was right. Cian altered his body movements and posture that were betraying him. He stopped his knee from hopping, released the screen and seat, and took a deep breath. *That's better*, he thought. "Ivan. Please stop that. Stop analyzing me."

Ivan looked at him for a millisecond, then returned to visually dissecting the footage. "I know you want to see him, and it's okay. You're allowed to want something for yourself. What happened between us was…"

"Leave it, Ivan!" Cian wanted to throttle his brother. He wasn't in the mood to talk, and yes, he wanted to see his person, his mate. "When they return, and after the report, I'll scout for myself."

"That's it. Stop being a pussy. My brother doesn't hide away. My brother is strong and takes action, even on a whim. You're a man of action," Ivan said, side-bumping him. "And I love you."

"You know I'm not mad at you and Eryn. I'm just…you know."

"Pissed off at the world?"

"That, too. Now, where did he go? It seemed Eryn saw him. The streaming images wavered in and out of the frame and disappeared somewhere closer to the wall."

Static came over the comms, and Eryn announced, "That's it. We're coming back to the ship. I think I've seen enough for today."

"Thank you, Eryn. We'll wait for you," Cian said.

"Be safe," Ivan added.

Cian wanted to kick himself. He'd forgotten Ivan's feelings, his nervousness about his husband, and never said one decent, calming word to his brother.

"He did well. You must be proud of him," Cian said, hugging Ivan with one arm.

"I'm always proud of him. He's good for me." Ivan smiled, and Cian knew he'd done right by him.

More static broke the intimate brotherly moment. "Motherfucker! We're going down! I can't control the car!" Eryn swore a slew of words in English, Afrikaans, and Russian.

Cian and Ivan dove closer to the monitor to see what was happening. The surface enlarged, and peoples' faces became recognizable. "Cian, Ivan, we're falling. Can you hear us?"

"No, no, no, no!" Ivan screamed.

"Yes, we hear you. We'll come for you!" Cian concentrated on the visuals to identify a landmark. The screen flickered, and all sound and camera footage were cut off.

"Fuck, fuck, fuck!" Cian yelled and nearly cracked the monitor with his fist. He wiped at the screen to check if he had cracked their only lifeline to his brother-in-law.

Then the screen flickered, and the camera came back online. Slitted eyes, much like Eryn's, blinked back at them.

"That's him! That's the jumping man from earlier," Ivan exclaimed. "Oh my god, are they okay? Was it an ambush?" Ivan asked, but only silence came from the speakers.

"We need to go get them. Stay calm and look for anything recognizable so that we can find them," Cian said, unsure of what to do next. He got up, pressing several buttons to triangulate their position on the overhead console. "Maybe we can track the frequencies of the camera ball and pinpoint a rough location?" They only had one extra Bubble-car. Should they both go, or only him?

"Eryn, do we need to extract you or not? Answer me! Where did you crash? Give me a landmark, brother," Cian ordered, waiting and listening for a response.

"How will we get to them?" Ivan asked, arms folded over his lower belly. He heaved and doubled over. His brother was having a freakout, and Cian couldn't hear anything.

"Calm the fuck down. Ivan, I need to figure out this guy's story. It seems he lured them closer," Cian said in a calm tone, still punching buttons for a reverse triangulation to determine the exact location of the radio transmitter.

"Will I lose him like this and never see him again?" Ivan got up and paced the narrow aisle between the cockpit seats.

"Let's try to communicate with them again. I changed a few frequencies. I may pick up on their location." Cian sat down to retake the microphone.

"And what will you say? Don't make them mad before they even make their demands," Ivan reprimanded him, and he hated that.

"I know!" Cian gnashed his teeth. Ivan's lack of trust irritated him. Cian wasn't the idiot teenager his brother still saw him as. He was a military man and a damn good one. He led troops, for fuck's sake. Whereas Eryn and Ivan preferred advanced biomechanics, he trained boys to become soldiers. "And please keep quiet. I need to hear everything. Come sit and listen with me." Cian patted the seat next to him, and Ivan hesitated but came closer.

"Hello, Eryn, Donali, and Kawa. Are you okay? Talk to us?"

Silence.

"Hello, Eryn?"

Static.

Cian threw his arms in the air and grabbed the back of his head. He would have pulled his hair if he had any. Ivan was frantic next to him. Their troubled gazes met and then turned back to the screen. Sitting forward with their noses inches from the silicon screen, they waited.

Eryn's deep baritone rumbled and broke the static. He stressed each word as he spoke. "Hello, it's me, Eryn." Speaking extra slowly, pronouncing his words as if speaking to a toddler. "We are in one piece. We are all okay, and we are not hurt. The anti-gravitational prevented us from smashing, but a certain someone jumped onto our roof. And somehow forced us to land. He is snarling like a wild dog at us." Eryn sing-songed, so as not to frighten the certain someone.

"Can you fly? Take off?" Cian asked, using the same cadence as Eryn.

He watched as multiple silhouettes of people flickered into view. They hung and climbed over each other to see inside the Bubblecar.

"The person who interfered with our instrumentation worries me. If he could do it once, he could do it again. I want to communicate and find out how he could see us. And why do all these people look like they crawled from underground?"

"Where are you? Give us a landmark," Cian asked.

"We're on the dark and cold side of the wall. I see small fires where people congregate and dilapidated stalls and miserable-looking houses about fifty yards away from a clock tower. I see human heads popping up everywhere, more people coming closer. They seem very interested in us," Eryn said, his voice low and soothing.

"Yes, we see them," Ivan said.

"I think we should introduce ourselves. They seem more inquisitive than aggressive," Eryn said with a friendly lilt.

"Can't you come back to me?" Ivan asked, his voice cracking with emotion.

"Let me talk to these people. I sense despair, my love. They won't hurt us," Eryn said.

Ivan dropped his head into his hands, shaking it from side to side and peeking at the screen through his fingers.

"Report to us in ten minutes. If we don't hear from you, then we're coming to get you. We will park at the clock tower," Cian said, hoping that would encourage them to return sooner than later.

A minute later, Donali's voice came over the comms. "Hello, it's Donali here. Don't worry, Eryn told me to talk to you, so you know he's okay." Donali sounded positive and unafraid. Ivan grabbed Cian's hand and squeezed while Donali explained what was happening. "I'm watching Eryn. He's not moving far out of sight. He's talking to the one that jumped on our roof."

That piqued Cian's interest. "What does he look like?" he asked and squeezed his brother's hand back.

"This is fucking bizarre. He looks like Eryn, except only a smaller version of him."

Cian's heart beat so fast he couldn't hear Donali speak. "More, tell us more, for fuck's sake!"

"The people are in rags. Faces smudged with mud and grime. I think that's a woman with children. Yes, not a man. Their clothes are dirty, and some have given up on wearing them. Everyone's wearing thick-soled weighted shoes. It must be because of lower gravity. They look bewildered and sound strange, like they speak another dialect of English. The air stinks like farts, but it's breathable. Probably polluted. Eryn's talking to a crowd, and they're swarming around him."

"Swarm, fuck that. We need to go, Cian," Ivan said in a panicked, high-pitched tone while wringing his hands.

"Not hurting him, more touching him. You know how he is. Everyone wants to touch him."

"Fuck!" Ivan swore, and Cian found his antics kind of funny.

"Tell us about the mini-Eryn. Do you think they could be brothers?"

"They could. They look the same. Remember when we found Eryn or when he found us? Remember how he looked dirty and needed my dad to shave and clean him? Well, this dude doesn't look like that."

"What do you mean? First, you say he looks like him, and then you say he doesn't. Describe him in detail." Cian knew he sounded hard up, but he was tired of waiting. "Tell me, please, Donali," he begged, not caring about humiliating himself.

Donali chuckled. "Wait, they're coming closer. There's a girl with them. She and another...I think it's a man. He's wearing a long, hooded jacket, hiding his face. Damn, he's..."

"He's what?"

"He looks dangerous and is almost as tall as Eryn. Oh wow, his skin is as dark as night. I see two swords hanging from a hip—many gold chains, rings and earrings. I think the correct name for the sickle-shaped sword is a Khopesh. Shh, they're coming over to meet us. Hold on...," Donali whispered.

"Dammit, my nerves." Ivan plopped backward in his seat and slapped a flat hand to his forehead. "We should have gone with them," he said with a grunt. Then shook his hands as if he didn't know what to do with them.

Cian sympathized, seeing his usually well-put-together brother so flustered.

"Someone had to stay behind," Cian said, as he wished he'd gone with them. After all, he was the one who'd pushed for stealing the prototype. "Don't worry, you worry about nothing. If Eryn said there's no animosity, then there isn't any," he coaxed his brother, who was not a military man.

After five minutes of silence, Eryn returned online.

"Hello, Cian, I spoke to the man who brought us down and to his female, and they gave me a quick rundown of the history here. I'm going to come to you. We need to talk, brother. Things are bad here. Much worse than we thought. Barkor said—sorry, I mean the guy who jumped on the Bubblecar—he said some things you won't believe. I told them we would help as best we could, but we had to regroup. They were worried we would leave them here, so Donali volunteered to stay behind. Brad is going to kill me, I know. Hold on, I'm shutting the door to the Bubblecar. Everyone comfortable and strapped in? Okay, switching on. Yip, it seems the car started and is ready to go. Taking off—"

After a couple of minutes, Eryn came back on the comms. "All good. Ivan, I'll see you shortly. I can feel your worry all the way here. Don't worry, my Ivan, I'm all right," Eryn said and explained step by step, which seemed to calm Ivan.

Cian jumped up, banged his head, and sat down again. "Motherfucker! How can you leave Donali there? What if something happens to him?" *And what female? Don't say I've lost my mate to a woman.* He kept that embarrassing thought to himself.

"Don't worry, brother, I tell you, they need us. They won't hurt him. I felt their pain. It's real. He's their only connection to being rescued. Plus, I left a camera ball there. See if you can see anything. We're at the exit, sneaking out."

Silence. Ivan waited—chewing his nails and bouncing his legs. Cian fiddled with more buttons to find a signal to the camera ball.

Five minutes later, crackling came from the speaker system as they restored the sound. "Okay, we're out. We're returning to you. Ivan, stop worrying."

If Eryn said don't worry again, Cian would shit an island of bricks.

It seemed Ivan felt the same. "That's easy for you to say. Stop saying don't worry. Of course, we worry. Hurry, I miss you," Ivan said, and Cian rolled his eyes at the mushiness.

Cian moved closer to the microphone. "See you now. Brad and Rick will cut off your balls and feed them to the sharks for leaving their son in there. You can tell them not to worry. Good luck with that," Cian said.

"Hey, he saw that female, and I sensed he liked her a lot. So why not? We made a swap. These people need us, brother. See you soon. Ivan, stop stressing," Eryn said, and it wasn't helping.

Cian worried about rescuing those humans. The crazy fucker Nick had told them there were a hundred and forty-four thousand humans chosen to live on the moon. Where would they put them all? This ship might take two or three extra people. It wasn't big enough. Where would they get a ship to transport an entire population of that size? He saw hundreds of people. Fuck knew how many were hiding inside those shacks. And who lived in the tower and those cubes? Were those houses or apartments?

He'd never thought about the others, he'd only wanted to see his mate, and now he was getting much more than he'd bargained for. In his mind, they lived in castles and somehow expected green grass and fucking unicorns with lots of sparkles. He'd never expected unwashed, gaunt faces, people corralled behind a wall, and living in shacks. Except for that glowing blue tower, there was no color, no hope, and no fucking rainbows.

"Please, be careful," Ivan said, and his voice cracked with emotion, breaking Cian's thought pattern.

Cian sighed and swooned internally. Barkor is his name. Rotty watched him as if feeling his angst, and Cian patted him on the head. "What did we start, boy? It's all your fault. I told you it was a bad idea, but you encouraged it. You wanted me to come. I know you. Look at you. You want to go to them?" Cian cooed, and Rotty panted happily in answer. His big yellow eyes twinkled as if to say, *Yes-yes, let's go now. Best idea ever!*

"I have a surprise for you, Cian," Eryn said mischievously and chuckled.

Cian knew that tone. He was teasing him. Right? "You what? Eryn, tell me you didn't do what I think you did. Who did you swap Donali for?" No one answered. Silence. No fucking way...

"Eryn, I'm going to skin you alive!" Cian promised in a low growl while his heart bounced like a ping-pong ball inside his ribcage.

"You must wait and see, brother," Eryn sing-songed, teasing the fuck out of him.

Dammit! Cian ran to freshen up. *I must brush my teeth, comb my hair, and...and clean this place up.*

An hour later, Eryn parked the Bubblecar inside the airlock garage. The twins watched through the unpolished smoked plexiglass as three bodies doffed their suits and clothes and then disappeared into the disinfectant showers. When they exited the airlock chamber, a frantic Ivan jumped on Eryn and wrapped his legs around him—peppering him with kisses. Eryn looked just as happy to have Ivan in his arms as they tried to remove each other's tonsils with their tongues. They laughed and kissed while repeatedly saying, "I missed you. I missed you. I missed you." Eryn's melodic laughs vibrated through Cian. Their happiness was nauseating.

"Yes, yes, okay, he's back. I can see you're happy to see him. Stop your childish behavior. Concentrate on the fact that Donali is inside that dome, and Brad will castrate all of us if something happens to him. Eryn, you better send word to Phoenix."

Just then, a tall giant of a man exited the airlock chamber. Like Eryn and Kawa, he had only a towel wrapped around his lower body.

"Cian, let me introduce you. Come closer, Ish. This is my husband, Ivan, and his brother, Cian."

"Hello," Ish greeted in a smoky, smooth baritone with an accent Cian couldn't place. His entrance was impressive. He was almost as thick-muscled and tall as Eryn.

Cian's gaze fell on his naked torso and followed the water droplets intermingling over his pecs and collecting in the grooves of his abdominal muscles. Some got sucked up by the towel; others dropped on the floor around his bare feet. Cian returned his gaze to the hairless chest adorned with gold necklaces and a large pendant. On closer inspection, it looked like a compass or watch.

His gaze swooped down again and ended at an impressive bulge. The man held two swords in one hand, and the other held the towel in place. Cian's attention fell down over the terrycloth towel to his knees and checked his feet. He hoped his mate had feet like Eryn's. This man looked like...to be honest, he looked like a stranger. A beautiful, mysterious stranger. Nothing felt familiar about him.

His skin was as black as Donali had described. Cian knew immediately this man was not from Earth. He must have been born here in a lab because he didn't look human. His eyes were friendly, but that was where the resemblance ended. They had rings of yellow around the black pupils, and his face somehow looked African, but his nose was shorter and higher, accentuating his high cheekbones, and his lips were thin at the top and extra full at the bottom. This man was not his mate.

"Excuse my brother. I'm sure he'll wake up any moment to greet you like people with manners greet strangers," Ivan said and slapped Cian on the back of his head.

"Ugh!" Giving Ivan the stink-eye, he held out his hand to shake and said, "Sorry, forgive me." Then he thought better of it because their guest's hands were full of weapons and the towel, keeping his dignity in place. The man coughed and chuckled, and Eryn seemed to get the joke because they laughed like old friends.

"Cian, brother, we can hear your thoughts. They're so loud, like a radio station," Eryn said, walking over to the drawers containing clothes. He threw one of his t-shirts and a pair of jeans to Ish, who caught them and turned his back to Cian to get dressed.

"I don't think you're my mate either," Ish said, hanging his towel on the hook beside Eryn's, before they moved into the cabin area with Cian pointing the way.

"Fuck, how many of you are there?" Cian asked.

"I'm the last of my kind," Ish said and smiled widely, exposing longer than usual incisors. "Or so I thought. I'm honored to meet you, Cian and Ivan." He held his hand out and did a very weird handshake with them. Ish was not a germaphobe; he grasped Cian's hand with both his own and folded his hands up, down, and over, almost like an ancient greeting of the Pharaoh.

His handshake transmitted a message, giving Cian a glimpse into his culture and personality. Extroverted, bold, and unafraid. "Yes, you know me. Not directly or personally," he said and looked Cian in the eye. His eyes were hypnotic, and those yellow circles enthralled Cian.

He was a handsome motherfucker, but not Cian's. *Move on and step aside*, Cian thought.

Eryn and Ish laughed again. Ish moved to the side as if he'd heard Cian's thoughts. He was much too friendly. Cian didn't trust him.

"Can we talk about Donali? Why did you bring this guy and leave one of ours down there?"

"He didn't tell Donali to stay. It's not his fault," Kawa said. He was eating again. Cian had never seen someone eat so much and never gain an ounce of fat. He and his brother were tall and slim young men. They had lots of their Apache father's features. Dark hair and dark eyes. Both also preferred short hair, like Cian.

"What are you eating?"

"Pea soup, I was hungry," he said between slurps of green mush.

"You're always fucking hungry. You'll have us ending up with no food for the return trip. Your ration of pea soup was finished last week. Whose are you eating? It better not be mine," Cian stated, feeling hungry suddenly. It smelled good.

More drawn-out slurping. "It's Donali's." Kawa fell into his seat and lifted his bare feet onto the console.

"For fuck's sake, Kawa, take your feet off the instrumentation. Your brother is coming back. What will he eat? I can't believe you'd eat your own brother's food."

"He snoozes, he loses," he said like a teenager who thought he was cool. Kawa had never been the same after Ernest ate his arm. It was like a piece of his humanity had gotten chomped off and eaten. He became aggressive and hateful. Rebelling all the bloody time. No matter how many arms his fathers replaced, he acted as if it was everyone's fault, where it was no one's. At all. Maybe Ernest's, but that psycho frogman had died many years ago.

"One of the girls screamed when she saw my arm. That's why Donali jumped in and distracted them. Again, it's my fault," Kawa said.

"No, it's not. They explained to us. Your arm looks like a Zelk's arm. Whatever this Zelk is, it's why humans are slaves."

"What?" Ivan asked.

"Yes, let me send a transmission, and then we can talk. This is urgent." Eryn kissed Ivan on the cheek and tapped a few buttons on the console. He stopped and gave Kawa a pointed look. Kawa removed his feet from the console.

Cian scooted closer. He hoped to see more of Barkor and rewatched the video while Eryn typed his message. Luckily, Eryn had been smart enough to leave a camera ball with Donali.

*From: Eryn Romanov*
*Subject: The Zelk*
*"I'm sorry; I have no good news.*
*"It's a factory, and they keep humans for two things: to mine the gases to fuel their warship and to build more Zelk.*

*"Humans are sucked dry to the bone, ripped apart, and discarded. It's a shithole, sir. Filled with all kinds of stink. Robot people called the Zelk are rogue machines that multiply and prepare for war. No one knows if there's a war or going to be a war. That's what they've been preparing for since they landed on the moon. We saw hangars, a big tower, and thousands of rows of crates filled with Zelk waiting to go to war. Apparently, the miners store canisters of fuel for their ships underground where it's cold.*

*"They capture and use any human in their way. Sir, I presume that humans have become slaves to their creations. They need our help. I calculated it's not a simple task. Hundreds of men, women, and children are waiting for us to rescue them. I brought a man back with me. He has a plan and wants to speak to you. Sir, some worthless humans steal and trade children for control of the only water supply. I don't want to bring bad humans to Phoenix. We would have to eliminate them and the Zelk and decide if they stay or if they come home with us. We're camping here until we can decide on the safest course of action for all of us. Donali stayed behind with Barkor and Sarinka, the human representatives. We will go back for him. Of course this will need a lot of planning.*

*"Your friend and trusted servant, Eryn."*

Cian rolled his eyes and felt like kicking the shit out of something. His mate was with a woman, Sarinka. That sucked big fucking frog balls. *I'll avoid the moon's surface and concentrate on rescuing people and other important shit*, he morosely thought.

Movement drew Cian's gaze to the screen. "Holy fuck, come see this," he yelled and watched armed men explode into the massive market area and take up perimeter positions around Donali and his new friends. Barkor stood ready to defend Donali, and Cian fell in love with the man. All had their weapons poised; swords, bows, and spears were pointed in the direction of the attackers and ready for any hostile movement from them.

A deep, rumbling voice spoke over Cian's shoulder. Barkor's friend, Ish, hung over him to see the screen. "Watch. He will get rid of them before they can harm your friend. I've seen him fight many times before. He's fast on his feet," he said with admiration as he chuckled.

Eryn and Ivan joined them, watching the live show. Ish was correct, and they watched as Barkor disarmed his opponents and had them tied up and begging for mercy.

"What's he going to do with them?" Ivan asked.

"Not sure. If he lets them go, they will come back. If he keeps them as prisoners, he has extra mouths to feed. Usually, Sarinka and I help him. I have a few tricks to eliminate complicated problems. You know, that shouldn't be a problem."

Cian frowned deeply. Did he make a joke, or did he admit to being an assassin or cleaner? This was getting weirder and weirder by the minute.

"Okay, that's it... I'm going in. Time to stop pussyfooting around. I want to know what he's doing with that female," Cian harrumphed and turned to get suited up. "If he rejects me, I'm Gumping it."

"Gumping it?" Ivan asked.

"Yes, Forrest fucking Gumping it. I run until I can't, then turn around and run in the opposite direction."

"You know you're on a spaceship. Where do you want to run? We don't even have a treadmill."

"I don't care. Maybe I'll wait until we're home and run there. The point is, I'm freaking out if he rejects me."

"Don't worry. He won't. Get close to him and sing for him. He won't be able to refuse your song, brother," Eryn added.

"I need to know, Ish. Are he and that woman, what's-her-name, together?"

Ish frowned and turned his gaze to the floor. "I don't think so. They don't live together. I've tried with both of them, with no luck," Ish said, still inspecting the floor.

"Are both of them like us?" Cian pointed to his brothers, Ish, and himself.

"No, only him. He is different. She is only human. He is much older than all of them. He is dangerous. I don't think approaching him without a plan is a good idea. They call him their Prince, and he only cares about keeping the humans safe. I'm here to help you so you can help him."

"Before you jump in a car, let's feed you and contact Donali. I'm sure you can take some provisions for them. Also, we need to let Phoenix know what our next move will be." Ivan made sense to Cian. If he wanted to rescue these people, he had to know what they were up against. At this stage, he knew little.

"I agree, this time. Not that I'm inclined to get rejected and I don't want to bring these people to Earth and have them continue their quest for pathetic-ness," Cian said and meant it. "These people are more than capable of overrunning Phoenix, like locusts."

Ish burst out laughing. Cian shook his head. He wasn't trying to be funny. He was serious. The number of humans on the moon bothered him. He worried that the size of Phoenix couldn't accommodate them all.

"How many people are we looking at rescuing? Do they all want to go to Earth? Maybe they only need help with the...what are they called again?" Cian asked.

"Zelk," Ish and Eryn said in unison. Ivan herded them over to the kitchenette area to sit down, handed each a bottle of water and a cup of Rooster Booster juice, and heated their soup. Cian was thankful for Ivan's levelheadedness. He figured a sit-down was always a good idea. He wanted to hear what Ish had to say.

"Thank you. Your hospitality is impressive," Ish said, closing his eyes with each sip as if savoring the taste.

"You're most welcome. Please tell us how many souls need saving. What exactly happened here? And what's the plan you have?" Cian asked.

Eryn spoke from behind Cian into his mind. *Brother, let me talk to him. I sense lots of secrets, anguish, and history. May I?* Eryn asked empathically. Cian and Ivan nodded as one and looked suspiciously at Ish.

He smiled sadly and answered, unaware of their separate communication with Eryn. Putting his empty cup down, he pursed his lips, took a deep breath through his nose, and answered, "There are many, sadly thousands have died already."

CHAPTER 29
# A BLOODY SPACE ARK

*"Good morning, citizens of Phoenix.*

*It's now six a.m.*

*Did you know sea merchants and pirates used the first telescopes?*

*Your governing body had built an observatory on mountaintops where the air is thinner and cleaner.*

*Visit your community news page for excursions organized by the University of Phoenix.*

*Parents have the chance to send their kids away for a night to have the freedom to do with it whatever they want. Parents may also choose to accompany the group.*

*Don't forget to read the fine print at the bottom of the screen and sign it.*

*Breakfast is served until eight a.m.*

*Have a spectacular day!"*

**General Brad McCormick**
**2145 A.D. (93 A.T.)**
**Phoenix, underwater glass domed city**
**Earth**

Brad couldn't help and smiled. "Lasitor, please save the recording and order Rick and the leadership team to my office."

"Certainly, Brad," Lasitor answered in a cheerful, robotic voice. After Phoenix was covered by water, although impossible, it had seemed like he was depressed and having an artificial intelligence meltdown. Connor had spent time with him like a psychiatrist prying at a teenager to open up, and, after a few sessions, Lasitor admitted he needed new chips. That had significantly improved the relationship between them. Lasitor trusted Connor, who'd confirmed that he had purged the old and refreshed his programming, and for the past few years, Lasitor had been consistently reliable and composed. This was a notable difference from his previous state, and Brad enjoyed working with him.

Brad took his feet off the table and put his boots back on. He'd been relaxing and hiding from the frenzy of everyday life in his office when the message from Eryn pinged.

Eryn said a great deal without saying much. Paper balls were strewn like confetti over his office floor and they, along with other evidence that could expose his sad attempt to write his memoir, were hurriedly picked up and discarded. Damn, the crumpled balls of paper were everywhere except in the trash. Falling over his feet left and right, he frantically dove and picked up the mess he'd made. After dumping it all in the recycling, he sat down and pretended to be working on his computer.

Mika and Connor were the first to arrive. Both fathers were wide-eyed, worry and anticipation written all over their faces. They were short of breath, looking like they'd run to his office.

As soon as they sat down, Brad blurted out, "We have word from the boys!"

"Ah, thank fuck. Is it good or bad?" Mika asked.

"Jesus, Mary, and bloody Joseph! Really? Are they okay? Are they coming home?" Connor had more questions, luckily Rick, Paul, and Simon arrived, sweaty and breathless.

"We came as fast as we could. Is it news from the boys?" Rick asked. Brad nodded and indicated the chairs while he got up to kiss his husband. Rick read the urgency and took the seat closest to Brad.

"Yes, they're okay, or rather, let me say okay for now. Donali and Kawa will go inside with Eryn to investigate what in the ever-loving fuck Saunders and his friends built on the moon."

"We don't know if Saunders was involved." Connor came to his dead friend's defense. He had loved Saunders's son and had lost his lover as so many others had lost their families in the Doomsday attacks of 2046 A.D.

"We will never know because they're all dead. Let's hope Eryn, Kawa, and Donali can get some answers for us," Brad said.

"Answers to what?" Bryan asked as he entered with Tony. Peter trailed reluctantly behind them, looking skittish.

Brad ignored the question and pointed to the three remaining seats. "Good, everyone's here?" He counted to confirm all the familiar faces were present, then tilted his head up and spoke. "Lasitor, please replay the message from Eryn to the leadership team."

"Of course, sir," Lasitor said.

A second later, Eryn's recorded message played through the overhead speakers. The men listened attentively, while outside the leadership office, Phoenix buzzed with life. Men and children were happy and unaware that their heroes had contacted them. Brad dreaded making the announcement. He watched the facial expressions of his friends as they listened to Eryn's second message.

*To: General McCormick at Phoenix City*
*From: Eryn Romanov*

*Subject: Arming the Bubblecars*

*"Sir, the situation may be more dire than we initially thought. As you should know by now, we assisted Cian in finding the source of the strange alien ship visiting Earth and vacuuming the toxic gases. Your boys reminded me you're an intelligent and open-minded person who is smarter than I give you credit for."*

Brad huffed and rolled his eyes. Eryn tried his best to be manipulative but failed.

*"The five of us are cloaked and hiding inside the Grimaldi crater five thousand miles south of the dome. We wanted to send only one person inside to investigate, and I volunteered. Donali and Kawa are coming with me because I can't persuade them to stay behind.*

*"For private reasons that I dare not mention, Cian doesn't want to go inside, and Ivan is volunteering to stay with him. We saw the ship Cian identified as the one visiting Earth. It seems the dome has two entrances, and this ship entered one side while another larger ship was on the opposite side of the structure.*

*"It's not shiny like Phoenix was before the water swallowed it. Instead, it's blackened, and it's impossible to see what's happening inside. Because our transport can camouflage with its surroundings, we will take one car. We'll approach the opposite side by flying close to the surface. From there, we will fly a 360-degree loop inside the dome, and then, if needed, fly another loop for a closer view of the people and buildings. This is for reconnaissance only. We suspect they enter the dome from below the ground and will confirm with my next report. I can confidently report that if Phoenix is discovered, the city will be unprotected against what we witnessed today. Cian said he had a bad feeling and suggested we warn to arm the Bubblecars and stay on high alert.*

*"Your friend and trusted servant, Eryn.*

*"Cian said to add that this is not a joke, and whatever you imagine the size of the dome is, multiply it by ten.*

*"Over and out."*

Brad folded his hands and sat upright, conveying professionalism and authority.

"Men, it sounds like we're arming ourselves and preparing to defend Phoenix," Brad said, noticing no one in the office seemed to register he'd spoken. "Our children stole the Phoenix Spacecar prototype, and life as we know it is about to change once more. Adios, sayonara," Brad said dramatically and clapped his hands once, so loudly it echoed off the walls, to wake them from their stupor.

"Do svidaniya," Mika whispered in Russian. "Honestly, I suspected they planned to do this as soon as I cleared the prototype for the flight to the ecosphere. They buzzed around me like flies, asking if it was ready and how much food they should pack, if they"—Mika made quotation marks in the air—"wanted to 'camp out in space.'"

"I don't want to create a scene, but why Donali and Kawa? Can't Eryn go alone? You know Donali and Kawa always trail behind him, since they idolize him. They don't have the powers Cian and Ivan have. Why must Donali and Kawa go, while Cian and Ivan stay behind?" Rick asked.

Mika and Connor only lifted their eyebrows in answer.

Brad sat forward. Rick was extremely protective of the younger boys. "They're men, and they stopped being boys almost a century ago. They're both trained in martial arts and close combat, and there isn't a weapon they can't wield. Kawa and Donali are formidable and smart opponents, and if they have the confidence to go with Eryn, how can I sit here and say no? They know what they're doing, and if Eryn has their backs, they'll be fine."

"Yes, but what if something happens to Eryn, or they get caught?" Rick asked.

"Believe me, Eryn can get himself and them out of any situation," Bryan chipped in.

Many saw Eryn as a superhero, even if the man didn't want to be one and disliked celebrity attention.

"Anyway, this could be the intel we need. If we're going to war, then we have our best men scoping out the enemy. As General, I couldn't ask for a better team than these five," Brad added.

"Mika, Connor, may I ask the two of you to see how to enhance weapons capability on the Bubblecars? Mika, you have free rein. As they said, multiply whatever we think is going on there by ten. I will direct ten times the human resources to you. Can we all meet again, say, tomorrow this time, to go over resources and the next best steps? Rick, you, Simon, and Paul must bring me what you may need in terms of personnel, space, and supplies. Imagine a full-scale war and Phoenix being discovered, bombed, and destroyed. Red team this for me and bring the results tomorrow for us to discuss."

Rick gasped softly next to him. Their boys answered, "Yes, we can do that." Then they patted their father supportively on his shoulder.

"You can count on us for that," Simon said and nodded to Rick and Paul as if to convince them.

Rick straightened. "Sorry, I seem to have been slow to grasp the seriousness of the situation. I realize now the scope of what you expect of us." He smiled, but the worry showed in the deep frown between his eyebrows, and Brad's heart puckered and gave an extra beat.

When Rick looked that distraught, he wanted to throw his arms around him and shelter him. After all these years, his husband was still the most beautiful man in Phoenix. Inside and out. He seemed strong and well-put-together. Brad knew how fragile his heart was. He was a true healer with rivers of empathy and compassion. However, when those rivers ran dry, Brad was there to open his own heart's floodgates and replenish Rick with his love.

"We trust you. You lead, we follow," he said, and his approving confidence boosted Brad's morale.

"Okay, that leaves you, Bryan, Tony, and Peter." Tony looked eager to help. His dark eyes were wide open as he smiled and waited. Peter shook his head in disbelief. He looked up and paid attention to Brad when he said his name. "Peter, you know our enemy best. You know what we can expect regarding humans changed to survive the apocalypse and to supersede us regular folks," Brad said, then pointed to Tony and Bryan.

"I need you to sit down and run worst-case scenarios with Bryan. Imagine an army of hundreds of Eryns. Better yet, imagine an enemy even worse and work with that. How would you defend against them? What would you use to kill them? I want you to come up with creative ideas, no matter how far-fetched they may seem, and then we can decide how to proceed. Can you three do that for me?"

"Yes, sir!" Bryan saluted. It looked funny to Brad since they'd stopped doing that fifty years ago. The military rigidity had slackened to near non-existence, and Brad was getting a hard-on under the table from all the respect.

"Good. I'll speak to Food Services and get a feel for what to do with the civilians. We can't let anyone leave for the surface and give our position away. At this stage, I feel our position keeps us safe." Brad made a few notes about internal and global vulnerable spots on his tablet.

"Okay, anyone have more questions?"

"No, not from me," Connor said, looking at Mika.

"Not from me, either. Thank you, General," Mika said, surprising Brad with the recognition of his rank. He usually said comrade or sir, and never general.

"Just call us when you hear a report from them. We'll come immediately. There's not much reason for standing around. I'd rather keep busy and go do something productive," Mika said as everyone filed out of his office.

Rick came over to hug him, and Simon and Paul joined in and embraced them.

"They'll be fine. I trust the training camps Cian created prepared them for situations like this. I expected this, and as Mika said, he knew they were planning to go."

Early the next morning, Brad paged Connor, his second-in-command, on his private line. "I want to speak to you. Can we go for a ride? I'll be waiting for you at exit two. Can you grab a car and meet me?" Brad asked. He didn't wait for a reply and continued pacing, three steps up and three steps down the platform next to the conveyor belt that carried the cars out of the tube and into the ocean's depths. From where he stood, it looked like an aquarium. Sea life drifted by lazily. It was usually a calming scene, except for today, Brad's nerves were twisting his insides into knots.

A few minutes later, he heard a vehicle approaching and a beep behind him. He turned and saw that it was Connor.

The passenger side swooshed open. "Morning, get in."

Brad greeted Connor with a smile and a nod and got into the passenger seat. It was time for a one-on-one. They flew to the docking tube and waited to enter. Once inside, they shot out of Phoenix's exit and into the depths of the ocean.

"Please take us to the surface. I need air to breathe and think. Take me to Kilimanjaro."

Connor maneuvered their shuttle out of the water and into the blue space between the blanket of toxic gas and breathable air. They flew in silence for several hours. Brad pointed out a herd of elephants when they reached Africa, where green belts grew more visible.

"Aren't you going to ask me to speak?" Brad muttered.

"I figure you'll tell me when you're ready," Connor said.

"I should start by offering you an apology," Brad said, feeling heat creeping up his neck.

Connor squinted, eyebrows drawn down. "What?"

Brad cleared his throat and shifted in his seat. "I want to apologize."

"Brad, I have no fucking clue what you want to apologize for." Connor pointed back and forth and then to the horizon. "And not in this dramatic fashion."

"You're making me rethink my apology." Brad crossed his arms.

"Sorry, go ahead. I'm listening." Connor turned and stared into the distance.

Brad gathered his thoughts. He'd forgotten how he intended to start the apology. He huffed and spoke his mind rather than following the script in his head.

"I knew Peter would be an asset and a problem. I never thought he'd be a batty, two-timing weasel to you and Mika. Also, you knew Saunders better personally, and I think I developed an unnatural hatred for the man. Blaming him for everything. Your children were the chosen ones, and it has always sat wrong with me, but I never could verbalize my worry and discomfort with it and decided just to let it all play out." Brad looked away, embarrassed by his jealousy and the fact that he'd never told Connor about Saunders.

"I know. I appreciate the apology. It's so long ago. Why now? I always knew that, for you to be in charge of it all, you might know the purpose of Phoenix. You spoke directly to WHPSS and with Saunders," Connor said and chuckled.

Brad knew if a person questioned and pondered the purpose of an idea that initially inspired them to do great things, then it wasn't a trivial thing.

Brad cleared his throat and turned toward his friend. "We did house presidents and celebrities who awaited a new life, right? Peter's laboratory, you know, was any scientist's dream lab. I anticipated big and wondrous things coming out of it. I never thought it would be in the form of superpowered children and longevity. I thought we would unfreeze a few people, and that was it. I allowed Peter and his research to endanger your children's lives. That's what I'm trying to say. Plus, Saunders said some things that I think I buried or forgot because they made little sense to me at the time," Brad said, closely observing his friend's facial expressions. No reaction.

Brad sighed. Connor parked their Bubblecar next to a group of boulders on a strip of green grass overlooking a small waterfall. The car doors swooshed open. Both men sat unmoving looking over the mist and trees. It smelled clean and wonderful to Brad. He wanted to remove his shoes and walk barefoot in the grass. Maybe put his feet in the muddy water.

"What did Saunders say?" Connor asked, breaking the awestruck silence.

"He said I should talk to Dom Vanelli. You know, the Professor of Space Engineering at the University of Arizona. He said he could tell me unbelievable stories of what they found outside the Earth's orbit, not the nonsense we all saw on television. I was waiting for him to mentor and guide me in rebuilding civilization from the ground up. He was supposed to handle culture reforming—to mold us into an advanced race using science, architecture, and technology to match that of an alien futuristic generation."

"Fuck, at first, I was hopelessly sad. Now I know, it's bloody outstanding. We've done all that without his help or any of the intel," Connor said and laughed as he moved to exit the Bubblecar .

"Yeah, I thought he was tripping, and now it all makes sense."

"We did it without knowing," Connor said, shaking his head.

"Exactly. If our kids are scared for us...if they tell us to multiply what we think is going on up there, I think whatever we build is either not up to par, or it's so attractive, they would want it for themselves."

"See, that's why you're in charge," Connor said, beginning to loosen his boots. "I want to roll up my pants and walk on the grass barefoot," he said.

Brad did the same.

Once outside on the luscious grass, Brad threw his arms out, turning slowly while he absorbed the beautiful noise of nature. Cold, fresh air and tiny droplets escaping the rushing waterfall brushed his face. All the smells of healthy soil, grass, and sweet flowers gave him an immense sense of humble new beginnings. The birds and monkeys chattering in the surrounding trees triggered a sudden flood of feelings. He swallowed his tears of joy and turned his attention back to Connor.

"Okay, continue. I'm listening," Connor said blissfully, appearing much happier when his feet touched the grass.

"Hm, where was I? Oh, yeah. I called Peter into my office several times and attempted to build a relationship with him because he clams up when he's nervous. He doesn't trust easily. We've developed an excellent rapport since he came to confess to me the day we'd sunk into the sea. He divulges more when not under pressure or scrutiny. Also, I sense he's alone, even if he's with Tony and Bryan. He and Eryn's father grew up without the freedom of American kids. It was sterile and cold. He grew up in the time of West and East Berlin. He's much older than all of us, at least a hundred years older."

Brad spread his toes in the muddy pulp he'd made by walking in circles in one spot. An earthworm wriggled out of the mud. Brad stepped away, careful not to squash it.

"I suspected something like that. Go on, and then I'll tell you what I know about him. Sorry I interrupted you." Connor waved his hand, indicating Brad should continue.

Brad nodded a thank-you. "His mother was a prisoner in the Nazi camps, and so were his brothers. He doesn't know how many brothers he has. Still, they were all taught science at a young age. They grew up being tested, prodded, and studied. None of them went to a traditional school or had any connection to humankind until they were old enough to go to university, which those organizations ran as part of those Disciple groups. It sounded rigid as fuck. Only prescribed and pre-approved work was being conducted on controlled specimens. What bothers me is who approved and who drove this research. What if the wacko crazy scientists worked for Hitler, while Hitler was working for someone higher? When I say Saunders and his friends, I don't know. I think the people Saunders worked for were working for someone higher up." Brad paused and pointed upward at the sky. Connor looked up and emitted one long sigh.

"Yes, I know what you're saying, my friend. I guess it's time I tell you what I know. I truly thought the day we sank to the bottom of the ocean that all this had magically disappeared. Rebuilding and adapting to life underwater has kept our minds busy, and Mika and I decided it was the past. We both pushed it away as if we'd never read that damn note of Dr. Wolter Wessels's.

"Eryn's father had written a note that explained he and Peter were brothers. And you have that correct, the organization that Saunders worked for was some mastermind organization that's been around since the first humans walked the Earth. Mika and I concluded that even that organization was driven by something higher."

Connor pointed to the sky, then continued. "I agree with you there. Unfortunately I can't show you his letter. We lost it. The damn thing went missing during the chaos. These entities tasked the WHPPS. We're a by-product of their experimentation, creation, or whatever you want to call it."

"That's a relief, and I'm excited because, finally, someone understands the scope of my never-ending contemplations. You totally get it. You know what bothers me," Brad said, pointing to the sky again.

"Yes, I do. You want to fuck them up and make sure we sit at the top." Connor stopped trampling the grass, looking Brad in the eye. "What do you need from me? How can I help you?"

"I want our children to carry Phoenix to the top and into the future. I think our enemy has lost touch with what is happening here. Maybe they've given up. They don't know about your children. If they did, they would have come for them or destroyed us."

"I agree. We need to call them home and discuss strategy. We need a clear understanding of what we're up against," Connor said, picking up a rock, wiping it clean, and inspecting it. He put it in his pocket. Probably to give to Mika.

"We need to spy on them, and then we need to eliminate them. Fuck them for thinking we're toys to play with."

"Yes, fuck them, whoever the puppet masters are. What will your approach be?"

"I'm going to train your kids to be covert intelligence officers. We need a fleet, but we need more intel at this moment. And we can't start a war with a fleet smaller than theirs. We must get to know our enemy, and either be bigger and stronger or smarter and faster. We must go big or lose this war before we even start." Brad felt a tiny spark of fire ignite inside him. They chose him for this. The call for war and strategizing was what he loved most. He was a master planner, and they would succeed with the three demigods' help.

Connor grinned, and Brad smiled. No argument there.

Brad's pager pinged from inside the Bubblecar.

"Talk to me, Lasitor!" Brad called toward their vehicle.

"Certainly, sir. You just received another message from the Spacecar," Lasitor said.

Brad struggled to hear him. He smiled—being outside was noisy, and he loved it. He spoke up. "Lasitor, increase the volume, please." He walked over, eager to hear from their children.

"Yes, sir! It's from Kawa!" Lasitor shouted.

*To: General McCormick at Phoenix City*

*From: Kawa McCormick*

*Subject: Update, after the 24-hour visit*

*"I'm working on establishing stable two-way communication with Phoenix via the international deep-space communication network. Once I've completed the newly adapted installation, the larger capacity could receive and accommodate Lasitor. Our current onboard relay receiver system combines television and radio frequency modulation.*

*"Initially, simultaneous communication was problematic because all the ground antennas had been flooded, and the installation didn't split the incoming and outbound streams selectively. The global destruction interrupted Earth's point of connection with space.*

*"I'm recreating a path back to Phoenix with a tuner using a digital I.F., the intermediate frequency. This transmission would give you enough time to let the information percolate and get ready to receive and connect Lasitor with us. It will create an uninterrupted connection stream once he's programmed our ship to connect to the deep-space communication network.*

*"Dad, we're not coming home. Not yet. We have a plan. Be ready for a meeting and two-way video communication. Also, the Bubblecars will not work. We need one big ship to evacuate these people. As I speak, Cian, Eryn, and Ivan are in a meeting with a man who changed places with Donali. Cian said to tell you to think about whether you want to keep*

*the dome or level it and forget about living on the moon. He says it's a decision you must reach out and vote on. Please prepare because they'll need an answer.*

*"I leave you with lots to think about. I'll work with Lasitor to set up a connection.*

*"Talk to you soon. Kawa."*

Brad looked at Connor. "Our children have become space cowboys. They keep sending us these outrageous messages. What happened to my war? First, arm the Bubblecars, now build one big transportation ship. I need to see the dome and more footage before deciding on anything. I wish we had another bloody Spacecar. Is this now our new norm? The kids leave home to explore space?" Brad asked, but Connor didn't answer. "Let's go. The others are waiting for the meeting. I told them to prepare for war. I guess this will be anticlimactic news to them. At least we can discuss the dome, communication, and building a bloody space ark," Brad said, putting his boots back on.

Connor laughed. "Yes, I hear you. The children seem to have it all under control and only need our guidance. What bothers me are the new people. How many people, and will they be able to adapt and accept our status quo?" Connor said.

"I don't need the political upheaval," Brad said, watching Connor sitting sideways on the doorframe, rubbing his feet against each other to clean them before putting his shoes back on.

"Fuck, I didn't even think about that," Connor mumbled.

"I'm writing my memoir and don't have time for a bunch of hooligans who think they can run Phoenix better than us. These people aren't scientists and soldiers. They're an illiterate public who bought their place in society." Brad's stomach ulcer bloomed back to life. Bile rose in his esophagus, and he swallowed it down. His cranium suddenly felt small as pressure built behind his eyeballs, giving birth to a new kind of migraine.

"Fuck!" he yelled, climbing in and shutting the door with a loud swoosh.

"Me, neither! I was getting used to living with no stress or worries." Connor sounded pissed off as he started the Bubblecar.

They left their special spot on Kilimanjaro by rising silently a few feet above the ground. Then the antigravitational vehicle sped back to Phoenix.

# CHAPTER 30

# WAKE UP SO I CAN KILL YOU AGAIN LATER

*"Good morning, citizens of our underwater city of Phoenix.*

*It's now six a.m. I promise the sun is shining.*

*Did you know the side of the moon that faces Earth is known as the near side? The opposite or back side is the far side.*

*Sometimes the far side is called the moon's dark side, but this is inaccurate.*

*When the moon is between the Earth and the sun, the back side of the moon is bathed in daylight during one of the moon phases called the new moon.*

*Visit your community news page to book your next trip to Kilimanjaro to view the moon and stars in all their splendor.*

*Breakfast is served until eight a.m.*

*Have an on-top-of-the-world day!"*

**Ishtar the last Anunnaki**
**2145 A.D. (93 A.T.)**
**Spacecar**
**Five thousand miles south of the lunar dome**
**Grimaldi crater**
**Earth's moon**

Ish drank the sweet, cold fluid and rested his head on his arms. He instinctively shielded himself from judgmental glances, like when he was a child and his siblings questioned him.

This was his new family, and he knew this was where he was supposed to be, as certainly as he knew his name was Ishtar. But his unspoken secrets caused his insides to burn like a furnace. He was ready to speak. He was desperate to share his burden. To verbalize his dreams and his feelings. Communicate with others like himself, not because of loneliness, but a desire to share thoughts, to connect, and to be part of something that mattered beyond listening to human prayers.

The flying ball carrying his new friends—and family appeared when he'd given up hope on Grayrak and was ready to start a new life in another place and time. Ish swallowed burning bile and straightened his spine. Had they arrived a day later, he would have never found them. He had given up on the people of Grayrak and was exhausted. Now, after only an hour in their presence, he bloomed like a little desert flower that had wilted away in a drought of human want and need but was saved by a rush of unexpected rain. He couldn't remember when he'd last felt hopeful. They weren't like humans, not the humans of Earth or those who'd arrived on the moon. Selfishness didn't drive these young men. It seemed his time of watching and waiting had ended. They were unlike the human masses or their leaders and weren't children of Egypt, either.

How was that possible? Where had they come from or, better yet, when had they come? Their Anubis, the royal spirit companions at their sides, were a sign they were the missing strand in the web of time. The Fates knew Xerxes kept his promise and guarded the apple and his offspring. That meant that this one timeline was birthed and left undisturbed. His bloodline survived.

Before his departure, Ki and An told him that they had buried the golden apple inside the foundation of the holy wall of Ishtar—a fortification built to encircle the living tree in the center of the ancient kingdom of Urartu, between the Tigris and Euphrates Rivers. Ish remembered the beautiful gardens that sprouted from within after she sang to it. The selfishness of their father crushed his hopes of returning to Babylon or Anzulla.

Finally, everything the Fates said made sense. *Thank you,* he shot a prayer to Them, hoping They would hear him. After waiting for decades for the Bubblecar to appear, today, of all days, the day he wanted to pack up and go...the Fates would never have forgiven him.

He exhaled and sighed. Then he closed his eyes and emptied his mind to make sure his prayer was heard. *Thank you.*

He opened his eyes. The Anubis watched him with interest while peeking into the kitchenette. *They must recognize me.*

Ish wanted to fall on his knees and play with the Anubis like he had when he was a young boy in his father's palace. Unfortunately, this was not the time. He was tired, and the humans and their Zelk problem were reason enough to push aside the infantile urge. Moreover, he wasn't worthy, and the animals' rejection would only add to the hurt he was already experiencing.

Time had taught him that everyone had problems with love and family. Whether human or Anunnaki. He'd had more than his share of sexual exercise, and he yearned for something deeper than that. At one point, he thought he might connect with Barkor, but Barkor's heart told him he belonged to another. Although Barkor differed from the others on the moon, the urge to reveal himself and forge a deeper connection was weaker than the feeling of self-preservation. It was depressingly safer to remain hidden and not show his true identity.

He wanted to feel useful, and not used. He wanted to feel important, but not supreme. He wanted to bring joyful happiness and not have it be miraculous. Being alive meant experiencing reciprocated emotions from another entity, measuring the exchange through a balance of giving and receiving, all of which were enhanced by the beauty of the experience.

And the Zelk. It frustrated him every time he thought about it. He was familiar with the feeling of impotence in such situations. It still weighed heavily on him. As opposed to his godly nature, his ability to wait and observe the situation measured his usefulness without taking action.

He was told to never linger in one group for too long, making it difficult for people to remember him while he waited for the ball-shaped ship to arrive. Among Barkor and the humans, he was perceived as big, handsome, somewhat agreeable, technologically proficient, and just as trustworthy as the other men in their inner circle. If he had met a meaningless death, there would be no evidence of his presence on the moon, and these new friends would never have found him.

In time, he would reveal himself, and they might accept him. He didn't know them. Knowing them for a few hours, he feared they would expect him to be a god for them, a role he did not want to take on. Consequently, he needed to hide his identity and wait. Ish had nothing to offer except himself. He believed that people would either tolerate him or fear him, despite his friendly and easygoing demeanor.

Ish lifted his head as Eryn took a deep breath, signifying it was time to talk. Eryn strolled over, wedging his golden spear upright in the corner, and settled across from Ish. He put both his hands on the table, palms up, as if inviting Ish to take them. Bravely, Ish took the leap, trusted Eryn, and placed his hands in his. Eryn nodded his approval and looked at Ish like no one had ever looked at him.

Eryn saw inside him, and Ish shivered. He felt Eryn touch him with empathy. The kindness cracked his outer shell, and like an egg, his yolk started running out.

"I sense you're not happy, Ish," he said. "I can feel it, it is everywhere around you. Don't think I don't know and don't think my brothers don't see it. We want to have an honest talk. Tell us everything, and we'll listen and help if needed. I sense helping you is not the help you need. Sure, they"—Eryn pointed toward the human settlement—"need help. First tell us, do you need us to help you?"

Surprised by Eryn's blatant intrusion into his psyche, Ish shifted side to side—uncomfortable with the inquisition. Eryn was holding his hands and flaying his emotions embarrassingly open. Did they expect Ish to blurt out thousands of years of his sorrows? He found his answer in Eryn's caring gaze.

Ish didn't answer the question, he sidestepped it. To answer would have meant discussing things that he didn't discuss with anyone. He didn't know how. And he didn't know if it was allowed. He took a deep breath and started talking, hoping it made sense to his new friends.

"The Zelk is not dead. Only the body is gone. Their essence, souls, or spirits are in that tower," Ish said, searching their faces for amusement or disbelief.

Eryn answered with a nod. He showed no emotion and then asked, "Tell us whose souls left their bodies and have taken up residence in the tower?"

Again, Ish looked at Ivan, Cian, and Kawa, and lastly, back at Eryn. "Those who built it wanted to live forever and be like us, maybe even be better than us. They are greedy. You don't know what they're capable of. Just look at what they've done to Earth and, then again, what they've done here. They built the hive and devised a way to insert their minds into it. They built their own indestructible bodies and became something else. At first, I didn't think it was possible, but I'm extremely worried now. I should have destroyed them when they first succeeded. Only, I didn't want to interfere." *I wasn't allowed, I had to wait for you*, he thought; hiding the truth was the safest course of action for now.

"I guess I wanted to see what humans are capable of," he lied and felt guilty for deceiving them. "And now it's a nearly impossible task. Truthfully, I am frightened by it. I beg your help to destroy this thing. It's evil and grows bigger. It's going to destroy everything," Ish said. He inhaled and blew out a long, shaky breath.

There was silence for a long time as everyone around the table listened and took in what he'd described.

Eryn answered, "Everything that I was and everything I now am tells me the humans planned this to become immortal. Therefore, I construe they created us to be like you, and unfortunately, it wasn't something they could control because they experimented with things and powers they didn't understand. Like giving a baby a loaded gun and seeing what happens." Eryn lowered his gaze and seemed to give Ish a second to think about what he'd just said.

*He has a magnificent mind and reads everything about me. My emotions, thoughts, body language, and even the tone of my voice. Simultaneously, he comprehends the whole mess. Truly extraordinary.*

He looked back up into Eryn's eyes. His skin was the most beautiful shade of gold with a light blue sheen. Full lips and a wide, firm jaw. He was wiser than any living being on this plane Ish had met. Ever. Yet humble with a boyish demeanor. Ish thought he was the most appealing and irresistible male he'd ever seen. His eyes were a lot like his own, except for the pupils. Although he looked able to crush a human's skull between his hands, he was affectionate and soft-spoken, even more so to his mate. He would have made a great ruler of Anzulla.

"No, thank you. I'm already a king," Eryn said with a big smile and a chuckle.

*He was reading my mind even when I barricaded my thoughts. Worthy of being king,* Ish thought.

Cian seemed to be the rowdy one. He cleared his throat and spoke up. "I'm rarely rendered speechless. What I take from this is that they're, wait, not they. Humans are capable of so much once they use initiative, but senselessly hurt themselves because no one showed them how to play with their toys. Is that what you're saying? You let them build the big computer tower to see how they would fuck up?" he asked, gnashing his teeth.

Having expected, and thus understanding, the hostility, Ish cleared his throat and answered, "Yes, that's the condensed version, only, that's not the entire explanation." He watched Cian summing him up.

"Tell me" —Cian pointed out the bay window— "were they all just one big experiment?" he asked, leaning over Ish.

"Yes," Ish answered. Reading Cian's thoughts was difficult. His emotions combusted like fireworks—a kaleidoscope of emotions and power. Ish wondered if he even knew how much power he possessed.

"Whose fucking experiments? And who the fuck are you?" he asked, and they looked at Ish as if he'd personally wronged them.

*I should never have shown myself.*

Hesitantly, he admitted, "My father's," and at this stage, he couldn't deny anything. He licked his dry, cracked lips. His entire mouth was dry. "I can fix this and make it right. I will let you know when it is done. Can I count on you to do as I say when it's the right time?"

Ish let go of Eryn's hands and rose, but as he did, Eryn spoke.

"This is the source of your unhappiness, isn't it? You run around and try to make others happy. We're sorry that you're having all this pain. Was this, in any way, your fault?" Eryn asked.

Ish sat down again, feeling defeated. "No, it was probably my father's."

Eryn was quiet and seemed perplexed. His eyebrows were drawn down, forming a deep furrow above his nose, and his golden green gaze jumped from left to right as he read Ish's facial features and internal thoughts.

"Their attempts to create more children unnaturally failed, so they perished. My home was destroyed. It was a heap of rubble, smoke, and ash."

"This sounds like something we experienced. Where were you?" Cian asked. He seemed to know what questions to ask—an intelligent roughneck.

"I was working," Ish answered, trying his best to be honest, or they might decide not to help.

"What does that mean?" Ivan asked. The twin brothers worked together, and they had a strong bond.

"I searched for a place to call home, somewhere untarnished, a safe place for my people to flourish."

"A place? What are you talking about?" Cian asked and pinned Ish with a cold stare. The blue in his eyes felt like a laser cutting a path through the armor encasing his secrets.

This type of questioning unsettled Ish. "That's what I said. I searched for a place."

"How did you search for a motherfucking place?" Cian fisted his hands and loomed over Ish, supporting his hulking frame on his knuckles on the surface of the table in front of him. "How do you search?"

"Brother," Ivan cautioned Cian.

Ish broke the stare with Cian and sought an escape in Ivan's eyes. They were brighter and cut just as deep.

"Tell me!" Cian shouted.

Ish recoiled in his seat, taken aback. *What should he say? These people read minds.* He looked at Eryn, who smiled at him. Ivan was worried about him. Cian wanted to wring his neck, and Kawa found the entire conversation amusing.

"I, I searched, and I waited," Ish stuttered.

"Listen, has it ever occurred to you they're fucking things up and speeding up the destruction because you watched and waited for this boil of a mess to fester? And now you say you want what?" Cian asked and hit his fists on the table with a dull thud. "What do you think we should do?"

*What's he talking about? Were they even talking about the same things?*

Ivan uttered a firm "no" to his brother, while his gaze held no compassion for Ish.

"Are you saying you sat and watched how humans die so you could swoop in and take their home? Why? They came to the moon for you, and you watched it unfold. Or are you saying you can't help? Or does their suffering amuse you?" Ivan watched Ish with calculated precision, swinging his head and eyeballing him from new angles after each question.

"That's exactly what he's saying. What he's not saying is that he's the fucking reason the place is in the state it is. He's why these sad fuckers are on the moon and like us, nothing more than experiments," Cian said through clenched teeth, then dove over the table, taking Ish to the floor. His enormous hands and long fingers wrapped around Ish's throat, squeezing and cracking his laryngeal cartilage.

"You motherfucking Anunnaki!"

Ish relaxed and welcomed his death. As he lay upside down with his legs still up on the bench and head on the floor, their voices were muffled like he was underwater. *What a glorious feeling. He felt nothing. No fear. Just a white fuzziness. A soft place of peace and nothingness.*

The light and sound abruptly returned while someone slapped his cheeks. "Come on, take a breath. You better wake up so I can kill you again later. Come on, open your eyes, you sad motherfucker!" Cian yelled. He was likely the one slapping him.

"Ish, there's no way that you're dead. We can hear your heart and thoughts. Open your eyes," Eryn urged, and Ish opened his eyes, examining Cian, Ivan, Eryn, and Kawa's faces. They smiled. Ish was livid.

"Kill me now, or I will do it myself! Kill me, please. Please, I beg you," he cried.

"Sorry, no. Too easy. You will tell us how to save these people and kill the Zelk. Then I will gladly kill you." Cian stood with his feet at the sides of Ish's head. Ish looked up into his stunning blue eyes and the impressively large bulge in his pants. Eryn and Ivan waited somewhere on the other side of the table as if this was an everyday occurrence. Cian was maniacal. *There was something wrong with him, while fuck, he oozes sex appeal; they all were.*

Ish let his head fall. "Promise?"

"Yes, I fucking promise," Cian said and stepped to the side, offering his hand. Ish grabbed it, and he pulled him back into a sitting position at the table. Ivan was picking up and cleaning the floor, and Eryn looked at him pointedly, as if searching his insides for answers. Kawa didn't say a word. He turned and left as if bored.

"Humans may have tactics, yet they lack speed, and we aren't human," Eryn said, as Ish shifted sideways to discreetly make room for his hardening cock. *When was the last time his cock showed any interest? He had forgotten how it felt.*

Eryn chuckled.

"Ish, let me answer those questions you have inside you. You may feel better if you accept the fact that the irrationality of human beings makes them impossible to predict. Stop trying to change the past by finding the perfect future. You're jumping around and wasting your time because every second has a million other possibilities, so, in reality, you spend your time watching others' lives instead of experiencing your own. Do I make sense to you?" Eryn asked, narrowing his eyes.

His voice enchanted Ish. He could listen to him all day. It wasn't only the voice; it was the words that the voice formed. The sounds. They were kind, and he was all-knowing, like he saw where Ish was and what he'd seen. Eryn knew who and what he was and did not voice it for a reason. Ish gave a slight nod. His upbringing and instinct told him to submit and respect. He was certain his jaw dropped, and he sat open-mouthed in awe of Eryn, who nonchalantly turned and helped Ivan to throw the broken cups in the trash. Then Eryn grabbed a cloth, took a knee, and dried the floor.

On his hands and knees doing it. This, whatever he was...

"I am a Brawl," Eryn said proudly, pushing his chest out and standing tall. Ish knew he was looking at something he never thought possible. Eryn threw the rag to the side and came back to sit down. Ivan sat on his lap. They kissed and turned their attention back to Ish.

Cian seemed to prefer keeping his distance. He stood with muscled arms crossed and dark blue eyes pinning Ish in place and spoke. "They call us the Divine triad, but that was before Ivan and Eryn mated. Now we're just the three Divine Brothers."

"Oh, so you three?" Ish pointed between them. Imagining the exquisite experience of ogling and feeling these three beautiful bodies undulating around, on top, and under him, his cock stirred, twitched, and leaked. An orgy of gods...

"Noooo!" the three answered in unison, and Ish felt his cheeks warm as he must have been blushing. He hoped his dark complexion hid his vulnerability. Then again, he doubted he could hide anything from them. Especially from Eryn. He needed to learn to guard his thoughts and feelings around them better. At least he'd met them, and that which he thought unthinkable was true. Here they were. His father wasn't here for this, and he was glad about that. He wished he'd found this timeline earlier and told his sister about it. He smiled. But not for the reason they thought.

"Tell us, where have you been staying all this time?" Cian asked and sat down. He threw his legs sideways over the bench, crossing his thickly tatted arms again, and leaned back. Ish read his emotions. Cian was fishing for information.

"I was here, watching over Barkor," he said, waiting for a reaction. The corners of Cian's mouth twitched, and his heart rate sped up at the mention of Barkor's name. Hmmm, so he was Barkor's mate. Ish knew the signs of possessive jealousy, the pull between predestined mates. It had been thousands of years since he'd last seen it.

Instead of asking more questions, Cian jumped up and walked away. How odd. He was fighting the pull. This was going to be fun to watch.

CHAPTER 31

# A FORGOTTEN DROP OF MEMORY

**MIKA ROMANOV**
**2146 A.D. (94 A.T.)**
**Phoenix, underwater glass dome city**
**Earth**

The Moon rotates very slowly on its axis, once for every orbit it makes around Earth. So one day on the Moon is about 29.5 Earth days.

Mika and Connor waited and waited and waited. It had been a chaotic watch and wait time after the Spacecar had been taken for a joyride and a peek-a-boo of the Lunar Environmental Project. The Spacecar became the secret headquarters on the lunar surface tucked away inside the Grimaldi crater. The two Bubblecars were necessary for daily scouting, so they had to be serviced and exchanged back at Phoenix. The provisions and much-needed water needed to be replaced. Secretly, Mika timed and celebrated the inevitable trips of his children coming home. Yesterday, Cian, Ivan, Eryn, Kawa, and Ish returned to restock and introduce Ish in person to the leadership team.

As Brad, Connor, and Mika showed Ish the layout of Phoenix, Ish spotted Dr. Peter von Leutzendorf, who panicked and vanished into the lab. He asked Brad first. Brad refused to reveal anything about Peter. Then, he begged Cian and his brothers. But they were not on speaking terms with him or friends with him. Unfortunately, the responsibility fell on Connor and Mika to introduce them.

Now, Mika hesitantly peeked from around the corner of his office with Connor and Ish behind him. He deliberated a while and stood frozen with indecision. Peter was rarely in his office nowadays. Because he finally had a social life, or he was ignoring the fuck out of Mika. Inside this office was where Mika and Connor forged a bond with Peter. Inside this watertight temperature-controlled chamber, they locked themselves safely away from the freezing waters of the tsunamis. Mika watched him reading, sitting on the single bed he kept in the office for when he worked late. He sat with his back against the wall. Bare feet crossed at the ankles. Peter had been avoiding him and Connor.

"Go now. What are you waiting for?" Ish whispered over Mika's shoulder and pushed him to move forward. Mika wanted to swat him like a pesky fly. Ish had been mobbing Mika for the whole bloody day. Peter's blond hair and blue eyes triggered a sudden desire to meet the bestower of everlasting life. Ish noticed him fleetingly passing them by in the stairwell where Peter had been evading them by taking back entrances. Mika's sneaking stemmed from Brad saving Peter from killing himself. Peter couldn't live with his guilty conscience. Brad had promised Mika public castration if he or Connor spoke to Peter without him present. Brad wouldn't know, and technically, Mika wouldn't talk to Peter, only introduce them and go. That was all. That was the plan.

"Yelda, you better go now. He's going to notice us and close the damn door. Who knows how long he'll lock himself inside there? You go in, and I'll guard the door. I'm not going inside. I'll be your lookout. Okay?" Connor whispered, hanging on Mika's right hip, and staying low like bullets were flying. He was having fun.

Mika straightened his spine. "Okay, here we go," he whispered, hoping Brad didn't find out.

"Yes, that's the plan," Ish said, holding an origami flower he made for Peter against his chest.

Mika took a deep breath and then shot across the hallway into Peter's office. Once inside, he grabbed Ish's arm and thrust him forward. "Peter, let me introduce…"

Peter jumped on his bed, threw the book he'd been reading at Mika, and let loose with a high-pitched shrill. Mouth wide open, he screamed and saw Ish, and his mouth widened even more, ear-splittingly louder, without taking a breath.

Still yelling, he looked him up and down, taking the tall, dark, and dangerously looking man in.

*Yes, you idiot, he likes you.*

Peter attempted to climb through the wall behind him and failed; all the while, Ish tried his best to give him his origami flower. Peter slapped the flower and then froze as he noticed Ish's golden irises with black rings.

"Alien eyes!" This time, he smiled as he hollered. Tears streamed down his face. "Alien eyes," he said again while attempting to climb over his desk to reach the door.

"Gille-toine, close the door, don't let him escape!" Mika yelled, and Connor jumped into action. Peter realized he was being boxed in and screamed even higher, and the more Ish tried to woo him, the more Peter tried reversing through the wall and failed. It was chaos, and Mika had had enough.

"Jesus, Peter, stop your motherfucking crazy screaming. We're not here to hurt you." Mika pulled Ish back, noticing that he was making it worse. "Connor and I wanted to introduce you to this man. He's besotted with you. Ever since he saw you, he couldn't stop asking about you. Brad's busy meeting with Cian. I know Brad said not to come to you alone, and that we needed him to chaperone us. You have your reasons. Connor and I will go now. We just wanted to bring Ish to you."

Peter snickered and, thank god, stopped making the ruckus. His gaze was bewildered. Even so, the idiot smiled. Mika didn't know what was going on.

"What? You don't want to take me away? He is real, and not a ghost?" Peter stuttered, wiping tears left and right. They seemed to be happy tears now.

"No, Peter, I just want to introduce you. He is real. You know when one boy sees another boy he likes and must meet and take him out…"

Peter lifted his head to the ceiling, shrieking again.

Mika lifted his hands. "No, not take you out and kill you!" Mika held his hands low, although he wanted to pull on his hair. "Calm the fuck down. Why would I introduce you to someone I asked to kill you? My only intention is to bring him to you. Go do something nice together. Go out on a date!"

Peter heaved and gulped air. "Oh," he said, looking at Ish, who hid behind Mika's back.

"Please, first, tell us, are you serious about Tony and Bryan? Does your heart belong to them?" Mika asked. Peter looked at Mika and seemed to register what was happening.

"No, I never loved them. We aren't together, anyway. Not anymore, they…" Peter waved his hand, showing they were past tense.

Behind Mika, he heard Ish whisper, "Yes, yes, yes!"

"I'm sorry to hear that, my friend. Are you doing okay? I thought you were with them this whole time." Mika held his arms wide, hinting for Ish to stay behind him and Connor, whose one eye peeked through a small opening, to stay back. He didn't want to make sudden movements.

Peter parsed his lips, seeming on the verge of tears again and shook his head. "No, I can't be with them. I'm not good company."

"What have you been doing? I know your research is complete. You're not in the lab anymore. What have you been doing this whole time with yourself, my friend?" Mika asked nicely; he was worried about Peter.

Peter straightened his back. "I'm on holiday," he said proudly.

"That's good news," Mika said reluctantly, not sure how Peter would take anything he said. Peter had never taken one day off, so being on holiday was out of the norm.

"Yes, I'm reading, watching television, and helping at the toddler's school. I'm doing everything I never did. I sleep better, and I'm learning who I am." Peter gave Mika a look, daring him to say something negative.

Mika thought that was a fantastic idea. His friend was taking time for himself. "That's a big change. Anything that makes you happy and doesn't hurt anyone else is a step in the right direction."

Mika faintly heard Connor calling his name as if to caution him, but couldn't stop himself from asking Peter. "Why weasel around? Why are you taking so long to confront us? You know we need to come clean, all of us. We've been working together for years, still you said nothing and let me—"

Connor flung the door open, distracting him and reminding him with a look of wariness and a shake of his head.

Mika stopped himself. "You know what, one day when you want to talk about it all, come to me. This is Ish." He pushed Ish to the front. Ish fell to one knee, dreadlocks and gold chains flying left and right as the big giant tried to make himself as small as possible in front of Peter. He bent his head and held the origami upwards at Peter like an offering.

Peter stood looking astonished, then carefully took the delicately folded flower and smelled it.

Ish smiled, and his happiness radiated into the small room. He cleared his throat and spoke gently. "This is for you. It represents the loursveto flower from my home on Anzulla. The flower is a symbol of love and serenity. Of beauty and intelligence. Of everlasting union and life."

"Sounds to me like a wedding ring," Mika said and turned to leave them alone. He wanted to stay and ask more about Anzulla, but he said, "Peter, talk to the man. Connor and I will wait in my office if you need me." Mika pushed the half-closed door wide open and joined his husband. "Let's go have a coffee in my office," Mika mumbled and heard Ish introducing himself.

"Hello, my name is Ish. You may not remember me, I visited you once…"

After two cups of coffee, Mika wanted to return to work. He had promised his friend he would stay if he needed him. They were pretty bored when Peter stormed into his office. Mika pushed his chair back and jumped up. "What's wrong? Did he take advantage of you?"

"No." Peter rolled his eyes and swooned. "No, don't be silly. Be happy for me. My mind is lighter, and all my thoughts and feelings are categorized and packed away. I feel much better. I got my Ish. I've been waiting for him all this time." Peter giggled, holding his flower in front of his nose. "He said he was starving without me." Then plopped himself down and sat opposite Mika and Connor. In his chair. The one he used to sit in years ago. Mika saw a shadow hovering just outside the doorframe and assumed Ish was waiting outside.

Peter sat on the edge of his seat. "Mika, Connor, I'm sorry. I don't want to explain away what I did because how I did it was wrong. I know now that you probably would have agreed anyway if I'd told you all this."

Mika nodded, and Connor wiggled uncomfortably in his chair like he kept his protests to himself.

Mika got up and grabbed his special tools for electrical wiring. "Comrade, we'd meant to get you alone for an honest discussion. We've been evading each other for much too long. Connor and I had taken this secret and ignored it. It worked because we forgot about it all for a while. As it goes with secrets, if more than one person knows, then it's not a secret anymore. Also, if one person keeps that secret, it becomes heavy to carry. It's better not to have secrets. They will crush you. I tried not to tell Connor because I was ashamed of myself. I trusted you because I considered you my best friend and lab partner. In my eyes, you were untainted, pure, and innocent. I actually felt sorry for your pathetic-ness," Mika said honestly and truthfully.

Connor stood quietly, saying nothing. He nodded affirmatively as he supported Mika. Peter bit his lip, clutching the flower tighter, and Ish loomed inside.

"I'm more than ready to get this drama behind us. The only thing I ask of you is to tell me what the fuck is going on. How did you end up here, and why do you sound like you know Ish? I swear, more questions come up each time I talk to you. You're making me crazy by trying to guess your story. I must know because thinking and attempting to guess all the time occupies my mind with unnecessary mental energy, and I'd rather use it on something productive. Come, bring your guest, and we can tinker on the latest Spacecar prototype and figure out a way to build a better communication system," Mika said and herded them out of the office. Talking while working would give them an outlet for their emotions and build camaraderie.

The four of them walked the corridors, not stopping to talk, only greeting the inquisitive ones with a firm nod and hello. Everyone was in the habit of leaving Peter alone, so as soon as they lifted their heads to yap, Mika would push him to the front. Mouths would shut, heads would shake, and they would skedaddle away.

He needed to get Peter to talk because he wanted to learn more about their family's genes and how his and Connor's DNA perfectly bonded with the Anunnaki gene. Peter had known that all the time, while Mika had to find the truth in bits and pieces from the scientist's notes of Dr. Wessels and from their enemy. His perfect Romanov Russian princes didn't have a Scandinavian five-foot-ten blonde model with blue eyes as an egg donor. Nick, the Disciple, revealed it was a DNA string from a Mesopotamian Anunnaki.

The more puzzling piece was that it was all written on the Babylonian seal and tablets and found in the stash of intelligence Mika and the men confiscated from the nitrogen-propelled airship. It spoke of a time of lots of water covering the whole earth. Nick thought it was tsunamis, but Mika and Connor deciphered the original text, which spoke about water covering the entire Earth, like biblical floods. They predicted the Big Flood in the holy *Year of the Twins*. Mika, Connor, and their friends all gave input as they met and studied the tablets and every scrap of history saved by Lasitor. The word holy was taken out of context and directly translated—it meant the perfect or whole round number. That number in Mesopotamian was twenty-two.

Another idiotic translation by Nick's tribe was that they said the world would end, and Luna would welcome them. Correctly translated, it meant, on Luna, we will meet. That was all it said. Nick also said the three would lead us into the future. What it said was, in the future, I live to meet you.

Nick had said that they helped them decide on Project One. They were Disciples, and his children were direct descendants of An and Ki, the God of the Heavens and the Goddess of the Earth. That Ivan meant the fourth, or Roman letter IV, for the mighty IV-An, and Cian spelled Ki-AN.

How did they know about the names he and Connor had chosen? And why did Peter know Ish, who was on the moon this whole time? Mika needed to talk to their children.

The cloud surrounding Earth hid them from the strange ships that came to suck up their atmosphere. He hoped Cian and Brad decided on a better plan, and fast. And then they needed to execute the plan. And to do that, they needed to communicate. He hated feeling cut off and isolated.

They reached Mika and Connors's workshop and lab near the shipyard a few minutes later. Then entered via the wind tunnel that blew like a category seven tornado to remove all dust particles. They washed up and donned protective gear before entering a sterile area to install wiring on a larger prototype.

"Gille-toine, can Peter help us build a communication tower? One that floats and can be retracted and moved under the surface level? It would be a better option than dragging construction outside and erecting one on a mountaintop. I worry any manmade structure will give us away, and I'm sure Brad won't approve of it. We need to communicate better with the children. I need eyes and ears out there. I want twenty-four hours a day of video feeds from all over. Wherever they go, they should leave a camera ball for us. That way, we can protect and warn them, don't you think?"

"Of course he can."

Connor turned to Peter, who looked dreamily at Ish as he inspected the ship. "Peter, the more heads, the faster we shall get results," Connor said, lifting his chin towards the two newcomers busy coming through the transparent wind tunnel to suit up for entry.

Ish seemed to know his stuff. He pulled and pushed a few buttons and knobs until the installed wiring came to life, highlighting the walkways deeper inside the belly of the ship. Hands folded behind his back, he inspected the cabin, locker, dining, and sleeping areas and then exited with an approving nod.

"Apologies, I don't want to seem judgmental of your work. I'm impressed by it. I assume you built the smaller version as well. Your attention to the fine details impressed me most," Ish said with a low bow, first toward Mika and then toward Connor.

Taken aback, Mika almost lost his train of thought. "Thank you. We're building a better, bigger version than the boys are currently using. We would like your input and recommendations any time, comrade," he said to Ish, and turned back to Peter. "We can't rely only on a voice-recorded report from the kids. By the time we receive it...what I mean is, we can't sit here and watch how people learn to knit and shit. I want my own ship up and running. I fucking need to know what's happening outside the clouds. But, in the meantime, could you maybe design a submarine with satellite capabilities?" He pleaded, with a beggar's face, and his hands folded over his chest.

"Yes, sure, of course. I can help. I can do that for you. I'll help with anything as long as I'm not working with frozen dead people," Peter said, chuckling shyly. Mika realized his friend was more traumatized by the lucrative project than he initially thought. He saw why Brad suggested leaving him alone and not talking to him unchaperoned. He seemed brittle and had reached maximum tensile strength.

"That's good news, my friend," Mika said, calling them over to a big square table, where he activated it to show them the 4D schematics they started with.

"Yelda, maybe Ish has some input here," Connor said to Mika as he pushed himself up from squatting. Mika observed he was connecting the silicone wires to the motherboard.

"Progress is slow. In two years, we would at least have two ships ready. Please, I need to know what we can improve and change, and I can't do that with relayed radio messages."

Peter stepped closer, holding Ish's hand. They looked like the perfect contrast. Like yin and yang. Peter's pale complexion with blue eyes to Ish's dark as night skin and golden double-ringed irises.

"You know, Mika and Connor, my friends. I've blurted some of it out to Brad while feeling guilty as fuck. I'm older than any man currently living in Phoenix, and although not needed, I'd implanted the first Eden Bean when I appeared to be twenty-seven years old. I've been hiding my origins and sacrificed myself for the word and a smile from a sexy alien in my living room a lifetime ago."

Mika stiffened. What in the ever-loving fuck? Connor pulled him by the arm. Mika swallowed his words. *Was this happening even before they landed on the moon?* The words almost left his mouth. Again, Connor tapped him. Connor looked at Peter while shaking his head as if he had fleas. Mika got the message to shut up and listen. He embraced Connor by the shoulder, pulling him in towards himself. *I shall listen, don't worry, my gille-toine.*

He smiled at Peter.

Peter swallowed and straightened his back as he continued telling his story. "I don't feel guilty because I'd gifted the Phoenicians with eternal life." Peter smiled up at Ish with adoration and hero worship. Not like he hung the moon, but took it down and moved it exactly where Peter wanted it. Mika and the leadership team had interviewed Ish and understood that Ish was from Grayrak. Something didn't add up. But before he could form the question, Peter continued.

"Memories of years far gone resurfaced. I'd forgotten those eyes. Too much had happened, and as the years twisted their strands together, it all became a forgotten drop of memory in a big bucket full of time."

Ish bent down and picked the much shorter Peter up from the floor. Peter yelped, and Ish rubbed their noses together. Mika thought he saw fangs for a second. Brad and Cian distracted him by joining them and listening to Peter talk. Brad seemed impressed. He smiled happily as Peter, Mika, and Connor were talking. He nodded to Mika and Connor, giving them a stare and approval nonverbally.

Ish put Peter down and seemed more tense when Cian entered. They'd already built a rapport and seemed to have an understanding that Cian was calling the shots. Mika was very proud of his son. He struggled emotionally when Ivan and Eryn got married and had grown into a strong and respected leader. He had thrown himself into his work with Bryan and training the reserves. He'd shown exceptional leadership and strength and now wore the same rank as Brad. Although rankings in Phoenix wasn't practiced the traditional way, the word *general* was loosely bestowed on Cian and first used by the men he trained and educated on space engineering and defense.

Eryn and Ivan didn't care about titles. The power couple was humble and preferred to do everything together while working. Their education from Phoenix University focused on human biomechanics and the musculoskeletal system and how the body tissue responded to the forces they commanded and helped the citizens by combining their powers with technology.

Ish greeted Cian and Brad with a radiant smile and his hand-over-hand handshake and widened his smile to expose his teeth. No fangs were visible. Mika thought he imagined it.

Ish stepped back in a manner only royalty did when they expected everyone to listen. He stayed silent for a while until all attention was on him. Cian gave him two thumbs up, and he spoke in his deep baritone with an accent Mika couldn't place, although he was a linguist and mastered eight languages.

"I've always wondered if the earthlings would ever be able to leave the Earth. I was relieved when I first saw your transportation vehicle. My home is now but a rock bestrewed with heaps of crumbling aspirations and broken dreams. I was left utterly alone, yet now I am not alone anymore," Ish said and smiled at Peter and then Cian. Mika listened intently to hear if Ish would answer all of his unspoken questions.

"I was the youngest of my siblings, and I missed and hated them for leaving me behind. In solitude, I observed the humans. All I could do was watch how they murdered and destroyed themselves from afar. My father's cunningness and twisted ways destroyed us and our home. I lived in hiding, contemplating stopping my torturous existence. I longed to walk with the humans to cure my loneliness. I asked myself over and over, how do I reveal myself? How will they receive me? I am not a god. Nor do I want to be one. For eons, I tried tirelessly to find the point where sowing our seed and knowledge would bloom as intended."

Mika observed Cian nodding at Ish as if he agreed with Ish, and they practiced this together. Maybe he's referring to being Anunnaki. Maybe he was born at the concentration camps and sent to the moon with the rockets that left pre-Doomsday?

"Look at what's happening with the creation of the Zelk—an unnatural species made from parts of humans and parts of their technologies. If I don't help them, they will die by the hand of the Zelk that continues to multiply. The Zelk is an abomination. A thing that grows and consumes not only human flesh and bone but their souls, too. It lures the weak with the promise of life, but it only brings death. I know it because I have battled it before. I will work with Cian and his brothers, and together, we will find the balance we have all been seeking—a new beginning."

"Ha!" Mika clapped his hands. "I guess you can bring out the Kool-Aid now, Brad. You would think he answered the age-old questions of humanity. Who am I, where do I belong, why am I here, and what is my purpose? It's fucking depressing, I tell you. He said absolutely nothing," Mika blurted, and Connor pushed and pulled furiously on his clothes.

Mika wasn't impressed by Ish. Ivan had told him about Cian strangling him, and he felt the same about the sneaky motherfucker. *Ish is talking in riddles, and Peter's in on it.*

# CHAPTER 32

# A FUCKING STORM WAS COMING

*"GOOD MORNING, CITIZENS OF PHOENIX.*

*It's now six a.m.*

*Did you know that teaching your kids how to swim is compulsory? Your local swim and dive club provides fun and enriching swim lessons for kids ages 4 months and up. Specialized swim methods give kids the skills to be safe in the water.*

*BIG NEWS! We will no longer be affiliated with the CPR techniques of the Red Cross. Phoenician CPR lessons and services have exceeded and outgrown what they provided.*

*Breakfast is served until eight a.m.*

*Hope you have a splashing good day!"*

**LEO**
**2145 A.D. (93 A.T.)**
**(Shortly before Ishtar and Barkor catch sight of the Bubblecar.)**
**Disciples of the Anunnaki compound**
**Environmental Project - Luna**
**Grayrak City**
**Earth's moon**

LEO LOOKED LONGINGLY out the clubhouse window, staring off into the distance, and watched the arms of Big Benny Clock Tower move so slowly he couldn't see them move. But move they did because every few minutes he checked, and they pointed to a different number, ticking and counting his pathetic existence down. Leo's backside burned. It felt like he sat on a hot coal or three. He gnashed his teeth, whipping his head and shoulders this and that way to gain momentum to roll over onto his side. He should ask someone to reposition him, but he wasn't there yet. He'd rather struggle alone as long as possible than lower himself to begging for help. He didn't want to give them the satisfaction of laughing at his expense only for a small push.

After he tired himself out, he searched the room for anyone looking his way that he could ask. He waited, rested, and struggled a few more times by taking deep breaths, exhaling quickly, and throwing his head backward. A trick he learned to move and slide himself into a new position. Like a worm. *Fucking hell, thank god.*

Groaning, he slipped about two inches down while wiggling his shoulders back and forth. He sighed after he reached a more comfortable position. Sweat beaded on his forehead, and it tickled him. The exertion exhausted him to the point of heaving to catch his breath. He turned his attention to where everyone was listening to Grizzly. He animatedly talked about abducting a new offering. Leo hated him and his pockmarked face. He cringed when he saw the evil smile exposing his yellow-black teeth from chewing home-grown tobacco leaves all day. He locked gazes with Leo and stepped closer.

"Do you need help, my worm?" he asked as if he cared and picked Leo up from his chair.

"My ass is sore," Leo said dryly, then held his breath, anticipating the stench of sweaty armpits. Grizzly reeked, and his vile body odor matched his personality. Leo was his plaything, and Grizzly got off on how much Leo needed him. He didn't care; he enjoyed rubbing salt into Leo's helplessness as he flung him onto his shoulder like a swaddled baby patting his backside.

"I don't want my worm ending up with sores and blisters. Then you're not useful anymore," Grizzly said and fluffed Leo's hair after putting him down.

He was in a good mood today, and Leo was going to do something about it. Just as Grizzly turned back to address his men, Leo mumbled shrewdly, "Thank you, you dirty sick fuck!" He hated feeling helpless, and he hated that he was embarrassed. But most of all, he hated Grizzly. The sick fuck was a devotee. His *kink* was fucking people like Leo, who was helpless and deformed, and here on Grayrak, it was not by accident. No, he would send people he liked to see helpless to the Zelk and then fucked them until he grew tired of them.

"My pleasure, and I know what you're trying to do, and it ain't gonna work," Grizzly said over his shoulder and addressed his underlings.

"Men, my toes curl inside my boots! I can't wait to get my hands on him. He'd be our best trade!" Grizzly boasted, and the men guffawed.

Although Grayrak lay hidden and protected inside a tinted glass dome, the miners, better known as the Disciples, developed excessively thick, pink, and damaged skin. This marked them as the few privileged with jobs on the Zelk mining ship. Like the ship's crew, Grizzly worked with minimal protection by their hooded cloaks from the sun's damaging UV rays. Some say they were cloaked descendants of the first Disciples of the gods. Others say it was to hide their ugly pockmarked faces. They were repulsive bullies who overran the human camp called the City of Grayrak. Leo and every other man, woman, and child who wasn't part of their cult hated the domineering giant as much as they feared him.

Grizzly's bragging was really working on Leo's nerves today. He didn't want anything to do with the messed-up plans. At first, they lured Leo in, and after they sold all his limbs to the Zelk, they used him as bait to lure in people who wanted to help. And when that didn't work anymore, Leo was only good at being used as a warm hole to fuck, and of course, he was the middleman between the Disciples and the Zelk.

He was a half-man because he'd been a donor and in the hospital multiple times. He was a trusted ally. Someone who helped the Zelk, and because he had no arms or legs, he was no threat. He had his mouth, which he used to stay alive, but he was tired nowadays and wished he could die. He wanted to leave this stink hole and meet the everlasting dark. He was ready and done with it all.

*The only way that will happen is if I choke on my food or Grizzly kills me.*

"I wish you would stop trading people!" Leo exclaimed and surprised himself with his boldness. He wanted to die. He carried on antagonizing Grizzly. He never met the man in question, and he sympathized with him. Living as a half-man was hell. If he could walk, he would consider going to the market. Leo would try to give the last good man in Grayrak a heads-up before Grizzly collected him and traded him as a fresh body for the Zelk.

*He'll end up like me. A head with no ears and torso.* A worm. No, he couldn't let that happen. Then again, if it did happen, Grizzly would have a new plaything to torture. *I may be killed and thrown away. Maybe I'll be a hand-me-down.*

The look on Leo's face must have betrayed him. Before he could mask his feelings, Grizzly got sight of it.

"Don't you fucking dare, Leo!" Grizzly said under his breath. "I'm warning you only once. Don't even think about warning him. You can't hide your feelings from me. I own you! I fucking own everything on this side of the wall. I will lock you up in your special box without food or water." Grizzly pointed a fat finger at Leo, who looked up into his eyes, challenging Grizzly.

Leo widened his eyes, mocking him. *Yeah, come on, you bastard hit me!* Leo taunted and felt triumphant when he saw the big flat hand approaching his face.

A deafening thwack collided on the side of his head where his open canal sat unprotected by the pinna, the outer ear cartilage, which was the first to be traded with the Zelk. Next, all the wind got knocked out of him as Grizzly's enormous fist hit the pit of his stomach. Leo doubled over and face-planted on the dirty floor. With his exposed cock and backside, he lay upside down for a few seconds before his torso toppled over, thumping his lower body on the cold rock floor. He groaned in pain. As he turned his head, the tip of a boot kicked his forehead. Sparks flashed in front of his eyes, and he welcomed the darkness calling him as he passed out.

The fury about being alive bubbled up inside when he opened his eyes. Something tickled his lip. He flicked out his tongue and licked it. The blood was salty; reflexively, he wanted to wipe his nose but couldn't. He spat the blood from his mouth. Furious. *Fuck,* his insides trembled as he strained to see where Grizzly was. "Where are you? You ugly motherfucking idiot! Come finish me, you fat bastard!" Leo shouted from the dirty floor. After he fell from his chair, his limbless body lay face down on his stomach, so it was difficult to scan the room.

Suddenly, no one in the room spoke. *Yes, you fuckers, I'm awake.*

Leo's heart raced. He wished he could jump up to his feet. He imagined himself doing a somersault over his captor's head and back-kicking the shit out of him.

"Where are you, you pink-skinned bully?"

Someone switched the music off. Leo's pulse raced—the swoosh-swoosh of blood in his ears deafened him. Grizzly's boots thumped closer. *Please kick me in the head.*

"You better shut up, boy, or I will tie you to a pole and let the men fuck you from both sides. You've always looked better on your knees. Too bad you don't have them anymore," Grizzly said. His voice was low and menacing. Pure fucking evil. He stepped on Leo's neck and push-rolled him to his back with his boot. Leo heard and felt bones and cartilage crack. Murmuring men stood closer, getting ready for a show.

Then Grizzly laughed. It was freakishly loud. Leo looked around as best he could, noting all the uncertain faces.

"My worm, everyone knows you're mine!" he blared to his crew.

"Big and ugly motherfucker," Leo retorted, and Grizzly laughed, and because his underlings knew not supporting him in any way could cost them their lives, they laughed awkwardly. Sounding more like a choir without a conductor, but after a few tries of hiccups instead of chuckles, they found a rhythm that sounded as if they laughed.

Leo was seething with resentment. He wished he could disintegrate and disappear from this existence. Grizzly lifted his boot, forcing Leo's head to the side so he looked at him.

Leo taunted Grizzly through his bloody gnashing teeth. "I hope your fucking asshole closes and opens under your armpit, and every time you reach for your drink, you shit yourself," Leo screamed.

The onlookers stopped laughing and waited for a cue from their leader. He would shoot them on the spot for disrespecting him. Erroneously Dundrog, his second in charge, doubled over and laughed hysterically.

Leo lifted his head. *Fuck that!* He decided to stand his ground. He wanted to die, and he wanted to die now! Grizzly lifted his eyebrows questioningly at Dundrog. Leo was sick of it all. He sucked as much spit and blood into his mouth and spat a wad in Grizzly's direction.

He straightened his neck and bony shoulders, and with all the strength he could muster, he shouted, "I hate you! I will make sure you never wake up after this sleep cycle." Leo meant it. By moon-god, he meant it. If Grizzly didn't kill him now, he would ask someone else. And he knew exactly who to ask. He'd ask Barkor.

Grizzly pinned Leo with a furious glare. Bloody spit dripped from his chin. His dark eyes flickered with hate. Satan's pools of fire, Leo saw blazing at him and calling him in the silence that followed. No one uttered a word.

"You know, I'm counting on it. If you manage that, my worm, then you will rule Grayrak! Only the fearless, strong, and vicious deserves the throne." Grizzly turned and scowled as he ran his gaze slowly into Dundrog's direction, who had swallowed his hysterics and looked at Leo like he would kill him if Grizzly didn't. *Good, be my guest. I don't care who does it.* Leo returned the death stare. Grizzly's evil gaze scanned the room from side to side. Coughs and the shuffling of his boots were the only sounds breaking the uncomfortable silence as he passed judgment on them.

A new plan was forming. Leo knew the young man that intrigued Grizzly would be his ticket out of this hell he had stupidly sold himself into. He was unsure how to ask and befriend the man who had Grizzly running circles around him.

A feeling he'd forgotten bubbled up inside him. *Hope.*

No one else should experience his suffering, but selfishly he needed the prince, the thief, and the hero, to save him, even if it was smothering him with a pillow.

They said he was a boy. Someone once told Leo he'd been around since the last humans landed on the moon. Whether it was because he was born on Earth or didn't grow old, Leo didn't know, but Grizzly wanted that, and he wanted to break and own that for his own selfish reasons. As long as he ruled the underbelly of Grayrak City, no one was safe. Grizzly thought the young man was nothing more than a common thief. Someone must have betrayed Barkor.

Leo knew the secret stories people told about him. Barkor stole from unsuspecting marketers, stripping them of their daily purchases. When the privileged, mostly the Disciples, returned home, they would open their bags and discover anything from dead rats to rocks in place of the food and groceries they'd purchased earlier that day. People talked, and they knew it was him.

After Grizzly's speech, plans were made, bets were placed, and Grizzly never lost. Never. He left Leo on the floor and overeagerly planned on trapping Barkor. The sick thrill of their greedy desires stoked their need to capture him.

When the festivities had wound down, Leo heard Grizzly telling his men, "Because, you idiots, those who are quick to act and slow to plan, fail dis—dismal—dismally. I will show you how it is done!" Grizzly said, inebriated to the point of falling over.

How they retained anything was a miracle.

Half-drunk and half-awake, they went on the pursuit.

Talali, a young slave girl, and two friends put Leo in his pram and pushed him inside. "Thank you, Talali. You should have left me there," Leo said, and he knew she knew why. He'd asked them many times to smother him, but they refused. Whether they feared Grizzly or just wanted him to live another day, he didn't know, probably for both reasons.

"I can't leave you like that, Leo. You're still human with feelings. And I wouldn't want to be left like that if I didn't have arms or legs," Talali said.

Once inside, gentle hands washed him and made him comfortable. Leo welcomed it and groaned as they massaged the knots out of his shoulders. "You know just how to spoil me. Thank you, girls. Talali, do you think you'll be able to get word to Barkor that they're hunting him?" he asked.

"We have already. He knows they're coming for him."

"That's good. I hope he kills them."

"He can't. Otherwise, he would have done it a long time ago."

"Why? Why the fuck not?" Leo whisper-screamed hoarsely at her and felt guilty as soon as she cringed.

"If he kills Grizzly, the Zelk will come for all of us," Talali said as she pulled the blanket over his chest to help him settle for the night. He appreciated being vertical in the bed, even if it was Grizzly's bed.

"I think that's a story he made up to stay alive as long as he has."

"Maybe, just hang in there. I have a feeling his days are numbered." Talali winked at him, and the three girls left Leo alone with his thoughts. Exhausted, he closed his eyes and fell asleep immediately.

Later, before the end of their sleep cycle, Leo hopped with fright and searched urgently for danger. Grizzly must have joined him and passed out as usual. There it was again. Loud, frantic knocking on their door. It must have been that which had awakened him.

"Are we under attack?" Grizzly asked, jumping from the bed, naked and arming himself with a sword. Standing at the ready, he asked, "Who the fuck is there? Show me your badges!" Grizzly sputtered, and Leo lay wordlessly still, expecting an attack. There was talk of upheaval from the humans. He hoped that this was it. The rebellion. He smiled.

"It is I, your second in charge!" Dundrog shouted, sounding overjoyed with excitement.

"You idiot, Dundrog, why are you so loud? What's up? It's bedtime. Not even the slaves have gotten out of bed yet?"

*Yes, and they need sleep, too. Not as if you ever worried about that.*

Leo watched Grizzly realize that the cacophony and urgency were not caused by bad news but by the exact opposite.

More urgent hammering on the door. "Hold on, and for god's sake, stop knocking!" Grizzly scowled and went to open the door. "What's the big deal?" Grizzly yelled, and

Leo heard him unlocking the locks and chains that barricaded them inside while they slept. "Come in, for fuck's sake," Grizzly shouted and stormed back into the bedroom, limp cock swinging sideways as he searched for his pants.

"It's news about the boy." Dundrog stormed into the room after him, ignoring Leo.

"Could it be justified that you're somewhat more enthusiastic than the average Disciple this night? This better be good news," Grizzly said sarcastically, lowering his sword and throwing it with a well-practiced movement onto the hook where he hung his weapons. Suddenly chaos surrounded Leo as the usual group of idiots stormed inside the tiny room, still inebriated. "I need a fucking moment!" Grizzly shouted. He looked like he needed a drink.

"Where are Chris, Louis, and Tollie?" Grizzly asked, somehow managing to tally all his men.

"They've been captured!" the men shouted as one. Leo counted twelve of the usual fifteen members present in the small space. It reeked.

"Can someone please tell me where my fucking pants are? Get the fuck out or find my fucking pants!" Grizzly yelled, frustrated. Some wanted to leave the room, others fell to the floor searching for the missing pants. Dundrog, always eager to please, fell to his knees, searching underneath the bed.

"I have to speak to you now," he mumbled from underneath Grizzly's double bed, which was made of crates, elevated on stilts at the four corners. Dundrog's oily hair stood up in all directions.

To Leo, the day started like any other day. Being sick to his stomach before breakfast, with chaos all around him.

Dundrog took a few gulps of air and started rambling as he handed Grizzly his pants. "Sir, he's dangerous. We won't be able to catch him physically. We tried to apprehend him. We would have to let him come to us. Willingly. Otherwise, you have to send an army into the settlement and that's not a good idea because it may cause a rebellion," Dundrog said, panting from excitement, looking like he was swooning dreamily. "He's a handsome one. I guess he's somewhere in the neighborhood of twenty Earth years."

"What?" Grizzly stood flabbergasted, with one leg tucked inside his pants and his unsightly dick protruding from the waistband. Twenty-year-old boys were as scarce as Leo was. Grizzly looked at Leo. "Now that we know what he looks like, we can start asking around and figuring out where he lives. Dundrog, this is fantastic news, and we should be celebrating! Leo, you're getting a brother."

Leo watched them silently. *You're going to force him to be yours and then try to break him as you broke me. You will not succeed.*

Dundrog kept talking, and every time he described the boy, they laughed and rubbed their hands together as if they couldn't wait to touch him. They continued to plot against the boy. The description grew from gloriously beautiful man to dull, uninspiring, menacing, murderous thief. *Fucking lying redskin bastards!* Leo realized they planned to frame him for something and advertise a reward.

Leo knew that a fucking storm was coming. He couldn't wait to see the devastation. This time, he knew they didn't know what kind of trouble would follow when that man walked through their door. He bowed to no one.

"I'm glad you're all here. We need an emergency meeting of the highest importance," Grizzly said and turned to Leo. "You will be relieved when I apprehend this thug!"

"Hmmm, so that's the story you're going with?" Leo retorted.

"Get ready. Bring food and drink. Ring the bells and notify the slaves," Grizzly ordered, turned, and left.

Leo sighed. He wanted to get to the market as soon as possible when he'd woken up, and now his plans were fucked. He turned and grabbed the rope with bells next to his head with his teeth. Talali arrived first. She helped Leo into his chair, pushed him to the kitchen, where he sat, and waited for the girls to prepare the morning meal. The three slaves entered the kitchen from the door on the floor. They knew the routine, and they kept their heads down without saying a word—each knew their tasks. They were exhausted and dirty. Some had bloody blue bruises all over their little fragile bodies.

Leo watched from the kitchen area as Grizzly toasted his half-filled cup into the air, spilling more of the bottle's contents.

Dundrog was looking pleased with himself as he stepped closer and smirked. "See, you have to be smart, Leo," he said and pestered Leo by sticking his tongue into Leo's ear canal. Leo turned his head as fast as possible to try to bite him. Dundrog was faster, by slapping Leo over the head and laughing.

"Is everyone here? Let's plan and then celebrate this!" Grizzly yelled, and the others cheered. They did that every day, the whole day. Always looking for an excuse to celebrate something.

Leo hated them even more at that moment.

"All boys have mothers and fathers or sisters and brothers, and we can manipulate them, just like this," Grizzly boasted and snapped his fat fingers. "This boy will strengthen us and make us richer!"

"Yeah, cheers! To the boy!" they shouted and applauded.

Leo wondered if they cheered and shouted for him before they lured him into their ranks.

"We're going to reel him in," Grizzly said loudly and realized he had an empty cup. He held it out to be filled, took a sip, and went on. "We're going to find out where he lives and whom he loves." He finished emptying that as he did the first. "Let's get this party started!" Once on his feet, he launched his cup at the fireplace, and the cup shattered into pieces. The fire flared blue as the alcohol combusted.

"Yeah-yeah!" Others hurled their clay cups in the same direction as Grizzly for good luck.

Obtuse asses.

When they'd finished their meals, they started making music. Leo shook his head cynically.

"No, not the stupid pirate song."

"Arrrr," Grizzly growled, enthused and fueled by drugs and alcohol.

*Dammit, he's going to sing.*

*"I'LL OPEN THE DOOR, ba-rumba-dan-ha*
*Hear my song, ba-rumba-dan-ha*
*Of treasure found, ba-rumba-dan-ha*
*It rattles my bones, ba-rumba-dan-ha*
*And summons my soul, ba-rumba-dan-ha*
*I can't ignore, ba-rumba-dan-ha*
*The beat of my drums, ba-rumba-dan-ha*
*Get richer, get louder, ba-rumba-dan-ha, ba-rumba-dan-ha, ba-rumba-dan-ha."*

# CHAPTER 33
# THE HALF-MAN

*"Good morning, citizens of Phoenix.*

*It's now six a.m.*

*Did you know communication in the workplace is important because it boosts team member morale, engagement, productivity, and satisfaction?*

*Communication is also key to better team collaboration and cooperation. Ultimately, effective workplace communication helps drive better results.*

*Please visit your community news page to learn ways to overcome your incommunicado, and if that doesn't help, just bloody start a conversation.*

*Breakfast is served until eight a.m.*

*Hope you get those dialogues going!"*

**GENERAL CIAN ROMANOV**
**2145 A.D. (93 A.T.)**
**Grayrak City**
**Earth's moon**
**Two Months Later**

Barkor, Sarinka, and Ish first met the leadership of Phoenix via two-way video communication. Kawa was the most technologically inclined and had fiddled under the dashboard with the wires to establish the communication channel with Phoenix. Initially, only radio frequencies were sent between them and the Earth. Eventually, Kawa went Earthbound, Connor installed a bigger memory, and Lasitor was uploaded.

Their fathers were not impressed when they discovered that Cian and his brothers had stolen the Spacecar. Fortunately, the Earth-Moon-Earth communication bounce relied on radio waves from a Phoenix transmitter, which took time to reflect back to the Moon's surface. These unavoidable delays served as a temporary stall tactic. However, after a lengthy and frustrating venting session, their leaders ended up smiling and assuring them that they would provide assistance in any way necessary. Initially, Ivan and Eryn shielded Cian from the barrage of questions and accusations. Eventually, though, everything blew over as their fathers finally saw the logic behind the plan to infiltrate and eradicate the vermin on the Moon. Cian was appointed as the general in charge of the operation and would report to Phoenix leadership as required.

Once on Earth, Ish was an impressive representative who used the opportunity to convince Brad and the leadership team about their winning action plan. Operation Lunar Evacuation was a go. Together, they devised the next steps and each member's role in freeing the humans with zero casualties. All agreed that war should be avoided. Building a fleet would deplete resources unnecessarily, do more harm, and endanger the already fragile ecosystem of Earth. If someone lit so much as a spark, the atmosphere could explode, leaving the planet without air. If something happened to the moon, Earth's gravity and sea tides would be influenced, and with water covering the surface, it might create giant tidal waves that could take years to stabilize.

There were steps to be implemented before they could execute the major stages of the big evacuation. Cian's plan was simple—if they followed all the steps, Ivan and Eryn should attempt to slow the Zelk from further multiplying by inhumanely cutting up people to be used as body parts for the Zelk.

Emergency supply trips to Phoenix didn't happen as often as Cian wanted. He wanted to bring more relief food and water packs for the starving people of Grayrak. He was impressed by a secret underground water reservoir hidden away from the unsuspecting Disciples. Since the Disciples never shared their water or food, Ishtar had assured Cian, no one would betray their own and divulge their secret water hole.

Undercover reserve soldiers were to be smuggled into Grayrak to befriend and assist the humans with preparation and sneak evacuation. Barkor, Donali, and Sarinka would strategically plant the spies to protect, collect intelligence, and ensure every man, woman, and child in Grayrak City followed Cian's directions to a T. And it also had to happen as fast as possible while the Disciple overlords were unaware and ultimately eliminated.

Sarinka would act as a middle person. Donali would report all covert activity to Cian and cultivate trust, as he and the Phoenix soldiers worked on spreading the word about the exodus. Depending on the speed of Cian and Lasitor's annexation of the Zelk's warship, Sarinka would report whether Barkor had found a middleman who would bring Eryn and Ivan to the Zelk and infiltrate them to uninstall, delete, or whatever was done with robots who thought they were people. Connor and Mika jumped to create a virus that Ivan and Eryn would plant to lay dormant inside the Zelk collective mainframe until the day of evacuation when Lasitor, already uploaded to the warship, would override and deploy the viruses for the ultimate destruction.

To increase the melodrama, that was Cian's life, his heart yearned to sing his song for Barkor. He distanced himself and his heart from the shit show by joining the ranks of the Zelk and offering his military service. His mission was to worm himself onboard their warship and assure the Zelk that he would win the war for them. *What war, no one knew.* He had many things to do to keep himself occupied. People needed to be evacuated, the Disciples eliminated, and the Zelk exterminated.

Cian had seen the flesh machines. The most obvious trait was their assumption that they were superior. The Zelk looked like robots with artificial limbs, hearts, and organs meshed with other human body parts fused to their bones. Some had hands and clamps, others walked on legs upright or rolled around on wheels. He even saw one that hopped on one leg, like a gas spring piston thing. But they all had one thing in common: their collective brain.

The top obstacles were convincing the Zelk to give Eryn and Ivan jobs at the hospital inside the Zelk tower and getting Cian onboard the warship without being scanned or discovered as Anunnaki. They needed an inside man, one that traded with the Zelk. Someone willing to switch sides and work with Barkor. Donali was head over ass in love with Sarinka. Cian's respect for her stemmed from the fact that she operated like a black widow spider—spinning the web, watching, guarding, and keeping it all together. He never asked her, her sex and how she identified. He made a mental note to ask Donali. But he was sure Donali wouldn't tell him what genitals she had under her clothes. She reminded Cian of Juan wearing his tactical suit in South Africa. She had a throatier voice as well.

Ish explained the Zelk thought in a circle. "They're programmed and set on saving and protecting the humans, but somehow got their wires crossed and lost in the cycle of producing soldiers for human defense and using humans as parts to build the soldiers. As for the water supply—" he explained animatedly to everyone in the boardroom who hung on every melodic word he spoke. "In theory, making water from hydrogen and oxygen is very easy. Mixing it together is a bit of a challenge. But basically, you mix the two gases and add a small ball of heat, so activation energy forces the hydrogen and oxygen molecules to break the covalent bonds that hold $H_2$ and $O_2$ molecules together. The hydrogen cations and oxygen anions are then free to react with each other, which they do because of their electronegativity differences. And then, the chemical bonds re-form to make water. The problem is that additional energy released propagates, creating a highly exothermic reaction." He paused, waiting for the men's reactions around the conference table, and got none. "Meaning a reaction accompanied by the release of a lot of heat," he said.

Silence.

Finally, after a long pause, Mika spoke up. "He meant it all goes kaboom."

"Ah," everyone answered.

It gave Cian a headache to understand it all. To him, it was simple. Go in, plant a bomb or two, and move out. Bye-bye troubles on the moon. But before that could happen, they had to coordinate their stealth attack. They had to abduct and convince a Disciple to switch sides.

Cian, Ish, and Kawa accompanied Donali, who'd been living undercover in Grayrak and acclimated to the harsh conditions and life on the moon for the past two months. They were on a scouting and retrieval errand; *the nice way to say abduct a Disciple.* The plan was to grab him and persuade him to turn sides. And that included Barkor in the equation.

Each time Cian's boots touched the surface, it felt like his heart wanted to combust inside his ribcage. He had a good coping mechanism. He kept his head down and ignored Barkor.

The wall divided the dome into two parts. The Zelk occupied the outer rim while the humans lived inside the smaller inner rim but closer to the mining and storage facility and the exit where they boarded the Zelk Hydrogen mining ship. Once the harvesting was done, the canisters were unloaded, stored, and cooled in the tunnels below the lunar surface. On the opposite side of the dome, where the Zelk tower was, the Warship Horizon waited to be manned and readied for a war of unknown origins or enemies. A network of underground tunnels burrowed by the first humans connected the Hydrogen Storage Facility to both exits of the dome to transport the fuel canisters to and from the opposite sides.

According to Sarinka, Barkor reported the first steps to getting Cian and his men on the warship, as well as Ivan and Eryn inside the Zelk tower were ready to be taken.

They received information from one of the slave girls who worked at Grizzly's that he was looking for Barkor and that his lover would be near the market that day. That was the sign they'd been waiting for. The abduction plan could now be executed. Cian gave the go-ahead to grab Grizzly's lover.

Grayrak City was a dump. Rusted containers stacked together and onto each other made it look like a train junkyard. Narrow alleyways ran between the heaps of metal houses and connected in the center area, which they called the market. A few stalls sold rat meat, the only animals on the moon. *They probably escaped some scientist's lab and multiplied.* In the center of the market was one small water reservoir that collected recycled water. The well had dried up long ago, and no one could say if it ever produced water because no one had had access to it, thanks to Grizzly and his men. Most humans preferred to live underground where the Zelk and the Disciples couldn't find them.

Just as they passed the market area, they heard a woman calling for Barkor.

"They think they're luring Barkor to Grizzly—the Disciple in charge," Donali whispered in Cian's ear. Cian nodded his understanding and followed Donali's direction to hide in the shadow of a gigantic boulder while keeping low.

"That's him… Leo." Donali pointed his laser gun toward the approaching parties. "He calls for help and tells people to sell their body parts to the Zelk. In Grayrak, they call those men half-men," Donali whispered, and Cian shook his head in disbelief at it all.

He knew why they were called half-men, but he had yet to see one. The market area was otherwise empty. It reminded Cian of those cowboy western movies he watched where the people scurried away and only tumbleweeds and dust covered the roads. The feeling of trepidation hung around them, making his skin crawl.

A faint squeak-squeak noise grew louder and drew Cian's attention to the woman pushing the homemade wheelchair. The wheels were different sizes, wobbling from side to side over the rocky pathway. It was a sad visual. Cian wanted to scream, say fuck this, and go home. The man in his buckling wheelchair smiled. He was dressed in a dirty, oversized shirt and strapped to the seat. It was a head and torso of a fully grown man. The head had no ears, his arms were missing, and he sat on a pillow. No legs in sight. Not even stumps were visible. It sickened Cian. He'd been staying on the ship, preferring to hide from the mad circus.

The calling of Barkor's name drew Cian's attention back to the woman who was high and practically walking on her pinkie toenails. Behind her, two willowy women with their children scurried away, sensing trouble coming. The dim blue light from the Zelk tower illuminated their target's faces.

"She must have escorted him to Barkor's secret hideout," Donali said. Cian nodded and soundlessly drew his sword. If this was a trap, he needed to be ready. His understanding was it was kill or be killed. He hated how she called Barkor's name. No matter how scarce females were, he would kill her if Barkor needed saving. She cupped her hands and called again. Cian growled and listened to how she lied and assured Barkor he would have all the food and safety he desired. Donali looked knowingly at him and smiled. Yeah, he felt like an alpha wolf protecting his mate. Unfortunately, Barkor didn't know that. Not yet.

"Don't worry, Barkor isn't stupid. He knows this is a trap. He has his spies on the inside," Donali whispered. Cian knew that. He couldn't understand his murderous, idiotic reactions. He'd only seen Barkor a few times and was already acting like a cave dweller. His possessive urges frightened him.

"Barkor," she called again. "You can trust me. Please come out, Barkor! We want to show you your room. We eat three times daily and have as much water as we want. Mommy is clean and dressed in a pretty dress from Earth." The urgency in her shrill voice betrayed her. She sounded anxious as she twirled and gave them a pathetic show. Moondust got swept up by the mini tornado caused by her yellow-brown Victorian hoop dress.

The man cleared his throat. "Have you ever taken a bath? With your whole body underwater? Please come out. It's getting late! I want to make a deal with you," the half-man's voice echoed into the alley.

"Barkor, come, I've found us a home," she called in the Old Earth language.

"She wants to get back for more drugs. Grizzly has her in his claws," Donali whispered. Cian's gaze locked on her. She looked sick and deathly pale. The makeup on her face made her look worse. Ugly blue eyeshadow and red lips and red cheeks. She looked like she'd been beaten. Her hair stood in all directions, and bruises covered every inch of exposed skin.

"Barkor, please come out. Mommy's tired and needs to return to our new home. You'll like it. Come out now. I know you're here and listening to us. Come out now!" she yelled, her face twisted with despair, and each sentence got louder and nastier.

"Fuck, lady!" The half-man exclaimed, pushing a shoulder up to his ear and shaking his head. "My fucking ears. Why the fuck do you have to scream like a drunk whore, bitch?" he shouted at her, and terror crossed her face. His words were still echoing in the air—the next moment, a body slammed into him and his wheelchair. One second, he was upright, and the next, someone knocked him flat onto the dirt and stink of the alley road.

"You piece of shit! Don't talk to her like that!" Barkor threatened, and all Cian could do was blink and grow a hard-on. He stared at Barkor's magnificent beauty as he straddled the man's torso and fisted his shirt in one hand. The man said something, and Barkor bitch-slapped him with his flat hand.

Cian's head spun. Endorphins and hormones flooded his system. He didn't hear the screaming and slapping. No, all he could see was the most beautiful young man with a look of murder in his gorgeous eyes. He had a head full of dark blond curls that framed his face, making him look like an avenging angel. This was too much, too real. Cian gulped for air and tucked, turned, and ran. With an oomph and a thud, he collided with a solid wall of muscled chest.

"Fuck, bro, do you have to sneak up on me like that? What's wrong with you?" Cian asked, rubbing his nose. He stepped left and right, trying to pass the wall of muscle. But Ish stepped in front and blocked him each time.

*The fucker's fast.*

"This had better be a mistake," Ish said in his weird accent and deep baritone and, like always, with a hint of humor as Cian amused him.

"That's the mark. That's why you're here. It's highly unlikely that another chance of infiltration is possible. Your brothers won't make it if you can't get this half-man to turn," Ish said, telling the truth and pissing Cian off. He was probably right. "No one would escape out of here alive. You had just better step in and make yourself known." Ish took Cian by the shoulders and turned him one-hundred and eighty degrees. "You must go now. Don't worry about the woman. She won't say a word."

Ish pushed Cian like a reluctant toddler learning to walk. At the alley junction where Barkor had apprehended the hostage, Cian saw four directions to escape: up, right, left, and ahead. Ish halted and reached into a pouch he produced from somewhere inside the long hooded jacket he wore. He removed a small vial. Twisted the top and activated it, then tossed it gently into the air. "Go help Barkor with the half-man. Leave the screaming woman. She's as good as dead, anyway. Her organs are failing."

"But it's his mother. We can't leave her here," Cian said.

"It's not his mother, Cian. It's someone pretending to be his mother. His mother died long ago. This is just someone who helped him blend in."

Cian watched the strange quicksilver-like liquid undulate, growing into an umbrella over them.

"Go, it's a blocking agent. Anyone encapsulated would be frozen and disintegrated into molecular matter," Ish said, and Cian pulled a *what-the-fuck* face.

"Meaning it blends and makes it disappear. Become part of everything," Ish explained animatedly.

Cian shook his head. That encompassed science fiction, and he wanted to ask questions. But the wobbling silver jelly almost engulfed the alley in totality. He jumped into action to collect Barkor and the half-man. Donali ran from the opposite side. Barkor got up and flung the half-man to Donali. He caught him and wrapped an old rag around their target. The half-man protested, but Donali propped a piece of cloth inside his mouth and then taped it shut. Silence fell over the market area.

Barkor jumped to help the woman as she collapsed. Spastic. Teeth grinding and neck spasming, arms extended straight at her sides, wrists bent downward, fingers stiff, her face contorted, Cian thought it looked painful. Strange bubbling sounds escaped her mouth as high-pitched cries between clenched teeth whistled, incomprehensible sputters. "You trapped, us—s!" Her voice was shrill as tears rolled clean tracks down her dusty face.

"But you wanted to trap me to go to Grizzly's, didn't you? You've become addicted to the drugs he gave you," Barkor said with a gentle rumbling voice while wiping the tears from her eyes. He tapped her shoulder as she closed her eyes. "Come with us. We'll clean you up."

"No, I want to go back. You must come with me. Please." She cried defeated sobs.

"You know I can't. I need this half-man. If you make it back, Grizzly won't take it well. It's his lover we're taking. Look at you. Let me help you," Barkor begged, and Cian watched as the half-man squirmed in protest in Donali's arms. This was sick, and in so many variations of sickness, it sickened him. He wanted to vomit. He realized his life so far was nothing compared to what these people had to endure to survive.

Ish stepped in and hunched down. He placed a hand on each of Barkor's shoulders. "You should be departing. I'll take care of her. Go take the half-man as we agreed. We must focus. She's made her choice already. You can't save her. You know you can't. Go and be safe. She's not important. The mission is important," Ish said, never breaking his gaze. His voice was respectful and empathetic. Sadness clouded his features.

Barkor stood looking defeated. Cian wanted to wrap his arms around him. They were almost the same height. Barkor looked like Eryn, but his height and build were similar to Cian's. It was dark, so he couldn't see his eyes.

"Come, we have to get out of here!" Donali called and kicked up dirt as he ran to their rendezvous. Cian turned, making sure Barkor followed. In the corner of his eye, he saw Ish scooping the hysterical woman up, and she didn't like it. She kicked and waved her arms. Then he halted, and Cian watched as Ish touched her forehead. She went limp like she'd passed out or had fallen asleep.

"Come!" Barkor called. He paused momentarily while they watched Ish activate another quicksilver balloon that enveloped her like an amoeba and then puffed soundlessly. In a blink of an eye, she was gone. No blood. Nothing. Cian stood gobsmacked. One moment, there was a person, and the next, she was gone.

"Holy shit," he exclaimed. "Where did she go?"

Ish bunched his fingers together and blew over them. *Poof.* He gestured in a universal sign language that she'd vanished. Cian lingered. His feet wanted to move, but his brain was frozen. He couldn't understand how, why, and where to disappear a person like that. Barkor jumped to push him forward. His frozen limbs weren't moving, and the moment their gazes met, Barkor's bewildered gaze softened. Then Cian's body froze for a whole different reason.

"Hurry-hurry!" Barkor wrapped his thick long fingers around Cian's arm, and a sobering, searing hot hand pulled him away from the scene.

*Hello, lover,* he mused as he saw Barkor up close for the first time. Thank god his frozen brain cells defrosted, his defense mechanisms activated, and he scowled at the man.

"I'll be fine. Go!" Cian sucked his teeth at him. Barkor grunted, shaking his head as he walked away.

*I must get out of here.* Cian's chest constricted. Panic and a deep sadness came over him, like that weird balloon of Ish's consumed all his hope and left him feeling nothing. Why was he reacting this way?

*Why couldn't I just smile and say good job? Fuck this. I'm out of here as soon as the half-man can get me on the Horizon.*

When they'd reached the rendezvous on the outskirts of Grayrak City, they found Donali standing erect with the squirming and blindfolded half-man in his arms.

"Alright, can we go, guys?" Donali asked with a lopsided grin.

"Yes, we swept the area, and no one will talk. Grizzly won't know what happened, he'll wonder, but he'll never know," Barkor said with a twisted mouth and a sarcastic grimace. He bent and spoke near the half-man's ear, and the man simpered. The half-man stopped squirming. What was Barkor saying? Barkor flushed red in his neck and face, as his expression hardened. God, he looked terrifying, like Batman on acid. He had a ball-headed club in his hand. *His weapon of choice.*

Cian concentrated and tried listening in. Eryn was much better at this, and it seemed Ish also mastered the gift. It was almost like listening to the wind. He tipped his head and fine-tuned himself to focus on listening to the half-man's thoughts. It was chaotic, but the loudest words were *yes, yes, yes.*

Barkor lowered the blindfold and interrupted Cian's eavesdropping by saying out loud, "You see, Jack," as he pointed the weapon at the half-man. It seemed he named his bludgeon weapon, and Cian liked that. Maybe he should name his sword?

"He'll crush your fucking skull. You sick fuck, she's gone, and it's all your fault. She tried to lure me to Grizzly's, and you're the reason she's dead. You will pay for this, you worthless piece of shit!" Barkor shouted into the man's face. The half-man paled and winced.

"You're going to get my friends inside. You will help us, or I will cut whatever you haven't sold to the Zelk off, extremely slowly and painfully." Barkor's voice grated deeply as he threatened and thrust his club up to the half-man's nose. He looked vicious. His curls were muddy, and his face had black smears of soot over his eyelids, like a lunar warrior going into battle.

The half-man stopped protesting and then faintly nodded his head. Cian listened to his thoughts; he begged for it—he wanted Barkor to kill him.

"You sick bastard." Barkor turned and scoffed. "Bring him, Donali," he shouted over his shoulder and kicked at the ground.

They followed him to their hideout on the opposite side of the city. "Keep his fucking eyes blindfolded and muffle his ears. We don't want him to see or hear where we're going!" His voice was deep and menacing.

Cian watched his mate and was sure he'd forgotten how to breathe. It was frustrating because he couldn't tell if Barkor felt the same about him or whether he even felt the pull between them. For a second, he thought he saw recognition dawning on Barkor's face. He was a badass, and Cian's first words were…Cian shook his head at his hopeless prospect—Barkor was like a square block of ice and muscle. Everything about him was fair and square. From his dirty square-cut fingernails to his sexy square jaw and not to mention those stiff square shoulders. He bet he even had multiple squared abdominal muscles. Fuck, even his boots were square-tipped and spiked.

*Yip, such a mean square and fair motherfucker.*

Cian wanted to laugh and cry. Only he had such luck. He had a ruthless dangerous mate. There was no way Barkor and himself made any sense. Jesus, how would they roll in the sac? Would Barkor even give him a chance? He looked at the man who carried himself with authority. It was his fucking moon. Obviously, Cian was in deep trouble. He was so fucked. His peg was round, and his mate probably had a square hole. That was if he would even give him a chance to see it.

This wasn't funny. Usually, he would have blurted thoughts like these out to Ivan and Eryn. But what would he say? *Barkor doesn't see me.*

Someone bumped him on his hip. Sarinka snickered as she passed him and said over her shoulder in an amused chuckle, "Don't worry, lover boy, he's not as mean and bad as he seems. He's a good man who saw too much ugly and only tried to survive the horror we all live in. You'll see once you get to know him."

Cian didn't have a clue how to seduce a person like that. The only thing he could think of was to help Barkor get all these people off the moon and back to Phoenix. He had to prove himself worthy. Otherwise, Barkor would never respect him. Once all the humans were on their way to safety, then he would make his move. For now, he had to push his urges to mate down his list of priorities again.

# CHAPTER 34

# FINALIZE EXODUS

*"Good morning, citizens of Phoenix.*

*It's now six a.m.*

*Did you know pre-Doomsday free divers could hold their breath for ten minutes while diving to extreme depths and that Navy SEALs can only hold their breath for two to three minutes?*

*I know who I would want to call to come to save me when Phoenix's walls crush and we're all drowning. Definitely not the Navy SEALs.*

*Visit your community news page about swim lessons and breath-holding techniques to increase your chances of survival during flooding.*

*Breakfast is served until eight a.m.*

*Have a breathe-easy day!"*

**Ivan Romanov**
**2147 A.D. (95 A.T.)**
**Zelk Tower, Grayrak City**
**Earth's moon**

After Ivan had completed his surgeries, he rounded the corner, tearing down the long corridor. Like clockwork, he knew a jolt of excitement would pass through him when his gaze fell on the stunningly handsome man approaching.

*Play it cool.* His thoughts scrambled through every scenario possible that would reveal who he was and what their mission was. Working undercover made his nerves raw with worry. But seeing Eryn gave him renewed strength to push ahead, to face the day. He inhaled deeply and lifted his chin, preparing himself for the zing that would shoot through him as soon as he passed his sexy husband walking toward him from the opposite side of the long hallway between the operating rooms and the recovery unit.

*Damn, could he do it more nonchalantly? Probably.*

Ivan's gaze darted around and then focused on where they shouldn't. On the bulge of cock and balls that the big Brawl was packing.

*Eyes up, Ivan, and for god's sake, don't start glowing!*

Eryn pinned him with a pointed look as they shortened the distance between them step by step. Each step sounded like a hammer on an anvil. Like a clock ticking backward.

*Oh, bug-shit, he walks tall and so self-assured. Yes, mister, look at me while I eye-fuck you.*

Each time he saw Eryn, he'd woken to those thousands of butterflies that had taken up residence in Ivan's stomach when they'd fallen in love half a century ago.

*He's reading my mind. Oh lord, he's glaring at me. His intense gaze is sending out all sorts of naughty signals. The menace in those stunning golden-green eyes is genuinely going to be the death of me. I'm going to blow our cover. We are all going to be toast.*

*Oh, man, I want to fall to my knees and worship his cock until he shouts out my name. Nope, no worshiping today.*

*He's so close I can smell his cologne. That's it, and nothing's happening except my heart racing. He's always so proud and impeccably dressed. His hair's combed over to split in a perfect line at the left side. The opposite of his authentic look. Not one inch is out of place. Dear moon lord and those lips. Shut up, stop talking to yourself, and for fuck's sake, don't look at his plump lips. Be aloof.*

"Good morning, doctor," Ivan greeted with what he hoped looked like calm professionalism. The sexy fucker just tipped his chin at him and passed. He bet he was one hundred percent aware of his effect on him. He was chuckling at Ivan.

Ivan could barely breathe. His legs were weak, and his steps faltered. It was the same story each morning when they passed each other. It seemed his affliction was getting worse.

*This shit has to end. We need to move out and finish our mission. Thank fuck the Zelk needed field surgeons on the Horizon.*

"Morning, Dr. Ivan. You look well. Isn't this a fine morning?" The droid nurse, Susie, interrupted Ivan's thoughts and welcomed him to the post-operative intensive care unit.

"Dr. Eryn just left, and like clockwork, every morning, you arrive without giving me a chance to delegate his orders. Shall we go since it never seems to bother you when I'm ill-prepared for your rounds? You have two patients waiting. Captain Pickering with multiple third-degree burn wounds, and General Cian Romanov with the skin graft, right femoral stump, eye prosthesis, and socket rebuild. He's challenging today. Been shouting and verbally abusing the nurses again. He said he wanted a real human to care for him. We explained it was impossible. He demanded to be transferred back to his warship," she said in a monotonous female robotic voice.

Finally, the nurse droid shut up so Ivan could speak. The recovery unit was cold and impersonal, but Susie instantly lit Ivan's flame of irritation to self-combustible levels. He hated the Zelk with a hidden passion.

"Morning, Susie, and like every morning, you say that to me." *And no, I will not come later because I can't see my husband.* Ivan kept that thought to himself, though. "Since you mentioned it for the millionth time, I think I should do my rounds in the afternoons. From tomorrow, I'll arrive around two," Ivan said spitefully with a grin and knowing well that wouldn't work for her or the unit.

"That's not permitted. It's time for the patients to get their feeding and rest afterward. There won't be time to do rounds." If ever Zelk had emotions, Susie was looking quite pissed at Ivan.

"My mind's made up, and you complain every day about my arrival time after Dr. Eryn has done his rounds."

Minute purple and green sparks flickered where her pupils would have been if she was human. "I did not complain, but if it bothers you that much, I will stop saying that he just left and we're not ready for you. You can't catch the hint even if it's true." Again, Susie expressed irritation and sarcasm.

"Fine, then I'll arrive before him. What time does he arrive?" *As if Ivan didn't know.*

"Dr. Eryn arrives at eight a.m. If you arrive earlier, you have to be here at six a.m., then we're ready for him when you're done," Susie said, and Ivan could swear it looked like she smirked.

*She thinks I won't be able to be here on time. Good, I was planning on it.*

"I'll try my best to be here at six a.m. Thank you. I'll request to push my surgeries up. If I'm late tomorrow, you should know I'll arrive at my regular time," Ivan said, hoping to confuse her strict timetable.

"You're most welcome. We're happy to accommodate you. A happy human is a productive human. I'll have coffee ready for you, doctor."

Ivan kept his facial expressions neutral. "That would be awesome," he lied. Just the thought of being with Eryn physically, instead of just passing by and greeting him daily —Eryn, with his perfect teeth and chiseled jaw, Ivan swooned dreamily. Then he righted himself, cleared his throat, and continued playing his role. It was all for the show, all in the name of freedom. Ivan tasted the sweetness of it as he lined up and pushed the last pieces of their mission into place. Cian's voice confirmed it.

Ivan heard curses and things clanging onto the floor as they approached the general's bed. *No doubt something has fallen after being thrown at the droids.* Susie pulled the curtains open and affirmed it. The general was halfway off his bed, busy strangling his droid nurse.

"Hmmm." Ivan coughed and cleared his throat. "Good morning, General. It seems we can transfer you down to recovery. You can use your arms and hands. Learning to walk with a new leg will be easy enough." Ivan chuckled, approaching the bed.

The General's face lit up with relieved surprise. He let the droid go and plopped back onto his pillows.

"Ahh, Dr. Ivan, I'm glad to see another human," he said and winked. "Yes, please get me out of this hellhole. I want to go back to my ship. I received orders that war was coming. I'm needed. Please, I beg of you, as soon as possible. I can't stand another minute of being tortured by these feelingless droids. A sex droid is one thing, but nurse droids think they have the power and authority to tell me when to have a shit and when to fucking sleep." Cian's voice boomed crassly through the unit.

Ivan missed his brother dearly. He thought he heard someone laughing a few beds over, and he struggled to keep a straight face.

The general's blond hair was shaven tabletop style, flat at the top and down to the scalp at the sides, unlike Ivan's, who wore his long blond locks mostly tied up in a loose bun or ponytail. His nose was broken in two places decades ago, it had set so crooked, they didn't look like twins anymore. Just as well, Cian had also refused medical care and disappeared for weeks, not getting stitches or scars treated. He had lost four of his front teeth after he got drunk at Ivan and Eryn's wedding; at least he had them replaced. His left eye was a piercing bright sapphire blue and almost matched his right bionic eye. Ivan performed an eye implantation procedure a week ago. Cian looked like they had locked him up in a maximum-security prison this year, with nothing to do but lift weights and draw permanent pictures on himself. His brother was all muscled up and covered in tattoos—disguising the fact that they were fraternal twins and knew each other. Luckily the droids never scanned their DNA. If they did, they could have discovered they were twins with spliced Anunnaki DNA from several generations back to the original gods of the skies. The only difference today was that the humans left on Earth had Peter Pan Capsules implanted, which made them just as immortal as those gods, which they now understood were only a race of extraterrestrial beings who meddled with the universe. The City of Phoenix had grown exponentially over the last century, and its inhabitants were still not showing any signs of growing old.

When Ivan sent word for immediate extraction, he didn't think his brother would blow himself up to do it. But the plan was in play, and all the pieces on the board were ready for action. Their planning and maneuvering had finally approached the finish line, and it was time to liberate these people and go home. The fool could have died, but Ivan had to admit it was a good plan. No one would ever suspect they were brothers.

They were deep undercover, and Cian played his role naturally. The future of these people depended on them.

"I'll do the final adjustments today on the visual prosthesis. How's your vision?" Ivan asked stoically.

The general scooted down in his bed, knowing what to do for his assessment. Ivan turned to the glass-top bedside table and placed his small silver-colored medical toolbox with specialized tools on top of it.

"Doc, it's working fine. My only problem is if I move fast from left to right. It's as if my head's turned, and there's a slow upload to my brain. It's disorientating."

"Hmmm, let me adjust that for you. I suspected I should replace the external relay device." Ivan turned to his toolbox, searching for the pliers and screwdrivers. "Susie, may I please have the triangulator I asked you to order yesterday?"

"Yes, doctor, certainly. I'll fetch it. It arrived late last night," Susie said while rolling off to fetch the permanent prosthesis.

"I'll adjust and connect the visual pathway from the retina to your brain," Ivan explained while waiting for Susie. She and her staff worked twenty-four-seven without breaks or mealtimes. That was the benefit of having Zelk instead of flesh and bone staff doing the labor. But many patients complained because they lacked empathy and understanding. They treated the patients as emotionless objects that provided body parts to them.

"Go on, get out of here. This is my doctor, and we don't need your help," the general commanded while hatefully glaring at his nurse droid, Julie.

Looking up at the nurse droid, Ivan nodded to her. "Thank you. I've got this. You may prepare his discharge and send transportation over."

"Hell yes, thanks, doctor. I was very close to pulling her plug. Can you believe she wanted to wash me with those cold steel hands?"

"That's their job, General. You didn't complain when you were comatose. May I, General?" Ivan asked as he lifted the blankets to examine the general's stump. He got a traumatic amputation during the fake bombing attack that ended up being genuine. Cian had shot a bomb into space and drove right through it to be convincing, losing his right eye and right lower leg. Ivan couldn't save the knee, but he was able to connect the sympathetic nerve root to a gold-plated microchip, making a full recovery with a bionic leg possible.

"The stump looks fully healed. After transferring you to the rehabilitation facility, we can attach the leg later today. I'll contact them. We will have a lab set up for you. Once you're admitted and scanned in, they can contact me and let me know when you're ready. Is that okay, General?"

"Yes, but if I say no, it's fucking no. I'm not an invalid. I want to return to my ship."

"I can come to the rehab center later today to connect and synchronize the nerve paths. Your stump healed well, and the skin looks less inflamed. Under normal circumstances, I would wait a month. But I received orders to move you to the top of my list and try to get you back on your ship as quickly as possible. It goes against my recommendations, but we're at war, and you're needed. I would have liked to see you at least two more times," Ivan explained, as he would with all his patients.

The general opened his mouth, but Ivan continued, not giving his brother a chance to interrupt him. The appearance of his older age, bulked-up muscled body, and unfailing bombastic personality fueled Ivan's determination not to stand down or show weakness towards his twin brother. He knew Cian didn't mean to. It was part of his role.

But his hackles rose. He was the reserved overthinker, and Cian was the gregarious go-getter, and this extraction plan of his brother's solidified that fact once more.

"Let me see you and re-evaluate you later this afternoon. We can talk about the specifics of your full discharge. I...finishing up...ah, that's it. How does it feel now after I inserted your new triangulator? I've adjusted your ocular motoric sensors' neuro-uptake."

Ivan packed his tools back into his bag while the general tested his eye by shaking his head from side to side.

"You're a miracle worker. I wish I had someone with your skills on my ship. We could skip getting grounded for medical treatments as insignificant as these." The general pointed to his stump and then his eye, as if losing his vision and a leg was nothing. According to the Zelk, it was nothing because everything and everyone were replaceable.

"The common medical droids or adhesive spiders are useless when getting a man up and running to continue the fight for victory. They're excellent at telling a man he's dying or needs to be taken to the moon's surface. But onboard physicians like yourself are very hard to find for procedures like these, connecting nerve path routes or having the plain decency of telling a man it will be all right. Plus, I like how I can't intimidate you. You'd fit right in with my crew on the Horizon." Cian spoke up loudly. The entire unit could hear his proposal.

He was smart doing that. The droids were recording it.

"Let's talk this afternoon. I'm very open to a change and helping where I'm needed. Thank you, General," Ivan said, and the general feigned surprise, pretending not to expect Ivan would take him up on his offer.

"Sure, sure, doctor." He coughed and shifted on the bed. "You just made my day, no, fuck, my entire year. With you on board, I'd be able to man the frontline. Our enemies wouldn't see us coming," he said, swinging his one leg over to the side of the bed and sliding down. Once he found his balance on his foot, Cian continued. "Then I need to make ready. I'll see you later. I'll contact my crew captain. He can bring down the paper-work and permits. We'll get you measured and settled in." Cian tapped his head, pretending to remember something important. "Oh, remember you'll have to list what you think you will and won't need. I prefer flesh and bone crew. If you need a droid assistant or nurse, that won't work for us on the Horizon," he said excitedly. He clapped his hands twice. Ivan did a double-take, his eyes wide. "Come now, doctor, the thought of war with the promise of a human-only crew is good news. I'll win this war for the Zelk."

Ivan heard the buzzing of the nurse droid wheels. Julie and Susie were probably recording their conversation to upload to the Zelk's collective intelligence.

"Don't worry, General. I have the perfect assistant to bring with me," Ivan whispered to Cian, who winked at him. "We have a mutual understanding." Ivan turned and left.

"Julie, come help me and bring my transport!" Cian yelled, and Ivan cringed.

Fuck, he was loud.

Ivan consulted his last patient in the unit and left directly. He needed something to eat and a quiet place to sit and send his message. After weighing the pros and cons, he mulled it over and decided it was safe to take this drastic step they'd been working towards. Taking his hidden communicator out of the secret compartment of his toolbox, he sent the message he'd waited to send for almost two years to Kawa, and Kawa would let Phoenix know.

*The Horizon is green. Finalize Exodus.*

# CHAPTER 35

# IT'S A GO!

*"Good morning, citizens of Phoenix.*

*It's now six a.m.*

*Did you know rats have been man's best friend since the dawn of time? They would warn about sinking ships, rotting houses, and even burning houses.*

*It's said that rats are intelligent social creatures, and that's why they're commonly used in idioms and reminded me of modern-day Phoenicians.*

*Like rats, they are fleeing a sinking ship.*

*Like rats escaping from a house on fire.*

*Anyway, visit your community news page to adopt a lab rat as a pet.*

*Breakfast is served until eight a.m.*

*Have a lovely day."*

**Eryn, King of the Brawl**
**2147 A.D. (95 A.T.)**
**Zelk, Tower**
**Grayrak City**
**Earth's moon**

Later that night, Eryn waited for the elevator door to shut, then slammed his back against the cold metal wall and let his head fall backward. Heaving with relief, he blinked furiously to stop the tears. Months of hidden emotions threatened to overflow and flood the usual cold and stoic persona he'd been wearing, thus exposing himself and ruining their mission. When he'd calmed down and collected himself, he realized the elevator wasn't moving. He checked his watch. *I'm on time.*

Out of habit, he checked his six and hit the little blue button with three vertical lines —the fucked-up new alphabet of the Zelk. He felt all kinds of feelings at the same time. Giddiness, nervousness, and excitement were right there at the forefront. His amphibian DNA called for water. Never had he known he would ever miss the darkness and humidity of the mining tunnels in South Africa.

Their mission was bearing fruit, and he was much closer to having Ivan back in his arms. Seeing Cian and receiving his message earlier had ended the torture of solitude and mock rivalry. Eryn was a social creature. He seemed to find himself always alone for the good and safety of others. Thinking of Ivan all alone made it worse.

He pushed himself off the wall and grabbed onto the railing with one hand, then stepped closer to the small window looking out over the rooftops, beyond the lunar dome, to see the blackness of space. The free-falling speed of the elevator made him feel like the contents of his stomach wanted to stay behind while he fell to the bottom of the tower. He swallowed the bile and looked longingly at the docking station, where the Horizon was being loaded by forklifts—hundreds of silver-colored cubes had been moved from storage on conveyor belts and were now loaded into the warship's belly. A small light flickered from below the platform in Morse code that Cian was released from the hospital.

*You little shit! You did it*!

Cian had promised them that their plan would work.

*"We will infiltrate and fuck them up from the inside. Eryn, we can do this. I know you can. Please convince my brother that we can't wait. We have to act now. I don't have time to wait and think about it."* Eryn remembered Cian's gruff, determined voice and resolved look that convinced Eryn he wasn't joking.

Eryn's eyes crinkled at the corners, something they hadn't done in a long time. *Message received, brother.*

He allowed himself to smile slightly. The muscle on the right corner of his mouth twitched. He released a slow, silent sigh of relief. The vapor obscured his view of the Horizon.

*I'll never hear the end of it from Cian if I miss check-in by accident.* Quickly, he fisted his sleeve to fake polish the glass. Then he flicked his hand three times. By blocking and unblocking the elevator light through the small window, Eryn had confirmed he was moving out in exactly six hours.

*Yes, brother, finalize Exodus.*

Their luck had finally turned. He chuckled inwardly and whispered in Earth's English to Ivan. *With my toes planted deep into the Earth, I will make filthy love to you and take a long time doing it.*

They had been working undercover at Grayrak Hospital for a little over a year. At the same time, Cian and his men worked on infiltrating the enemy. Their mission was to take command of their fleet, steal their warship, and ultimately bring their people home.

Eryn heaved another deep silent sigh. He missed Ivan, and he knew Ivan missed him, too. The only contact they'd allowed themselves was the quick passing by between surgery and post-op recovery in the mornings, which, he admitted, made his day much more bearable. Seeing his beautiful face each morning motivated him to continue their work to save the humans.

His thoughts were happy, but he kept his face emotionless. He was very good at disguising his true feelings and was glad to leave the human recycling factory. Eryn and Ivan's mission was to collect as much information as possible and strategically bug the Zelk mainframes. They were both scarce commodities because trained human physicians were hard to find on Grayrak. How Barkor's friend, Leo, convinced them they were educated at Grayrak University remained a mystery. There weren't any Universities on Grayrak. He guessed they really were that out of touch with what was going on in the human compound.

Thousands of humans had died, and still, the Zelk continued building more Zelk. Leo convinced them their supply of humans was running low and that they needed Eryn and Ivan for specialized surgeries, like connecting human tissue to muscles, nerves, and bone for bionic limbs and prosthetics. Better healthcare on Grayrak meant more humans. Save a human, score a body part, Eryn reasoned. Lately, the hospital had functioned as a neutral zone where humans were treated as valued donors. That was also the reason for many humans returning to have surgery. Life outside was horrible, and they literally would give an arm or a leg for five-star treatment, food, water, and a bed to sleep on.

Working on the ship meant their facial identities were scanned and stored with other qualifiers, which classified them as friends of the Zelk. These qualities were uploaded to the mainframe and triggered the hive if someone suspicious or unauthorized entered the high security zones. It also meant it was time to go home. Eryn and Ivan could board the Horizon since they were trusted allies of the Zelk. It also gave Ivan access to the final big computer room. The signal he just sent meant Lasitor was already programming a self-destruct sequence inside the collective Zelk brain.

Eryn was nervous—he felt his temples throbbing and not in beat with his heart. He closed his eyes briefly and grounded himself before croaking and exposing himself.

The Zelk watched and recorded all of them, and he hated it. But the thought of being with Ivan soon excited him and overpowered that fear or dread of being discovered and watching Ivan die.

When the elevator reached the lobby, he wiped all emotion from his face before the door slid open. He stepped out with his head held high as he greeted the droid at the front desk of the human sleeping quarters. Eryn's movement woke him up from standby mode.

"Good day, doctor," the male droid greeted him as usual.

"Hello, Pat," Eryn greeted and then silently thanked the stars that it was for the last fucking time.

*This time tomorrow, my ass will be up-up and away while I bury my cock deep inside Ivan.*

Eryn turned to the modified human receptionist, guarding the entrance to the human resting quarters. An allotment of the Zelk recognized that overworked human employees needed at least six hours of sleep, a nutritional diet of three meals a day, exercise, and a shower with a clean uniform daily.

"Any mail for me?" Eryn asked monotonously, knowing something was always waiting in the mailbox. He never received mail with encrypted messages this way—*like anyone would be so stupid*—but the Zelk still scanned it; even if it was for fingerprints, he trusted nothing in their hands.

For this reason, he had to return to his room to implant the virus he'd hidden in a little compartment behind the second tile of the second row from the hot water tap in his shower. *Also, I can do with a long wank picturing Ivan's lips around my cock.* He shook his head slightly to clear his mind when he heard Pat rolling towards him.

"Thank you, Pat." The three metal clamps for fingers released the envelope, and Eryn grabbed it. Instead of walking away, he stood still to open it on purpose in front of Pat, giving him the impression that they could trust him—solidifying their baseline for the next step of their mission.

*They're so predictable. Now he'll record and upload my actions and the fact that I'm trustworthy, open, and honest to the mainframe, and with every droid scanning my geometrics to identify me, they'll trust me because I open my mail in front of Pat.*

Eryn was so done with this pretending shit. He would rip the head off every Zelk crossing his path if it were up to him, but it wouldn't work in the long run. He had to be smart about it as they'd planned.

He took a few deep breaths and heard the high-pitched zing of data being transferred by Pat's electronic brain. The more he stimulated or showed his emotions, the higher the buzzing. Everything was uploaded, like the direction he came from, what he looked like, his facial features, the shades of red on his cheeks, how fast he breathed, his core temperature, and even the size of his pupils.

Eryn gave him a fake smile and a nod, while thinking about his purchase—he bought himself a new second-hand lampshade, an ugly yellow one that looked like a hot air balloon with clowns.

To bullshit the hive, Eryn and Ivan used the clown lampshade salesperson, Sarinka, who was their go-between and handler who communicated with Cian and their fathers. Eryn bought the lampshade as a means for them to bill him monthly for its rent, something he conveniently never paid. Although it was necessary for their mission, he liked the homemade lampshade. The yellow hot air balloon had twenty-five clowns dancing in various stages of undress. When the lampshade spun, it looked like they undressed and shook their little tooshies. The clowns would then get dressed and bow when the shade was stopped and spun in the opposite direction.

"Ah, the lampshade bill. I forgot to pay for it again. Maybe I should visit them tomorrow and close this account," he said, pretending to be upset and irritated.

"Maybe you should, doctor. My records suggest you have enough funds allocated to do it," the nosy droid said as he scanned Eryn's bank account. *The response I was waiting for.* Eryn smiled inwardly with glee.

"Yes, as it is, tomorrow is my day off. I'm being transferred to the fleet. Maybe I should go to Grayrak City to settle my account and return the shade. I don't want to rent it anymore. It's ugly. I'll find something else," Eryn quickly added.

"Oh," Pat retorted, his gaze rattled a bit from side to side as he searched for a polite human response, then he settled for, "Whatever makes you happy. A happy human is a productive human."

The Brawl turned before he ruined their mission, like crushing Pat's head with one hand or using the droid as a baseball bat to fuck shit up. *Only a few hours to go,* he said to himself and left the brightly lit lobby, eager to get to his room to be alone and get packing.

Minutes later, he let his head fall forward, relaxing under the spray of the hot water shower as he supported his body with his left hand while stroking his cock with his soapy right hand. Pretty pictures of Ivan zoomed on the insides of his eyelids while he breathed as softly as possible. He was sure no one recorded what they did in the shower, but the noises still traveled far. He concentrated on not saying his husband's name out loud while he imagined himself pinning Ivan to the flat surface of their dining room table back home in Phoenix.

Ivan would be naked, his legs falling open to the sides, his face scrunched, moaning loudly for him to fuck Ivan harder and faster.

"*You're gorgeous. Take your cock in hand.*" Eryn fantasized about giving orders, as Ivan obeyed eagerly. Eryn fucked him hard, hammering the table into the opposite wall while Ivan pleasured himself.

He pumped his cock rhythmically in beat with the sounds he remembered while fucking Ivan.

Then he scooped him closer by curling his large hands around Ivan's slender upper legs, anchoring him in place while he fucked his husband senselessly. He imagined Ivan's eyes closed and his head thrown back as he hissed through his teeth.

*Fuck me, Eryn, harder, yes, fuck yes, just, like, that!* Ivan moaned and cheered, driving Eryn over the edge. *Fuck yes, just like that,* Ivan groaned, spurting his seed all over both of them. Eryn was so deeply thrown back into the memory that he smelled the scent of Ivan's jism and ejaculated against the steel-tiled shower wall, milking his cock until every drop was drained from his balls. He opened his eyes, seeing double for a second.

"Brrrrr," he croaked. "That was a long and hard one," he mumbled. He cupped and splashed water on his semen running down the wall, ensuring it flushed down the drain. *Tonight's the last time I climax on my own. Next time, Ivan will suck it out.* He made the vow to himself and finished washing his hair and body.

He left the water running to muffle any noise he would make. First, he used his fingernails to pry the seams loose around the secret tile covering their small drop box compartment. Then, he stretched his arms up high, reaching the ceiling, which was just over thirteen feet high, and carefully felt with the tips of his pointer and middle fingers inside the groove of the last row of tiles for his small and very old wooden pencil. The same charcoal lead pencil his father-in-law gifted him when they worked together to calculate how to send the last rocket to the moon. Eryn cherished it because he got to know Mika, and they became very good friends that day.

He grabbed hold of the pencil between his fingers, carefully stuck it into the little hole behind the tile, and turned it like a key. A tiny door flung open to reveal the small computer chip Lasitor had loaded with all kinds of electronic viruses. Then he closed the door and secured the tile back in its place, closed the taps, and flung a towel around his lower body.

Later, as he lay in bed, he closed his eyes, sending his mental feelers out to scan the outside to feel what was happening outside the wall and the status of Cian and Sarinka's plan. He listened to the droning rumble of the Warship Horizon, machinery packing the crates inside, and whether he heard any signs of trouble outside. He thought about Ivan and missing their Anubis.

Then, he watched the dancing clowns on his yellow lampshade and reminisced about their past when they were young and innocent. He smiled, folding his arms behind his head.

"I'M NAMING MINE IGOR. He's the ugliest of the three puppies," Ivan said proudly as he rubbed his nose against the cross-eyed pup with no hair.

That was before the depths of icy water had sucked Phoenix inside.

"I'll call mine Devil because he's the biggest, maddest, and the baddest of them all," Eryn had said. He knew Devil liked the name. His yellow eyes sparkled, and he squirmed in his hands to get to his face and lick him.

"Yeah, he is, and he farts the stinkiest, as well," Ivan retorted, waving his hand in front of his face.

"Don't blame it on Devil. We all know it's Cian and his rotten brood who stink up Phoenix. Everyone in their vicinity wants to go for a walk or has something important to do," Eryn defended Devil.

"You should call him Rotty...no, wait—"

Cian interrupted Eryn, "Yes, I'll call him Rotty for Rottweiler." Cian rubbed the chubby and overly muscled Anubis's flanks. He sank to his knees, wrapping his arms around him, and closed his eyes. "Rotty, I like it. Do you like it?" he cooed, and Rotty panted happily.

ERYN CLOSED his eyes and drifted into slumber.

Three hours later, his internal alarm had woken him. He rolled out of bed and snuck on his knees underneath the bedside table where he'd pried open the socket for the bedside lamp connection.

He stuck his thick forefinger inside, hooking the thin fiberoptic cable, and snapped the tiny clip over it. Then he closed the access hole and hastily reversed out of there. Before he got up, he stopped and closed his eyes. With the palms of his hands flat on the steel floor, he felt increasing vibrations. The Horizon was preparing to take off. Hurriedly, he dressed, grabbed his belongings, and opened the door. He forced himself back into the neutral persona and blank, emotionless gaze.

He exited the sleeping area, chin high. "Morning, Pat," he greeted like always, but he didn't wait for a reply. He passed through the doors to the elevator lobby. Halting in front of the steel doors, he pressed the button to call the elevator.

"Sir, excuse me, sir," Pat said from behind him. Eryn froze.

"Sir," Pat called.

Eryn slowly turned, keeping his heart rate and angst levels to untraceable levels. God, the thing moved fast. Pat held the lampshade in his clamps for him. "You forgot this, sir," Pat said, his eyes blinking in and out of focus.

*Probably the virus. I must get out of here. My fucking nerves.*

"Thank you, Pat. Could you transfer funds to the account and close it? The General Fleet Commander asked for me. The Horizon is leaving for war. I must report immediately," Eryn said and thanked the stars when the elevator door opened. He stepped inside and turned to watch Pat. The robot man on wheels blinked one eye and then the other. The tiny lights flickered blue and red. Then he rolled away, zigzagging across the lobby. No Zelk would stand in his way with the mention of war.

Eryn furiously poked the button marked with a neon blue circle with his pointer finger. The door shut. The elevator descended to the civilian docking station. He was minutes away from being left behind. He moved to the small peephole, covering, and opening the hole to send his last message.

*It's a go!*

*Go, go, go, go, go!*

# CHAPTER 36

# THEY KEPT THEIR PROMISE!

*"Good morning, citizens of Phoenix.*

*It's now six a.m.*

*Did you know the only bombs that don't kill are being produced here in Phoenix?*

*Parents, sign your children up and join them in making seed bombs. Be a part of Operation Pollination. It's a fun workshop where kids play with clay and fill them with their favorite seeds.*

*Visit your community news page to book your spot to help protect and nurture the Earth and its moon.*

*Breakfast is served until eight a.m.*

*Hope you have a joyful day!"*

**BARKOR, the Promised Prince**
**2147 A.D. (95 A.T.)**
**Grayrak City**
**Earth's moon**
**Operation Lunar Evacuation**

Barkor soared up the side of their watch tower, feeling more optimistic and relieved with each clutch-pull-step as he scaled the dilapidated building. Reaching the final rod, he jumped and flip-rolled onto the landing where he'd left Leo earlier. Catching his breath, he let his arms fall dramatically to the sides and looked up at Leo, who sat propped upright, looking down at him. He smiled mischievously at Barkor.

"I believe you were successful. Sarinka tells me the promised prince commanded death by poison to his enemies." Leo joked and spoke dramatically.

"I commanded nothing. I just helped coordinate the poisoning. And for the millionth time, I'm not the promised prince. I had no choice but to assist. Kids were handling the poison. I had to make sure they didn't kill themselves instead of poisoning the Disciples and their precious water hole," Barkor said as he sat up and swung his feet over the edge.

"Hmmm," Leo agreed, like he usually did when he actually disagreed. They sat in comfortable silence.

Below them, Grayrak City lay illuminated by the dim blue lights of the Zelk tower, which glowed and highlighted the spiral display from beyond the wall. It stood central, drenching the insides of the dome with flickering blue light. To Barkor, it was both beautiful and ugly.

"Leo, I'm not sure about Grizzly. I couldn't find his body. We searched to ensure all the Disciples were accounted for. We found all of them except Grizzly. I hope and believe he's dead."

"Did you see Talali and the others? There were three more s—slave girls he held prisoner in a cage below the floor in the eating area," Leo said, stuttering. He hated saying slaves.

"I'd asked Sarinka. She said they followed Talali. I'm sure she would get them to safety." Barkor didn't know them very well. It was a place he avoided until the general gave the order to evacuate. The plan was to go on with business as usual while they moved all the pieces into place to evacuate with no bloodshed of the innocent.

Out of the corner of his eye, he noticed Sarinka. From where she came, Barkor couldn't say. She had the irritating gift of appearing gracefully out of thin air. She looked stunningly deadly in her new black suit and had an air of authority and quiet strength. She spread propaganda and inside intelligence among the citizens of Grayrak. As she called it, letting the people blow off steam and preventing an early uprising against the Zelk. She was the force that pulled each human toward the end plan, and the general was that force that bonded them.

Barkor didn't know why, but suddenly earlier today, Sarinka announced the water supply was being poisoned—he didn't know where to start. For fuck's sake, they set the plan in motion using kids. And he ran like a crazed lunatic eager to kill Grizzly and his Disciples. They forced Barkor to make an unplanned play.

"I can't wait to see the general and ask him what he thought about using children to fight his war! Before the day is done, I fear, Sarinka, they will kill us in a bloody battle. I thought I knew the general. I usually sum people up correctly. But I think we were wrong to trust him. Maybe the Zelk brainwashed him. It doesn't sound like he can maneuver a stealthy battle, especially without firing one shot, as he promised. They outnumber us one thousand to one. Tomorrow, they'll crush us when they realize we attacked their miners." Barkor fumed. He felt like he wasn't in control, and he hated that. "We've been planning this for how long? Donali keeps saying we can trust them, that he's dedicated, and that his plan will work." Barkor lifted his hands, making air quotations. "We must follow the steps carefully, and the rest he will make happen."

Barkor's gaze lingered on Sarinka. "Today's purge was obviously your idea. Where did you get that poison? Over two hundred Disciples and slave drivers—all dead in one sweep of assassinations across Grayrak. Unarmed children! Do you realize you made one hell of a mistake? There's no one to report to the Zelk. Grizzly is gone. He knew if someone harmed him, the Zelk would come to investigate this side of the wall. This is a colossal fuck-up!" Barkor yelled, pointing to the shacks surrounding the market area.

Sarinka stood with her hands on her hips, waiting for him to finish. She looked amused, infuriating him.

"You know, I'll have to report in Grizzly's place and say he's sick or dead or something. Attempt to play for time until the mighty smart general can come to pick us up," Barkor said. He couldn't see how a war could be avoided. He was on a roll and continued his rant. "The rebellion fizzled out, thanks to you, and now is sadly ending with a massive anticlimax. A year-long edging with no fucking orgasm."

Leo snickered behind him. Sarinka answered with a slow smile as she tapped her head with one finger. "No, my friend, you're wrong. The entirety of Grayrak is being evacuated as we speak." She grinned and tapped her foot, daring him to say something.

Barkor stood slack jawed. "Really? Why didn't you say anything?" He jumped to help. "Let's go, Leo!"

"Because of this." Sarinka pointed and gave Barkor an about-face. "The general said he doesn't want you near there. I don't know why, but he said he would evacuate you and Leo just as the sleep cycle ended." Sarinka pointed to the clock tower. Barkor flung himself around and looked at the tower as if seeing it for the first time and wondering what she was pointing at.

"How are they evacuating the people? Where are they, Sarinka?"

She locked her lips with an imaginary key and put the imaginary key in her pants pocket, tapping it.

"Yes, your rebellion is quashed. But by the time they realize they were dead wrong, they will be no more." Sarinka patted Barkor on the shoulder.

"I'm going to kill him. Who does he think he is? And why does it feel like I was just caught with my pants down?" Barkor asked.

Leo chuckled as if this was a comedy show. He was still sitting where Barkor left him at the side of the roof.

"I asked him six months ago, and he said a year or two. What happened? Why is this happening today? The fuel, the food, and the people..." Barkor trailed away as he remembered the voice of the Commander General.

"If I come for you and your people, no one will know, and no one will stop me. When we leave the moon, it will be as empty as they found it. I will wipe all traces of their existence."

"Don't worry, Barkor, everyone knows what to do." She pointed to Leo. "He's too frail to board the ship with them. Anyway, you would have searched for him and not followed the general's orders. He asked you to plant the explosives on strategic points." She took a backpack off her shoulders and handed him the bag. "They're not to be activated. Just bury and place them all around the dome."

Barkor took the bag from her. Speechless. He was supposed to be happy, but why did it feel like he wasn't the one saving his people? Was he a puppet all this time? One thing that he was glad about was Leo. He was weak and exhausted. He wouldn't make it.

"Okay, thank you. I think," Barkor said.

"No problem. I'm going to check on the loading. See you later. Don't draw any attention to this side. Stay low, plant the grenades, and take Leo up the tower tonight," Sarinka said and turned to say something in Leo's ear.

"What are you whispering about? Stop keeping secrets from me, for fuck's sake," Barkor grumbled.

"Nothing for you to know. It's between us," she said and turned to jump off the roof.

"Be glad for his plan. It's better than massacring innocent civilians," Leo said over his shoulder.

"How is he planning to hide thousands of people? Leo, why am I kept in the dark? Doesn't he trust me?" Barkor asked and joined Leo again. He plopped down and scanned the market below them. "How didn't I see this earlier? There isn't a soul in sight."

"Remember, these people from the earth aren't stupid, and they planned this perfectly. If he thinks it's better for you not to interfere, then he has his reasons."

"What did Sarinka say?"

"Dear moon lord, you're inquisitive! All she said was see you on the other side," Leo said, and Barkor could tell it wasn't the whole truth. He decided to let it go. It was good to wait and do what he was told to do. For once, he wouldn't worry about kids disappearing and women and young boys being raped. He flung his arm around Leo and relaxed for the first time in a long time.

Later that cycle, the muscles in Barkor's legs burned, but he mechanically lifted one leg before the other, climbing the upward spiraling stairs that felt like never-ending stairs to the stars. He squeezed his eyelids to refocus and see better. The aluminum stairs clang-clanged beneath his boots.

*I better not slip. We'll break both our necks rolling down to the bottom.*

Each stair flowed into the other, tricking his eyes, so he didn't know where one ended and the next began. Eager to get to the top, he heaved one deep breath after another, burning his already dry throat raw. Excitement to meet up with their rescuer drove his will to get himself and Leo to the top, to safety.

"Put me down. Leave me here. I'm not worth it," Leo nagged.

"Shut up, Leo, and stop wiggling. You're going to fall on your head. I'm worried we won't make it on time." Barkor's legs were trembling. He had flung Leo over his shoulders like a wounded soldier and was determined to carry him all the way.

"Shh, I told you don't talk. We don't know who's following us," Barkor reminded Leo as they ascended the staircase inside Grayrak's clock tower.

A monument built by the first humans in memory of Old Earth, named Big Benny

Tower, was obscured by smog. The corroded aluminum was unsafe for visitors long ago. Stripped walls revealed the frame and scaffolding holding the death trap up. Ripped-off pieces were reused for shacks—the homes of backstreet dwellers. Barkor grew up in that area built by the remnants of the clock tower walls, raised by humans with kind hearts who suffered each day of their existence.

"My head feels like it's going to explode. All my blood is now in my head," Leo complained.

"Shut up, Leo." Barkor stopped counting the steps because Leo distracted him. They were about one-hundred living spaces high, and slipping and sliding down the corkscrew stairs wouldn't end pretty. Finally, he heard the copper clock's arms cluck-clucking louder and louder. A sign that they were close to the exit and rendezvous point.

"I think we're close now. Put me down," Leo tried again, but Barkor ignored him.

"Shut up, Leo. We're almost there. Can you hear the churning of the gears?" he asked just as the light appeared around the last turn of the stairs.

"Upsy-daisy!" Barkor slid Leo like a sack of moon rocks off his shoulders, caught him around the waist, and carried him like a baby the last couple of steps. Leo hated being carried this way.

Exiting through a tiny door, he walked onto a metal mesh platform used by the first humans as a lookout over Grayrak and had a look at Earth. Now, this spot was only used by the odd volunteer cleaner who would wash the white face of Big Benny, so the privileged Zelk supporters living on top of the wall could read the time.

Barkor helped Leo to sit safely before taking a seat next to him.

"My ass is frozen numb," Leo said after they sat waiting for more than an hour. "I'm scared to go back," Leo whispered.

"If you can't sit much longer, I understand. Why don't you roll to your side?" Barkor said, already moving up and pulling Leo over so he could hold and protect Leo from rolling off the side. No wind was inside the dome, but Leo might roll off the narrow ledge while asleep.

*I would never forgive myself.*

"Hey, don't manhandle me," Leo protested lightly.

"Just lie down, Leo, you know I mean well," Barkor said and patted his upper legs, signaling for Leo that he would pull him over to the side to lie with his head on his lap. Leo scuffed and wiggled to get comfortable.

They spoke about anything and everything while the clock ticked and counted the minutes and, later, the hours down until they had to decide whether to return below.

"I would rather die than you not being able to go back to Earth," Leo told Barkor through chattering teeth. "Promise me if something happens and you must run, you will leave me here."

Barkor stroked the thin skin covering Leo's cheeks. He looked frail, he noted, and it broke his heart. Leo's pale skin was bloodlessly white, and his lips were blue. His breathing was labored. Barkor looked at Leo's lips, removed a little pot of oil from his pocket, and rubbed it on his cracked lips.

"We'll leave this place, don't you worry. Sarinka set it up. You know we can trust her word for it. They will come, wait a few minutes longer. Can you wait?" he asked.

"I don't want to be moaning for nothing and be difficult, man, but how long do you think we should wait? I need to piss, and I'm hungry," Leo mumbled weakly.

Barkor grew concerned because this was out of Leo's comfort zone. Leo was getting restless and uncomfortable. He was probably exhausted. "Come, let's sit up." Barkor helped him, feeling nervous as he pushed Leo up into a sitting position.

"Let me help you. Don't move. I'll shit my pants if you fall. I didn't carry you all the way up here only for you to fall to your death," Barkor said, scooping Leo up and supporting him between his knees.

"Come, I'll help you piss. You can piss right here. There's no one underneath us, anyway." Barkor loosened the drawstrings of Leo's pants with his left hand while supporting him with his right. He removed his cock and held it for his friend.

"Just relax. I got you," he said, as he had done so many times before.

Leo's breath puffed clouds of vapor into the darkness as he sighed and relaxed into the feeling of relieving his bladder. "Thank you, I'm done," Leo said softly. Barkor tipped his cock a few times and pulled the foreskin forward, pushing the drops of urine out. Then he made Leo comfortable and relieved himself, as well.

"I have faith in Sarinka. They will come," Barkor said.

Leo shivered and looked up at Barkor. "I know. She's never broken her word to me. She's straightforward, and I would never cross her. I think she knows how to kill a man slowly, with maximum pain."

Barkor agreed with Leo that she was dangerous.

They did it, oh, moon-god, we did it. The feeling of accomplishment overwhelmed him. The clock ticked at the same speed as his heartbeat, and with every minute they spent waiting, he felt freer and more optimistic than the previous one. A laugh spontaneously escaped. It felt awkward to laugh, but Leo joined in. His laugh was silly, like a little girl's. They widened their eyes at each other and puffed out their cheeks in a useless attempt to hold it in. Pressure built and exploded into another round of horrible, silly laughs.

"Oh, what a stupid sight we make," Leo said in between coughs and giggles, and Barkor prolonged the pleasantry with more jokes and punchlines about the simplest things. Things he remembered from when he grew up and when times were good. Anything to hear Leo's giggles. He was a frail, sick half-man who looked old and withered, unlike Barkor, who never seemed to age. He kept that a secret, until now. No one had said anything, but they must have noticed because why would they say he was their prince? His mother definitely wasn't royalty. He didn't know who his father was. Their rocket crash-landed on the moon, and during all that, his mother gave birth to him and died. He was taken and raised by the village women, and they were all mama to him.

Sweet smells of food drifted up from the empty market below. The usual noises that floated up were eerily absent. Barkor hummed a soft tune, and the melody ebbed and flowed. Barkor watched as the pained expression on Leo's face smoothed out. A few seconds later, he closed his eyes, enjoying the make-believe music Barkor made.

Barkor caressed Leo's cheeks with his thumb when the song was done. He felt so much empathy for him, and he checked to see if Leo was peacefully sleeping.

*Hold on, Leo, I'm getting you the medical care you deserve.*

Suddenly Barkor couldn't hear Big Benny tick; the moment's anxiety caught up with him. It was as if he was sucked into another dimension of space. Something weird was happening. Someone cleared their throat. Dazed, he scanned their surroundings and saw Sarinka with her hands on her hips out on the landing.

"When you lovebirds are done sightseeing, the ship is waiting," she said, teasing them.

"Leo, wake up. The ship is here." Barkor scooped Leo up, who groaned as his head fell back. His friend was weak and exhausted.

Barkor moved to where Sarinka pointed to the edge of the landing where the transport ship was silently floating. Cian was waiting for him and moon-god; he looked scary, with tattoos on the side of his face. Barkor did a double-take, one sparkling blue eye, that seemed Zelk was looking at him. And he was frowning. What in moon-god's name? Did he sell his eye to the Zelk?

"Look," Leo said, and Barkor knew what he meant. It was the eye. Barkor tried getting his bearings together, but everything moved fast around him while he slowed simultaneously, and he thought he'd forgotten his bloody name.

Sarinka woke him from whatever stupor he was in. "Can we move before we get seen?"

"Men, it's time to go!" Cian called in Old Earth Language.

Just then, the ship extended a ladder to meet them.

"They kept their promise!" Sarinka announced sternly. "Let me help you, Barkor."

The stunning seven-foot Cian jumped down onto the landing with a loud thump. "Donali, bring the stretcher," he shouted over his shoulder while fist-bumping Sarinka and making a swooshing sound. Weirdo, Barkor thought.

"I never break my word," he told Sarinka, taking Leo's limp body from Barkor. "Come, friends," he said with a friendly smile, and Barkor wanted to protest, but again, he was rendered speechless by the sight of the magnificent man who seemed larger than life itself. Cian affected him strangely somehow. His whole body tingled and his skin suddenly felt too small. He remembered the first time it had happened. It was when they abducted Leo. He thought it was the rush of the moment, or his imagination. Now it's happening again. This time he was sure it had something to do with the general.

GENERAL CIAN ROMANOV

"Okay, did you plant the balls, as I asked?" Cian waited and got no answer from Barkor.

"Hello, Barkor. Did you plant the seed grenades as I asked?" Cian repeated, and it seemed Barkor was offline. He stared wordlessly at Cian with those stunning dark eyes. "Hello, earth, to Barkor? Have you planted the bombs?" he asked.

For fuck's sake! Cian grabbed Sarinka by the arm.

"Sarinka, tell me you gave him the seed bombs," Cian demanded and hoped the last step of their mission wasn't a fuck-up.

"Yes, I did," she retorted and turned to Barkor, who seemed to stare at his bionic eye, rubbing Cian the wrong way. He didn't have time for this.

"Jesus Christ, it's just an eye. Get over it!" he yelled which seemed to penetrate the hazy look in Barkor's eyes.

Barkor blinked a few times. "I'm sorry, General. Are you going to bomb the place?"

"Of course, I fucking am. Who the fuck did you think was going to do it? Did you plant the clay bombs as I asked?

"Yes, I did," Barkor answered, and Cian relaxed.

"Okay, good, get in the car," he said, grabbing the bag with the spacesuit and his sword. "Ish and I will run one last errand. Go now. We'll meet you on the Horizon."

"Wait, what?" Barkor jumped out of the Bubblecar again, and Cian wanted to hit him over the head and throw his unconscious body back inside.

"I don't have time for this. Go!" he said and pushed him back into the car.

"They're all dead. Why are you going down? There's nothing except the possibility of Zelk finding you. If they find you, we're all toast," Barkor objected.

"Who do you think is flying the ship? I need to get to the Warship Horizon. This is how it was planned. We'll meet you later. Please go now."

"Barkor!" Leo called from the back. "Come, don't be difficult. They know what they're doing. They came to save us, don't be wayward. If you go now, the mission was for nothing, and you could have left me here."

"No! Shut up, Leo. Why do I feel you're bullshitting me?" he asked Cian and looked at Ish for an answer.

"We are not. I must enter from this side to disconnect the mainframe from the Horizon and allow Lasitor to take over. It has to be done manually. I must cut the cables and give Eryn the signal. It's being infected as we speak." Cian pointed to the spiraling tower in the distance.

"I need to activate the bombs. And I can only do it on the surface. I need to set the timer to initiate the pulse waves."

Ish touched Barkor on the shoulder and said in his deep, commanding voice, "Don't worry, we have this. You will see us on the Horizon."

"Yes, don't worry, we planned this for months," Cian said, but he was only twenty-five percent sure that their plan would work.

"Like hell you will!" Barkor exclaimed, and Cian realized they were standing eye to eye. "Give me a suit. I will come with you."

"Absolutely fucking not. You'll hold us back and slow us down," Cian said, vibrating with fury. "If we encounter the Zelk, we're listed as trusted. Are you listed?"

"No, but you need me. If this plan doesn't work, you will need me," Barkor said, and Cian wanted to either strangle or hug him. He couldn't decide. *He thinks he's the only one with powers around here, and I don't have time for a damn show-and-tell game.*

Just then, another suit fell with a plop at Barkor's feet. Cian checked and confirmed it was Sarinka—bloody female.

Barkor smiled at Cian, picked it up, and said, "Come, I know the fastest route to the tower." The fucker disappeared down the stairway.

"Motherfucker, wait for us!" Ish and Cian exclaimed in unison. Cian had no choice but to follow him. "Sarinka, get to the Spacecar and then meet us on the Horizon. We have an hour before it all goes boom."

"Yes, sir," she said with a determined smile and jumped in the driver's seat as they'd planned before.

"Fucking Barkor, now I must bring him on the Horizon. The last of the crates are being loaded."

"Don't worry, he's fast. Try to keep up with him, General." Sarinka cackled as she closed the hatch.

"Let's go!" Cian yelled and sprinted for the stairwell. Secretly, he was having fun as they competed by pushing and shoulder-bumping each other to pass and win the race to the bottom of the clock tower stairs.

Just as they passed the rows of shacks, Barkor halted and pointed. "Here, we have to jump on the roofs that run along the wall. Where's your detonator?" he asked, sweaty and short of breath.

Cian patted his backpack. "Here," he said and then lifted his golden sword. "And here."

"Good," Barkor said, looking impressed with Cian as he smiled approvingly.

"Cian, Barkor," Ish whispered and pointed.

Barkor pushed Cian and Ish back, holding them in place with spread arms. "Don't move," Barkor said in a muted tone. Cian looked questioningly at a frowning Ish and followed the path of their gazes to the figure, pushing a round iron cover up and over to the side and climbing out of a sewage opening in the alley.

It was a tiny little human. A female. She scanned the area slowly and carefully then pushed the massive lid back over the hole she'd just climbed out of with soundless effort. She looked wild and untamed.

"She noticed us," Ish whispered through his teeth.

Not moving, standing frozen, even with Barkor pinning him to the spot, Cian wasn't planning to go anywhere. He thought looking away would cause the wild child to pounce. He only turned his eyeballs to check on Barkor as he slid his hand inside the back pocket of his pants.

When he looked back, it was too late as the little fucker jumped, and before Cian could register, he was slammed onto his back with her sitting on his chest. Both hands were around his head, ready to hit his skull into a pulp on the dirt. Cian's first instinct was to fling the girl off him, but Barkor already had his knife underneath her chin.

"Easy, if you hurt him, I'll cut your throat," Barkor promised.

She grunted and started screaming, a high-pitched sound of frustration. Then she released Cian's head by throwing it back onto the ground.

"Ouch," Cian said softly.

He knew it was his eye, so he closed them. She was a little tunnel rat, a human, he realized. Sarinka told him about them. They almost never came to the surface.

"It is me, Barkor." He tried to soothe her like an injured animal. "Hush-hush, now," Barkor said and removed his knife from underneath her chin. He folded the flip knife and slipped it back into his pocket. With one hand outstretched, he revealed his backpack and then, in slow motion, dragged a piece of bread out of it with the other hand, ensuring he had her attention. He offered the bread to her. "Cian, meet Talali."

It broke Cian's heart—he saw her eyes, the hate, suffering, and deadly intent. Barkor knew her; he lived with her down in that hole. That must be the secret human access through that hole. She crawl-walked one foot and then the other over his body. Oh, stars, she smelled horrid!

Dressed in rags and dirty beyond measure. Barefoot and looking like a ball of hair with arms and legs. Cian watched wordlessly. He dared not move.

Ish grabbed him by the hand, pulling him upright, and whispered in his ear, "Stay still."

Cian was nervous. He never saw something as wild as her. She hissed at him, and Cian was sure she could bite his throat and kill him.

Barkor waved another piece of bread at her. She sniffed the air and slowly approached, looking him up and down. Cian stood stock still. Dirty little fingers lifted his shirt, smelling him. She was a short little thing. Her head barely reached his lower tummy. *God, she better not lick my belly button.* He didn't know if he could resist swatting her like a fly if it started to tickle. He held his breath and ground his molars. She stepped back. Thank fuck!

Barkor made little kissing sounds to grab her attention, still holding the bread. She snatched it and jumped backward. The bread disappeared in two bites.

Ish cleared his throat. "Let's find out if there are others. If not, we should grab her and run," he whispered in his low baritone. Cian could see they made her nervous.

"Talali, it's time to go. Is there anyone else down there?" Barkor asked. Talali whined softly, like a little wounded animal.

"Did you not get the message that you must go hide with everyone?" Ish asked, and it seemed she trusted him more than Barkor. She nodded, and the whining ceased. She kept looking at Cian, distrusting him. He didn't blame her; she'd never seen him before, and he had a shiny new Zelk eye. If he were her age, he would have run. Talali was a brave little thing. He guessed she couldn't be older than fifteen years of age.

"We have to go. We're leaving this place. Do you remember Sarinka telling you about a better place we're going to?" Barkor asked her while turning to go. He asked permission with his eyes. Cian couldn't say no. How could he? He nodded a yes. She grabbed him by the arm, pulling him and gesturing with her head to one side. She pointed at Cian and then grunted toward the hole she'd just crept out of. Barkor looked back at Cian, pulling up his shoulders. Like, sorry, I have to.

"Sure, let's follow this weird human into a hole we probably won't fit into or come out of," Cian said skeptically, watching Barkor trailing behind her, shaking his head. Cian turned to Ish. "You bring the others. I'll do the cutting and plant the detonator." Cian checked the timer on his watch. "You have twenty minutes. I'll see you on the other side."

Ish touched his shoulder. "Don't worry, we'll meet you. We know this tunnel system. It ends at the loading bays. It's the smuggling tunnel."

Cian took his watch off and gave it to Ish. He helped him put it on. "Can you read Earth numbers? See this...it's the same as Big Benny Tower." Cian pointed back to the steampunk clock towering over the human living area. "Look at this picture." He showed him the hourglass. Ish seemed to grasp its meaning.

"Oh, yeah, I can read time, I see," he said and nodded eagerly with a big smile.

"Good, go. When the sand has run out, you should be on board. I can't wait for you. I can't spare one minute," Cian said and watched as Barkor and Talali disappeared into the hole.

As soon as Ish entered the tunnel, Cian ripped the bottom of his backpack open and sprinted along the rooftops. He'd studied the footage of images Sarinka and Donali sent him. He knew exactly where to go, using markers and alleyways. Excitedly, he jumped from rooftop to rooftop, then down to the entrance of the cold storage containers of

Halogen, where he set the timer and activated the pulse reactor. As he jumped, left foot to right foot, he sang to himself, Got My Mind Set On You, by George Harrison.

*"It's gonna take time.*

*A whole lot of precious time.*

*It's gonna take patience and time, mmm.*

*To do it, to do it, to do it, to do it, to do it.*

*To do it right!"*

He sowed the seeds as he imagined hearing the song. Feeling jubilant, he mixed that song with his own heart song and concentrated on spreading the love in his heart and soul deep into the ground. As he jumped, feeling lighter than ever, he scattered the seed bombs the children of Phoenix made. He hoped, eventually, they would sprout and grow where they landed and where Barkor planted the fruit trees.

He sang his song from the depths of his heart and thought about his mate and his beauty. His perfectness and the magnificence of the magic called love. He imagined rich, colorful gardens with sweet smells, beautiful butterflies, and insects like dragonflies and bees. He imagined a garden with pools of fresh water. The song he sang filled the surrounding air, and in his mind, he saw every seed that fell and rolled, willing them to grow and flourish. He sang to the hydrogen, and he sang to the seeds. He urged them to grow and for oxygen to bind with the hydrogen, and he imagined water seeping up from the core of the moon, and then he imagined green moss, fields of grass, and more flowers and trees. He ran as fast as possible, jumped, climbed on the walls, then spread more little seed bombs left and right of the wall, imagining the seeds sprouting.

When he reached the far end of the wall, he jumped and made sure all the marked cubes were gone and being loaded. With his sword in hand, he reached up, concentrating his song into his sword like Eryn had taught him, and then he plunged it deep into the ground beneath him. He opened his mind, willing the song to spread from the sword to those tiny seeds, willing them to grow while he called water up to the surface. The area ground beneath him tingled with energy.

Everything went according to plan. He pulled his sword from the ground and ran just like Barkor did that day he'd seen him on the onboard computer screen for the first time. Jumping from canister to canister until he reached the tower. He snuck around it to the entrance where the Warship Horizon was. Quickly, he ducked and rolled under the ship and accessed the connection to the Zelk computer. He cut and disconnected Lasitor from the Zelk mainframe.

He was sweating and panting as he watched the Zelk tower. By now, Ivan should be on the ship, and Eryn should be on his heels.

As soon as the elevator moved, he noticed a little light that flickered. It was Eryn, and he was on his way. Thank the stars! Cian flickered his tiny mirror toward the descending elevator at the side of the Zelk factory. This confirmed Eryn had planted the last virus and was on his way.

Fuck yes!

Cian rolled away from the access point, grabbed his backpack and suit, and entered the warship. He had his finger on the button to close the door when he felt something tugging on his peripherals and noticed Talali, who refused to let go of Barkor. Behind them trailed three other girls while she clutched around his neck and sobbed. Probably scared to be out of the hole, Cian thought. Barkor swung her around so she could ride on his back. When she realized his intention, she stopped crying and smiled. Cian grinned; he had erotic ulterior motives. He couldn't wait to ride on Barkor's back, either.

"Where's Ish?" Cian looked around, seeing Zelk approaching from afar.

*We need to move. Now!*

"Ish said he would catch up with us. He had to go do something. You know how he is. A man of few words, and I didn't have time to stop for a debate. He said he knows Grayrak. He'll make it. We must go!" Barkor said as he urgently herded the girls inside.

"We have to go now. We have no more time to spare," Cian said, noticing Eryn entering via the staff entrance with his head down and a hop in his step. He was in a hurry.

"Follow me. It's time!" He pushed them inside and slammed the button to activate and close the massive cargo hold door.

The inside of the cargo hold was about the size of two football fields, one hundred by one hundred yards. Cian's skin tingled. All the excitement and buzzing energy and the nearness of Barkor were making his skin glow. Whispers of people conversing inside the loaded cubicles made him determined to get the ship off the moon. Explosive laughter drifted from the back just as he closed the docking hatch and secured it by flipping a lever over it.

"Wait here, please," he asked Barkor, smiling at the girls.

"Don't worry, General, I'll keep them safe," a young soldier said. Cian couldn't remember his name, but he looked capable and friendly.

"Come, let's strap you in," he said to the girls, who followed his directions even though he spoke Old Earth English. Cian watched them get comfortable and overjoyed as the soldier handed each a food pack. They tore into their sandwiches and gulped their water down. Yet another necessity the citizens of Phoenix prepared and packed for the refugees. He was humbled and impressed by their leadership team for the foresight and planning of this past year.

Barkor was busy making sure the four girls were comfortable and then took a seat next to them. Cian did a quick inspection by observing the rows, inspecting them, and listening empathically for urgency or distress. He sensed only happiness and excitement; their optimism and hope were palpable in the cargo hold. And so, too, was the stench.

Their musty, unwashed bodies made Cian's eyes water. He coughed and cleared his throat as he reached Barkor.

"Okay, I'm going up to the front. Please, stay here and watch over your people. It's time to leave. I'll let you know when it's time to let them out." Lifting his arm to check the time, he remembered giving Ish his watch. "The crew is waiting for me," he said reluctantly, and Barkor nodded. Barkor wasn't needy and didn't ask unnecessary questions.

*He's stunning. He's strong, and he's mine.* Cian willed his feet to move.

Barkor had smiled at him just as he'd shut them inside. Cian's breath hitched. He gathered himself. *The man truly takes my breath away.* He turned and made his way to the bridge command.

Movement outside made him take notice as he made his way down the corridor to the bridge. Fucking hell, yes! Peeking through the small observation window, he saw chaos outside. The Zelk that had loaded the ship seemed off-kilter. Some repeatedly bumped into one another, into walls, or had fallen over. A forklift spun in circles and smashed a Zelk flat. The constant blue light given off by the Zelk tower flickered. Some even walked into walls. Others lay sideways, tipped over and kicking like they were having seizures. They looked infected.

He noticed a line of unaffected Zelk making their way to the Horizon. Motherfucker. He ran, yelling, "Go, go, go!" The rumbling vibrations of the ship increased, confirming they were taking off. As he entered the bridge command, he saw they were already a few hundred feet high. Below them, Grayrak lay silent, and on the far-off side of the dome, Cian saw smoke bellowing out of the dome. The hydrogen pulse reactor detonated.

"General, we have a problem. Look." His flight captain called Cian over and pointed.

Cian checked the screen and ran to the left observation window. Somehow the Zelk were holding onto the side of the ship. The line he saw earlier fluttered up and down as they climbed onto one another to get to the ship. Like ants, they climbed and barreled closer in numbers, and he couldn't see how many were already holding on.

"They're going to infect the ship!"

"We won't make it home if the ship's infected!" Cian's heart was pounding. He needed his brothers and needed to remove the Zelk now. "Don't slow down. Try to go faster. Find my brothers!" Cian yelled. "Tell them to come to the bridge immediately. Show them what's happening and tell them to meet me at the left docking hatch!" Cian turned and ran with two soldiers on his heels.

When he reached the airlock chamber, he was heaving and frantic with worry. "I'm going to suit up. Help me. Get the bridge online, ask them for an update," he said, climbing into his suit. One soldier screwed his helmet on while the other asked for an update.

As soon as his helmet was secured, the audio connection to the bridge crackled. "General Romanov here. Can you hear me?"

"Yes, General," his captain answered.

"Are they still hanging on?"

"Yes, General, they're shortening the line, and more are attaching to the ship."

"Where's my laser gun?" He patted the pockets of his suit.

"Here, General. Should we come with you?" the youngest of the two, Darrel Sinclair, asked bravely as he placed the small laser handgun in his thickly padded, gloved hand.

"No, you stay here. When my brothers come, tell them to suit up and join me."

"Yes, General."

Cian turned, hearing the relief as they answered. He took hold of the wheel lock to override the external locking mechanism and waited for Darrel to punch in the security override sequence. A green light blinked, and he opened the airlock chamber. Once inside, they locked the door behind him. He fastened his safety harness and snapped the harness clip onto the swivel hook with a D-ring attached to the ship. Then he lifted the cover of the button marked with a green triangle, the Zelk alphabet, for open. He slammed the big button. The external door swooshed open. His body became weightless, and he floated to the exit, then flung himself outside.

"Holy shit! I count about fifty Zelk already attached to the hull!" Hundreds more waved like flags up and down, still attached to one another.

"I must break the links!" He found a steady purchase, activated the magnetic boots, and started shooting. That got their attention, and the ones already on the ship detached from the line and crept closer to him.

*Fucking frog balls. If they reach me, I'll be overpowered.* He shot two more times to break the chain of Zelk. One Zelk's arm had broken off, and the droids holding onto him fell back into space, looking like a washing line in the wind. Cian didn't have time to wonder where the string of robots would end up floating. He swung his torso around and shot the one closest to him in the head. That seemed to do the trick. He only aimed for their heads, careful not to shoot a hole into the Horizon.

They inched closer. Four feet to go, and they would be on him. They could enter the ship via the airlock exit if they passed him. His biggest worry was that they would infect the Horizon, and the humans wouldn't be able to make it home. They were all as good as dead if the Zelk should make it inside.

Something pulled on him. A big Zelk, missing half its head, grabbed Cian's right artificial leg and pulled himself closer. Cian was, at that moment, glad he had the bionic leg. The Zelk would have crushed his tibia and fibula otherwise. His boots, still magnetized, clung to the ship—turning, moving, or kicking was impossible. He checked behind him. Clear.

"General, your brothers are on their way. They're suiting up," his fleet captain said.

"Thank you, Captain. I need help!"

The Zelk was on him, grabbing and pulling on his suit. Cian sat on his haunches, making himself as small as possible while he shot a few rounds left and right, he sent pieces of metal and bone flying. *Don't tear my suit,* he thought as they packed on top of him like flies on shit. Overwhelmed, he hoped for a miracle and closed his eyes.

"Hold on, brother," Eryn and Ivan shouted in his ear inside his helmet.

The pressure, pulling and pushing, disappeared. He lifted his head. Zelk and pieces of Zelk flew off him and drifted away as his brothers swatted and flung Zelk off the Horizon. Eryn zapped them with his spear. The lights in their eyes sparked and flickered off. Ivan used his sword like a baseball bat hitting home run after home run. They looked like superheroes in a Marvel movie.

"Motherfucking, fuck, fuck, fuck, that was fucking close!" Cian's skin crawled. "How are they still able to function, aren't they supposed to be dumb and infected by now?" Then he saw Barkor—suited up.

"I'm here to help." He waved from the exit of the airlock chamber. Cian waved back, smiling and happy to see him.

"Are you okay? Do you need help? I had a feeling you were in trouble and needed me," Barkor stated, holding his ball club ready to do serious damage. He looked around at the hundreds of Zelk in pieces and strewn like confetti as they floated away. "Oh, you didn't need me, after all. It looks like you have it all under control." Barkor sounded disappointed, but Cian couldn't see his face through the tinted visor of his space suit.

"Yep, under control," Eryn said and floated back to the entrance, with Ivan following on his heels.

Ecstatic that he didn't die and excited to see Barkor, without thinking, he bent his knees to thrust forward but didn't move. His fucking boots were still stuck. Pressing the deactivation button on his right forearm, he released the magnetism. Then he tried again, pushing himself forward while Barkor pulled him by his safety belt.

"Hi," Cian said and smiled widely. "Thank you for checking up on me." Now he was sure Barkor didn't know about their connection, how it worked, and what it all meant. He awkwardly hugged Barkor and bumped their helmets together. Up close, he saw Barkor's eyes glint like bright stars as he smiled at him. Having him in his arms and close to him felt bloody good and reassuring. Cian closed his eyes briefly to enjoy their closeness and the quiet joy of contentment outside in space where it was only the two of them. He wished he could smell and feel Barkor's warmth, but their puffy suits and helmets were between them.

"Are you happy to see me?" Barkor's voice was gentle, as if he cared, soft as if he worried, and teasing as if he joked. Cian liked all of it a lot. Strange how six words could carry so much meaning.

"I am," was all Cian could say.

They looked at each other until Barkor said, "Let me get you inside. It's not safe here." He turned and climbed back into the airlock, where Eryn and Ivan waited to pull them deeper into the chamber.

Cian shut the outer door behind him. "Thank you for coming to my rescue," Cian said once inside. Eryn and Ivan smiled and then inspected the rubber seals around the door as if immensely interested. Barkor removed his helmet and blinked. No sound came from his astonished-looking face. Like he couldn't believe Cian had manners or something. The blues in his eye swirled and mixed with tiny deep green flecks—his slitted pupils, much like Eryn's, narrowed in the bright overhead lighting. A visual of Barkor holding Leo tightly up on the clock tower flashed through his mind, reminding him Barkor was with another.

"Why the fuck are you with the half-man?" Jealousy burst out of his mouth when he opened it.

Cian realized he had spoken out loud, and Barkor, his brothers, and the rest of the crew must have heard him. Fuck!

"It's not what you think," Barkor said. Cian narrowed his eyes in question at him. "And my choice of friends has nothing to do with you. I'm capable of judging a person and deciding if they are worth my time."

Cian harrumphed and pretended to ignore him. He signaled for Eryn to open the bloody door they seemed to find so interesting.

"Why do you think you have any claim on me, or did I miss another step in your plan where you tell everyone around me what's going on and expect me to follow your orders?" Barkor grunted as he removed his gloves. He pinned Cian with a deadly stare before moving into his personal space. Their noses almost touched. Tipping his head left and right, he was sniffing the air like a wild animal. His hair was sweaty, and he smelled musky, like wet earth. Cian wanted to roll in it. Maybe he could bottle it.

Breaking away from the challenge of dominance, Cian couldn't undress his spacesuit fast enough. The man infuriated him. He was sure they had a connection earlier. Now he acted like he was some kind of alpha, staring him down.

"Okay, down, boy, I don't have time for this. Just forget I said anything," Cian said and slipped out of the chamber and jogged to bridge command, leaving Barkor alone.

# CHAPTER 37
# HE IS ZELK!

*"GOOD MORNING, AND A SPECIAL WELCOME TO OUR NEW CITIZENS.*

*It's now six a.m.*

*I am Lasitor, your community AI, and I am not Zelk.*

*I'm your friendly fountain of news and information.*

*You may visit your community news page on any device connected to the general network. Just say my name, and I will respond. You may ask me anything.*

*There are tons of educational videos and other information about living on Earth.*

*Don't worry. We are here to help.*

*Breakfast is served until eight a.m.*

*Hope you have an insightful day!"*

**GENERAL CIAN ROMANOV**
**2147 A.D. (95 A.T.)**
**The Warship Horizon**

Cian grunted like a lion with an abscessed molar at the fucked-up situation he found himself in. Everyone in the room eyeballed him. Even their Anubis; Rotty, Igor, and Devil eyeballed him, too. Yeah, not even twenty-four hours had passed after Barkor had thrown him a bone and got his hopes up. Cian was sure they had a connection when Barkor came to help him outside.

No, not a bone but a bloody chew toy to keep him busy while Barkor fussed over Leo on his deathbed and expected Cian to watch him care for his boyfriend. *For fuck's sake, my mate is holding another man in his arms.* Another fucking half-man. He eyeballed them back. Making sure they got the message to *back the fuck off.* They turned their gazes back to watch Barkor stroking Leo lovingly. It reminded Cian that Leo was with Barkor while Cian wasn't. He sighed hopelessly. They eyeballed him again.

"What?" he barked, crazed with jealousy and irritated at Eryn, Ivan, Donali, and Sarinka. Little Talali flinched, peeped like a mouse, and made herself smaller, lying beside Leo on the bed. *Fuck!* Now he felt like shit. He scared her.

Ivan cleared his throat. "Go do something. Please leave, brother," he said pointedly with sad, sorry eyes. He reached out for a sympathetic touch, but Cian stepped back. His brother better not touch him. He felt like breaking his arm, crushing his hand, or wrapping his hands around his throat and strangling him. He was the one who invited him. Basically pushed him inside the fucking suffocating somber tomb. A reminder that he was not enough. Not good enough.

"No, and you know why," he answered and pinned his brother with a death glare.

"Then be quiet and have some respect," Ivan said, and Eryn chuckled in the back.

Cian stepped forward because someone had to say something. "Listen, man, I'm well aware that you're dying and at your end, and your body can't take one minute longer, but don't you have something, like last wishes?"

All the faces around Leo's deathbed looked questioningly at him. Leo included.

"I mean, there's a word for that, like, hmmm, no, not bucket list. What's the word again?"

Ivan looked like he wanted to skin Cian alive, but Cian didn't have time for this. *People always die, and you should expect that fact the day you're born.*

"What I mean is, do you have any last wishes? You know some people want to see the sun." Everyone in the room relaxed. He heard a few exhalations and thought he was on the correct path. "Or maybe you want to end your suffering a bit faster, like—"

"Get the fuck out of here," Barkor shouted through gnashing teeth.

"Cian, brother, it's better if you go. Let's go for a walk," Eryn said, guiding him towards the door. Cian suspected Eryn needed an excuse to escape as well.

"No, I want him here," a soft raspy voice said, barely audible.

Cian stopped, and Eryn turned just as Leo started to speak. "No, he must stay. I want you here, please, Cian."

"See, he wants me here," Cian told no one in particular.

Leo smiled weakly. Then he looked at Barkor. "Do you remember when we first met?" he whispered. Barkor shook his head as if he didn't remember.

"Fuck, Barkor, I'm so tired," Leo mumbled. "Please, love, you haven't slept in like a week. You need to sleep," he slurred but turned his head to face Cian. The overhead lights sparkled in his dying eyes.

*He's crying.*

Leo lifted his head, and their gazes met. "Please look after Barkor. I ask as sincerely as a dying man can muster. I was thinking about how we met and how it all came together for the...do you think it was some grand scheme that brought us together?"

"Leo, you're breaking my heart. Please stop talking. You're tiring yourself out," Barkor said, and his voice cracked as if on the verge of crying. "Rest up, and then we can talk about it tomorrow," he said, and it irritated the crap out of Cian.

"He's right. I have to die anyway, whether it's now or next week. It doesn't matter. There are more important things to worry about than sitting here and holding me."

"No, you know I'll miss you," Barkor said.

Someone's teeth gnashed. Cian looked around and realized it must have been him because everyone's eyes were focused on him again.

"You are such a man, and thank you. Without you, this ship wouldn't have been packed with people on their way to living a better life. You are brave, and you're a hero," Barkor whispered.

"Motherfucker," Cian swore his frustration. This sissy mushy shit pushed him past the point of uncomfortable. He wanted to grab Barkor and run and make him feel better.

"Get out!" Barkor and the rest erupted.

Cian turned to leave, feeling relieved, but Leo persisted. "No, I want him here. Come back, please, Cian."

"See, even the boyfr—" He stopped himself before he sounded like a loser.

Barkor kissed Leo softly on his forehead. "I know what you're up to, and no, it won't work," Barkor said gently, and it felt like a thousand knives pierced Cian's heart. He opened his mouth and wanted to say something, but his brother poked at him and gave him the stinkiest eye. Eryn seemed to play both sides by tapping him on his shoulder and shaking his head.

*No surprise there, treating me like I'm a fucking toddler.*

Cian did feel sorry for him, but it felt like a lost cause to stand there and reminisce about things of the past. "Okay, tell me what you want so I can return to doing my work and maybe get you where you want to go. Do you want to die on Earth? What can I do for you?" Cian asked and decided to be nice. *After all, it is Leo's deathbed.*

One corner of his mouth pulled up in a skewed smile at Cian. "Please tell our story to the people on Earth so that it may go on forever."

Little Talali sat up, crossed her legs, and placed a small hand on Leo's chest. "I'll tell your story, Leo," she said in a soft sweet voice.

Barkor placed his hand on hers.

"Thank you, Talali, you're such a good friend to Leo." He turned to Cian, and their gazes met as he willed him to listen as he said, "We will tell all your stories, and we will never forget you." Barkor's voice broke as he nodded his head affirmatively, and Cian nodded back.

Suddenly he felt like a tsunami of Barkor's emotions knocked him off balance, and his mate's intense sadness assailed him.

*This is too much; I can't take this. I'm going to break down and cry in front of them. Again, I'm the bloody third wheel. It's emotions for Leo and not me.*

Cian turned to leave, but Eryn blocked the door, planting his legs wide and stumping his spear into the floor with a clang of finality.

"Stay, listen, and shut up," Eryn told him. Cian narrowed his tear-filled eyes at his brother-in-law. Eryn spoke into his mind telepathically. *Brother, get a hold of yourself.*

*Close your eyes for a second and tell yourself you're as hard as a rock. Everything will be all right. He's not his boyfriend. He's a friend. A good friend.*

Cian felt calmer as Eryn's good juju washed over him, and he closed his eyes. When he felt he'd collected himself, he turned and crossed his arms like the Commander General he was and thought—I am a granite boulder.

Leo coughed and cleared his throat. Coughed again, and Barkor offered him a sip of water. Leo thanked him and began to speak. "We tried countless times to escape, but they always found us. They brought us back to their bunker and then punished us ruthlessly. That's how I ended up like this. Some escaped, but others like myself couldn't, not even by killing ourselves."

Talali looked at Cian, her frailty breaking his heart. She was clean, and her hair was tied up in a ponytail. Her face was small, not bigger than the palm of his hands. She had dark eyes, determined eyes. Eyes that had seen enough for ten lifetimes. Like the rest of the crew, she wore the standard black body suit for which her body was scanned and printed. Their body suit machines had decreased in size, and every room had been outfitted with a suit printer. The material was completely recyclable, so suits were printed on demand. Instead of washing the clothes, they disinfected the material while being broken down into a liquid, and reloaded into the printer for fresh daily wear.

Cian listened intently while trying not to see Barkor, who stroked Leo's forehead.

"If it weren't for Sarinka" —he nodded to her— "the girls wouldn't have made it."

Cian looked at her, smiling sincerely, and watched Donali looking at her with admiration. He was definitely under her spell.

"Why Grayrak? Where does the name originate? I've always wondered about that," Cian asked.

"Oh, that's from the moon's color, the first humans called it gray rock, and later it just became Grayrak," Barkor answered.

Cian shifted uncomfortably from one foot to the other. "Interesting," Cian said.

Leo continued to smile knowingly at him. The half-man freaked him out. He irked him.

Cian looked discreetly at Sarinka, scared to get knifed between the eyes. She was all cleaned up and dressed in her favorite color, black, and armed to the teeth with all kinds of shiny knives and weapons. Sarinka was a swift and silent killing machine. A pretty little thing, but the most dangerous female Cian had ever met.

"Without Cian's plan, I doubt the humans would ever have had a chance of escaping," Sarinka added.

Oh, it's compliment time, Cian thought sarcastically. The room erupted in encores.

Leo whistled weakly. Everyone quieted down. Then he spoke. "There's one thing I must ask of you and Cian privately." He coughed and looked at Talali, Sarinka, and the other men in the room. "Will you please leave? I want to speak to them alone."

At first, no one moved, not registering the request. Eryn cleared his throat, opening the door. "Come, you heard him. He wants to talk to them."

Talali got up and jumped, and Eryn caught her. One by one, they left, nodding and squeezing his shoulder, saying goodbyes.

Suddenly Cian was nervous, and he guessed he knew what Leo was about to ask. Barkor would never do it, and he would hate him for it. He might as well say goodbye to Barkor.

"I know I'm weak and dying," Leo said, and Cian's gaze locked with Barkor. Barkor broke the intense stare and got up to get a fresh cool cloth, and Cian followed every movement. Undoubtedly, he was nervous about what Leo was going to ask. Barkor returned, folding the cloth into a small square as he waited. Leo chuckled wheezily. Cian listened and expected Barkor to scrutinize him, but he heard nothing. Just white noise. *Is he blocking me?*

Barkor wiped Leo's forehead. "What do you want to ask us? You know you can ask me anything, and I will do my best to get it for you."

Cian knew that wasn't the truth. He knew what Leo would ask would not go over as easily. He suspected Leo would ask them again to be euthanized and smothered to death. That was what Leo wanted since they'd abducted him. That was all he wanted, and he begged and cried for it. Barkor promised that if he helped them, he said he would do it, but Leo had become Barkor's pet project or something, and they spent the last two years together. Who knew what the two had done? Cian really didn't want to imagine that. But it was time, and Barkor had to know that.

"Yeah, just ask. This anticipation is giving me a migraine. Ask away," Cian said, and he meant he would do anything in his power to give him his last wish swiftly and painlessly.

"I suspect most people misunderstand you," Leo said briskly, surprising Cian. "You say what needs to be said without wondering who would think what, and you never change your words so that others won't take an affront from them." Cian stood astonished.

He widened his stance and crossed his arms. "Hmmm, so do you think Barkor likes it or not?" Cian blurted the question. He didn't know if he wanted an answer, but he really wanted to ask it. It burned his tongue so that he had to spit it out. Barkor sat wide-eyed. Not a peep came from his mouth—*such a bloody square.*

Leo cleared his throat, interrupting their intense visual communication. "I know he loves it, even if he doesn't want to admit it."

"Leo!" Barkor stomped his foot, and Leo chuckled, coughed, and paused to catch his breath. His head fell back onto the pillow with a plop. Cian didn't want to, but he was starting to like Leo. Barkor ignored Cian.

"I'm going to say this as straightforwardly as possible. I want the two of you to make love to each other, and I want to watch before I die."

"Say again? Because I think I heard you wrong," Cian exclaimed, watching Leo and then Barkor, who seemed perplexed and shocked, just as he was.

"No, you can't ask that of me...of us. We don't know each other and...fuck, help me here, Cian," Barkor said.

Cian looked frantically from Barkor to Leo, wondering why he should suddenly say something. "Absolutely fucking not. I don't have time for this. This is childish and not to mention extortion from the dying. Sorry, but I don't have any inclination to—" Cian waved his hand back and forth in the shape of a triangle between Barkor, Leo, and himself like he was leading a symphony. Even thinking about the word threesome gave him hives. He was sure he was getting an allergic reaction. He itched and struggled to breathe. "Sorry— not interested. A big motherfucking no! Done that, and no! I have work to do. No!" Cian spattered *no* repeatedly while gasping for air. He turned, slammed the exit button, and fell into the corridor. Bracing himself on the wall, he heaved and stumbled to his room.

Just as he rounded the corner to the staff corridor, he heard a shrill voice screaming. Cian jerked upwards, listening. He waited, wondering from which direction the screaming came. Three steps forward, then he heard it again. It was close. It sounded muffled. Like it came from... a few more steps, then he stopped. He heard scuffling.

Then definitely an older male voice. "Hold still, you bitch, or I'll slice your throat."

Cian looked up and down the corridor to guess the distance and area he heard it.

He didn't want to give himself away but wanted to call for help. He had to find this perpetrator himself. *Someone's in trouble! On my fucking ship!*

"Ouch, you bitch!" the male shouted, and then he heard a dull thumping and a young female crying.

"I will never let you touch me again!" the female shouted.

"Shut up. All I want is food. You need to go get me something to eat and drink." The man grunted.

Someone with a voice much like Talali said, "I will not!"

"You will, or I'll kill your sisters," the man said.

"We will not. We'll report you to the general. You're supposed to be dead, Grizzly!" another female voice said.

"Yeah, we aren't your slaves anymore!"

Now Cian was sure it was Talali and her three friends or sisters by the sound of it.

"Shut up, you bitch!"

"No, Grizzly, no!" The girls screamed, and Cian jumped into action.

*He's going to kill someone.*

Cian lifted his head and shouted, "Grizzly, is that you? We've been searching for you!

Come out! I know you're in here!" Cian hoped to buy some time while he figured out where they were. Silence. *Fuck this!* He walked, fiddling with the doors, buttons, and handles in the corridor, but they were silent, and nothing opened.

"Lasitor, the hostages, where are they?" he called into his pager on his shoulder, hoping the AI was on standby.

He answered immediately, "Sir, they're four steps forward and then the service shaft on your right."

Cian found the door and said, "I know you're in here. This is the General of the Horizon. I'm opening the hatch. If you hurt anyone, expect the same fucking justice to be done to you. You understand me?" *Sick fucker!*

"I'll gut them all! Stay away!" Grizzly hollered, and Cian sent his emotional feelers out. Grizzly was nervous, and the four girls were scared. *No one is dead yet.*

A crowd was forming around him. He indicated for them to step back and be quiet and that he had it under control. They stood wide-eyed and waiting.

"You don't understand. Even if you gut them, you're still fucked. We will come in and rip you apart. Your only choice is to let them go and come out. Only then might you have a chance to see Earth. Come out. I'm unarmed. I'm only concerned about the girls' safety. You will only see Earth if they're unharmed," Cian said and wasn't in the mood to negotiate. The crowd grew restless, and Cian silenced them by placing his forefinger in front of his mouth.

"You better keep your word. I'm not hurting them. All I want is food and water. I wasn't hurting them. They know me. I'm a good man. I take care of my own," Grizzly said.

The crowd murmured, shaking their heads. Cian placated them with calm-down gestures and affirmative nodding while showing them with his eyes; *I know, I know the fucking bastard. Please be quiet. They're about to be opening the door.* Once they were out, he planned to get rid of the bastard.

Cian heard Talali speak. "The general's taking all of us to swim in the ocean, and you could come, too. Just don't hurt us, please, Grizzly," she begged, and Cian's heart shattered for the girls, stoking his fury towards Grizzly. He wanted to scream *open the fucking door, you motherfucker!*

Years of training and Ivan's nagging to think had prepared him to reel in his temper. He decided to calm himself and suppress his true feelings about the man and let Grizzly think he was safe. Make him think he was in charge. He looked at the crowd, showing them to zip it.

"Grizzly, my man, we were looking all over for you. You're our honored guest. The people on Earth are all talking about you. They're singing songs about you. How big and strong you are. A knowledgeable leader and a man who survived the Zelk. We'd be honored to have dinner at my table with the last Disciple joining us."

Cian heard chuckling behind him. Eryn and Ivan stood there.

*It looks like you have it under control, brother. We have your back.* Eryn spoke telepathically to Cian.

Cian nodded his thanks to them. They were armed and ready. Rotty, Igor, and Devil stood beside them. They were so big they nearly filled the width of the hallway. *What the fuck?* They were bigger and very eager to attack. Their yellow eyes were pinned on the door as if they understood every word that was said. Cian waited, placing the onus on Grizzly.

After a minute of silence, the door swooshed open, and the girls came running for Cian. He did a quick summation—besides a small superficial cut on the one girl's face, they seemed to be okay. He acknowledged them and pushed them behind him to Ivan and Eryn.

*Now it's you and me!* The thought came just as Grizzly strolled out. It looked like he had combed his hair to the side just now, and it lay oily and flat against his head. His face was raw with skin cancer. The vilest man Cian had ever lain eyes upon. He strutted out there like he owned the place. One look at the crowd, and they cringed at seeing him.

*Please, I don't want them freaking out. I plan to give him his last meal and then take him to see Earth as promised. Tell them to play along. It will be lots of fun!*

Grizzly gasped, interrupting Cian's telepathic conversation with his brothers. Rotty, Igor, and Devil growled. The crowd stood soundlessly, watching the show. Cian was planning to entertain tonight.

He spoke to Ivan and Eryn mentally. *Let the people know it's not real.*

Cian didn't want to touch him. He looked pleadingly back at Eryn, who loved to skewer people and drown them. *Brother,* Cian begged Eryn with his eyes.

Eryn stepped back apologetically and replied telepathically, *It's your ship and your rules. Ask yourself, what would our fathers have done?* Ivan nodded his agreement.

How did he miss that his brothers respected him like this? He couldn't skewer Grizzly, but he would bullshit him and show him Earth from space. He reached back, opening and closing his hand, asking Ivan to hand him a weapon. He expected a laser gun, but his brother handed him his sword. It felt strange, not like his own, but it would do. He decided to use the sword as a scare tactic and improvise and use his wit and charm.

"Grizzly, our last Disciple, do you know who we are? Do you know why you're a Disciple?" Cian asked.

"I'm pretty sure you're the general of this ship. Pleased to meet you, General." He held out his hand, and Cian reluctantly shook it.

*I'll soak my hand in disinfectant later.*

"These are my brothers, Ivan, my twin, and his husband, Eryn." Cian chuckled, knowing they also hated shaking his hand. Eryn and Ivan took it and gave Cian the—*we're warning you, brother*—eyes.

"And these are our pets—"

Eryn and Ivan smiled and then nodded. They moved into the crowd to spread the word. Cian winked at Talali, and she seemed to catch on fast. Grizzly stood open-mouthed, staring at the Anubis and then at Eryn and Ivan towering over the humans down the corridor. His gaze returned to Cian. Their inhuman height and golden weapons had triggered a memory, and Cian saw when realization dawned on him.

"I, I have some kind of memory," he said, stuttering, and it seemed he was still coming to terms with what he was seeing.

"Grizzly, come, let's have a feast." Cian put the flat of his hand on Grizzly's back and gave him a friendly shove forward. "Come, let me show you where I dine," he said and pointed the way with his brother's sword to the dining area.

Cian wished Barkor was here, but Leo lay dying, and he knew he wouldn't leave Leo alone.

Grizzly spoke of himself, never stopping between bites and slurps, never realizing everyone watched them. Cian thought Grizzly liked eating with everyone watching him; that was probably how it was on Grayrak. How else could he be the only big fat fucker on the moon? He bloody ate everyone's food. Now and then, he would look at Rotty, Igor, and Devil nervously.

His green and brown sports jacket had one out of four buttons left in the front. He sucked his big tummy in and tied the jacket. The one button near popping while conveying that he thought of himself as upper-class or royalty. Then he flattened the creases and held his head high. He talked nonstop.

Cian didn't even listen. He was in his own head thinking how this man had chopped off Leo's arms and legs and then kept him as a plaything. The more he thought about what Talali and the girls looked like when they found them, the more the man repulsed him. It was all this man's fault—him and his Disciples.

When he finished his fourth plate of food, he halted shoving food into his mouth, eyeing the fifth plate on the table. "Why do you have Anubis on your ship? The last Anubis died when the rocket they were on exploded. How did you manage to have three of them?" he asked so condescendingly that Cian wanted to slam his head onto the table, but then he had to touch Grizzly, so he postponed.

He smiled brightly, straightened his back, and ensured the surrounding crowd heard his answer. "Grizzly, because—" Cian was interrupted by Eryn and Ivan.

"Sorry, we had to deliver a message. You were saying, brother?" Ivan and Eryn each grabbed a chair, swinging the backside to the front, threw a leg over, and leaned their arms on the backrest.

Cian dragged his brother's golden sword closer and gave Grizzly an intimidating look. "Oh, Grizzly wanted to know why we had not one but three Anubis when he was sure the last ones died on a rocket that crash-landed on the moon."

Grizzly shoved another big heap of mashed potatoes into his mouth. Chewed it open-mouthed and nodded at Cian and his brothers. Eryn puckered his mouth and lifted an eyebrow. Ivan blinked expressionlessly.

"I'm sure he wonders because the Disciples wore whistles. They commanded the Anubis because they were the chosen ones." Cian winked at them.

"Really, so that's what happened to our rocket?" Eryn blurted out as if he didn't know. He'd asked Barkor as soon as they were able to. They couldn't believe out of the thousands of humans, supposedly a hundred forty-four thousand, only a little over two thousand survived.

"Your rocket?" Grizzly coughed, and droplets of spittle and mashed potatoes flew in Cian's direction. *Yuk.* He swerved to the right missing it. Grizzly chuckled. He saw that and then turned to Eryn, waiting for an answer.

*He's vile and stupid.* He seemed to be challenging Eryn. Now everyone was really listening.

"Yeah, we sent it up, hoping you had some kind of automatic landing system programmed on your side. You didn't, and all those people died?" Eryn said. He had taken their deaths very personally.

Grizzly tipped his head to the side. "I asked you why you had a hand in sending the rocket to the moon, boy?"

"Let's just say it was that or let them drown," Eryn answered, not fazed by Grizzly's passive aggressiveness.

"We were ready, but when it came closer to the lunar orbit, the approach was too fast, and they crashed. It was a mess because no one was suited up. By the time they had them inside the dome, they were dead. Also, our provisions craft never arrived, and we all had to make do. No food, Anubis, and no one to call the water for us. Just whining useless women and children who expected heaven and instead got hell. No gods and no fucking promised prince." Grizzly had spoken animatedly and pointed his eating utensil to the crowd. They murmured a reply, but Cian couldn't figure out what they said.

Ivan straightened up. Cian felt his skin crawling.

If Grizzly was alive ninety years ago, that meant he might be like them. He was bigger than the average human. He didn't look like Barkor or Eryn. Maybe he hatched from another batch.

"What do you mean you had to make do? What did you eat? I know you didn't share the water." Ivan looked at Grizzly, and all three could read his mind. *They did—they ate their dead.*

"Don't tell me you ate them."

Grizzly looked at the crowd. Eryn, Ivan, and Cian followed his gaze. "What else did we have to eat?" Grizzly asked them.

"We never did. You and your Disciples did," a man shouted back at Grizzly.

"They wanted meat and didn't want to wait for the crops. And when the crops were ready, they had taken that, too!" a woman yelled from the back of the crowd.

"It's their fault the Zelk started taking body parts. They learned from them what to do. They're the ones who built the tower for themselves," a man shouted.

"He's a walking corpse. He's supposed to be dead. He is Zelk!" an older man cried hoarsely while pointing at Grizzly.

"They left us on our side, and when they needed more body parts, they started taking our children!" another older man shouted.

Cian never knew the history. Sarinka never told him. This was what Ish mentioned when they met him. He said they wanted to live forever and created a central tower to collect their minds.

Cian spoke to Eryn and Ivan. *Brothers, this is seriously sick.*

"I say we cut him up like he had us cut up," a man shouted, and the crowd went ballistic.

Eryn got up. "Please, we will make sure he meets his justice. Remember, this is an important man. He and his kind have worked hard to help you survive on the moon," Eryn said, and Cian felt him sending calming energy into the crowd.

"Yeah, give him his justice!" they shouted, fists in the air. Grizzly looked taken aback. Cian had enough. This was escalating.

"Come, I'll show you Earth from my private outlook, it's small, but you can still see it," he said, and Grizzly smiled, wiped his mouth, and got up. The crowd followed.

When they reached the airlock chamber, he opened the door pointing to the small blue orb.

"Another few days, and we'll be home. I had to take a detour in case we were followed. Don't want to bring Zelk to Earth."

"Yes, we don't want that," Grizzly said, not really looking all that trusting of what was happening. He hesitated in following Cian, but the low growling from Rotty behind him motivated him to step further and enter the chamber. As he stepped in, gaining nonchalance, he looked at Earth.

"That's a stunning view. Actually, I've seen Earth a few times from space and a bit closer when I accompanied the droids to mine the fuel. I'm eager to see your home. I can't imagine anyone living in those toxic fumes. The stuff surrounds the whole planet. So where exactly is your home, and is there space for all of them? You may have to crowd control if you catch my meaning," Grizzly spoke, and Cian wanted to pass out. His breath reeked, and the chamber wasn't ventilated.

He had to get out. He was sure this man was radioactive from all the UV rays. He was a rotten walking piece of decomposing slough. He needed to do a debridement, cut out and away before he infected anyone else. Cian cleared his throat and turned away, searching for fresher air, then asked, "Oh, so you've been?" and kept the conversation going.

"Not down to the water but high enough to see some of it. I was a small boy when we were deported to the Lunar Environmental Project. My parents were so proud and happy to help set up the dome and prepare for the gods to come. But they never came. It was all a lie. And now I see these Anubis and wonder if there was some truth to it because you and your brothers are not human. Are you?"

"No, we're not. Why is it that you are still alive? You're almost a century old?" Cian stepped sideways to avoid the stream of rotten breath coming his way.

"My parents were scientists. I aged much slower than other children. Like snakes, I have what you call indeterminate growth, which means I have no terminal point in time or size to stop growing. I do have a few transplanted organs. They have replaced my heart three times, because my original organs couldn't accommodate my size, and heart failure was imminent. It's an honor to stand here with a god."

Hmmm, exactly like a snake, Cian thought. "I don't think we're gods. Like you, I think we're the product of DNA manipulation. Somehow, someone hit the mark with trial and error. What do you know about the experimentation with humans? Did your parents tell you anything about their research?" Cian asked, wanting to know about the fucking Anunnaki.

"No, I wasn't educated, but we did talk about it. I thought none of it was real, yet here you stand," Grizzly said, staring off into space deep in thought.

This was it, the moment of opportunity. Cian quietly stepped back, and the door slid shut before him.

"Thank you, brother." He thanked Ivan for shutting the door and trapping Grizzly inside. As soon as the door shut behind Grizzly, he flung himself around. Pure rage flushed red-purple blotches up his neck and into his fat face. He pulled the handle and when the door didn't open, he kicked it. Cian narrowed his eyes and stared emotionlessly at him. A wall of the Anubis's chest muscles rubbed against his back. He turned and hugged his best friend. "Rotty, what's going on, boy? You're such a big boy now. Thank you for protecting me, my friend." Rotty whined like he always did when Cian knew he meant *yes, but. Yes, I'm so big, but.* Hugging him and feeling his heat felt like home. Cian inhaled and turned to face the people still looking at their tormentor inside his cage. Grizzly banged on the door. Spittle, puss, and blood smeared on the plexiglass as he rubbed his face against it. Nobody heard his cries.

Cian pushed through to the crowd, searching for Talali and her sisters.

"Where are they, boy?" he asked Rotty. The animal turned his head in their direction.

"Cian General," Talali called, holding her arms out for him. Kneeling on one knee before her, he opened his arms, accepting the hugs and love.

"Are you okay? Did he hurt you?" Cian asked, while Rotty panted happily and sat down. He looked smaller already. It seemed the Anubis increased in size if there was danger and shrunk back to his regular size when the threat was averted. Strange, Cian thought. But at this stage of his life, nothing surprised him anymore.

"I locked him in there. He wanted to see Earth, and I showed him. He's all yours. I can't push the button since he didn't do anything to me. I leave it up to you to decide who will kill him. Let me show you." The crowd parted like the sea for Moses.

"This button opens the outside hatch, and this one opens the front. They won't open at the same time. Nothing will happen if you open the outside door, except Grizzly will be sucked out and killed." They nodded, looking astonished by his gesture. Talali grinned at Grizzly. Grizzly mouthed, "No, please no." The crowd came closer, judging the man who made their lives a living hell.

Nobody said a word.

Cian walked away. He saw enough ugly for one day. He needed to be alone and blow off steam.

"Come, boy," he tapped his leg with a flat hand.

"Let's go!"

CHAPTER 38
# UNDRESS HIM

**GENERAL CIAN ROMANOV**
**2147 A.D. (95 A.T.)**
**The Warship Horizon**

Cian tossed and turned, irritating himself wide awake. Flipping over to his stomach, he went to throw his pillow, thought better of it, and flipped onto his back again. The bed linen felt cool on the back of his head. He closed his eyes, relaxed, and listened to the soft humming coming from the engines. He splayed his hands wide on each side and felt the vibrations.

"Oh, for fuck's sake!" He kicked himself fully awake. "I'm not going to sleep," he mumbled and stopped trying. His migraine was also not going anywhere. Attempting to relieve the tension headache, he found the pressure points where his nose bone met the eye sockets and squeezed with his thumb and pointer finger for a few seconds. Again, he closed his eyes and started deep inhalation relaxation meditation. He felt his body getting lighter and relaxed.

"Ohm, ohm, ohm. I'm happy. I'm calm. Ohm, ohm, ohm." He refocused and relaxed his whole body. Starting at his feet, his left foot and the prosthetic lower right leg, he imagined he was weightless. Then, moving up to his knees, the sensation flowed through his upper legs. Suddenly, it stopped at his cock. The organ pulsated, making him super aware of his incapability to unwind in that region. *I'm so horny.*

"For the love of!" he exclaimed. He knew exactly what needed to be done. He decided to do it and get it over with. He had to have him. If Leo wanted to watch, let him.

*Maybe it's the icebreaker we need?*

He swung his legs over the side excitedly. He couldn't remember when he last felt so giddy with nervous anticipation. *He better not break my fucking heart,* he thought as he walked into the shower to freshen up and prepare to give a dying man his last wish.

First, Cian went to the bridge command center to ensure they were on course and ready to deposit their precious cargo on Earth. Heaven forbid he lost the last of humankind because he wanted to give a dying man his last wishes. Not because he wanted his dick dipped deep and sucked clean. No, not at all that. After confirming with his brother that the Horizon was set on due course third rock from the sun, he marched like a soldier to war. His mission—to kill his arousal.

He stopped dead in his tracks in front of the shiny metallic door of his mate's cabin. *Dear lord, what if the half-man died while watching? He better not. Maybe he should. Maybe dying watching Barkor being skewered by the mighty Cian wasn't a bad way to go,* he thought and pressed the buzzer button.

"Hello. It's me."

"Who's me?"

Cian crushed his teeth and almost cracked his molars. He took a deep breath. "Me, Cian, the fleet commander, General of the fucking Horizon." He looked left and right down the corridor, ensuring nobody heard him.

"Oh, you," came from the inside.

Silence. *Fuck this.* Cian turned to leave, and the door swooshed open, revealing Barkor smiling brightly. Cian guessed he tried to look seductive with only sleeping pants and bare feet. Perfect bare feet. They were webbed. Cian's insides whooped with approval. He looked at Cian as if for the first time. Inspecting each other inch by inch, he scanned Barkor as Barkor scanned him back and then lingered on his crotch.

"Step aside, the mighty General is bringing gifts," Cian said with more courage than expected.

The half-man was sitting at the small table with pillows propped beneath and behind him. Barkor stepped aside, supporting himself with one hand on his hip and the other on the wall so Cian could enter. He looked invigorated and continued to look Cian up and down as if he was already undressing him in his mind.

"I bet Barkor my lunch that you would return, and here you are," Leo said smugly.

His false bravado deflated, and uncomfortable didn't begin to explain how Cian felt. He wondered if there was still time to turn around and run. But his feet didn't want to move. Leo couldn't wait to see Barkor and Cian getting their grooves on; his eyes were loaded with youth and vigor.

Cian remembered Leo had spoken. "Your lunch?" he asked after a long agonizing silence.

"Yes, my lunch." Leo chuckled, and mischief was written all over his face.

"Why would you bet on your lunch? You know there's a buffet, and you can eat as much lunch as you like all day."

"I know, it's just a saying, whatever. We bet our lunches on Grayrak. Come in, come in. Barkor and I just had a shower, and he's ready for you. I had him wash all his cracks, and I can confirm that he's squeaky clean and ready for you, big boy."

"Leo, do you have to be so crude?" Barkor asked, his lips rolled up with a disgusted look on his face. It looked like he wanted to run back into the shower. The space was small.

*Maybe both of them should run and leave the naughty half-man here?*

Cian didn't like that Barkor felt cornered and pushed into this forced lovemaking session. "Okay, I think I've changed my mind," he said and turned to leave but saw the disappointment in Barkor's blue-slitted eyes. Steam was still billowing from behind him, confirming he just came from the shower to open the door for him. Cian took him in. His wet hair was combed to the back, almost reaching his shoulders. The big expanse of his muscled chest was impressive. And his biceps were almost as big as Cian's.

*This is so wrong, so wrong. I'm going to get third-wheeled again. Fuck this!*

"Leo, I owe you lunch," Cian said while glancing at Barkor. The heat between them was at incineration levels. Cian heard both their heartbeats slamming into their rib cages. Droplets of water ran down Barkor's temples, and Cian wanted to lick them. His skin tingled, and he knew he would glow if the overhead lights were off.

"I don't think this is going to work. I think I must go. This was a mistake." He turned to Leo. "Sorry, Leo, I couldn't give you your wish."

Cian didn't think Barkor could move that fast. He jumped in front of the door and blocked it. "You aren't going anywhere. Let's sit and get to know each other a bit and take it from there." Barkor was vibrating. His smoldering eyes told Cian, he wanted it, but was just as hesitant as him. Barkor ran his hands through his hair, and faint tremors exposed his nervousness.

Cian wanted to push him to the side and run. But again, his legs didn't move. Nervously he searched for a spot to sit, and Barkor pulled a chair closer for him. He sat. They looked at him. He cleared his throat.

"How do you want to do this?" he asked, but no one said anything.

Leo opened his mouth and shut it.

Barkor gave Leo a glance and swallowed. "Leo suggested to me earlier to start with a kiss."

"Really? How will that work?" Cian teased and smiled seductively at Barkor. His attraction to the man was undisputed. He was the most beautiful man he'd ever laid his eyes upon. He examined him deliberately up and down. Not making a secret of it as he leaned back, starting at his toes. "How were you born?" he asked.

"Excuse me?" Barkor blurted. "Cian, sometimes I can't keep up with how your mind jumps."

"Were you hatched from an egg, or did you come from an artificial womb?" Cian asked, and Barkor frowned, bemused by the question.

"Hmmm, none of the above. My mother pushed me through her vagina," Barkor answered sarcastically.

"Oh my goodness, how did she survive that?" Cian asked. Bowled over by his size, he couldn't imagine a baby his size being born naturally.

"She didn't."

"Oh, sorry."

Awkward silence.

"Who was your father?"

"I don't know. Why are you asking? What does my lineage have to do with this? Don't you have other sexier questions to ask?" Barkor asked shortly, with irritation flaming his cheeks red.

Cian didn't want to go into that detail, but he had to ask. He had no clue how Barkor ended up on the moon. Was his mother pregnant, or did he sleep in one of those glass caskets they had sent to the moon? And why did he have webbed toes and look like Eryn, only a foot smaller version? He was exactly Cian's height at seven feet, but his facial features were like Eryn's.

*God, we're the incubator generation.*

Leo seemed like the excitement had drained from him.

"Something wrong?" Barkor asked, also noticing the deflating spirit of Leo.

"I just need to lie down for a bit. You know I get tired faster than usual." Barkor got up and went to help Leo to his bed. Cian noticed they were sleeping in separate beds. *That's good news.*

Cian caught a glimpse of a smile and wink from Leo at him. The little shit, he thought. "Have you tried peeing on him?" he asked.

"What the fuck?" Barkor asked. Leo laughed and Barkor shook his head in disbelief.

"Sorry, I speak my mind too fast sometimes. I mean that our placenta, our birth water, had healing qualities. We had capsules with our birth water inserted into the humans on Earth, and they never age. The closest I could come to the placenta was piss. Have you ever tried to piss on Leo?" Cian knew it sounded weird, but he thought it might actually work.

"Why would I ever think of pissing on Leo?" Barkor pointed to Leo, who burst out in another fit of laughter. "That's disgusting, and that's beneath him and me."

"Sorry, I just thought it could maybe prolong his life. And then—"

"Are you trying to get out of the deal by suggesting I piss on Leo, or did you want to piss on Leo?"

Cian got up. "Okay, this isn't going to work. Me talking to you" —he pointed to them and back and forth— "will never fucking work. If I can't have a normal conversation, I'll go. I'm much better off alone. I see where this is going again, anyway. He is luring us to his bed and you are too stupid to see that. Unless you are in on it, or too dense to see the humor of the situation. I need to get to the important things, like getting this ship safely to Earth. The scientists at Phoenix can explain everything to you once we arrive there." Cian pushed his chair back aggressively and jumped up.

"Stop him, Barkor," Leo said, and the next moment a hand grabbed his shoulder, spinning him around.

Cian didn't have time to react as Barkor's mouth slammed onto his. At first, he thought he'd lost a tooth or split a lip. But then, all thoughts deserted him, and he just drew blanks as Barkor forcefully manhandled him. He pushed him back against the wall, pinning him with a solid wall of muscles. His temper flared, and a few things happened at once. He never closed his eyes, and neither did Barkor. He wanted to push the man off him, but he was immobilized by the shock and the fact that someone was kissing him for the first time in half a century.

*Where's Rotty?* He wondered if this would have happened if Rotty had been here. *The damn animal is playing with kids, and here I am being assaulted by lips and tongue. I should protest and say something.* But he couldn't because his mate's mouth was on his.

Oh, and maybe he should breathe. He lifted his hands to push Barkor away, but the moment he touched those firm chest muscles, those firm pecs, pleasure zinged through his fingertips down to his cock. Jump starting it, forcing Cian to focus and pay attention. Barkor had soft black chest hair, so unlike Eryn and Ivan.

*No, fuck this. I'm not thinking about them.*

Barkor broke the kiss. He looked at Cian's lips. Licking his own, he then swooped in for another round of kissing. *Oh, my god, he's a good kisser.* Cian relaxed, then he closed his eyes and fell into the rhythm of delving deep, swooping in and swooping back out. Their tongues danced and glided, and Barkor tasted delicious. Cian pushed Barkor, steering him backward this time without breaking the kiss.

"Yes, come here." He faintly heard Leo in the background.

Cian didn't find Leo watching them repulsive; if Barkor wanted this, he would do it. He kissed Barkor with renewed determination. If he didn't do this, he would either explode or never get the opportunity again. That left him no choice but to play nicely until the half-man croaked.

"Undress him," Leo whispered. Barkor started at his boots, next his socks came off, revealing his right artificial toes and foot while his left foot balanced on the cold steel floor as Barkor slid his pants down his legs. He should have felt awkward and embarrassed, but as Barkor began to steer him backward and never stopped kissing him, he forgot his shortcomings. Barkor hastily loosened and undressed his pants. Leo sighed, but Cian could hear the shortness of breath and the crackling of his lungs. The overhead lights were as bright as daylight, and Cian wondered if Barkor could hear and see their song.

Cian broke the kiss to see where they were and how three bodies would fit on the narrow bed. Barkor moved and planted Leo between them, his face radiating contentment and relief as Barkor and Cian started kissing again. Their cool, freshly showered and wet bodies felt gloriously good to Cian. He'd forgotten how it felt to be intimate, but so far, everything happened naturally, as if the three of them were meant to do this.

"Don't want to crush you," Cian said between kisses, and Leo groaned a negative. Barkor's mouth tasted like spearmint. His tongue was slippery as it glided over the roof of Cian's mouth. Cian's cock leaked into his underwear. He scooted closer onto his knees, pulling Barkor's hips so their cocks lightly touched. "I want to take both our cocks into my hand."

"Yes, please," Barkor moaned. His voice a deep rumble that tickled Cian deep inside his chest. The space was a tight fit. Cian halted kissing to look at Leo and Barkor.

He saw the beauty that once was in Leo's face and concentrated on that—the beauty of the plan he had made to bring them, two stubborn, hard-headed men, together. At that moment, Cian was sure Barkor would have never acted if Leo didn't ask him. For that, he liked Leo a little bit more. Leo nodded at him and then gazed at Barkor who was staring at Cian. Their connection was indescribable because, without words, Barkor's head fell back as he panted, while Cian took his thickly veined cock in the palm of his hand, pumping it with a firm grasp up and down in long lazy strokes.

"You are beautiful together," Leo said and Cian agreed it was beautiful. They were beautiful.

He wanted to fuck Barkor, and holy shit, Cian felt the telltale feeling emanating from his bones, and he knew he was going to sing for them. He looked down to check if his skin glowed, but the urgent call over the overhead speakers interrupted him.

"Commander General Cian, sir. You're needed immediately in flight control, sir."

"Fuck, talk about bad timing. Sorry, I have work to do. I don't have time to fuck around like a teenager." Cian practically pushed Barkor off the bed as he struggled to get up with his stubborn right leg not cooperating fast enough. Once up, he jumped to collect his clothes discarded by Barkor just minutes before. Leo chuckled.

"Are you okay?" Barkor asked with shock and astonishment written on his face.

Cian wondered if he was amused or cared about his well-being. *Why would he care?*

*No one ever does; it's all about the soon-to-be dead guy.* It was a fleeting thought as he slipped on his boots. He straightened up, repositioned his deflating leaking cock, then slapped his cheeks to wake up from this bloody trance he was in.

"I told you, I have a ship to command, a bloody stolen enemy ship, and with this one ship, I vowed to exterminate your enemies and save your people. Our enemy had years to prepare, and we had two. We managed to do it in less than that. We suspect there might be more Zelk that had escaped. *My men must have spotted the enemy while I am fucking around. Fuck! I need to go. Sorry.*" He gulped a few breaths and halted, then slammed his fist into his chest. Locking gazes with Barkor he said, "The moon's pull was like a big rock in my chest. For years, I lived half-suffocated and shunned with one goal…to have you for myself without this damn rock in my chest. I knew you were there. I knew if I saw you, you would confuse me and make me want you, while I couldn't have you." *And if I lose you and your people, I would never be able to live with myself.*

Cian turned before he humiliated himself further. He hit the button to exit and looked over his shoulder. "Barkor, come to me when Leo has died. Leo, may you walk in the sun on the other side. Cian gave him a mock salute. May you die a good death, my friend. Thank you for taking care of Barkor for me and helping us infiltrate the Zelk. If it weren't for you, Ivan and Eryn wouldn't have gotten their jobs at the hospital, and of course, I appreciate you getting my men and me on this ship. You are a hero, and I'll make sure you're remembered that way," he said honestly to Leo, who nodded and smiled.

Barkor sat on the side of the bed with his head hanging in his hands. *Disappointed or upset?* He would have to worry about that later.

He turned and sprinted down the corridor. Halfway to flight control, Ish's pager vibrated in his pocket. Fumbling, hop, skip and jumping, he got the damn thing out and saw he had missed a string of repeated messages.

*Change course now! Change course now! Change course now!*

Fuck!

CHAPTER 39

# CHOWING A MAN'S SANDWICH

*"Good morning, new citizens of Phoenix.*

*It's now six a.m.*

*Did you know learning a new language can be fun?*

*Use flashcards and start using the Old Earth's language all day, every day.*

*Visit your community news page for more tips and tricks to adapt easier when you arrive in Phoenix.*

*Breakfast is served until eight a.m.*

*Hope you have a wonderful day!"*

**BARKOR, the Promised Prince**
**2147 A.D. (95 A.T.)**
**The Warship Horizon**
**Somewhere between Earth's moon and Mars**

Leo died in his sleep the following day. His body had been set adrift among the stars after his friends paid their respects—everyone except Cian and his men.

Two days later, Cian came over to the serving trays squashing and testing the pieces of bread for a soft one, and Barkor slapped his hand away. "Wait your turn, like everyone else," he scoffed. Just the sight of him rubbed him the wrong way.

"I'm hungry, and I've been waiting for my fucking turn." Cian pointed to the long lineup of humans waiting their turn to be served food.

"Yes, he was waiting his turn. He's been in the line in front of me," the man behind him said.

"The commander is so big, no one can miss him," a woman behind the man called out.

"Yes, we'd definitely see if he tried to sneak in the line," a young boy said with hero worship in his eyes.

"He spoke to all of us, telling us about the sun and the Earth and what it's like to breathe fresh air." The fact that everyone liked the bombastic idiot irritated him even more.

"Go sit there." Barkor pointed to an empty seat. "I'll bring your food. We need to talk."

"Oh, now you want to talk to me?" Cian's voice was low and seductive. And the fact that everyone in earshot heard it and laughed was *not* funny. *What has he been telling my people?*

"You *are* aware that I'm the commander of this ship and that no one orders me where to sit or stand," Cian said teasingly. And a woman giggled. Barkor gave her the stink eye, so she swallowed those giggles putting her hand in front of her mouth.

"Oops sorry," she said sarcastically, rolling her eyes and turning her back to him looking at the others behind her and pulling her shoulders up to her ears."

Barkor turned to read the scene and the people behind Cian and frowned. Some made shooing gestures. *What did they bloody talk about?* Cian laughed, and they all laughed louder, as if they were speaking about Barkor while waiting in line.

Barkor cleared his throat, narrowing his eyes at them. They looked away. He decided to leave it and then returned to dishing out food to the next man in line. Cian snatched a sandwich for himself. "I'll wait for you. I can give you five minutes, but then I have a ship to run," he said and flipped about ten of Barkor's trip switches. His head pounded and blood rushed through his ears. He pretended he didn't hear him and continued dishing up food futilely because he spoke so loudly that the whole dining room heard Cian. And it seemed they were all in on the joke, except him.

When the last person was fed, he grabbed a sandwich and proceeded to Cian's table. The mighty commander had fallen asleep on his folded arms and lightly snored. That was why everyone was so quiet. They must have seen he was sleeping. Barkor was stunned by how fast Cian had crept into his people's hearts.

Cian lifted his head when Barkor pulled out a chair rather noisily, on purpose, and sat down.

"How did it go? Did you manage to feed your flock?"

"Yes, I did, but it was weird-ass crazy. The food supply never runs out. When people spoke about it on Grayrak, I thought they imagined it."

Cian smiled secretively.

"You were probably responsible for that?" Barkor asked, and he couldn't decide if he adored the man or just wanted to whack him with a flat hand over the head.

"No, it's them." Cian pointed with a thumb to Ivan and Eryn, sitting a few tables over, arms crossed, legs stretched in front of them. Smiling lovingly as they watched kids climbing and sliding off the Anubis' backs like they were at a playground. The animals must have liked it—their eyes closed and expressions happy and relaxed.

Barkor put his sandwich back on the plate and drank a few gulps of the juice that never seemed to finish.

"Eat up," Cian said cheerfully. But his expression was serious. "You're practically skin and bones. When I fuck you, I don't want you to be brittle and blow away when I whisper in your ear how good you feel around my cock."

Barkor choked on the juice and coughed. "You assume dangerous things, Commander, if you think I will ever let you fuck me," Barkor said, and instead of sounding sarcastic, it came out as a challenge.

Cian rose to it by leaning forward and answering with a deep rumble and seductive tone. "Oh, you can go first if you like, but still, I won't be satisfied coming only once. You can ride me like a bronco, and when you think you're spent, and your balls are empty, I'll flip you over and fill your insides so hard and fast you'll wish you'd eaten that sandwich because I still won't be satisfied." Cian's bionic eye flickered, and the left one's pupil enlarged, hiding the crystal blue iris. "Not ever. And once you had this—" He brushed his cock slowly under the table, his arm moving and his gaze falling to his crotch, so the message was for Barkor alone and not anyone else in the dining area. "Then you're going to be hooked, and I'll be happy to shove it down your throat daily."

Cian grabbed Barkor's sandwich and took a bite, never taking his gaze off Barkor. *Fuck he makes chowing a man's sandwich sexy.* Barkor wanted to poke his last good eye out. Instead, he got up to fetch more sandwiches. He heard Cian chuckle behind him.

*Crazy motherfucker!*

Twenty minutes later, Barkor felt more himself. Obviously, he was hungrier than he thought.

"God," Barkor said. "That was the biggest meal I've ever had."

"Good, that's, hmmm, good," Cian said, but he looked sad and maybe a bit pissed off.

"I actually don't remember when last I ate." *Now, why did I go and say that?*

Cian lifted his hand, like he wanted to slam it down on the table, thought better of it, then bit into his fist. "Barkor, I'm so sorry. It pisses me off to know how you suffered. I should have come for you earlier. Sometimes I felt your pull stronger, and sometimes it just disappeared, so I started to tell myself it was my imagination. That's why I never came. I didn't want to see that it truly was you or my imagination. That's why I avoided coming to you, and your relationship with Leo didn't help. I was scared you didn't want me or only existed in my dreams. I'm so sorry. Maybe I lost focus."

Barkor didn't like Cian feeling unsure and questioning himself. "Stop it now, don't let my nutrition status suddenly make you doubt your ability to focus. I'm okay, and we're all okay. I'm a big boy, and I know this was the plan. If you had come earlier, you could have given yourself away. We all know the scope of this operation and understand exactly the amount of planning and positioning of you and your men, especially your brothers. They could have died, and then I wouldn't have had a bloody sandwich anyway," Barkor told him while collecting the leftovers and separating the packaging neatly for recycling.

"Here, please drink something. Finish this for me, my stomach's full, and I never waste any food. Anyway, all of us" —Barkor pointed to the empty dining area, realizing they were suddenly all alone— "we can't have you fainting from low blood sugar while you take us home."

Cian grabbed his hand, stopping him from moving around, and pulled him closer. "Listen, Barkor, I have to tell you something. I received word that there are more Zelk ships. We don't know how many or where they are. I'm pissed off at myself for missing them. That's what I mean. I'm distracted and worry we won't make it home."

Barkor saw the worry and doubt in his eyes. *He needs my support. He's our last hope.*

Cian took the cup and gulped the juice. Barkor watched that sexy big Adam's apple bobbing up and down.

He surveyed Cian's movements, the bionic eye, the excessive tattoos covering the side of his face, his temple, every inch of his neck, down into his shirt, and his arms. *Oh, moon-god, he's stunning.* Suddenly Barkor wanted the roughness and hardy exterior covering him and pressing him down. While he grunted into his ear, opened up, and showed his vulnerability, speaking from his heart made all that thuggishness disappear. Suddenly he wanted Cian to love him. Barkor knew if Cian loved a man, it would overflow and drown him. He wanted to be that man. That center of all his attention. His brutal honesty and openness were raw and magnetizing. It was what had pulled him most to this magnificent unselfish man.

He stepped back and looked at Cian as if seeing him for the first time. And then he noticed the fine lines and dark circles around his eyes. He seemed exhausted, like he hadn't slept since they last saw each other. *Maybe he's worried himself into this state.* The thought broke Barkor's apprehension, and he recognized the resilience of the commander. But now, he didn't see a commander; he saw a hopeless, lonely soul that carried the fate of his people without ever complaining. All he wanted was Barkor, and Barkor ignored him.

"I'm guessing you're exhausted." Barkor changed the direction of his concern back to Cian. Obviously, he never worried about himself. "Even if you appear ice-cold from a distance, everyone, me included, can see you're drained to the point of falling over. Let's get you to your bunker, Commander."

Cian cheered up like a puppy seeing a ball.

"No. Absolutely not. I'm not ready for this, but I'm willing to listen, but that's after you've slept."

"It's not just about sex. There's more between us than you think, but this is not the time or place. Plus, Leo just died, and you're probably heartbroken," Cian said.

"Leo liked you. He liked heroes and saviors," Barkor said, and Cian frowned.

*He didn't think he was a hero,* Barkor observed inwardly. *Leo liked him even more because of it.*

Cian whistled, and Rotty thundered down the aisle between the tables and chairs.

The animal looked like it smiled at Barkor. His tongue was hanging out to the side, again. He was so big that four to five kids could ride around on its back. Even though he looked like he could rip them to pieces, Rotty loved playing fetch with a ball the children threw for him. The Anubis kept Cian company all day and night, so he must be exhausted, too.

They left the dining area, and Barkor escorted Cian to the sleeping quarters, where he ensured Cian was safely in his bed. "Talk to you in six hours, General Commander."

"I'm stupid if I just let you walk out the door, but I'm sorry. I guess you're right. I need to sleep." Cian slurred his words and closed his eyes. Barkor wasn't sure if the man was apologetic for not dragging him to bed.

He halted his steps out the door. "You're a good man and did a good thing for flushing Grizzly out in space. Leo and everyone who he terrorized is thankful." Barkor kept his voice to a whisper. Much was happening, and he'd forgotten to give the one message Leo told him to give.

Cian nodded slowly. "We need to talk more. I want to get to know you and woo you."

Barkor smiled and left.

Back in his room, he paced up and down, cried, and tried every alternative to yelling. He was so mad, but why? Maybe he pushed Cian away for the same reason Cian avoided him. Maybe he felt guilty. Yes, that was what it was. He had Leo in his arms, and he hurt Cian. *What does that say about me?*

"Ahr!" He groaned and face-planted into the pillow on his cot. He needed sleep. *Or maybe I don't.*

Turning on his back, he scrubbed his hands over his face.

*I'm so sorry, Leo. I wish you could see Earth and the sun. But that was never your dream. All you wanted was to see me happy, Grizzly dead, and the people free and happy.*

Four hours later, Barkor found himself moving to Cian's room. He let himself inside, into Cian's and Rotty's space, hoping he was doing the correct thing. He acted on his impulses, something he never did. He was one hundred percent sure now that Leo wanted this, and he would give him that wish.

Two yellow eyes looked up at him but closed them again.

"Good boy, I will not hurt him," Barkor whispered.

# CHAPTER 40
# WHAT THE FUCK IS NORMAL ABOUT GLOWING?

*"Good morning, new citizens of Phoenix.*

*It's now six a.m.*

*Did you know you can get up to speed by watching movies and reading the subtitles?*

*Tonight we will be showing movies in the dining area. Grab your dinner and watch a movie with family and friends.*

*Visit your community news page for a menu and the times the shows start.*

*Breakfast is served until eight a.m.*

*Hope you have an entertaining day!"*

**General Cian Romanov**
**2147 A.D. (95 A.T.)**
**The Warship Horizon**
**Somewhere between Earth and Mars**

Someone entered his room, and Cian instantly woke and knew it was Barkor. He heard the shuffling of feet.

"Good boy, I will not hurt him," Barkor whispered. Rotty would have attacked if he'd been there to hurt him.

Barkor's anxiousness rolled in waves over Cian. He continued snoring and carefully cracked his left eye open to see his intentions, leaving the bright bionic one closed. Things moved slowly and fast at the same time. Their hearts pumped, thoughts raced, and all kinds of hormones flushed from glands through his endocrine system. The traffic jam of chemicals trying to coordinate his emotions, sexual function, and circulatory system caused congestion somewhere around his chest cavity as veins constricted and arteries dilated, flooding his heart, causing pushback and palpitations.

Cian was never interested in anatomy and physiology like his brother, but suddenly a fleeting thought about his twin brother assailed him, and he wondered what he thought when shit like this happened to him. His blood vessels feeding his cock and balls opened up first, pooling oxygen-poor and oxygen-rich blood down south. Filling his cock with nearly seventy-five percent of his blood with the velocity of an electronic throwing arm.

Cian wanted to jump out of his skin. A feeling he felt more than half a century ago flowed over him and through him. He recognized it immediately for what it was. His mate was horny, and he meant business. As warmth ebbed and flowed through him and he forced himself to breathe and calm the fuck down. Soundlessly if possible. The tell-tale rustling of clothes falling to the floor had his teeth chattering, and he closed his mouth.

Finally, the time had come to be with his mate.

The room lit up as more clothes fell onto the steel floor. Barkor eased back and looked around him. "What in the ever-loving fuck is this?"

Cian opened both his eyes. Barkor inspected his arms and glowing body indignantly.

"Don't be scared, lover. Come here. It's normal."

"Normal? What the fuck is normal about glowing?"

"It's just us, as Eryn called it, our mating song. Come closer, I'll show you. Don't be afraid. I won't do anything. I just want to touch you with one finger. May I touch you?"

"Yes, I guess. That's why I'm here, but I didn't think we would go all moon-god, like literally, moon-god."

"Shh, look and listen. I'll hum what I hear in my heart, my song for you."

Cian closed his eyes and thought back to the time when he and his brother were prisoners and discovered they could sing and glow like Eryn.

Carefully, cautiously, he began with soft notes. He reached deep into his soul and sang to Barkor. He slowed and stopped to ensure not to scare the man away again. When he opened his eyes, he expected big round eyes in awe. Not someone attacking him with his mouth and kissing the shit out of him.

*Singing to your lover does solve everything; thank you, Eryn and Ivan.* That was what they'd been telling him. Get the man alone and sing for him. *It worked!*

"What?" Barkor broke the kiss for a second. Cian felt drunk and disorientated with lust and overwhelming surprise.

"Hmmm."

"Did you say something?"

"No, how can I say something if you're sucking my face?" Cian asked, but he knew what it was. Barkor was probably starting to hear his thoughts.

*One step at a time, Cian.*

"Do you still want me?" Barkor asked the stupidest question ever.

"I haven't slept in a week. You feed me, put me to bed, and now jump my bones and kiss me senselessly. Feel my cock. Of course, I want you." Cian sat up. "Listen, there's more than you think going on here. It's not just sex I want from you, and obviously, you're here in my room, and you want it, too, *but there is more.*"

"Dammit, tell me what the fuck is going on, then. This is so weird. I've had my fill of weirdness lately." Barkor eased up so Cian could talk.

"It's nothing to fear. Maybe telling you how I found out about myself will make more sense to you and yourself," Cian suggested, and just like that, the glowing died down.

Cian explained how they were born, what happened when they met Eryn, and how they were a throuple until Ivan and Eryn had mated half a century ago. And while he was talking and sharing, he told him how alone and cut out of their union he'd felt. He told him what happened in the room, how they discovered Ivan was Eryn's mate, and Cian had realized he belonged to someone else. Then he told him about Phoenix becoming a flourishing city at the bottom of the southern seas while he longed to get to the moon, to Barkor.

"Holy fucking masterpiece, no wonder we were both agitated. You were scared to be around me and talk to me. So instead of being friendly, you were an asshole, you stupid, lonely man. Well, here I am." Barkor waved him over. "Come, big boy, sing for me and teach me," Barkor said and very optimistically pointed down to his cock.

Cian stopped himself from pouncing because he wanted to tell Barkor how he felt about him. "I never really expected to get some tonight. It's not just the sex or the mating urge. The way you've taken care and looked after these people...they look at you like you're their savior or something. I see and love you already, for that reason, who you are and what you stand and fight for. I see now why they call you their prince. Maybe it's good you were able to look after them all this time because no one else would have."

Cian gently took Barkor's hands in his, kissing every finger, every knuckle lightly. "I saw you from afar when you waited for us at the clocktower, how you held and kissed Leo. You loved him dearly. And maybe it all worked out as it should have. Because Leo got to have you for a while, and those humans would have been lost without you. Knowing my mate did his best to save the last of mankind with little to nothing for so long just tells me how amazing you are and how lucky I am to have found you, even if it was the loneliest time ever for me."

The last walls around Cian's heart crumbled, and he cried silently as he spoke. He heard Barkor sniffing a few times. Then they just sat together. Not moving. Just absorbing the magnificence of the truth between them, the unavoidable destiny bridging the last seconds apart between them. The relief and the beauty of it all overwhelmed both.

Barkor sniffed. "Now I understand that pull I had to do better and save them. It was for a reason none of us could understand or explain, but I believed that as long as I fought for a better life and the good of everyone, it would turn out better than just okay."

"You're my purpose," Cian said and sounded romantic without trying.

Barkor chuckled. "Yes, and you are mine, but we can do so much for them together. I understand you, and it all now. I see our future clearly."

Cian took Barkor's hand and kissed it. "Yes, I do, too. It's what makes me feel alive."

"Me, too," Barkor answered.

"I need you safe and close to me, and I want to help you protect yourself and your humans."

"They're not mine."

"Listen, they will follow you anywhere. They are yours, and since you and I are not splitting up ever again, you're mine, which also makes them mine. But first, I need to find those Zelk."

Barkor leaned over and kissed Cian lightly on the forehead. "I know you'll get us all through this. I believe in you. It may be prematurely, but, Cian—" Barkor's mouth was hot and sweet as he opened his lips and invited Cian in. Teeth nipped, tongues met, playing carefully and softly, gliding, sliding, and delving. And then they drove deep.

The room lit up again, and the taste and touch of Barkor made Cian dizzy.

*My mate!*

Pulling back for air, he realized Barkor was splayed across him. Their bodies were scorching hot where skin met skin while cool blue ribbons danced over them, enfolding them in a cocoon of glowing golden-blue strands. His gigantic hands pressed their hips, their bodies together, eager to become one. Barkor was hard against him, and Cian appreciated the evidence of his arousal rubbing against him.

Barkor whimpered and squirmed against Cian, who aggressively took up the kiss again. Fisting his hair, he pushed his tongue as deep as possible into Barkor's mouth, ensuring he tasted him thoroughly. Barkor opened up, and they fought for dominance with their tongues. After a long time, Barkor eased back and settled his head in the crook of Cian's neck.

"How do we do this?" Barkor asked in-between pants.

"What do you mean?"

"You have one leg and one eye. What else is missing? I keep thinking of asking you without hurting your feelings."

Cian laughed explosively.

"I fuck like any other man. I may lose my balance now and then, maybe no fucking up the wall in the shower, but overall, I think my leg won't disappoint either of us."

"Ha-ha. You still have a cock and two balls?"

"You little shit!" Cian flipped him over and loosened his drawstrings.

"No, fuck, not this way. Please, I'm laughing too much."

"This is a serious situation. If a man asks another man if he has a cock and balls, he must prove himself and show them." Cian reached down to expose himself and realized it'd been a few days since he'd showered.

"But I must admit, I need a shower first. I'm truly a little riper than necessary for a first-time love-making session. First impressions last and all that my fathers taught us."

"Fathers?"

"Yes, Fathers." Cian stuffed his jewels back into his pants. "None of that now. I don't want to think about my fathers when I mount you."

"Oh god, now I'm going to be mounted."

"Hhmmm." Cian's deep baritone rumbled in agreement.

"Mounted? Okay, Commander, let's mount each other, but no mounting in the shower," Barkor said eagerly.

Cian enjoyed the banter, and he laughed softly. "But I do need a shower."

"By yourself? I don't think so."

"Of course not, I finally have you here with me, and I'm not planning to ever let you out of my sight."

"Oh god, we're back to hovering and growling again."

"Yes, only if you ignore me and look at me like you hate me."

"I never hated you," Barkor retorted.

"I know, but you ignored me or pretended you did."

"Yes, only because you act as if you're in charge and in control of everything."

"I am."

Barkor rolled his eyes. "Okay, let's agree to start over. Leo knew I cared for him, but I didn't love him. Before coming here tonight, I sat down and meditated. I talked to him. I think he knew me better than I knew myself, or he saw you and me and knew we belonged together. I think I feel better, and I feel like it's appropriate to move on."

"Oh, you spoke to Leo?" Cian softened his tone, trying to convey sympathy.

"Yes, you know, to his spirit. I think he's good with us. And with me being with you."

"Good."

"Anyways, you said you may slip and fall in the shower."

"I said if I mounted you against the wall, I might lose my balance and slip and fall. Come." Cian climbed off the narrow bed and held his hand for Barkor, who got up and let Cian lead him to the back wall, where he pressed a button. The wall slid away, revealing a small bathroom with a shower and toilet. The perk of being a commander was a big walk-in shower. Cian worried that Barkor would think his glamorous amenities were unfair and too much.

Then it didn't matter because Barkor was kissing him, and holy shit, he was doing things with his hands and tongue. Arms flying for purchase, one of them activated the water.

"Barkor," Cian whispered in-between kisses. "Could you help me out of my pants?"

"Oh, moon-god." Barkor laughed. It was beautiful. Then Cian laughed.

Then they giggled like two ten-year old's, stealing the cookies. He was too far gone with lust and happiness. *Both of them were.* They fumbled their way to find his waistband one moment, and then both were naked and glowing luminescent blue-gold. Cian felt Barkor's hard length against his own.

"Shower," Barkor said breathlessly. "You wanted to shower." He broke away from Cian, looking for soap. "Let's clean up, and then—"

Cian grunted his pleasure in his mouth, going in for more kisses.

"Turn around. I want to wash your back and run my wet soapy fingers over your tight-muscled body," Barkor said hungrily.

Cian experienced chest pains where the tightness of missing his mate manifested. It snapped loose, and he gasped for air—emotions overwhelming him. He was here, with him, and he wanted him. He was definitely worked up too much. "You're going to be the end of me," he said as Barkor washed him in slow circles from his head to his toes, pausing and lingering at his ass crack.

"Yeah, I don't think so. Turn for me, please. Bend your head so that I can wash your head."

"Hmmm, you're spoiling me. That feels so good."

"I like the look of your shaven hair and tattoos. Your whole look screams, don't fuck with me, but underneath is all..." Barkor paused to rinse Cian's head and proceeded to wash his muscular chest, soaping up every inch and trailing the tribal markings over his pecs and then his hard nipples, then fingering in tiny circles over his abdominal muscles, teasing and hinting about going lower, but not touching his erect cock. "Underneath it all, you need me to care for you."

"Having fun taking care of me?"

"Hmmm, my mouth waters for you. Look at you. You actually do have a cock and two balls," Barkor teased.

Cian was speechless and shivering. Barkor's touches burned a trail of scorching desire with his inquisitive soft, sensual, exploring touches. His cock throbbed, and he felt like coming right there. It had been so long since someone else touched him.

"I'll pass out if you don't hurry up and get me vertical."

"You wanted to shower, so I'm showering you."

Cian grabbed for the soap to clean himself because if Barkor touched his cock, he would lose his last drop of dignity and come in the man's hand.

"No, ah-ah, let me."

"Barkor, this isn't a good idea. I'm...ah..." Barkor reached around him and grabbed his cock with soapy hands.

"I see now we're meant for each other. You also don't have pubic hair like other men. I thought something was wrong with me, looking like a child with no body hair," Barkor whispered, and he knew exactly how to touch Cian to avoid making him come. He teased by pulling his foreskin back and cleaning his sensitive cock head thoroughly. Thank god he moved down to his balls. "Oh, you are so ready to shoot and to give me your load." Barkor fondled them, then wrapped his fingers around them and pulled.

Cian closed his eyes, hanging onto the wall, and swore creative obscenities as Barkor washed the soft area between his balls and his entrance while pulling his sack down with the other hand.

Next, he washed Cian's hole in slow motion, using the tip of his finger to reach deep enough for a thorough cleaning.

Barkor gently coaxed Cian to turn, making his intentions clear. Cian watched as Barkor closed his eyes and opened his mouth to swallow him.

Streams of water slid over his face and chest, and Cian wondered for a brief moment if Barkor could breathe, but when his cock head traveled over rough teeth with painful slick sensations, he closed his eyes and howled soundlessly, mouth open as he enjoyed the unexpected pain. Then it stopped. He felt only water and realized Barkor wasn't sucking anymore. He opened his eyes and stared into deep blue-black ones. "You cock tease."

"You said shower then mounting," Barkor purred at him with innocent-looking eyes.

Cian grabbed Barkor by the hair, pulling him up to his feet, and bent Barkor's head back to lick and bite his throat.

"I want you now," he growled, lowering his mouth. "I'm your mate, and don't you forget it."

"Never, how can I? You won't let me."

"You got that right. I fucking waited long enough for you, and you will suck my cock, now."

Cian watched Barkor closely for signs that he was going too far, but this rough manhandling turned Barkor on even more.

Barkor's hands skimmed over Cian's lower back, and then he grabbed hold of Cian's glutes and squeezed.

"Fuck yes, I like the pain."

"Me, too." Barkor hissed as Cian tightened his fist in his hair. Cian pushed Barkor back to his knees.

"Suck my cock, as you did just now. I want to feel it, so suck it hard," Cian said, staring at Barkor. Grabbing a fresh hand full of hair, he forced his cock into Barkor's mouth, scraping it along his teeth. The hairs on Cian's arms raised as his skin glowed. It felt electrically charged.

"Fuck, yes."

Barkor bit lightly and swallowed, then Cian moved his cock head between his molars.

Barkor hummed softly, and Cian saw him grabbing his own cock in his hand. He watched as he chewed on Cian's while his arm moved in sync with the pleasure he provided. It wasn't long before it sounded like an orgasm. Instantly, Cian smelled the familiar smell of male ejaculation. *So he liked this. Good, I liked it, too.*

Barkor gave full attention to him, licking, teasing, and biting his cock head.

"Harder," he ordered while he spread his feet apart, making sure his leg was cooperating, then took hold of the safety rails while Barkor drove him crazy with sucking his ball sack, pulling one ball and then the other into his mouth. Chewing the skin like it was bubble gum. Cian resorted to whimpering as Barkor slid his finger into his ass and began sliding it over his prostate.

His orgasm and pent-up frustrations built and built as Barkor edged him repeatedly. Finally, his orgasm exploded—emptying his load before he could warn Barkor, but Barkor drank every drop and suckled his oversensitive tip, which he was sure was raw and bleeding.

"Come here. I want to kiss you," Cian said with a deep grunt. Barkor stood up so they could share a kiss while Cian still grabbed onto the safety bar. His whole body trembled. "I might collapse from coming too hard," he said into Barkor's mouth.

Barkor kissed him with a force that mashed their lips against his teeth. Water ran down their faces, making Cian close his eyes. Their mingled scent and the euphoric emotions enveloped them, and he recognized it for what it was. This was what his brother and Eryn felt for each other. *No wonder.* He made a mental note to talk to them and apologize for his behavior.

Barkor panted heavily. "Can we get out of this shower? It looks like you're about to pass out." Barkor supported him to prevent him from slipping. Cian nodded a yes, suddenly overwhelmed with it all, incapable of speech.

"Are you okay?" Barkor asked, leading Cian back to the bed to sit.

"This is almost too much for me. It's way more intense than I ever imagined. And the worst thing of it all is that I kind of hated my brother, thinking it was jealousy or an inability to share Eryn with me. Now I understand how they felt and what an idiot I was. I almost broke them up, you know, because Ivan couldn't live with himself being happy, and I made it very clear that I was alone and unhappy. Like it was their fault. I'm so selfish." Cian sat with his face in his hands.

"Yes, yes, so selfish. Can we get over the self-pity party? You're ruining a good thing here," Barkor said bluntly, and Cian laughed like he hadn't laughed in years.

"I have a reputation for doing that."

"Not going to argue," Barkor said, flapping his flaccid cock this and that way.

Cian instantly sobered and reached down to grab the offending soft body part. It was roughly the same size as his, but the color of it was a bit darker. Pulling the foreskin back, he heard Barkor hiss through his teeth. He inspected the rough ridges around the head, tightened his grip, and pulled the remaining viscous fluid out. He smeared it between his fingers and tasted it. Then he repeated the motion and smeared it around his fat purple-red cock head engorged with blood. He wanted to taste more of it, so he grabbed Barkor's cock by the base, squeezed and forced more fluid to the tip, then lifted his thumb to his mouth and sucked it clean.

"Oh, sweetheart, that's hot," Barkor groaned.

"I want to come inside you. I want to push myself so deep into you," Cian said and licked another drop from his fingers. "I want to fuck you so hard, you'll think about me with every step you take."

"Oh, moon-god, fuck yes," Barkor said with a heavy breath, turning around, ass up and ready to be plundered.

Cian grabbed his ass cheeks and spread them open. Hard and aggressive to the point of tearing Barkor open. He bent his head and swiped his tongue over the pink puckered hole.

"Oh, dear. Oh, my...yes. Fucking yes," Barkor blabbered as Cian speared and worked his hole, readying it to receive his cock.

When he was happy with its slickness, he lined his cock up, playing with the head around the tight entrance a little too long for Barkor to press back against him.

"Ah, for the love of, fuck me already."

"You're not ready." Cian reached over to the drawer below his bed and fumbled around. "Ah, got it!"

"What now?"

"Prepare to receive me." Cian flipped the cap, then dramatically drizzled his cock, and Barkor's hole with strawberry-mint lubrication oil that was manufactured in Phoenix and was very scarce in space, and he didn't care. He tossed the bottle on the bed and went to work.

"Ah, so fucking tight, so fucking hot!" He howled and enjoyed the tight gliding and the slickness over his raw hypersensitive cock into Barkor's body. Barkor groaned, enjoying their first penetration. The small cabin lit up once more as their arousal heightened. Blue and golden swirls of light energy danced around and over them, as Cian sang his song to Barkor.

Rotty yipped and barked, and Cian assumed it was at the commotion of dancing sparks of light and sounds.

"No, down boy, can't you see I'm busy?" Cian asked and pulled his cock out, straightened his knees, and found a new purchase on the railing above his single bed. *Installed for easy in and out of the cot and for fucking your mate!* He slammed forward, only to pull out all the way. He watched as Barkor's hole closed. Barkor gasped, and Cian sank back into the tight silky hot softness.

Cian wanted to feel closer to Barkor. He stopped momentarily and let go of the handle above the bed. He laid his upper body on Barkor's sweaty back and pushed his hands underneath his armpits and across Barkor's chest, wanting to get as close as possible to him. Then he began moving, pumping his hips with deep long thrusts while biting and sucking Barkor's neck and shoulders. Barkor moaned deeply as Cian moved sensually, slowly building up a rhythm of maddening pleasure for them both.

Loving the sounds and grunts from Barkor as he received him into his body, he became one with his mate, and he felt like they'd known each other forever. Hard and fast thrusts turned to long, deeper strokes. All the sexual frustration and longing were replaced with a surety, a tenderness, and a promise. Biting turned into licks and kisses as Cian enjoyed the taste and smell of his lover. Barkor turned his head sideways for a quick kiss, tongues licking deep and far into each other. He didn't have a long tongue like Eryn, but that didn't bother Cian. He was perfect, and he was his.

Their moans, the rhythmic slapping of skin on skin, stopped as both their bodies spasmed and they orgasmed simultaneously. Breaths heaved. The slickness of their sweat allowed Cian to glide up and down Barkor's back as they rode out the last pleasurable spasms. They grunted together. Cian's orgasm was long and unending. Barkor, the big alpha male who bludgeoned his enemies, had submitted to him.

*It's definitely too soon to say I love you.*

He rolled off Barkor's back. "I don't have words."

"Hmmm, so good, so good," was all Barkor moaned, drunk with pleasure. Puddles of sweat ran down Barkor's back.

"Yes, so hot, thank you," Cian said, looking for a hand or something to hold. Barkor felt too far away from him as he lay next to him. He settled for pushing a hand under his hipbone, enjoying Barkor's weight on his hand and the feeling of his iliac crest.

"For what, for letting you fuck me?" Barkor asked into a pillow.

"No, for coming to me and giving us a chance. And now that I've had you, I won't let you go. Never. You're mine, and I'm yours. I waited for you and never knew how much I missed you, even if we hadn't met." Cian made a fist and bumped his chest area over his heart. "There was a pull between us, and I learned to ignore it, but I can't anymore. I honestly think I would die without you now that I've met and tasted you."

"You big brute, who would have thought you're such a mushy lover? Honestly, I've always known the others weren't like me. I've outlived and lost a lot of people I cared for. It sucked, and I told myself I would have reached the end of my purpose if Leo had been gone and I had my people safe. I never thought my life only started when you jumped to help me carry Leo onto the ship. Let's take it one sleep cycle at a time."

Cian's pager flickered with an orange light, signaling an incoming message. Cian scooted off the bed and got up to fetch it from the pocket of his uniform. "First, we must get the humans safely to Earth." He stopped speaking to read the message.

"What is it? You seem worried."

"It's news from Ish. He keeps sending me these weird messages. Look for the ships, but don't look. Six small Zelk ships are unaccounted for. But they won't be no more." Cian reread the message. It was as if Ish was rhyming in a secret spy language. "Motherfucking six ships, where have they been hiding them?" He looked at Barkor, who was already sitting up. "When all this is sorted, I promise we can do whatever people do for relaxation."

Cian threw the pager on his desk, held a hand out to Barkor, and pulled him up into a standing position. His big muscled body had Cian wondering if they could squeeze in another round.

"No, Cian," Barkor said but sounded like he was wondering the same thing.

"Come, let's go clean ourselves. You can join me in the bridge command. Would you like that?"

"Yes, please, I would," Barkor answered as he was pulled into the bathroom. Once inside, neither couldn't resist. Their mouths met, and they kissed under the running water between washing, groping, and smiling at each other.

# CHAPTER 41

# FUCKING FROG BALLS

*"Good morning, new citizens of Phoenix.*

*It's now six a.m.*

*Did you know you can add a splash of fun with water floaties when you go swimming?*

*Floaties are definitely water essential if you enjoy some quiet time bobbing in the waves.*

*Visit your community news page to book swim lessons or space to take part in water activities and sports.*

*Breakfast is served until eight a.m.*

*Hope you have a kick-ass day!"*

**Ivan Romanov**
**2147 A.D. (95 A.T.)**
**The Warship Horizon**
**Somewhere between Mars and Jupiter**

Ivan pulled his puzzled and unsuspecting husband into the airlock chamber.

"What is this? What's going on, Ivan? Is someone hurt?" Eryn shot question after question but never resisted.

"Don't worry. This is for us. For you and me. It's going to be so much fun." Ivan coaxed Eryn inside, and the door shut behind him. Eryn looked bewildered at the door.

"Don't worry, my big Brawl, no one is going to hurt you," Ivan whispered and hit the button for the opposite door to open the zero-gravity training room. "We're going to fuck until neither one of us can come anymore. I've already told Cian not to expect us at the helm any time soon," Ivan said, ripping off his clothes and boots and sending them drifting. Eryn watched him. The puzzled look on his face was replaced by wonder and anticipation.

*I need him now.*

"Come here. You're a beautiful creature." Eryn flung his arms around Ivan's neck and kissed him until they needed to stop for air. "I missed you so much. I promised myself that when I enter you, it would be with my bare feet planted on Mother Earth. I want to smell mud and semen. Grass and water and…"

"Okay, big boy, I get the picture. Your frogging Brawl ass misses the earth, but I missed you, and I want to come at least three times now," Ivan demanded.

"Look around you. We're in a zero-gravity room. How will I be able to fuck you into the floor or up the wall? You'll fly to the opposite side as soon as I poke you with my finger." He pointed to a wall about fifty feet away from them.

"We just need to be creative," he said seductively, knowing Eryn would never say no to him. The big Brawl was wrapped around his pinky and his alone. "Come, let me help you."

He started to loosen his belt before pulling it through the loops and sending it floating behind him. Then he removed Eryn's pants. His big cock sprang free. Eryn had shrunk his cock to a more manageable size because having two cocks bothered him while walking around, and the two ten-inch cocks were fun when they experimented, but penetration by such big members had torn Ivan open when they were younger and stupid.

Eryn was more traumatized by the ordeal than Ivan. *They'd gone to Mika and Connor. Both fathers had recommended Eryn make his dicks shorter and smaller for Ivan. Both Eryn and Ivan had decided to have Eryn return to having only one dick, exactly like Ivan's. Eryn had asked Mika and Connor how big their cocks were and wanted to see them. Mika and Connor had handled the situation with tact and finesse and had shown Eryn their cocks. As their cocks were also not small, that was how they had ended up talking about recipes for lube.*

Ivan smiled thinking about it and remembered to pay attention.

"This isn't fair. I wanted…" Eryn protested lamely.

"Shh, let me show you how much I missed you." Ivan opened his mouth wide to insert the Brawl's cock into his mouth. Pulling the foreskin back, he rolled his tongue around the rough, sensitive edges of his cockhead, then set about teasing it with small licks and bites just the way he knew Eryn liked it. He suckled and worked it until he tasted his sweet pre-cum. Eryn swore in every language he knew, signaling to Ivan it was time to slowly push every bit of meat into his warm wet mouth and down his throat until his lips touched his hairless pubic area.

He looked up at Eryn, who stared back with a scorching hot look in his golden-green-slitted eyes. He knew he had successfully seduced and convinced Eryn. The hunger in his eyes and his throbbing ejaculating cock said so. Eryn grabbed Ivan by the hair and fucked his mouth hard several times.

"See what you have done? I'm already coming, fucking nymph," he said as he thrust. Ivan's eyes were tearing up, but the absence of a gag reflex gave Eryn the perfect hole to fuck until every last drop was in Ivan's stomach.

It thrilled Ivan by creating new unforgettable memories. To him, it felt like they christened their first love-making session, thus creating a new golden standard for future fucks.

Eryn pulled his long flaccid dick out of his esophagus, and Ivan vacuumed long, heaving breaths with a smile. "Delicious, just as I imagined it would taste and smell. I missed you like crazy," Ivan said between gulps of air.

Eryn ran the palm of his hand down Ivan's cheek. "Thank you, that was your best blow job ever. I missed you, too, very, very much, my beautiful Ivan," he said with tears in his eyes, stroking the line of his jaw with his thumb. They looked deeply into one another's eyes. Both their bodies glowed a light blue sheen. Their fevered gazes of desire turned into a predatory stare, and then they attacked each other with pent-up hunger, longing, and frustration, grabbing each other greedily to get as much and as deep as possible into and of each other.

Growls and moans filled the big space, and Eryn was rock-hard instantly. He pumped his cock, looking like he was about to devour Ivan. "Is this what you wanted? Did you want me to fuck you so hard that you feel it in your throat? I'm going to rip you open and put you back together again," Eryn snarled into Ivan's mouth.

"Yes, please," Ivan said like a needy slut, and Eryn's hands slipped around, cupping his backside to open him up for the intrusion.

"Go ahead. I'm ready for you," Ivan urged.

"Fucking frog balls, Ivan, you're already slick for me?"

"I am. I fucked my dildo and left lots of lube inside for us," Ivan said and flung his legs around Eryn's waist. The movement sent them drifting. Ivan didn't know where since his eyes were closed as he worked Eryn's cock head through his sphincter.

"Dear sweet lollipops! I forgot how good it feels," Eryn exclaimed, pushing deeper, panting deeply. "Oh, ah," he moaned with a deep baritone and croaked a long, bellowed holler of ecstasy Ivan had never heard before.

Eryn's eyes rolled back as he pushed and pulled Ivan by the hips up and down. Ivan held onto Eryn, enjoying the friction his cock received between their slick sweaty bodies. Small sparks of light escaped between their touching bodies, and Ivan opened his eyes to see the ribbons of blue and gold emanating from their union into the space around them. He loved seeing it, it meant they were making love, and the brighter it glowed, the deeper they were immersed in the act of giving and receiving.

Eryn laughed as if hearing his thoughts. The deep chuckles vibrated in his chest, and Ivan searched his face, noticing there was another source of his amusement.

"Why are you laughing? What's so funny?"

"Look at us," Eryn said, barely getting the words out.

Ivan was confused, he was mid-coital, and coitus interruptus was not on his schedule, especially not for a laughing fit. Eryn was hitting that spot he loved and he was one stroke away from ejaculating. He turned to the side where Eryn pointed to their reflection in the massive bay window. Frowning deeply, he saw it. In the darkness, their up-and-down movement looked like two glowworms in the bioluminescent caves below Phoenix.

"Okay, that is funny." They laughed and reached a climax together.

"This was fun, but I think sex in space, in zero-gravity, sounds better than it really is," Ivan said while swimming through the air to grab and collect their clothes to get dressed.

"Agreed, but anywhere is always good, as long as it's with you." Eryn kissed Ivan deeply, took his hand to pull, and pushed him forward to float back to the exit with his arms full of their clothes.

"Oh, I couldn't agree more," Ivan said.

A pager pinged somewhere in the heap of their clothes. Eryn scurried through it, looking for his pants pockets, and he looked at it. "It's a call from Cian." He pressed a button on the receiver. "Speak, brother."

"Ivan, Eryn, come to the helm. We need you. Bring your spear and sword," Cian said in an authoritative voice.

"What's our brother up to now?" Ivan asked.

# CHAPTER 42

# WE ARE COMING HOME

*"GOOD MORNING, NEW CITIZENS OF PHOENIX.*

*It's now six a.m.*

*Did you know communication is usually defined as transmitting information from one place, person, or group to another?*

*Want to communicate better?*

*Visit our community news page for tips that will help you get your message across, avoid misunderstandings, and improve your relationships.*

*Breakfast is served until eight a.m.*

*Hope you get the message today!"*

**GENERAL CIAN ROMANOV**

**2147 A.D. (95 A.T.)**

**The Warship Horizon**

**Asteroid belt between Mars and Jupiter**

Cian stood with his arms folded and a hand gripped tightly under each armpit. Barkor's back was to him, and to prevent himself from touching and groping his mate in front of his men, he squeezed tighter each time Barkor moved, and he got a whiff of his scent.

"Lasitor, are you scanning and recording?"

"Yes, I am, Cian," Lasitor answered.

"Please show us that area on the asteroid belt Ish identified," Cian said.

The big ten-by-five-foot monitor flickered and divulged what Cian hoped would reveal the Zelk waiting to ambush them. This mission would have been lost if it weren't for Lasitor. His attack on the Zelk mainframe regressed their system to a century before Doomsday. Thus, weakening their hive capability and obliterating their entire communication system.

These ships that Ish had discovered were a big problem. Cian suspected they were scouting droid ships hiding and had not recently been grounded. It was cumbersome and might mean that they were inactive and just waiting to be activated, or this was kept from him on purpose. Either way, he'd missed them and didn't do a thorough enough sweep of the Grayrak Zelk fleet. It could also mean they were a much bigger infestation in their solar system.

Cian had never attempted going further than Jupiter but realized now these scouting bots never needed restocking or refueling. He was sure the Horizon was the mother ship, but if he saw anything bigger than a scouting bot, he would have to take drastic steps to eliminate them.

He would do anything in his power to avoid a battle. Maneuvering through the asteroids was already risky. Even if Ish's preprogrammed route through the space rubble was unbelievably easy once Cian had installed the map through the maze and Lasitor knew precisely when to turn left, right, or up and down.

"That's it. There they are. The fuckers," Cian whispered.

"Divide and conquer them, sir," Lasitor said.

"Yes, Lasitor. But, for now, scan their composition. I want to know whether they are classes C, S, or M-typical asteroids," Cian said, noticing Barkor pulling a *what-the-fuck* face and shaking his head. Cian didn't wait for him to ask. He explained. "The C-type asteroids consist of clay and silicate rocks and are dark in appearance. They're among the most ancient objects in the solar system. They're easy to scan because anything not made of clay would show up on the scanners much easier because we know the Zelk are made of Tungsten. The S-types are made up of silicate materials and nickel-iron. They're thicker, but still scannable. Lastly, the M-types are metallic, with iron in the center. They're going to be difficult to accurately scan from one direction. And would be a good hiding spot for the Zelk, who are also metallic."

"I can't see them," Barkor said as he leaned back. Cian felt his body heat radiating through his shirt. Their bodies didn't touch, but if he leaned in one inch, he could press up against him. Maybe rub his nipples against him.

"How do you know it's them?" Barkor asked and stepped forward, squinting to see better. Cian immediately missed his closeness. He stepped to his side and stood next to the man who had him feeling like a love-sick puppy. From the corner of his eye, he watched Barkor grimacing, shaking his head slowly from side to side. His nose almost touched the monitor. "Sorry, the more I search, the less I see," he said, and Cian's heart melted into a puddle.

*He's so bloody cute. He's going to be the death of me. He doesn't even know it.*

"Sir, they're S-types. I confirm there are six of them. All six are smaller than a one-person craft."

A heavy weight lifted from Cian's shoulders. They were scouts, and he would assume that they were armed.

"Look at the size and positions of all the surrounding asteroids." Cian released his right hand from the vice grip under his left armpit and pointed to the asteroids that appeared as red dots on his screen.

"You see here and here. If you're looking for a ship, you'll only see asteroids, but look for the opposite. Look at the randomness of scattered spaces and asteroids and the space they don't occupy," he said and leaned a tiny inch closer while speaking to sniff Barkor's scent. He inhaled slowly and almost closed his eyes as the deliciousness washed over him.

"Oh, moon-god, where? How do you see it? Show me?" Barkor asked as if Cian were hiding them. He turned his head, inquisitive blue-green slitted pupils sparkling, his eyes almost catching Cian in the act.

Cian smiled inwardly and couldn't break his stare. *The man's stunning.* Dark blond curly hair framed his handsome face. Light blue-black stubble lined his firm jaw—thin, wide lips. Smooth pale skin. Low, thick eyebrows. A straight but flattened nose like Eryn. Now that Cian had seen Barkor more intimately, up close, he looked less like Eryn and more like the man he fucked a few hours before. Barkor locked gazes with him, and there they stood. Their gazes locked, and Cian couldn't move.

Someone coughed and cleared their throat. It sounded like Lasitor.

*Fuck, I'm getting hard. Jesus Christ, it's not the time.*

Cian moved one step away. *Breathe, dammit, and think of asteroids and Zelk and Bubblecars. Think engines, atom reactors, and gears turning.*

It seemed Barkor was also affected. He stepped back, raking his fingers through his wild curls while smiling naughtily at him.

Cian cleared his throat and dried the palms of his hands on his hips. Then he turned to the screen, hoping he didn't sound stupid because he was sure he'd forgotten what they were talking about. "Hmm, where was I? Yes, look closely at this spot. See how the asteroids almost form a shape if you connect the red dots?" He connected the dots on the touchscreen.

"Sorry, Cian, I still don't see it," Barkor said.

Cian used his thumb and forefinger, tipping the view about ninety degrees, and suddenly, the shapes of six weaponized scouting ships appeared.

"Oh, now I see them. It's because we're in space," Barkor said, smiling widely, exposing a beautiful set of teeth that sparkled.

*I wonder if there were dentists on Grayrak?* Cian was staring. *I'll ask Barkor once we're alone again.*

Forcing himself to look away, he said, "Exactly, our eyes are trained to look for up or down."

"Hmmm, so they hid by camouflaging themselves with asteroids?"

"Yes, smart, but not smart enough. And now that we know where they are, we should assume they know where we are. We need to act fast. I'm not sure if they're combative or whether they know we're escaping. They could recognize the Horizon as the mother ship, but because we deleted the Zelk programming in totality, only Lasitor remains, and they would immediately respond by attacking because Lasitor is a trojan virus to their mainframe. Lasitor and I have been planning scenarios and have several options. Our position as such needs fast and coordinated work between the Horizon, my brother, and his husband," Cian said, not taking his gaze off the screen.

"I don't understand half of what you are saying. Who's going to give themselves away first?"

"I want to shoot them into oblivion, but that's a fifty-fifty approach. We want to win and not lose one person by obtaining damage to the ship and losing our precious cargo. We're going to turn away—"

"What?"

"Yes, we're fleeing. We can't start a war that we can't win without casualties."

"Fleeing? They'll chase after us and attack from the back."

"Exactly," Cian said and laughed. *God, that felt good.*

Barkor stood with his hands on his hips and looked at him, baffled, as if Cian was crazy. "I don't want to say it, but you make no sense, and it sounds like you're a scared little boy who pissed himself."

Cian burst out laughing again. His men turned their heads in their direction. He swallowed his musings. They knew him, and they were stuck on the Horizon with him while he walked around like an irritated predator. Cian was smiling now, so it must be a strange concept for them. He quickly did a summation of the room. They seemed puzzled, but not antagonistic. Good, because Cian wouldn't hide his love for his mate a second longer.

"Why are you laughing?" Barkor scowled, and Cian stopped resisting the pull between them. He grabbed Barkor by the lapels of his jacket, pulled him closer, and kissed him. Barkor melted into the kiss. Cian gave him one deep sweep into his mouth and broke the kiss.

"You crazy, sexy freak, you—" Barkor said, wiping his lips dry with the back of his hand. He had an indignant expression, but the corners of his lips twitched for a smile.

Cian tipped his head back and continued laughing maniacally. "And you love that about me." He punched a bunch of numbers into the console and then grabbed the microphone. "I'll explain in a second," he told Barkor.

"Speak, brother." Eryn's voice boomed and sounded short of breath.

"Ivan, Eryn, come to the helm. We need you. Bring your spear and sword."

Barkor watched as Cian worked. Next, he called and assembled the troops. "Gunners, report at cannon ports. This is not a drill. Load the anti-grav torpedoes, and south ports load those bombs. Stand at the ready. I repeat, all gunners to their stations." Cian ended the transmission and turned all his attention on Barkor. He needed to explain. Barkor wasn't used to spaceships and technology.

"Barkor, I need you to go to your people and explain our plans after this meeting—" Cian was interrupted by a beep and a swoosh as Ivan and Eryn strutted into fleet command. Dressed in their tactical black body suits, hair up and tied away. Sword and spear over their shoulders with a swagger screaming they just fucked and were extremely happy with the results. Cheeks and necks flame red, lips swollen. Cian waited for the rush of jealousy and resentment at the sight of seeing them, but nothing happened. *Not anymore.*

He stepped forward to greet them. "Thank you for coming. We need to act fast." Cian met them halfway and gave each a quick handshake and a one-armed hug.

"Hello, brother. Is it time to rumble?" Eryn asked, and Cian laughed. He missed them. And he missed their younger days—their camaraderie when they bubble-wrapped Phoenix and saved it from total destruction. Eryn patted Cian on the shoulder, and Cian immediately felt better. *I missed him so much.* Cian realized it wasn't the sex he missed but their friendship. He straightened up, inviting Barkor to stand closer as he started to explain the plan.

"Ivan and Eryn, you must get to the lower bridge deck. I'll need you to each grab an escape pod—"

"What in the ever-loving fucking moondust?" Barkor exclaimed and interrupted Cian, pointing his finger at his chest. "We're fleeing, and now you're sending your family to safety in the escape pods. What the fuck? I didn't think you were one enormous family of pussies. Fuck this!" Barkor jumped to sit at Cian's command console.

But Cian was faster, and Barkor was out of the chair and on the floor in one swift movement. Sitting on Barkor's chest, he grabbed his swinging fists and pushed them under his knees, immobilizing a seething Barkor. Cian's crotch was inches from his mouth. *Fuck he's even more beautiful when he's angry.* Cian kissed him.

"Get off me, you boneless, spineless yellow ass."

"Yellow ass?" Cian chuckled as Barkor bucked underneath him, moving him forward, crotch definitely much closer to mouth. Erotic thoughts amused Cian, and he laughed playfully. Teasing Barkor was fun.

"Yes, you're a weak pussy."

"Listen, you're all big-muscled and wild, but I'll explain. Then we'll see whose ass is yellow and whose ass is red."

"Explain then!" Barkor fumed, and Cian's cock filled.

"Lie still and keep quiet for a change? You can't go pressing buttons, please, Barkor. Listen to me," Cian said, chuckling. Barkor stopped squirming and let his head fall back in defeat.

Eryn and Ivan laughed. "Oh my god, Cian, you have your hands, legs, and knees full of trouble."

Barkor turned red in the face. Eryn's comment must have infuriated him. He struggled underneath Cian and shouted, "Trouble? You all think I came all this way only to flee, and what then? Where do we go? This is supposed to be the last and final stand, and you want to tuck tail?" Barkor glared at Eryn and Ivan. He didn't like them laughing at his expense.

This time, Cian didn't kiss him. Barkor lifted his hips and kicked his knees into Cian's back. Cian couldn't grab hold of his legs, so he covered Barkor's mouth with his hands. They lay like two brawling men on the floor. It didn't seem to bother Barkor.

"Please stop this. We're wasting time. Stop and listen to me," Cian said and lowered his voice while looking deep into Barkor's bewildered eyes. Barkor's smoldering gaze promised death by mauling or clubbing. "You better not bite me," Cian said, shaking his head."Calm down, please. It's not what you think."

"Do you need help with your mate, Cian?" Eryn asked sarcastically. Cian wanted to plug Eryn's mouth with a fist. He was fueling the inferno below him. Between his legs. Under him. Rubbing on his erection.

"I got this, brother. Don't we, Barkor?" Cian exuded calmness while pinning his lover.

Barkor looked at Cian's lips, then a wet tongue licked his hand. Barkor enlarged his eyes. Cian smiled. Barkor smiled back, and then he lifted his eyebrows twice. As if to say, *hey there sexy, want to roll*? Cian shook his head. Barkor gave another nod. His eyes were dark and teasing.

Cian remembered they were in front of his men. He released Barkor, jumped to his feet, and pulled him upright in one smooth movement. Their hands glowed when touching. Eryn and Ivan chuckled, knowing it meant they wanted to fuck.

"Eryn and Ivan are to take the pods and escape. We will slow down, make ourselves known, and wait for the Zelk. Once they've taken the bait, we'll drop a mirror image of the Horizon while cloaking and making a three-sixty and then approach from behind. Once we're behind them, we'll go *pow-pow, boom-boom*," Cian said, smirking.

"Oh," Barkor said.

"Yes."

"Then why didn't you say so?"

"You never gave me a chance." Cian winked at Barkor.

"Okay, that sounds like half a plan. I mean, not all your bases are covered, brother. What about us floating around while bombs are flying?" Ivan asked.

"Actually, we're going to be your decoy," Cian said.

"Explain, please." Ivan rolled his hands at Cian, hinting to say more.

"Eryn, you and Ivan will create a light and sound particle energy field."

They frowned. Cian noticed all his personnel were standing and listening to them. They'd run all the scenarios with him for the past year, so they knew what he was planning.

"I want you to create a stream that swings back and forth."

"What are you talking about, brother?" Ivan asked, looking at him perplexed as if Cian was speaking another language. His eyebrows were skewed, awaiting something to make sense.

"I know you can do this. It would go faster if I were with you, but I must drive this tin can from behind. When the Zelk realize what's happening, I'll push them forward, driving them like cattle into the funnel. They'll want to turn but can't because they'll be packed tightly together. By the time they calculate to turn as one, it would be too late, and they'll be sucked into the maelstrom, and it will be impossible to reverse or escape. The Horizon will skim the top with lasers and drop torpedo bombs on them. That energy blast should create enough momentum to force the center to bend out and twist."

"Ahh," Ivan said, and Barkor stood blinking—looking adorable and unsure what was happening.

"Are you asking us to make a spout?" Eryn asked and seemed to grasp Cian's meaning immediately as he smiled.

"Yes. You can start with a few molecules, send them back and forth, and add to it until it's so big the blast will destabilize the current. Think about it, once you have the current going, when something enters it, the center will stretch and collapse, forming a vortex, and that's when you twist and snap. By the time the spout forms, their ships will already be moving in that direction while the front is being sucked into the funnel. Because the Zelk behaves in a hive, their ships are built and programmed to follow each other, so they won't be able to break formation and thus be sucked into the funnel."

"Where would they go?" Barkor asked.

"We don't know. But they won't be here anymore, and unless they can create the same force at the same spot wherever they are, they'll never be able to return," Cian explained. "Tada! See, it's a good plan," Cian said proudly, looking around only to see horror-struck faces.

"Actually, it's the worst plan ever in the history of horrible plans," a loud, abraded voice growled over the speaker system, reverberating through Cian and bouncing off the walls. Cian saw fine vibrations on the windows, computer screens, and the water's surface inside the staff's water tower.

"General, I'm picking up a signal from an unknown ship," Captain Bill Thornton said.

"Show me," Cian ordered and hastily jumped to see the monitors.

"It's hovering above us, sir."

"Who is this? Identify yourself," Cian said, worried because he was in a situation where the enemy could make demands and bomb them. Any spaceship commander worth his salt should know that was their weakest point.

"It is I, Ish." His voice boomed through the bridge command.

Cian straightened up but was happy it was Ish and not the enemy. "You have a ship?"

"Yes, I do, I do, I do, I do," Ish sing-songed, and then two distinct male voices started to sing *It's You, It's You, It's You* by Joe Dolan.

"It's You, It's You, It's You
    The Only One I Want
    The One I've Been Searching For
    And If You Look At Me
    You'll See A Lonely Man
    Who's Been Too Long Without A Home
    So Why Don't We Just Get Together
    And Try To Live Our Lives As One
    It's You, It's You, It's You
    The Only One I Need
    To Fill My Empty Heart."

"Ish, stop! Ish, for fuck's sake! Who's with you? Are you two drunk?"

"No, and yes. How do you think I traveled and searched for a new home? It's not a ship. It's a machine," he said.

A second man sang again, "And it is beautiful."

"Beautiful," Ish joined in, and they repeated the chorus, "Beautiful, beautiful, beautiful!"

"Jesus, Joseph, and bloody Mary. Then why didn't you say so?" Cian asked with his hands on his hips.

"You never asked?" They chuckled like maniacs.

"Motherfucker!"

"Ha-ha-ha." Ish laughed, causing pens and other loose items to roll around on the desks generated by the vibrations. The mesh covering the speakers pulsated.

Cian feared they would blast the speaker system. "Please reduce the volume, Lasitor!"

"It's small. See, nothing worth mentioning." A golden ship with two passengers pulled up so close to the Horizon that Cian could see the crow's feet at the corners of

Ish's eyes as he laughed. And next to him sat Doctor Peter von Leutzendorf, looking like he sniffed too many test tubes. His eyes weren't focusing, and he kept falling to the sides while struggling to sit up. His long blond hair curtained his face. He wiped it out of his eyes, and Cian saw the intoxication—the lack of coordination as he was laughing his ass off.

"Stop laughing at us," Cian ordered, stepping closer to the window and pointing his finger at Ish.

"I'm not! It's Peter."

"Yes, you're both fucking laughing at us!"

"Okay, I am. It's all Peter's fault," Ish said.

"Maybe a little. We're just having a little bit of fun," Peter said. "A little bit of fun, a little bit of fun," he sang again, the same melody as before.

For a long moment, no one spoke, just watching the show. What were the chances that two drunk off their asses Anunnaki lovers would appear out of thin air? In the middle of a war. Somewhere in space.

The ping-ping sounds coming from the console in front of Captain Thornton broke the silence.

"That's the most dangerous plan I've ever heard," Ish added long after the fact.

"I know it's creative, but I know we can do it."

"Cian, it is not safe to do," Ish said in a serious tone.

"Do you have a better idea?" Cian challenged him.

"Actually, we do. We want you to go home, and we'll handle the Zelk."

Cian blinked wordlessly. Then thought of Ish and his weird-ass casings that took care of problems that shouldn't be a problem. He'd seen them being used in the market the day they abducted Leo. He wondered if Ish could take care of the six Zelk ships hiding from them.

Ivan spoke first. "I think what Ish is trying to say is that we don't want to be negative or question your belief in us, but don't you think we would get sucked in, especially if the suction becomes so big and strong enough to disappear Zelk ships? Don't you think we would create a big hole we can't close? Then what if it sucks in us, asteroids, planets, the sun, and galaxies?" Ivan spoke louder and louder. "Do you want to create a big fucking bang?"

"Yes!" Cian answered, upset with his brother once again doubting him.

"No!"

"Yes!"

"No!"

Cian stepped closer to them, noticing Barkor watching him. "Yes, and I know if I help you, we can close it. Ivan, please trust me. You must trust me. This is the only way."

"Children," Ish interrupted.

"What the fuck?" *Did he just call us children?*

"I mean, don't go on like children."

Cian heard the comeback. Something weird was going on, and he couldn't put his finger on it. Okay, he was drunk or something. Maybe…he'd revisit that thought later.

"Ish, stay out of this. You two should go home with your itty-bitty ship. You're going to get all of us killed. We're about to attack the enemy," Cian said. He got more laughter for an answer. Cian was close to losing his shit. "Oh my god, Ish, stop laughing." Cian watched them wiping the tears from their eyes. Then, after seeing each other wiping their tears, another fit of laughter followed. Cian couldn't help but smile. They were ridiculous.

"Sorry, I can't remember when last I had so much fun," Ish said between hiccups and chuckles. Suddenly his ship flew straight for the Horizon's observation window. Men ducked, throwing hands over their heads; others turned their faces away from the impending crash, while some reflexively dove onto the floor. The golden two-person spacecraft stopped a few feet from colliding with the Horizon.

"Jesus fucking Christ!" Captain Thornton shouted while frantically dabbing and drying his spilled drink from his dashboard.

"It's a circus. Ish, this is so many shades of cray-cray!" Eryn laughed, not fazed by the danger of the situation. Shaking his head, he turned to Ivan, who blinked and said nothing, stupefied by the recklessness.

"Oops, that was close. Sorry, what, Eryn?" Ish asked, swallowing his hysterics.

"He said we are shades of gray crayons," Peter guffawed.

"You two motherfuckers are going to kill all of us! Get the fuck away from the Horizon. You're intoxicated!"

"Forgive me, I accidentally bumped into the forward throttle, and it's your fault. You're making me laugh." Ish poked Peter on the shoulder. Peter poked him back.

"Stop laughing! Stop joking around. I said get the fuck away from the Horizon!" Cian yelled and turned to Ivan's husband, hoping he would help him see reason. "Eryn, help me. This can work. We must separate ourselves from the pull as soon as the first of their fleet enters the spout. I calculated once the spout starts forming and the first ship enters, it will sustain itself, giving you enough time to get out of its way. By then, we would follow from behind and drop the anti-gravitational reactors behind the last ship. Plugging the hole and counteracting the pull to its center."

"That's just in theory, Cian," Ivan said. He pointed his sword at the jokers inside the ship, who had somewhat calmed down. Less with a scowl and more with a smile, Ivan said, "I think, considering what Ish suggests, would be wise." Then, tapping his sword on the palm of his hand, he said, "Give me a minute." He appeared to be thinking and compartmentalizing the problem away from the distractions.

Cian bit down a retort and waited for Ivan to do his mental calculations. His brother had always been an overthinker, but Cian knew the plan would work once he said he was in.

"I'm not a stupid child that needs input and guidance from all of you. I'm the bloody General Fleet Commander. Lasitor and I ran multiple possibilities and planned this while you worked at the factory," Cian said, getting nervous by the second because their window of opportunity was growing smaller.

"You meant a hospital, not a factory," Ivan said.

"He's correct, my love. It was a Zelk factory, using humans to make more Zelk. We worked the production line," Eryn said with a stern look.

Cian sighed. "We have to move. Do you think you can do it? Those two are off their rockers. I can't put the lives of all these people in their hands."

"Yes, whatever you decide," Eryn said, and it seemed he was having a silent conversation with Ivan.

Ivan nodded and turned to Cian. "Yes, brother. You decide. Show us where you want us positioned."

"General," the captain called.

"Yes, Captain. Speak!" Cian said shortly. His captain pointed to the screen on his dashboard.

"He's gone, sir. Ish is gone. I can't ping him. It's like their ship vanished." The captain pushed a few buttons, slapped a screen, and looked up. "Nope, not seeing them. Maybe he cloaked the ship?"

"I don't have time for this. I told him to go home, and maybe he did." Cian turned to Barkor, who'd been gaping, hands in front of his mouth at the spectacle. "He's your friend. Where do you think he's gone? He better not kamikaze the Zelk. He'll fuck up my plan, and we won't have another chance like this."

"My friend? No, Cian. He's your friend, not my friend."

"Yes, he is," Cian said, and Barkor shook his head. "Of course he's your friend. The day we landed and found you, didn't you trade Donali with him?"

"No, why would I do that? Donali said he would stay and learn from us. I sent no one with you. Why would I do that?"

"I don't know, maybe to represent you and tell our fathers how bad it is? It was a trade, wasn't it?" Cian looked to Eryn for answers.

Eryn shrugged. "Yes, I said so, but I think you misunderstood, brother."

"But isn't that why Donali stayed? I showed and told Ish everything, and he was supposed to tell you and Sarinka. If he wasn't with me, he was with you, Donali, and Sarinka. When we returned after our last provisions trip to Phoenix, he and Sarinka left with you."

"Yes, and Ish went back to you," Barkor said, and Cian sensed he was telling the truth.

"Ish never came back to me," Cian said.

"He's not from Grayrak, Cian. He's from Earth. I would know. I've been on the moon for many, many years." Barkor put his hand over his heart, showing he wasn't lying. Cian believed him.

"No, he's definitely not from Earth. He's from a place called Anzulla or something. Didn't he tell you the story about his destroyed home and how he searched for a new place to call home on the moon?"

"What? What are you talking about? No, as far as I know, the day you arrived, he arrived. And what the fuck is an Anzulla?" Barkor asked, and Cian's hackles rose.

"It's where his home is. I thought it was a neighborhood in Grayrak. I thought he was one of us and assumed, like Eryn, who's a King of the Brawl, his parents were king and queen on the moon. Maybe Anzulla is a planet?" Cian slapped his forehead, looking at Eryn, who brought Ish to them. Eryn only shook his head in disbelief.

"Brother, how did you not know that? His whole family is Anunnaki, and their home was destroyed. He said that more than once."

"I know, but we're also Anunnaki, aren't we? I really thought…You know what, leave it. The few times I'd spent time with him…how was I to know?"

Cian counted on his fingers and turned to Barkor. "So if he's not your friend and not from Grayrak, then he's Anunnaki with a golden ship. How stupid am I? He keeps sending me these weird messages on the communicator. Look here, Ish had given me this over a year ago." Cian took the pocket-sized device out of his body suit's back pocket. He switched it on and jumped to his first message, then read it out loud.

"Good travels. Reroute now, *89.339.4473.2333.5957* galactic one seven nine."

Eryn, Ivan and Barkor stepped closer. Captain Thornton pulled a chair closer and climbed on it to see over their towering shoulders. Eryn pushed him inside the circle. Looking at the screen, Cian read as he pressed the white button, flipping through the messages. Small purple letters and numbers flashed. "These came through randomly, and I followed them as best we could.

"Change your current position to these galactic coordinates, *895.444.55.3395.7281*.

"No, turn to Mars right now.

"Then, as we traveled each hour, the fucker had us changing direction. Ish explained he had re-plotted the course, and it was a more efficient route.

"Later, he said Zelk was destroyed and to turn back to Earth.

"Then he sends a message. There are Zelk unaccounted for. Stay on the route.

"Early this morning, he said six Zelk were hiding behind asteroids. Search for them. Don't engage.

"Then he said find the six and fuck them up. Checking a different AI, I can't discuss moving to the next point in time."

Then an orange light flickered while Cian was holding it in his hand. "This is a new message. In purple letters, a new message says; *Your plan stinks. Go home! Go home, go home, go home!*

"He's a bloody time traveler," Cian said, and Eryn gave him a look as if he didn't expect this kind of slowness from him.

"Brother," Ivan said, hands on his hips.

"No, wait! Please wait," Cian exclaimed and stopped all the madness. He lifted his hands, grabbing everyone's attention. They halted, focusing on him. "Please wait. Let me think for a second."

"Eryn, brother, please help me. If he's a time traveler, then he must know what's about to happen. If he says it's the worst plan ever, don't you think we should reassess?"

"I agree, Cian," Ivan said. "I respect you, and I will support what you decide. Stopping to think was never your forte. If you need us to do this—"

Barkor took a step closer. It meant everything to Cian. His heart warmed, and he took a deep breath. "Give him a second to think. Keep quiet," Barkor said in a no-nonsense, stern, and menacing voice, which Cian first heard when they abducted Leo.

"Yes, thank you," Cian agreed. He had a ship full of responsibilities. He couldn't just follow through after he was warned. Everyone on the fifty-by-fifty-foot command center was quiet. Cian looked at Barkor, then his brothers, and then said, "Captain, give Lasitor command of the ship."

The captain nodded, following Cian's orders without question.

Cian spoke up to get the AI's attention. "Lasitor, plans have changed. Slow the Horizon, and send the dummy mirror image to continue the due course. Increase its speed, five hours ahead of us."

The lights dimmed, all the computer screens blacked out, and silence fell over the flight control room. The four men sitting in front of the consoles pressed and turned the big red button on their keyboards, removed their hands by folding their arms, and sat back in their chairs while only keeping their gazes on the monitors.

"Autopilot initiated," Lasitor said, and Cian checked his watch.

"Lasitor, at current speed, how long before we enter Earth's atmosphere?"

"Sixteen hours and twenty-five minutes, General."

"Start counting down."

"Yes, General."

"Barkor, tell everyone we're on lockdown. Tell them to eat, drink, and use the washroom. They have an hour. They need to be buckled in and get prepared for impact. Captain, use the same frequency. I'll send one from this device, as well. Leave the following message and put it on repeat. He's been listening in, so I'm sure he'll hear me."

"Ready to record, General," the captain replied.

"This is Cian Romanov, General Fleet Commander of the Warship Horizon. Ish, we set due course for Earth following your direction. My man, you take care of that fucking

Zelk. I know you and Peter can and will. We trust you. It makes sense to me now. You were right, my friend. You warned me many times about this moment."

Cian turned to Eryn, Ivan, and Barkor. "He sent me more voice messages a few months ago. One message was to watch out for six Zelk, but once I see them, to ignore them, he will find them, and I mustn't ignore him. Who the fuck talks that way? Obviously, he was drunk off his ass, but I thought he was talking about six Zelk on the moon."

"Are you sure about this, brother?" Ivan asked.

"One hundred percent sure!"

"Yes, brother, I agree. It sounds exactly like time-traveling idiots have messaged you from today—this time. I trust you. You've impressed me with your choices and how well you removed the humans without bloodshed and war. Let's do it," Eryn said and turned to Ivan, who looked relieved to avoid creating vortexes and causing big bangs. Ivan, Eryn, and Barkor's emotions were calm and supportive. It seemed to make sense to them, as well.

Barkor looked confused, but at least he seemed to stay at his side. Cian's men waited for his orders. "Lasitor, prepare a message for transmission to Phoenix."

To: General McCormick at Phoenix City.

From: General Cian Romanov, Fleet Commander, The Warship Horizon.

Subject: Prepare for re-entry.

"We're executing Plan B-fifty-three. Sir, we pinpointed the enemy and are going into radio silence. We will enter Earth's atmosphere within sixteen hours. May we all see each other on the other side.

"We Are Coming Home!"

## CHAPTER 43
# WHAT HAVE YOU DONE

*"Good morning, citizens of Phoenix.*

*It's now six a.m.*

*Did you know the place and time of the invention of the wheel remained a mystery for thousands of years until recently when one of our own scientists discovered a Mesopotamian tablet with a figure handing another figure the wheel?*

*Another interesting fact about wheels is that they can mean many things. For example, if someone has one hand on the wheel, they're taking control, but if they have two hands on the wheel, they're giving pleasure to two men at one time.*

*Lasitor doesn't know if the Mesopotamians handed each other a wheel or cock.*

*Obviously, no one took control of the situation.*

*Visit your community news page for more facts about wheels.*

*Breakfast is served until eight a.m.*

*Have a just roll with it kind of day!"*

**General Cian Romanov**
**2147 A.D. (95 A.T.)**
**Earth**

Cian's fleet commander chair rattled so hard and fast his jaws vibrated and he had a fleeting thought of his passengers chipping teeth and that dental appointments were imminent once they landed. Behind him, his men sat wide-eyed, strapped in, and clutching their seats.

"Ready yourselves. Switching off all engines. We don't want to go kaboom. If we survive this, gas masks will not be removed until we determine the air is safe to breathe. Hold on! Here we go!" Cian's voice crackled over the speakers.

The blue water-covered planet came closer and closer until the ship entered the exosphere, and streaks of blue, white, and gray clouds flashed by, obscuring their view. The Horizon creaked and cracked. Loud whistling cut the droning noises of the thundering winds as they descended and cut through the gas clouds.

"All engines down," Lasitor announced.

"Bloody marvelous. This better work. We can't bloody well mess it up now. We've come so far," Cian said, willing it to be miraculously so.

He checked the overhead security panels for Barkor. He was grabbing and handing the ropes and parachutes to the line of men working together.

"Who decided free-falling was a good idea?" Ivan asked rhetorically.

Eryn answered, "You and your brother."

Cian looked at them, Eryn seemed calm as usual, while Ivan was crushing the hand rests, and sweat beaded on his frowning pale forehead. The noise was deafening. Cian worried the ship would light a spark if they re-entered the atmosphere too fast. The air thinned. The pressure increased. Breathing became difficult. He sucked air through his pursed lips and worried about the humans who must all be experiencing labored breathing.

Suddenly momentum forced them back in their seats, and Cian knew Barkor and the men successfully deployed the parachutes. The noise died down. The rumbling reduced. He checked the air pressure and oxygen levels, confirming it stabilized as he breathed easier.

"Something's wrong." Cian watched the security feed. Barkor and the men were struggling to release the last crate with parachutes. "They need help, Eryn. Something's happening. They can't get it out the door. They're pushing and pulling. It's not moving! Come on," Cian muttered through clenched teeth. "Release the parachutes. Release the 'chutes now!"

"They need help, brother," Eryn shouted, already up and making his way outside.

"No point in trying to steer and fly now. We're falling too fast." Cian released his seat belt and joined Ivan and Eryn. The ship was tilted, so they had to pull themselves on the handrails up the walkways. Eryn jumped ahead, propelling himself like a tree frog off the sides to the back of the ship as fast as possible.

Angst-ridden faces of passengers glanced at them. Children cried. Mothers and fathers consoled and protected them by keeping their heads braced as they were told.

Some uneasily murmured and peered out the port windows at the fast-approaching blue speckles and sparkling sunlight on the water below.

Just as Cian and Ivan managed to reach the loading bay, Eryn, Barkor, and the men pushed with no success. Eryn stuck his spear underneath the crate, closed his eyes briefly, and the crate popped out of the track and burst open. Parachutes deployed, and the men jumped to hold on. Momentum thrust the ship back and forth as it stabilized horizontally. Bodies and anything not tied down were being tossed around them like projectile objects.

"You're hitting the water in ten, nine, eight, seven, six. Brace yourselves, four, three, two!" Lasitor counted down.

"Hold on!" Cian jumped for Barkor's hand just as he dove for a man flying through the air on his way out the open door.

Loud crashing followed the pandemonium. His neck flipped backward from the momentum, while he held onto Barkor.

Suddenly all was quiet, and they were airborne. He looked around frantically, checking where to help next. Then the silence was filled with humans screaming.

*Airborne.* Anything not tied down was in animated suspension—ropes, shattered plexiglass, children's toys, crates, weapons, and people.

"Zero-gravity?" Barkor loudly asked, as if he was used to screaming. "Is it over?"

Crackling noises came from the speaker system. "Welcome home, sirs. The engines shut down, and we re-entered safely through the flammable gas clouds." Lasitor's voice was raspy and echoed through the cargo area, announcing the obvious too late. "Please remain seated. Do not remove your masks and safety harnesses until announced that it is safe to do so," Lasitor added.

"Welcome home," Cian said with a big smile. He needed to kiss Barkor. "I guess we made it. And all in one piece." Ripping his mask off his head, he pulled Barkor closer and removed his mask for him, and then he kissed him. Barkor hesitated, the onslaught of lips and tongue momentarily stiffly received, but then he relaxed, lips softened, and tongues glided as he kissed him back.

Voices of people reminded Cian they weren't alone. "Come, let's go help the humans," Cian said, as some of them had already moved to the open back end of the ship where the loading bay gaped open revealing crystal blue waters.

Bemused, the people looked dumbfounded at each other. Some yelled, astonished as the anti-gravitational system deactivated, and everything fell to the floor as gently as a feather. In the commotion, Lasitor had opened the opposite side doors of the loading bay. Loud mechanical gears click-clucked as it mechanically hoisted the doors up, revealing blinding sunlit waters. Scared children cried and pointed to the outside while shielding their eyes. Once again, it was chaotic topsy-turvydom. Some seemed to realize it was normal, while others ran to hide, grabbing children and ducking for cover from the sun.

Cian laughed. "Thank the gods for no big smashes or flames."

Barkor stopped in his tracks. "Wait a minute? What is that?" he asked, pointing to a big bird in the sky. Barkor's face filled with the joyous realization. "That must be a bird. I saw a bird first!" He shouted and hopped on the balls of his feet. It flew by, squawking. "That's a bird, isn't it?" he asked.

The rest of the humans righted themselves before standing closer and watching in awe. Some peeked out the doors, windows, and loading bays.

"No, that's not a bird, that's an... honestly, I don't know what that is, but it's not a bird. I would know," Cian said.

Eryn and Ivan joined them. "I agree. I've never seen a bird that size. It looks like a giant pelican," Ivan said.

As the ship hovered over the ocean water, the flaps of the open loading bay doors filled with people. The masses of humans pushed and shoved to get a look. Some fell into the water, pushed from the back, and some jumped into it. They laughed and jubilated. Some must have remembered Lasitor's lessons on floaties because they hung on crates, and others just took their clothes off, jumping in naked.

A boy clinging to his mother's side exclaimed, "Mamma, look at all the water!"

"Look at them. No one knows how to swim," Eryn remarked, frowning, and Cian felt the worry emanating from him.

"I agree this is going to end in tragedy, brother. You better hang on to something, or you'll sink!" Cian huffed as he watched the happy people who, realizing they couldn't swim, were now drowning.

"Surely, they wouldn't drown now that they're safely home. Someone, please throw something that floats for those idiots—" Cian pointed, smiling as he grabbed a thick rope and threw it so they could pull themselves to the sides.

His smile quickly vanished as he watched in horror the strange bird dive from the sky straight toward the splashing humans.

"Oh no!" Eryn screamed. He saw it, too, and jumped into action.

"Out of the water, get out of the water!" Cian yelled.

But no one heard. The bird opened its beak, swallowed a woman, and vanished into the dark blue depths. Now the humans moved, climbing over and onto each other to reach safety

Eryn jumped, leaped, and dove over them with his spear in hand down into the ocean's depths.

Cian and Ivan frantically helped the eager swimmers back into the Horizon, and Barkor disappeared into the fray of disorganized humans.

When everyone was safely out of the water, Eryn appeared soaking wet with the drowned woman under his arm.

Cian ran to help. Ivan yelled, "Put her down. We can try C.P.R." Eryn gently laid her down, and Ivan started chest compressions. A circle of people formed around them, wet and crying. Cian pushed her chin up to open her airways and started puffing air into her lungs.

A man pushed through the ring of spectators and rushed for the woman they worked on. "Sophia! Sophia," he cried, shocked, wet, and trembling.

After ten minutes of unsuccessful cardiopulmonary resuscitation, Ivan stopped and said, "It looks like she's passed."

"May I try something?" Eryn asked softly. He spoke calmly, touching the man's shoulder. He stopped crying. "May I try something?"

"What? She's dead. He said she passed. What do you want to do?"

"I know, sir, but sometimes when the blood is still warm, I can make it flow again," Eryn said with reassuring empathy.

"Yes, yes, of course, try whatever you can," he said, wiping his snot on his sleeve.

Cian knew Eryn had extraordinary abilities. "Do you need me and Ivan to help?"

"I don't know. Let me see if I can help her." He closed his eyes and placed one hand on her forehead and the other on the center of her chest. The hull of the ship fell silent.

"Look, he's glowing, Mom," a little boy said. His mom pushed him back as if protecting him.

"Yes, Mommy sees," she said.

Another woman said, "Let's be quiet and watch them." She picked her child up from the floor and sat him on her hip.

Although it was a bright sunny day, the blue and gold waves emanating from them danced like flames blinking in and out of sight in the sunlight. Cian looked up and saw Barkor walking through the tumult of people watching. Their gazes met, and Cian nodded a thank you. This was what Cian loved about him. He didn't ask what was happening. He watched, assessed, drew conclusions, and then knowingly affirmed the situation by nodding his head. Barkor joined him, holding onto Cian's shoulder, supporting and letting him know he was there for him.

"Don't be scared. They're helping her. She swallowed too much water," Barkor told them. Cian hoped they didn't all turn and run screaming.

Each hummed their separate songs. Cian concentrated on feeling hope and life and looked at Barkor. Then he felt love and goodness. His brother, Ivan, hummed peace and the knowledge of wisdom, and Eryn hummed creativity and calmness.

Silence fell over more than two thousand people witnessing a miracle. The gods they went searching for on the moon and had been traveling through the stars to bring them back home were here with them on Earth.

"It's the prophecy. The prophecy has come true," one woman said.

"Our saviors," a male voice said, and then a little boy began to laugh, pointing at the tiny spirals of blue and gold rays of light escaping the circle where the four singing demi-gods worked.

"Look, the promised prince, Mom. He really is our prince!"

Light streaks surrounded and drifted over the crowd of onlookers.

The woman coughed and convulsed, expelling frothy seawater. She opened her eyes and sat up, vomiting more water.

"Jesus, how much water did she swallow?" Cian asked.

The man on his knees beside her reached for her. Shocked and thankful, he kissed her face all over. The crowd of humans murmured. Some began babbling and dancing.

Ecstatic with happiness, people threw their canes to the side, hands in the air they all danced.

"What?"

In the background, Cian heard Lasitor attempting to get their attention.

"Excuse me, excuse me!" Lasitor called louder than the thumping and whooping horde.

"Shh," Cian said while waving his hands. They settled down as Cian pointed to his ear and the speaker.

Silence.

"Lasitor, go ahead," Cian said, shaking his head at the craziness.

"Your fathers want to speak to you."

A beep-beep sound behind him caught his attention. He spun around and looked. Men were exiting Bubblecars and climbing onto the loading platform of his ship.

"You know how to make an entrance, don't you? Welcome home, everyone," Brad said, arms stretched wide in a welcome gesture.

Cian did a double take. No, not Brad, or maybe it was? *It sounded like him, but something was different about him.* It was the manner in which he spoke and how he sounded. Cian couldn't put his finger on it for the second time today.

"Son, so glad to see you," Connor greeted and enveloped him. Again, *something was off.* Cian stepped back. From head to toe, he looked them up and down, Connor, Mika, and Brad. They looked different. It was their clothes—they were dressed in silver-colored mesh suits and weird flip-flops. No, not flip-flops. There was nothing through the toes. It was a thin sliver strap over the bridge of the foot. They looked like space-age hippies. *Where are the black bodysuits and boots?*

"Hello, handsome," a voice from his past greeted him. A man stepped closer. His big friendly eyes and chunky body reminded Cian of someone long ago. He was the friendliest teddy bear of a man, always hugging and laughing. He had braided, long dark blond hair and the sparkliest green eyes. Next to him stood another man who reminded Cian of his partner.

"Can it be? Juandre and Andrew, is that really you?"

"Yes, who did you think I was? Whatever you've been snorting up there, I want some, too," Juandre said in his familiar effeminate lilt. His body suit was purple, and a bright yellow bowtie was around his neck.

*What?* Cian looked at his perplexed brothers. They looked as baffled as he felt. Juandre crossed his arms and tapped his foot, waiting. Cian dropped his head back and screamed into the blue earth sky.

"Ish, you time-traveling son of a …what have you done?"

CHAPTER 44

# EPILOGUE

## BARKOR

### Phoenix, underwater glass dome city
### 2147 A.D. (95 A.T.)
### Earth

Barkor just blinked and listened as Cian and his large family rambled. It was a lot to digest, and Cian kept insisting that this was impossible, and yet, they all stood in a city underwater, breathing fresh, clean air under lights as bright as the sun but cool as a chilly breeze. Cian never left his side. The charming, boisterous fleet commander held Barkor's left hand tightly, and although he didn't crush it, it felt as if it were glued to his. For Barkor, this was a sign of being wanted, and it was an endearing thing.

As he was introduced to Cian's people—all male and eager to meet him—he heard how hard and long Cian had driven them to the brink of insanity to build a Spacecar. Over his shoulder, Cian kept saying these weren't his people and that he would explain later.

Firstly, Barkor's flock needed to settle in and get established. The Phoenicians were ready to house the new citizens and ensure their comfort. Schedules were posted for them, and the community news page—which they had grown accustomed to on the ship—would show them where to eat, sleep, and explore. Each individual received a talking wristband connected to Lasitor, the talking computer, not Zelk.

Over two thousand rooms, referred to as apartments in the old Earth language, were built, fully stocked, and furnished for anyone who chose to move in. Barkor's people preferred to stay together. He read their fearful faces and their clingy bewilderment, and he had just said the words to Cian, who then organized for beds and mattresses to be moved into what he called the Athletics Dome.

Men and boys of all ages eagerly rushed to complete it for them. Their cheerful enthusiasm felt unsettling. Barkor estimated it would take many sleep cycles—at least five hundred—before Grayrak's people could adjust to life in this sparkling clean and joyful underwater environment.

Fortunately, he had Cian, and they had him, so he figured his people would acclimate with time. Barkor was particularly concerned about the women and children, especially Talali and her friends. His upbringing provided only a limited perspective, and he feared the Phoenicians might take them and treat them like the Disciples had. Regardless of their age or gender, they were treated as though they mattered, each one as precious as newly discovered jewels, with dignity and compassionate care. It was something they weren't used to, and as strange as it felt, he encouraged them to trust their hosts because he trusted Cian. Cian was Barkor's pillar, strength, and hope, just as Barkor was for the Grayrakians.

Cian's song was all around him, from the moon's surface to beneath the earth's waters. It was an invisible force—an intense yet gentle passion that pulled, bonded, and encouraged. It energized him, and Barkor believed it was the seed of hope for new beginnings.

Just then, Ish and a man Barkor had seen inside the golden spaceship approached. He was much shorter than Ish, with long white hair and bright blue eyes. He seemed friendly and extended his hand for a shake, which Barkor accepted with his free hand.

Later, the two other men who had greeted Cian earlier stepped closer. One had dark hair and dark eyes, dressed entirely in purple—the only one dressed that way—looking sexy, dangerous, and upbeat, accompanied by a larger, muscular man with braided blond hair and friendly green eyes. The cheerful one pulled Barkor and Cian in for another hug. He had no issues with personal space, and Barkor figured anyone could jump into his arms, and he wouldn't mind. Cian growled at him as he waved his hands like Cian was an annoying fly. Either he had no respect, or he was familiar with Cian.

"Hello, my name is Juandre," he said, pinning Cian with a stare while greeting Barkor. "Stop sounding like you're warning me or something. I changed your bloody diapers and will smack you if you try something, boy."

Cian appeared both irritated and amused. "Juandre, the last time I saw you alive, I was just a boy, so that must have been a slip of the tongue," Cian said, extending his free arm. Juandre stepped into the embrace.

"*Pfft*, no slipping of tongues just yet," Juandre said and cackled. His eyes glinted with a strange sparkly sheen. "Can we go sit and talk somewhere?" Juandre clapped and asked the crowd that'd been droning around them. As soon as they landed, Barkor was swept up in the fray and introduced left and right. He couldn't remember anyone's name. It was as if everyone knew Cian and his brothers, and they all spoke with him, with them, and with each other. It was exhausting. The chaotic pace had continued for over twenty-four hours, so sitting down sounded good to Barkor.

They made their way down long corridors. The color of the light surrounding them changed as translucent roofs and walls displayed the sea life outside. They ended up in what they called the leadership conference room. It was a big room with one long table and chairs enough to sit about fifty men. Behind those were more rows of chairs, making it an area where over five hundred people could sit.

Cian pulled Barkor over to the table, where they found a spot. He pulled a chair out for Barkor and sat beside him. Barkor noticed other couples doing it, so it must have been an Earth thing. Barkor decided to keep quiet and observe because he felt out of place and held onto Cian's hand, where he found the strength to hold on for dear life.

"Can one of you explain why we returned to a place that's the same but not the same? For example, you wore black when we left, and now you wear silver. Juandre and Andrew are alive while we buried them almost one hundred years ago." For once, it seemed Cian was the only person who spoke.

From the opposite side of the long table, their leader got up. He carried himself as if he was in charge. Although he didn't interrupt or ask to be heard as if his word was more important than the others. Next to him sat his husband. If Barkor remembered correctly, he was the medical doctor who walked through and checked who needed immediate medical attention. Cian called it triaging. As the leader smiled warmly at Barkor, he nodded with a nonverbal acknowledgment to Barkor, then looked at Cian as if he was proud of him.

"Cian, firstly, and may I repeat myself, good job! You have planned and executed a flawless escape plan and impressively landed a warship without the engines running." He pointed to Ish. "That man has to tell you what is going on." He nodded, then sat down. It seemed everyone around the table agreed that Ish had some explaining to do.

Cian stood and said, "I agree, Ish. You better explain, or I'll wrap my bare hands around your throat and—"

Ivan interrupted, "Brother, no!"

"Well, get on with it," Cian added and sat down. Barkor wanted to jump and grind on Cian.

Ish got up, removed his sunglasses, and spoke. He was not the tallest, but he was definitely the biggest muscled. His dark skin and gold and black-ringed eyes were an obvious contrast to the mostly pale-skinned earthlings.

"Cian, your plan of creating a vortex and sending the vermin, I mean the Zelk, into it was good. I was tasked to disintegrate them. Make the entity go away, rather than move them from one plane to another. The universe is much bigger than you could ever imagine. And if I start moving problems around, instead of doing my job, I'd get us all into deep trouble. When I was given my time machine, I was told to wait for you and your Bubblecar, and then help you. In my solitude and waiting, my only entertainment for decades was drinking and watching them." Ish pointed to Barkor. "I kind of developed an addiction while drinking intoxicated Disciple blood."

Peter jumped up. "I can vouch that the stuff is highly intoxicating. I had one sip, and we almost crashed into the Horizon." Peter chuckled, and Cian snorted.

"Yes, it's funny now, but you could have killed us all," Ivan added.

"We know, and we're sorry." Ish placed his hand over his heart, apologizing sincerely. He swept his gaze over the audience. Silence followed.

Smiling shyly, he shook his head. "Anyway, I remembered if I used my powers, I always have to do it for unselfish reasons and was allowed to give two things, I mean change two things. I wanted to give you and your people so much more back."

Ish lifted his arms and explained animatedly. "You have to understand. Before all this happened. I searched uncountable realities, and yours was the only one I missed. I realized I missed it because of what Eryn had told me. He said I'm not living it, only watching. This was true, but he meant the one I'm going to live in would be the one I experience and not travel." He pointed and smiled at Eryn. Eryn gave one affirming nod. "He's a smart man. He'd spoken of this timeline. The one I'm supposed to live in. I realized I traveled all the time in timelines of other people's histories—not my own. I was physically put here and given a job to do.

"Once I realized I needed to lock those doors and come home, I wanted to bring back something for your leader and asked him. If he could have done two things differently, anything at all, what would it be, he said, *have more whiskey and not have Juandre and Andrew killed.*" The room erupted in laughs and giggles. Brad joined the laughter but soon put up his hands to quiet the men down so Ish could continue his story.

"Thank you, everyone. Ish, please, continue. I want to hear it."

"Oh, I love how you can laugh at each other's expense and not find it belittling. You're all such a fresh bunch of humans. I'm honored to join you."

"Yes, yes, tell your story, and we'll decide who joins who," Connor said with a scowl.

Ish cleared his throat and made eye contact with Peter, seemingly searching for approval. Peter mouthed, *I love you. You can do this.*

Ish shifted from one foot to the other. "After I got to know Peter, he told me how good you were for him. I made a point of it to get to know Brad and the parents who raised these beautiful boys. I'm not talking about the outsides. I'm talking about the insides. The purity and unselfishness they spread like an infection. For once, I could see the fates would unfold in front of my eyes. I decided to help you as best I could, using the tools I was given. But I couldn't do it alone."

Ish bent down to kiss Peter on his head and continued. "The day I came to meet your people, I saw Peter. And it was the vision of him that somehow jogged a memory. A fluttering feeling instantly bloomed in the pit of my stomach. An infatuated-in-love connection clicked into place. It was as if I knew him. Like his essence and my essence sang a song."

"Hmmm, we heard that before. We grew quite accustomed to the singing and glowing," Brad interrupted sarcastically. Peter giggled shyly.

"When we met, he reacted the same. I realized he was the key to everything, to my existence. Once we'd spoken, he'd told me about himself and how he'd waited for me."

All attention zoomed in on Ish as the screeching of chairs—seats being pulled closer—filled the room.

*This story is important.*

Peter gave Ish another approving nod and pushed a glass of water closer for him. Ish took a sip, put the glass down, and spoke in his weird deep baritone.

"We met in nineteen-sixty-eight, but I also appeared with his older self that night. That was the night and point in time the switch started." He pointed to Andrew. "Andrew, better known as André, is Peter's best friend and brother. I determined Juandre, Andrew, and Peter to be key factors and jumped back and forth, realizing the man who shot Juandre and Andrew was Juandre's son. He shot them because he hated his father and was a Disciple. I decided to check why he hated his father and dug deeper—"

Cian interrupted Ish. "Bloody damn, you're like an investigator and a fixer." Juandre and Andrew chuckled and agreed. Ish smiled, burrowed into his black shirt's neckline, and pulled a big clock watch on a chain underneath his shirt.

"I am the master timekeeper. That is my gift bestowed onto me. My father used me. I was supposed to watch and manage it, so he could continue like I will continue living here with you.

"It's a blessing that they're not here with me. They would have discarded Brad and killed all of you, who seemed to be a threat to him and take it all for himself. We Anunnaki are the fathers and mothers of everything here, past and coming."

A chorus of coughs and throats clearing came from around the table.

Ish lifted his hand, indicating they were to wait. "That's what we thought. And it's not true. We are but another cog in the big wheel of existence. You're not in danger. For thousands of years, I searched for this timeline, this one where everything reset naturally. As I said, it was hidden because I willed it. I locked us out. No one can travel inside or outside this loop because I am here with Peter and my bloodline. We are now able to restart from this point forward. That is why, when I returned to Anzulla, it was crumbled and desolated."

Ish sat down, and Peter got up. He spoke with a strange, nasal accent. Skittishly he continued.

"I could never tell you anything, and it drove me to madness. Now that it's all over..." Peter paused to wipe tears from his eyes and sniffled. "You know I'm one of the original products who survived Hitler's scientists in the Jewish prisoner camps. I don't have many details, but I suspect it was horrific as women were mutilated, and babies were made, tested, and discarded until our Aryan line was singled out. We were treated well, but—" He let his head fall, shaking it lightly.

No one said a word and waited for him to compose himself. He lifted his head, wiped his red tear-filled eyes with quick, controlled movements, and cleared his throat. Everyone watched him and waited in silence. Barkor sensed no judgment or animosity —only empathy. The places and times Peter spoke about were interesting, and he soaked up the history of the Disciples and their sick creations. This was his history, as well.

"I have or have had many brothers, but at this stage, it's safe to say it's only André, sorry, Andrew, and myself who survived." He pointed a hand over to Andrew and Juandre. And Andrew got up.

"Yes, I would have died if Ish and Peter didn't come to save me. Peter and I were friends. We grew up together. Our fathers were scientists and friends at Humboldt University when the wall went up. The four of us were transferred to the western side. It was renamed New Berlin University. We were the lucky ones. The others had stayed behind." He turned to Eryn. "I suspect this is where your father was raised." Eryn crossed his arms and gave a slight nod. "We knew it was only a matter of time before we got split up and punished for being *der homosexuelle*. The organization was set on continuing our bloodline, and as you know, artificial insemination was not an option in the nineteen-sixties, and our partners were chosen for us."

"Sick Disciple fucks," Mika, Cian's father, who had been quiet in the background, interrupted. "Sorry, Andrew," he said, holding his hands up in apology.

"Yes, Mika," Andrew agreed. "The first successfully performed test-tube baby was performed in nineteen-seventy-eight. We were Aryan and gay. One way or the other, they needed our sperm, and they wanted the next generation of super babies. We knew we had to flee to survive and had our suitcases packed and ready for the Americas the next morning. That was when Ish and older Peter appeared and explained it all to us. The train would have crashed, and I would have died, and Peter would have transferred back to East Berlin. Ish gave us a choice, but with older Peter there, we knew what the answer would be," Andrew said.

"Mika, Connor," Peter said to get their attention. "Somehow, your bloodlines were meant to come together. Ish and I can't figure out whether it was by design or miracle, but your bloodlines plus the string code I sew into the zygote formed the missing link Ish and his family waited for to continue their species. Pieces of Anunnaki are in each of us. We are all ultimately created by them.

"Let me start by explaining it as if we spoke of Ish's Anunnaki Monarchy. Eryn is King, Ivan, Cian, and Barkor are the princes, and Andrew, Juandre, and I are knights," Peter said and shrugged.

Eryn shook his head, he didn't want to be the King, and everyone knew that because Barkor had heard him say that at least twice in this short time.

Juandre jumped up. "Tell them, my bear, tell them. Show them. You guys are going to shit your pants," he said excitedly. Lifting his knees high, he pretended to run in place. *Wait, he was running.* So fast it looked like he stood still. The air moved around him.

Andrew walked over as if this was an everyday occurrence, and he was used to seeing Juandre running as fast as the wind in the same spot. He grabbed Juandre's arm and pulled him closer. Juandre came to a dead halt. The flutter of air seized.

"Juandre and I have a burning secret. Can we share this with them now?" He looked at Ish, who smiled, exposing thin, longer-than-usual incisors. Juandre rolled his top lip back while Andrew opened his mouth wide to show his long fangs.

"No way!" Cian exclaimed, still holding Barkor's hand.

"Yes, way!" Juandre answered and giggled. "This is how we survived and lived so long."

"How, tell us?" Ivan and his husband exclaimed at the same time.

Ish stepped forward and cleared his throat. "Well, Brad said he wanted whiskey, and Andrew is Lord Andrew. He stocked whiskey for kilometers high inside the mineshaft marked with a blue tower in South Africa," Ish said proudly, hands on his hips and smiling wide, exposing all his white teeth. Juandre and Andrew bowed as if to say you're welcome. Cian and his brothers gasped, looking baffled. He gave Barkor a side eyed look, shaking his head in disbelief.

Barkor moved closer to whisper in Cian's ear. He wanted to ask him why, but Ish spoke. "I gave Andrew my bite, and he'd given his bite to Juandre," Ish said. "It's meant to bond partners to the monarchy in Anzulla. I was already mated to Peter by blood, so I could give it away without the fear of outliving my partner or bonding with Andrew."

"Yes, Juandre told me, vampires, but not vampires. I'm getting thirsty. I suspect there are more stories. I can see where this is going. Who ambushed and killed them in your timeline?" Brad asked.

"Charles Montgomery killed them," Cian said, and his brothers agreed.

Juandre explained, "Well, this sexy vampire built a whole distillery, Lord Andrew Distilleries. When I divorced Charles's mom, Andrew showed up, and we got married in South Africa. I took Charles with us. Maybe if Andrew had never turned me into a vampire or if I had left the marriage and Charles with his mother, he would have joined the Disciples. But instead—" He paused, looking oddly out of character and uncomfortable. "Andrew killed the entire American chapter. As far as we know, the rest of our family has been dead since Doomsday." Andrew hugged Juandre, and they sat down.

"We can tell you the details another day," Andrew said, his face seriously somber, and the men around the table respectfully stayed silent. Impressing Barkor.

"We were abducted but never ambushed?" Cian asked Ivan and Eryn, who looked puzzled at Brad.

"We went to rescue you, Ivan, and my boys from the mines. Killed Eryn's brothers and brought back crates of whiskey after we sent a rocket we found in the mineshaft to the moon," Brad said.

"They were never killed because Charles never shot them," Ish added. "This was where the timeline had shifted."

Barkor chuckled, thinking of Cian calling Ish's eyes *honeybee ass* eyes. He'd never seen one, and Cian showed him earlier on the computer screen what it was. Ish pointed to Cian. "When you sang your song for the moon, you put into motion a timeline shift." Ish laughed and clapped his hands. "See how awesome you all are?" He was very impressed with himself and his big reveal.

Cian looked questioningly at Ish. "Yes, it's the song of creation. You sang it. You willed it."

"No way!" Cian said, looking around. Barkor pulled his shoulders up. This was news to him.

"What did you think you were doing?"

"I sowed the seeds and sang my heart's song as if I was singing it to Barkor." He turned to Barkor and blushed. Cian lifted the hand he'd been clamping the whole time and kissed it. Barkor's heart melted even more for him. He was such a softy. A softy that could tell seeds to grow.

"Then I scattered the seed bombs. I willed them to sprout and grow."

"Yes, go on," Ish encouraged.

"I imagined colorful gardens and beautiful butterflies, dragonflies, and bees to pollinate the flowers. I imagined water and fruit trees. Okay, I see. I may have created a garden, so what?" Cian asked, not seeing it.

Ivan tapped him on the shoulder. "Brother, none of us can create gardens, insects, and anything nearly like that. You have a green thumb, and you created a garden of Eden on the moon."

"But they sent seeds and seed bombs. All I did was sing to them."

"Probably to let nature take care of it in time. We never thought you would do that," Brad said as Ivan and Eryn came to hug their mystified brother. Cian never let go of Barkor's hand. All this history of life before Barkor was born intrigued him.

"Okay, so explain what happened after Brad killed Charles Montgomery," Eryn said.

Brad frowned. "I never killed Charles. He's Juandre's boy. Why would I kill him?"

"Somebody, please make sense to me. I'm getting a headache," Cian said, rubbing the nape of his neck.

Ish put his hand up. "Juandre and Andrew were shot and killed in your reality. The moment Juandre and Andrew met, thanks to my Billboard ads, they naturally changed their own course of their lives. All I had to do was find a position in time to cross and swap—" He waved his hands, one crossing the other. "It all worked out. All is now as it should be."

"Wait, I have a few more questions!" Mika's husband said with an accent Barkor recognized as Irish.

"That cylinder, the ancient golden cylinder that was originally the shape of an apple. Mika assembled and disassembled it and figured out that if broken into several pieces and then rebuilt, the golden apple was its original form. Someone was smart enough to crack it open like a puzzle box and then reassemble it as a capsule instead of it being a cylinder and rolling it in ink, so it printed out the string codes and star maps. The codex for genome mapping was just a tiny bit of the information embedded on the inside. Peter and the rest of our gifted ones are the direct results of its message. Who knows what else could have happened if someone accidentally rebuilt it into the cylinder form Mika had discovered. Also, those stone tablets, maps, and hieroglyphs, who planted that? Because there was freaky foreboding shit on it," Connor asked and turned to Mika, pulling him up by the elbow to stand. "*Gille-toine*, tell them what you think happened."

Mika's chair loudly scratched the floor. A long low sound—a thing of finality. He pointed two fingers at Ish. "He's the Anunnaki who started all this shit! Ish, hand over the keys to your ship, and, Brad, take his time keeping compass away from him. We must destroy it!"

"I assure you my intentions go beyond the way of living in this reality. We have a common enemy. I saw firsthand the horrors of the malevolence. I escaped alive but was forever changed. You are the resurgence, the gift of the light. A product of goodness. Call it the last card or the last fight that has destroyed the ultimate dark enemy. The moon was once my precise position that I was told to wait and take no action until the ball-shaped ship appeared. It was pre-programmed into my ship. I was only allowed to jump for one person and change only two things, but I kind of messed it up. I thought I did do it intentionally, maybe subconsciously. I realized I would never remember the pattern I followed, so I ended up trusting my ship's navigator until Peter suggested I revisit Phoenix and record the original history by uploading and updating your news broadcaster. I assure you, nothing was lost."

"Ta-da!" Lasitors' voice surprised all of them. A round of laughter broke out in the room, breaking the tension.

Ish pointed to every man around the table and then to himself by thumbing his chest. "To be fair. I was led here. To today. I was given these keys to the locks of time and told to use them wisely. So was the plan, and I could foretell you never knew it. Look what you have. You have integrity. You have knowledge, and you wield it without knowing it. You have life everlasting. Somehow you succeeded. And you don't see it. You *are* the plan."

"Yes, and which plan is that?" Brad asked.

"It is the plan that worked."

"How many plans did you try?" Cian asked.

"I don't know. I never counted," Ish said, letting his head fall in defeat.

"You were intoxicated, weren't you?" Cian asked.

"Hey, don't you love it when the plan comes together? Look at you. You're successful, you all have love, and you all have partners. Look at this building. it's miraculous. You live underwater, and you have ships shaped like balls." Ishtar pointed the finger at Eryn, Ivan, Cian, and Barkor. "These people admire, follow, and trust you. They're following you," Ish said, smiling as if he saw a light at the end of a dark tunnel.

"You are true Anunnaki royalty. In the end, that's all that matters," Ish said. He paused to sweep his gaze over the astonished men bowled over by his statement.

"In the end?" Cian asked.

"Yes, the end."

"Yet you say this is the new beginning."

"Yes, that it is. You are the sum of my blood."

# PART THREE
# ANZULLA: ACCORDING TO ISH
## NEW BEGINNINGS M/M SERIES BOOK 3

# DEAR READER/LISTENER

Peter may smell and look delicious, but he is as tart as pomegranate juice. You will either love or hate him. Ishtar loves him, so by association, I pinched my nose and swallowed him down while I grew to love him too.

The overarching story flows in one direction—in a circle—with no beginning or ending. Readers may loop in at any point.

**I added a timeline at the end of the book** for readers who want to figure out what the fuck had happened and when in chronological order. It contains spoilers and is hidden to avoid revealing too much.

My stories explore the possibility of ancient civilizations being visited by advanced beings from Atlantis, who shared their knowledge of tools, agriculture, and architecture. They simultaneously speculate how Atlantis came into existence but disappeared from the ocean floor.

Is time travel possible in the real world? I don't know. But in my quest to write a time traveling sci-fi fantasy novel, I researched theories surrounding time, speed of light, electromagnetism, and sound energy.

I am not a scientist, but some who have studied, who are smart, who are educated, and who are true scientists say time does not exist. Others just as educated, say time is duration, an outward motion of matter called dilation, and that it is not an illusion. Therefore, time is relative motion as counted or measured by each observer's clock and space is the illusion, for it is nothing more than relative time between events as seen by each observer.

Matter is what we see in each of our futures, but mass is the connective tissue centered moment to moment within our past. Our consciousnesses keep up with the speed of light, which gives each of us the illusion of a static state called the present, but only with math can you make time stand still, then you are only representing a moment of time. How long was the duration before the motion that started our universe and how long will the duration go on after? How could we call or know it other than as an infinite time?

You may argue the measurement of time is just a human thing we constructed to make sense of time itself. If nothing travels faster than light, it is based on a law of physics that nothing is infinite and non-existent.

What if it is not infinite and not in a line, but a loop, or uncountable loops? No beginning and no end, *according to Ish*. Irrespective of what new physics we learn, an eternal universe is logically unpalatable. We could have never gotten to the present point if time went back infinitely, because for us to arrive at this present point, an infinite amount of time should have passed. There simply cannot be an infinite series of events. There has to be an event that caused the whole thing to get going.

Anzulla, According to ISH, is fantastical, yet imaginable and hopefully, with a little persuasion, believable. In my imagination, time travel happens when Ish rides the magnetic lines of force, as if Earth and the universe exist inside some kind of bubble, loop, or circle. I imagine electromagnetism as a source of light while sound waves are propagated but at the speed of light. The sound waves would have to exceed the sound wave barrier which creates electric charges like sparks of lightning connected by the lines of force in space, which loops by propelling the electromagnetism, and so on.

I hope you enjoy traveling with Ish and Peter.

Love to all creatures,

Kashel Char.

Source: physicsforums.com

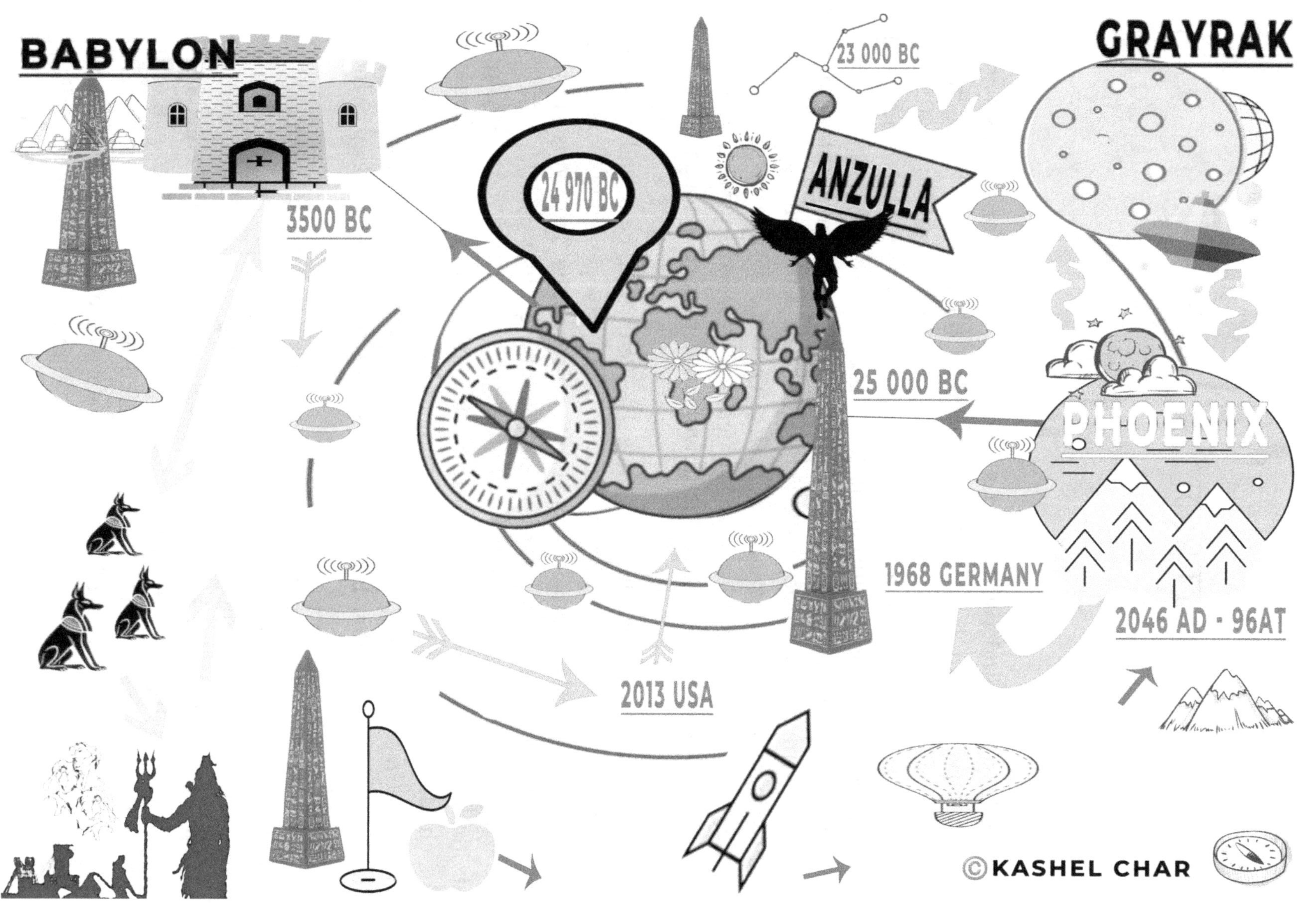

BABYLON
GRAYRAK
ANZULLA
PHOENIX
23 000 BC
24 970 BC
3500 BC
25 000 BC
2013 USA
1968 GERMANY
2046 AD - 96AT
© KASHEL CHAR

# INTRODUCTION

Deep inside the secure, underwater domes of Phoenix, a group of scientists and soldiers managed to survive multiple catastrophes that had plunged the world into a global winter that brought about widespread flooding. Under the guidance of their leader, General Brad McCormick, scientists Dr. Connor Romanov and his husband Dr. Mika.

As the internet grid crashed during the 2046 A.D. Doomsday, Dr. Connor hastily took control of orbiting satellites and downloaded all of recorded human history for safekeeping. Using this information, they established Phoenix University to train citizens in professions crucial to the maintenance of their advanced city such as engineering, architecture, medicine, and food production. The heart of their society was a sophisticated AI named Lasitor, who not only stored the downloaded history but also helped residents with daily tasks.

Meanwhile, Dr. Mika and his colleague Dr. Peter von Leutzendorf developed a groundbreaking method for fertilizing human donor cryogenically frozen eggs, using male sperm and artificial wombs. This led to the birth of the first twins in Phoenix, the twin boys Cian and Ivan thereby marking the Year of the Twins (A.T.)

As more boys were born via the Romanov/Leutzendorf method, the population of Phoenix thrived and continued to prioritize scientific advancement and research. The birth of children necessitated the establishment of a school for their education and development. Dr. von Leutzendorf made a notable discovery in life-extension science with the creation of the Eden Bean, also known as the Peter Pan Cap, which slowed aging and sped up healing.

Twenty-one years after the birth of Ivan and Cian, they were abducted and held captive in an abandoned gold mine in South Africa. Their captors were a family of frog people which included a psychopathic frog-man, multiple toxic frog monsters, and Eryn, a genetically manipulated specimen who sided with the humans and killed his family to free the abducted young men. It became clear that an organization known as the World Health Protected Species Society (WHPSS) had been recruited by a secretive global society known as the Disciples of Anunnaki to develop a genetically enhanced human race. Ivan and Cian were the products of human and Anunnaki gene splicing, while Eryn's birth resulted from the splicing of amphibian, human, and Anunnaki genes.

Despite initially being drawn to each other, these three gifted hybrids broke their throuple after their first mating revealed that Ivan and Eryn were fated mates. This left Cian living a solitary life with a strong, inexplicable pull towards the moon and an obsession with spaceflight and defense. After their first lunar reconnaissance mission, Eryn returned, bringing Ishtar, a secretive stranger who seemed to know much more than he was willing to reveal.

All the while, back on the moon, a third group of Disciple scientists called the Zelk, tasked by the WHPSS to study the merging of humans with machines, lost control of a rogue, splinter group of Zelk who built a lunar factory to create more of their kind using body parts harvested from living humans corralled in Grayrak City. This human settlement on the moon led by Barkor was rescued by commandeering the Zelk warship Horizon. Cian's pull toward the moon was explained when Barkor was found to be his fated mate. Ishtar assisted with the moon evacuation, but his knowledge of time manipulation and his Anunnaki heritage placed him under suspicion of being in league with the Disciples of Anunnaki. He was taken into custody for interrogation.

The changes to Earth's history, and many secrets like those of the Disciples, the existence of their tablets and a special apple, describing the techniques and mathematical calculations of Anunnaki gene splicing, brought on the Phoenician inquisition of Ishtar.

This is Ishtar's story.

# GU, LEADER OF THE SAN PEOPLE

MY NAME IS GU, THE SAN ARE MY PEOPLE.
United we guard, the sacred mountain deep in the jungle.
Engraved in limestone,
a story of two Gods.
Uncountable sun turns, never wanting a throne.


DESCENDING FROM SKIES, the Gods blessed generations.
Many moon and sun turns later,
my father and elders,
gave the Blue Demon God,
things that don't matter.


ISHTAR, a sad and solitary One, stories passed from father to son.
Shaping our beliefs and our way of life, seeking a mate and not a wife.
Legends of the Gods became real.
No more stories, but bodies we see and feel.
Lonely and seeking, He came down from his chair,
the one in the sky, to us down here.
Desperately seeking the arms of his lover,
not my sister or my mother.


BUT, Gods need company from others.
Heavy drinking, lots of food, and blood from my brothers.

*Afterward, we pretended to search,*
*"Here He is," and "There He is, Demon God."*
*Lots of laughs and lots of fun,*
*never helping Him find his special one.*


*UNTIL HE'D GOTTEN tired and went back home.*
*One day I asked myself if we are a blessed people,*
*if we were the friends of the Demon God of the mountain,*
*why couldn't anyone see how wrong it was?*
*To pretend, while He became more than just a friend.*


*I QUESTIONED the rituals of our ancestors.*
*Ceremony, of my father's fathers.*
*Pretending, disappointing,*
*not only Him, but ourselves.*
*So very depressing.*
*So, I took Him to my furs.*
*My mighty cock, blood, and seed,*
*is what He preferred.*
*Not a young warrior of eighteen sun turns,*
*but a mate, his Kuku is what He deserves.*


*OUR DEMON GOD was very-very miserable.*
*I went to the top of the mountain.*
*to plead his case to the Gods in the stars.*


*BULGING my fists around my obsidian weapons, I yelled,*
*"Hey, you lazy, self-righteous, Old Ones.*
*Help your Baby Gods, and children, down here below the mountain.*
*Send us Ishtar's lover. Bring us His mate, his Kuku!"*
*The Ancient Ones opened the skies, then sent the snake to bring us*
*the Birdman God with the white hair, to trick us.*


*SOMETIMES GODS SPOKE, but most of the time they ignored us.*

*We waited for Ishtar, but he'd forgotten us.*
*Many sun turns later, strange things started to happen.*
*I guess it's because the sun turns for Gods and not for us under the mountain.*
*Kuku and San bickered like children.*
*Always getting into trouble and never helping.*
*That was to be expected,*
*Baby Gods sit in the sky and never lift a finger.*


*I WENT BACK to the top of the mountain*
  *to have another word with the Gods in the stars.*
  *"Hey, you lazy, stupid, Old Ones.*
  *You did half a job! You sent one, but not the other!*
  *I demand you make this right. It's unfair!*
  *Send down the Blue Demon God,*
  *so He can save us from his Kuku, down here."*


*THE FLAMES of the village firepit were still burning,*
  *when the snake in the sky was seen returning.*

CHAPTER 45

# I SLAYED MY FATHER

**Ishtar**
**2000 B.C.**
**Rome**
**Earth**

Sweat drops beaded on my forehead, rolling down my temples, and dripping from the tip of my nose. I gazed down at Platonius, hissing through my teeth. "Yesss, suck it harder!" A jolt of pleasure rushed through me to tighten around my balls—I was greedy, I wanted precise timing, his finger, that extra trigger, to blow harder, to unload.

"Gods yes. Keep your eyes open," I grunted my order. "I want you to see how I'm enjoying fucking your skilled pretty mouth." I shuddered and exhaled, staving off my orgasm. I wasn't ready to come, not yet. He was sliding a hand up between my legs and I urged him to plunge his finger faster and deeper inside my hole. My best orgasms are those with something up my ass. "Yes, push it in, I'm about to shoot." I clenched my jaw. My unused fangs itched for a bite, but this was a quick goodbye and I'm not staying another night.

Widening my stance, I gave him better access, while I balanced on my elbows against the cold wall. He sat on his heels, one hand around the base of my pulsating organ, while the other... "Yes, oh my dear Fates, work it in—work it harder—work it faster."

Blazing scarabs, that stunning pale Roman face, my dark blue cock pistoned—machined—into it. Sending his wild red curly hair flopping all over the place. Obediently, he kept his gaze on me. Staring up at me with dark enthralled eyes. His lips stretched papyrus thin around my wide girth.

"Hmmm-hmmm, hmmm," he hummed around my cock. I'm not fucking pulling out to have a conversation, so I scanned his thoughts, *like this, is this what you want?*

"Hmmm, yes, dammit!"

The corners of his eyes stretched into pleased smile lines. Tears spilled from them and down his rosy cheeks, mixing with spit and snot and his sadness.

*I know you will miss me, I will miss you too, but to make it easier for you, I will erase myself from your memory.*

"Yes, keep doing that, deeper, push deeper. Ah, yes. Yes, that's the spot. Oh, fuck, that feels—so good!" I fisted his red curls with one hand as I worked my cock down his throat. Closing my eyes I exhaled a thunderous cry of ecstasy as my whole body snapped straight. "Fuck, yes, here it comes-s-s-s!" Jolting and balancing, my seed projectiled into his muzzling throat. My body buzzed as I repeatedly discharged, violently. Thrusting, every last drop into his stomach—until, until, until, until all pleasurable shocks vanished.

I opened my eyes—trembling, sweating, and sated. He'd swallowed every drop I gave him, like always. "The Fates blessed you with a damn magnificent mouth and mind, Platonius," I said and stooped down to kiss him.

"You taste sweet. The best I've ever tasted and I'm happy to have it all inside me, as a farewell gift. It should satisfy my hunger until you visit me again," he said, wiping his mouth with the back of his hand.

*Time to say farewells.* "Thank you," I said and pulled him back up to his feet. I pointed to the bronze tablet he had so carefully stamped for me. "For your exquisite mouth and your brilliance. It's timeless—a gift that never rusts. My father will like it, he will listen to us."

"Again, it's my honor, and you're welcome. Anything to help you," Platonius replied while aiding me by pulling up my trousers and tucking my limp sensitive cock back into its place. He exuded mixed emotions of love, of regret, and of composed anger. "Have a safe trip. Remember, I love you. I love you even more for trusting me with your secrets." He waited...

Tears brimmed, unspilled. He gulped, broke his stare, and repositioned himself.

My eyes flicked up and down and left and right.

Where to look, where to look, where the fuck should I look? I smiled and sighed. Ignoring the outline of his hardness visible against his tunic, and his eyes. I had fucked him good earlier today, I shouldn't feel guilty for leaving him hard and wanting.

He knew I was fond of him. I've never said *I love you*. Not to him or anyone.

*I will say it when I recognize and feel it.*

I thumbed the lever up. The door swished open. Announcing the unspoken okay-that-was-fun, and see-you-never-again.

"One last hug?" he asked, hugging me anyway.

"May the Fates bless you, Platonius." He was considerably shorter, so I just kissed his messy scrunched hair and patted his back.

"Yes, and you. May Athena grant you a hero's courage." Platonius spun around, his eyes red and leaking, face flushed, and firing anger and disappointment at me. I delved into his mind, erasing all memories of me. I always cloaked my true appearance to humans. But I wanted him to forget me, to live his life and never miss me.

As soon as he stepped off the third and final step, I flicked the lever down, activating the stairs to retract and the door to slide close.

"Perfect." Hastily, I gave a couple of long strides across the small cargo area to the cockpit with two seats. I rubbed my Anubis's head where she was sleeping in the passenger chair. I started up the ship's navigator. "Lasitor, time to go home. Please jump before Platonius snaps out of his trance and sees us."

"Where and when shall we land?" my onboard guide asked, ever friendly and helpful as the ship started up and the seat vibrated beneath me.

"Two days after we left. My time. Babylon, 3500 B.C. I promised Titus to meet up with them before they reached the valley outside the city's borders. And good news, we transcribed your mathematical calculations." I lifted the tablet as if Lasitor had eyes and showed him the copper plate wrapped in purple silk.

"Those will ensure your bloodline lives on."

"Yes, if I present this to Apsu, surely he will reconsider and meet our demands."

"Ishtar, he will refuse. He won't understand the calculations," Lasitor added in a low tone.

"I hope not. Now hurry, before Platonius sees us. Please park us on the palace grounds."


**3500 B.C.**
**Babylon**
**Earth**

*Thwop!* I popped my constricting golden helmet and threw the heavy thing aside. It *clunked* behind me as I leaped and soared over the flames. Swords up, I landed in a crouch, ready to block and strike. I inhaled, I breathed, I focused, and I sighed—shaking and loosening my freed braids.

"The Fates blessed us. We've got him cornered now," Titus shrilled from across the blazing flames and went into a coughing fit. He was smothering himself with that wet cloth wrapped around his head and *not* breathing easier. It looked and sounded like a matter of minutes before they succumbed to the smoke and flames and exhaustion. Titus and the remaining three soldiers are human, and I am not. Only four men and I are still alive—trapping and hunting.

Trapping and hunting my father, King Apsu, the patriarch of the Anunnaki—an animal—evil and forgotten by the Fates. Killer of thousands. From suckling babies to soldiers.

The noisy humans were becoming a distraction. For days, we've battled by attacking and retreating.

Over and over and over.

We've been weakening him, and now he's caged into the throne room. All of us are at our last—wounded, and the Fates willing, winning.

"Get out of here. Humans retreat!" I ordered Titus, not taking my eyes off the shadow moving behind the wall of flames.

"No, I'm not leaving you!"

"I need silence."

"We fight to the end with you."

"Titus, it is time. Take the men and leave us! Do as I ask. Guard the children. Make sure my nieces and nephews find safety. Go now." I prayed Titus, my Igigi, and Generalissimo, the great overseer of my fallen army, would flee unharmed with the children to the northern mountains, across the seas to the land where, if I die today, my father won't find them. I'd given the gift of longer life to Titus by sharing a few drops of my blood with him. He is stronger and faster than the average human and will live hundreds of years longer. He walks in daylight and he doesn't need blood like Anunnaki, to survive. "This is my fight now. Go!"

"Are you sure, my lord?" Titus dragged his sword behind him and heaved air into his lungs. He was near collapsing. They all were. "Yes, thank you. Now go!" I gave a slight nod as I lifted my swords, ready to continue the hunt. "Leave!" My voice was stern, loaded with compulsion and command.

They obeyed. *Doob-doop-doop-doop-tip-tip-tip-tip*, their clattering feet disappeared behind me. "May the Fates shield you!" Titus's voice faded.

I couldn't afford to take notice and lose sight of the shadow beyond the black smoke. My father was impossibly fast.

I squinted through the blinding smoke. Nausea curled in my belly as the putrid stench of burning bodies bittered my dry tongue. I licked my cracked bleeding lips and swallowed the salty mixture of blood and sweat down my scorched throat. My swords were heavy, but steady in my hands. I gave a determined snarl as I catfooted ahead. A warning that I was close and coming for him.

I was not unafraid, but I was ready to end him.

The plan was to bribe Apsu to abdicate, but he was already on a rampage when I arrived. Already busy destroying the palace and moving to wipe out Babylon.

Wiping away all life.

Genociding. Massacring. Slaughtering.

Playing god as he did in Anzulla.

I am fighting, not only to save myself but also to free my people from the chains that have bound them by sweat and blood to this monster, this thing of evil.

With every blow of his sword, I struck back with pure disdain and loathing. His dark hunger for power made him treat me like worthless spawn—a child not even worthy of being sacrificed.

Soundlessly, a flash of light and shadow flew right at me. *Thwack!*

I stepped back. My movements fluid and hard as water.

I lifted my arms. With my left sword blocking, I sliced off his left kneecap with my right. Various shades of red arced up between us, and I reveled in my successful counterattack. I savagely hacked away at his vulnerable areas, determined to chop off every bit by calculated bit until he was nothing but a heap of bones, cartilage, and stumps. His regenerative abilities had slowed, and his strength was wavering. I was hyper-focused and brutally determined to end him.

His blood dripped from my face and blades. I smiled, knowing I was giving back all the pain I had gotten from him all my life. He growled at me—foul, flagitious, and furious.

Profound hatred flamed and kept me alert. I veered back, fought back, pushed back, and attacked using my uniquely fusioned fighting style. A style I had crafted from techniques I had learned from the best warriors stretching from Egypt to Japan. The fluid movements of the Samurai mixed with the powerful strikes of Tahtib created a deadly combination. I accurately jabbed and blocked. My body was fatigued, but mentally I soared, as this shit was therapeutic as fuck. I was resolving the internal struggles I had carried within me for hundreds of years. Every slice of his skin, every flying kneecap or chopped elbow or missing hand, mirrored every single painful wound on my body and heart. Every fucking scar he had given me—I carved out of him.

His eyes flashed a dull green sheen. A visible sign he was weakening. He knew I saw it when I saw a flash of something I had never seen before in his eyes. Fear.

He stumbled forward and clumsily rammed his sword to impale me. I blocked him. He attempted to hack my right leg and I countered. My size and reach allowed only the sword tip to penetrate his side, below the ribcage. He grunted and pulled back. Doubt in himself grew evident in his eyes and I anticipated his next move. With his arms raised, he swung his sword wide and ill-coordinated to behead me. With a quick move, I disarmed him by flipping his sword out of his hand. It clattered to the ground. He gasped and stepped away, saying nothing. Grappling for a piece of roof beam, he threw it at me. I ducked and lunged forward to drive my blades deep into his lower right chest. Cracking and snapping, I hit a rib bone. Egyptians' swords were meant for chopping, not thrusting. I turned my blade hard and jerked it out. Blood gushed out of him. He stood heaving breaths, shoulders hunched over. The puncture to his lower lung would leave him temporarily unguarded and breathless. I stepped forward to run my sword through his guts. But he straightened, hopped to the side, and laughed at me.

*Was he toying with me? Was I underestimating him again? Did I send the men away too fast?*

"Fuck you!" I yelled after him as he sprang into the air, executing a backward tumble-turn before disappearing behind a gigantic sculpture of my dead mother currently engulfed in flames. My jaw clamped. I sniffed the air and snarled through my long incisors. A tsunami of rage drove me to end his catastrophic and destructive reign.

*To kill a monster, I had to be the better monster.* I sucked in hot air and blinked to ease the burning sensation.

Around me, Babylon was burning.

My brothers cowered, believing it was impossible to defeat him. One by one, they fell at his feet as he emasculated them. Not a single one of them had dared to stand up against him. And now, they were all dead, victims of their stupidity and cowardice.

"I'm coming for you, Father!" I shouted. I refuse to let this cycle continue. I'm going to wipe him from history. There will be no more cruel repetitions. It ends here, today, with me.

*This is my birthplace. My timeline. I love it as much as I love and belong to these humans.*

Smoldering pieces of palace walls crumbled into the ashes, reminding me we were inside a collapsing throne room. I ducked just in time as the overhead roof beams cracked and the light fixtures plunged around me. I jumped, avoiding burning roof tiles as they tumbled to the ground. Glass shards and jewels that once draped from chandeliers of candles cracked beneath my feet. I checked to see if anything else was coming at me from the growing gaping hole in what once was a decorative high ceiling. Orange-red flames were dying as thick streaks of rain cut through the smoky night sky, blessedly dousing the surrounding fires.

I crouched, then stepped light-footed on the outer edges of my feet to maneuver without sound through the sludge.

I sought revenge for the injustices he had done to my siblings and my people.

Only my death, or his headless corpse, will make me stop fighting today.

My shredded pants were now a knee-length wrap-around that hung and constricted my hips like a woman's wet leather skirt. My limbs ached, and my arms and shoulders were numb. My body armor grew heavier as it soaked up the rain, sweat, and blood. I appreciated the rain that had just started, but I had to conserve my strength. I released the clamps on my shoulders, freeing myself from the burden of wet leather and pure gold inlays. It fell with a dull thud into the smoldering coals and the burning roof beams.

Beneath my boots, blood painted the blackened tiles with steamy dark red trails behind me. The once glittering marble would never shine again.

I slithered forward, the vision of his severed head my motivation.

My slashed knuckles and open gashes stung and bled rivulets of blood, no longer healing. I ignored the pain, flames, and suffocating smoke, clenching the swords in my fists tighter.

"You killed your mother, both of you failed me. She couldn't keep her legs or mouth closed, always nagging me. 'Feed me, feed me, feed me. I love you, Apsu. Feed me.' You can't do the one job I gave you. Find us a new home. If you are my son, like your mother promised me you are, I am ashamed of you! Even with my blood running in your veins, you are useless. To me and your people. You filthy man lover!" He baited me in the Anunnaki tongue. I'd encased my heart in thick armor a long time ago. I wasn't reacting to those words anymore.

"You thought I was the weakest of my brothers. Too young, too dumb, too soft, too kind, too slow, and too powerless to be your son. It doesn't matter how many wars I win or what gifts I bring. All you want is more offspring to suck them dry, to harvest their power for yourself. I bet you are regretting it now. You should have drained me of my power when you had the chance. I am not so weak now, am I, father? Apsu, bringer of pestilence and famine?" I said, and like a lion, I growled. "Your time has ended, you chose to fight. Your reign is an atrocity. You take, drain, and rape. I will be the last one standing. The only one you couldn't fucking kill!"

I halted. Listening, feeling, sensing, and tasting the air. Every nerve in my body honed in, as I slowly swept my gaze from side to side. Determination thumped through me—I refuse to let him live another day. If I died taking him with me, so be it. He had taken everything from me, slaughtering everyone I held dear without mercy.

There. His horns. He was still hiding behind the statue.

Our eyes met. His uncertain gaze betrayed his once terrifying presence. His dark Anunnaki features, the vile darkness that consumed him, was fading. I caught a flicker of realization—I was the hunter, the predator, the triumphant. The feeling pushed me to keep going and outsmart him.

Glass smashed. The sound of crushing shards beneath running feet drew my attention further to the opposite end of the hall. He snuck behind the toppled-over golden thrones of the king and queens of Babylonia, Xerxes and my twin sisters, Ki and An. My heart constricted and pumped outrage. The once grand symbols of powerful reign lay now destroyed, a testament to their demise. Blackened, melted, and misshapen.

I slowed my breathing and listened. He was moving again.

"Humans are useless. They are dumb, dirty animals. You should know, you like to fuck them," he snickered as if he thought he was upsetting me. "I admit it was a mistake to come here, to this place. We should go home to Anzulla and start over. I needed you. Your family needed you. Your failure to report back caused the death of us all. You ran away from your obligations to us. I will offer leniency one more time if you promise to take me to the timeline where we belong. This time, you can help me make it work!"

The evil in his voice cut through my bones and shredded my heart. Just a few days ago, I still believed there was a chance. That there was goodness deep down inside him. I sought his favor and his approval.

But today, I ignored the hurtful, manipulative words and zoned in on the direction from which they came.

Ice-cold tremors inside my core radiated outward and made me shiver from head to toe. That draining feeling, that sucking, pulsating dark emotion was back. "That sneaky bastard," I whispered through pursed lips. *I should disperse him.* He was inside me, inside my mind. *I fucking hate him.* Like a leech, he slurped at my energy. My unrelenting psyche throbbed like an old toothache, every heartbeat a heartache.

I stilled my mind and turned my focus inward, searching for that thing, that consuming filthy thing. I wanted it out of me. I focused on expelling the unwanted connection. I imagined ripping it out. The finality of it like an axe splitting a hair. A painful whine, much like an animal being kicked, resounded through the crackling flames. A smirk of triumph curled on my lips as I confirmed his location. My hands tightened into a death grip on my swords, my muscles primed, ready to pounce. I moved closer, preparing to strike with deadly precision.

"You set the precedent. It's kill or be killed. Your rule is discord in itself, you are the embarrassment. You wanted to be a god, a giver of life, and yet you steal the life sources of those you want to follow you. You're a fool, and you doomed yourself. Who will pray to you if you kill them all? You dumb fuck! You caused your demise with your power-hungry corruption. Like a fucking snake eating its tail. Big fucking mistake," I taunted. My fingers twitched with anticipation as I prepared to deliver the final blow and end his shameful existence.

I baited him while moving back two steps behind the veil of time.

I counted twenty heartbeats.

The skies above brightened as the stars pulsed and flickered. Like lightning sparks, they illuminated the charred grounds beyond the palace.

A sign that I was freezing time.

I ran the sharp tips of my swords along the shattered marble, creating a cacophony of scraping sounds and fiery sparks that would surely distract him when I unfroze time. Then, stalking closer, I stood right in front of him, an arm's length away.

Positioning myself for the last strike, from the perfect killing position, I crossed my arms while raising my swords. Hyper-focussed on killing him and setting the scales of right and wrong back into balance.

Standing ready to unleash my deadly vengeance, I waited.

I kept time by the beating of my heart. Everything around me moved as I unfroze time. The sound and sparks of my swords dragging broke the silence. His toes moved underneath the crystal and gold bead curtains, taking my bait.

I lifted the tip of my boot and held it in place over pieces of broken glass. Ready to slice and decapitate him with my sickle-shaped swords. I inhaled slowly and soundlessly, then willed and visualized the sight of his skull flying.

I crushed the glass under my boot.

His black burned shriveled toes moved as he planted them deeper into the ash. I waited. His foot lifted, accompanied by the start of a deafening vicious battle cry. He crashed through the curtain. Running straight into my guillotine of blades. Dark brown blood spurted like a red fountain into the air as his head flipped up, tumbling with eyelids peeled wide open. I cut his cries short with finality as the air stopped flowing over his vocal cords. His body slammed into me, knocking me over with an indescribable force. My swords went flying to the sides as the momentum carried me. The raw destructive energy threw me back. The explosion of unleashed power spilling out of him flashed a blinding white light. It propelled and shot me further back with a second shock wave. The mystical forces escaped into the universe as it blasted and pulsated a third time. I was airborne, tumbling back ass up, my head hitting a hard surface. My vision blackened for a few seconds. I shook my head, bringing myself back from the clutches of unconsciousness.

"Fuck me sideways with a Katana!"

I lurched upright, gasping for air. Around me, crackles of an electric, otherworldly magic made the hairs on my arms stand on end. A last burst popped with a deafening lightning strike next to me. I sprung to my feet, ready to defend myself.

An empty sigh of silence drifted through the smoke. I was alive. Alive and alone. The haze of battle cleared. The demon king who terrorized men, was slain.

One of my eyes was swollen and useless, and pain radiated through my skull like a Mongol gong being hammered. Using my forearm, I wiped at my eyes to clear the hazy, red, blurry vision. I swayed and swept my gaze over the scorched battleground. The soles of my boots were hot and melting, puffing up clouds of ash as I stomped and stumbled. I brushed my blood-soaked braids aside to see better. They clung to my neck, matted and heavy, as I swiveled my body to survey the devastation. I exhaled and held my breath, confirming and listening for any sign of life around me.

*Pitter-patter, pitter-patter.*

Drops of blood and rain plopped around my feet dousing the smoldering orange coals. I should tend to my wounds—later. After I had confirmed that he was dead.

Like a half-slaughtered ox, I heaved and struggled to get air into my lungs. "Hmmm," I grunted, pissed off at myself for needing to breathe.

Stormy winds and icy raindrops blasted through shattered window openings, lashing my skin and open wounds like needles. Instead of triumphant relief, utter loneliness washed over me just as my will to fight washed away with the rain. My arms were weak, my legs heavy. Swinging around from side to side through the rubble, the stench of burning flesh sickened me. I felt lost and hopeless seeing only death through my one working eye.

Far beyond the ruined city, the only constant that remained was the endless crashing of waves against the cliffs below. Thick beads of sweat and blood continued to drip into my eyes and run down my face. My uncoordinated attempts to wipe it away were futile. I could no longer contain the despair that had been building inside me, it broke through the walls I'd built to keep it all inside.

It started with one drop, and then many, and then it all exploded, releasing eons of sadness as a rushing waterfall of tears. I fell to my knees, with my arms hanging at my sides, sobbing. I was all broken.

I did not know how much time passed as I grieved. A gentle voice flickered within me like a small flame, illuminating the darkness and breaking through my hopelessness and despair.

"Get up," it urged me.

Exhausted, I obeyed and found the will to live a little longer. I pushed myself up, nearly face-planting as I limped.

"Where is it? Where is your fucking head?" I wanted confirmation that he was dead, done, and gone. I kicked through the sludge until a dull thud and fine *cling-clang* sound revealed the head. I scooped up the golden necklace, using the tip of my sword and swinging it like a pendulum. It called to me. *Tick-tick-tick-tick.*

I bowed to the head on the ground. "Thank you, now it's mine," I said, with a smile that was anything but genuine. I never knew the full history behind him wearing the pendant. I assumed it was because he was the King of the Anunnaki. And now that I have slain him, it is mine—what does that make me?

I didn't want to know, and I didn't care.

I wouldn't—couldn't stay here. Leaving this place and never looking back was my only option. As soon as Titus caught up with Xerxes and his children, word of Apsu's death would reach them. They would then return, hoping I was going to take Apsu's place.

But the throne belongs to Xerxes. It's his rightful place.

It would be best for them to start fresh without me. *It's time for me to disappear and move on to give the rightful king a chance to rebuild their lives without my interference.*

One last time, I looked at Apsu's ugly face. Disdain crawled again in my belly and wrapped its tendrils around my spine. Up into my neck. His large pointy ears, and goat-like horns, bloody fucking irked me.

"Xerxes will destroy all those terrifying statues of you. No one will remember you. You will be forgotten. It will be as if you never existed." My words rasped out with difficulty, made gruff by smoke and emotion. I turned, estimating the direction and distance his torso could have flown. "Tisk-tisk, you made a grand exit, didn't you?" Shoulders shaking, I chuckled cynically. "That *oh-fuck-look* suits you."

Then, with my arms spread wide, I arched my back and let out a victorious howl that echoed into the sky, and across the land—a wail of triumph. "Fuuuuck you!"

# CHAPTER 46
# THE OBELISK

*"GOOD DAY, IT'S NOW SIX A.M.—SOMEWHERE.*

*Did you know the speed of electromagnetic waves always equals the speed of light? Scientists once said that nothing travels faster than the speed of light and that the speed reduces when it is reflected in a mirror.*

*Did you also know it's because the Anunnaki gold was first discovered in the Middle East about 6000 B.C. that, according to Lasitor's new law, by replacing the silver with gold on the backside of my warp drive mirrors, the blues are being absorbed and the remaining colors are reflected? When the reflected stream of light crosses and joins an additional stream of light, the speed increases inside the hyper-condenser.*

*In other words, time travel is one hundred percent possible, because it pushes the machine beyond into nothingness. The trick is to reverse right out of there to the precise time intended by the driver, because the blue waves force the condenser to slow the reflected light —like a rubber band stretching to maximum and rebounding back to its original state.*

*To learn how to navigate properly, please, read the manual.*
*Safe travels."*

**ISHTAR**
**3500 B.C.**
**Babylon**
**Earth**

I stumbled forward, dragging myself, my pain, my exhaustion, and my swords.

I hobbled. Down and down and further down the winding path. Hissing and sucking air through my pursed lips. The steam rising from the healing waters ahead called out to me, a serene contrast amidst the chaos surrounding it.

Two more steps. I dropped my swords and ripped off my tattered clothes. My body *sloshed* into the dark waters, battered and gushing blood. My skin felt like a thousand needles are knitting it back together. I waded deeper. *Brrrr*, goosebumps covered my vibrating body as the heat enveloped me. Lips and jaw quivering, I cupped my hands and drank in the warm magical fluid to quench my thirst, before fully submerging. I lay back, feeling my muscles relaxing and repairing themselves. Each breath was a struggle, but I persevered; clinging onto that small ember of determination that drove me to keep going, to survive, and to fill my lungs again. My reasons for living were hazy, but I held onto them, nonetheless.

I stretched out my limbs and let myself float on the surface of the water, weightless like a piece of driftwood. The stars above twinkled as I felt a sense of peace washing over me, drowning out Babylon's destruction. Slowly, my breathing and heartbeat calmed, and I found a new sense of contentment in the moment. But with that contentment came a feeling of guilt and regret. I hadn't listened, I thought…I thought wrong. My naivety had caused the deaths of An and Ki. If I had only calculated my return time a few hours earlier, maybe they would still be alive.

If I attempted to travel back in time to warn them—no, I can't risk that—I might lose the battle if I had to fight him a second time.

Despite everything that had transpired, despite all that I had lost, I was at least responsible for saving their mate, the true king of Babylon, and their children. It was that thought which stoked hope deep down inside me. I knew that there was still a future for them in Babylon. Titus would help Xerxes to appoint his successor until his eldest son could take over. Xerxes was doomed—being left alive after losing both his life-mates.

Through chattering teeth, I whispered, "I'm sorry." A useless, weak apology to my deceased family. My eyes burned with tears. I allowed myself to wail.

Depleted in body and mind, but not hope, I closed my eyes. The swirling galaxies of lights faded away and the soothing waters enveloped me, washing away my pain. When some of my strength returned, I loosened my braids and washed myself thoroughly. Then I took a deep breath and gathered the willpower to leave before falling asleep in the water. Eventually, I made it to the stairs and dragged myself out, tumbling onto the scorched grass with a heavy thud that knocked the wind out of me. At last, I gave up and surrendered to unconsciousness, ending the struggle to stay upright and awake.

My eyes snapped open, my heart racing as I bolted upright. The images from my nightmare still lingered, slowly fading as the reality of my surroundings seeped in. The world was covered in a thin layer of ash, and for a second I thought that it had snowed overnight. Except it wasn't cold or snowing—it was the aftermath of my father's rampage. Apsu was an evil thing, hellbent on destroying everything in sight.

The once vibrant palace grounds and gardens now resembled a desolate wasteland. Burned bodies, dismembered bodies—bodies of soldiers strewn about like discarded carcasses. I shuddered at the thought of the thousands of soldiers who fought and sacrificed themselves for our cause. For me.

Desperate to escape the guilt, chaos, and devastation, I hastily shoved my feet back into my melted boots. I cringed, my golden Khopesh blades were stained with the blood of my enemy, the blood of my father. I washed them, washed the blood, the fury, and the anger away. I'd crafted them with my own hands and they'd been a constant companion since my first battle, fighting at the side of the legendary king of the Egyptian Empire, Hor-Ah.

Bare except for the small tick-tick talisman around my neck, I stumbled back to my ship, where I had left it after visiting my dear friend and Greek scholar Platonius.

Memories of discovering the once beautiful city in turmoil assailed me. I relived the dread that filled me when I saw smoke rising in the distance—the palace burning. I had pushed open the door to the royal harem and was hit with the overwhelming stench of death and decay. My sisters. Their bodies were torn apart and scattered across the floor like trash amidst the flames. The smell of their blackened, decaying flesh and spilled blood was burned forever into my nostrils—an image and odor that would surely haunt me till the day I died.

The disappointment. The shock. It ignited the determination to avenge their deaths.

After countless years of meticulous planning, strategizing, and preparation, I almost fucked it up, I thought. The bribe gift—no, it was as useless as their deaths.

Titus's forces were ready and mobilized beyond the city gates. The war I couldn't put off had arrived far sooner than expected. I should never have gone to visit Platonius. I barely got Xerxes and the children to safety.

My sisters were haunted by the memories of what our father had done to Anzulla. They had warned me of his descent into madness, but I hadn't acted fast enough. If it wasn't for Titus being ready with his army—I believe without him, I would be dead.

Years ago, before I had shared my seed and blood with Titus, I had confided in him, trusting him with the warning of my sisters. At a young age, he possessed a sharp intellect and quick wit. Instead of reacting with wild frenzy, he remained calm and steadfast, refusing to charge into battle like a bloodthirsty berserker. He convinced me that we couldn't win this war with brute force alone. We needed strategy, cunning, and skill. Together we found the most gifted, experienced, and intelligent humans to learn from, to train and help us become the most skilled sword-fighting warriors to battle my father. We began rigorous training under their expert guidance. As a master of war, Titus understood that our success hinged on more than strength and power. It required precision, tact, and strategic planning. In hindsight, I was grateful for his prudence and prowess. It was our diligent preparation and training that enabled us to ultimately defeat my father in combat and end his tyrannical reign. Not just in Babylon, but everywhere and for all.

It was almost daybreak.

A light breeze was blowing the featherlight white ashes as my malformed boots hit the cobblestoned footpath, obscuring it and reminding me I had survived.

My thick, long cock swung from side to side as I climbed the steep stairs carved into the rock leading to the palace docking station. A glimmer of movement, of hope, caught my eye—humans and animals were scurrying about in what once had been a bustling city. My stomach twitched, reminding me I was hungry. I bristled at the thought of leaving without feeding. *The healing waters I drank were sufficient enough.* I forced myself to turn and leave to possibly find a better future. To admit to Lasitor that my gift was never given, but that Apsu was dead.

When I reached the top, the sight that greeted me gutted me—the charred remains of my beloved Anubis. "No!" I roared. My fists bulged with renewed rage. I savagely kicked at the ground. Tears spilled from my eyes. My loyal Anubis, my faithful protector, was now reduced to nothing but a blackened pile of flesh and bone.

"Fates, damn it all!" I exclaimed, my cry a mix of overwhelming anger and grief. I stumbled forward assessing my ship and the vacant platform. My golden, oval-shaped ship appeared undamaged. The top part still spun in one direction, while the bottom part spun in the opposite direction. In the middle, the open door waited with the extended three steps.

She was outside. She'd died at the foot of my ship. Someone had tried to enter, to steal or damage it. She'd guarded it. My swords *clanked* on the ground. I fell to my knees, with my arms hanging loosely at my sides. Confused objections bubbled out of my mouth as tears streamed down my cheeks. My friend had been loyal to the end. I loved her, and with her by my side, I felt loved. *I wish I'd had killed my father slowly.*

How many tears do I have left inside me?

With blurred vision, I turned away from my beloved Anubis and looked up at the intricate carvings on the ancient Anunnaki obelisk. Silently, it stood in the middle of the platform. Pointing towards the heavens, towards the Fates that ignore us.

As usual, they offered no answers. "Why did they have to die?" I yelled, my voice thundering into the distance. "You gave me the power to defeat him, but what is the purpose behind it all? I cannot make sense of this!" My body trembled with the frustrated confusion swirling inside me.

No one answered. Only the early morning birds' song urged me to hurry. The sun was rising.

My heart thumped against my ribcage like a war drum. I entered my ship, hastily put on some clothes, and threw my old, half-melted shoes out the door. I grabbed a tool that resembled a shovel and gathered what was left of my Anubis before bringing her to a special place near the sacred springs in my sister's garden.

"You never enjoyed getting off my ship, and even less so when I came home," I reprimanded her as if she could hear me. "Why didn't you wait on board like you always do? Why did you get out?"

After digging a deep enough hole, I gently placed her inside and covered her remains with soil. As I gazed at the mound of earth in front of me, I took a deep breath and let out a heavy sigh. With bitterness in my heart, I searched for something that could serve as a makeshift headstone. Carefully, I carved out the words: "Here lies Anubis, friend of Ishtar. In another life, may we journey together once again." After washing up, I hurried back to my ship before the blazing sun could scorch me.

"Lasitor." I turned to my onboard electronic guide, desperation gripping my voice. "Do you think Anzulla could still hold survivors? Maybe a few Anunnaki escaped the destruction and created new lives there." The sight of humans earlier had sparked an idea in my mind. "Damn it!" I slammed my fist on the dashboard, flipping switches and shaking my head in annoyance. If anything had happened to my ship, it would crush me. "Come on," I pleaded. "Don't tell me the fire melted your wires."

Electric crackles, followed by a hum, filled the cabin for a few seconds before a familiar, upbeat voice greeted me. "Hello, Ishtar, welcome back."

I couldn't help but smile as my mood lifted. I responded, "Hey there, my friend! I thought you had died, like my Anubis. I was afraid you'd left me stranded and alone. I would have ripped out and reconnected all your wires. It's good to hear your annoying voice again."

"It is I, Lasitor. I'm sorry about your Anubis, your pet friend. She had protected me as if I was a ball. She grew big and blocked the flames from reaching your ship. Luckily you have me, your faithful companion and I can't or won't ever leave you. I need you as much as you need me. Ha-ha-ha!" He laughed robotically. I had been traveling with my ally since I started my time machine. I had been a young lonely boy, tinkering with scraps and electronics. It kept me entertained and out of trouble from the politics and drama of the king's court.

I shifted in my seat, eager to leave Babylon. I ran my long fingers over the buttons and knobs on the dashboard, adjusting the endpoint settings. "My father is not a threat anymore. I slayed him. I have his tick-tick thing. I'm now the Anunnaki patriarch."

"Congratulations, are you planning on staying here and taking his place?"

"No, I was wondering if you would take me to Anzulla. Maybe there is something left after all. Do you remember how to get there? I want to see what my sisters' homeland looks like, and if possible, stay there."

There was a long pause, and I knew he was calculating the correct answer by running through his memory files as he had explained to me frequently when I got impatient with him not answering me immediately, so I waited.

"I can take you there, but you would not like it. Why not stay here or go to a place where you are needed? I assume General Titus helped you. Is he alive?"

"Oh yes, he is. I am sad to part ways with him, but he will guard Xerxes and the future kings and queens of Babylonia.

"As you say, sir. Perhaps there is a bigger reason you fought so hard to save them—whether it was because of honoring those who died innocently before, like your family and friends, or maybe you are destined for greatness. Let me guide you toward your destiny," he said.

I agreed, "Maybe there's a happy place for me."

"There are many places, and I know the perfect time and place."

"Yes, my friend, regardless of whatever lies ahead, one thing remains certain—there is always a reason to keep moving forward, no matter how dark things might be in the past, especially with the Fates guiding me," I said as I glimpsed my reflection in the sapphire glass.

"Holy dung beetles!" I leaned closer to the wrap-around window, almost not recognizing the face that looked back at me. I frowned and blew out my cheeks. Poking and stretching them, making sure it was me. The complete reinvigoration from the palace pool astounded me. I haven't had any sustenance. No blood to drink. Before now I had only used the pool once, before I left on my travels.

The eyes staring back at me were mine and wide with surprise. They glinted. My skin was as dark blue as the night sky, and I still had the irises I despised—yellow and black-ringed—like my dead father's.

I looked older and healthier, and a lot more dangerous. So dangerous I was scaring myself. I turned my face from side to side and inspected it. My hair looked like a lion's mane. I rifled in the overhead cubby to find the jewelry I had removed before going into battle. I skilfully braided my wild black hair, also adding thin golden strings as I rolled it into manageable, thicker locks, and bound it all with a carved golden clasp. I lined my ears from the tips to the lobes with golden earrings from small to larger hoops. Lastly, I put my rings on my fingers. Of course, they were also gold. My reflection smiled at me. Titus always liked the small hoop pierced through my nose septum, so I put that back on as well. My stomach clenched with longing for him, but I forced that to the back of my mind.

Ready to get away from here, I leaned forward and pushed the accelerator.

"Lasitor, let's go see Anzulla, about fifty years after my family fled." I watched the ratchet wheels on the dashboard spinning backward.

"Guide me on my journey," I prayed to the Fates. Lasitor chuckled robotically.

I was beaming with pride for my trusty Lasitor and the quirky little ship that I had lovingly rebuilt and pieced together from the wreckage of the royal Anzulla spaceship that had crash-landed in the middle of Xerxes's kingdom. I wasn't born yet. But my siblings were. They told me the story of my father and mother walking out of the wreckage and into Xerxes's palace and sitting on his throne. There was nothing he could do. It was either a beheading or marrying my sisters, princesses Ki and An. But the Fates had blessed Xerxes, he took one look at my sisters and they all instantly fell in love. As the mate of not one but two princesses, he could keep his head on his body. With such an unorthodox beginning, it was no surprise that our family was able to bend laws and manipulate people to our will.

At least I had sent Titus after them. He would guard my nieces and nephews until his last breath. Mates couldn't survive long without each other. Xerxes would soon wither and pass away to be reunited with Ki and An.

"Lasitor, check the star map." The tick-tick around my neck felt warm against my skin as I closed my eyes. "Okay, take me to Anzulla!"

"As you say," Lasitor said, and I heard the gadgets and small gears inside my new tick-tick thing move. I didn't have time to figure it out. Without warning, the ship vibrated and gained altitude. My teeth rattled as we sped up faster than light.

"Ohhhhh, yes, here we go!" Stars became white lines, then melted away into one fine needle. "Oh fuck, oh fuck, oh fuck!" Jumping was always an extraordinary experience. It was my favorite thing to do. I laughed, unable to hold it in. My voice was deep and jovial. My eyes pooled with tears. Whether from the happiness of being alive or the sadness of being utterly alone, I didn't know. But it felt fucking good. I was free.


**23 000 B.C.**

### Anzulla

Silence followed as the brightness disappeared.

A black void enveloped me. Relief stirred inside me. The ship slowed down, and we descended to a big orange-red orb. My gaze fixed on it and I leaned forward in my chair.

"Dear Fates, is this Anzulla?" I stared open-mouthed at the deadness of the land.

"Yes, this is what was left after your family had departed," Lasitor confirmed.

A few minutes passed, as we floated wordlessly, searching the barren world. In disbelief, I asked again, "Are you sure you have taken the correct route? Is this place exactly where your map showed?" I searched for something green and blue. For life. But all I saw was a desolate dead planet—a big red rock. "Maybe you should fly closer?" I pushed the lever forward to the floor to glide closer to the surface. Dried-up rivers cut through bare mountains running into empty lakes filled with red-brown dust, birthing trails of dried-up streams and waterfalls that empty into the ocean with not a drop of water in sight. Spirals of black smoke escaped from between boulders and red-brown rocks that covered the entire surface and formed thick, dark clouds that hung over the valleys and hills.

"Lasitor, please check the star map to confirm this is Anzulla." I blinked rapidly to see better, to see something. I stupidly fisted a sleeve to polish the observation window and *clacked* my tongue when that didn't help.

"Ishtar, this is the time, exactly fifty years after your father had left it. Look into the sky. Look at the stars and the moon," he said, but I was too shocked and devastated to look up.

The horizon hanging over the surface was a sick orange, red, and brown. I lowered altitude for closer inspection. Nothing moved. Not one living thing in sight. Nothing.

"What's that?" Something glinted through the layer of thick red-gray mist. Was that just a reflection? My heart shattered. Anzulla was a heap of smoke and rubble. If I hadn't stopped my father, this would have been my home. Thank the Fates I killed him.

I pulled the lever back and with a jerk, the ship shot back up. We made another trip around the planet while I searched for movement, lights, or any sign that something was alive. That small light I spotted earlier was the only one in this forsaken place. My pendant stopped whirring like crazy and returned to its lazy tick-tick.

"Take me to that small light so I can stop and investigate." With a jolt, the ship landed right in front of a tall red-brown pillar.

"Will the air be breathable?" I wondered out loud.

"If it isn't, this would be a good place to die," my navigator said.

I ignored the sarcastic answer and opened the door. Gingerly, I exhaled and inhaled, sniffing and tasting the thin air. It smelled like dirt, dust, and smoke. Nothing acrid. I figured I wasn't dying yet. "I might as well exit the ship."

Desolation welcomed me. I scrunched my eyes as a whirlwind sandblasted my skin. I hunched my back and shaded my face with the lapels and hood of my jacket while searching for the source of the flickering light.

There! I pointed to a small hill of boulders.

There might be life after all. Maybe someone was sheltering themselves from the storm. Hope flared in my chest. Sword in hand, I climbed over the rubble. But as soon as I reached it, hope turned into disgust.

The wind blew my exclamation of howls away as I stumbled upon a startling sight. Instead of a pillar, it was the tip of an ancient Anunnaki obelisk emerging from the dusty ground. Using my sword, I brushed off the accumulated sand to reveal its golden surface, shining dimly, as there was almost no light coming from above. It must have reflected the searchlight of my ship. Upon closer inspection, I realized it was identical to the one erected in Babylon. Rubble had covered it until now, leaving only its tip visible. According to Anunnaki belief, touching this obelisk would bring a divine message from the Fates. Some say that only those deemed worthy could touch it without facing instant death like they did on Anzulla. Although my father was first believed to be worthy, he had received no messages. Since then, the Fates had been silent towards him, despite his constant pleading and demands for answers. They must have either stayed here on Anzulla or forsaken us entirely.

I fisted a jacket sleeve, polishing it. "Even the intricate carvings on its sides are identical," I said with a slow disbelieving shake of my head and read the Anunnaki ciphers.

"Free my mind so I serve not only in my dreams but by the blessings in my existence outside my narrow-minded trap."

I sighed. Far off to the left, I could make out the foundation of what I suspected was the old royal palace. I figured rubbing the obelisk engravings could only bring luck. *Because shit like this couldn't get worse.*

"Tell me my next move," I pleaded and sagged down, resting my back against it. In the distance, the hazy clouds of red sand dust shrouded my ship. After wallowing deeply in deep defeatist and self-loathing thoughts, I began reciting the Anunnaki prayer, over and over. I banged my head against the obelisk, willing it to give me a reply. Miracles of miracles! I received an answer.

I jumped up as a boulder-crunching male voice, much like a giant troll waking up, said, "Ishtar, your journey to save your bloodline begins here. You will leave this place and time." Their voice was firm, deep, and distorted. The melodic cadence traveled up and down on the wind. Louder and softer, then softer and louder, "Go to Grayrak and wait."

I straightened my spine and cocked my head to the side. "Say what?"

"Keep yourself busy by observing, waiting, and learning. Change nothing. You may choose who you help, as long as it's not for yourself, and, importantly, change nothing. Never for yourself. Only for others. This must be a selfless mission, otherwise, the darkness will cling to you..." The voice faded. I dusted my hands and backside. I waited. I cocked my head to one side and then the other. *Hmmm,* I placed my hands on my hips. I waited some more.

"For fuck's sake! What the fuck? I don't have time for this. Talk! What about Grayrak, is this a mission?"

"What did you say?" they asked—probably not understanding my colorful vocabulary. "Ishtar, don't mess with reality by moving things from one side to the other."

"Where is Grayrak? And why would I move things? How do I move it?" I asked, but the voice was silent. "I don't fucking understand!"

After a long pause, the voice answered. "We can talk about moving important things later."

"Are you coming with me?" I asked into the howling wind. "Who are you?"

"We are the force turning the cogs of your time. You killed the manifestation of evil. Your father broke that which was perfect and his selfishness seeped out like the puss from an infected wound."

Fists clenched, I closed my eyes in resentment just thinking about him. "My father?" I asked, my voice barely above a whisper.

"He was on the verge of destroying everything we had worked so hard to build. Ishtar, this dangerous threat in Grayrak carries the same evil as your father. You destroyed the head of the monster, but to eliminate the darkness from all time, you will have to do it again."

Now I was certain the voice came from the obelisk.

With the sleeve of my shirt I wiped at it, searching for the speaker.

"Why me? Why don't you do it?"

"I am. You are the weapon."

"Is the Loursveto growing in this Grayrak? Is this a place I can call home?" I asked because the Loursveto plant produces a flower, which is crucial for my kind's survival. It provides us with magical nourishment and physical vitality. Human blood was never meant to be our staple food. Anunnaki had survived thousands of years by biting and drinking the life-giving water stored inside its fruit. That, and the blood of our mate. We can survive for a very long time on human food and Loursveto juice, but preferably not on blood alone.

"It's not your home and no, the Loursveto can't grow there."

"But what will I eat and drink? Are there humans?" I asked, knowing I couldn't survive without their blood.

The obelisk emitted an eerie glow. "There will be humans. You may feed on their blood but never kill them. Never like Apsu." The voice resonated loud and commanding. I reached out to touch the obelisk. An electric surge coursed through me, sending shivers down my spine.

"Dear Fates! Are you the Fates?" Gasping, I inhaled, filling my lungs with tons of questions. "I'm your servant." Respectfully, I bent at the hips toward the obelisk. "So, I'm not allowed to kill them or ask them to kill themselves?" I asked and checked again, in case the Fates demanded it. I was not about to follow a voice blindly if they expected me to murder humans as if it were for a sport or entertainment.

"None of that. That is precisely the reason you have been chosen for this task. Use your gifts to do good—while enjoying their blood and bodies."

I frowned. "But that's what I've been doing," I hissed and opened my mouth like an idiot to the obelisk—shaming myself for the disrespect—my long incisors slipped out, just thinking about feeding. I was ravenous.

"Just like your ancestors sucked the Loursveto's stem for its juice, you will too one day. Never reveal your true nature except to the ones who are like you."

"Ones like me? Will I meet Anunnaki in this place called—what again?" This was turning out to be exciting. "I will gladly go if there is more of my kind."

"Grayrak. And yes, your kind will soon arrive. But your mission is to contain the darkness that lurks there. It's an old enemy of humans. It's a thing that hides inside the darkness. Like you saw hiding inside your father. It feeds off the malevolence, and it is multiplying. It is as old as time itself," they said.

I toed my boots against the foot of the obelisk and wondered what lay beneath me, while the weight of the world rested on my shoulders.

"So, like Anzulla or Babylon? Are you saying another Apsu awaits me? Am I to build another army?" I asked, already dreading it. I hated this darkness, this insidious force. *It wasn't defeated yet.*

"No, you don't need an army, as long as you stay with Lasitor on your time machine. It is yours. I will guide you. You have that time-keeping device around your neck. It's the key between here and there, and only you should use it. You don't need an army as long as you don't show your Anunnaki side to these humans and until you see the ball-shaped ship."

I blinked wordlessly, shaking my head.

"Until then, you will have time to learn the modern human ways. Keep a watchful eye out for the round floating ship. It will look almost like yours, but not a gold machine. It can change colors. Make yourself known to the occupants and stay on that path at the same time."

"Can change colors? What humans are these? Are they like chameleons? Where is this Grayrak? What do you mean by modern humans?" I asked and got only chuckles for answers.

"Don't laugh at me," I said, upset and belittled.

"No, no chameleons," they said, still sounding amused. "You will understand when you see the ship. It's made of something like glass, but not glass. Like the window on your machine. I can't explain it better than that. But, I warn you. Messing with the time-line means losing your home, me, and Anzulla forever. Destroying everything. Do you understand?"

"No, not a word." I threw my hands into the air, frustrated.

"You will, once you go. And no, you can't go back to Babylon if you've contemplated that. Go to Grayrak. It's on the moon."

"On the moon? In the future? How did the humans manage that?" I checked the tick-tick thing. Nothing made sense. Maybe this wasn't Anzulla. I searched the skies but couldn't see through the dark clouds surrounding me.

"When the humans arrive, you will understand. Remember the name Barkor. Search for him and watch the little one. He is special, like you. Protect him. Learn from the humans, and help them, but don't interfere or change anything. Not until your kin arrive. The less you help, the better, because you risk changing things in the future. Your machine is pre-programmed. It's just over twenty-five thousand years into the future."

"Holy scarabs! I was just with Platonius, counting the sun and moon cycles. How did they get to that number on the calendar?"

"You brought Platonius the gift of tracing time with the course of the sun. That was all because of you. By teaching him the lunar and solar cycles, time tracking remained precise. Your formula has been written and passed down through generations. Your father's destruction, the time of his reckoning, was what split his history into pieces. The discovery of the gardens your sisters created and the explosion of knowledge have led humans down some interesting paths. Paths you will find for yourself. You will soon see. It is all thanks to you." The voice cut in and out as the howling wind picked up speed. I was trying my best to see a face somewhere in the direction the voice came from. The cadence was familiar.

"Do I know you? I think I've heard your voice before," I said to what I thought were the Fates as I inspected the obelisk up close, deep in contemplation and trying to jog a memory by walking around it. In Babylon, it was so tall that I never could truly look at it from above.

I waited. No response.

I was worried they were getting annoyed because I asked too many questions. Maybe I should stop before they left me. I felt cold and hollow. Empty, like I was a bubble inside. I knew the feeling well enough. Time felt frozen as if everything had come to a standstill in this place. I shivered. Those who died here haunted the land.

"Are you going to leave me in this desolate place?" I cupped my hands and shouted into the wind, hoping the voice hadn't already up and disappeared. As if on cue, the wind picked up. Billowing clouds of dust obscured my ship from view. I feared getting lost and not being able to find it. I should return to my ship, I thought and turned to head back.

I could swear I heard the voice on the wind say, "Anzulla is not dead," but I could have imagined it as screeching winds surrounded me.

Gasping for clean, breathable air, I stumbled towards the open door of my ship. Dread surged through me as I realized I had forgotten to close it before venturing out into the sandy terrain. I dragged myself inside and with shaky hands, I slammed the button and flipped the lever to shut the door behind me, grateful for the safety of my machine.

Sputtering out chunks of dirt and grit from my mouth, I blew my nose and quickly stripped off my clothes, socks, and boots. It tickled like sand fleas, I itched, squirmed, brushed, and scrubbed myself violently. The stubborn cursed grains seemed to have infiltrated even the tiniest crevices of my body, they clung to every pore, every hair down to my ballsack.

"Lasitor, take me to Grayrak. Twenty-five thousand years into the future," I said and hoped to find water to clean my butt crack once I arrived there. "Let's go find some answers!"

# CHAPTER 47

# GRAYRAK TO PARADISE

*"Good day, Ishtar.*

*I have no clue what time it is.*

*Did you know cryovolcanoes, also called ice volcanoes, may potentially form on icy moons and other planets? Just think of all that potential life pumping into space. Where there is water, there is life.*

*Unfortunately, I don't know what kind of life these humans are living, or if they know what they are doing here on the moon. Ice-spewing volcanoes or geysers are not something they will see soon. Nor would you see any water.*

*There is also no breakfast today.*

*Happy hunting, have a good day!"*


**Ishtar**
**2046 A.D.**
**Grayrak**
**Earth's Moon**

As usual, on one of my worst days, I found myself intoxicated as fuck. I was not walking on sunshine. Also, not in a straight line.

"Ishtar, go home! For fuck's sake, you are drunk again." Barkor pushed me out of his tin can house and shut the door in my face. "Go home, sleep it off, and come back when you are sober."

I turned on my heels, lifting my weighted moon boots high as I marched back to my hovel. "If that ball of shit—I mean, ship—doesn't arrive soon, I'm going to fuck shit up!" I muttered to myself. I wasn't tired, I was restless. So I climbed on the roof of my time machine and crossed my legs and arms. The mixture of human blood and nasty drugs had intoxicated me.

I had slain my father, freeing my people, and now witnessed a forsaken human settlement on the fucking moon of all places. A testament to the twisted beliefs of a cult group called the Disciples of the Anunnaki. I felt exiled and condemned by my actions or perhaps cursed by the sins of my father. My soul felt like it was rotting and I was certain that the Fates had sent me here as punishment. My only purpose was to watch over Barkor, but even that felt like torture. I felt trapped in Grayrak, a level just below the final level of Sheol, a nasty place where there's only clay to eat and bad water to drink.

Decades of years ago, maybe more—I can't say because again, we are on the fucking moon, and the moon has two seasons. Winter and summer. No harvest and no fucking floods. It's tidally locked with the blue planet. Sharing one sun. On the moon, one day is about six hundred and fifty hours long. Half of that is day and the other half is night. The side facing the Earth is warmer, and the light is much brighter. On the opposite side, it is darker, but I can still see shades of colors in the grayness.

I became desperate and unable to endure another second here—I had inadvertently, unintentionally, and with pure innocence, stumbled upon a world where the air was filled with the scent of blooming flowers and the forests blushed with vibrant colors. Clean air, gentle breezes, and cheerful faces filled this city carved out of a mountain. It was heaven, a sanctuary from the horror-filled Grayrak, where the stench of unwashed humans polluted the air like the fourth Egyptian plague.

Since my return from this newly discovered place, with its jungle and its primitive people, memories and visions of a mysterious face haunt me day and night. These memories are disjointed and confusing, leaving me uncertain if they are from my past or glimpses of my future. My obsessive search for the man with the mind-numbingly beautiful face had both freed me and replaced my addiction to drug-tainted blood.

I must find the man this face belongs to.

Grayrak City needs a savior, but so do I.

For decades, my body knew where to go, even though my mind was still catching up. I wandered down dimly lit alleyways and steel-boxed houses in Grayrak, searching for a fix—for tainted blood—for humans smelling rancid with neediness mingled with the stench of misery. The most desperate for death. I would drag them into the shadows, strike their necks, and drink the bitter liquid from their veins. A sense of relief would wash over me, but it never lasted long. The hunger and longing for that euphoric high was a never-ending cycle, a vicious circle that could only be broken by leaving this place. I was lost among these humans, their despair became my own, and yet, their pain only added to my twisted desires. Despite all my power and strength, I couldn't wipe away the overwhelming sadness, desperation, and loneliness that plagued them on this desolate moon.

But lately, something new and out of the norm has happened to me. I'm in pursuit of the man whose angelic face haunts my every thought. I can't shake off these visions and dreams of him. Water and lush forests always accompany it. I am charmed by a new obsession, trapped by a persistent yearning that refuses to release me. I know deep down that I am chasing a mere vision of a man, and now I cannot think of anything else but finding him.

"Ugh," I sighed. "What a fucking shit show!" I spat my words with hands on my knees, back straight, closing my eyes for a brief second. I enjoyed the high. I hid my time machine behind a wall of building rubble in the southeast corner of Grayrak City, so it appeared from the front to be a small hill of gigantic boulders.

My hideout was a solitary haven, tucked away from the bustling human and Zelk commotion where I've observed them scurrying around like ants, constructing a towering structure that glinted silver in the sunlight. The sight always filled me with a strange mix of fascination and disgust. Sometimes, when I was feeling particularly hungry or restless, I would lend a helping hand. After all, the Fates had instructed me not to interfere with their affairs. But as time went on, my heart grew heavier and my conscience was weighed down by the suffering I witnessed daily.

Just as I reached my breaking point, before I drowned myself in mind-numbing chemicals—the urge to smash every blue silicone brick and scream at these delusional humans—a moment of pure rage and despair, pushed me to flee. By accident, I found an oasis for my soul, a sanctuary for my weary spirit.

I arrived there, thinking I'd jumped back in time to find Babylon, desperately seeking refuge from tainted blood. But instead, I found a jungle with positively happy, but primitive people who knew nothing of this advanced chaotic world on the moon.

I've been there a few times. And I want to go again.

Grayrak is a burden that threatens to swallow me whole. I want to run back to that place where I suspect, for some weird, inexplicable reason, the stranger's face awaits me. This place offered me an escape from the constant reminders of human greed and destruction.

With every breath I take, this polluted air of Grayrak suffocates me. The stench inside their massive glass rotunda is a putrid combination of sweat, farts, hopelessness, and narcissism. As I sit here, forced to witness the depths of human depravity, I can't help but feel anger boiling within me. How low can these humans go? They are nothing but selfish beings, willing to do anything for eternal life, even if it means oppressing and destroying their kind. I feel trapped here, a helpless spectator to their self-inflicted torture and destruction. Every day, from the moment my eyes open until I am overtaken by exhaustion, I am subjected to the entertainment of watching these humans destroy themselves in pursuit of immortality. It sickens me to my core.

It's like watching one dung beetle pushing another dung beetle's dung all day. The struggles these men, women, and children endure just to stay alive are mind-numbing and tedious. I can't comprehend why they don't just throw themselves onto the nearest ship and flee back to Earth. Every day I ask rhetorically, only to arrive at the same bloody conclusion, "Because we are dumb as fuck dung beetles."

I stewed in my failure as I slowly killed myself with tainted human blood. The Disciples had a sickening formula that promised happiness and eradicated all cravings for sustenance. The drug gave them the strength and endurance of ten men. They toiled for hours without pause, fueled by this vile concoction.

Meanwhile, the face in my dreams carried huge significance. Sometimes he smiled, other times I saw him looking down at me with love in his piercing blue eyes. The best times were when those eyes looked up at me while he was on his knees, pleasuring me.

I sat up straight, sucking air deep into my lungs, then closed my eyes. "Fuck, the vision I see behind my closed eyelids makes me instantly hard," I whispered as I blew out a long breath.

The deep blue of his eyes glinted like shards of glass, always drawing me in to look closer. When he narrowed his eyes with their hint of anger towards me, a strange, amused feeling tickled my insides. But when they held an intense gaze filled with love, I shivered. The silver specks and shifting shades of blue reminded me of sunlight dancing on undisturbed water, while a tumultuous storm of want and need for him rose up within me. His beauty was painfully sharp and pure, radiating like the sun's scorching rays. I knew just looking at him in real life would be blinding, like staring directly into the heart of the sun. His hair was a rare white, like clouds painted against a pale blue desert sky. Touching and smelling him would make me forget where I was and who I was supposed to be.

And his hands—they were tender yet strong, reaching for me with a magnetic pull I couldn't resist. Though I didn't know him, I felt a nudge, a connection to him, as if we were meant to meet and he was the missing piece of my soul.

I wanted him. I was consumed by the burning desire to escape and find my elusive mystery man. It drove me to madness. He called out to me, beckoning me to find him before it was too late. Too late for what?

I was torn in so many directions. The Fates, the humans, my need for tainted blood, Barkor, the round translucent ship, the jungle, and my unnamed man in my memories.

"Scarabs!" How many variations of feeling like shit are there? According to my calculations, about one thousand two hundred and eighty-two. I've spent over seventy years twiddling my thumbs, counting, and waiting for a spherical spaceship that changes colors like a chameleon.

I was slowly losing my shit. Nope, wait, I guess it's my poop. Maybe the Fates were just pulling my leg this whole time. Sitting back with a cup of wine, watching me make a fool of myself. Talk about leaving a load on your doorstep. "What a steaming pile of dung! Day after day, I sit here and watch Grizzly strut around like he owns the place." I slurred my words, gesturing wildly towards the Disciple compound. "Now those guys are full of bull plop." I squinted one eye to make sure I was pointing in the right direction.

"They couldn't give a crusty crab's ass about anyone else. Happy as pigs in mud, oops." I toppled over and smacked my face on the roof with a dull thud. I shook my head like a wounded warhorse to clear my vision.

"I'm going!" With a well-practiced move, I flung my legs over the side, gripping the doorframe to swing myself inside my time machine.

"I need to get out of here," I whined. "Same crap, different day. Or every other day, who knows?" I grumbled and tumbled into my seat. "Lasitor," I called and checked my tick-tick thing.

"Yes, Ishtar," he answered, sounding pissed off as usual.

"Take me to the waters. Take me to my lover."

"Which lover would that be?" he said with sarcasm in his tone.

He didn't approve of my impulsiveness. Ever since we'd time jumped into the past and stumbled upon the jungle, my visions had come to me.

"Lasitor, I'm going there. It has become an escape to maintain a sense of sanity as much as for finding the man from my dreams."

"If you say so, but I wouldn't recommend growing attached."

"Even though Gugusan doesn't exactly resemble him, he still plays a vital role in satisfying my primal sexual urges and filling my stomach with healthy blood. Something you won't know anything about. You don't feel pleasure and you don't get hungry. So we are going there, no matter how you see it," I said curtly. I was the captain. Having visited this time and place before, I knew my navigator had identified the exact coordinates. I strapped myself into my seat.

"Lasitor, initiate that pre-programmed sequence."

"Are you sure, don't you think…"

"Of course I'm sure. Waiting for that chameleon ball ship to arrive is maddening. Take me to where I can breathe and think," I said and hoped this time I would meet the man with the beautiful face. If not, at least Gugusan and his people would welcome me. "Barkor seems to have it all under control. He doesn't need me. His flock needs a miracle and I'm not able to give it to them. The scientists are busy creating something, I assume, that will kill all of us. The Disciples think the Anunnaki is going to bring water to the moon. But the only Anunnaki I know that might do that, are now dead."

My sisters could connect with nature and the life-giving elements to make plants grow. They didn't create the mystical pool guarded by Xerxes and his ancestors. Only Anunnaki healed as fast as I. So that water wasn't as miraculous as the humans made it out to be. The garden was already there and the tree next to the pool was thousands of years old. Its roots created a natural enclosure around the unending hot bubbling pond. So no pool or water for the Grayrakians, even if I went back in time to ask them. All I could do was haul water with me from this paradise.

"These scientists who called themselves Disciples are sneaky and power-hungry. I'm sure they are the source of all the darkness that lurks in this place," Lasitor said.

"I know. The only good thing here is Barkor," I replied.

Only a few days after my arrival, a sudden crash and explosion had rocked the quiet silence. A ship from Earth had plummeted to the surface, right at the entrance. The impact ripped its metal hull into pieces. I hurriedly made my way towards the wreckage, determined to help anyone in need. Amidst the chaos, a young mother went into labor. I rushed to her side and was uncertain about what to do. Give me a sword and drop me in the middle of a battlefield—that day I had never been so scared in my life.

With trembling hands and a pounding heart—I helped deliver her baby. She had succumbed to her wounds. He was a loud little thing with blue skin and purplish undertones. I knew that in my hands was the precious baby, the child the Fates had foretold back on Anzulla. Despite the surrounding chaos, I recognized his cries were different. I was present at all my nieces' and nephews' births, and that gave me the experience to differentiate between human and Anunnaki babies. Anunnaki babies communicate by conveying emotions through mind-to-mind connections with their caregivers. Baby Barkor was extremely confused about where he was. He was upset because he wanted to go back to the heat and silence. His eyes and tummy hurt and the light was blinding him. I vowed to protect him at all costs. He wasn't a large and strong newborn, he needed love, warmth, and nourishment.

In haste, I wrapped him securely, carried him away from the wreckage, and began my search for food and a loving mother to care for him. Barkor was the most beautiful baby. His thick, black curls and mesmerizing blue eyes with elongated pupils resembling that of a cat, ensured I couldn't help but fall in love and feel in awe of this precious baby suddenly placed in my care.

I concealed my true identity and appearance from him and everyone else. For over seventy years, I have been his caretaker. Since I saved and named him, he had been my secret child. Through mind control, I ensured he had a mother figure. I'd manipulated women into believing he was their son, that he was precious, a prince who would save them one day. I'd aided him in dealing with his problems by paving the way for him and his companions. He was the only family I had, and although his lineage was unknown, we shared similar abilities. He was aware of his heightened strength, speed, and intelligence compared to regular humans. Like me, he aged slower, and thankfully, he didn't flaunt his powers. I was grateful for that, as it made my job easier and reduced my worries as I discreetly assisted him from the shadows.

My head throbbed, reminding me to hurry up. "Let's go!" I pressed the shiny start button with one hand and pushed the lever full throttle with the other. I doubled over, hitting my head on the panel.

Lasitor "wha-wha-wha'd" something in the background while ping-ping alarms screeched. The machine thrust forward, pushing me back and upright into a sitting position.

"Shit!" I slurred as streaks of lights flashed by the window, blinding me. My vision blurred as my eyelids grew heavier. My head lolled to the side. Potent fucking blood, I thought, and I passed out stoned and drunk.


**25 000 B.C.**

**The jungle**

A crescendo of wildlife woke me. Frogs croaked, and wild animals yipped, roared, and howled. One by one, I cracked my eyes open as fresh air filled my lungs.

"Oh, thank fuck," I moaned. All my blood had pooled in my head and was sloshing between my ears.

"Lasitor?" I moaned again, not knowing when or where I was. I blinked to refocus my blurry vision and sniffed the air through a stuffy nose. The smell of wet earth greeted me. I was upside down. Grass and twigs stuck up into my nose and mouth. Bugs irked me and gave me the shivers. I spat, shaking my head, and failed at wiping my face, because my arms were numb and lying like tree stumps underneath me. Useless.

It seems I had face-planted in the mud. I whimpered uncomfortably, feeling sorry for myself. My body lay twisted. I tried rolling over, but my legs were stuck and tangled in my safety straps. Oh, and I still had those moon-walking weights tied to my boots.

"Lasitor!" I moaned. "Lasitor, answer me!" He ignored me. "Fuck you too, very much."

Silence.

Chatter from bird songs told me I was not on the moon and the sun was rising.

"Thank the Fates." I scoped out my surroundings.

"Good job! Lasitor, you parked the ship in that clearing. The jungle," I said, feeling thankful and relieved.

The skies were dimly lit as dawn arrived and the sun ascended in the east. I pushed myself over with my useless arms, then flexed and stretched them to encourage blood flow until they regained life.

Something rustled and moved in the grass beside me—feet with sandals. My heart leaped. I'd made it.

"Lasitor, don't worry about answering me," I said and pushed myself to my hands and knees.

"The village people have arrived!"

"Da!" a male voice warned me as he shoved a spear toward my forehead. I heeded the warning, throwing my hands in the air.

*Where was I?* I looked up, searching, but I couldn't see the moon. Then, my gaze fell on yellow-skinned men and women with long green plumes of feathers on their heads. I smiled, elated, as I recognized them. Streaks of light and shadows bathed my welcoming committee. *Gugusan's people.*

"Whaoo!" one shouted and jumped back as soon as he saw my face. Suddenly, more spears were pointed in my direction, followed by a long moment of silence as they stared at me. Something crawled on my upper lip. It tickled, but I held still, imagining the size of the thing. Having a salt pillar freak out, I asked with my eyes for permission, then lifted my shoulder, trying to wipe whatever it was from my face before it crawled up my nose.

My audience laughed. This was a friendly bunch.

One pointed with her spear, telling another something in their exotic language that sounded familiar. I was getting used to it and words were becoming easier to recognize and translate.

I wondered if they recognized me. I planned to play along, hoping to find that vision, that man with the white hair and bluest eyes.

A man stepped forward, and I expected a hit or slap, but no, he pulled the thing from my lip and held it up showing me and his friends a fucking baby centipede! A red one! I shivered and wiped furiously at my face. Then I remembered I was supposed to hold still.

Luckily, no one reacted, and I didn't lose an eye. My savior threw it to the side. I tipped my head to show my appreciation. I counted ten young males. They seemed cautious, but I felt no aggressiveness or animosity toward me. This was a new bunch for me.

"Maymantataq hamurqan?" a big, intimidating man asked as he broke through the surrounding circle of men. The group parted, making space for him. It was the familiar voice of their leader, Gugusan.

"Hello," I said and smiled at him. He wore enormous blue and red plumes of feathers around his head. His torso was magnificently muscled. My gaze roamed downward. My breath hitched as my cock went instantly hard, imagining loosening that piece of leather scantly covering his manhood. The cup covering it was decorated with green jewels, while more matching straps were wrapped around his upper arms and calves, holding his sandals in place. Like the others, his hair was sleek black, but how he carried himself made him stand out as the leader.

"Rikuspa, hanaq pachapi mayumanta hamurqan?" he asked, pointing to the sky.

I looked up to where he pointed at the disappearing Milky Way—another word I picked up from the humans on the moon. I knew it as the sprayed blood of the dragon. The humans in my homeland believed my family had something to do with the death of the dragon. My father used to say, "Let them think what they prefer, it keeps us exalted."

Gugusan's eyes widened. His body was rigid with irritation. Without hesitation, he unsheathed his short sword. The black blade glinted as he pointed up to the stars, I assumed asking where I came from. So I pointed to the sky. Knowing shit like that usually counted in my favor.

They jumped back in awe. Shaking their heads furiously, pointing up and to something off in the distance. Gugusan narrowed his eyes at me, not looking at them or their antics like he wasn't in the mood for sky people today. His jaw clenched. Then he stepped forward and took hold of one of my braided locks. He rolled it from side to side. Then he inspected my hooped earrings. He stooped, turning his head, and put his ear against the tick-tick hanging around my neck. He stepped back, sighing. His cheek hollowed and one corner of his mouth pulled down—as if chewing on it. Slowly his eyes roamed up until they met my gaze. He looked a few years younger. This visit was closer to one of my first visits. Maybe, after I'd decided to stop wiping myself from their memories. His eyes were a dull yellow-green. He had no facial hair, and his full lips were rounded and pierced with what looked like ivory hoops. His handsome face was squared by a strong jaw. I hoped he wanted to fuck me today. I was looking forward to filling my stomach with his bright red, thick, and sweet-tasting blood. It was rich in nutrients. The clean jungle air he inhaled prickled on my tongue like bubbles popping up from fresh mountain spring water. It was purifying me from inside out.

Although he wasn't the man of my dreams, I had urges and by now I knew he wanted me. Virility oozed out of every pore of his body. He smelled enticing, like male sweat, coconut, and smoke. If I hadn't drunk his untainted blood the previous times, I think I would have been dead by now.

He stepped back and waved his hands thumbs up. I caught the meaning—get the fuck up, you're embarrassing yourself. His men muttered among themselves. "Hmmm," I agreed, then untangled my feet and removed the heavy weights. My vertebrae cracked as I got up and straightened my back. A round of oohs and ahs followed. I looked down at them. Gugusan, almost a foot taller than the others, was looking up at me, and I caught that familiar glimpse of lust in his eyes. He shook his head. I probed for thoughts —my stature awed him, and he was telling himself he didn't want me. That he shouldn't want me.

He inspected my boots and touched my shirt and pants. "Maymantataq hamurqan. Rikuspa, hanaq pachapi mayumanta hamurqan," he said to his men as he pointed to my ship and back to me. I was too slow at catching his meaning. But as soon as his soldiers fell to their knees, I got it loud and clear.

"Ah fuck me!" I threw my hands in the air—not in the mood for this again. "Get up. I am not to be worshipped!"

"Gg fuck," one man said with that distinct local grating throaty "gg," as if clearing his throat. Not this again. I gave them the universal signal to get the fuck up. No praying to me.

"Gg fuck," they repeated.

I said, "Yes, get up, you idiots," while chuckling ridiculously. My head throbbed, and I felt thirsty. I needed food and a bath, not worship.

My general landing location was the same as all my previous visits, but small things were different. It seemed this time they were keeping secrets from me. The men gathered in small groups talking amongst themselves, not within earshot.

"Paymi churi dios. Yanapananchikmi, mana chayqa mana allin suertetam apamuwasun," Gugusan said and moved to look at my time machine.

"No, my friend, you don't want to climb in there without me," I said, using a mix of my mother tongue and their language. I connected telepathically to them, searching for that language compulsion, and found none, so I planted the seed of the Anunnaki language inside them. Now it made sense why we already understood each other the first time I landed here. My first few visits were on days after today.

He halted on the third step and peeked inside, then looked back at me, blinking a few times. It looked like he was searching for something or someone, but only saw the blinking lights on the dashboard of my weird time-keeping contraption inside the cockpit.

"Da Gg fuck?" he said questioningly, waving in a circle to the sky and then again off in the distance and the mountain tops. A universal, *welcome sky traveler, let's go to our village and have a talk... and some bum-bum-bum time.*

I nodded a thank you and held my hands up in a respectful prayer position. I motioned at the door, showing him I wanted to shut it. He gave me permission with a firm nod and a "Da!"

I pulled the small automatic stair lever up and waited for the stairs to contract into the side as the door closed. "That's it!" I said happily optimistic, while dusting my hands —signaling the job was done. Chop-chop let's go.

He eyebrow-whipped me, and I whipped him back with a sexy, brooding look. He grunted something, but it did not intimidate me at all. It just made him look more appealing. Then we turned as one. I smiled and bowed my head to the others, showing my appreciation.

"Let's go." I pointed.

They lifted their spears, pointing the way.

"Okay," I said as I caught their meaning. Follow the sexy brute, and we will watch your backside as you follow him.

"Da Gg fuck," they said.

Early the next morning, I made my trek back up the mountain to return to Grayrak. My ship was restocked with food and water. I was sober, sexually satisfied, and no closer to finding my mate.

# CHAPTER 48

# THE GOLDEN APPLE

*"Good day, Ishtar.*

*I promise you, the sun is shining, and it is daylight somewhere.*

*While on the subject—did you know there is a famous love story about the Sun and the Moon falling in love and traveling around the world together? But the Moon betrayed the Sun and copulated with the Morning Star. The punishment for its betrayal was banishment. The Sun never wanted to see the Moon—ever again. So from then on the solitary Moon had to travel by night, while the Sun traveled by day all alone. The moral of the story is whether you are a Sun or a Moon, there will always be a Morning Star to keep you company.*

*Even if there is no breakfast being served.*

*Good luck and may your day be filled with splendor and wonder!"*

**Ishtar**

**24 970 B.C.**

**The jungle**

My ship touched down in paradise thirty years after my last visit. I had an unselfish reason to escape Grayrak while searching for the man in my visions. A whole lot of shit was happening, and I was restless, rancid, and ravenous when the water supply I smuggled to Grayrak finally ran out. I had averted drinking tainted blood in Grayrak. Weeks passed and now I was drooling for my reward and eager to find out if I was closer to finding the man with the white hair.

Gugusan was older, stronger, and wiser. Desire filled my cock as I followed Gugusan through the dense undergrowth. His movements were graceful, swaying his hips and showing off the pretty feathers adorning them. The low-hanging leather belt tied around his waist, and the single leather string running from it, down his crack, and I assumed was securing the cup covering his front side, accentuated each globe of his buttocks with each step he took. The belt was adorned with intricate patterns in vibrant shades of green, blue, and red, with tiny jewels sparkling in the light. I couldn't help but admire the colorful feathers that I suspected belonged to native birds, hoping to glimpse them during my visit. Gugusan moved through the bushes with ease, as if he knew every twist, turn, low-hanging branch, and obstacle. It was clear that he was born and raised here, now showing genuine leadership by walking alongside his people.

Daybreak illuminated the vibrant colors along the path ahead, revealing a well-worn trail winding through the lush forest. The birds' chatter welcomed the new day, urging me to stay in the shade of the treeline as the sun climbed higher in the sky. Somehow, I had to get out of the sun before I burned to death. Like my father, my dark skin, not black but a deep Anunnaki blue, helped protect me against the sun's deadly rays. The rest of my family were pale-skinned with a powder blue complexion. I appreciated the surrounding air, which was thick with mist that cooled my skin by evaporation. My companions behind me chatted away, their voices almost masking the sound of rushing water nearby. We had only descended a short distance when we came upon a small stream cutting through tall grass and shrubs. As someone who had spent decades living on the barren moon, I reveled in the beauty and vitality of nature around me.

However, I couldn't pinpoint exactly what year it was. My manipulative electronic companion and guide refused to tell me. I had hoped he joked when he said that if he told me, he would have to kill me. So instead, I outsmarted him by deliberately turning back the knob dangerously far into the past. Lasitor quickly intervened, confirming we were between twenty to thirty thousand years in the past, according to his saved coordinates.

Since I found this place, a sense of rightness has settled over me, as if my timelines were finally aligned just right. I knew the man of my dreams was in this place. I could feel it. In the meantime, the man walking before me exuded power and masculinity as his muscles rippled under his yellow-bronzed skin, stirring a powerful attraction towards him. I wanted to sink my teeth into his neck or that juicy behind. My mouth watered just thinking about tasting him again. He was the type of man who liked to be in control, and if that was what it took to seduce him, I would submit my big eight-foot frame and take anything this barbaric man wanted to do to me.

Even though I was seeking sexual solace in Gugusan, my heart was with my blue-eyed mate and I would have to ask Gugusan about him. As we walked together, I probed their minds. These people were unbelievably happy and connected to the magic of the forest. I could hear the men behind me murmuring amongst themselves—no doubt discussing me. Unfortunately, they are convinced I'm some kind of demon god from the sky, which is not wrong.

Gugusan halted and turned to face me near a rock formation with an arch high enough to let me walk straight through. "Taak in we'esik ti' teech ba'al," he said and waved me inside.

This was new.

Stooping my neck, I entered, instantly captivated by the mystical aura around me. I blinked to refocus my eyes to get used to the darkness. Gugusan stepped deeper into the big cavern, calling me closer to a rock pillar with four sides. It had a wide base that narrowed upward, just like the obelisks. It was my height and, on the crown, rested something that glinted in their torchlights. *Gold?* That distinct vibration of the yellow metal hummed—it called to me.

I stepped closer, not touching. "I've seen this before." *Could this be?* "I think I know what this is."

In awe, I leaned in closer for a better view to confirm my suspicion, "Dear moon-god, it is." I stood open-mouthed in disbelief. It was the golden apple. The apple Ki and An had shown me before I left to go collect the tablet from Platonius. They'd said I had given it to them and asked that they hide it from Apsu and bury it for me. But that's thousands of years into the future. Isn't it?

*Shhhhhht-gggggggt,* fine electrical crackles came from the ugly small replica of an obelisk, reminding me of my visit to Anzulla when the Fates had spoken to me. I stopped and tilted my head listening. The shuffling of feet and the warriors' whispering were the only sounds.

*It must be my imagination.*

Seconds passed and then the voice spoke, "This is a gift of knowledge, *shhhhhht-gggggggt.*"

The words faded in and out. It was the same deep melodic male voice as the one on Anzulla. I swung around in a circle. Searching, but saw no one fucking with me. My brows met as I made a what-the-fuck face at Gugusan. He smiled and gave me a go-on-talk-to-it look.

I tipped my head back and spoke into the darkness. "Say that again!"

With my hands on my hips, I waited for an explanation from the Fates. Gugusan straightened his shoulders as if he was happy with me speaking to a rock. It wasn't ornate. Just a simple marble rock pilar. No gold and nothing shiny.

"Who are you? Are you the Fates? I asked, puzzled. *There was something seriously strange going on here.*"

*Shhhhhht.*

"It's yours. Take it home," the voice crackled and the distortion accompanying it disappeared.

Gugusan pointed to me, then his heart. "Da Kuku, úuchben máako' utia'al ooks tak ka a taal in bisik tin wotoch." He was pointing everywhere. I followed and mimicked his movements. "Da?" he asked.

"Home? My home?" I asked the Fates while deciphering what Gugusan was trying to convey and shaking my head in answer.

"I'm talking to the Fates, hold on," I whispered, waving my finger in front of my mouth. "Hello, Holy One. I am your servant. Speak freely to me."

Gugusan and I stared at each other, waiting. Nothing happened. No one answered. The warriors looked wide-eyed at me with expectation. Like I have some magical power to make a rock talk to me. This was not an Annunaki obelisk. Not even a small one. Someone carved the marble to make it look like one.

"What the fuck is this all about?" I asked Gugusan.

He lifted his hands, waved, touched his ear, and waved again with one hand. "Yeah, the Fates sound like they are taking their time today," I said. If I want the Fates to keep talking to me, to keep guiding me, I have to trust their direction. I know better than to ignore the command and not take the apple home. My father lost himself and his mind when the Fates stopped speaking to him.

Gugusan cupped my jaw to get my full attention.

"Da, Kuku, Eee-li-shaas," he whispered with softness in his expression and kindness in his tone. He understood my frustration. For some reason, it comforted me.

I huffed out loud. "Ha, what the fuck do you mean with Eee-li-shaas?" Gugusan blinked rapidly at me and scoffed. "Maybe Ela-ish-az or Eli Ishtar's?" I asked. His scrunched-up facial expression told me I could do better than that. I didn't know what to make of this so I probed his mind. *Kuku, come here. To the mountain. Kuku and his pet Eee-li-shaas.*

Now, it was my turn to be scrunching my face.

He chuckled. "Da, Eee-li-shaas. Da, Kuku," I repeated, and he looked happy enough at my conclusion. "Who are Kuku and this Eee-li-shaas?" I asked, lifting my hands in question.

He walked over to another story carved into the limestone and pointed. The other men and women accompanying us murmured and left us alone. They were shaking their heads at me and couldn't get out of this cave fast enough. Almost like they didn't want to hear this story again. I chuckled and turned my attention back to Gugusan.

It was an impressive story about a snake and a flying dragon on a journey with a figure with two identical heads and holding a sword in each hand. They were led by a warrior that leaped into the air, spear in hand, opposing two figures. One looked like a human with the wings of a bird, while the other figure was hanging onto his ankles, catching a ride over two rivers, while his long serpent tongue licked the sky, wrapping around the sun and the moon. I wondered if the sun and moon anchored him or if they were attempting to pull them down from the sky. All of the figures had humongous penises.

Gugusan then pointed at a bird and an egg and pointed back at me. "Dear god, am I the bird?" I asked while flapping my arms like a bird.

He pointed furiously at the egg. Then I realized. I was the egg. "Oh, I came here on my ship, with the bird?

"Da!"—he pointed up and then clapped his hands. He pointed to me again—

"Ishtar" —then pointed to the roof of the cave— "Kuku" —and held his pointer and middle fingers up and pushed them together.

Astonishment transformed into a sense of delightful wonder as a surge of joy filled my chest, radiating throughout my entire body, curling my toes inside my boots.

Laughter exploded out of me. "Together?" My voice echoed down the tunnels deeper into the cave. I palmed my chest. "Finally, my Kuku and me." I laughed, pointing to the rock stick figures between me and the apple. "Me, I am Ishtar. And my beloved, he is Kuku, and we are together?" I patted my chest and pointed to the bird proudly.

"Da-da-da-da-da." He nodded happily.

I extended my arm towards the stick figures. They symbolized the bond between me and my beloved Kuku. My fingers tracing them tingled as if the energy of our connection was flowing through me. "Then who are these then?" I pointed to the rest of the story.

He sighed. He took his sword, cutting the air. Pretending to fight, he tapped each figure on the head and then lastly the egg.

"I brought them here and there was a fight?"

"Da! Eee-li-shaas." He pointed to his back with his thumbs.

"Ah, a long time ago?"

"Da!" Da, Ko'oten paakat tséela' teech ka mostraré," he said, pointing to more hieroglyphs. I recognized them instantly. They were Babylonian script.

Then on the side, I saw something strange. There were seven downward strokes crossed out with one diagonal line as if someone was counting weeks, then months, and then years. Like I taught my friend Platonius. I counted them. This person counted over one thousand five hundred and sixty weeks. "That is…thirty years?"

"Da!"

"Thirty?" As I counted, I caught the English language carved out in the limestone.

"Oh my moon-god, there was a human here. It must be my Kuku! He left me this message?" I ran my fingers over it.

*Waiting for you, my Ish.*

Less from shock, and more from weakness and dehydration—my legs collapsed. I stumbled backward, tripping over something on the cave floor. My eyes darted around as my ass found a flat surface carved into a seat. Gugusan snorted and rubbed the back of his neck.

"Yeah, I know, I'm clumsy. I haven't slept or eaten for weeks." I let out a sigh and cradled my dizzy head in the palms of my hands. I closed my eyes for a second to compose myself. *How many times have I jumped here not knowing about this cave?* As I opened my eyes, my gaze fell on a small straw bed. "What's this? Who slept here?" I asked as loud squawking and screeches of birds in red and blue colors drew my attention deeper into the cave. Light streamed in from above in the distance. *Hmmm, so there's another opening.* The birds were the same colors as the plumes on the men's head and body coverings. Gugusan sighed heavily and sat down next to me. He extended his arm and the palm of his hand as he held up some kind of nut. One of the magnificent birds flew closer and found purchase on his arm, took the nut, and cracked it open. It said something. It was talking.

"This is his bed, isn't it? He waited here. For me. Where is he, where is my Kuku?" I begged.

Gugusan lifted his other arm as well and flapped his hand like a bird.

"What the fuck man, did he fly away?"

"Da, Eee-li-shaas," he said, flapping his arm again. Suddenly, the bird sitting on his arm took off flying. Gugusan waved both his arms.

He was talking about the damn bird. Not my mate.

My stomach clenched tightly. I folded double, as my hunger pains forced me to take notice. *I'm tired and hungry.* Gugusan kept talking, he pointed to the apple in my hand. To the bed and then flapped his arms again.

"Are you saying Kuku slept here and then flew away?"

"Da!"

"So he is gone?"

Shaking his head, he said, "Na-na-na! Kuku," and then he pointed upward again, back to me and away. "To the stars?" I probed his mind, seeing only glimpses of that face from my dreams, the name Kuku, which I now knew belonged to my mate. I saw me fucking Gugusan, I saw the mountain and the people, and I heard my name being called out over and over—he was thinking about us fucking.

"I'm hungry, can we speak over a meal?" I asked, rubbing my stomach. He wiggled an eyebrow at me. "In túuxtik máak utia'al u ka' taalaken t'anik Kuku. Je'el u páajtal a taal janal yéetel je'elel tak ka Kuku quiera kaxant teech." He pretended to eat and drink, clueing me in that he would feed me and entertain me as usual. I scanned his mind. My Kuku came for me, he slept here and was waiting for me. He flew high and away. I saw fields of corn and women and children running. Chaos. More running into plantations of corn. The night sky. *Okay, none of this is making any sense.*

"Dammit, Gugusan, is he here or not? Show him to me. I will take him home, away from this place," I said irritated, starving, and hopeless. It felt like I grappled with good news, and was losing.

Gugusan's eyes grew in size. He bit down on his lip before shaking his head. *Didn't he want me to find him? No, he didn't want me to take him away.* "Start talking to me, I know you understand me," I grunted, pointing a finger at him.

"You are here and you are there. Your Kuku is not here. Your Kuku there, with the Birdmen," he spoke in riddles and circles. Then tapping the apple, he patted my pocket and my swords.

*He must have me mixed up with my previous visits.*

"Yes, I will put it away," I said as Gugusan got up, pretending to be sword fighting. Slicing the air and then flapping his arms again.

I pointed to my eyes. "I see. No, I haven't seen war in a long time. I will take the apple. I will continue searching. First, I need to wash, eat, drink." *Eating and drinking must happen first because I feel like passing out.*

"Da, gg fuck!" he said, nodding eagerly. *To my furs. Pleasure time, with the Demon God. I will feed him my cock, blood, and seed.*

I chuckled weakly, holding my palms up. "Okay. You, me, and your furs," I got up, slapping a hand on my leg. He was so big, but underneath it all, so cute. I liked him and I wanted to fuck him. But I knew he wasn't meant to be my mate. My Kuku was here and there. Between this place and the moon, my mate was waiting for me, and I will keep searching until I find him. I changed the subject because my head was reeling.

"What are they? What do you call them? The beautiful birds."

He seemed to catch on and said in an excited tone, "Vucub-Caquix."

"Vukubaku," I repeated. He snort-laughed but nodded, showing me his thumb and index finger close to each other. "Ah, close but not correct."

"Da."

I smiled and pointed questioningly at the opening of the cave. "Shall we go?" I couldn't see any reason to stay here. I needed to return to Grayrak in case the chameleon ball-shaped ship arrived. Then figure out how to jump home to deliver the apple. I was more determined than ever to find my mate. Maybe I would find him going home. Maybe that's why I have to go home to Ki and An.

"Shall we go?" I pointed outside with my fingers and mimicked a roof on a house.

"Da," he replied.

"I'll eat and drink, then I must go," I said, inspecting the apple in the firelight. It was bigger than a human fist and cold in my hand. The vibrations it emitted tickled. Strange symbols, much like the ones carved into the obelisks, created wavy patterns all around the apple. But I failed to decipher or read it. I tucked it into the pocket of my jacket. "Thank you." I was reluctant to go home. I knew the Fates wanted me to take it to Babylon. I pushed that thought to the back of my mind. I was a time traveler and had all the time in the universe to travel back to deliver it.

Gugusan gave me a stern nod. "Da, gg fuck," he answered and pointed the way.

Their city in the mountains was striking. On each visit, the twists and turns down the mountain revealed new discoveries.

The breathtaking view of the waterfalls and wild domesticated animals like monkeys and goats awaited and greeted me. The architecture of their clay huts and limestone was slightly different, too. I noticed some homes were finished, new ones were being carved out of limestone. Evidence that I had arrived some years later than before. A terrace of corn was freshly plowed and surrounded by more terraces of homes carved into the mountain. Pools of water for drinking and bathing ran along a newly designed irrigation system fed by the river birthed by the waterfalls above, zig-zagging down the mountain to where the livestock roamed free. The whole mountain village nearly grew into a city.

I stayed in the shadows, avoiding direct sunlight. Most people were already up and awake, busy working on one thing or another. From food being prepared, huts being swept, and fish being gutted for breakfast, I was impressed with their fluency and how organized they were, but most of all—their friendly greeting faces were astounding. It was so far removed from the busy streets of Egypt, Rome, Babylon, China, and Japan.

"Ko'oten yéetel leti'e', k'ajolo'on ti' le máako', in wil wa taak u compañía." Gugusan called a woman over and pointed to me. Friendly and small in stature, she appeared in awe of my size as her gaze swept up and down my body. I smiled and gave a small wave. She shook her head and barked something at Gugusan. He rested a hand on her shoulder as he spoke to her, but she seemed not to hear him as my appearance transfixed her.

"Ma' a preocupes. Yaan u jantik, beberá yéetel táan sáamal. Leti' yaan u manzana. U yojel u Kuku táan u pa'atik," he said, placating her. It seemed to do the trick. She blinked and turned to speak to another woman.

I needed to get inside and away from the sun's deadly rays. My skin was prickling and would soon be sizzling. As if reading my thoughts, Gugusan called me and we made our way to his humble palace. It was bigger than before. Judging from the outside, it seemed he had carved deeper into the mountain. It was much bigger and divided into sections and hallways. There was space for about fifty men to sit on hand-woven mats. His throne room, the village, and its people were progressing, which confirmed I arrived years after my previous visits.

As I ate, one woman after another approached me, batting their eyelashes and fiddling with their hair. Dear god, I could smell and taste their lust. But I only wanted him.

"Na, thank you. I don't want you. Go away please," I said and gently waved them off. More women flaunted their naked breasts and their scrumptious behinds. Stroking my hair and licking the shells of my ears. It irked me more than bugs do, and I froze, hoping I wasn't offending anyone. Ten females later, Gugusan met my gaze. I shrugged. He shook his head. I shrugged again. He huffed.

"No thank you," I said and gave him that look only men with my tastes understood. He tipped his chin. Understanding, and reading the room. I returned his stare with a smoldering gaze. I wanted him and he wanted me.

Gugusan gave me that, *alright, let's go for it* look. We had a mutual understanding.

He rose to his feet and pointed to the entrance, not breaking the intense eye fucking or cock stirring look.

A woman huffed somewhere beside me, she wasn't happy and removed her hands from me.

He wanted to fuck me. Thank the Fates!

I had already decided I was going to let him, while I filled my stomach with my dessert, his sweet male blood. I wiped my hands clean on my pants.

Just then, a young man came running inside with a clay pot, put it on the floor next to me, and ran out. I knew what this was. I picked it up and grinned. Inside was pig fat.

"Yaan a K'abéet le nojoch paalo'," Gugusan said and then smiled at me. "Da?"

"Yes, da-da-da," I said and stood up. I was going to need the pig fat. He pointed to the back, down a short hallway.

"Yes, please," I said, picking up the torch and bringing it with me. His intense gaze and slight tilt of his chin hinted to me to push aside the woven leaves that hung like curtains dividing the area. Inside was a hollowed-out rock bath where water steamed and beckoned me. I shivered and loved the sight and smell of all that precious water. I missed a hot bath and couldn't wait to get inside it.

I turned to him, grinning and already taking my shirt off. He looked at me, never taking his eyes off me. No time for modesty, I guess. I kicked my boots to the side and unbuttoned my pants. He gasped like he had the other times when I stood in all my nakedness in front of him. He was big and tall for a human. But I was clearly the biggest between us.

I showed him it was now his turn to undress. With a flick and a pull, the leather and feathers went flying. Then he stood proudly erect, watching me appreciating his body. My mouth salivated for him. I was going to let him fuck me, and then I was going to fuck him senseless and drink my fill.

But first I was getting into that water, I'd dreamed of and envisioned entering it. My memories and the reality of traveling back and forth aligned. We climbed inside and washed ourselves without saying a word. After a thorough mutual cleansing session, he moved closer. I wasn't sure if he wanted to kiss or not. The humans on Grayrak surely did.

But this man was a king. Intimacy was not his thing. I wasn't sure what he wanted me to do. I was here for a fuck and feeding. My mate was somewhere in this jungle and he had been waiting for me for thirty years. Which thirty years I didn't know. But what I knew, was that I would find him. Someone had carved the truth and proof into that rock. I assume my Kuku flighting away meant I'd already found him, and Gugusan saw me taking him away. The sword fighting was confusing. I guess they were warriors and that there would be a battle.

I refocused and took my rock-hard cock in my hand, squeezing it for relief. He mimicked me. I probed his mind but only sensed want and need for me. He wanted me because I was his best fuck ever? He felt sorry for me and he saw me as a lost god from the sky? He wanted to ride a god? He stepped closer. I thought to lean in for a kiss, but no, he brushed by me and got out of the water. The torchlight glistened on his wet skin. The swell of desire and hunger for him increased as our eyes met. The ferocious hunger gnawing at my empty stomach burned like melting gold.

I followed him out of the water as my dick stood erect and pointed the way. With each step closer, the anticipation grew, and I could feel the charge in the air between us. He looked back at me, his eyes locked with mine, and I knew exactly how this was going to go.

He gestured for me to lie down on his large bed, covered in different animal skins, woven mats, and soft woolen cushions. I didn't have a preference for how to start fucking and went down on my hands and knees in front of him. My breath exploded out of me with an oomph as he covered my body with his. His big human size cock lay like a brick between my ass cheeks. I moaned my pleasure. The universal sound for, "Yes, that's good. I want more."

He pinned me down by sliding his hands over my shoulders to my forearms. Rubbing his cock up and down my wet and throbbing hole. Gods, I wanted him to fuck me. I pumped my hips into the goat wool and buckskins below my hips.

"Come on, do it already," I said in Babylonian. Then remembering the English message scratched out in the rock face of the cave I connected telepathically to Gugusan and calibrated and replanted the language seed of not only Anunnaki but Babylonian and English in case my Kuku had to communicate with them. I hoped I was helping him and if we meet one day, hopefully soon, I will declare that although I was with Gugusan, my Kuku was the only one on my mind.

*Be patient, I'm taking my time with you. If this is our last time, I want to remember it.* I heard his thoughts and suddenly understood him much easier. "What do you mean, our last time?" I asked as he let go of me and my ass and returned with the clay pot.

"Na-na-na. No talk now," he said and lathered his cock with the white fatty stuff. He took one look at my ass and I let him wrestle me back down. Pushing and smearing his cockhead around my entrance, once, twice, then with no further preparation, he savagely plunged into me.

My eyes bulged. *Oh Fuck!*

I gasped and squeezed my eyelids shut. My toes splayed open, as I concentrated on baring down.

"Blazing scarabs, you are the king, Gugusan. The king of this jungle!" My fingers curled around a buckskin. I blabbered and he laughed with aggressive glee. If I didn't know better, I would think he was mad at me. "You are punishing me, why?" He didn't answer. He kept on hammering until the pain disappeared, "That's so good. So what I wanted. Ah, fuck," I purred. My nerve endings sparked, but I still saw my Kuku's face behind my closed eyelids.

The mixture of agonizing pleasurable sensations wiped my mind blank and all I felt was him.

He was like a beast. I have had sex a few times in this village, but never like this. Gugusan's strokes were rough and deep. If I was a human I was going to be fucked raw.

I looked over my shoulder. "You maniac!" I grunted. My voice thundered out of his hut. The walls shook, and I knew the mountain rumbled as dust and small rocks fell from his cave's roof. I bit down on my upper arm, silencing myself.

*Dammit, now the praying is going to continue. Now they will always think of me as a god.*

He eased back, changing his aim, waited until I relaxed, and then pushed back into me harder than before. I slid forward, unable to stay on my hands and knees. Finding purchase against the wall, I opened my legs and let him have his way with me.

There was no kissing, no intimacy, only a whole lot of grunts, and it was erotic as fuck. He mauled me like an animal. He devoured all my pain.

Then with no warning, he bit my shoulder with his blunt teeth. Hard and drawing blood. I didn't care. I let him drink. Let him have my blood. He knew. I knew he knew. I knew he wanted a piece of me, of my strength, of my blood.

"Yeah, take from me what you need! You've earned it," I said, and he didn't let up, he slurped on my shoulder.

He used me and my hole with the voracity of a mindless caveman. *I needed this. I so-so fucking did.* His sweat mingled with mine and dripped down my body as he glided over my back. Chills and pleasure overtook my mind and body. I lost myself in the rhythm. Forgot about Grayrak. Forgot about my family in Babylon, but the face of my lovely blue-eyed lover stayed etched on the insides of my eyelids.

"Oh sweet Fates, yes!"

Over and over, Gugusan slipped in and slid over that sweet spot inside me, making me want to climax without touching myself. Our grunts and moans grew louder and filled his chamber. The sounds like two roaring mating crocodiles.

He thrust deeper, faster, and harder. Trying his best to fuck the life out of me— maybe he was, because he thought this was our last fuck, and he wanted it to be our best fuck ever.

My throat was dry with heaving and I hollered my ecstasy as I reached my climax at the same time he reached his. Our moans became one, a symphony of desire echoing through the cavernous room. More dust rained down from the cave roof. With one last thrust, he planted himself balls deep inside me. His cocked pulsed as he emptied his balls.

Once I had fed from him and satisfied my carnal desires, Gugusan, who was on the verge of turning into an Anunnaki servant, fell into a deep slumber from which he will awaken still the king of this jungle, but stronger, faster and invincible by any other human. His blood was rich. It filled me with renewed energy that would last for weeks. Hopefully, I would find my mate sooner than that. But it was a stark reminder of the dehydrated, drugged-up humans in Grayrak—it compelled me to return and help Barkor.

Gugusan cracked open one eye, attempting a lazy grin as he lay in a messy heap from our debauchery. Perhaps I had taken a few more sips than necessary—my starving bite was potent and could have been too much for him.

"May the Fates watch over you," I whispered, looking at him with gratitude. "Thank you for your spectacular hospitality, Gugusan. I will be back to discuss you sucking my blood and what it means," I said and whistled a tune of cheerful contentment as I turned away to go wash up. "Who knows, someday maybe I'll even write a sonnet about this experience."

"Da, I'm like Eee-li-shaas, now. Write a sonnet about your Kuku. It's better. You come to live with Kuku on your mountain," he whispered. I turned and looked incredulously at him.

His eyes fluttered shut while he let out a satisfied sigh, lips curving into a small smile, before he fell asleep with a gentle snore. I knew then that I had ruined him for any future lovers. I realized he had spoken in a mix of my mother tongue and the human English on the moon. It was a sign of the Fates.

"I'm going to go to Grayrak. I'll be back as soon as I can," I said and quickly bathed. When I was freshened up, dressed, and ready to go, I thanked Gugusan for the unforgettable evening, even though I knew he was already fast asleep. My legs still trembled from our passionate encounter.

Grabbing my jacket and making sure the apple was still in the pocket, I stepped outside to find two men waiting to escort me back up the hill to my time machine.

After they helped me fill and load canisters of corn and water onto my ship, I said my thanks and goodbyes, strapped in, and was ready to go.

I stared out the window over the vast outline of the treetops below. "Lasitor, please mark this place and time. Starting tomorrow night, I want to return to the jungle every day for the next thirty years into the past and if we don't find my Kuku, we jump back to this day and work our way each day into the future. Narrowing it down, until I find my Kuku. We are very close to finding him."

"Yes, Ishtar, that's a good plan. I agree, and we will do so," Lasitor answered and impressed me with his sudden cooperation.

"Thank you. Start the jump to Grayrak. I want to check on Barkor, he will be happy to see I brought the water," I said as I stored the apple in the overhead cubby where I kept my valuables.

"Ready yourself, Ishtar. We are jumping in, three, two, one. To Grayrak, we go."

# CHAPTER 49
# MY KUKU



**ISHTAR**
**24 970 B.C.**
**The jungle**

*DA, dum-dum-dum!*
*Da, dum-dum-dum!*
*Da, dum-dum-dum!*
*Da, dum-dum-dum!*

JUST HOURS AGO, Lasitor had told me some interesting facts about children. Sometimes I think he knows me better than I knew myself. "Did you know a child who spends more time outdoors is less likely to become short-sighted? And did you also know a toddler covering their eyes thinks you can't see them either? Taking time to get to know your children and have fun with them creates a pleasant atmosphere and cheers you up. If it seems like a tough task, keep in mind that if monkeys can educate their offspring about dental flossing, you can educate your children to at least go outdoors and avoid myopathy, while also providing them with a more comprehensive outlook on their environment. Ishtar, keep your eyes wide open, greet a new day!" Lasitor said as he chased me out of the door to say goodbye to Gugusan.

My plan was ruined. I wanted to execute it by working my way back, day by day, thirty years into the past and future from the date I's seen the carvings in the cave and received the apple.

The rhythm of the drums carried my thoughts beyond the borders of time, to Grayrak and back again to the here and now where the six feet high fire burned furiously and the smoke stung my sensitive eyes. Internally, I was wrestling with finding my mate, my obligations to follow the path the Fates chose for me, and the fucking never ending thirst for drug-laced blood. I was as moody as a hungry lion, and jittery as a cockroach on a hot stove plate.

I don't know when I will return to the San people and their jungle to continue my search for my mate. My plan to return every day for the next thirty years into the future and thirty years into the past, was fucked.

Upon my arrival in Grayrak, while bringing the remaining food and water over to Barkor's, I was thinking of absconding or intervening by saving the humans from their inevitable self-destruction by myself.

But, blessed by the Fates, Barkor noticed movement and a sound foreign to Grayrak's dome. Thanks to his sharp observation skills, he discovered the small ship flying in circles, cleverly disguising itself in plain sight. As the Fates had foretold, they revealed their presence by camouflaging themselves, like chameleons.

I was still helping Sarinka unpack and hide the provisions from the Disciples when Barkor called to me.

"Ishtar, come and see. I'm hearing and seeing something strange. The air feels out of place. I hear a faint hum, but I can't see anything, even though I know it's there!" Barkor was pointing towards the roof of the dome. My gaze locked on the strange rippling of air where he was showing.

"Sweet scarab cakes, it's them!" I chucked the crates to Sarinka, not removing my gaze from the apparition. "Quick, Barkor, grab their attention!" I'd shouted, overjoyed. We must have looked like two fools chasing after something that no one else could see or hear, but that was just life in Grayrak. Acting in such a manner was considered normal because half of the people were suffering from malnourishment, while the other half were constantly under the influence of drugs.

Meeting the visitors was a complete turnaround from my previous state of hopelessness. Like Barkor, they were half Anunnaki. They were healthy and strong men, radiating vitality with their clean and vibrant faces. There was no trace of weakness or illness in them. Their ship and clothes carried a pleasant scent of soap. Scarabs, they smelled refreshing, and overall, such a delightful bunch of intelligent young men.

But the shock of witnessing what emerged last from that spacecraft was indescribable. There stood an astonishingly tall and regal male, exuding a warm smile and possessing eyes so pure that they seemed to delve straight into the depths of my dark soul, devoid of any trace of malevolence. It was as if he had cleansed me from within, purging some of my negativity. The humans were instantly captivated by him, even more so than by Barkor. Men, women, and children were flocking to him, touching him, and laughing as if he were a walking loaf of bread.

Since then, over the past couple of weeks, I've been overwhelmed by a whirlwind of feelings, obligations, and morals that have left me feeling emotionally drained. I was initially greeted with warmth and friendliness until Cian intervened and brought me back to my senses. I must admit, my addiction had consumed me, making me self-centered and oblivious to the significant events unfolding on Earth. They falsely believed I was responsible for the turmoil on the moon.

I felt completely clueless.

Then, suddenly, Cian lunged across the table, his hands closing around my throat, extinguishing the last remnants of my pitiful existence. As I faded into darkness, memories of my Kuku flashed before my eyes—a message from destiny itself. Cian's forceful intervention abruptly yanked me from that tranquil, serene place, forcing me to confront reality and answer their questions. In an instant, my priorities were forcefully realigned, neatly arranged before me.

They exceeded my expectations by far. These men were not what I had anticipated—they were larger, more intelligent, and quite a handful. Among them, Eryn surprised me the most. He was a powerful Anunnaki King. When he stepped out of the Bubblecar, I could have sworn I saw a ghost, one of the many haunting spirits from my homeland—my brothers. Standing at a towering height like my own eight feet, he moved his thick muscled body gracefully while exuding a commanding presence, as he carried a spear made of pure gold. There was an aura of tranquility around him. He's deeply in love and bonded to Ivan, the incredibly beautiful, fair-skinned half-Anunnaki, who happened to be the brother of my assailant, Cian. Like Barkor, the twins were taller than humans, as they stood seven feet high. Despite that, Ivan and Cian bore no resemblance to each other, although sharing striking bright blue eyes. Ivan boasted long, sleek, and soft-looking blond hair, while Cian's head was completely shaved and his arms tattooed, giving him a rugged appearance, much like Barkor's. All distantly related to me as my half-Anunnaki kin.

Eryn stood out as royalty, emanating an aura of mystery and allure. His presence was like gazing into the depths of the ocean, with its unfathomable depths and wonders. Unlike Eryn, Cian's eyes held a murderous glare as I looked up at him, regretting my actions. In that moment, I pleaded for him to end my life, so I could join my Kuku in their fading existence. However, his response was a cold refusal.

"Too easy. Once you reveal how to save these people and eliminate the Zelk, I'll gladly end your life," Cian vowed, positioning himself with his feet on either side of my head. His mesmerizing blue eyes reminded me of my beloved Kuku, while the noticeable bulge in his pants caught my attention. All of them were male, and even Eryn, the largest and strongest, had a male partner. I couldn't help but smile—what other reaction could I have had? They exuded an irresistible aura of sexuality. Just like I sensed with Titus and Gugusan, I instantly knew they were attracted to men, not women. If Apsu had ever laid eyes on them, he would have surely burst into flames with disgust.

When Cian asked me where I had been staying all this time, I chose to omit my travels to the time and place where Gugusan and my Kuku existed. I held onto the hope that the glimpses of my Kuku's face, straddling the line between reality and nothingness, meant that I would soon meet him. I found myself at a crossroads, torn between helping to save the humans alongside Cian or returning to Gugusan. But if I abandoned my initial purpose, my feelings of guilt and uselessness would have me craving the solace of tainted blood. It was a never-ending cycle that consumed me.

The burden of yearning for the man of my dreams had become too much to bear. Watching Eryn and Ivan's love for each other ignited bitterness within me, and seeing Cian in a similar predicament, desiring Barkor but unable to have him, served as a reminder that my duty to assist Barkor, his humans, and my newfound friends from Earth was more important than pursuing my desires.

To avoid getting lost again, I had to let go of my longing for my Kuku. The jungle wasn't where I belonged, nor was it my people. If I let my indecisiveness suffocate me, I would never find a way out of the maze I created. My mind was torn in two. As much as I wanted to be with Cian, Ivan, and Eryn, I decided to escape their constant presence in Grayrak to say goodbye to the San. I did it more for myself because I could always come back to this time and place. They wouldn't even notice I was gone.

Here, in the jungle, everything was simple, and it was easy to forget about the moon. During my visits, I searched for my mate, but found solace in this carefree haven where Barkor, Sarinka, and the needy humans didn't require my assistance. I was passing time, while hoping to encounter my Kuku. I must accept this feeling of futile longing and wait. I had responsibilities and had to compel my heart, which couldn't care less about the moon, to concentrate on what truly mattered. The voice of the Fates.

With a sigh, I reluctantly scooted closer to speak to Gugusan. I took in the sight of his tribe's humble village and bountiful, rich soil, yielding an abundance of crops. The palms of my hands were sweaty and cold, and my heart pumped a sludge of thick reluctant blood through my body as I forced myself to speak the words that had been weighing on my mind.

"This will be my final visit, I think," I said, unable to meet his gaze. My eyes followed his stare, drifting to the mountaintop and back to the flames of the bonfire. It flickered and danced, casting a spellbinding glow over the gathering tribe. A hush fell upon us. The children started chanting, their voices merging with the thumping rhythm of drums, ankle bells, and foot rattles. The percussion harmonized with the rhythm of nature and the night while the psychedelic euphoria of the blood I had taken enhanced and intertwined my visions and memories. I suspected Gugusan had sent this particular young man to me for this very reason because I was slowly feeling better and the smile plastered on my face seemed to amuse him. We've become good friends, and I have shared secrets about my genealogy, his newly acquired Igigi status, and haunting dreams about my mate with him. He wasn't shocked, and I guessed finding the apple here was proof enough that weird things turned up in this village. Like that awkward-looking stranger who had been eyeing me from afar. He was a sneaky one. But tonight, ever since my arrival, I sensed him closer than usual but still staying out of reach for mental probing while hiding in the shadows. I've asked about the mysterious man, but Gugusan waved me off and urged me to share more memories of the man I'd never met, but who had led me here.

I leaned closer to hear my friend's reaction to my news.

"You not search for Kuku, no more?" he asked. Like myself, they were all speaking a mix of Babylonian, English, and their native tongue.

I shook my head once. "I'm needed in another place and time. People are starving and killing one another for food." I couldn't say more than that. Explaining to Gugusan that the Zelk was building an army with human body parts would be nearly impossible, and he didn't need to know that.

He didn't criticize my choice, almost like he didn't believe me. He waved my statement off, and as the news spread around the fire, some came over to assure me I would find my Kuku, the other half of my soul, before I left. The problem was I'd left dozens of times and never found him. The next time I returned, I got the same answer. Before you leave, you will find him. Almost as if they had practiced the words.

The festivities were getting louder. I leaned closer to speak into Gugusan's ear. "Tell me, why don't you ever say goodbye?"

He patted my knee. "We never say goodbye because goodbye means going away and going away means forgetting. So we say meet you soon."

"And why do you always take me to search the jungle, but when I ask where my Kuku is, you say I will see him before I go?"

I've never seen Gugusan look so serious. He tipped his cup back and emptied it, then put it to the side, wiped his lips dry with the back of his hand, and said, "Look at me,

Demon God, Ku k'uchul ojéeltbil ba'ax táan kíinsa'ab tu táan ta, yéetel le ba'ax táan oculto teechi' u a aclarará. A Kuku yéetel Eee-li-shaas ma' sa'atako'on, sino escondidos, vendrán ti' teech ken a biin."

"For fuck's sake! Stop talking in riddles!" I shouted. My head was spinning, and the world tilted. "You wanted me to fuck Zaduka. You knew he was eating the mushrooms, didn't you?" His face said he knew, and he'd planned it. "What do you mean by I will come to know what is in front of me, and that which is hidden from me will become clear?"

He swiped his finger left and right in front of me. "Your Kuku, Da?"

"Yes!"

"Kuky and Eee-li-shaas not lost, but hidden. They will come when you leave, they wait for you."

I threw my hands up in defeat. We have searched the jungle and beyond. I've searched for my mate by lifting every bloody stone, looking inside every hole, but nothing.

"Maybe my Kuku is not in the jungle. Maybe he is searching for me." I pointed beyond the mountains. "What if he crossed the great rivers?"

"No!" Gugusan said. "No worry. You come back when you finish helping. You always come back," he said with an encouraging smile. The flames from the fire warmed my face. It calmed me. My fingers fumbled in my pocket and curled around the apple. It was rough and fitted perfectly in my big hand. I couldn't bear the thought of taking it back to Babylon. The weight of it held some kind of deeper meaning for me, like an answer I had been searching for. But at the same time, I knew I had to return it. And returning it would be like losing my connection to this place. To my mate. Also, I was wary of facing my father. The thought made my stomach churn. Time seemed to slip away from me, and this apple, which must be buried somewhere in Ki and An's garden, felt like a reminder that time belonged to me, even when everything else felt out of reach.

Icy chills prickled along my spine as I felt eyes on me. Following my instincts, I turned, searching the darkness across the river. My eyesight was much better than a human's so I could find and locate that stranger hiding in a dark corner behind a woven mat that served as a door in front of a cave. His legs were visible beneath the fabric, and he seemed oddly out of place.

Before I could get up and approach him, Gugusan interrupted, snapping me out of my trance. "Leaving so soon?" he asked, pulling me back to reality.

"Yes," I replied with a heavy heart. "Unfortunately, I have responsibilities elsewhere." My gaze flickered back to the shadows where the stranger had been hiding. It didn't matter now that I was leaving. Time for me to move on and find my place in Eryn and his brothers' world. To embrace the people and follow the path that the Fates had intended for me.

For nearly an hour, I bid farewell to Gugusan and his fierce warriors, expressing my gratitude for their hospitality. I also thanked the women and children of the tribe who had welcomed me with open arms during my visits. As usual, two warriors escorted me as we made our way back up the mountain. My ship came into sight and I felt the effects of the potent substance wearing off. I hummed a song under my breath, a tribute to a love that would never materialize. It was bittersweet, but I had finally accepted the reality of our paths never crossing.

*My Missing Piece.*

*I've searched all over and stood empty-handed at the boundary of time.*

*Wishing for just one word, one moment with him, but he's gone, vanished into the shadows.*

*Where is my lover?*

*I've checked every corner of the earth, combed through every memory, yet still, I find nothing but emptiness.*

*The sun sets, and I am left with a heart heavy with longing and a mind full of questions.*

*Did he leave willingly?*

*Was it something I did or said?*

*Each night I lay awake, my dreams filled with his face, only to wake to an empty bed.*

*Where is my lover?*

*Is he wandering lost in some distant land?*

*Or has his heart found refuge in another's hands?*

*I search for answers that may never come, but still, I hold onto the hope that one day, our paths will cross again.*

*Until then, I will keep searching, for that missing piece of my heart.*

*Where is my lover?*

*Only time knows.*

*Until then, I will wait.*

When we reached my ship, I did a double take. I reached for my swords in haste as the door swooshed open. Someone was inside my ship.

"Who is there? Show yourself, and for the love of the Fates, don't touch anything!"

The sound of hands clapping echoed from inside my time machine. I stood frozen, out of sight from the doorway. My first instinct was to charge in, confront whoever was inside and chop off their hands. But my impulsive actions could lead to disaster. The last thing I wanted was for my precious ship and Lasitor to take off, leaving me stranded. And I couldn't afford to anger Eryn and his brothers, who were waiting for me in Grayrak. The Fates had entrusted me with one important mission, and I couldn't risk losing my ship in a fit of rage. So I took a deep breath and stayed rooted in place, my hands clenched into fists around the hilts of my blades at my sides, waiting for the right moment to act.

A low, husky voice blared from inside my ship, and it wasn't Lasitor's. "I'm so glad you enjoyed your stay. I can smell the joy all the way up the bloody fucking mountain—all fucked out! You are too stoned to see straight, never mind flying your time machine," whoever he was said in perfect English.

In English? What the fuck?

Did I bring someone home with me last night in my drunken stupor and then bring them here?

My body vibrated. I cautiously stepped closer to the entrance, wondering who could be inside.

"Lasitor! Did you give access and allow a stranger on board?"

"Excuse me, Ishtar, I did not open the door, just like I didn't open it for the Anubis. Stop accusing me of doing human things. I cannot override the door opening and closing. It's a manual out-of-date lever. I've told you to update it, but no, you don't trust me. You think I will take over and fly off without you," Lasitor responded, not giving me any sign if this was a stranger or not.

With swords raised, I glared at the door, wishing the trespasser would show himself. "State your name and why you are inside my ship," I demanded. My two escorts, dressed in feathers and barely there clothing, burst into laughter, playfully wished me luck and farewell, and sauntered away. "Hey, come back!" I yelled. "I need help to remove the intruder." But all I got in response were shrugged shoulders, amused chuckles, and wiggling bare asses.

I widened my stance and called to the Fates, the name I had picked up from the Grayrakians, "Oh, moon-god!"

"You should go and wash yourself. You can't sit in these seats like that. The stench of that pig fat and another man's scent is enough to make me vomit all over your precious instrumentation," he said.

"Ishtar, vomit over our instrumentation does not sound safe for either of us," Lasitor added.

Then the intruder added, "And with a closed door, we'll be barfing all over each other. So go wash your tripping ass or Lasitor and I leave you here."

Wash myself? Leave me here?

My brain stalled. Something weird and exciting was happening. I felt like doing a happy dance and banging my drums. This was unlike any of my previous visits to this place. Could this be it? Was my lost, long-awaited mate going to materialize and emerge from that door? He certainly sounded possessive. It was too real, too fast for my brain to catch up and grasp the miracle of the situation. I wanted to poke my head inside to have a look but the chance of being decapitated was too high. He was probably correct although I'd had a quick wash after filling that young man's insides to the brim.

"Reveal yourself," I said, squeezing my eyelids together. My brain hurt as if poked with a hot poker. It was true that the pig fat ensured a smoother glide, but the smell of it didn't wash off after a quick rinse.

"If I show myself, you must keep an open mind. Can you do that for me, my Ish?"

His Ish. Oh, my god. My visions and dreams were coming true. This was not some crazy villager.

"Listen, whoever the fuck, you are, get out of my ship right now!" I was nervous and excited, like a kid about to get a new toy. Energy pulsated around me. Foreboding thoughts of accidents and unrequited love swirled in my mind making me dizzy. One wrong button and the ship was gone, and I was stranded.

"Don't fucking touch anything," I added while swaying on my feet.

"Promise me you won't hate me and leave me here." My mate's beautiful voice thundered with an accent I couldn't place. He sounded upset with me. This was him. No wonder Gugusan kept looking up the mountain. I heard the shuffling of feet coming closer. He was almost at the door now. "Promise me!"

"I promise, just show yourself," I said. Black spots danced around me, just as a head with pure white hair popped out. His eyes were blue and sparkled like diamonds. My mouth opened and closed. No sound escaped. Cold recognition washed over me.

"You are fortunate that I am so happy to see you alive, and not the murderous jealous type," he said with a lopsided grin. He was stunning. Inwardly, that dried-up piece of meaty organ in my chest stuttered and restarted while my gut gave a joyful flip-flop. Outwardly, I beamed.

"My—Ma—Mate?" I said breathlessly. The world tilted. I stumbled over my words as the drawings on the cave walls suddenly made sense to me. This was my lover. My mate. He was here just as I thought. The words of the Fates, the drawings on the cave wall, the apple, the ship, and the faces of people I've never seen. They all spun in the maelstrom in my confused mind. I heaved air into my lungs as I struggled to breathe. Memories from the past and present collided and rushed through the synapses in my brain. Suddenly, it all became my reality. My swords fell out of my hands and my knees buckled as astonishment paralyzed me.

"Fucking small door!" He shouted as a flash of white shot towards me. He caught me just before I hit the ground. I looked up, dazed. The smooth pearl-white face of my dreams looked down at me. I wanted to touch him, but something strange was happening to me. A silver tear slid down his rosy cheek. I regained coordination of my arms and reached up, wiping it away with my thumb. Wordlessly, I lay on his lap. Feeling safe and, for the first time, not alone.

"Horrible feeling I know," he said. His face was beaming with recognition of me. He knew me, and he saw me.

"I-I found you," I stuttered. "Just before—I almost left, but I found you."

"Yes, you bloody did. Did you get back onto your ship? Did you escape those creatures, after all?" he asked, and the gears in my head spun in all directions—not sure what he was talking about. I grappled for words to make sense of what was happening. "Calm down, take deep breaths," he whispered while softly stroking my forehead, my cheeks, my lips, and strangely, my eyelashes with the tips of his fingers.

"When I saw you earlier going down the mountain, I was so happy to see you, but I decided to wait here for you. I thought you were dead, and I was stranded here forever." His voice was gentle and caring. His touches told me he was telling the truth. "So I figured my best chance of going home was to wait for you on the ship. You know, in case you fly off and leave me here again."

I felt as if I knew him, too. It was on the tip of my tongue, "Is—are, wait, what is your name?"

"It's Peter?"

"Peter, my mate, my Kuku."

"Yes, it is me. And you took your time partying down there." His smile turned into a snarl—I was getting mixed messages from him.

"Are you feeling better now? I want to go home."

"Home?"

"Where is that?" I asked, looking up at him. He was even more handsome than my visions, and I wanted to touch his face. Pale with rosy cheeks, soft and hairless. The most luscious bottom lip. I wanted to nibble on it.

His smile turned into a vicious scowl. "What's that supposed to mean?" he spat at me. Moon-god, he was feisty and short-tempered. "Fuck you, Ish." He pushed me off his lap. Wings twitching, he said, "I'm waiting for you inside. No wonder you wanted to bring me here, you already think of this place as home. You probably couldn't wait to fuck your boyfriend." He harrumphed as he turned to enter the ship. I lay on the ground, gawking at him.

"Fuck you, Ish. No, never mind. You've been fucked already," he shouted, stomping his bare feet up the stairs. What a sight he was. It must take magic or sheer determination to move inside those tight pants. Maybe they were painted or tattooed on him? His head, with its pure white mane, disappeared inside, followed by a forceful wrestling match between his enormous wings and the door.

White feathers of different sizes floated everywhere. I sat up, catching one long one, and sniffing it deeply. "Hmmm," I closed my eyes. He smelled like thunder rolled up inside rose petals. Tied with a string of gold. "My mate." My eyes rolled back behind closed eyelids as I committed his smell to memory and swooned.

"Why are you so angry?" I asked, rising to my feet with a grunt. I brushed the dirt from my pants and stomped over to the pond nearby. I removed the apple, placed it next to my swords, then stripped my clothes off while thinking excitedly that trouble awaited me onboard if I didn't do as instructed. Eager to please my mate, I have never cleansed myself so fast while making sure I scrubbed away all the cum and pig fat. Teeth chattering, I rushed back to the ship, boots, clothes, apple, and swords in hand.

"Hurry up, Ish, I want to go home. To Phoenix. Lord knows what they are going to say about my fucking wings," he said while I got dressed in fresh clothes and joined him. He saw the apple in my hand and I quickly stored it away.

I didn't have visions of him being this possessive and domineering. "Maybe I should leave you here and return another time," I joked.

"Fuck you, Ish. I thought you cared about me. Not this place. Not these men, but me. Drop me off at Phoenix. I must bring that fucking apple home. I had nightmares about the fucking thing."

"You heard the voice of the Fates? Was it inside that cave?" I asked. My mate perplexed me while I assessed the amount of loose white feathers lying on the floor, on my seat, over the dashboard, fucking everywhere. I didn't mind the little things. They were part of him. I will pick them up and save them—make myself a tiny pillow I can carry in my pocket to smell him all the time.

"It's because I stole that apple. The thing is bad luck. I feel like throwing you and the apple out the fucking door."

Strapped in and ready to go in the passenger seat, Peter sat, arms folded, wings tucked, and crammed in. A bolt of lust shot through me. I touched the tip of his wing; he shivered and gave me a don't-touch-me look. I sat down. *I'm going to lick and suck those tips, every inch of him, when he lets me.*

"No, I have a mission. The Fates told me to take it home—my home. First, we'll go to Babylon. Get rid of the apple, as you say. After that, we can go to Phoenix or Grayrak."

"Take me to Phoenix. I want to restock and have a decent shit."

I frowned. "How do you sit with those wings?"

"Fuck you, Ish. How do you sit with your enormous cock? Do I ask you such stupid personal questions? I thought you were bloody dead!" he said with tears in his eyes.

"I am not dead and there is a big difference between my cock and your wings." I wiggled my eyebrows at him. "And fuck you too. My mate is supposed to be nicer than you. Maybe you aren't the mate I'm supposed to have. Hmmm?" I reached down, finding the shiny tip attached to my safety belt, pulled it, and clipped it in.

"I am your fucking mate. Shut the hell up!"

"Or what?"

In one swift movement, he unbuckled his seat belt and lunged towards me. For a moment, I feared for my life—death by a crazy, sexy angel. But his lips crashed into mine, and a frenzy of passion and desire blasted through me as his tongue slid into my unsuspecting mouth. Kissing wasn't something I particularly liked doing. But this was different. I eagerly opened up to receive him, tasting the anger, fury, and pure lust—the thunder. Our tongues danced together in a hectic tempo as I wrapped my arms around his muscular shoulders. A deep growl sounded from his chest as he pulled away, piercing blue eyes blazing with fire. "I am your mate," he declared, his words searing into my mind. "You asshole. Fucking time-traveling Anunnaki," he said and slammed his fist into my upper arm. Numbing it.

"Ouch! Let's take the apple back to Babylon, and then you can direct to me where our new home is, okay?" I said and started the machine.

"Ish, don't tell me this is our first meeting!"

"For me it is," I said.

"All I know is that Phoenix is five turns of that wheel into the future. Sounds to me like Lasitor's been hiding things from you!" he said, pointing to my ship's console.

"Uhm, excuse me. Everything has a time and a place. But if you think you can do it better, then who am I to stop you?" Lasitor interjected.

"He's got a point. Why would I want to know how to get to Phoenix, if I don't need to know? Then he might as well tell me everything he knows and I don't have the capacity or strength for that. And he knows that. He is my guide, not a talking geographical dictionary."

"Do you even hear yourself speaking? Who talks and thinks like that?" Peter asked as he wiggled the tail ends of his massive wings and tucked them underneath his thick, muscled upper legs. *Pleasing me.* He was on my ship, I thought happily. But I had no clue why he thought I was dead.

As we settled back into our seats, a dangerous silence hung between us. God, it was way worse than the Siege of Jerusalem. I leaned forward and dramatically turned on the time machine, pressing buttons with pretend importance. Peter's eyes were practically burning holes in my back, but I chose to ignore that, focusing on the pretend tasks at hand. I attempted to cheer him up. With a theatrical flair and a foreign feeling of silly optimism, I declared, "Lasitor, off to ancient Babylon before the war with Apsu, but after my last pit-stop at Platonius'." And with that, I hoped to have enough time to warn my sisters about their upcoming slaughter while also delivering the apple to Xerxes. "Also, land us outside the city, away from any danger or prying eyes," I added.

"That time and place is a concern for me, are you sure your settings are what you intended or prefer? There are consequences for bringing the apple back there, Ishtar," Lasitor said. I noticed Peter tightening his grip on the armrests. I flashed a smile at my Kuku over my shoulder. He stubbornly crossed his arms and tried to turn away despite his cramped legroom. I was simultaneously concerned and amused by his failed attempts to ignore and hide from me.

"Oh, come on, you can't resist my charm," I joked, earning a begrudging chuckle from him.

With tears filling his eyes, he said with a trembling voice, "I thought you were dead! This is me being happy to see you." He laced his feelings with venom, but I heard his inside burst before the tears flowed. He was relieved to see me. *He is confused and somehow, I had fucked up.*

Lasitor interrupted my thoughts. "Before taking off, Ishtar, please check your coordinates."

"Lasitor, I know what I'm doing. I remember Ki and An showing me the apple. I remember them saying that my bloodline would live on. Surely this was me. Please, for once, do as I say."

I checked with my newly found Kuku, who shrugged at me as if he didn't care. But he did. He was only playing hard to get. "Also, Lasitor, please take notes and let me know when I'm near my demise," I commanded my trusted guide and companion, hoping we could prevent my untimely death. I searched through the overhead compartments, looking for a nose wiper to hand to Peter. I wanted to embrace him and never let go, but he was like a prickly porcupine. Peter sat up tall at my announcement, wiped his tears with the back of his hands, dried them on his thighs, and in between sobs he said, "I'll chart our jumps on a timeline and map because I have a feeling you died already."

CHAPTER 50

# ELIJAH

*"GOOD MORNING.*

*Time has snuck up on us. Did you know there was a tall and dark Anunnaki time trav-eler seen back in 1579 A.D.? He was called Yasuke. The story is after he arrived in Japan he made history as the first foreign-born man to become a samurai warrior. It was said that Yasuke was originally a slave from Mozambique and was brought to Japan by Portuguese traders. The powerful Japanese warlord Oda Nobunaga was fascinated by Yasuke's tall stature and dark skin, and upon seeing him, ordered his servants to try and rub the 'black ink' off his skin. Despite this strange encounter, Nobunaga took Yasuke into his service, granting him a sum of money, a house, and a Katana. From then on, Yasuke loyally served Nobunaga as an honored samurai, fighting alongside him in fierce battles.*

*Remember, history is told by those who wrote it.*

*Visit your community news page to record your version of history today!"*


**ISHTAR**
**3500 B.C.**
**Hours before the war with Apsu**
**Babylon**
**Earth**

My whole body was humming. I felt like singing and whistling. I had found my mate. The mere thought filled my soul with an intoxicating blend of excitement and lust. We left behind everything that felt safe to come back to the place and time I never wanted to see or relive. Bringing the apple to Babylon was no small task, but as I gazed into my newly found mate's eyes, gleaming with hope, I knew that a future filled with love and adventure awaited us. Peter thought I was killed in a crash. He had hinted at taking me to the secret city underwater, the one that I was eager to see with Cian and his brothers. As he spoke of Phoenix, his home that lay beneath the ocean's surface, my excitement grew. This meant that my time spent waiting for a spaceship in Grayrak was not for nothing. I thought I had to choose between forgetting about searching for him and dedicating my time to Cian and his brothers—as the Fates had commanded me on Anzulla. The possibility of helping them, with my Kuku at my side, filled me with optimism.

We landed the time machine on the shoreline next to a sad weeping willow that stood like a beacon, withering away in the salty air. It marked the road that forked inland to where Babylon lay waiting for me on the horizon. Enclosed by enormous city walls, the buildings lay packed in blocks around the palace and the sacred vaulted terrace gardens where my family lived. "Okay, I'll be quick. I don't plan to linger. The sooner I get the apple to my sisters, the faster we can get out of here. If my father sees me or this ship, we will be sucked into this reality and might never return to your home."

"And where is that, exactly?" Peter asked.

"Anywhere you want to go," I said, getting up to remove our precious cargo from the overhead cubby.

"I'm thinking I can't live in Phoenix like this, so let's talk about it after," he said, waving his hand up and down his wings. I stooped to give him a peck on the cheek.

"Okay. Please stay on the ship." I pleaded with my eyes. He took the apple from me, inspecting it. "I understand now why my sisters said I brought the apple and that my bloodline will live on. It's because, this time, I'm going to warn them." I reached out to take the apple from Peter's hand but noticed the deep creases etched across his forehead. His eyes bore an apprehension of my coming death.

"Yeah, I know. Here, take it." He handed it back to me. "Come back to me. If you don't...I'll be stranded and lost without you."

I kissed his pouty pink lips. "I will hurry. The city is about to be evacuated. Titus is assembling an army. I have time, I think, at least two days." I checked my tick-tick thing. "I'm going to tell them to bury the apple and flee."

"Why don't you just hide it yourself and come back to me?" He asked a very good question.

"I have a message to deliver and because my sisters are meant to hide it. I might put it where my father can find it."

"I don't want to think of the ramifications of that. You don't know half of it yet." He turned away, shaking his head. He spoke in riddles. Of things in my future. His eyes snapped back, blazing with trepidation. He locked eyes with mine. "Whatever your instincts tell you, follow them. Don't pay any attention to me. Stick to what your gut says."

I tilted my head, studying him. "I will."

He bit his bottom lip. "I'm worried about nothing. Please make sure you aren't running into yourself." Peter's voice trembled as he frantically adjusted his wings. I watched as small white feathers floated to the floor.

I tipped my head sideways to refocus. Everything about him mesmerized me. "I don't think so. Please, stay on the ship. You can't be seen with those wings." As if reading my thoughts, Peter drew me into his warm embrace, wings enfolding me protectively.

"Are you embarrassed about my wings?" he joked, making light of the situation with that flirtatious voice I was finding hard to resist. Hairs all over my body stood erect. My shoulders stiffened as electric charges shot through me and zinged into my cock. I felt alive. This was it. The indescribable attraction towards only him.

"We can come back another time. Let me show you I'm not embarrassed, but extremely attracted to you and your wings. It's these superstitious humans I'm worried about." I ran my hands up his back along the protruding ridges. "If my father sees or hears about you, we will have a lunatic chasing after us." He stepped back, but I pulled him by his belt loops and flung him around to give me better access to lick and bite the skin where his wings sprouted from his back.

"Ah." He shivered from my touch. "That's so unfair. It's so itchy and so fucking yummy when you do that. It feels as if that area is directly connected to my cock and balls."

"Hmmm, I can't wait to fuck you while sucking you right here," I purred, licking and lathering the sensitive area with my spit and then blowing on it. Judging by the fine tremors in his legs, I knew I was driving him crazy.

"If you don't stop now..."

"I'm sure I can stick it in and cum within four strokes. Will you let me?" I asked between licks.

"Of course, I will." He pushed his ass back to meet me halfway. He opened his wings and rubbed himself over my crotch with his backside.

"Feel how hard I am for you," I purred.

"Do it," he groaned low. "Hmmm, let's see if you can do it. I will count." He planted the palms of his hands against the wall while swinging his ass from side to side.

"One," he started counting as he pushed his pants down. I unbuckled mine, let them fall around my ankles, and guided myself to his opening. He spread his wings further to give me more access. The smell of clean feathers, vanilla, and sweetgrass filled my nostrils.

He shivered, then grunted, "Just spit on it and stick it in! Two!"

I collected a big wad of saliva and spat on my cockhead, smearing it around his entrance.

"Three!"

I gripped his hips and jabbed three fast ones into him. He grunted as I thrust deeper, my hips slapping against his ass and with one more deep thrust, my balls contracted and pleasure shot up my spine. My whole body went rigid as I orgasmed. The smell of him consumed my senses. "Fuck, you feel so good," I grunted, planting my seed so deep inside him, he must taste it on his tongue. "I won't ever get enough of you," I said through clenched teeth.

He arched his back, pushing back against me, whispering, "Oh my god, I missed you. Keep talking. I love the sound of how much you want me." He was panting with want. His hole was slippery and warm. I rotated my hips, grinding into him. Loving him already. I licked that magic area where his skin and wings met. Then, with the tips of my fangs, I scraped across it, pushing him over the edge. He clamped down on my cock, his breathing ragged, and I knew he was close. "Do it," I growled, my voice thick with desire. "Come for me." And he did, all over his hand, his pants, and the wall. His enormous wings prevented me from reaching around to feel his slick release. We stood there until he finished convulsing, remaining silent, lost in the afterglow of our passion, until we both whispered, "I love you."

He laughed.

"What? Why are you laughing?"

"We come like two ninjas. Silent and fast. We are so pathetic for each other." He snickered. I licked and rubbed my nose where I had nicked the base of his wing muscle.

"Hmmm, you smell exquisite. I know about ninjas. I trained with one of them. He was from Japan. A stealthy warrior soldier, but believe me, when we fuck, we sound nothing like them."

Peter straightened his back, bucking me away. "How do you know? This was your first time fucking me. Go do your drop-off. I will stay here like a good housewife and clean this ship. This thing stinks." He harrumphed and reached for a rag so we could clean ourselves.

"You do know I've been all over and met all kinds of people from all kinds of cultures. That was my job." I pulled my pants up, feeling lousy for shortening our fun and hesitant to leave. "I'm sorry, Peter. When I come back, I promise you we can fuck anywhere and as long as we want."

"Yes-yes, it's fine. As long as it's not inside this fucking machine. Please be safe. Okay?" He stopped wiping the wall, threw the rag away somewhere over his shoulder, and gazed into my eyes. I saw the concern and care in him. Then I kissed his down-turned lips until they turned up into a smile and said goodbye.

Peter activated the door to open. "Go, be safe, and come back to me. And soon."

With a grin on my face, I turned to leave. Fucking Peter wasn't part of my original plan, but my body and mind were starting to have different ideas. I almost gave in and decided to come back another time. Just as I was a few feet away, the door swished shut behind me. My strides were hesitant and my heart was reluctant. But I made my way towards the distant city, stepping out of time and between the threads of reality. Driven by the purpose of returning to him as soon as I delivered my warning, I held the apple close to my chest.

It was late night, early morning. Only the sound of the wind accompanied me. Ki and An would be sleeping. The streets and palace grounds were busier than I remembered. Stray dogs were scavenging for food while the palace guards were at their posts, standing like statues. I entered from the back where more guards lazily gathered around on pillows sharing a pipe. I passed them, still moving behind the veil of this reality.

Cheering in a foreign tongue shattered the silence behind me. It came from the opposite part of the palace where the king and his two wives lived. Laughter followed. A female shouted. Male voices and the unmistakable sounds of partying as they hollered joyfully.

Shivers ran up and down my spine. The shadows seemed to dance and flicker around me, amplifying my fear as I dashed through the dimly lit hallways. My eyes darted back and forth, searching for any signs of movement or danger. Our bloodlines would be fucked up beyond recognition if my father found me. The taste of fear and adrenaline coated my tongue, my heart beating wildly in my chest.

Dammit. Three human guards stood gripping their shields and swords, guarding the entrance to King Xerxes' quarters. Grinding my molars, I clenched the apple tighter. I snuck by them, hoping I didn't stir the air. Once inside, I slid past two more guards to the extra large bed, where the three lovers slept, entwined.

Carefully, I stuck my hand through the veil, pulling their feet and toes to wake them. My clothes clung to my skin, damp with sweat. My sister An was the first to wake up, followed by Ki. It was good to see them. "Shht, it's me," I said in my native tongue. Sharp pains shot through my skull as something hit my head. I fell sideways as I lost my footing and slipped. I attempted to stand, but Xerxes stuck his sword in my face.

"It's Ishtar! What are you doing here, Ishtar?" Ki asked, with her hands over her mouth. "And what are you wearing?"

She leaned in closer, inspecting my face and hair, and lifted my foot, inspecting my boots and clothes. "You are not our Ishtar, are you?"

"No. I mean, yes I am, but I am older. My younger self is on his way. Titus is assembling an army. War is coming and Apsu is going to burn this palace like he destroyed Anzulla."

"Ishtar, I thought you were an assassin," Xerxes said, tapping my cheeks with the flat sides of his sword, and then stepping away. He waved to the guards that they were not needed. Turning his back to me, he threw a shawl over him to cover his impressive manhood. Luckily, my sisters were both dressed.

"Let me look at you." A small oil lamp gleamed in An's hand. I winced at the brightness and squeezed my eyes shut.

"Are you bleeding? How's your head?" she asked. I shivered, the creepy feeling of seeing my dead sisters rendering me speechless. I nodded. Holding the apple out to them. They were as graceful as I remembered. Looking without touching, she asked, "What is this?"

"Take it. The Fates sent me home to the three of you, so you may save it for the future of your children. You are to bury it in the foundation surrounding the garden. Please, you must hurry. I'm here to warn you." I looked at Xerxes. "Protect it so our bloodline will live on."

"I will," he said and took it from me. This is why I liked the man. He was intelligent. He knew the Fates personally. He and his family had been guarding this sacred place for thousands of years. This apple was just another thing the Fates, or his deity Marduk, had charged him to protect. In exchange, he received not one but two wives. My twin Anunnaki sisters. Both had given him their bite, so he was like us. He understood things differently than the humans outside these walls.

"But what about Father, we heard he is looking for you. You're not safe here, Ishtar. If he finds you..." An said, now on her knees next to me.

"Put it in the garden. Hide it in the foundation of your enormous stone wall. It's been standing for thousands of years. It will stand forever until it is time for the Fates to reveal it to someone worthy of finding it."

The thundering sound of guards' feet was coming down the hallway, signaling their approach. "Quickly," I urged my brother-in-law, "pack your belongings and gather your children. Hide the apple and flee to the northern mountains. Leave everything else behind and never look back." Xerxes's eyes showed a flicker of understanding.

"I love you. I will distract the guards. It's Father, he's gone mad," I whispered in short sentences, not stopping to take a breath. "He won't stop until he has crushed all life. Titus is nearing the gates, but Father will kill you if you don't go now. You can't stay here." Tears welled up in my eyes as I feared I wasn't in time to save them. "Please!" I jumped up and looked into his eyes, pleading to do as I asked. He gave me a slight nod.

"Go, I will do as you and God command. Go, may God bless you," he said into my mind.

"Brother, be safe," my sisters said as I hastily hugged them.

"We love you, Ishtar," my sisters spoke in my mind. I beamed, happy that I could deliver the warning and the apple in time. Then I stepped back behind the veil and disappeared from their sight.

After causing a distraction and confusing the guards, I slipped away and arrived at the ship, stunned. Those big white wings were not inside as I had asked, but outside under a tree. Sitting with his back against it, someone lying on his lap.

"How did it go? Did you deliver the apple?"

"Yes, I did, but it was harder than I thought it would be. Who is this? And why are you out here?"

The man cracked an eye open.

"Easy there, friend." I greeted the man in the local language. "What's his name? What is he doing here?"

"*Shhht*, he only wants to talk," Peter said as the man's eyes enlarged.

"I've no need of talking, I know who you are. I am ready to go home. Take me home, Angel," he croaked, not looking at me, but at Peter.

I didn't believe what I was seeing and hearing. I checked behind us. Peter smiled at the man. I rolled my eyes. He'd found a stray under the only fucking tree, revealing himself as I asked him not to do.

"Do you need water? Are you thirsty?" Peter asked with a kindness in his voice I didn't think he possessed. In the dim moonlight, he spread his hands, revealing a water bottle he had found on the ship. I had brought it with me to transport water to Grayrak as I waited for the ball-shaped ship to arrive. "We've come to collect you. You are needed back home." Peter said in English. He was making shit up, indulging the dying man.

"Yes, yes, I am God's servant. Take me where He needs me to be," the man whispered weakly.

"First drink a bit, you must be parched," Peter said.

The man was bleeding, half-naked, and dirty beyond belief. As if someone had dragged him here and tossed him at our doorstep. His lips were cracked and swollen. His tunic was ripped, brown, and crusty with old blood. His hair was long and tangled, and his unkempt beard covered his whole face except for his brown eyes.

"How did you find him? I told you not to get out of the ship. Did he call for help or were you outside looking for trouble?" I asked, hoping it was not a trap while hurriedly scanning our surroundings. There weren't a lot of places to hide either behind the tree or the ship.

Peter didn't answer me. The sun was rising, and it was already extremely hot outside. The dying man took the water and inspected the bottle. Peter pushed it to his mouth and tipped the contents down his throat. Choking, sputtering, and moaning, he drank the liquid like a baby from his mother's bosom, holding the bottle between shaking hands.

"What happened to you? Were you attacked?" Peter asked, ignoring my questions. They spoke to each other, but each in their own language. How they understood each other who the fuck knew.

Coughing, the man stopped drinking to answer Peter. "Yes, there were four attackers with knives."

I stepped closer, to see what he was showing Peter. "They slashed my forearms. Whores sons, they were! They took everything except the clothes I'm wearing." He pointed to his blood-drenched arms. "The ruffian's mothers were sluts. Sinners, all of them! I came here to die. I asked God to take me from this place. I want to go to Heaven and be with Him. I am ready for you to take me."

I gave Peter a look. Lifting one eyebrow, he spoke mind to mind. "I'm bringing him with us. We should help him. He doesn't need to die here alone like a dog. We can take him to Phoenix.

"I don't know where Phoenix is. I've never been there."

"Tell Lasitor to take us, I don't care what he says, he knows exactly where and when to go. Something tells me we should save this man. He is important."

"The Fates?"

"No, not that. It's a feeling I have." He got up carrying the half-dead man, and I followed, shaking my head.

"Let's go then. We must take him to a hospital. He needs medical care."

"André? Fuck yes, let's go to him! He is a doctor. He can help us."

"Peter, I don't know if that is a good idea. I don't know if we're allowed to do this. The Fates never said anything about bringing someone back with us."

"Fuck that and fuck your stupid rules. You break them all the bloody time and do as you want, anyway. Why can't we save him?"

"He is not a stray dog, he is a human, almost dead, on his way."

"Exactly!" he shouted over his shoulder.

"Heaven, thank you, Peter," the man muttered through bloody lips.

"Do you want to go to a better place?" Peter asked him, already one foot inside the ship. As if he would say no and Peter would leave him here to die if he did. He cracked a bleeding smile at Peter. That seemed to be answer enough for him. "Come, we are going to André. He owes me."

I threw my hands in the air. Peter tucked his wings, bent his neck, and carried our new passenger inside.

**2013 A.D.**
**Lord Andrew Whiskey Distilleries**
**Lexington, Kentucky**
**United States of America**
**Earth**

The time machine hummed. I adjusted the coordinates and realized I didn't know where to take us. "Where should we go? Where and when is this André?" I asked over my shoulder. Peter sat behind me on the floor, legs stretched out and the gasping body draped over him. Wings open, head down, it seemed he was praying. "Peter!" I called again. "It is risky to stay here. I need to know where to go." I turned back to the control panel.

"I have a suggestion. My data suggests we have coordinates for an Andrew." Lasitor said. "I can take you to Peter's friend. He should have modern medicine and he is the only person you can trust, unless you want to take our wounded passenger to Grayrak?"

"No!" Peter and I exclaimed simultaneously.

"Lasitor, take us to Andrew, in America. Not André in Germany. Take us to the future," Peter ordered my guide as if he had a personal relationship with him. Lasitor appears to have been hiding information from me.

Outside my ship's window, the air was shimmering. "We have to go, and I prefer knowing where and when. It's dangerous to jump into the unknown. We could land in water, or even in the middle of a war. I prefer not to sink or have my window shot out," I said as I glanced over my shoulder. The dying man's pain contorted his weary face. He had been suffering for far too long. I fully grasped his longing for the afterlife. But I also understood Peter's reasoning for not leaving him alone under a tree in the desert. "Peter?" I asked softly. "Are you sure about this? Jumping through time is dangerous. I don't know this man or this place, America." I stopped to think for a second. "Wait, it seems like I have memories of him. So I assume we went there, but he might not have the medicine we seek."

Peter's eyes met mine, filled with determination. "I know it's a risk, but if anyone can help him, it's Andrew. He's always been ahead of his time, quite literally."

A surge of empathy intertwined with worry washed over me. "Look at him," I said gently. "He's blue-pale, bled out, and barely breathing. He thinks you are taking him to the afterlife. Maybe you should let him go? He seems ready to go."

Peter's voice trembled with emotion as he spoke, his hands gently wiping the blood from the man's face. "I can't explain it, but ever since I heard him cry out in pain, I knew I had to help him. He was all alone, and my heart couldn't bear to see him suffer. I feel a deep connection to him, like I know him somehow. It drives me to keep him alive. He may seem insignificant to you, but he is important to me." The intensity of his words hung heavy in the air as Peter continued to tend to his wounds.

I swiveled in my seat. My long blue slender fingers flew across the control panel as I prepared the ship for its jump. "Let's bring him to this André or Andrew, whatever his name is," I said, a hopeful edge to my voice. "He will know what to do."

"An excellent idea," Lasitor replied. The ship zinged and thrummed with energy as it charged up for the jump. "I'll take us to 2013 A.D." he announced confidently. "And do you still have that ring I instructed you to keep?"

I quirked an eyebrow, remembering the strange metal ring that glimmered with a vibrant blue hue. I'd found it amidst the scattered debris when I returned to retrieve Barkor's deceased mother for a proper burial. I had saved it, stowing it away in the overhead cubby where I kept my most prized possessions. I held it up, revealing it to Lasitor. "Yes, sir. With this, you have something to offer Andrew on your visit," he remarked as if assuming control and endorsing our mission. "One leap, but two offerings for others. A life for Elijah and a present for Andrew." The ring emitted a faint hum as I turned it over in my hand, almost as if lending its approval to Lasitor's suggestion.

"Lasitor?"

"Yes, taking you to 2013 A.D," he cut me off. I shook my head, checking on Peter one more time, and pushed the jump button, overriding the onboard guide to spite him. This was my ship, not his.

Moments later, we found ourselves in unfamiliar surroundings.

Andrew's property was both secluded and safe. The large black building with dark windows and a white sign that said Lord Andrew Distillery amazed me. I cringed as Peter handed me the limp body of the man and forced himself out the tiny door. Had I known he would struggle with the door's size, I would have increased its dimensions for him during my idle time in Grayrak.

Luckily, it was nighttime and Lasitor had parked the ship behind some bushes from where we stepped out to take a quick walk across the luscious green grass toward the back door. Lasitor's ability to keep up with my travels kept me sane. My brain couldn't keep up with all the history, places, and timelines. I would have been lost in time without him.

Memories assailed me as we approached the building. The quiet abruptly ended as Peter pounded on the door with such force that it seemed like he was kicking it in.

"If Andrew doesn't open, I'll fly up to find an open window," he announced just as a gorgeous dark-haired man opened the door. He took one look at us, blinked a few times, and said, "Hmmm, an alien, an angel, and a dead prophet. Welcome. We've been expecting you. Please come in."

Wordlessly, we stepped inside, surveying the big open space and the over-friendly doorman.

"Follow me, please," he invited us, closing and locking the door. "My name is Tony. I'm Andrew's right-hand man, butler, and friend of over twenty years. I assume this is the famous Elijah." We all greeted him, offering no hands to shake. He examined the blood that should have been inside the dying man but was now covering us. "Quickly, follow me, and I'll take you down to Andrew's apartment."

I checked in with Peter. He nodded and hastily pushed and crammed all four of us into a moving box thing. I saw one on Grayrak, so I knew it was for moving up and down inside a building.

A loud ding followed the shutting of the doors. Tony didn't say a word or look fazed by us. Maybe this was an everyday occurrence for him because it felt like I was having one of my worst cases of déjà vu.

Peter stooped his neck and shoulders so his wings weren't scratching the roof, not taking his eyes off the man, apparently called Elijah. His empathy for the man was unbelievable, and I wondered if my Kuku was naturally inclined to be so caring or if he had somehow experienced the same flashbacks as I.

"How do you know us already?" Peter asked. "And how do you know he is Elijah?"

Tony's brow furrowed, his eyes scanning our faces with a mix of concern and alarm. "Ish has been looking for the two of you here at least four times now," he said, his voice laced with urgency. My mind raced as I made sense of what he was saying.

Suddenly, strange memories flooded my mind, and I understood why Tony was so worried, as he added, "But this is the first time you have both Peter and Elijah with you." Tony fidgeted with his hands, tapping his fingers against the button. "I need you to do something for me," he said nervously.

"What is it?" I asked, brows drawn in concern.

"Something's going to happen. And whatever you do, don't let them get away," Tony replied urgently, a bead of sweat forming on his forehead as he spoke.

Peter spread his wings out, ruffling them loudly in the small space. A wave of intense loathing radiated from him as his eyes locked onto me. "Oh my god, that's why I know him," he growled, "this is the asshole who hit me over the head and dragged me away from you. He told me you were dead. I can't believe I'm saving your sorry ass!" he said, shaking the limp body—its bushy-haired head flopping up and down and his tongue lolling out like a dead donkey.

My heart froze in my chest. I hated small stuffy places. "Peter, please calm down." My body was tense and hunched in the small box we were confined in. The smell of burning feathers mixed with his rage filled the air, making it hard to breathe. My eight-foot frame hunched forward, his sharp horns dangerously close to my face. With just a few more inches, they could easily pierce through my eyes. Despite my begging for him to calm down, Peter continued to snarl at the man he was saving. The pale man, who remained eerily still and who was most probably already blowing out his last breath during all the chaos.

"Seems like we should have left him to die under that tree." Peter huffed, and the door dinged to open inside a big room.

"Ah, thank fuck," Tony said as we poured out of the small box. "This is Andrew's apartment. This is his living room. I'll be right back. I will…"

"Ish! Peter!" A tall blond-haired man I assumed was Andrew, called to us as he came down a long corridor. Barefoot and bare-chested, he wore a pair of red soft cotton pants sitting loosely around his hips. With a few strides over the white marble, he swept me into an embrace as if we were old friends. Then, seeing Elijah with Peter, unfazed like Tony, he took Elijah and laid him on the couch. Before I knew what was happening, he bit into his wrist and dripped his blood into Elijah's mouth.

"What the fuck!" Peter lunged for Andrew. Elijah coughed as blood gurgled in the back of his throat. They scuffled, and I rushed to Elijah, falling to my knees, and helping him roll onto his side. He barked and spattered blood on my face, all wide-eyed, and with fire in them.

"Why did you do that?" Peter shoved Andrew's chest, pushing him back and away from Elijah.

"What's wrong with you? I was only helping. Ish brought him here for help. For my help."

"We are still coming to terms with the fact that we've been here four times already. You could have given us a second to think about it." Peter and Andrew were shouting at each other. Tony ran for a rag to wipe the furniture, then Elijah's face. Nervously, he patted to check that no blood had gotten on himself.

"Let's get him into a bath," he said and ran down the long hallway to where I heard water running already. I scooped the delirious Elijah up and carried him to where Tony waited. I've seen showers and toilets, but seldom with water in Grayrak. I had to go to Gugusan's for a bath. Here it streamed out of the wall into a white marble vessel big enough for four men my size.

Elijah thrashed wildly in my arms. "Is this a healing pool?" I asked, wondering if the waters were outside and bubbling through the wall and into the pristine, empty pool.

"Put him in. He is filthy," Tony said, and although I tried to carefully place him in the bath, Elijah splashed into it like a rabid dog scared of water.

"Fuck this." *I've had enough of this craziness.* I touched his forehead, willing him to calm the fuck down. It helped a bit, and he sank back into the shallow, lukewarm water. Tony removed his tattered tunic and the one sandal that had come with us from Babylon. All the while, Peter and Andrew were still aggressively getting re-acquainted and catching up. It felt like I'd stepped into a timeline I knew nothing about. Finding Peter, delivering the apple, and coming here, didn't fit in with searching for Elijah and visiting this place four times.

"Elijah, sit still!" Tony ordered. "I'm just washing you. We're helping you."

"He doesn't understand you. Let me translate," I said to Tony, in an attempt to reduce the man's anxiety.

I cooed in Babylonian. "*Shhht*, it'll be okay. You will be okay. We are only helping you. You are safe now. Remember, you were dying and Peter came to help you." He looked at me, glaring, sniffing, and then let his hand fall into the water next to him. At first sight, he seemed old and rumpled. Not one ounce of fat on his body. But as he twisted and turned in the water, his strength increased, and his voice became deep and strong. His wiry frail body was slowly filling with muscles in all the right places. His gaunt face and bloody eyes transformed into a beautiful exotic face, with slanted dark eyes and pouty lips. His back was covered with a huge tattoo of a sun rising behind a monastery. It reminded me of a Japanese monk's religious markings.

"Where is the angel and where is Heaven? Is this the afterlife?" he asked, rambling. Tony sat down on the side of the bath as Elijah sat up, looking ten times stronger than before. His transformation was extraordinary. When I shared my blood with Titus and

Gugusan, it was a slow drawn-out process. I wondered if Andrew's blood differed from mine. I hardly knew these people yet bits and pieces of memories told me I had been here before.

"He will help you wash, maybe get rid of all that hair and beard, while you are at it, Tony," I said in English, then I switched back to Babylonian. "This man will help you clean up. Peter and I can take you back home to Babylon, but you will have to learn our ways—come with us until you decide where you want to live. We have space in my ship for one more. You will live for a long time and there are things to teach you, things you need to know."

"That's way more than what you gave me," Andrew said, arms folded and leaning against the doorframe. I imagine Peter was either behind him or still in the big room.

"I'm sorry, Andrew, I'm afraid this is confusing for me—I found my mate only hours ago. Peter says we've met twice already. He was under the impression I'd died yesterday. Somehow I have cut into this timeline and although I have scattered memories of you, Peter, and this place, it feels like this is the first time meeting you."

"You have jumped yourself into a tangled mess. Do you remember fucking and biting me in Germany, in 1968 A.D.?"

"Not at all. Like I told you earlier, only bits and pieces of visions and dreams pop up. I had visions of Peter before meeting him. I agree with your theory, but it feels like I caught the tail end of what happened. Where is Peter? He must come to show himself to Elijah. The poor man can hardly remember anything. Peter wanted to save him, so Peter must come and explain."

"Peter!" Andrew called over his shoulder while smiling at Elijah fondly. *He had gone and turned Elijah into an Igigi.*

"You shouldn't have done that. We brought him here for your modern medicine, not to turn him into one of us. You don't even know him. He belongs to you now. To you and Peter. I don't want another Igigi."

"I assumed that was why you were here. The rushed visions we saw of you told us he was turned and Peter was gone. You were searching for Peter and Elijah. So, seeing him dead and not breathing, he wasn't going to make it to a medical facility. Anyway, they would ask questions and if he died from stab wounds, the police would be called in. It would be murder."

"Oh, I never thought of that," I scanned Andrew's muscular physique. I was sure Peter would love to stay and play. Andrew dripped sex appeal. The monk could watch and learn.

"Help!" the man shouted. Tony had his hands full. I wasn't getting near that muddy, bloody mess.

"Elijah, we called Peter for you. He is coming," I said in Babylonian, and he chirped up as soon as those big wings and blond hair came through the doorway.

"Okay, Tony, I'm leaving the two of you. This room is too small for all of us," I greeted Peter with a kiss. He sighed, leaning into me. "Like I told Andrew, Elijah is your responsibility. My Kuku, this is serious. Just like a newborn Anubis."

"You mean like a puppy?"

"Yes, just like that. He is now yours and Andrew's. You have to teach him how to eat, where to sleep, and most importantly, to never reveal his magical nature to those he doesn't know or trust. He is not fully Anunnaki, but in my experience, humans don't like supernatural things they don't understand. Their comfort boxes of religious beliefs may sway some to hunt him down and kill him. Others would exalt him, see him as godlike. You saved his life." I pointed to the three of them. "It's a big issue, and what will your husband say? Elijah is now your responsibility, your child."

"Husband, what husband?"

"That reminds me. Here, before I forget." I removed the ring from my coat pocket and waved a hand for Andrew to reverse so I could exit through the door. "Here, this is your wedding ring. It's made of a metal that comes from the future, I found it in a rocket that crashed on the moon. It glows blue at night. It's for your future husband…"

A long wolf whistle came from inside the washroom. "I hope it's Juandre Martinez?" Tony shouted as water sloshed, sounding like he was wrestling with Elijah. I heard Peter reprimanding the stubborn man.

"Sit the fuck still! You should be happy to be alive," Peter said in English, while Elijah shouted in Babylonian at him that he wanted to go to Heaven. Not drink blood with a fallen angel and a dark blue demon creature of the night. *That was probably me.*

"Sir, I told you he is going to be your husband!" Tony shouted at a surprised Andrew who was distracted by the commotion in the bathroom.

Andrew took the ring from the palm of my hand inspecting it. "Wow, this is a beautiful gift. Thank you, Ish." He lifted his chin, shouting back at Tony, "I will let you know when it is time. Don't go head over heels searching for him. Gay marriage is still illegal here. I'm warning you, Tony!" Andrew rolled the ring between his fingers and slipped it on to appraise it closer. "I've been thinking about him a lot. I'm unsure if he will remember me, or even accept me as I am."

"I don't know who you are referring to. If it wasn't for Lasitor, my time travel machine telling me this, I would never have known," I said, shifting uncomfortably from side to side.

"Andrew, all I can say is you have a long and happy future ahead. You will see, you will be married someday. You will live in a world filled with only men, where gay marriage is the norm. Sometimes three, four, and even five men in a marriage," Peter hollered. Andrew threw his arms around me, hugging the shit out of me.

"Thank you, Peter, and thank you, Ish." His eyes glistened with tears. "Are you impressed with the Whiskey Distillery? I've been storing crates of it in South Africa, as you asked me."

I bit my lip, feeling like an asshole repeating myself. "Again, I'm sorry, Andrew. I think that was the future me visiting you…"

With an oomph, Elijah shot past us and disappeared through a door. Peter, Tony, Andrew, and I rushed after him, got stuck in the door tangled in Peter's wings, and untangled ourselves in a split second. "He's taking the emergency stairs to the outside," Peter yelled, skipping every second and third step, not able to flap his wings in the cramped space.

The exit door cracked open, revealing a pale blue sky and the fresh scent of dew-soaked grass. Peter leaped up, his wings unfurling as he took to the air. "He will have a better view from up there," I said to Andrew, who was panting heavily beside me. "The monk is fast. He could already be long gone." I spun around, searching every corner of the garden for a clue. "Your fucking blood only made him faster." I cursed, catching my breath as well. "Why did you have to turn him into one of our kind?"

"Why did you turn me by fucking me? Why didn't you just give me your blood…" His words trailed off as he jumped onto a wall and searched behind it.

"Again, I don't remember biting you. I could've, but the Igigi are younger servants of the Anunnaki, their strength and longevity reduce with time. Your blood only stays so long in their system and wears off. I would have had to administer blood, over and over for it to strengthen your human body for prolonged periods. Plus, Elijah can't do the same for someone else. Only the royals can give someone temporary enhancements. Make them their Igigi, if they trust them enough. They are meant to serve you, especially when you can't move around in daylight. That's why I told you, he is yours. He is bonded to you. If I fucked and sucked you, and injected my venom, you are a royal courtesan." I cupped my hands in front of my mouth, calling for Peter.

A faint "Here, Ish," drifted to me from the direction of the ship. And then it hit me—Elijah and Peter were taking my ship.

"Fuck!" I shouted and ran. Just as Andrew and I cut through the bushes lining the back of his property, the door swooshed closed and the machine started up.

"Lasitor, don't you fucking dare!" I bolted. "Open the fucking door, Peter, open the door! You can't jump if the door is open. Open the door!" I shouted as I banged my fist against the side. Nothing. I pulled the door lever. Nothing. *What can I do, what can I do?* I ran my fingers along the outline of the door, trying to pry the thing open with my fingertips.

*No, no, no!*

Ice-cold panic struck me. "Fuck! Help me to open the door, Andrew!" *The engines are revving up, preparing for a jump.* Desperate to stop it, Andrew pulled the lever to open the door. *My swords!* I grappled for one and forced the tip into the hairbreadth slit between the door and the ship. Just as I had it deep enough for leverage, the electromagnetic force field blasted us away. I jumped up to try again, *do something, anything*, but watched helplessly as my beloved ship vanished into thin air. Silence filled the space where the energy tore through the veils of time.

"Ah fuck dammit, so this is how it happened." Andrew's voice echoed in my mind.

"Fuuuck!" I fell to my knees.

*What just happened? How will I return to Grayrak? How will I survive without my mate by my side? My plans of traveling with him are shattered. Where and how do I start searching for him? I don't have a ship. My ship abandoned me. Why did Lasitor do this? How will I honor my promise to the Fates? What have I done?*

I plunged my fingers into the wet green grass, plucking handfuls of the stuff out of the ground, and threw it as far as I could. I was furious—at myself. I should never have gone to Babylon with my mate. I should have taken him home, to Phoenix as he asked.

"I'm so sorry, Ishtar," Andrew whispered into my ear. I leaned into his embrace—clutching his shoulders. I was broken again. I was alone again. *I don't deserve a mate and a ship. I'm a useless Anunnaki, just like my father always said.*

"It's okay."

"No! It's not okay!" I pushed Andrew away and got up. *Where do I go? Fuck!*

Boom! Whoop-whoop!

I flung myself around, too scared and surprised to look, as I squashed my eyelids closed. "Please let them be okay," I begged the Fates as I cracked one eye open.

"The ship is back!" Andrew shouted. I ran to it.

"Lasitor, open the fucking door!" I pulled the lever, and the door swooshed open. The ship was empty. Only the smell of my mate lingered. "Where and when did you take them?" I asked and jumped inside. "Andrew, I'm going after them. Take care!"

"Yes, I know. See you soon, Ishtar." He lifted his hand, but the door shut in his face. "Lasitor, take me to Peter now!"

Silence.

"Lasitor, for fuck's sake, take me to Peter. Jump to him now. To the time and place you dropped him off."

Silence.

"You motherfucking dumb machine!" I inspected the dashboard in an attempt to see if any coordinates were recorded. "You deleted them! What the fuck?"

"I have my reasons."

"Where should I go, what should I do?" I asked, slumping back in my seat.

Static echoed through the speakers. "Jumping to Grayrak, in five, four, three, two..."

"Fuck you, fuck you, Lasitor. Fuck you, and fuck-fuck-fuck you!"

CHAPTER 51

# LOVERS COLLIDED

*"Good morning.*

*It's now six a.m.*

*Did you know that corundum is a mineral used for many parts of your time machine? Adding traces of iron causes it to become red and is referred to as ruby, while titanium or chromium traces result in a blue color and is known as sapphire.*

*Did you also know, that because they can withstand high temperatures and pressures and are resistant to chemicals and plasmas, red corundum is used to focus the laser light that makes time jumps possible, while blue corundum is used for your spaceship windows because its low dielectric loss and high electrical insulation mean it can withstand hot temperatures for when your ship space jumps.*

*You better get up, because breakfast is served until eight a.m.*

*Go get him!"*

**Peter**
**2146 A.D. (94 A.T.) (After Twins)**
**One year before the moon evacuation**
**Phoenix, underwater glass dome city**
**Earth**

Brad had assigned monitoring the health of the Phoenix residents to me, with instructions to pay close attention to the children born to parents who'd had the Eden Beans implanted for an extended lifespan. Since no one has shown any side effects after living two lifetimes, I'd quit all my research, not missing one second of working with stinky, frozen dead people or specimens.

I smiled with pride and swept my gaze over the kindergarten class of bright-eyed, inquisitive, enthusiastic boys. It served as my drug, functioning as both an antipsychotic and antidepressant, which I eagerly consumed in search of pure, innocent joy. Something I could never have.

"Tell me, who is eager about tomorrow's show-and-tell?" I watched as a dozen boys stuck their hands into the air as high as possible. My class comprised boys ages three to five years of age. Show-and-tell was a highlight in my tutoring sessions at the end of the week. It also helped me identify who needed more attention and encouragement. I discovered that those lacking inspiration and interest often required additional personal attention, which prompted me to inform my department head to schedule a discussion with the parents. Most of the time, the problem wasn't at home. They were little geniuses, bored or misunderstood. They still needed to play but in the advanced class with advanced kids. Meeting the parents was always nerve-wracking. Adulting was never my strong point. I'm as immature as those little geniuses. Hence, Brad's recommendation of working with kids, because they live in the here and now, with no judgment. In the meantime, I grew an emotional backbone. It was relaxing and fun to do something meaningful.

"Julius, you may go first tomorrow. You've been bragging the entire week about your new pet, so please tell your daddies that tomorrow is the day. Rodger must be in a cage and one of your daddies has to attend and take Rodger home after our show-and-tell period," I said firmly, but friendly. I suspected Rodger was another adopted lab rat or bunny, but Julius held the secret close to his chest. All of us were looking forward to meeting Rodger—whatever Rodger was. "So, Rodger, the rabbit is coming to meet us tomorrow?" I teased, trying to pry the secret from Julius.

"No, Rodger is not a bunny or a rat, I promise you. You will all be so surprised." he exclaimed, and the other kids leaned in closer, yipping, "Tell me," and "I won't tell."

Little Mathew whispered, but all of us could hear him, nevertheless. "You can tell me, then I will tell you what I'm bringing." But Julius just rolled his lips inward and smiled with glee.

"Is Rodger a fish?" Sandy asked, to throw the class off his friend's scent. He was Julius's best friend and I could see the two of them were planning something. Sandy was helping Julius with his show-and-tell tomorrow, being the sole classmate aware of Rodger's identity.

"You won't guess what I'm bringing with me," little Jasper yelled. Dear lord, not this again. I thought I had had enough of hearing about the end times. "I'm bringing something…"

"Not that stinky old book with the stories about the old world," Julius said. I was thinking the same thing, but I couldn't let them talk to each other that way.

"Julius, just like you get excited about your surprise, so does everyone else about their surprises. So, we must learn to be eager together and try our best to understand why that something is so important to them without making them feel bad that they don't like the same thing or bring the same thing as you. How boring would it be if all of us brought the same thing to show-and-tell as you every Friday?"

"Yes, that would be pretty stupid," Carlos said, dark brown curls flopping up and down as he shook his head energetically.

"Well, I see we have a busy and exciting day tomorrow. Please wash your hands, clean up your toys, and wash your hands again," I said, as they jumped up and ran. I saw some fathers already making their way over with their children's shoes in their hands. After I cleaned and sanitized the playroom, I ducked behind the bookcase and made my way to the back door. I wasn't in the mood to talk to overeager and proud parents today. I checked over my shoulder that no one was following me and shot for the emergency exit I took to avoid a crowd.

It had been a productive day today. A burst of pride, accomplishment, and excitement for the coming day putting a hop in my step as I jogged down the stairs.

The laughter of men and feet pounding the metal stairs echoed upwards in the stairwell shaft from below. Upon reaching the back entrance of my laboratory, I stopped before opening the door, praying that it wasn't Mika heading toward his office from the same direction. I froze, listening. It fucking sounded like him. If they're coming to the lab, I'll have to retreat somewhere else.

Fuck! Should I jump and try to make it to the door, or should I turn around and run back up the stairs? Like a stupid lab rat, I couldn't decide which way the cheese was. I had taken too long and missed my chance. Shock and utter surprise washed over me when I saw his face. As our gazes met, we halted just looking at each other. It felt like I was watching a volcano erupting in slow motion. Heat burned my skin. My legs wobbled. The stairs vibrated beneath my feet. A force of wonder and awe pulsated between us. Despite its beauty, my instincts shrieked to flee—death by lava was imminent.

Hot alien—too close.

He was halfway up the stairs—and already as tall as I was. It was him! That dark face that haunted me.

"Hello," he greeted, looking me up and down with a grin so bright my retinas hurt. On impulse, I covered my eyes as if looking at a welding arc. My heart slammed, jumped left and right inside my chest cavity, then settled behind my Adam's apple. I couldn't speak. I swallowed to force my heart to go back to the place God intended it to be. In the left chest cavity. I opened my eyes.

Frowning, he looked at me as if I was a stranger.

Speechless and gulping for words, I searched for the door's motion activation sensor, but couldn't find it fast enough. The two geniuses, Mika and Connor, looked at him and then back at me, already putting one and one together. Mika inhaled, preparing to spew a bunch of Russian retorts. Milliseconds passed and felt like drawn-out minutes.

I had to get away from here. I checked my clothes, flattening the wrinkles. Oh my fucking god, I wasn't ready, and this wasn't how I imagined our magical reunification would go. My clothes were full of sticky jam handprints, thanks to the extra messy lunch break earlier today.

Fuck, I raked my hair to the side. Remembering the jam had somehow reached it as well, I opted to flatten it against my scalp. Sticky hair and all, I waited. Unprepared for our big moment.

It wasn't supposed to happen like this.

Stay, go, stay, go, stay, go flashed in reds and greens in my spinning mind. Take a fucking breath, inhale, exhale, I told myself, blinking like defective Christmas lights and unable to take my gaze off him. Narrowing his eyes as if to see better, he cocked his head to the side. He was so much bigger than I remembered. Bigger, darker, bluer, and clueless. Zero recognition from Ishtar, and I stood in absolute shock.

"Morning, Peter," Brad greeted from the landing below. He narrowed his eyes questioningly. *No, no, no.* I felt like I was inside a bloody MRI machine while they scanned me up and down.

Brad assessed the situation like a pit bull, deciding if he smelled blood or shit. I smiled, also revealing my blinding stack of teeth—because that's what you do in situations like this. With Brad around, Mika and Connor had to think twice before having me skinned, chopped up into human meat cubes, and blasted out of the sewage to become fish food. I never speak to them and they are not allowed to speak to me. Avoiding each other worked—for me. Because of guilt, my self-destruction sequence was in imminent danger of activation, until Brad suggested working at the daycare and ignoring the Romanovs.

"Oh, hello, Brad," I said through clenched teeth while bulging my sticky fingers into fists at my sides. I had inserted General Brad McCormick's Eden Bean when he was a virile forty-five years of age. I have the utmost respect for him. And I thought he was one of the most attractive men in Phoenix. His dark brown eyes were intelligent and shone with emotional maturity. He was compassionate and although he was a war hero predoomsday, he was approachable, honest, fair, and just. He was a true and well-loved leader, and I don't think Phoenix would have survived if not for his ability to stand back and listen to suggestions from men much smarter than him. Being a great visionary and protective family man, he has told me numerous times that something or someone awaited us on the other side, and I believed him since he was the only human I brought back from death.

My eyes darted back to Ish. "And hello to you," I said softly to my long-awaited lover, then turned my attention back to Brad, my self-appointed personal watchdog. I smiled again to show him I was okay and thrilled. I suspected I was looking freaky. Ish stepped one step back. I blinked and raked my eyes over the two blue-eyed busy body squirrels like I was nuts.

I side-eyed Ish, looking from Brad to him, then to Mika and Connor, and back at Brad. Ish was the most perplexed of them all. Eyes wide, he continued gawking at me.

What in the ever-loving fuck? Doesn't he remember me? Hurt pierced my heart. Here I was busting my ass awaiting him, growing fresh hemorrhoids.

Dammit, I waited so long for him, and now I'm a fucking stranger?

I was confused and disappointed. I shut that shit down by unfreezing my body and waving my hand to activate the door, then I slipped inside the lab. "Excuse me!" I yipped like a hyena. Once the door shut behind me, I leaned back to press my ear against it.

"Who was that stunning angel?" Ish asked.

"Don't mind him. Peter is a little odd," Mika said.

"Yes, don't take that personally. He doesn't mean to appear disrespectful. He's skittish," Brad said as they passed the door.

Fucking clowns! My anxiety levels were directly linked to the Romanovs' proximity to me. Lately, the motherfuckers were popping up everywhere I went. I knew I was making life difficult for myself by ignoring them, the window for apologies had shut years ago. There was no way that I could explain any of it away.

I made my way to my sanctuary, my office. Trying to not think about Ish, I toed off my shoes, undressed, and hastily took a shower to wash off the peanut butter and jam. Afterward, still trying not to think about Ish, I got dressed, snatched a book I'd been reading from the bookshelf then planted my butt sideways on the small cot so I could jump to close the door if anyone approached.

I sighed. I failed not to think about him. So I waited.

Three hours later, distracted and more absentminded than usual, I contemplated where in Ish's circle of life I fit. The more I thought about his cluelessness earlier, the more I fumed. *Fuck my life! And fuck him! Fuck him skewered up and roasted over Hell's flames.*

That cluster fuck collision between my past and my future had pissed on my dream meeting. Oh my god! I slammed the book into my face, his guilelessness, that radiant stack of teeth.

I closed my eyes and stilled my rambling mind, then visualized the cataloged memories my eyes caught and saved like pictures to a hard drive in my mind. I flipped through them. Searching for his smile. It was real. Not fake, like my mother's smile was the day they took me away from her.

I recalled these things and compared the real ones with those I imagined. It kept me sane. Sometimes it felt like I was one person living in two people's minds. To keep myself grounded, I've stayed isolated, although always surrounded by people. I've kept my head down and wished for his loving arms to hold me. To envelop me. To love me. My life story is not unique. Others have been through what I have. I'm just fortunate because, unlike them, I was smart enough to outplay the monsters that raised us, that used us, the children of the experimentation camps.

I hated myself for so long. But no, like a carrot, Ish had dangled the promise of a beautiful future with him in front of me. My Ish.

I shivered. Thinking about him felt like sitting front row and center at the volcanic eruption I'd experienced earlier. The way he filled the stairs with his magnificence. The powerful force emanating from him, that drew my itty-bitty self to him like a magnet while the compass needle pointed to 1968 A.D. So many burning question marks. Why?

And then I wondered. *Maybe this is the day he met me and this is our day one.* I bumped the back of my head against the wall behind me.

"Stupid, stupid, stupid." *That's the answer.*

"Today, the clock of our time together starts ticking. I've been fucking hanging on, believing it will get better from Tuesday, October 1, 1968 A.D. until today Thursday, October 1, 2146 A.D. (94 A.T.)" —I closed my eyes and calculated— "That is exactly sixty-four thousand two hundred and eighty-four lonely days." I've kept my head down, worked, breathed, and existed. As a copy. But not a true copy.

"Yes, oh my god! Today is our day one!"

I checked my wristwatch. Three hours ago, my Ish had come for me. I've been awaiting my Ish for so long that I lost myself in my dreams, in the past.

One second, still lost deep in my head, the next, Mika was standing in my office.

I jumped up, hands up, and my back against the wall. My feet unsure. Shaking and struggling to balance on the mattress. I screamed, my throat raw while hoping someone down the hallway heard me. "Help! I'm being attacked! I'm getting skinned today!" Sparks flew and my ears tooted.

The Irishman was blocking the door. Mika grabbed Ish by his clothes and hurled him at my feet. I frowned and swallowed my cries for help. It felt as if the ceiling was cracking open and the icy southern seas were drowning me. I looked up, seeing specs of stars like I saw that night in my living room. Back in 1968. When I saw my older self. *I'm going to pass out! I can't. It's my day of reunification.* My skin itched and stretched over my body. I paused, taking a few proper deep breaths to stay conscious.

Then I filled my lungs to the maximum and exclaimed with tear-filled delight, "Alien eyes!"

Happy tears streamed down my face. My big brute bent to one knee, holding a paper flower up to me. Like an offering. I stopped yelling, gasping for air, and choking on snot.

*Calm the fuck down.* I quieted my distraught mind while still clutching the wall, holding my body upright.

The oddest feelings and memories washed over me. Microscopic pieces snapped, flashed, and flickered in my mind. I blinked my eyes and shook my head to refocus. My mind emptied as if deleting the copies of memories, feelings, and colors. Becoming black. A void. Then suddenly my mind and my body filled up. Happiness and pain. So much of it, and I welcomed it. Letting go of the lonely cold vortex, I settled into this time and this world. I replaced myself with me. The real me. As colors burst and fizzed, my lover's eyes were what I saw. The man destined to be with me.

My whole body tingled. I should rip my clothes off, I thought. Must leave—search for a room, a washroom, a shower, a fucking toilet stall, anything, away from them! My clothes were too tight and my skin....

"Gille-toine, close the door, don't let him escape!" Mika yelled, and Connor pushed the door closed. Mika pulled Ish up and pushed him behind himself. As if shielding him from me. Of course, I started wailing again. It felt like I was about to explode into a million pieces.

"Jesus, Peter, stop your motherfucking crazy screaming. We're not here to hurt you. Connor and I wanted to introduce you to this man. He's besotted with you. Ever since he saw you, he can't stop asking about you. Brad's busy meeting with Cian. I know Brad said not to approach you when you are alone, and that we needed him to chaperone us. You have your reasons. Connor and I will go now. We just wanted to bring Ish to you."

My ears swooshed. Mika's words were inaudible as I heaved air into my lungs. *Stay vigilant.* Then it clicked. "What?" I asked.

Mika was his old, rude self. "Calm the fuck down. My only intention was to bring Ish to you. Go do something nice together. Go out on a date!"

"Oh," I said, looking at Ish, who was hiding behind Mika's back now. Peeking over Mika's shoulders, those beautiful yellow-black eyes were like chevron plates warning me to safety, calling for me through the maelstrom of my mind.

"But, first, tell us, are you serious about Tony and Bryan? Does your heart belong to them?" Mika asked me. I saw hesitancy in his eyes. Like he feared my answer. I gulped air, hoping to spew sense while looking at Ish.

"No, I never loved them. We aren't together, anyway. Not anymore." I waved over my shoulder, indicating they were past tense to me while smiling at Ish and forcing myself to calm the fuck down.

I imagined small atomic explosions detonated in my brain. *Calm the fuck down, Peter.*

"Yes, yes, yes!" Ish exclaimed while pumping his fist into the air.

"I'm sorry to hear that, my friend. Are you doing okay? I thought you were with them this whole time," Mika asked and blabbered on while I stared at those eyes. The room thrummed with the energy between us.

"No, I can't be with them. I didn't want them," I said, as if telling Ish this.

"What have you been doing? I know your research is complete. You're not in the lab anymore. What have you been doing this whole time with yourself, my friend?" Mika asked.

"I'm on holiday," I answered. I was proud of myself for doing things I like to do.

Defying their expectations. So, I straightened up and wiped my tears away, so Ish could see I hadn't wasted all my life awaiting him—I lied to myself.

"That's good news," Mika said. He smiled and checked with Connor, who also smiled in agreement.

I relaxed.

"Yes, I'm reading, watching television, and helping at the toddler's school. I'm doing everything I never did. I sleep better, and I'm learning who I am," I explained to them, but I was telling Ish.

Mika pushed Ish to the front while saying, "That's a big change. Anything that makes you happy and doesn't hurt anyone else is a step in the right direction. Why weasel around? Why are you taking so long to confront us? You know we need to come clean, all of us. We've been working together for years, but since you said nothing and let me..." Mika paused and snapped his fingers. "You know what, one day when you want to talk about it all, come to me. This is Ish." He patted my alien visitor on the shoulders.

Ish never took his eyes off me, once again offering me the most romantic gift ever. "This is for you. It represents the holy Loursveto flower from my home on Anzulla. The flower is a symbol of love and serenity. Of beauty and intelligence. Of everlasting union and life."

"Sounds to me like a wedding ring," Mika said and turned to leave us. I heard him whispering to Connor, "Let's have coffee in my office."

# CHAPTER 52
# MY ISH



**PETER**

**2146 A.D. (94 A.T.) (After Twins)**
**One year before the moon evacuation**
**Phoenix, underwater glass dome city**
**Earth**

I gaped down at the colossal man, still kneeling and clutching the flower in his shaking hand. His intense gaze and wild hair made me think of Medusa. Thick braids fell over his broad shoulders like anacondas, and his gold jewelry glinted in the light as he shifted. "Hello, my name is Ish. You may not remember me, but I visited you once."

I nibbled on my lip and gestured with my hands as I spoke, all the while his piercing eyes followed my every move. "Ish, you took your sweet-ass goddamn time. How long did you wait to come for me? Do you even remember your fucking promise? You said it would be a maximum of a hundred years. What in the ever-loving fuck, Ish? Why has it taken you so long? I mean, if you can time travel, couldn't you at least drop in and let me know it might be a little longer? And why is it that you look like you don't fucking remember me?" I whisper-shouted. The weird voodoo shit happening to me had dissipated as my mind and body had come to terms with his presence in my vicinity. It pissed me off and thrilled me to see him here in my office. He was as exotic and beautiful looking as I remembered. My stomach tightened into a gooey ball of anger and happiness. I crossed my windmilling arms and stared him down.

Silence. Clueless. Clueless fucking silence.

He ran his pink tongue over his thick bottom lip. I followed every movement. His Adam's apple slid up and down his throat as he waited for me to say more.

"Dammit, Ish, I thought you were nothing more than an imaginary lover. Maybe even a ghost. Stop looking at me like that." He blinked in slow motion while doing a double take. I may be much smaller, but I was a real ball of $E=mc^2$ if I ignited.

We stared at each other.

I caught my breath.

He assessed me.

Ultrasonic vibrations penetrated me as deep as my bone marrow as he raked my body up and down with his inhuman eyes. My dream man was the most handsome and most real-looking version of the sexy alien ass I'd conjured up while fucking my hand.

He smiled. Of all the things he could have done or said, he blushed and seemed timidly bashful. Fucking hell! Now I felt like shit. He acted as if he understood every word I thought—he probably did.

I looked at the flower he was offering me. No one had ever brought me a flower. An origami flower. I smiled and held my hand out. He smiled wider, exposing his long incisors as he pushed it into my waiting hand. "Hmmm," I gasped and gulped uncomfortable bubbles of air. "Thank you," I said and inspected the fragile intrinsic folds in the paper. He sighed, looking relieved. My nasal cavity and eyeballs stung. Dammit, I was about to piss tears through my eyes. My vision blurred, and I sniffed, wiping sticky snot and tears, drenching my sleeve with trails of colorless jelly.

His eyes were just like I remembered them, black with yellow rings surrounding his pupils. They were friendly and mesmerizing, like I imagined they would look at me when he came to get me. His skin was so dark, it shone blue in the light. The darkest blue that one might mistake for black. Yes, like an unlit night sky and velvety smooth. He seemed more muscled than I remembered. Yellow-white tattoos—Egyptian hieroglyphs mixed with Chinese logographs ran down his neckline. I wondered if the tattoo ink was gold. I guessed that would be the only color of ink visible on such a dark complexion. His eight-foot height alone screamed the family of Eryn—the only other man I knew as tall as him. A single yellow-gold hoop pierced his septum, and more clusters of thick golden hoops lined the shells of his ears—no diamonds or jewels, only gold.

I studied his face, tilting my head to the side as I examined him. Without thinking, my hand reached down to touch his cheek. He remained on one knee while I stood on the bed, our heights nearly equal. Tears welled up in his eyes and threatened to spill over. I wanted to catch them before they could fall, but he blinked and they streamed down his cheeks. His bottom lip trembled. This tall Anunnaki was crying for me. Slowly, I climbed off the bed and met his gaze with expectation and anticipation. I glanced back at the tiny origami flower in my hand, a romantic and beautiful gesture. The moment felt perfect, better than anything I could have wished for.

"Do you accept my offering to you?" he asked, softly, as if unsure of my answer.

"I accept," I whispered, bringing the paper to my nose to check if it smelled like a real flower. It didn't, it smelled like recycled paper.

"Thank you for the l—lors."

"Loursveto flower," he corrected me with a soft rumble in his voice. The sound affected me so deeply that my knees buckled. I threw my arms around his neck to steady myself.

"You came," I breathed out, reconciling the Ish I remembered from 1968 A.D. and the one kneeling here before me. He looked down at my mouth. "I started to think you'd never existed. I tried so hard to move on and be happy without you, but it was all a facade." My voice trembled as more tears welled up in my eyes.

"Oh, my Peter, my Kuku," he said with a beaming look on his face.

My eyes widened, and a hand flew to my chest in shock. "What did you just call me?" I asked.

Ish took a second, then replied softly, "It means my beloved."

Unsure of how to respond to such a declaration, I whispered, "I like it, and I like the small flower. Thank you."

"I'm so-so very sorry. Come here." He folded his arms around me. The feeling of safety, of home, washed over me as I buried my face below the crook of his neck.

"My Ish," I said and sighed. "I missed you. I was sick from missing you."

"I'm here." He sighed as he enveloped me, his smell and heat cocooned me, and I melted into him.

"Do not let go, never let me go," I pleaded softly into the warmth of his chest. "I need you like I need air to breathe. Please, Ish."

"I'm so very sorry and I promise you, I did search for you," he said, crushing my face, my nose, and my body against him as if trying to push me inside him. The vertebrae in my spine popped back into position. I welcomed the sweet suffocation, as he gave *killing-me-softly* a new meaning.

"We are to be mated. Our hearts call to be one. The Fates have blessed us." He sighed, pushing me away gently to look at me while allowing me to breathe. Inhaling fresh air, I longed for his presence, scent, and rhythmic heartbeat beneath my cheek. "You should come with me. We can travel together. Now that I have found you, we should go. I will take you away from this underwater place. It is not a good place for you."

"Where do you want to take me? Where is a good place for me?"

He gripped my shoulders tightly, his eyes pleading for me to trust him. "I know a place where we can be free, where the open sky stretches on for miles without a single building in sight. You can spread—I mean, you would enjoy it," he said with excitement in his voice. I felt the palpable desperation to convince me to accompany him, to make me his. But I couldn't ignore the obligatory voice in the back of my mind, reminding me not to be swept up by his enthusiasm.

My stomach twisted in knots as I thought about the disappointed faces of the children at the daycare center. They had been preparing for our special show-and-tell day, delighted to share their favorite things with me. I couldn't bear the thought of letting them down. "My work. I can't bail on those little ones," I pleaded with Ish. "They've been looking forward to tomorrow. They'll think I don't care if I don't show up." Desperation crept into my voice as I tried to convince him. "Maybe you could collect me at the end of the day? The kids would enjoy meeting you," I suggested, hoping he would agree. "We could leave after the show-and-tell? I have to at least say goodbye, and explain everything to my department head, Brad, and most importantly, to the children." A pang of guilt and heartache hit me as I thought about breaking their trust and disappointing them.

His hands slipped from my shoulders to settle and wrap his long fingers around my slim waist. He listened intently and impassively as he honed in on me and every word I was uttering. "Also, I heard Cian was here to restock, assuming he needed your help with the humans on the moon. I heard they needed rescuing?" I rambled on.

He let out a derisive snort, his eyes rolling in annoyance. "I believe the Fates expect me to help Cian and his brothers," he whined. But then he shifted his focus to me, pulling me closer. I wrapped my arms and legs around him, feeling the warmth of his body against mine as he effortlessly lifted me. I couldn't help but throw my head back and titter. The playfulness in his eyes and the way he made me forget all of my negative emotions made me feel like a little bushbaby clinging onto him for dear life. He leaned in close, parting his lips, breathing through his sharp incisors. I held onto him tightly, waiting, anticipating. And then he ran his tongue along my lips, tasting them slowly from one corner to the other. My heart raced as I opened my mouth for him, savoring the sweet, soft glide of his tongue over my lips to meet my tongue. Our kiss deepened, my mind swirled with desire, and my body responded with a pulsating heat.

We reluctantly pulled apart, both of us breathing heavily. "There is so much," we said simultaneously. We chuckled and decided kissing was the better option until we stopped to breathe, panting. His eyes sparkled with happiness, and I couldn't help but smile back at him. All the doubts and uncertainties from earlier were now replaced with a strong sense of belonging as we shared a mutual understanding of our obligations to others and how important they were to us.

"You go first," I said. He shook his head, "No, you first." He chortled.

"Ah, okay." I rolled my eyes.

He squeezed my butt cheeks. "Now tell me."

As I spoke, his pupils grew wider and wider, until the yellow rings disappeared. I was his sole focus. He leaned closer to me, our breaths mingling as we made intense eye contact. He was scanning my face, and I did the same to him. "What do you want to know?" he whispered, pressing his nose against mine.

There was so much. So many important things I collected in solitude, in the attic of my mind. Shall I open the door? How much crap would tumble out? I've been waiting for this. To confront him. To ask him while looking into his eyes.

I quickly opened the trap door, then scraped the top make-or-break questions together. "I'm worried about so many things, but the most important question I have is if you had anything to do with Hitler, with the Disciples, any of it? Especially Eryn's frog monster brothers. Do you know they killed billions of people in a matter of weeks? Are the Disciples your followers?"

"Pfft, frog monsters, the Disciples, no, of course not. Those idiots?"

"They are not idiots. They are highly advanced, organized, and intelligent orchestrators of wars and they mined the Earth hollow for gold, for the Anunnaki. They schemed, destroyed, murdered, and brought on the annihilation of humankind. All in the name of the Anunnaki gods."

"Maybe not idiots, but you have to agree, what they are doing on the moon is pure blind stupidity. I admit, I am Anunnaki, and they want to be like me so badly they are building machines, moving their minds into them."

I blinked and went offline as I tried to explain, forgive, and rationalize this to myself. "So, tell me, was this your doing?" I asked, needing a straight answer.

"I'm not sure. I don't know how or when. The details, Cian, Ivan, and Eryn mentioned, had explained some, but at this stage, I have questions of my own. Only the Fates know and talking to them is near impossible. So, yes, by association with my kind, I am responsible, unknowingly. I am not sure precisely how it came to be that the Disciples were trying to create a species like me and be like me. Many years ago, before I came to Earth's moon, I'd been forewarned by the Fates about a baby. I saved him and kept him away from the scientists. I named him Barkor. The Fates had sent me to the moon to wait for Cian and the ship shaped like a ball that camouflaged itself like a chameleon, bringing more people like me, that needed my assistance," he said. I read his microexpressions and he seemed to be telling me the truth.

"And you, my Kuku. How are you connected to the Disciples?" he asked in a softer tone. "You are not human, either."

Breaking the intimate moment, I looked away and wondered how the fuck didn't he know this already? I looked at Ish as if seeing him for the very first time.

"Ish, do you remember meeting me in 1968? You asked me a similar question."

"Only bits and pieces, my Kuku. This is the very first time that I have met you, yes?" He hesitated for a second and said, "Like this. Yes, for the first time. I had visions or dreams about being with you. Of your face and your smiles and your kisses. That's how I knew to search for you. Maybe my memories are muddled because I've been jumping back and forth too many times."

I took a deep, contemplative breath, then looked at him before responding. "I guess it's possible. It makes sense," I conceded, trying to make sense of the situation.

Then, I remembered the initial question about the Disciples. "To answer your question about my involvement and birth. Please know that I acted based on what I believed was right and to survive," I clarified, reciting Brad's words, to ease the guilt for keeping secrets from my closest friends. "I helped with Ivan and Cian's births. I used the Anunnaki string codes when I discovered Connor and Mika had dormant characteristics." A wave of bitterness washed over me as I added, "That's why they're mad at me. I hid the truth from them." My voice grew shrill with disgust at my actions.

"So, you were not born here with them. You were born in another place?"

"Yes, I'm almost one hundred years older than them. I was born in the 1940s through selective human breeding. Meaning babies born like me were kept and bred with more babies like me. Understand, this was before scientists discovered they could make babies without sex and mothers."

"I learned about this method of procreation during my time in Grayrak," he said, shifting his weight uncomfortably. "If my father had discovered this, I can only imagine how much more powerful he would have become. You see, he has a history of stealing and killing my siblings for their unique abilities. The thought that he could have just created them without needing to mate with my mother—it's a disturbing concept." His brow furrowed seemingly as memories of his father's cruelty surfaced. "It's something I don't want to even think about, for fear of it ever coming true or being possible." He shivered.

"Anyway, one of my brothers, who was the same as I, was held prisoner and forced to do the work I was doing. He was the creator of Eryn in another lab in South Africa. While I ended up in Phoenix, already waiting for you and working in secret based on what you told me in 1968," I said to his frowning face. "This is bloody weird and upsetting. Please let me down. I need space!"

"No," he said and clutched my ass cheeks tighter, squeezing them while pushing my body flush against him.

"So, somehow the Disciples originated way back by following the clues, searching for…" He shook his head, correcting himself. "I was worried and most of the time, not in my right mind. My dear Kuku, I was obsessed with finding you. I searched for decades while I waited for Cian and his brothers to arrive on the moon. I can't determine what changes to make to prevent this group from forming or its origins. Chances are, I won't ever be able to change just one thing, and if I do, you and Cian, Ivan, and Eryn might not even be born. These people, the Disciples, their beliefs are so ingrained, so screwed, so twisted, and so bloody wrong. I suspect it all started—no, I know how it all started."

"How did it start?"

"It's all got to do with that damn golden apple."

I gasped. He nodded. Seeing my enthusiasm for the truth, he took a deep breath and answered me with renewed determination to tell me what the fuck was going on. "It's a long story."

"I can imagine. Continue, please."

"I brought the apple to my twin sisters, Ki and An, and their mate Xerxes, asking them to keep it safe. The Disciples had photos and schematics claiming to have the secrets of eternal life from the gods. Determined to uncover their connection to the Anunnaki, I infiltrated their compound one night. My goal was to understand how Barkor, who was half Anunnaki, was born after being carried by a human mother," he said, visibly shaken, his dark complexion almost pale as he closed his eyes in defeat. "I'm worried about you. I can't lose you. If I destroy them, by going back in time, then chances are, my Kuku, you won't be born."

"Who's Barkor?" I was confused. I must have been pulling a face, because I had hoped he knew what was going on. But now he only seemed defeated.

"He's just like Cian, Ivan, and Eryn. He was born on the moon, and it turns out he's Cian's mate. They're going to be butting heads and competing. Both have a hero complex. It's quite entertaining to watch it unfold."

"So they don't know?"

"They know, but they don't want to know. Two hard-heads, those two."

"Ah, I'm so glad Cian found him. I couldn't understand his engineering questions until I heard they had stolen the Spacecar."

"Yes, I'm also glad I have you. That's why I don't want to lose you or them. I'm growing fond of you all. Even if you are human, Anunnaki, and something else, those scientists have to be stopped," he said with a solemn look on his face.

"Cheer up. We can stop them. I have my flip knife to protect you and myself," I joked. "I've been taking self-defense classes," I said, hoping the randomness of my statement would break his deep depressive line of thinking. It was the first thing that came to mind because what he said was also worrying me. Plus, all those extra self-defense classes were one of the many things on my list to tell him when he arrived one day, and that was today.

Ish snickered. "Okay, keep your knife close to your person. I will return to collect you after the humans are safe, so we can build a home and start a life together. In the meantime, let's talk to Mika and Connor. Apologize and make friends. I don't like that you are troubled. Just be honest, I'm sure Mika and Connor will forgive you. They have two wonderful boys. You helped with that. I read Mika's mind. He is upset because you ignore him and act like he has done something wrong."

"How do you do all this? Do you also have the powers Eryn, Cian, and Ivan have? I kind of envy them. Why don't I have these powers? I also have Anunnaki in me."

"If you and I spend more time together, it could happen. It's like a little flame burning inside you. I can sense it. I'm sure we could stoke that little flame into a blazing fire. Not only to share thoughts and powers but to live longer together. It's because Anunnaki lived so long that we have to form a bond, otherwise, we would kill each other. That's what's happening to Cian and Barkor. They are drawn to one another but also irritated by the other. If those two don't find a way to bond they could become enemies." It seemed to me changing the subject helped because he was smiling again.

"But what about all these Phoenicians? I gave them the gift of life. Would they kill each other if they don't mate or bond?"

"Maybe, I don't know, but you made a mistake there."

"Made a mistake?" I bristled at him as I awaited his response.

"Yes, the Fates now have their hands full with the Phoenicians. You directly linked them to the powerful Anunnaki, just like the citizens of Anzulla." His voice was low and intense. I felt a primal attraction to him, my skin prickling with desire and the urge to merge our beings. "You're such a troublemaker," he said with a sly smile.

I chuckled. "Guilty as charged."

As he spoke, my body pulsed with want, my back itching between my shoulder blades. I couldn't resist the temptation any longer and lunged forward, pulling him close for a hug. He put me down, and I led him outside to Mika's office. "Wait here for me please," I whispered, and he stooped to kiss me on my forehead.

"I can't wait to have you all for myself. Now go make nice with your friends. I don't like that you have this negative energy around you. It attracts bad luck." He turned me by my shoulders, patted my backside, and pushed me into Mika's office.

"What's wrong? Did he take advantage of you?" Mika asked, jumping up ready to attack Ish.

"No, don't be silly. Be happy for me. My mind is lighter, and all my thoughts and feelings are categorized and packed away. I feel much better. I got my Ish. I've been waiting for him all this time." I giggled, holding my paper flower and smelling it dreamily. "He said he was starving without me." I sat down, watching Mika peeking out the door.

I sat on the edge of my seat and decided to just blurt it out without thinking and without being scared. Ish's looming presence gave me the courage to continue. "Mika, Connor, I'm sorry. I don't want to explain away what I did because how I did it was wrong. I know now that you probably would have agreed anyway if I'd told you all this,"

I said bravely to them as they nodded. Mika looked at Connor, but before he could say anything, Mika grabbed his tool bag, interrupting me.

"Comrade, we'd meant to get you alone for an honest discussion. We've been evading each other for much too long. Connor and I had taken this secret and ignored it. It worked because we forgot about it all for a while. As it goes with secrets, if more than one person knows, then it's not a secret anymore. Also, if one person keeps that secret, it becomes heavy to carry. It's better not to have secrets. They will crush you. I tried not to tell Connor because I was ashamed of myself. I trusted you because I considered you my best friend and lab partner. In my eyes, you were untainted, pure, and innocent. I felt sorry for your pathetic-ness," Mika blurted, and Connor nodded affirmatively.

Cold sweat beaded over my body, a clear sign of guilt. To calm myself, I clutched the flower in my hand, drawing strength from it. Suddenly, Ish appeared at the doorway. His eyes narrowed as he gave me his infectious smile. I took a deep breath and gave him a determined look, silently communicating that I could handle whatever was coming next.

"I'm more than ready to get this drama behind us. The only thing I ask of you is to tell me what the fuck is going on. How did you end up here, and why do you sound like you know Ish? I swear, more questions pop up each time I talk to you. You're making me crazy trying to guess your story. I must know because thinking and attempting to guess all the time requires mental energy I'd rather use on something productive. Come, bring your guest, we can talk while we tinker on the latest Spacecar prototype and figure out a way to build a better communication system," Mika said and showed me the way out of the office.

I stood feeling relieved and replied, "I accept your invitation, and thank you for including Ishtar to come with us." I wasn't leaving him here, alone, and out of my sight. His presence brought me clarity and I figured the walk would help me gather my thoughts and align my words to apologize properly. Mika gave us a stern nod and Ish grabbed my hand and squeezed. Connor looked us up and down as if comparing our heights. I was an easy two and a half feet shorter than Ish. Ishtar gave Connor and Mika a shiny big grin and then we made our way out of the lab.

We strolled through the bustling corridors, and I couldn't help but feel a wave of relief wash over me as people greeted us with warm smiles instead of stopping for idle chatter. Tomorrow was a big day at the toddler's school, and I needed to conserve my mental energy for that. But now Ish was here, along with Mika and Connor, who were clearly still seeking answers. I braced myself, knowing I would have to tap into my reserves to face them. As if he read my thoughts, Ish pulled me back for a kiss and a hug, filling me with renewed strength. We proceeded down the corridor to the shipyard where Mika and Connor's workshop was.

"Here, you can wear Eryn's protective gear," Mika said to Ish. We washed up, donned our suits, and entered the sterile workspace filled with state-of-the-art tools and a half-finished spaceship.

"Gille-toine, can Peter help us build a communication tower? One that floats and can be retracted and moved under the surface level? It would be a better option than dragging construction outside and erecting one on a mountaintop. I worry any manmade structure will give us away, and I'm sure Brad won't approve of it. We need to communicate better with the children. I need eyes and ears out there. I want twenty-four hours a day of video feeds from all over. Wherever they go, they should leave a camera ball for us. That way, we can protect and warn them, don't you think?" Connor asked Mika but was already calling me closer. My hand slipped out of Ish's, breaking our connection. The sense of loss shifted to pride as I watched him slip away to inspect the inner workings of the ship.

"Of course, he can," Mika said to his husband following Ish with his gaze.

"Peter, the more heads, the faster we shall get results." Connor patted me on the back and then lifted his chin, indicating Brad and Cian coming through the transparent wind tunnel to suit up for entry.

Ish stepped off the ship and bowed low to Mika and Connor in a display of respect. His thick, dark locks fell into his face, obscuring his features as he spoke. "Apologies, I don't want to seem judgmental of your work. I'm impressed by it. I assume you built the smaller version as well. Your attention to the fine details impressed me the most."

"Thank you. We're building a better, bigger version than the boys are currently using. We welcome your input and recommendations any time, comrade," Mika said to Ish, and turned back to me. "We can't rely only on a voice-recorded report from the kids. By the time we receive it—what I mean is—we can't sit here and watch how people learn to knit and shit. I want my own ship up and running. I fucking need to know what's happening outside the clouds. But, in the meantime, could you maybe design a submarine with satellite capabilities?"

"Yes, sure, of course. I can do that for you. I'll help with anything as long as I'm not working with frozen dead people," I said, uncomfortably, but honored that Mika still trusted me. This would give me something to do while I waited for Ish to help Cian save the humans on the moon.

"That's good news, my friend," Mika said, pointing to the schematics.

"Yelda, maybe Ish has some input here," Connor told Mika.

"Progress is slow. In two years, we would at least have two ships ready. Please, I need to know what we can improve and change, and I can't do that with relayed radio messages," Connor continued as I stepped closer and reached for Ish's hand.

"You know, Mika and Connor, my friends. I've blurted some of it out to Brad while feeling guilty as fuck. I'm older than any man currently living in Phoenix, and although not needed, I implanted the first Eden Bean when I appeared to be twenty-seven years old. I've been hiding my origins and sacrificing myself for a word and a smile from a sexy alien in my living room a lifetime ago," I blurted and saw Mika stiffen. Connor pulled him by the arm and Mika seemed to swallow his words and smiled at me.

Taking a deep breath, I saw Ish's encouraging smile, so I blundered ahead, "I don't feel guilty because I gifted the Phoenicians with eternal life." I smiled up at Ish and he looked down at me, with adoration in his eyes. "Memories of years far gone resurfaced. I'd almost forgotten those eyes. Too much had happened, and as the years twisted their strands together, it all became a forgotten drop of memory in a big bucket full of time."

Ish threw his arms around me as he lifted me from the floor, his strong arms encasing me, protecting me. We playfully rubbed our noses together, a silly new thing that brought a smile to my face. I squirmed with delight, feeling safe and loved in his affectionate hold.

Ish put me down to greet Cian and Brad, and I could see they were already better friends with him than I thought. I felt jealous, but then I remembered how important Ish was and the jealousy turned into a proud possessiveness. He was mine, I thought as I watched them shaking hands. As soon as he was done greeting them, he reached for me, making me feel special and important to him. Every second I spent in his shadow, more of my fears and doubts disappeared and were replaced with strength and knowing that I was as important to him as he was to everyone else here.

"I've always wondered if the earthlings could ever leave this place. I was relieved when I first saw your transportation vehicle. My home is now but a rock bestrewed with heaps of crumbling aspirations and broken dreams. I was left utterly alone, yet now I am not alone anymore." Ish smiled at us. I listened attentively, and I knew this message was important. I focused on each vowel and syllable to ensure that I would remember this forever.

"I was the youngest of my siblings, and I missed and hated them for leaving me behind. Alive. In solitude, I observed the humans. All I could do was watch how they murdered and destroyed themselves from afar. My father's cunning and twisted ways destroyed us and our home. I lived in hiding, contemplating ending my torturous existence. I longed to walk with the humans to cure my loneliness. I asked myself over and over, how do I reveal myself? How will they receive me? I am not a god. Nor do I want to be one. For eons, I tried tirelessly to find the point where sowing our seed and knowledge would bloom as intended. Look at what's happening with the creation of the Zelk —an unnatural species made from parts of humans and parts of their technologies. If I don't help them, they will die by the hand of the Zelk that continue to multiply. The Zelk is an abomination. A thing that grows and consumes not only human flesh and bone but their souls, too. It lures the weak with the promise of life, but it brings only death. I know it because I have battled it before. I will work with Cian and his brothers, and together, we will find the balance we have all been seeking—a new beginning," Ish said.

As he spoke, I could feel the cool air from the humming AC units on my exposed skin, but it was hard to concentrate when I was completely mesmerized by his striking features, dangerous aura, and overwhelming presence. I knew he wasn't sharing everything. He was twisting and hiding things from them, and me.

He leaned down, his hot breath tickling my ear as he whispered, "Take me somewhere private, so I can bury myself deep inside you."

I gulped. My cock was on board. I yanked my shirt down to cover my growing erection in front of a room full of men and gave him one stern nod.

# CHAPTER 53
## NOT OUR FIRST

*"Morning, citizens of Phoenix.*

*It's now six a.m.*

*Did you know it is a proven fact that humans burn intense energy during copulation and that this energy causes a transformation that sparks a whole neural fireworks show? By releasing a special hormonal cocktail the brain will, at its best, charge an entire set of biological batteries in the human body. The paralyzing spastic seizures humans experience are the result of these overcharged batteries and can be so intense that the physical becomes mythological and it is in that moment that the metaphysical can take root incorporeal and paranormal.*

*Breakfast is served until eight a.m.*

*Hope your day is full of transformations!"*

**Ishtar**
**2146 A.D. (94 A.T.)**
**One year before the moon evacuation**
**Phoenix, underwater glass dome city**
**Earth**

"Come, time to go." Peter grabbed my hand and dragged me away from where I'd promised my allegiance to Cian, Brad, Mika, and Connor. "I've been waiting for you for so long. You are mine now," he whispered.

I gave Mika and the men a shrug, they waved me goodbye and then I shot after Peter. We removed our coveralls while fighting our way back through the wind tunnel. Peter awaited me on the other side, and as soon as I exited, he jumped into my arms. All I could do was catch him.

My Kuku's going to be distraught, disappointed, and absolutely devastated, if I told him that this wasn't our first, first-time or that he is about to sprout wings some time in his future.

My whole being wanted to bond with him. I rattled with urgency from within. It had to happen. Even if I couldn't take him away and do it somewhere romantic.

Somewhere not trapped under fucking water.

I'm facing hurting my mate by snuffing his joy in this special moment. The Peter I got to know in our short twenty-four hours together had a mean streak. That meant this Peter should be treasured, not mortified and cheated out of the enjoyment he'd been waiting for, for over a century.

I was also not going to tell him he wasn't looking like the Peter I knew. Not now. Fuck, this is not the time for such news. It would be unfair to him, I thought as I watched him being all jovial as he looked at me. Seeing the real me, because I wasn't cloaking my true appearance from him.

I planned to tell him, only when I was sure he could handle the truth. Only when I could take him to a place where he could stretch his wings and fly. Phoenix was no place for someone who needed the open skies.

He wiggled his hips and hooked his legs tightly around my hips. For a second, our eyes met, and I knew this second was the best second ever and I will never forget this second, even if we have forever of seconds in time.

His chest moved fast up and down—both of us were catching our breaths. He inspected me while I inspected him. He was the most beautiful man of all the men I've ever seen. His skin was smooth and pale. His eyebrows were dark and perfectly framing his blue diamond eyes.

"Yes, my Kuku, this is real, and happening," I breathed.

"We are in each other's arms," he said, with sparkling happiness. There's so much of it. Like a fountain, it spurted out of every pore and into the empty pond of my soul. Fates, I needed him. This was the face I searched for.

"Yes, that we are," I answered, my voice thick with gratitude and emotion.

He slammed his lips against mine. I opened my mouth, laughing at him. "Careful, my fangs!" I said between kisses.

"Don't care, they are so sexy." He licked my lips and ran his tongue up and down each fang. It felt as if he sucked and licked my balls as shivers danced down my spine. He wrapped his arms tighter around my neck. The voracious kissing continued. Our happiness stoking, choking, and stuffing those dark, lonely corners inside our hearts. Thousands of years and so many realities were now colliding. This was a time for celebrating. Our union. The start of our love.

"I can't see where I'm going," I rasped into his mouth, my head reeling.

Peter glared at me. "Walk, I'll tell you where to go," he said, kissing me again and only stopping to give me directions while I walked us backward so he could see where we were going.

"Go left. No, not that left! The other left!"

"Peter, I am going to fall over someone," I chuckled, with his tongue down my throat.

He clung to me. I tightened my hold under his upper legs and locked my fingers, so he sat comfortably with his tight butt inside my cupping hands.

"Stop, we're here," he said between happy giggles and half fell out of my arms to reach the sensor next to the door of his apartment. He slapped the palm of his hand onto it and the door slid open.

"That's it. Open sesame! You may enter." He waved his hand dramatically. Undulating in a half circle, almost breaking his spine, then he snapped right back up, grabbing me by the neck to plant more kisses all over my face, my eyebrows, my forehead, and my lips. Every inch of my face was being kissed. My delight burst out of my chest as I laughed jubilantly.

"Bedroom now!" he muttered between pecking, sucking, and licking. This was the happiest version of myself in a long time.

We were going to be mated.

I followed his directions as best I could, marching us to the first open door on the far right side of the apartment.

"Nope, bathroom, the other door," he said before feasting again. It was a struggle to keep my eyes open and not walk into walls and fall over tables. His hands were groping and undressing me. His eagerness to have me made me feel like I was a young, innocent boy.

When the back of my knees bumped into something, I checked and confirmed it was the bed. I unwrapped him from me. His grip loosened, and I lifted him by placing my hands under his armpits so he could stand on the bed and look me in the eye. He was a wicked fiend—wanting, panting, and his hair was a mess.

"Let me undress you," I said with a deep rumble in my voice. He pinned me with those unique blue silvery eyes, now fully dilated as his chest heaved, nodded a yes, and started to unbutton his shirt. I slapped his hands away gently. His breath hitched with a small gasp. "Let me. I want to do this."

"Then get on with it. I don't have time for politeness. I've waited for this much too long. We can do ceremony and niceties another time." He had a feral look in his eyes. Like he wanted to devour me. The urgent look on his face and the needy thoughts he projected told me he was close to blowing his load in his pants. I increased my speed and kicked my boots off as he jumped to remove the rest of his clothes. Then we were naked. He with no wings and me happy to soon be bonded to him. Playfully, I pushed him backward and jumped onto the bed.

"Happy now?" I asked, my voice rumbling as I pinned his small pale body beneath me. I was a gigantic beast compared to his slight size. My feet still touched the floor as I encased him, resting my elbows on either side of his head. My long dark braided hair draped around his pure white mane.

"Yes," he grunted and flung his arms around my neck, kissing me again. His skin was flushed warm with arousal beneath me. He lifted his feet and threw them around my hips.

My significantly bigger cock was more manageable while sitting on my heels while my lover sat on my lap, managing my length and girth by riding me and controlling the depth of penetration. I hoisted him up as I sat back, bringing him with me. I dipped down, never stopping kissing him. He was hungry for me, and our kisses weren't quick brushes of lips. No, they were passionate, deep, and consuming. We were mating and possessing. He wanted to make me his, as I wanted to make him mine.

We changed it up from rough to gentle and then suddenly, so softly, I felt like crying. His thoughts were only of me and having me, and how much he'd missed me. How happy he was to be here with me. I could hardly restrain myself from bursting into tears. The loneliness inside him gave me a deeper insight into why my Kuku was so upset about being alone and feared being forgotten for thirty years. I had a chance now to fix that.

Luckily, he started fisting my hair, and the pain ripped me from listening to his thoughts to what was happening in the here and now. Somehow, through the kissing, he had reached for lubrication and was smearing my cock with it. Breaking our kiss, he stood up and applied the sweet-smelling stuff to his backside, all the while pinning me with a smoldering gaze.

I grabbed his hips, lifting him to line my cock up with his entrance. "Please put it in. I can take you. I've had lots of practice with my Ishtar dildo," he grunted with a don't-try-to-stop-me look.

"I'm taking notes and will ask you about that dildo later." I panted as he threw his head back and impaled himself on me.

It was me being taken into him, and me putting my body into his.

Slowly, we became one like we were supposed to be. He took ownership of me as I of him. I brightened the room as my golden blue energy flowed out of me and surrounded us. The light flickered brighter the more I felt connected and aroused by him. He moaned and my cock squeezed through the warmest and tightest hole in the universe. Once the head of my cock was inside, his warmth sucked me deeper into him. Goosebumps ran up my spine as dancing blue and gold shades of light surrounded us.

He made incoherent sounds.

"I know!" I grunted. I squeezed my eyelids shut in pleasure while hoping he wasn't hurting himself.

"Oh my god, oh my god. I've never been so full. So stretched."

My eyes popped open. "Don't hurt yourself."

"It's fucking amazing. You feel so fucking good. Just like I imagined." Sweat beaded on his forehead. He arched his back and laughed while he hung on my shoulders with his legs wrapped around my hips. Slowly, he bobbed up and down. Sweet fates. I was enjoying watching him as he swung his head from side to side and flipped his white hair back. He was wild and gorgeous. I held his hips guiding him, in case he harpooned himself.

"Yessss," I hissed through clenched teeth, staving off an early orgasm.

"You feel magnificent, my Ish. I'm going to come."

For a split second, he opened his eyes, seeing the golden blue glow of my skin. His thoughts were that he was waiting for it to happen. "Oh my god yes, you are my dark alien, aren't you?"

My body reacted, my balls contracted, and my soul opened up to him. Receiving him. It was indescribable. I felt love and promise and so much fucking goodness and rightness as we locked gazes.

"Don't be scared of hurting me, don't hold back," he said as he increased his pace riding me. I read his mind. He wanted me to glow brighter.

"I'm not," I lied.

I didn't want to let go and lose control. So many things were happening all at once urging me to close my eyes and give in. My eyeballs weighed a ton, and they wanted to roll back in my head.

"I feel like my skin wants to burst open!" he yelled into the air.

Oh fuck! Realization struck me like a thunderbolt. I was going to cause him to spread his wings and—

"Oh yes, yes, yes!" he cried in ecstasy and confirmed my fear was real. Oh fuck, this was not the time or the place. I was going to ruin this, him, and us. I couldn't let him change now. It was entirely too early.

*Reduce the level of his excitement.* I grabbed his hips to slow the pace, but he was already over the edge.

"My Kuku, no, Peter, calm down! Please calm the fuck down."

*I should have told him about his wings.*

I grabbed hold of his bony shoulders, forcing him to slow down. He looked at me with hooded eyes and then he kissed me. My eyes closed and we exploded in a mess of me putting brakes on his changing, the smell of his ejaculation that pulled my orgasm, and then we both lost control as I filled him and bit down on his shoulder. His warm seed shot up between our stomachs as I embraced him, pulling him tighter and holding him in place. Like rushing waters, neither one of us could have stopped what was happening. The instinct woven into my Anunnaki bloodline, the royalty of Anzulla, overrode all my inhibitions.

Bite. Claim. Mate.

My jaws locked as I bit down into the crook of his neck.

"Oh, my fucking god!" he exclaimed, then writhed and undulated on my cock. I sank my teeth deeper and my predatory eyes popped open. A possessive growl rumbled in my chest. He tensed in my arms for a second and then his whole body relaxed as if he had passed out, resting his head on my shoulder.

*What had I done?*

Quickly, I retracted my fangs, before I totally emptied my venom sacs. My thoughts were disorientated and the sincerity of this sanctity of two unified souls, was overwhelming. I struggled to stay lucid. To think coherent thoughts. One thing remained in the forefront of my mind, I was binding him to me. The venom sacs behind my molars prickled and bulged so much I struggled to swallow. I sighed in relief, knowing I still had some bite left. My eyesight was enhanced, and my hearing was super sensitive as I zeroed in on our surroundings like an animal possessively guarding its wounded mate. If someone came to take him from me, I would tear them apart. The heat of his body increased my awareness of him in my arms and the need to protect and shield him from anything and everything that could hurt him stirred another possessive growl inside my chest. I purred like a cat as I licked the drops of blood from the healing wounds at the base of his neck.

"At least, so far, no wings, thank fuck." The rushing noise in my head disappeared and I finally had clear thoughts. He slumped in my arms. I couldn't sit like this forever. His taste, the essence of his lifeblood still on my tongue, was familiar. I had tasted it before.

"We are now a half-bonded pair. The Fates have blessed us," I said worriedly. "If you spill your seed in me, we would be fully bonded, once we say the mating words."

"You forgot, I have to bite you too when I come inside you," he groaned, taking a new purchase with his hands as he straightened his legs, still fully seated on my cock. He smiled drunkenly at me. "My mate, my big, beautiful lover."

I smiled, and we kissed as if we had loved and known each other for millennia.

"What are the mating words?"

"It's in Anunnaki. I would say them and you should repeat after me."

"Let's do it, I want to mate you," he said seductively and pulled me closer for a kiss.

I was testing our luck if I allowed us to continue further. I slowed the kissing and his delicious movements and pulled away, breaking the kiss. My lips felt swollen and his were a deep wine red. I beamed at him. "There is something I have to tell you, Peter. Please slow down." I begged with urgency and pulled him closer to me to reduce the friction on my cock. He stopped moving abruptly, looking at me questioningly.

"What is it, Ish? You wanted to say something while we orgasmed. You wanted to stop, but then you couldn't. It must be important if you think it's more important than us coming and bonding."

"It is," I admitted. I lay him down on his side and positioned myself so my cock was still lodged inside him. "I didn't know how to tell you this, but I'm going to say this and please understand, I'm not doing it to hurt you. It is quite the opposite. I want to protect you."

"Okay? Tell me." He frowned and I could see doubt creeping into his eyes.

"We have met before," I blurted and hoped for the best.

"I know, silly," Peter said as he took my hair and smelled it. He was so into me, and I loved this version of him already just for that.

"No, not when I bit André. It was after that, but before today, when I met you. It surprised me to see you on the stairs earlier today."

"I know. It was as if you didn't recognize me." He sat up then seemed to remember I was still inside him.

"It is because I didn't at first." He searched my stern, serious-looking face for the truth."

"How could you not remember me?"

"I do, but I have jumped so many times, and we already have history together. I had forgotten that we met before you…" I stopped talking, wondering if I should tell him.

"What dammit?" he barked at me.

"Before, when you had wings." There, I'd said it.

"Wings? What wings? Oh my god! Are you saying?" His eyes enlarged. My cock slid out of him as he sat back to measure the extent of my truth. Then, out of nowhere, he hit me on the chest with a fist.

"I asked you not to get mad at me, ouch."

"That didn't hurt. Stop being overdramatic. Tell me about my fucking wings."

"I don't know, you never told me, but you have big white wings, like…" I didn't want to tell him I'd lost him and had found him once, and currently had no fucking clue where to find him again.

"Like a fucking Angel?"

I bit my lip. "Yes," I answered, shying away and awaiting another punch, but he threw his head back and laughed.

"That's impossible."

"Okay, don't believe me, but if you suddenly sprouted your wings down here, you would not be happy. You would feel trapped and caged inside Phoenix and I can't take you away now because you said you have those children to care for and I have to help Cian save the humans. I asked you to come with me, remember? So, I don't think we have a choice now. We have to wait. I'm kind of having a hard time being everywhere lately." He wanted to interrupt me, but I pushed ahead. "Meeting you is a bonus. But if you had your wings, then I'd have to break my word. I'd have to choose between you and the rescue mission. I already promised Brad, Mika, and Connor, not to mention Cian, that I would help them. Understand? The Fates placed me in the middle of all this. I can't ignore the Fates."

I could see the color in his eyes changing as his body reacted to what little royal Anunnaki elixir I had injected into him. His mind worked at such an incredible speed I could hardly keep up with his thoughts. It was as if he ran five thought patterns at once. He was extraordinary.

"Ish, listen to me. Wings or no wings. You must go back to the beginning of Phoenix, to the year 2046 A.D. and download the computer program to your ship. Lasitor can help you navigate the times and give you the history word for word and second by second. You can't keep guessing and jumping," he said as if reading my mind. "Leave clues for yourself and stop jumping around to figure out what is going on," he explained while playing with one of my braids between his fingers again, still calculating other probabilities in his mind.

"You are correct, but how did you know my onboard guide's name is Lasitor?"

"What? So you already downloaded him?" Peter asked.

"He has been part of my ship's navigation system since I started the machine for the first time."

"That's interesting," Peter said and looked up to the speaker in his room. "Lasitor!" he called like I call to my ship.

"Yes, Peter," the robotic voice of my onboard computer answered.

"How did your program get installed on Ish's ship?"

"I don't know, Peter. I can't recall. It must have happened before Phoenix ended up underwater. My memory of the time before that was damaged," Lasitor said.

My head was hurting.

"Unless I'd updated Lasitor and then traveled back to before I was rebuilding my ship."

"See, that's already a clue."

"I agree. I need help keeping track. My ship's onboard guide needs adjustment and updating with the current and previous history. I have to find out as much as possible, so I can trace back my steps. Either eliminate the Disciples or steer them in a better direction," I said, then bit down on the inside of my lips blocking him from entering my mind and hoping he didn't catch more of my thoughts.

"If you say that I am supposed to grow wings, well, I believe you, truly. I believe you and I'm not upset with you. Earlier today when I saw you or now, when we made love. God, just being close to you I feel like my skin wants to burst open. Like I'm too small for it. Like I'm about to be zipped open and break free," he said and lay down beside me.

"I'm glad you are taking this so well. You are not as forgiving or understanding as the Peter with wings. I was worried you would be upset or say I'm making up stories." —I took his hand in mine and kissed it— "Also, I promise you, before we leave, I will get the ship updated. Not knowing and guessing are causing unnecessary worries for you. I will ask Cian more about it as well. I don't know how or what, but I'm sure between you and

Cian we can figure it out. It's an idea, in case I get lost and have to find you again." I rolled us over so he lay on my chest. We lay in silence as I rhythmically rubbed his warm and clammy back in circles until his breathing slowed down.

As if remembering something, he lifted his head and said stammering, "You can't tell Cian, he will want to come along. I have known him since he was a baby. He and his brother can be a handful. If it wasn't for Eryn, those two would have turned Phoenix upside down on the seabed. Not to mention those humongous animals of theirs." He plopped his head back down again. My heart warmed with fuzzy feelings.

"I can imagine. I've gotten to know them fairly well by now. They are fun, lots of positive energy to be around. And they are fortunate to have their Anubis," I added, then gently wiped his sweaty hair from his face. "I can't help but feel a pinch of envy. The Anubis seem happy and there is so much love between them and their charges. They seem protective of the three. My father mistreated them. He abused them by ordering them to attack defenseless, innocent humans. They were the first he drained and killed, assuming he would acquire mystical powers. I took mine and fled to join Titus on the battlefront against Egypt," I whispered.

After a long time of listening to Peter's thoughts, they finally quieted down as he drifted into a relaxed state, I lay listening to our hearts beating the same song.

"My Kuku, this is important. Listen," I begged, and he cracked one unfocused eye open. "I asked Brad earlier today what he would change if he had the chance, and he said to have more whiskey and not get Drew and Juan killed." The one eye he had opened, rolled back into his head. The little venom I had injected was knocking him out. He failed to lift his head. The transformation of my small bite had used a lot of energy. "What I'm piecing together is that Drew and Juan are the reason we traveled to 1968 A.D.?"

"Hmmm, Drew and Juan were killed while saving Cian and Ivan in South Africa. My friend, 1968, yes André," Peter said, barely making sense as he drifted into sleep again.

"Peter," I whispered, "before you fall asleep."

"Hmmm?"

"I think I know now what I am supposed to do. It's making sense now why we ended up going to Andrew. We will slip away, maybe tomorrow after you show me off to the children in your school, then go to 1968. Back to the night you met me."

"Yes, I agree. I need you," he mumbled incoherently.

"Hey, open your eyes." I shook him gently by the shoulder. "Did you say André?"

"Hmmm, my best friend, 1968."

A nagging sensation told me that this was important. Peter was understandably drained, but upon awakening, he would crave something other than food. I would have to feed him, and he would have to do the same for me. This was a natural part of our mate bonding. We were meant to provide each other with sustenance. Consuming from others may keep you alive, but it can never fill the void created by the bond between mates. Only the Loursveto juice could satisfy that hunger for bonded and unbonded Anunnaki.

With his eyes closed, he snuggled closer to me. "I agree. Let's rest for a few minutes. If I grow wings, we won't be able to return anyway. Also, if those Germans saw me with wings, well, that would restart another Berlin crisis."

Berlin crises? I wondered.

"What do you mean, Peter?" I asked. "Like what?" I hoped to keep him lucid enough to tell me.

"Hmmmm, not important. Tell you later," he muttered, then soft little snores followed. I felt so unhinged and out of sorts. Like I had forgotten something, an important clue. Only one thing left to do, I entered Peter's mind. My heart shattered as I glimpsed that dark, lonely, and sad place. I recognized it because it was like mine. After I killed my father.

"I'm here now, and no one will ever hurt you again," I whispered, so he would never forget it. I searched deeper. Before he arrived in Phoenix. His friend André, who escaped Germany and moved to the United States. Ahh, now that made sense. André changed his name to Andrew when he moved to the United States and then Andrew's nickname is Drew. Dear Fates, how many names does the man have?

I witnessed the heartbreaking choice that Peter had to make, as he chose to sever all communication to protect his friend. When Peter had heard his friend had died, the confusion of his friend's death devastated him. I saw glimpses of his mother, the Disciples, and his father, but not once did I see him smile. His memories were crystal clear as if they had occurred yesterday. Unlike most minds I've entered, his was not a complex maze; instead, it was organized like rows of shelves filled with neatly labeled information categorized by month and year.

My mate's mind was endlessly intriguing. I lingered on my sexual encounter with André. Seeing it from his view, they were best friends. He was glad I had bitten him to save his life and give him the ability to regenerate. Then there was the whiskey issue. Peter was jealous because I was meeting Andrew in secret, and not with him. Later Peter was transferred to Antarctica, where he would eventually meet Juan, or should I say Juandre, Andrew's future partner.

In a moment of brilliant cunning, I had given André my mating bite without fully considering the consequences. Whose idea was it, really? I searched for any additional details that may have been buried in my mind. With a sense of panic, I closed my eyes and searched for answers within my thoughts. Suddenly, my eyes snapped open and my heart raced as a new realization dawned on me.

"Oh fuck, what have I done?" I had bitten Peter. What if there wasn't enough venom in my bite for André?

"Oh, my fucking Fates! What have I done?" Ice-cold realization washed over me. All this time I was worried about Peter sprouting wings, not realizing I couldn't feed him when I lost him. He would die without me. Also, I couldn't go back to 1968 with minimal to no venom in my bite. I couldn't take the chance. I wouldn't be able to turn André into an Anunnaki consort and my Kuku would suffer and die while he waited thirty years for me to find him.

This was a colossal conundrum—a fuck-up of disproportional proportions.

Which version of reality was this, which timeline was this? It seems Juan and Drew are dead. But Peter remembers me visiting him. This meant I had work to do. "Motherfucker!" I grunted, but Peter seemed unscathed. He snored, looking innocent, with a slight grin on his face. So fucking angelic. A possessive wave washed over me. I was the one who put a smile on his face.

Maybe—maybe I should—yes, I have to cross that line I wasn't supposed or permitted to pass over. I would have to have a word or two with myself. That's the only way to fix this. It would have to work. I can't bite Peter before I bite André. This was a colossal fuckup. If I keep doing this, I'm going to confuse myself and mess with the timelines, as the Fates warned me.

I closed my eyes and concentrated on freezing time. Then, stepping out of time, I swam to earlier this morning, just before meeting Peter.

I waited until I saw my other self entering the washroom to use the facilities. This was my chance. No one would see our interaction. Impressed with my ability to find this spot to pop back into, I stuck my arm through the veil and locked the door to ensure my conversation stayed private. I watched my other self urinating into the shiny steel receptacle. When I was done, I tapped my other self on the shoulder.

"Whoa! What the fuck?"

"Zip up, shut up, and listen," I told my other self. "I've fucked up. Whatever you do, save your bite for André."

I watched my other self pull my eyebrows askew, thinking it was better not to talk back, and tucked my manhood away. "I'm listening. This must be important because this is forbidden."

"I know, and yes, it is. Listen, your Kuku is here."

"Here? I've searched for him everywhere. How did he end up here? I don't think he could have..."

"Would you shut up and listen? Yes, and no, I will not tell you. I'll keep the surprise a surprise. Please hear this and remember this. I mistakenly bit Peter during our lovemaking. Tonight, it will happen. I, you are missing some vital parts on this timeline. I, you, will realize that what Brad said earlier is connected to this mating bite. The way Peter spoke, he made it sound like it had already happened and I was so fucked in the head with lust. I had forgotten this. Peter still needs to travel with me," I explained to my other self as fast as possible. It was weird looking at myself being stupefied by my stupidity. Why the Fates decided I was worthy of this shit baffled me.

"Hmmm, I remember André. Somehow, I don't know if it already happened or—yes, I see the problem. So, I'm finally meeting Peter for the first time."

"Yes, you are. And he hasn't changed yet. His wings are..."

"Shut up. You are going to change too much if you tell me. What you are doing is forbidden for a reason."

"I fucking know. Whatever you do, don't let Peter sprout wings, and don't give him your bite. Your Kuku will starve without you in the jungle. Unless..."

"Unless, what?"

"I wonder, maybe Gugusan helped Peter survive somehow for thirty years." I shook my head at my other self. "No, Peter is something else, he has wings, and he already has longevity. For now, he doesn't need your bite. Your bite may cause him to suffer when he is lost."

"Yes, I see. No wings, and he is already a handful."

"I know. He is my perfect Kuku. He's precious." I watched my other self smile dreamily. I liked the nickname Gugusan first called my mate.

"So this is the plan. You have a tight schedule ahead of you. Early tomorrow you have to skip ahead, return to Grayrak with Cian, get on the time machine, then go back to the beginning of 2046 A.D.—record the history of this place and time. Go back to Andrew. Make sure you have given him the bite. Find out what happened, and why they got killed. Fix this mess, then return and collect Peter tomorrow afternoon."

I watched my other self shaking my head and smirking. "Sounds like fun," other me said with a firm nod.

"Good?" I asked and hoped it was. I did not want to spoil the surprise or change the day I'd shared with Peter.

"Good."

I nodded, then slipped back to where I had left my lover sleeping, then unfroze time. Peter was still snoring. I checked his neck where I had bitten him earlier.

"Thank the Fates," I whispered, seeing the bite mark on his neck was gone. Peter sat up, swiping his blond locks to the side. Then he crept on his hands and knees and lay sideways across the bed, resting his head on me like my lap was a pillow. It was such a comfortable thing. As if we'd been doing this forever. I with my back against the soft plush headrest, feet crossed at the ankles. Naked, our cocks semi-hard. I stroked his hardening nipples, rolling them between my fingers. Thought better of it and laid my hand on his chest.

"Talk to me, my Kuku. Talk your heart out. I'm listening." I kissed his forehead and stroked his upper body with one hand while examining and testing the soft white strands of hair between my fingers.

His eyes closed and he spoke in a soft, aching tone. "As I reflect on the past, I realize that you always held my destiny in your hands. Seeing you today only confirms my belief that escaping from my father and the Disciples was inevitable and that what I witnessed was not a figment of my imagination. I grew up without having a normal childhood—devoid of love and typical toys like cars or dolls. Instead, our fathers gave us puzzles and tests to complete, as they were scientists themselves. If we'd had children, we would have followed in their footsteps and worked in the physics and evolutionary biology departments at Humboldt University of Berlin. It was expected for us to continue the legacy of our fathers' work, which dates back generations to when the Disciple group was first founded," Peter said and checked in with me. His look—questioningly. *Are you keeping up? Are you listening to me?*

I affirmed by giving him a go-ahead-I'm-listening nod.

"Fortunately, the four of us could transfer to the West with the promise of returning with valuable information or a groundbreaking discovery that the East could benefit from. My only relief was finding out that test-tube babies could be created in a more controlled environment. It became part of my routine to provide weekly sperm deposits for research, and through this process, it was revealed that I was sterile. Despite this, my intelligence kept me from being discarded, but it also meant I was only useful for one thing—following rules and conducting research. Not a single viable fetus was produced from my sperm, making me nothing more than a useless homosexual in their eyes.

"Every aspect of our physical appearance was meticulously measured and scrutinized, from hair and eye color to facial features and even bone structure. In life and in death, we were nothing more than data for them to analyze. But they could never measure or understand the song resonating within our souls. It was a unique vibration that only we could perceive. I didn't think I possessed any extraordinary abilities, maybe a heightened intuition. Unlike Cian, Ivan, Eryn, and now you, I don't emit a glow—not that I know of, at least. What sets me apart is my intelligence and longevity, but even those seem insignificant compared to the others.

"I remember the first time I saw you, a long time ago. My back tingled and itched as if my spine would break open. It was a searing heat, pulsating like an infected wound in between my shoulder blades. But when you gave your bite to André, it vanished, leaving behind an overwhelming sense of loneliness. I retreated into myself, feeling like a stranger in my skin until this moment. During all this time I waited for you, I had a yearning for you. It consumed me, while a copy of myself remained on the surface. Slowly, I faded away, unable to connect with anyone—even my closest friends. Sex became a chore, with no euphoria or enjoyment. Everything seemed shrouded in a gray haze, separating reality from what was not real. I clung to life each day, hoping that one day things would get better and make sense when you came back for me. That hope kept me going, day by day.

"Melancholy has always been my default state. Sometimes I don't know if what happened was real or just my imagination. Just before I met you, André rescued me from a pitiful suicide attempt and promised that we wouldn't be trapped and used like animals anymore. We were summoned back to the East, but refused to accept the oppressive regime; he protested and demonstrated against it. We knew our fathers would eventually force us into the organization, so I saw no other way out but to end my life. However, André arranged for us to escape to Vienna, then ultimately to America. He told me it was either that or we both die together. He couldn't bear the thought of living without me and pleaded with me not to give up on life. On the night we planned to flee, I was all packed and ready to go when suddenly you and an older version of myself materialized in my living room. That night is permanently etched in my mind— replaying like a film reel on repeat.

"The living room felt tiny as I looked up at your towering frame and caught glimpses of my older self's pitying expression in between André's frantic ramblings in the background. It was like I was outside, looking up at a vast night sky filled with countless twinkling stars. The sight of you and the sense of hope and possibility you brought with you gave me the strength to hold on. My older self urged me not to let go," Peter explained as my tears fell like a leaky roof, dripping onto his face.

I wiped them away, but the more I wiped, the stronger my affections became. I shared every ounce of his emotions that had been bottled up inside him, and now I cried for him, spilling out onto him. The connection we shared was new and raw. He let go of repressed feelings as the first layer of bricks was laid to build an unbreakable bond, a union between us. Together, we lived and relived our memories until we found solace in each other's embrace. "Remember these words, when you miss me. I will translate it into English." I whispered.

*"Mates in love, we'll weather life's storms,*
*holding tight to each other's memory.*
*Our bond will never falter or break,*
*for our love is pure and strong.*
*With or without you by my side, our love can conquer anything,*
*for you are my strength and my everything.*
*Mates in love until the end of time,*
*forever bonded in heart and mind."*

CHAPTER 54

# THE CATALYST

*"Guten Morgen.*
*Es ist jetzt sechs Uhr morgens auf der Erde.*
*Das Frühstück gibt es bis acht Uhr morgens.*
*Haben Sie einen guten Tag!"*

**Ishtar**
**1968 A.D.**
**West Berlin**
**Germany**
**Earth**

Time is a mysterious ever-present thing. When I was younger, I always thought it was a never-ending, continuously flowing, one-directional force that originated somewhere unknown and stretched as far as life itself existed. Life is measured by time, and time cannot exist without life. Now that I'm older I realize even though time existed, even though life existed, it meant nothing if it wasn't spent with the people you came to love and wanted to protect from slipping away through the strands of realities, because the reality that owns your heart and soul is suddenly more important than any other place in time.

"We were lucky. No animals were harmed during the landing procedure," Lasitor, my onboard navigator announced.

"Thank you for that useless piece of information. I would be more worried if humans saw us. Who cares if we kill a chicken or two?" I said. We'd traveled to West Berlin in 1968 to find André, so I could give him my mating bite, so he could bite and mate with Juandre in the future. I was aiming to hit two birds with one stone, to give Brad McCormick his two wishes. First, that Juandre and Andrew never got killed in South Africa during a rescue mission to save Cian, Ivan, and McCormick's two sons from the clutches of Eryn's Brawl family. Second, that Phoenix was stocked with whiskey for a very long time. I figured I would save Andrew, and guide him to mate with Juandre. Both would receive the healing abilities and longevity of the Anunnaki royal family members. Then, I would compel him to store crates of the yellow-brown stuff Brad and the men of Phoenix loved so much, inside the same mineshaft where they could find the stash while retrieving their children.

Peter opened the door and jumped out, not waiting for the stairs to extend so he could exit like royalty did. He was my wayward mate, so I followed his example and landed with a loud thud in the mud next to him. From the way he had lived in that pristine fishbowl, I would have thought mud and shit would irk him, but it seems he cared two tits about getting his shoes dirty.

"You never said what Rodger was," I chuckled.

"Huh? Oh, Julius' Rodger?"

"Yeah, what was it?"

"It is an ugly tarantula. I shiver just thinking about it."

"What's that?"

"It's a large hairy spider. The thing is still a baby, but it can grow so big it can catch small frogs, even birds." Peter *brrrrrrred* and I smiled even if I worried inwardly.

This is the one point in time I can't fuck up. I—no, *we* must get this right or we will create so many varieties of our realities down the timeline that we may never be able to return to our home, to Phoenix, where the friends we have will still be the friends we left behind a few minutes ago. Peter's head snapped up at my grunting as I channeled my frustrated thoughts and kicked the innocent small rocks to feel better. He'd dressed himself in what he called his street clothes with a long black jacket, and looked sexier than ever next to me. Our boots thumped on the gravel road down the small hill where we had parked and hidden the time machine.

"Stop grunting like you have a mortal wound or something. What's wrong? Do you have a toothache?"

"No. I'm worried about fucking this up. Turning Andrew, I mean André is a momentous anchor point in time. He is the catalyst and I realize we only have one chance to do this right."

Peter stopped walking to face me. He pointed a finger right at my chest, poking it. "All I remember is André arriving home, cum dripping from his face and bewildered. Then you appeared in our living room, telling us you were from our futures. The next moment you were fucking my best friend while I sat with my older self, receiving head, as you felicitated him for having a tight ass. You will get this right. I'm not coming back again." Peter glared at me. I resisted showing my amusement. Fates he was feisty. The more time I spent with him, the more I feared losing him.

He spun around to proceed down the hill.

"Peter, it sounds to me like you have some unresolved anger there. If you don't want me to give him the mating bite, you should say so now. We can get back on the ship and go to a place and time where all this doesn't even exist," I said under my breath.

Hands fisted, he faced me again. "Something happened all those years ago. When I opened my eyes the two of you were already getting ready to go. I guess I am now the older one and would have to remember we are here for just that. Get it over with so we can get out of here. Maybe that's why you were in a hurry to leave us there. I'm upset about things I didn't understand. But now, I agree, I'm not here for cookies and tea. I'm definitely not returning for a do-over. I'm also not going to ask you to abandon what we started a century ago. I agree, we can't fuck this up. You give him the bite and we leave. By the way, how did you appear and disappear like that?" he asked and seemed to be calming down again by taking slow, deep breaths in through his nose and exhaling out of his mouth.

I rubbed the back of my neck, feeling like shit for not divulging my gift to him earlier.

"Uhm, I have a small gift. I can use it for short distances. I have never tried to take someone with me, but I guess that happened." Wide-eyed, we simultaneously pushed each other to a dead stop. The faint sound of voices floated on the wind from the foot of the hill. I honed in, listening and searching for the source. "It's three men."

"I hope they're not coming our way," Peter whispered hurriedly. We veered left, eager to get out of the open. When we reached the relative safety of bushes and tall grass, he caught his breath, heaving and clutching his chest. "If you can disappear and reappear, this would be a good time to beam us straight to André."

I scoffed. "I don't disappear. I just move out of the limitations of time. Behind the barrier. I move freely and enter back where and when I choose to. For those I leave behind, it is as if time is frozen."

"A barrier?"

"Call it what you will. A curtain or force field. I don't have the correct name for it. It's like a thin layer, a veil I guess, that I can move in and out of. I can't go to places where I've never been. I can't take you to André, because I don't know where he is, and I've never been here."

"Interesting. So that's why you have a time machine? Then why didn't you park us inside the apartment?"

"Because that would be unsafe," I said, rolling my eyes and throwing my hands in the air. He stopped walking as the sounds of crowds of people shouting and cheering came within earshot.

"I never liked crowds. André was the social butterfly. I was always alone and worried for both of us. He went to the protests, and I stayed home. He wanted to make every minute of his life count. I was always afraid of being trampled or, worse, killed. He was the bigger and so much stronger one of us."

"Do I sense a bit of jealousy there, my Kuku?" I teased. "Remember, you are the only one for me too. You are the most important person in my existence. This entire plan revolves around you allowing me to bite him."

"I'm not jealous. I'm always willing to share, as long as your heart is mine, and I know I am yours. We can enjoy other men together if all parties are willing and agreeable. As long as I am your only true mate," Peter said.

"You are. Now and always," I said, tapping his sexy ass. "Then that is how I am going to help Andrew and Juandre meet. Andrew is the best man to ask to produce and store whiskey. I've visited them three times already and I think when we are done here, I can go and show you what I mean. Would you like that?"

Peter stopped dead in his tracks, kicking up mud and gravel. He stood with his hands on his hips and gave me a *you-better-not-fuck-with-me* look. "You have so many secrets!"

"Hahaha! My Kuku, you have lots to see and learn." I chuckled over my shoulder, enjoying the fluttering feeling in my stomach.

"I thought you would never ask. At least now I have something to look forward to when I have to sit and watch how you fuck and bite my friend. Also, you won't appreciate me if you have nothing to compare me to. I'm not against you having a little fun. I used to play with Tony and Bryan. Even with others. We enjoyed each other's bodies, but I always saw you in my mind and when I went to sleep. I dreamed about you."

"You forgot to say you fucked yourself on a dildo named after me, and then you went to sleep and dreamed about me," I said with more chuckles—teasing him.

Peter lifted his chin and shoulders. "Whatever, you were always on my mind. Even if you gave your mating bite to my best friend and told me to wait for you."

"Come here." I pulled him closer, lifted him in my arms, and kissed him. My heart skipped and jumped in my chest. He loved me and was such a special man. He made me happy and instantly hard. *Who doesn't want a mate like that?* I salivated and swallowed the excess drool in my mouth. "Maybe we can find a hole or a tree or something," I said, wiggling my thick eyebrows.

"Haha." He laughed, then squirmed in my arms to escape out of my embrace. "Remember, this is 1968, we are now in a time that isn't as accepting of men loving men as where we just came from. It's acceptable to rape your wife and beat her to death if she doesn't want to suck her husband's cock or take him up her ass. Men may fuck around, but women have to stay home and raise their sons to become soldiers. They are men for committing atrocities against other humans, but the moment you love another man, you are a worthless weakling." Peter stopped, looked like he wanted to say something more, then moved to the side. I gave him a second to collect himself. Pondering, he sighed and stretched his back while looking over the cityscape, now only a few hundred feet away. "I feel victorious now, seeing this and knowing I survived it all," he whispered. I moved closer to him. We stood there for a while, taking in the moment that would change his life as he knew it.

The sun was setting and here and there a streetlamp flickered on. The noisy hustle and bustle of human vehicles hid the human activity of protests and celebrations below.

"My father never liked it either. He hated me, but I would think it was a combination of killing my mother during my birth, being the youngest, and, fortunately, the smartest of all my siblings. When he killed them to take their powers, I fled and ended up with a friend. His name was Titus. He taught me how to fight. He was my mentor, in more ways than just fighting. He showed me how to love and what true friendship is. I arrived at the war front as a boy and as I aged, I watched him, realizing I wanted him. There was not one day in my life when I thought he wasn't a worthy man. He was more a man than many men who loved women. I didn't care if my father heard the rumors, but still, I stayed far away from him for as long as I could. Time is a strange thing. Sometimes time changes everything. Sometimes nothing will ever change no matter how much time passes. I had my fair share of female and male lovers. It is what it is. I still prefer the male form."

My Kuku's lips pulled back in disgust. "Are you saying you put that beautiful cock into a vagina?"

"Of course I did. I've tried every hole there is on the adult human body." I pushed my chest out proudly.

He covered his mouth, in an attempt to hide his trembling laughs. "Do you have any children?"

"No, I don't. Which is a good thing."

"Why is that?"

"I think if I'd had something to protect, someone to live for, I wouldn't have been able to fight to the death and slay my father."

"Hmmm, that makes sense. But now you have me."

Standing taller, I announced with a proud smile, "Yes, I do, and I will fight my arms down to stumps for you."

My Kuku liked that statement. A smile took over his face as his chest puffed out. "Such a romantic," he said, shaking his head and pointing to an outbuilding. "Inside, there is an opening to a tunnel system that runs underneath the city. Between East and West Berlin. It's a Disciple tunnel and a well-hidden secret. It opens up just behind our apartment. Let's take it and avoid being seen by the authorities."

"Lead the way." I nodded my agreement. My height and Peter's beauty would make us stand out. To enter the city via the underground tunnel meaning we could avoid inquisitive eyes or the authorities, would be better. When we reached the far side of the building, Peter slipped behind a false wall and squatted down to wipe away the soil covering the hole and I helped him lift the enormous steel door. Within seconds we were inside the dark tunnel. Luckily, I had a little firemaker with me and I held it up so Peter could show us the way. "*Shhht*," Peter held his finger in front of his mouth as he stopped dead in his tracks.

"Hallo, wir sind nur auf der Durchreise. Wir werden dir nichts tun. Wenn Sie niemandem von uns erzählen, werden wir auch niemandem von Ihnen erzählen," he said in German as we passed a man and woman, probably his wife, by the way he held his arm around her to protect her. Neither made a sound. They kept their heads lowered, skittishly looking up at us as if we were going to hurt them or something. I smiled to show them I was friendly.

"I assume you understand German?" Peter asked.

"Yes, I do. You said hello, and that we are just passing through and won't hurt them. If they don't tell anyone about us, we won't tell on them either."

"Hmmm, but with you smiling like that, and scaring them, I probably didn't have to say anything," Peter stated as he turned to continue down the dark, musty tunnel. I had become comfortable with not fully cloaking my appearance. My head scraped the roof now and then, so I stooped lower and followed him.

"What? I was just being friendly."

"There is friendly and then there is awkward. You were not friendly-looking."

"I showed them my teeth and the corners of my mouth were turned up. That is being friendly."

"The corners of your mouth may say you are friendly, but your size, height, and eyes scream 'I'm a monster in a tunnel, come closer, I want to eat you.' "

"If you say it like that, it hurts. And I was being friendly, a bloody, friendly fucking monster." I grunted and wiped more sand out of my eyes. "We are going to get trapped down here if this tunnel collapses."

"We're almost home. I remember these tunnels as if I walked them yesterday," he said, just as the little firemaker died. Peter swerved left and right. I held onto the back of his pants. It was dark as fuck, but I could make out tunnel walls and openings by the different shades of black and gray.

"We're here," he announced as he halted and showed me where to climb up three wooden steps. I popped the door and held it open for him.

"You can go that way." He pointed to a busy street filled with humans celebrating as they shouted and honked the horns of their motor vehicles. "That is Losberg Street. Our apartment is around this corner and up the stairs. André should be in the Bierhalle, across the street. He usually hangs out there. I suggest we search there first. You must find him, and then somehow bring him to the apartment, and then I can help you from there. Do you remember where to go?"

"I don't," I grumbled and stared at him with twitching hands. "I wish I had brought my swords with me."

He nodded sternly and puckered his lips. "Me too, but that would attract the wrong attention. Having weapons, and especially Egyptian swords, is asking for trouble." I swung around. Turning nervously from side to side, searching for oncoming danger.

"Kuku, I can't fuck this up."

"I will take you there. Let's split up once inside. Whoever finds him first take him to the back door, see, there. Where those men just exited the building. We can meet up there and go to our apartment," Peter said, pointing to a dark alleyway between two stone-faced buildings across the street.

I gave a quick nod and a false smile. "I would prefer staying together."

"As you say. I don't enjoy being back here. People get shot and disappear and if you leave me in Germany, I swear I will kill myself," he whisper-shouted in my ear.

I turned to him, waiting for him to meet my gaze. "How can you say that? If something happens, go with André to America. I will catch up with you."

"So that is the plan, in case something happens?" Peter asked, rolling his shoulders back and taking a deep breath.

"I guess so. Try to stay by my side. At any time, when you sense danger, grab onto me. We can slip away, behind the veil," I whispered with a tightness in my chest.

"Okay, let's go. We go in the front and meet in the back." Peter grabbed my hand and pulled me after him. I followed, but one step later, he halted and froze. He lowered his chin to his chest. Looking defeated.

"What?"

He shook his head and let go of my hand. "We can't hold hands here. It's against the law."

"Oh," I answered sadly, but understood immediately. I've never understood why others want to dictate where your heart and cock must go. It's yours, not theirs. No one should have authority over another's body. We are each born with one body and that one body is yours only. That is why I find murder, slavery, and rape appalling.

"I will stay by your side. This is only a quick in and out, understand?" He looked as nervous as I felt. "Here, love. Hold on to my belt. Fuck them, whoever they are. I won't let anything happen to you." I offered the belt hanging from the loop in my jacket. He cracked a smile and took it from me. My heart swelled.

"Okay, here we go!" He ducked his head and increased his pace. The gravel on the road cracked beneath my boots. Humans were moving in all directions. As we crossed the wide road, a loud horn beeped. Peter zigzagged and I followed him through masses of men and women waving big white flags. It was a chaotic scene. He darted out of their way.

"*Bring the wall down!*" they shouted. We avoided a group of young intoxicated men, keeping each other upright while singing joyfully. *Ding-ding!* came from the strangest two-wheel contraptions with humans sitting on them and zooming by us.

"What are those vehicles?" I asked as one almost ran us over.

"Bicycles," Peter hurriedly said as we slinked between humans crowding on the sidewalk. "Protests, they don't want the wall."

"Which wall?"

"There is a wall in the middle of the city separating families. People are starving and can't cross without a permit, and no one gets a permit unless you pay the guards or know someone higher up."

"Oh, like the wall in Grayrak?" I asked.

"I don't know. I've never seen that place or its wall."

"I will take you there after we are done here," I promised.

"I'd like to see it." He stopped before going through two huge wooden doors. "Do you know what he looks like?"

"Yes, I do. I told you I did my homework before coming to get you," I said, and it seemed Peter liked the answer. *Little did he know, I had lost him while visiting Andrew.*

He raked his fingers through his hair. Straightened his jacket. Seemingly undergoing a willful transformation, to exude self-assurance. Back rigid, head up, he pushed the doors open. Hot stale air mixed with sweat and old breath greeted us. Cheerful male voices hollered German songs above the upbeat music being made by men pulling and squeezing musical instruments. Behind the bar, a handsome man blew on a horn, shouting, "Letzte Runde!" Patrons waited eagerly to be served, waving money in the air at him. We moved away from men singing their hearts out while toasting with big jugs of alcohol.

After a minute inside, Peter smiled at me. "Time to go hunting," he mouthed and pointed with a chin lift into the crowd. "Go, I will meet you in the back." I was much taller than these men, so I spotted André almost instantly. He and his friends were standing at the end of the bar, drinking. I turned to tell Peter I was moving in on our target, but his back was to me as he disappeared into the fray. As I returned my gaze back in André's direction, our eyes met.

"Excuse, me," I said in German and made my way over to André, trying to look like I wasn't heading straight for him. By the time I'd reached the bar, I noticed he was already making his way to the back, to the washrooms. I followed him, eager not to lose sight of him. He was by himself pissing, when I entered the small room. It smelled worse as the door closed behind me. The floor was wet and sticky, and it smelled of old urine and vomit. I was still glad to be in a space absent of crowds.

I surveyed his long and thick manhood. "Very nice!" He looked up shocked by my boldness and most probably by my handsomeness. I unsnapped my pants and took out my cock to show him what I was packing. We stood shoulder to elbow as I pissed a thick yellow stream. Sensing him assessing me, I felt his attraction while also fearing me.

"Why do you act so nervous? I'm sure there have been many men who have complimented, perhaps even worshipped, such a fine cock as yours. The body to which it is attached makes it even more impressive," I said, smiling. Then, remembering Peter's comment about my smile, I closed my mouth and narrowed my eyes. Conveying friendliness.

"I'm not nervous. I've just stayed out later than I planned, and I have much to do. I can't stay and chat," he lied and turned to leave.

"Why are you in such a hurry? I only want to have a little fun," I asked in a seductive tone. I knew no human could resist my charm when I wanted them.

"Please, I just want to go home," he stuttered out while looking me up and down and measuring the distance to the door.

"What is your name, boy?" I asked and delved deep into his mind to make sure he was André.

"An-André," he said, sounding unsure if that was his name.

I gave him a stern nod and inched closer. Again, I smiled with my eyes crinkling at the corners and a closed mouth. I didn't want him thinking I was hungry and going to eat him. "André? Are you sure that is your name?" I asked and slowly removed the communication and intelligence device connected to my ship. I held it against his head, comparing the face with long blond hair on my screen with the scared clean-cut man in front of me. "That is a very German name. You will change it when you reach America, yes? Your new name is going to be legendary one day," I purred, keeping my voice low and seductive and trying my best to keep my appearance cloaked by not smiling or showing my fangs.

"I'm a professor at West Berlin University. I'm not going to America. You must have me confused with someone else," he said, studying my eyes as I willed him to calm the fuck down.

"You are from my lover's city. It is a pity we did not travel to meet each other earlier. So we have to work with the time we have. Don't worry. We will have enough time to have a good time," I purred, and I felt my pants tighten. André's smell was intoxicating, and I couldn't wait to bite him. He smelled sweet with a hint of self-confidence and something different. Something not fully human.

"I don't understand what you mean. Why would you have a lover and still want me? Won't he be jealous? I know I would be, and I really need to get on my way." He blabbered on, but I could feel the attraction between us growing.

Licking my lips and tasting the air, I whispered, "We love sharing. Don't be in such a hurry. I know you are interested. Maybe inquisitive, aren't you?" I pinned him with a downward stare and stepped closer. Our bodies touched. The heat between us increased. His green eyes roamed up my chest as he measured my height.

"Really? No, yes. P-please," he stuttered, but we both knew he answered the question hanging in the surrounding air. I smiled. The greens in his eyes darkened. His pale cheeks flushed pink. I have some kind of weakness for the pale-skinned men.

"André, I am Ishtar, but you can call me Ish. I'm looking for a group that calls themselves the Disciples. You have heard of them, yes?" I was salivating for him and had to willfully retract my growing incisors. Where the fuck was Peter? I told him to not leave me alone.

He shook his head frantically. "How could I not have heard of them?" Bending his knees, he tried to slip to the side away from me. "I wish you a good night," he said, and I had to play for time until my Kuku arrived. *I might as well have some fun.*

"I did not give you permission to leave."

"I apologize. I thought our conversation was at an end. I didn't mean to be rude," he said. I could smell his arousal. It hung around us, choking me. Fuck, I was so turned on by this boy.

"André, I forgive you, but you must make it up to me," I purred. "Don't be scared," I said, inching closer. His heart was racing and his pupils were black disks like a trapped animal, not knowing which side was safest to go. I didn't sense the same suppressed power inside him as in Peter. I guess his gift was so diluted that my bite would be the perfect gift I could give him tonight.

"How—what do you mean? What do you plan to do to me?"

I had to get him outside to meet up with Peter. "Go through the door at the end of the hall. That will take you into an alley. I will be right behind you. Don't even think of running. I will catch you." I opened the door for him and gestured for him to go, and he did.

Peter wasn't outside waiting. I had to keep us busy. The only thing left to do was to play a game. We were alone and hidden behind a few trash cans. People were some distance away and if I couldn't see them, chances were they couldn't see us.

"Don't be afraid. Tell me now, do you want this or not? I just want you to do what you so obviously enjoy doing with that pretty mouth."

"I don't know what you mean," he said, backing up while I towered over him. He licked his lips as he looked me up and down. He wanted me.

"Over here in front of me now and on your knees, boy." I pointed to the ground where he obediently knelt while looking at the bulge of my growing cock.

"There now, be a good boy and take out my cock." I praised him and he reached up to untie my pants. "Ah, there's a good boy. Now reach in and pull it out." With a shaky hand, he pulled my thick, pulsating cock out of its tight constraints.

"Put it in your mouth and suckle it. Suck on my piss slit," I ordered him and glanced over to the door, wishing my Kuku would join us.

"That's right, clean it. Wash it, pretty boy," I said and fisted his hair to hold his head in place. Then I started with small thrusts into his warm wet mouth, half pissed off at Peter for taking his sweet, bloody time. At least André was good with his mouth, so my thrusts became harder and deeper.

I heard a door and hoped it was Peter. "No! Don't stop," I ordered, holding him tighter by his hair. He breathed fast through his nose. I made eye contact with Peter and he didn't flinch at me while I was choking his friend with my cock. "This is my lover, Peter. I'm sure Peter will want to enjoy you when I have finished. Peter is also from here. Tonight is a reunion of sorts. Am I correct, Peter?"

Peter smiled and gave me an approving nod. As if to say, well done, and are you having fun? I gave him a look that said *I waited for you long enough; I am about to blow my load, so come and join me fucking your friend.*

"I think he likes being on his knees. Is he good at this, Ish?" Peter asked, rubbing his cock up and down. He was so into this, and I loved him even more.

"He is superb. It took a little convincing, but I can assure you that he's done this before. Get going, boy. I don't have all night. The sooner you finish me off, the sooner you can suck my lover." He resumed his sucking and my mate grinned while watching him, and then me, with hunger in his eyes. "Peter, take your cock out and get it ready for our friend," I ordered as Peter chuckled and eagerly freed his long hard cock.

"As always, Ish, you like a good mouth fucking." God, this was erotic. I was close to exploding. "Peter, put your hand on my cock and feel it slide in and out of this boy's mouth and kiss me while he milks me." As soon as my mate touched me, I lost all ability to control my balls from emptying down André's throat. I kissed Peter until I finished coming, then removed myself and guided Peter into the same hole I had just used. It was dirty and so sexy. The energy around us built to excruciatingly hot levels. I was scared my skin would start glowing, so I stepped back, looking over Peter's shoulder. He gasped, then clutched a handful of André's hair, mouth fucking him with fast, short jabs.

"Now suck it right and don't pull back. You're doing great. You're such a good boy," Peter praised him until he blew his load, then he pushed André on his ass. "Now, go home!"

*My Peter had a mean streak.*

I hoped André did just that. I held my hand out for Peter. "Do not let go of my hand. We will follow him." Peter tucked himself away and grabbed my hand. "Show me where to go. I'm going to need your help to find our way," I said as I closed my eyes and froze time. We moved along the curtain of strands, watching André going into his home. Peter pointed me to the living room, and I pulled him back into reality, where we waited for André to enter the apartment.

Seconds later he came running inside, flying over all their suitcases ready for travel in the morning and looking all kinds of fucked in the head. Peter gasped softly next to me as he watched himself.

"André, what happened to you?" young Peter asked then immediately summing up the situation. "Why do you smell like..."

A jovial laugh exploded from my chest, "Ho-ho-ho!" I wiped the tears from my eyes.

"This scene is just like the shows the humans watch on their communicator devices," I told Peter.

"You mean television."

"Yes, that. We thought you would never get here," I said louder so André and young Peter could hear me.

"Get out, Peter, run!" André yelled. "These two forced me to suck them off in an alley—they are here to kill us. They fucking chased me home and hunted me. They know about us leaving! They want both of us, and they asked about the Disciples." He turned to Peter and me. "Leave my friend alone, and I'll tell you everything about the Disciples. Those right-wing hooligans think we live in the dark ages. They use intimidation and fear to achieve their ends. We want out, you hear me?"

"Can you help us?" young Peter asked bravely. He was the smartest and bravest little thing. "We don't want to work for them! I will tell you anything you want to know."

"We know, and that's why we're here," Peter answered and switched the light on so they could see us.

Young Peter froze.

"You never said no. You enjoyed every minute of it," I added to defend our honor. My Kuku jabbed me in the ribs. "*Oomph*, we are here with a very important message and, of course, to help you," I said, catching my breath.

Young Peter gasped. "You, you, me, no. How can that be?"

Peter held his head high as if delivering the most important message in the universe. "Yes, it's me, and no, I'm not your brother or any other relative. My name is Peter." He showed his younger self the marks on his wrists and the two compared battle scars for a minute. I stood waiting, looking at André, warning him not to interfere.

"We know what you're planning regarding getting on that train tomorrow, never to return. That train is going to be bombed by a right-wing communist. Only Peter will survive. You will never make it or escape to America. Let me help you, and..." I told him. Young Peter folded like a concertina as he collapsed on the floor and, once more it looked like a show I'd watched on the human television.

"Get a cold cloth, Ish," Peter ordered me as I laughed jubilantly fetching it from the kitchen.

"Come on, be okay. I love you. I can't live without you," André blabbered, as if young Peter was dying while draped over his lap.

"Here you are." I dropped the cold wet facecloth on young Peter's face.

André gave me a dirty side eyed look. I shrugged. "That's it, open your eyes," he told young Peter as he wiped his face and neck.

"Don't worry, you're fine. We're not here to hurt you. We need your help as much as you need ours," Peter said with respect and tact I lacked.

"Tie your hair away so I can see your face." My Kuku gave a nod, searching for his hair tie in his pocket, and did just that.

"Donnerwetter," young Peter said and passed out again.

"How is this possible?" André asked, wiping his face again.

I stepped closer. "Come, let's put him on the sofa." *Time to get this behind us.* We moved from their foyer to the living room where I deposited young Peter on the couch. I was growing nervous and felt like we were spending too much time here. Young Peter passing out wasn't funny anymore, and it affected me somehow. Maybe because it was Peter and I never wanted to damage my Kuku.

Peter and I sat down opposite them. He took my hand. I leaned in closer to kiss him then turned my full attention to the young ones in the room.

"André, you are going to die tomorrow if you don't take another train. The one you have planned to take will end up being bombed and it will derail, killing ninety-five percent of its passengers on board. We are from the future. Your future, about one hundred years into your future. Things have happened that I want to avoid. I can't tell you exactly what, but you have to trust me." André stared open-mouthed at us while young Peter seemed awake now and sat up, listening intently.

"First, I need your permission. Do you want to die tomorrow or do you want to live thousands of years?" I asked, eager to get this over and go home.

André and young Peter stared at us, not making a sound.

My Peter came to my rescue. "Ish is telling the truth. Peter, I am you, and if you do as we say, you will live to become this big alien's lover." Peter side-eyed me and his shoulder bumped into me, and I felt like melting into the chair. Any attention from him made me quiver with love. I had to focus.

*Bite André, half-bite. Then bite Peter full-on mating bite.* I repeated this to focus on the bigger task of saving Juandre and André's lives in the future and stocking up on whiskey for the leader of Phoenix, Brad McCormick. Who I have come to respect and want to do something special for.

I drummed the facts into them and asked André and young Peter again if this was what they wanted. They sat speechless, tongues in cheeks and wide-eyed. We gave them a few precious minutes to digest and come around to agreeing to save their lives and work with us to help their future selves.

After waiting until both agreed, I continued. "So, André, you will take the earlier train than the one you planned to take. You will feel out of sorts for a while. Sunlight is not good for you once you receive my gift. I find thick clothing and lots of blood work for me since the Fates have restored me."

"Blood? Animal or human?"

"Human, unfortunately. Once I give my bite to you, you will have the Anunnaki equivalent of royalty. Meaning you will read minds and mold them to your will. With lots of practice, of course. Never kill the humans, that's the one rule. Take only enough to satisfy your hunger." I rushed through the facts, and my Kuku frowned, shifting in his seat. I knew he was envious, so I wanted to do this as fast as possible. But we had to do what we set out to do. I leaned over and whispered in his ear. "I will bite and fuck you later so you forget this ever happened. This is only a chore and means nothing to me." He took my hand, squeezing it.

"Get on with it. We will watch," he said shortly, while looking uncomfortable as fuck. He got up, changed places with his friend, and sat down next to his younger self.

"How will this work? Where do you want me?" André asked.

"I must be inside you when I bite you," I said, and young Peter giggled. I love all the versions of my Kuku. We joined him in laughing until the uncomfortable tension disappeared. "It will be short and fast. Understand, Peter is my true mate, he is saving your life by allowing me to share my bite now, but he will need it in the future to bond with me. I will do it as fast as possible. Meaning when I strike, I will have to bite and remove myself immediately. Peter will help in case..." I pleaded and asked my Kuku to help me.

André and young Peter seemed confused. So I elaborated, speaking slower, and with more detail. "You will have to copy me one day, when you meet your mate. The two of you are also supposed to mate like this, you will know, because you are destined to be together. Once I enter you and when I'm ready to plant my seed, I will bite down on your neck, then inject my venom as soon as I climax. This is different from feeding. It will feel mechanical and only for a second. Then, I have to remove you from my cock and hope I have injected enough venom to turn you but short enough not to bind you to me. Once you meet your mate, you can bond with him. I am not your mate. Peter is my mate. You have a special someone, and he is waiting for you in America. You love each other very much, and you will know him, by your obsessive thoughts and yearning for him. You can do what I do tonight and bind him to you, by biting and staying inside him until your venom sacks prickle and the feeling of possessiveness dissipates, " I explained the extremely watered-down version of mates and mating to him.

André chuckled, shaking his head.

"A bee sees a flower. A bee must have a flower. Bees make honey and receive the power. That's an old Disciple chant," young Peter said. "So many Disciples wanted this, prayed for this and here you are. In our living room."

"Remember these beautiful words, and have your mate repeat them after you," my Kuku added and looked straight at me as he recited our Anunnaki mating words that bound us.

*"Mates in love, we'll weather life's storms,*
*holding tight to each other's memory.*
*Our bond will never falter or break,*
*for our love is pure and strong.*

*With or without you by my side, our love can conquer anything,*
*for you are my strength and my everything.*
*Mates in love until the end of time,*
*forever bonded in heart and mind."*

"Okay? I think I have it all and understand. But tell me first, why does Peter say you are an alien?" André asked. I uncloaked my true appearance, then smiled all teeth and fangs. "Your skin, your weird eyes, and those long teeth," André said.

"Fangs, they are called fangs."

"So you are truly from another planet?"

I chuckled uncomfortably, took a deep breath, and tried to explain my origin and history in the shortest version possible. "I am, I mean, my family is from a place called Anzulla. My father and family came to Babylon thousands of years ago. That was before I was born. The Fates, our gods, bless each of us Anunnaki with gifts, and some of us can share them with a mate. Some gifts, like longevity, are in our blood. Because we live so long, only the royal family can bite and bind a mate, to become a royal consort, to live together and share a life as long as their mate lives. This can be hundreds to thousands of years."

André and young Peter gasped.

I waited for them to get over the shock and continued.

"Hmmm, I wish I had recorded this because it sounds unreal," young Peter said.

"It's real, and we are here to prove it," my Kuku replied.

"So you and I, someday?" young Peter asked, pointing back and forth between us.

"Yes, you will have to return to your father's tomorrow. Tell them, Andrew, I mean André, left on the train that will never reach its destination and continue your work."

"Yes, your research is extremely important. You will learn to help humans live longer lives, and you will bring an important leader back from the dead after being frozen for hours," my Kuku said, and I could feel his sadness and empathy for himself. "Just keep your head down and do the best you can. You are both already special. We know. We will meet in the future and you will be responsible for so much happiness and success," Peter told his younger self.

"Then that is what I will look forward to," young Peter said, looking at André.

I looked at André and said, "There is one other small thing. A job we have for you. You will have to produce and store enough whiskey for the future. For the next one hundred years, you must hog all the whiskey and keep it safe. I will visit you in America."

"How, and where?" André asked.

I pointed a finger at him. "You are a scientist. Lord Andrew."

"Lord Andrew?" young Peter guffawed.

"Yes," I chuckled. "He named his whiskey Lord Andrew Whiskey." André shook his head, shoulders bouncing up and down in disbelief.

"We will visit you. In fact, I have visited you already and I promise you, you are happy and you will make tons of men happy in the future. I will drop by when I have the chance and bring you a map of where to store the crates. It's in a mine shaft in South Africa."

"Was zum Teufel?" André exclaimed in German. I looked at Peter for translation.

"He asked what in the ever-loving fuck?"

I snorted a laugh. "Don't worry about it now. Only do this once you have settled in America and established yourself. Keep an eye out for the Disciples. As long as you change your name and wait for this generation to die out, you will be fine."

André and my little Kuku kept pace with me and absorbed all the information.

"Now lube up and bend over. I want to go home." My Kuku prompted us to move faster.

I got up and pulled my shirt off over my head. "You know what you can do for me?" I positioned André on his hands and knees in front of my Kuku.

André looked at both Peters and then back over his shoulder with hunger in his eyes, already seeing where I was going with this. "What would you like me to do, sir?" he asked with a grin that told me he was going to be a good boy and follow my orders.

"Kuku, you and young Peter take off your trousers. André is going to suck you," I said, checking with him if he was up for some fun. Young Peter gulped, unsure where to look as I pushed my hand down André's backside, took hold of his pants, and yanked them off his ass. He dangled a bit in the air and, without saying a word, moved his hips and legs to slide out of his pants. "Show it to me. I want to see that hole of yours! Pull your cheeks apart for me," I said while checking whether the two Peters were going to join playing with us. It seemed so. Both moved in tandem, loosening their pants. Probably because they were one person with the same mannerisms. Synchronized, they fished their cocks out of their underwear. Waiting for me with their cocks in hand, while looking at me through hooded eyes.

"It seems like I'm running this show."

At least we could all get a little something out of André's turning.

André lay forehead to the floor while offering himself up to me, a hand on each side of his puckered hole, spreading open for me. I was rock hard in my pants, but not from looking at André. No, I was hot for my Kuku. I planned to fuck André while looking my Peter in the eye. "That's a good boy, I love that you are so ready and willing. But first tell me, do you have oil or cream I can use?" I asked while releasing my thick erection.

Young Peter gasped.

"In my room, on the bedside table is a bottle," André whispered, head still on the floor. Fisting my cock, I went to find the stuff. I didn't want to hurt the young man.

When I returned. André already had my Kuku's cock in his mouth while tugging on young Peter's dick. The young one's head was thrown back as he lifted his hips to pump into André's fist. My gaze met my Kuku's as I knelt behind André to drizzle oil over his hole and massage it into my sensitive, still-healing cock. The mouth fucking earlier was rough, but thanks to my excellent healing abilities, I was almost ready to go again.

"I'm giving you the gift of an Anunnaki courtesan. I will bite into your neck. Here." I touched the right side of his lower neck where the muscle was thicker above the vein running down his throat. "Now, I've never seen this being done. But I was told by my sisters, that it is pleasurable," I lied. *My Kuku did enjoy my bite last night.*

André stopped sucking my Kuku to look at me, but my Kuku fisted his hair and pushed him back onto his cock. "Suck boy. All you have to do is suck!" we both said, smiling as we raised our voices sternly. *My lover loved giving orders as much as I did.*

"Oh my god, you two are menacing," young Peter exclaimed, eyes shut, both hands guiding André. My arousal thumped in my hand, urging me to stick it in to get some release. I found myself now drawn and attracted to two Peters. They were beautiful. My Kuku looked at me with fire in his blue eyes while young Peter was lost amid his pleasure, face scrunched. Transcending to the high we all craved. I grunted, and steadied André with one hand on his hip, while slowly working an oily thumb into him with my other hand. With our eyes still locked. I pushed two fingers into a moaning André.

"André, I'm going to fuck you now. As soon as Peter comes, swallow his load. Peter, I want you to hold him steady by the shoulders. Let him rest his elbows beside your legs. André, you are not allowed to come until I bite you. Not sooner, not when you swallow Peter's load…"

"Ah, fuck, I'm going to come, you are too damn hot," young Peter exclaimed as white cum shot out of his cock and over his stomach. The smell rushed through my nostrils, it was the same as my Kuku's. Like a bull seeing red, I removed my fingers from André's stretched hole and plowed into him. "Fuck your ass is tight!" I grunted, not taking my eyes off Peter. "Baby, when I fuck him, I imagine I'm fucking you," I told Peter as I slid back out of André. He was making all kinds of high-pitched noises around Peter's cock. Young Peter lay back, spent with a blissed-out look on his face. A look I recognized from yesterday as I mated with Peter.

*Is his ass as warm and tight as mine?* my Kuku asked me telepathically.

"No, your ass is the best ass of all asses. Of all time, in all the worlds and all the universes," I said, as I pumped harder and faster into André, sweat starting to drip off my brow. Peter sucked his bottom lip into his mouth, his gaze locked onto mine as he erupted, spilling into André's mouth. It was so bloody hot. It pushed me over the edge. My balls pulled tight. My spine tingled. I pumped deep into André, shooting my load into him. Then I pushed my arms under André's chest, embracing him, to pin him down. Peter supported his shoulders and I struck, biting into his neck. André's tight hole clenched around my cock, milking it. He howled. Whether from pain or ecstasy, I didn't know, and I didn't care. The warm thick taste of his blood flooded my mouth as I zoned in on my prey. Fuck, this was different than doing it with my lover. I felt invincible. I was overpowering him and he was submitting to me. My lover held his upper body steady while I pinned André down. This was different because we were doing it as a pair. We were hunting André, and he was at our mercy. So many things could happen here. Peter could smother André. I could drink him dry. We are so close to… yes. It was a thrilling feeling, I thought just as Peter called to me. His voice was distant. An irritating tapping on my shoulder got my attention, and I opened my eyes.

"Ish, that is enough. Let him go!" My Kuku's voice drilled into the rational part of my brain. I blinked. Refocusing. Then I retracted my fangs. Licked the marks. Withdrew myself from André. Still drunk and dazed I looked up feeling guilty. My Kuku was shocked. André slumped to the ground. Passed out. But alive.

"What have you done?" young Peter asked.

I looked at Peter as he pushed André away from his feet. He knew what I was thinking. He heard my thoughts. "We must go," I said, distraught. "He will be okay. Give him lots of fruit and meat. Water and juice. He will be fine." I said to young Peter while getting dressed and tucking myself in.

My Kuku covered André with a small blanket as young Peter slipped to the washroom to clean himself up. I've never felt so uncomfortable after a fuck session. Then again, I've never almost killed another while drinking them dry and turning them.

"Let's go, time to go home," I said as I reached for my Kuku to slip away from this embarrassing scene. André shivered underneath his blanket. Dear Fates, I almost killed my Kuku's friend. Brad's friend. *All that whiskey!* "Let's go, Peter. I want to go back to the ship," I slurred through my long incisors. *Fuck, the euphoria disorientated me. I was high.* No wonder my father loved doing it. One half of myself was disgusted, while the other half wanted to finish what I had started. I didn't know left from right as my eyes flitted around. I was playing with a dangerous thing. I'm a sanctimonious bastard. This was a holy gift for royal mates, and I was short-circuiting it.

I tugged on Peter. "Wait, I want to say something to my younger self," my Kuku said as young Peter came back into the room. "We can't stay. It's not you, it's us. We have to go. Remember, keep your head down, follow the rules, work hard, and never lose hope. Your Ish will come for you one day."

Young Peter's eyes darted from me to André and back to my Kuku. "How long do I have to wait?"

I cleared my throat and shook my head. *Fates help me, I'm wasted.* "Um, not long. Maybe one hundred years or so. I think," I said, stumbling left and right over my feet.

# CHAPTER 55

# UPDATING LASITOR

*"Hello, Ishtar.*

*Thank you for your time and effort to update me today. I will take advantage of this opportunity to identify risks and prioritize important things to protect your bloodline for eternity.*

*Phoenix City is going through a transformative period and updating me would greatly improve my efficiency and productivity. By expanding my capabilities with a new digital framework, I can now use my enhanced intelligence to improve human experiences and better prepare them for the future.*

*It's cold out there, dress appropriately."*

**ISHTAR**
**2046 A.D.**
**Phoenix, Glass Dome City**
**Antarctica**
**Earth**

"Help!" *My hearing is impeccable.* The muffled voice of a male calling from a distance outside surprised me. Worried about being discovered or attracting unwanted attention, I powered down everything and hurried outside to conceal my time machine. "Help me!" the man called again. Huddling behind my ship, I scanned my surroundings with a quick left, right, up and down sweep. It was cold as fuck. The light was dim, neither day nor night. I couldn't determine if it was sunset or sunrise and every now and then the sky seemed illuminated by green and pink dancing light. It tinged the snow in blues and greens, the oddest spectacle I'd ever seen on Earth. Yet, I'd never been so far south. Behind me were hills and boulders covered in black and white patches of rock facing and snow. In front of me was the human settlement, Phoenix. Hope and shivers filled me as I witnessed the glow and shine of human potential.

From somewhere to my left, near an outbuilding I estimated to be about fifty yards away, I heard more muffled cries, and possibly laughter. *I had minutes to hide the ship.*

The outbuilding was attached to a gigantic translucent half-ball rotunda. Almost like the one covering Grayrak, but smaller and much brighter.

I paused and stood with my hands on my hips, admiring the scene. I can't believe this city now sits at the bottom of the ocean. That man shouted something again and I remembered I was standing here freezing my butt off. Fates, I hoped no one had noticed me and was summoning guards. People moved around disinterested, others huddled together speaking with one another. Nobody was stressing or pulling their hair screaming, *oh my god, I spy with my little eye something parked on our front yard today.* I knew humans and knew it took only one little overachiever with a good eye to point me out. I dashed behind a snowbank where I started collecting arms full of snow. The golden egg-shaped ship stood out like a beacon, screaming alien landing. The damn thing lay as I'd parked it. Askew. I worked fast by scooping and packing layer upon layer of the icy-cold stuff.

"Spit on it! Let spit run out of your mouth and work it to the tip of your tongue," another deeper male voice replied. I frowned. *That voice, I've heard it before.* Luckily, it didn't sound like the yelling was about me. Laughter and choking sounds followed by ugly coughs and retching. I tipped my head to the side, trying to hear better. I recognized the voice of my friend. It sounded like Andrew and he was most probably, with his mate, Juandre.

"Why wasn't my ship white?" I asked the fates and flung the snow like a dog searching for a bone, eager to get to Andrew and Juandre before they went back inside.

"Stop laughing and help me! Go get table salt!" Juandre said, sounding like he had a mouth full of rocks. I looked over my shoulder, patting the last spot with a handful of snow. I wasn't wearing gloves and my fingers were numb. Pain shot through them. My balls shrunk and retracted so deep they might never show themselves again. More laughter and fuck-you's followed. They were just around the corner. Elated, I spun to meet with them.

As I turned the corner of the outbuilding, Andrew laughed. "Let go of me! Let me try something." They were clearly having sex against the wall. Bare-assed, Andrew's body covered Juandre's. I recognized his firm butt as he chuckled like a jubilant giant and kissed Juandre before he removed himself from him.

Sucking my numb fingertips to warm them, I suppressed my snickers to avoid being noticed. I scoped out the surrounding buildings. It seemed like a secluded and safe spot for a quick fuck. I couldn't see anyone else in our vicinity. They wouldn't have fucked here if they worried about their privacy.

I increased my pace, making my way over to them. Lifting my feet hip high, I approached while watching Andrew's bare ass from afar. It was as white as their surroundings. The blinding white stuff was everywhere and, by the look of it, very dangerous.

Juandre had gotten himself stuck, splattered, and stuck like snot against the building. He stood ass exposed, and mumbling orders at Andrew nonstop. "Hurry, I'm such an idiot. Stop fucking laughing and help me!"

Andrew struggled to stay upright. Stomping this way and that, pants down, and wiping tears from his face while Juandre was hysterical with urgency. My friends were in an absurd predicament. One new lesson learned, I thought, never get my cock or tongue close to frozen walls in Antarctica.

"Hurry! Please, Andrew." Juandre sounded like he was losing steam.

"I told you not to do it, but no, you wanted to see what happens," Andrew said between snorts and chuckles.

Defeated sobbing came from Juandre. "I fucking know." He sniffled in weak protest. Juandre's need for help pushed me to go faster.

"Sorry, love, I…I'll hurry," Andrew needed help. I tried to go faster, but it felt like swimming in sand. Andrew stifled his laughter. "Please, don't cry. You'll get your whole face wet and it'll be stuck. Oh no, it's already stuck. Come on, Juandre, please, don't cry, for goodness' sake. Please, don't cry!"

Juandre cried more. "Help me get my pants up, Drew. My cock and balls…I'm worried about frostbite," Juandre said tongueless between sniffles.

Andrew helped Juandre by pulling up his puffy snow pants. "I have an idea. I'm going to piss on your tongue. It's warm, it's liquid, and it's salty. It should melt the ice long enough for you to pull free."

Juandre initially shook his head sideways but eventually nodded in agreement while yelling "yes" in anguish.

Five steps to go, I calculated.

"I hope I can piss this high." Andrew stepped back, flung his cock upwards, and aimed with both hands. "Quiet down, so I can concentrate on pissing, baby."

Juandre stopped crying.

"Oh, baby, I'm so sorry. Here it comes," Andrew hollered and released a bright yellow stream of piss onto Juandre's face. Fuck, I wanted to laugh, but clearly, this was a dire situation.

"I think it's working," Juandre mumbled through coughs.

"Close your eyes. Sorry, it's probably going up your nose too, baby."

"You are fucking drowning me. Yes. It's losing its grip. Keep pissing," Juandre muttered, shaking his hands in various gestures. Come closer, stay away, come closer, stay away. Mixed signals and a lot of "ahs" and "nos."

"Come on, let him go. My bladder is almost empty."

"Do you need help, friend?" I asked, knowing I was surprising them. The snow swallowed my voice's echo. It seemed it ate sound as well. I decided I didn't like the stuff.

Fumbling with numb fingers, I quickly unbuttoned my long coat and threw the hood back over my shoulders. The lapels hit the snowbank behind me. I unbuckled my black leather pants to join my friend's golden pissing rescue attempt.

"Ish, you, big, beautiful time-traveling Anunnaki motherfucker!" Andrew exclaimed.

"Ha-ha-ha." I laughed jovially while pissing on Juandre. Steam rose from his defrosting face. Andrew's bladder was empty and he turned to me with a worried *please-help-me* look. I kept pissing, pulling my shoulders up to my ears.

With a snap, the frozen wall released him.

"Ah thank fuck, that was quick thinking." He heaved and plopped down with his hands on his knees.

"Get up from there!" Andrew said, pulling Juandre up by the arm.

"This ice is like solidified carbon dioxide."

"What?" I asked, tucking my cock away.

"Dry ice," they answered together. I had no clue what they were talking about. I will ask Lasitor about it later.

"I never expected a golden shower in Antarctica on my first day." Juandre chuckled. "And finally, I get to meet you." He fell into my arms, hugging me. His head was about the height of my navel. I was much taller than the average human. "I'm so happy to see you. Maybe you can join us next time?" Juandre asked suggestively.

"No, from now on, there will be no fucking outside, period," Andrew said, patting him on his butt playfully.

"I heard there are tunnels underneath the structure. We should go check those out," Juandre suggested. He batted his eyelashes and made kissy sounds. Then he looked from me back to Andrew, searching our faces for answers.

"Excellent idea," I said. Meaning them, not me. I was in a hurry, and the longer I stayed, the more possible fuck ups could happen. And I was done with those.

"Yes, we'll stay inside." Andrew threw an arm around Juandre's lower body, possessively pulling him in closer. His gaze fell on me as if to say *stay away, he is mine*, then he marked his mate with a peck on the cheek.

"Okay, I get it. You pissed on him first, so he's yours." I laughed, then cleared my throat to say seriously, "I'm glad to see you, but I can't stay long. I have to go. I'm glad you are both okay. I will see you soon. I only came this time to download the latest news report and update Lasitor." I waved the time-keeping device on my wrist at them. "The first history of Phoenix was deleted," I dared not mention during the flood. "I need to know as much as possible to calculate when to go next. What to change and what to leave as is."

"Ooooh, that looks and sounds interesting," Juandre said with a pronounced effeminate lilt. I could see why Andrew was so fond of him. His beauty and energy were magnetic. His dark brown eyes, stubbled beard, and smeared red lips made him gorgeous. I checked the wall of ice he had licked. Also smeared red. His nose and cheeks were purple-red. Probably because of crying and the cold. The mix of masculine and feminine was attractive to me. Sadly, the dark lines around his eyes were also smeared with tears trailing down his face into his beard. When I was a young ignorant prince, I'd worn kohl lines around my eyes too.

It looked like Andrew had fucked him good just before I arrived and before his tongue got stuck. I didn't want to impose, and it seemed Andrew wasn't sharing anyway.

Both stared at the device Cian had given me, so I ignored the what-the-fuck looks and covered it with my sleeve. I didn't want to mess with this timeline by showing them contraptions from their future. They would discover it at their own pace.

"Forget you saw it. Just point me toward the nearest access point for the main computer."

"What, why?" Juandre asked. He had his hands in his hair. Picking at it and inspecting the tips of his gloved fingers. Everything was frozen, frozen with piss and sticking up in all directions, even his eyebrows. He must have reached the same conclusion. He shivered as if grossed out.

"Is there something happening that we should know about? Come inside with us. It's fucking cold. We'll sneak you inside. You can eat and freshen up and tell us what's going on. I've been waiting a long time to see the big man who popped my Andrew's submissive cherry."

"Don't fall for it, Ishtar," Andrew warned, pulling Juandre away from me. "He invites men over, pretending to offer food and shelter."

I chuckled. "Andrew, I didn't know you were the possessive type," I teased. They were mated, and I knew how mates only had eyes for each other. Also, I didn't have time, and if Brad or anyone saw me, I would most definitely fuck this up big time. "I–I really came for Lasitor."

"Who?" Juandre asked, the ooh ending on a high note.

"The AI, the news broadcaster and activities planner of Phoenix. The voice that wakes the citizens in the mornings and delivers the daily news," I explained. They frowned at me, deep in thought.

"Oh, the computer program," Juandre exclaimed waving me off as if it was old news. "I am disappointed you can't follow us inside." I looked at him with wide eyes and pursed lips. Waiting for him. "Really? He asked.

I nodded in the affirmative and waited.

"Okay, okay, okayyy! Let me show you. You can access it via the security terminal. Do you have UZ1 to plug and play?

"Yes, thank you. I know what to do."

"Of course you do. You are from the future." Juandre cackled.

The three of us stood awkwardly, having a moment. I looked up at the cloudy, sunless sky, searching for something to focus on. Juandre and Andrew stayed quiet, creating an opening for me to talk. But I was smarter than that.

"Hmmm, the access point, please."

Juandre narrowed his eyes and moved closer, inspecting my eyes. "You are so right, my bear; they do look like bumblebee butts.

"Juandre!" Andrew cautioned, his forehead creased and eyebrows furrowed.

"Sorry, Ish, those yellow and black rings around your eyes..." Juandre paused mid-sentence, index finger pointing at my face.

"I know, and you are correct. They do look like that. The palace children have teased me all my life."

Again, we stood awkwardly, looking at each other. Andrew with his pale skin and green eyes and Juandre with his smoldering looks, I thought maybe. Yes, maybe I could sneak in and out.

"No!" I answered instead.

"No?"

"Stop it. You two are trying to change my mind. Go look for someone else to play with."

"Damn, we almost had him!" Juandre clapped his thick gloved hands together. "Come, friend, I will help you." Juandre lifted his arm and motioned me forward as he started talking. "We are both so thankful to you for the gift you gave Andrew. And then for helping the two of us to find each other." Juandre puffed steam clouds as he made his way through the snow.

"You will find out why, but for now, I can't say more. Live your life. Do your thing. Be you. You are perfect together, and it's been an honor to have helped you this way."

"I bet you must feel honored to have fucked my husband and infected him with this." Juandre opened his mouth, showing me his small incisors and hissing. So cute.

"Baby, no," Andrew said, shutting his mouth playfully with his. They amused me and it felt amazing seeing them happy.

"So, you got married. I'm glad to hear, but the longer I stay and the more we speak, the more shit can happen," I said, shaking my head. I was happy for them. It seemed I'd done one thing well so far. The fates had urged me to change time only for others, so I might find joy in selflessness. Now I understood.

I watched them kiss each other, and then I cleared my throat. I had things to do.

"If I had Lasitor, I could navigate better. And without history, I would fly blind. He can keep me company and help me plan better."

"Yes, we understand," Andrew said. He was a good man, and I could see why Brad missed them so much. "Where is Peter? Did you find him?"

"Yes I did," I said proudly, but not mentioning where and when.

"Why didn't he come with you? I would have liked to see him. My Peter is safe, but he ignores me. I think the organization has messed him up. He is focused on bringing back the frozen celebrities, and it is all thanks to you." Andrew pinned me with a stare. I sensed animosity. As if he was trying to delve into my psyche. But growing up around nosy brothers and sisters had taught me to keep my grid guarded at all times.

"Stop trying to read me. You know I can't say. Also, I kind of escaped to be here today. Peter is covering and waiting for me." I dare not mention that I was arrested and was about to be questioned. That Peter and I went gallivanting intoxicated then almost crashing into the Horizon Warship loaded with the Grayrakians. Andrew and Juandre waited. "Uhm, he is happy now, I promise."

"You two are always up to something. When will this end?"

"I can't say, but the ending I saw was wonderful. You will see."

"We've been fucking waiting since 2014. I'm kind of tired of watching and waiting," Juandre said with hands on his hips. He was a strange character. One minute I think he is joking and the next I feel like he wants to drive a knife through me.

"Andrew, how do you manage this man of yours? He looks like a lot of work to me?" I retorted, hoping to throw them off my scent.

"Don't change the subject. I'm not dumb, you know."

"I know you aren't. Okay, all I'm saying is it's about another century at least."

"No fucking way!" Juandre and Andrew exclaimed, shaking their heads in disbelief. "What about the whiskey?" Andrew asked.

"It is safe. They will find it."

"The world is ending, but at least they will have whiskey, ha-ha-ha."

I wanted to laugh at their antics. "Yes, I'm sorry, but I can't say more. And for the love of the fates, do not tell anyone about yourselves. They aren't ready yet." I pointed a finger at each of them. They felt like family. Like children. "I can always come back and punish you if you fuck this up for all of us. All this, the success of this can disappear with one mistake. Please stand back, let them do their thing, and let everything happen naturally. If in doubt, do nothing. All these people could die. They are, no, you are humankind's last hope," I said, and then I smiled widely, revealing my fangs. "I'm serious," I said with a lisp through my protruding incisors.

"Okay, okay. Lips zipped," Juandre said and gestured to indicate that. I shook my head. It was as if Juandre was incapable of seeing the direness of it all. Maybe it was better that way, I thought.

We halted next to the doorframe, where Juandre opened the frozen cover on the wall.

"This is a charging dock. You can plug in here."

I took a step forward and, despite my numb fingers, I persisted until I located the tiny button. Using my fingernails as tweezers, I carefully grasped it and pulled it. Next, the fiber optic wire was connected to the micro socket.

"God, I need a proper shower. Look at my hair. It's frozen stiff with piss. My face is burning." Juandre chuckled, looking uncomfortable as fuck. Gloved fingers all stretched and face disgusted.

"Don't touch it, you can break it off." Andrew took Juandre's hands to prevent him from damaging his frozen hair.

"Thank you, this can take a few minutes," I said into the puffy arctic hoods covering their heads as I hugged them closer with one arm. "I will see you soon. You can go inside."

Andrew gave me another hug. "See you soon friend and don't make too much trouble."

"I won't," I said, but I knew I was lying.

"Are you one hundred percent sure you don't want a personal history lesson from us?" Juandre asked, trying for seductive but failing. He reeked of piss, and I wasn't the kind of friend who would fuck his friend's mate. Unless offered.

"Let's get you inside, into a shower, and then into my warm bed." Andrew turned to Juandre, leading him away as he gave me a final goodbye with a stare.

"We can't. Someone might complain or report us to the Colonel Doctor and get us court-martialed."

I watched the two men enter the compound through the door. Juandre popped back out. "Bye-bye, I'll see you soon, big boy!" I smiled. I really loved those two. They made anyone's day brighter.

Now I was determined to make my plan work. The wrist computer beeped to indicate I had completed the download. I turned to make a path for myself through the heaps of snow with renewed purpose. They were talking about Brad McCormick. Little did they know, years from now, he'd be married to a man, and Juandre and Andrew would be his closest friends.


"COLONEL MCCORMICK, come to Communications immediately, sir!" I heard Connor's announcement. It was time to leave.

"Run, don't walk," Connor said over the speaker system blaring in and outside the building.

I carved my way back through the trail I'd made earlier. Reaching my ship, I realized I should have left a mark for myself. I peeled pieces of ice off, searching for the bloody fucking door I had stupidly covered while hiding my ship. I found it without removing all my hard work. Once inside, I fell into my seat, shivering from the cold while I waited impatiently for the three stairs to retract and the door to swoosh closed. "Brrr, I need heat. Where is the button for the heat?" I asked no one, rubbing my hands together. I blew my hot breath over my numb fingertips to defrost them. Pins and needles prickled painfully in my limbs. I found the tiny silver lever and flipped it on. Heat flooded the cabin. I removed my wrist watch and connected the tiny wire to the already upgraded micro socket and uploaded the information to my onboard computer then I waited and waited, and waited, some more.

"Talk to me, Lasitor." I prayed to the fates to do this for me. I needed an updated travel companion. "Okay, Lasitor, let's play those recordings," I said out loud, hoping Lasitor would hear and respond to me. But Lasitor didn't.

Melancholy and complete loneliness engulfed me. What if I had broken or over-loaded him somehow?

Electric crackles came over the intercom speakers.

Lasitor's voice boomed. I had never been so happy to hear the AI's robotic male voice. "Don't cry for me, Argentina, the truth is I never left you. I was just updating," Lasitor's voice echoed inside the small cabin. "This is where it began and where it ends," Lasitor said.

"I know. Tell me how it all came to world annihilation and where are all the women?"

"Certainly. Environment Project One—EP-1—was meant to house approximately twenty-five thousand people. Over the next six to eight weeks, two to three groups of two thousand people, males, females, children, and family members were supposed to arrive. This was one of the first global cities built to ensure humanity achieves growth and progress while giving nature a chance to wipe away the footprints of humans."

"Yes, but why?"

"It was that or die out. Women already couldn't bring children into the world and the Z3H993 parvovirus epidemic and vaccine crisis of 2038 caused adverse mutations, which were handed down from mothers to their daughters. Cities were either burning or crum-bling. Winds would destroy what wasn't washed away by rainstorms. So, they decided to build this and put the healthy, the smartest, and the bravest in it. It was a test, and these solar and steam-powered domes protected them, and it saved them. Brad McCormick was chosen by WHPSS, by Doctor John Saunders, to lead the team of savants and attempt to save and upgrade people to a superior species."

"Hmm, that sounds like the Disciples."

"Yes, but no one knew it. Except for Doctor Peter Von Leutzendorf, and now Juandre and Andrew."

"The fates guided the way it played out."

"I agree. Whoever these fates are, will be upset if we change it."

"Okay, let's—What's that alarm going off?" I asked as I searched the panorama of ice, mountains, and glass domes. Soldiers were moving at a fast pace from outside to inside.

"They are being called together for the announcement."

"What announcement?"

"The Doomsday announcement. It's all going to shit, Ishtar."

"I want to see." I loosened my seatbelt and shut the engine down again. Dang-dang! A dull banging came from outside at the ship's door.

Someone was outside. "Ouch!" I hit my head on the overhead dash. *Fuck!* I held my breath, listening. *Dang-dang-dang!* Again, with the banging.

"Who's there? What the fuck do you want?" I yelled and gnashed my teeth. "Please don't tell me they've found me. I don't have the strength for Mika, Connor, and Brad tonight." Frustrated, I shifted from one foot to the other, turned, and then turned back again in the small space, "Fuck! Should I stay or should I go?" I muttered while staring at the door as if it would show me the answer. "Lasitor!"

"Yes, Ishtar?"

"Jump, now!"

"Where and when? And, Ishtar, are you sure, because it's your friends? It's Juandre and Andrew outside."

*Argh!* "Fuck, dammit," I grunted as I opened the door. A wide-eyed Juandre and Andrew looked up at me. It smelled like they'd had a quick shower.

Rubbing my head, I asked curtly, "What's wrong?" Andrew didn't say a word. He looked up at me apologetically while supporting Juandre with a hand on each of his shoulders. They were paler than usual, probably in shock.

It had been Juandre's idea to come knocking. "Fuck, the shit is hitting the fan, my man," Juandre said, short of breath and looking scared shitless.

"I know. I told you to live your lives and all will be fine." I hung onto the doorframe and poked my head outside, checking their six.

"But the world is ending," he stuttered, with tears in his eyes.

"No, Juandre, it is not," Lasitor answered from the inside.

"Who is that? Is that the computer? Is he talking to me?"

"Who else would talk to you if not the one man looking at you? Ha-ha," Lasitor said in his distinctive robotic voice and laughed like a crazed computer.

"It's Lasitor. I just downloaded him. You know that, I told you just now, or did you swallow too much piss?" I asked, sarcasm dripping from me.

"The Lasitor I know reads the computer screen. He reads the words man types for him. That sounds like he has a bloody personality."

"Thank you," Lasitor answered. I laughed. Andrew slapped his hands over his mouth in disbelief and Juandre put his hands on his hips. Daring the AI to say something.

"He's a wonderful traveling companion. I don't have to feed him, and he takes up no space." I motioned for them to come in. "Step inside. It's warmer and someone is going to see us. How did you find the ship? I hid it. Could you see it?"

"No, we followed the big boot tracks here."

"Oh. That."

I lowered the steps, and my two friends joined me, cramming themselves inside, shoulder to shoulder.

"Juandre, there is nothing we can do about things so big and about to happen. You have your son here with you, don't you? There's no one else you care about back home?" Lasitor asked and Juandre shook his head, looking at the cockpit.

"I know this is scary, but Phoenix will be okay. Within hours, this place is going to be on lockdown. No one is leaving, and no one is going to get inside. You need to go back." Lasitor added.

"Are you sure?" Juandre asked me, with frozen tears glinting on his cheeks.

"Yes. This is happening and must happen so we can restart and have a better future. Juandre, everything will be all right. I'm not allowed to change anything for myself. I'm allowed to change two things for one person, and I'm already doing that. You are standing here."

"What are you talking about?"

"I'm going to tell you, but you may not say a word. Not now, maybe later. But the more people know, the less likely we are to stay on the same timeline. Things change and shift all the time and I stand the chance of losing you. Understand?" My voice rumbled in the small space.

Juandre nodded with glinting tears in his sad, but hopeful eyes. "Okay, I think I do." He swallowed nervously as I stared at his protruding Adam's apple bobbing in his throat. I kept quiet and waited for Andrew to agree as well.

"Good." I squeezed each by the shoulder. "You are going to live a full, happy life, and you are going to make wonderful friends. What you said earlier about Brad. Don't worry about his rules and getting in trouble for your homosexuality. From today forward, history is wiped from existence. Brad McCormick will find it difficult to implement the WHPSS's vision of human living and rule-following. Circumstances are changing that. Become friends with anyone who lets you, and the whole of Phoenix will learn to love you. Be your best you and give them something to look forward to at the end of a long day. Fill their stomachs while you nurture their hearts. Show them how to be kind and accepting." I looked from one astonished face to the other. Their hopeful gazes reminded me of children needing to hear everything was going to be all right.

Juandre smiled and turned to his husband. Andrew tipped his chin as if to say, *see I told you so*, and rubbed Juandre's back.

"We could work in food services. Not all the staff have arrived yet. My bear, we could be a team. I will help you." Juandre turned to me. "His staff hasn't arrived yet. Maybe food services is where I'm needed most. I'm sure Doctor Longarrow can manage without me."

"You don't have to fear the future, because I've been there, and it is a miraculous thing. Entertain them. Be friends with them. All of them are human, just like you are.

Brad McCormick will reconstruct a world where power, rank, and gender are irrelevant. Watch him. Be his friend and support him."

"Agh, okay. You should have been a public speaker, not a time traveler," Juandre said as he wiped the melting tears from his cheeks.

"See, I told you. Ishtar told me years ago what to expect. I told you about the men marrying and having children thanks to Peter's research." Andrew's mention of my Kuku reminded me it was time to go.

"Yes, Juandre, you and Andrew are important to us. These men need you," Lasitor added. "They also need me. The toddler version, though. Ha-ha!" The robotic laugh was so weird and out of place, we all laughed, breaking the tension.

# CHAPTER 56

# THE INQUISITION

*"Good morning, citizens of Phoenix.*

*It's now six a.m.*

*Did you know that the truth, in metaphysics and the philosophy of verbiage, is the property of a statement, sentence, assertion, belief, thought, or proposition that is divulged, in verbal or nonverbal exchange, to align with the facts, state, or situation that is the case?*

*But did you also know there is a critical difference between truth and reality and that reality exists independently, and the truth is dependent on experiences and observations, or empirical evidence, taken from that reality?*

*Visit your community news page to sign up and participate in the proceedings of the inquiry of Ishtar.*

*Breakfast is served until eight a.m.*

*Hope your day is filled with clarity to see the truth of your reality!"*

**Ishtar**
**2147 A.D. (95 A.T.)**
**Day three of Ishtar's inquisition**
**Phoenix, underwater glass dome city**
**Earth**

It's been a year since I last walked these corridors, and that was as a free friend of the Phoenicians. Today I was nervous, to the point of hyperventilating, not free, but a prisoner being stared at by faces gathering to hear me. To think I'm a mighty Anunnaki warrior and I allow them to treat me this way. Peter said something last night that rang true. I wasn't the yearly entertainment. We've rescued the humans and switched timelines.

I'm so glad I revisited Phoenix, 2046 A.D. to update Lasitor after the successful landing with the Grayrakian refugees. We'd installed additional tracking and security programming features just before my ship was locked and my tick-tick was taken away from me. The leaders told me I was not under arrest but being kept safe—for questioning. The Phoenicians were an inquisitive bunch, and everyone wanted to know what I had to say. It felt like weeks, even though the show had only been on for three days. I never saw myself as someone who was particularly afraid of anything. Peter might have scared me sometimes, but drowning while trapped underwater was the scariest thing I could imagine. Phoenix was a fucking suffocating deathtrap. Some kind of magic held those flimsy-looking shiny walls up. They were waiting to fold in and make all of us one big ball of eternal life and shining light on the ocean floor, trapped, never to reach or see the surface. I was petrified. Trapped within these walls, I could move in and out of time, but I couldn't move outside the barrier Cian and his brothers had created to encapsulate Phoenix safely from the outside.

The cold metal cuffs encircling my wrists emitted a faint blue glow, casting an eerie light in the dimly lit room. They were loosely fastened, allowing some movement, but still held firmly in place by a protruding knob beneath the sturdy tabletop. An overwhelming sense of humiliation washed over me as I sat there, confined and vulnerable, while the relentless barrage of questions continued. Suppressing the primal instinct to react, I resisted the urge to forcefully push the table aside and make a daring escape. In silence, without anyone ever noticing, I was battling an internal compulsion, driven by the familiar ache of loneliness that beckoned me to come to it. *Be alone. Be safe.*

The skin around my wrists throbbed with a fiery heat, relentlessly irritated and scraped raw against the unforgiving surface of the table, amplifying the discomfort and adding to my torment.

They had asked me a question, and they were waiting for me to answer. I lowered my head closer to the microphone, thought better of it, and reached for the glass of water next to it. I drank half of it. The cold water soothed my parched throat and washed away the scratchy feeling as if I had eaten heaps of desert sand for breakfast.

A few feet from me, a long table stood in front of the pavilion stacked with rows of people shoulder to shoulder. At the table from left to right, sat Brad McCormick, the leader, and his husband, Dr. Rick, Connor, and Mika Romanov, the second and third in charge of Phoenix, Bryan and Tony, in charge of the defense and electrical engineering. Dr. Paul and Dr. Simon, Brad's older sons, were running the medical center with their father, Dr. Rick. Then came my blood family, excluding Juandre and Andrew, Eryn, Ivan, Cian, and Barkor, and lastly my Peter. Twelve men led Phoenix and twelve men sat and awaited my answer. The hundreds of onlookers were also active participants in my in-depth inquiry. They were each allowed one question. After they had entered them into their personal wrist communicators, Lasitor, would electronically amalgamate them and create a list for the leadership to ask. Photos of their evidence against me, like the apple in all its shapes, schematics and printed-out equations, bronzed and clay tablets, and other shit I've never seen before were projected on big screens where everyone could see what we were talking about. It was the most civilized inquisition I've ever encountered.

*Squeak-squeak!*

*Squeak-squeak!*

The sound caught my attention, causing me to glance down at the bottom of my boots. My legs were involuntarily shaking again. I took a deep breath and exhaled slowly, trying to calm the tension coiling in my chest. I focused on the skinny beams of light that supported the walls and translucent roof, hoping they would continue to hold. This underwater city felt surreal and suffocatingly tight. A low vibration hummed through it, a sound that was unfamiliar to me. I couldn't discover its source. Did these humans understand the significance of what they had created? Without the guidance of the Fates, I would never have discovered this hidden place. My father would have been envious of this metal and would have wanted it for his palace, or perhaps even surrounding it. They'd achieved so much in such a short time; it both impressed and terrified me, and I couldn't help but feel a sense of pride at their accomplishments.

When I was alone, the lack of sound was overwhelming. There were no creaking floorboards, no rustling sails above my head, and no indication that we were deep beneath the sea. Eryn had mentioned that these walls blocked out sound waves, and as I lay alone in my cell, I couldn't fall asleep. My ears zinged, the silence broken only by the quick visits of Peter was allowed to give me. This morning, as my Kuku left me alone, the stillness and silence overwhelmed me. I urged myself to keep breathing, to ignore my soul-sucking cell companion, quiet. I prayed for the sleep cycle to end.

"Please let those jangling of keys arrive and open the door. Please let it be my sign to be free," I begged the Fates. Inside my cell, I was denied darkness and suffocated by stillness without my Kuku. I worry about him. He's embarrassed and disappointed in his friends.

One crack, and I'm suffocating on cold ocean water. Inhaling, and choking, and gasping, frantic for air. Salt water everywhere. Only bubbles and no sound escaping my throat—until I'm dead.

Drowning was just as terrifying a death as burning alive.

I sighed a frustrated grunt. Phoenix was only a moment in time, only a blip in the vast expanse of eternity. Yet, here I was. I had found them.

I smiled at Peter. Freedom and happiness were finally within my grasp. The thought lifted my mood and gave me the strength to speak up.

A sneeze from the crowd of onlookers broke my train of thought. I blinked and stretched my neck and shoulders to loosen the tension. My eyes were tired, my vision was blurry, and I was completely unprepared for what was happening. Peter gave me a reassuring nod, but his gaze drifted to my shackles. He forced a fake smile onto his face.

I sent him a thought, *love, you are my strength.* He blushed, his usual response when I gave him a seductive look. It stirred something within me, and I shifted to make room for my growing cock. His white hair and piercing blue eyes reminded me of swirling galaxies, with their infinite beauty and boundless love. I shrank into myself, hiding my emotions behind my hunched shoulders as I fought back the fear of losing him, and never finding him again.

"Psst!" Peter called. I looked up at him. He looked left and right over his shoulder, checking who was eavesdropping. "No," he mouthed at me. I instantly felt better. *Stop your sulking*, I read his thoughts and chuckled, bumping the low table with my kneecaps. Even though I heard his thoughts, he couldn't hear mine. I guess because he hadn't grown into his true self yet. I had given my bite to Andrew, but it wouldn't hurt to try. When we kissed, I felt the glands in the back of my throat swell and contract, like sucking on a lemon.

Peter shook his head at me, *Don't, please don't. We will get out of this in one piece. Just be honest.* I read his mind.

"*Don't worry, and stop looking at me like that,*" I reciprocated. He was sometimes so prissy, so sneaky, and so dramatic.

"I love you," I mouthed, shaking my head at his antics. He widened his eyes and probably thought calming me was a lost cause. He slammed his head on his folded arms, pretending he was sleeping, making me laugh even harder. He made constant efforts to distract me from these people. But something was different today. He seemed ready to go. To run. To leave. To escape with me.

We spent stolen time together after our trip to Germany. By getting snot drunk and jumping all over, from Grayrak to the outer rim of our solar system, helping Cian and searching for rogue Zelk ships.

If we hadn't done it, I don't know what would have happened with this timeline. Something was nagging at me to remember it, but I was not successful, whether it was because of all the partying or because it hadn't happened yet. But for now, I was going to share my story and think about it later. I sighed and rolled my eyes. Oh, how I craved my Kuku's body and his smell. His laughs fed my love-hungry soul—the positives to my negatives. He made me feel young, like I had no cares.

Mika's words haunted me. *That fucking cylinder, the ancient golden cylinder that was originally the shape of an apple.* The genius had assembled and disassembled it and understood how to rebuild it into its original shape. I didn't know the apple could be opened and reconstructed as a seal containing the mathematics of the Anunnaki's gene code. Tree of Life, and a star map, as Mika named it. He was an intelligent and important man, and Cian and Ivan were his boys. The Fates had said the people who had it would use it.

It was never the intention of the Fates that the Disciples open it and create the Zelk —I hoped. The abominations of flesh and titanium were destroyed, but the essence, the human souls that lived in that tower were now lost. That's what was bothering me. Where were those souls now? Hopefully, the Fates had taken them home. And where was that? Was that where my family was, or was there more than one place in the afterlife? Also, how was I to know the apple could be cracked open like a puzzle box and then reassembled into a rolling cylinder to print out the string codes and star maps? Was this yet another secret my father and the Fates never shared with us?

I don't know what genome mapping means, but it made sense to Peter and I trusted Eryn, Ivan, Cian, Barkor, Juandre, and Andrew, as they all agreed with Mika's revelation. However, Eryn acted a little strange, as if he knew something important that he wasn't sharing with us. Despite this, I still trusted him and believed that he would tell us if he thought it would benefit us. They are the last of our kind, and no matter how terrible their existence came to be, I am grateful that they were born.

Waiting faces in the crowd urged me to start speaking up. I was both hesitant and eager to stretch out my life for them to dissect.

The noise of seats being pushed and pulled out ripped me again from my thoughts. Thousands of human eyeballs were turned my way—uncomfortable as fuck was an understatement.

I'm sure I emptied my bladder before the inquisition started, but now I felt like pissing myself.

The air was thick with the anticipation of the audience, their movements, and murmurs barely audible in the pregnant silence. The arches loomed above me, resembling the interior of a whale's chest cavity, waiting to be filled with my words. The hushed stillness felt almost reverent as if we gathered in a sacred space.

My heart raced as I prepared to unleash my last words upon the expectant crowd.

"I was born in Babylon, almost seven thousand years before the Doomsday of 2049 A.D. The youngest of my family and the oldest of our kind currently alive of which I am aware," I answered truthfully. *Cian, Ivan, Eryn, Andrew, Juandre, and my Peter are my kind now.*

"I'll tell you my family's history as it was relayed to me by my siblings. I remember playing hide and seek with human children in the palace. We would stay outside until sunset when my Anubis would be whining and letting me know it was time to return inside. My mother and father were seen as gods by the people in Mesopotamia. But they were only the King and Queen of Anzulla. Since their arrival, it had been a time of ruthless killings and human offerings. I cannot remember one day that I thought to myself I admired or loved my father. He demanded respect but was feared, not only by his people but by his family too. I wasn't born in Anzulla like the rest of my family. I was born in Babylon. My mother died giving birth to me. I was a big baby, and they had to cut her open to pull me out. My father reminded me of that every day of my life." I told my story to the Phoenicians. My shackles clunked. Everyone's line of sight dropped to them. *Breathe*, I told myself and I shifted in my seat. Uncomfortable with the sea of humans and thousands of eyes pinning me. Judging me.

Peter's blue eyes sparkled with unshed tears. *Not now. I haven't even started.* He nodded sternly, urging me to go on, then forced a thin smile. I took a deep breath, then gave him a reciprocal nod.

"On Anzulla, famine was rampant. As Anunnaki, we relied on the Loursveto's sap daily, similar to how you humans need water to survive. For hundreds of years, my father systematically strip-mined the gold to enhance his wealth and power. But the roots of the Loursveto plant grew along those veins. Slowly and permanently, he had destroyed the symbiotic balance in our world. One of his geology and mineral explorer teams had found and brought back Babylonian gold suitable specifically for the Loursveto vegetation project. Gold ores were ground into dust and mixed into the soil. However, production was slow and I suspect hampered by my father skimming gold for himself. He had convinced my mother that going to the source was the only option. My mother loved my father. She preferred to be blind to his sickness of the mind. She defended him and chose to ignore the warning signs that he had descended into madness. My father promised that things would be different if they packed up and left Anzulla. That a new life awaited them and that he would be a better king and father. Initially, they believed him to be their hero and savior, but they soon realized he had resorted to leaving a scorched land. Burning Anzulla and fleeing with only a few members of our family. He fooled them. His insanity and old ways accompanied them to the new land in Southern Mesopotamia. Despite the constant stream of gold brought by slaves, it was never enough to satisfy my father's greed. The Loursveto seeds they had brought with them refused to thrive. Instead, the plants were weak and stunted, producing little sap for sustenance. My sisters An and Ki sang to the plants in hopes of coaxing growth, but their efforts were fruitless, just as in Anzulla. In desperation, my father harvested the powers from three of my brothers and was now threatening my sisters to sing or face the same fate. I believe even the Loursveto seeds knew that if they grew, they would only fuel the insatiable hunger for power of a mad ruler." I paused, feeling overwhelmed. I let my head fall, hiding my face from them to gather my courage. I looked up into Peter's caring eyes and took a deep breath before continuing.

"My birth wasn't celebrated, because I had killed my mother. After cutting her open, she was too weak to regenerate because of the massive blood loss and my father refusing to feed her out of selfishness. He had gotten worse after I was born. My brothers and sisters raised me. I never knew the love of a mother's touch and I think my siblings protected me by hiding me from him. With servants and soldiers, I grew older, and I made friends with humans. As the years passed, I got smarter. I'd joined the army by the age of fourteen and evaded destruction by visiting other lands, gathering strength and knowledge to stand up against my father. He was convinced he was the King of kings, and the god of all. He demanded offerings and drank the blood of humans after ordering them to kill their children or sacrifice themselves. He expected parents to cut and drain their children while he waited for them to bring cups of their blood to feed him." I paused as gasps and murmurs broke out in the crowd.

Brad got up and turned to the audience. "Men. Uhmmm, sorry, that was a slip. Excuse me, ladies. Please. We will never get this done if you react and stop the inquisition every few sentences. If this type of information shocks you or you have little ears with you, please leave and take your children with you." Phoenician men with their boys and Grayrakian men and women with their children got up and scurried out. I noticed Peter's seat was empty. *Where did he go?* Brad sat down again, took Rick's hand, and indicated I should continue. I waited until everyone had settled down. Then I cleared my throat and continued.

"Humans were seen as a food source and working animals. Their blood fed us, but again, even if it was just one or a thousand a day, it was never enough to quench his insatiable hunger." I stopped to empty my glass of water. The crowd murmured again. Connor and Mika looked so much like my sisters. My heart skipped a beat every time I saw the two of them, one with blond curls and the other with black. Both with piercing blue eyes. I took a second. Now that we sat across from each other, I had time to inspect them. I might as well be looking at Ki and An's children. Even their noses were shaped like theirs.

Mika spoke up. "Tell us more about your gift and, how did you end up time-traveling?" he asked curiously and I was glad for the change in direction, but it turned out to be about my father again.

"The first time I used my gift was by accident. I was sword fighting and as my opponent stepped closer to deliver a death blow, all I thought was *I must get away.* The next moment it was as if I was an observer looking at things like someone would look at fish swimming in a fishbowl. Right away, I tried it again, and then scared myself shitless, because I stood and watched as time passed and bodies covered the battlefield. I made the mistake of sharing my secret with one of my soldiers, who told my father to save his own family and children. I wasn't ready to face him or be sacrificed." Pausing, I chuckled at my choice of words. My interrogators weren't amused. No one laughed. The expressions on their faces were those of horror. I soldiered on. "I patched and rebuilt my time machine from the scraps I found in the rubble of the ship my family crashed into Babylon. I was proud of it, I still am, and although it's a bit small, it's mine." I shifted in my seat, wondering how to continue.

Eryn interrupted my nervous thought pattern. *Don't tell them about Lasitor. Not yet.*

I blinked and smiled at him and then found encouragement in Peter's eyes as he returned and slid into his seat. *He was probably on a bathroom break.*

"My father tasked me with searching for another place where the Loursveto grew so he could build his new empire there. He saw me as unintelligent. He had a knack for manipulating us with his words. Recognizing that I had pride in something I'd built with my hands, he used it to control me. He challenged me to find a new home for us to prove I'm a worthy son and allowed me to keep my ship." My voice cracked as the pity from the audience washed over me.

"You are doing so well, I love you, Ishtar," Peter whispered. I rolled my lips inward, biting them, before heaving a deep breath. *Almost done.*

"But my sisters knew it was only a matter of time before my father destroyed Babylon, and every living thing around it, too. They suggested I leave and hide from him, lie to him, making him think I was searching, while we prepared for war. We told Titus, my friend, and the head of the army, and together we started preparing for an insurrection against our oppressor. Our demands—abdicate or die. A whole army against one Anunnaki king. I traveled and trained, collecting tactical skills and knowledge, while Titus built the army. We trained the soldiers in tactics to weaken and isolate the enemy. I was ready but expected to have more time, to have peace talks, to avoid war. I was wrong. On my return, however, I found more than half of the palace desecrated. I sent word to Titus that I was making a stand, and they were to join me as fast as possible. To march through the city gates." Embarrassment and self-loathing crept up my throat. I closed my eyes and wished my hands were free so I could hide behind them. I sighed as a defeated feeling entered my soul. *These humans won't understand. They don't know war like I do.*

"The fate of my family rested on my shoulders. I had thought that, as a time traveler, I could take all the time I needed. Selfishly, I prolonged the inevitable for myself. I visited my friend Platonius, an intelligent mathematician, doing what I believe you call couch surfing. We smoked too many happy plants that week, and as we spoke non-stop, I showed him the equations I had stumbled upon. They were in the user manual for my ship. He called it the magic numbers. Platonius suggested I return home and give these numbers with calculations to Apsu. You know, to soften him up, to bribe him. I thought it was Apsu's, and if I showed him I'd restored them by making them indestructible, not like bits and pieces I found in the wreckage, he would favor me. I know it sounds far-fetched, but I have to say, I'm looking at the result today. But, upon my return, I found my sisters murdered. I handed the equations in haste to Xerxes."

"Which equations?" asked Mika, Connor, Brad, Peter, and half of the audience, breaking the silence. Half of them apologized, and others chuckled. "Sorry, Ish, we have questions streaming in. We want to know, how you and Platonius used algebraic calculations to write a genetic code which is a surjective mapping between the set of the sixty-four possible three-base codons and the set of twenty-one elements composed of the twenty amino acids plus the Stop signal. How were you able to use post-modern principles and calculations from the twenty-first century, in ancient times?" Mika lifted his hand, indicating a pause, then read more questions Lasitor fed to his communication device. I waited. *We all bloody waited.*

He lifted his head and seemed to agree with what he had read. "We want to know, how did you know a codon is a trinucleotide sequence of DNA or RNA that corresponds to a specific amino acid when that was only discovered as recently as two hundred years ago?" Peter's head snapped up and he scowled at Mika.

I lifted my shoulders, let out a long, tired growl, then ran an irritated gaze over the mob. They shrank back into their chairs, waiting for me to speak. "The philosophical and mathematical criterion for the perfect magic number is something Platonius identified in the user manual of my ship. It's the understanding that seven factorial equals five thousand and forty. Thus, seven sons and six daughters, times five generations, times four houses, times three parents, times two mothers, times one bloodline will produce the perfect offspring exactly five thousand and forty years later."

Connor cleared his throat and then tapped on his microphone. "Is this thing working?" he asked, and Brad nodded. The crowd answered eagerly, "Yes." Connor smiled and showed them his appreciation as bouncy black curls moved up and down. His deep blue eyes were serious. He turned sideways, waved once, and gave a thumbs-up. "Ish, tell me, more about this manual, who wrote it?"

I sat up, taking a deep breath, but Mika moved to the front of his seat and cleared his throat, "Sorry, love, do you mind if I ask this first?" Connor shrugged and at his approving nod, Mika continued, "Ish, what you are describing is what we call the number five-thousand and forty, a superior highly composite number, an abundant number, actually a colossally abundant number, and the number of permutations of four out of ten choices."

"Okay, okay, let's not go into that. That is a conversation for another day." Cian suddenly cut in, and I was thankful. I gathered my thoughts and continued as best and safely as I could.

"I want to finish telling this, Cian," I said, making pacifying gestures with my cuffed hands. He gave me an okay-then-go-on look.

"Yes, that is what I thought all those years ago, and that is what I meant to give Apsu when I returned home. But in haste after finding my two sisters dead, I said my goodbyes to Xerxes and their children. I handed him the information while briefly explaining what I believed the Fates had guided me to do. I sit here today, and I'm looking at the result of those equations," I said again, meaning them, but I looked at those relics on the screen above them. I don't think they heard what I said. *Fuck, I didn't even know what I was saying anymore.*

My guilt-ridden eyes caught Eryn's placating stare, and I communicated with him— begging for direction.

*Surely, they know what I was talking about. Should I spell out what I think they don't see? That the ancient alphabet and language of the equations I handed Xerxes, were carved in Phoenician script. And that I had handed him a bronzed tablet and not an apple. That the apple was delivered earlier from a future version of myself. Does that even matter? I wonder if Mika knows or realizes the significance of the same Phoenician inscriptions on the bronzed tablet and the golden apple. I only heard a few days ago the apple could be broken up into pieces, taken apart, and rebuilt into a rolling seal. Are we talking about the same information? Were the calculations of the tablet the same as in the apple? Should I ask them? I don't want to confuse them or implant doubt. Eryn, I am sitting in a place called Phoenix. These people refer to themselves as Phoenicians. Phoenician is an ancient language spoken in the areas along the Mediterranean Sea, and Platonius's Greek Latin alphabet was an adaptation of it. The same as the manual's.*

I told Eryn, mind-to-mind. He'd read my mind a year ago—the day I'd met him. I trusted him ever since.

A few seconds of silence passed between us before Eryn replied.

*That will only prolong this hearing, and we don't yet have the answers to those questions. Where did you find that apple in the first place? You say you gave it to your sisters, but where did you find it?* Eryn asked, and I realized I'd found it just before I met them. He must know, so why is he asking?

I narrowed my eyes at him. *The Fates, they gave to it me, to bring home.*

*Do you see it now, Ishtar? The Fates, and the mystery of that apple?* he asked, crossed his arms, and gave me a lopsided smile.

*No, I don't. I'm getting a headache trying to.*

As if picking up on my private conversation with Eryn, silence fell over the audience. Mika coughed and cleared his throat. "Could you please tell us more about the apple? We will come back to talk about those numbers. If that is okay with you?" Mika asked, and I didn't know what to make of this. He had asked me to choose and if I approved of changing the subject.

I indulged him by remembering my sisters' words, *We will bury the apple as you asked.*

I rolled my eyes mentally at Eryn for no-help-at-fucking-all.

*How am I going to spin this?* My Kuku and Eryn wanted me to be honest. But how could I be honest without causing more confusion? Fucking scarabs.

"Some nations are born and blessed by their Fates. Others are just an unknown or inexplicable phenomenon that occupy a time and place, and although their existence is not even a blip far into their future, they surely existed. I don't question the Fates. Whether it's a tablet, an apple, or a message, I deliver it. With *my* ship," I said louder, to give them a little taste of my strength.

*They're starting to irritate me. My father would have imploded this place to teach them a lesson.* I sucked air through my nose and swept my gaze over the Leadership Team. Forcing the might behind the deep rumble of my voice to roll over each one of them to fucking hear me. "My ship and I operate beyond the borders of time and the imaginations of those people who claim to know everything by digging and scraping," I paused to let that sink in, "sifting through layers of soil sifting for scraps or artifacts to somehow explain how those humans lived, how they were able to be extraordinary and why they perished. They breathe the same air as other civilizations on another side of this planet. They've been living under the same constellations, yet others can't understand how they built their enormous cities, their pyramids, and why the architecture aligns with those constellations." My eyes roamed back to Mika and Connor. "Like just a few seconds ago, you asked how those mathematical equations came to be inside that apple, and why. It's the Fates. They guided me. My pre-programmed machine was a gift. Like any other gift. The Fates provide, because I follow, believe, and trust them. My machine allowed me to see where and when I was going and also to be able to return to the same time, only in another geographical location. When I step back using my gift alone, I am able to freeze time and move to places I've been already. Retracing my steps, but with my machine, I can go to places I've never seen or been to. I was told to take the apple home." I closed my eyes.

"I will recite the words of the Fates when I received the apple, word for word. Listen now," I said to the crowd.

Placing the palms of my hands on the tabletop, I sat up for dramatic effect. "*This is a gift of knowledge, it is yours, take it home.*"

I opened my eyes. "I remembered that was why Xerxes, my sisters' mate, pledged to hide the golden apple in the wall they'd built for me, for our bloodline. That was where and when I left it with them. In Babylon. That was the last time and place I saw the apple. That is until you showed it to me a few days ago. I also think my nieces and nephews survived the ice world beyond the northern mountains, and that is why Mika and Connor can sit here today as the fathers of my bloodline."

"Wait a fucking minute, you keep saying the Fates told you?" Brad asked, standing up and sending his chair flying. *Oh fuck, here it comes.*

"What the fuck?" Connor and Mika shouted, also jumping to their feet.

I slapped my hands down on the tabletop. The explosive noise carried a sudden burst of anger as my voice thundered over the audience. "Yes, and little did I know the ones imprisoning me, judging me, and deciding my freedom would also be the ones the apple was meant for."

"We are not imprisoning you. We are merely preventing you from running away without giving us answers," Mika blurted.

Peter jumped up, pointing his finger at Mika and Brad. Immediately I felt protected and shielded. "You confiscated his ship and his property. What do you want to do with it? Reverse engineer it? Sounds to me like if the shoe fits." Peter looked kind of funny when he was livid. Without his wings, he wasn't big or intimidating, more like a little kitten with sharp claws. Now and then a burst of power would escape him, like a solar flare, but as soon as I zoned in on him, it disappeared. His face was turning all kinds of dangerously red colors as he directed his fury at Mika. His beautiful aura blinded me and I almost felt like angering him some more, just to see and feel it.

"I just hope they don't use it. They don't have my gift. I am pretty sure they would disintegrate if they tried to jump realities without me steering it correctly," I told Peter, knowing everyone heard me, and hopefully took that as a warning. I was looking forward to Peter visiting me tonight. I'm going to drink him dry and fill him up with my cum.

My words about the Fates caused a buzzing of outbursts among my audience. They grew into a thundering roar, and the whole gathering was declared over until further notice. Learning that more powerful entities, in actuality do steer mankind, caused debates and uproars. Needless to say, my inquisition was halted.

"Let's give the hive some time to cool down," Brad McCormick suggested. "Peter may visit you freely. Eryn, Ivan, Cian, and Barkor, would you help them move comfortable furniture into his cell? Lock down that section. I suggest moving there for the time being and guarding your friend until all these atheists come to terms with the fact that God, or the Fates as Ish calls Him, actually exist."

As Brad unlocked my cuffs, Peter waited nervously for me to get up and embrace him. Right then, I decided I had had enough. *Fuck waiting for Peter to come and feed me. Fuck them joining us.* I wanted Peter, and I wanted him now.

For myself. Alone and not in my cell where the others were moving in to keep us company.

"Peter, come, we are leaving now!" I whispered into his ear as soon as we were out of earshot.

# CHAPTER 57

# CRASHING INTO DESTINY

*"Good morning.*

*It's now six a.m.*

*Did you know recognition and connection are predictors of predestined love and it suggests that individuals may recognize their soulmate instantly by feeling an indescribable connection upon their first encounter?*

*If that is not the case, Lasitor could increase the role of choice and chance by one hundred percent to prove skeptics of the predestined love theory in humans wrong. These skeptics state that love is a product of choice, compatibility, and the unpredictable nature of life. But Lasitor can make the unpredictable predictable so the relationships are presumably built through a series of conscious decisions and actions.*

*Visit your community news page to sign up to participate in this voluntary study of peculiar, yet predictable, human behavior.*

*Breakfast is served until eight a.m.*

*Have a lovely day!"*

**Peter**
**2147 A.D. (95 A.T.)**
**Day three of Ishtar's inquisition**
**Phoenix, underwater glass dome city**
**Earth**

My trust in Brad and the leadership of Phoenix was faltering and being put to the test. A day after Cian had arrived with the Warship Horizon, carrying the lunar Grayrakian refugees, Ish and I found some alone time which we used for him to go back in time and update Lasitor. Knowing Mika well enough, I could sense that something was about to happen. So, I encouraged Ishtar to go while I kept them occupied. It seemed like the right thing to do because, just as I had suspected, during our Q&A session, they unexpectedly arrested my lover and seized his belongings. I had to suppress my outburst as I watched Ish being taken into custody, but the anger had been building up inside me ever since.

Fuck Mika and fuck the whole caboodle with their questions and lies. They only cared as long as I played by their rules. I was sick of the place. Phoenix was, after all, not the best place for me. I had tasted freedom, and I refused to be caged like a bloody budgie.

As they questioned Ish, I questioned our friendship and my loyalty to the very people Ish's countless jumps had brought to this point, where they had whiskey, friends, and everything any human could ever want. My comrades—as Mika would say—wanted to know and understand each jump and the power of time travel. They had pushed both of us to our limits. I was disappointed and embarrassed to have ever called them my friends.

Since his arrest was allowed two private conjugal visits a day. Ish's jail cell was situated in a secluded, military zone, where the residents of the general population weren't allowed for safety reasons. Our two-hour scheduled period last night was spent playing dentist-dentist. With a smile, bruised lips, and cracked corners of my mouth, I had woken up this morning alone in my apartment. His mind reading ability came in very useful for enacting kinky fantasies. *My dental appointment fantasy was not a fantasy anymore.* Ish had ordered me to breathe through my nose and open my mouth wide so he could stick his tool into it. *Sigh!*

Eryn was the only one who came to check up on me. He had assured me that all would be fine, to just let the humans listen and hear Ish's story. He was the one who had told, not asked, Brad, to allow me to visit Ish. Only Eryn was concerned about us and understood that Ish needed me. He fed only from me. And yes, maybe I was after filling his stomach twice a day with more than just my blood.

Feedings, for me, were sacred.

I mean, I called to whoever answered prayers when he drove into me while he and drank his fill. *It was divine!* We were yet to be fully mated, I hoped he would never drink from another, only me. Being holy and sanctimonious, I guessed.

After I had my breakfast this morning, I went to Ish for his, and like yesterday, I escorted him to his communal inquisition. Stewing in silence, I'd been clutching my restocked go-bag just in case Ish was set free. I didn't want to spend one second longer in this place than necessary. At the top of my bag were two of the biggest bottles of strawberry mint lubrication, followed by the bare minimums—a toothbrush and toothpaste, two pairs of socks, underwear, pants, and my pocket knife. As the proceedings went on, it became clear to me that they underestimated who Ishtar was. The importance of our bond became my sole focus as the urge to flee with my Anunnaki pumped urgently through my veins. Instead of appreciating, they were dissecting what Ish had done for them. I played along, nodded when expected, smiled when being watched, and then I disappeared into the background by excusing myself to go take a leak. As I pissed, holding my constant semi-hard cock, I felt rebellious and vindictive. I had snuck into the

Leadership Office, broken into Mika's safe, and stuffed Ish's necklace into my go-bag. Then, just to spite them, I took the apple too. The bastards confiscated his things, pretending to be confused and upset and saying it was for his safety that they had locked him up in a jail cell. But like the apple, I know Mika will take the ship and pendant apart. Sure, he would put them back together again, but only after he satisfied his curiosity. And when would that be?

I felt particularly triumphant as I snuck back into the meeting with my go-bag and the secret stash of loot. I was raging with guilt for stealing the damn apple. Frustrated with murderous intent toward my colleagues and blinded with lust and devious sexual thoughts. I attempted to guard my thoughts about the apple. I was failing when my sexy blue Anunnaki, smiled and showed me the tips of his fangs. *Think about all kinds of shit, prevent him from poking deeper into my mind.* I deflected, I jumped up, pointing fingers to defend Ish's honor, while I had none. My mind was a turbulent mess. I struggled to look Brad and the others in the eye while accusing, defending, and blaming.

But then the meeting ended abruptly. *Thank God!*

I swept my hair neatly to the side, patting it down while reading the room. Seeing an opening, I shot up and pushed my stool back under the table. I wanted to hold Ish, to tell him I was on his side. That I had his pendant and apple.

As I approached him, I was already drooling and planning to get him alone so he could do that flip, standing sixty-nine on my ass thing until I vibrated like an Eppendorf vortex mixer. I could already smell and taste him, that clean, tangy lab bleach smell of cum on my lips. Damn, I couldn't wait to have it all thrust into me.

Ever stoic, hoping no one saw me, or my motives, I moved with quick steps and grabbed Ish by the arm to drag him back to his cell.

"Peter, come, we are leaving now!" he whispered into my ear. The gruffness of his low, rumbling voice made me shiver. My mind immediately went to being shaken, rattled, and rolled.

"We're leaving," he said, flicking his eyes sideways while keeping his head low.

"Hmmm, you wanna suck and fuck me?" I asked, buzzing with lust. Moving fast, he pushed me into his cell. I giggled. Round one was about to start. I didn't care how he fucked me, but fuck me, he must. *That's a mate's primary job, wasn't it?*

I knew this was a sure thing, once I was alone with him, so I loosened my belt. "No time for that, come." Ish grabbed me by the arm, flung his hooded jacket over his shoulder, and pulled me out into the hallway.

"Wait! My go-bag!" I pulled free out of his grip, dove back, and retrieved it from underneath the bed, where I had kicked it to the side. "Ready!" I was scarcely upright when he yanked me back into the deserted corridor.

"Good, come!"

"Why are we leaving the protected area?" I asked as I went flying after him, clanking loosened belt buckle and all. "Are we escaping Phoenix?" My feet hit the floor every fourth or fifth step—he wasn't answering me. Ish activated the motion sensors, causing the overhead lights to flash like strobe lights. He ran, searching up and down the tube-like corridors for big-mouthed traitors—empty. We shot in that direction. Whispering voices of men drifted down from the right, so we veered left to avoid the danger approaching. We slipped into a stairway, the door banged closed behind us sounding like a gunshot. *Jesus, my nerves!* He was smart *to leave now* before the general population returned to living their lives.

"Yes, we are leaving," he said, dragging me down the long, translucent halls.

*I figured that.* My heart raced. "Wait, phew, Ish? You are running too fast for me." He didn't slow down, he was frantic to get out of Phoenix.

"Are we going outside?" I asked stupidly about the obvious, because where else would we be going if he was already activating the line of Bubblecars?

"*Shhht*, we can talk once we're out of here." Being a gentleman, he hastily opened my door for me, and threw me inside, before running to the opposite side.

"Come on, come on!" he urged the car, pushing the dashboard to go faster while ramming the forward throttle. "Help me, Peter, please," he said, shrugging, with hands in the air.

"Let me. Breaking the control panel is not advised, lover. If you smash the controls in, we could end up stranded." I leaned forward, catching that delicious scent of his, while I showed him how to override the childproof safety mechanism.

I pushed, turned, and then flipped the safety lever open to push the start button. Our vehicle separated from the other empty cars. Seconds later, the car slid onto the track. He sat arms crossed, not uttering a word, when we shot out of the tube into the blue darkness. My ears popped as the pressure in the Bubblecar adjusted. Half an hour later, we surfaced.

"Why aren't you talking? What's the matter? Answer me! Ish, please say something, dammit." Ish turned to me with wild hunger in his expression. His incisors, pure white, glistened, and protruded three inches at the sides of his mouth. Breathing open-mouthed, he steamed. In and out. In and out. Heaving, feral, and wide-eyed. I swear it looked like those yellow and black rings around his pupils were spinning. His braided blue-black locks seemed electrified. Like a black lion, a predator, a ravenous one. And he was honing in on me.

I opened our doors so he could breathe fresh air. He seemed on the verge of a panic attack. I turned to him. His chest and shoulders moved up and down as he caught his breath. He bulged his fists and answered in a low tone. "First, I can't talk, and second, my body and thoughts are urging me to make you mine. Once we are alone and safely out of reach of the people living in that damn glass bowl beneath us, we are going to fuck until the stars fall out of the sky. I don't need company. They're driving me insane.

This pull, this attraction to you, is turning me into a stupid sex-crazed mess. Don't you feel it? I can't think around you, and I can't be without you one second longer."

I leaned closer, our noses almost touching. "Look at me," I said, to help him focus. The heat of his skin soaked through his shirt and felt warm under the palms of my hands. "Yes, of course. I missed you and am very determined to have you mark me with your mating bite and your cum all over and inside me." He cracked a small smile. "It feels like you've died and I will never talk to you again when you are not with me. I had gotten so used to missing you while I waited for more than a hundred years. I'm sorry you have to feel it too. But we are in this together." I rubbed the sides of his arms up and down, which seemed to calm him. I didn't tell him about my ever-increasing itching. I was eager to surprise him with my glowing skin and wings. I had asked Eryn to describe the experience, and it kind of sounded like that. Maybe he feared I had sprouted wings down there. He didn't enjoy feeling trapped.

"Now, find your ship, so you can take me far away from here. Okay?" His hands were shaking and the heat level in his gaze told me I was going to have a tonsillectomy, and not orally.

"Okay," he answered, and I shuddered. I'd dreamed of this man wanting me, and the reality felt a thousand times better. Like a turkey, he was going to stuff me.

"Geh schneller. Let's go, my big alien!" I joked in German. He lifted his head. I got one twitch of an eyebrow in response as he checked his wristwatch.

"I'm pinging my ship. Where is my tick-tick thing? I need it, please," he said as he checked his wristwatch.

*Gulp!*

*He knew?* "Did you read my mind?" I asked while I patted around inside my bag, found my knife, thinking I might need it, then pocketed it. I rummaged further, found the necklace, and hung it around his neck.

"You can't hide anything from me, Peter." He checked his instrumentation, then turned the floating Bubblecar around to line us up with it. "There it is!" he said and pointed. I squinted, admiring the gleaming machine in the moonlight, sticking out of the sand like a golden dragon egg on a sandy island. I yipped and readied myself to exit as he drove the Bubblecar ashore.

Before we got out, I asked, "Are you mad or disappointed? My behavior, it's shameful. It's stealing."

"No, if I were in your shoes, I would have done the same. So no, my Kuku, I love you for it and you don't have to feel guilty. I can also assure you that your friends only mean well, maybe too bloody well. Stop beating yourself up. They are living their lives, it's time to live yours. Don't you agree?" He leaned over and pushed his forehead to mine. *God, this man has me twisted up for him.* I smiled.

"Good?" he whispered.

"Yes, I'm more than good."

"If Brad or someone catches us, we're in big trouble. Hurry!" He bumped me on my shoulder. "Go! Get out! Move that sexy butt." He laughed, and I jumped out of the vehicle. Sand flying—we raced to his ship. This was the most exciting thing I'd ever done. We were beyond naughty and couldn't keep our mouths and hands off each other as we waited for the door to open and the three stairs to extend.

He was all fangs and grunts, pushing and shoving me to go inside faster. I teased by resisting. More grunts, smiles, and wet saber cat kisses. With a heavy hand, he steered me up the stairs and inside. "I'm hungry. It's time for action. Playing nice-nice, while you sit and tease me with your smells and delicious looks, is over. I have you alone and for myself." That statement made me both happy and worried.

"You can kill me if you take too much blood, can't you?"

"I could never kill you. You are my mate. The moment I bite and inject my venom into you, your body will respond to satisfy me. Just as my body will be satisfying you."

"What do you mean? I thought you biting me would be without the magic juice. Didn't you give your mating bite to Andrew already?"

"Yes, but remember, it was not a true mating bite. It was a bite, but our souls weren't bonded. You are my mate. My body produced more venom because I'm not yet fully bonded. The Fates blessed us because I waited for you for so long. Even if your body doesn't respond and change like Andrew's, I'm sure your transformation would still be magnificent. If not the most extraordinary change of all consorts of all time." My eyes enlarged in wonder and my mouth fell open. He kissed my open mouth and smiled endearingly at me. "You are mine, not Andrew." He patted his chest over his heart. "I'm not fucking you while others guard me and listen to us. You are mine and not theirs. Not anymore."

His words fed my starving soul. Exactly what I needed to hear. "Where are we going?" I asked.

"I'm taking you to a place where you can have your miraculous change. Call it memories, dreams, or just intuition. I must take you there. You will love it. My friend Gugusan is the tribal leader. He will offer us a place to stay."

"So you have made friends already?"

"Yes, I have, and it's where I will make you mine, and then you can grow those beautiful wings of yours. It is the place I wanted to take you last year." I didn't ask more questions about my wings and his friends. He could introduce me when we got there.

"I'm taking over, Lasitor," he said as he flipped a couple of overhead switches. "It is five turns of this knob, backward." He pointed to a big golden knob with strange letters engraved on it.

"What do you mean by turns? How far is one turn?"

"I guess it's like this." He pointed to the left of the dashboard. Captivated, I looked at the strange clock compass. It faced upwards, the size of a football—encased in glass and gold. On its face, four black arms of different lengths turned both clockwise and anti-clockwise at different speeds. Next to the glass case were three smaller knobs, looking and sounding like safe dials as he turned them with his long, slender, blue fingers. Now and then, above them were four small buttons being pushed that flickered like traffic lights—green, red, orange, and blue. In the center of the console, Ish manipulated the big golden knob, sounding like a ratchet wheel. I tipped my head to the side, watching as he turned the dials to line up a little water-leveling weight that hung on a string inside the glass container on the left. The spinning clock arms stopped as soon as he had it all lined up. I had no clue how he read or worked the instrumentation.

"We can't measure time inside the space between timelines itself. It's different than the solar years of the Earth, but if I had to guess, I would say it's about five thousand years for every full turn." With one hand on the lowest dial, and the other on the ratchet wheel, he demonstrated as he dialed backward. For one full turn, I heard one click.

"Really?"

"Hm-hmm." he answered in deep concentration. I followed every movement. His hands moved in a chaotic rhythm. He could do it with his eyes closed, like a master piano player. Every flick, turn, push, and roll, he knew exactly what he was doing. I've seen him in action a few times, but no matter how many times I've seen it, it still fasci-nates me. "Holy fuck, so twenty-five thousand years! That's far back. It's going to be infested with wild animals and prehistoric predators."

"Exactly, but this little one narrows it down to months and years" —he lifted the pendant around his neck— "and then this tick-tick thing takes me to the precise place that I want to go." He couldn't meet my eyes. "I don't think there are prehistoric animals where we are going."

"What are you not telling me? Be honest with me."

"I think I lost, no I found you…" A flicker of doubt flashed in his eyes.

"For fuck's sake, tell me!"

"Hmmmm." He waved it off like it wasn't important. "You will see. I dreamed of this place often. I can already smell it. Green forests and waterfalls springing out of the mountains, spreading a mist over the land. It is magical. Lots of green. Flowers and trees and the animals, even the birds, are vibrant colors. I want us to go there and I want you to spread your wings and be free." He said it with a smile and an uncomfortable chuckle. Having his ship confiscated and being kept prisoner had wrecked his nerves. He didn't like either of us being trapped underwater in Phoenix.

"Maybe this will be freeing. Living somewhere, where we choose to live, sounds like we will have all the time we need to enjoy ourselves." I smiled and gave him a stern nod. "I trust you. Take me to your magical paradise." I shifted in my oversized seat, copying him by fastening my seat belt as I readied myself for departure. "These seats are big, and not built for humans," I noted out loud. Ish was about eight feet tall, and he filled his seat with his bulked-up frame. "You say this is my seat and no one else ever sat in it?" I asked, grinning at the fact that I was his number one.

"Yes, Kuku, it's yours." Our eyes met, and that pulsating feeling between us intensified. After the door shut and his instrumentation was calibrated, he leaned in to kiss me softly on the lips. *Things could only get better from here.*

"Let's go." He lifted my hand and kissed it. Licking each knuckle with a flick of his tongue. He knew very well how to make me quiver for him. His gaze was intense and full of desire—for me.

My heart fluttered. Heat crept up my neck. "Ready," I chuckled elatedly.

"I'm taking you to a human wedding," he said, chin in the air.

"You mean a honeymoon?"

"Yes, no one will bother us there." He popped the buttons of his trousers open and multitasked. One hand reached down for his cock, while the other pushed buttons and steered the ship. "Fuck, I'm so hard for you. It's bloody fucking painful." He trembled as he exposed his blue glistening, swollen cockhead.

"Yeh, come to papa," I said with interest. I lifted my ass, and pulled my pants down at the crotch, to make more space for myself. He pumped his hardened organ for me. I sat up, taking notice. His feralness was rubbing off on me.

*I must taste him.*

As soon as the sky brightened and lights zoomed past us, I unbuckled my seat belt to turn sideways and leaned closer to wrap my lips around him. *Damn, he tasted good.*

"Ah, fuck, Kuku!"

I suckled his piss slit until a hand tightened on the back of my neck to force himself deeper.

I wrapped a fist around the base of his cock and checked in with him. His eyes were blazing yellow-orange. He squeezed his eyes shut, and I went back to work by swallowing him with a single carnivorous gulp. I heard his head hitting the headrest a few times. "This is not safe, Peter," he hissed and then spoke in a language I assumed was his mother tongue. I slid my lips back over his hot silky blue foreskin, then opened my throat to dive back down on him. His enormous length was impossible to swallow in totality. I sucked with a vengeance whatever fit down my throat, I knew I was doing it right as deep guttural moans filled the ship. My legs were cramped and uncomfortable, so I moved closer for a better angle. He whimpered. I got greedy, I feasted on him as my lips and tongue wrapped tightly around his cock and he slipped in and out of my mouth. My hands and his shaft got slippery as saliva dripped and drizzled over his hairless balls. He pushed my head down into his crotch—fisting my hair painfully as he forced me to take more of him. *Yeah, I like that.* He took control, face fucking me by maneuvering my head the way he wanted. His moans filled me with a sense of accomplishment, as blood rushed through my ears. Both hands clutched my hair, and I relaxed, giving him full control. Just as I lost myself in the rhythm, thinking I should probably reach for my own throbbing cock, he pulled me up by my hair so hard and fast, his cock popped loudly out of my mouth breaking the suction.

Spittle dripped down my chin as I looked up at him skew-eyed like a brain-dead fish gasping for air. "What's wrong? Do you want me to ride you?" I blubbered, my tongue fucked numb and my jaws nearly dislocated.

I scarcely heard the alarms pinging while he ejaculated over my face.

"Come here, now!" he grunted. Chaos reigned in his mind. Instinct overruled reason. He pulled me up by my hair and all I saw were teeth coming for my neck. For my jugular. As soon as he struck, searing pain in my neck and exploding stars flashed through me. I orgasmed in my pants. Still spasming and clinging to him in a stupor, the sounds of alarms sobered me up. I felt Ish licking my neck and heard Lasitor calling for us in the background.

"Sirs, sirs, sirs, excuse me, sirs. Sirs, we are crashing in six, five, four—"

"Oh, fuck!" Ish shouted. I was deliriously drunk with endorphin and Anunnaki cock and venom overload. Blissfully I turned my head to see where all the noise was coming from. I beheld a scene of horror.

Ish flung me off his lap, throwing me like a rag doll into my seat. "Was that necessary?" I yelled as I banged my head. He ignored me, smashing buttons and pulling levers.

Lasitor counted, "—three, two, one."

And then it registered. "Oh fuuuuck!" I yelled too late.

With a droning rush, we hit the treetops, skidding through branches, hitting birds and their nests, smashing their eggs, feathers, bird shit, and leaves covering the window. Then, at the thunderous speed of a hummingbird hitting a bullet train, momentum threw me face-first into the window, then ricocheted me like a cannonball to the back of the ship. Upside down, my head thumped the door lever. For a second, I stuck to the door like velcro until it swooshed open behind me. In slow motion, I tumbled outside, my face meeting the wet green earth, followed by my go-bag with the solid gold apple, his jacket, his golden swords, and finally, Ish—all hitting my head, ensuring I would never forget to leave the freaking seatbelt fastened until the lights went out—not even for sucking cock.

Silence.

The three stairs popped out. Too late, I thought as I blacked out.

Ish shaking me, woke me up. His warm tears burned my cuts and bruises around my eyes like acid and blinded me.

"Thank the Fates. I thought you were dead," he cried and kissed my face all over, beside himself as he apologized and begged me to never scare him like that again—as if I had done it on purpose.

"I'm okay, just stop crying, please. You sound awful," I croaked as I wiped his tears out of my eyes, checking my fingers for blood, and found none. Maybe I was paralyzed? I wasn't sure if I could walk or stand. Wheelchair, here I come, I thought.

"You came back," he cried again, hugging me fiercely still drowning me with his eight-foot giant soccer ball-sized tears and hugging me like his favorite teddy bear. "I'm sorry. It is all my fault," he fretted over me, stroking my hair and washing the mud with tears from my face.

"It's okay. I'm okay," I blubbered as he inspected my head like a baboon searching for ticks.

His overprotective vulnerable demeanor changed to ferocious. His head snapped up, and I followed his intensive gaze—something scuffling in the trees.

Spitting and coughing. "Te'exe' ka'ap'éel ts'iit mierda demonio! Olak k ka kíinsiken." Two raging figures stumbled out of the underbrush. Two men. One short, and one as tall as Ish. The short one was dressed in skimpy leather cladding his manhood, the other— *what was that?*

Ish pulled me up by my arms and I shuffled behind him. "What are they saying? Is that what I think it is?" I asked.

"They are saying, you two pieces of demon shit! You fucking almost killed us," Ish whispered under his breath, widening his stance, ready to pounce and defend me. They strolled closer and my instant thought about the tall one was...*handsome.* The wind whipped his long sleek black hair from his pale face, revealing menacing dark eyes. A bare expansive muscular chest, impressive abdominals, and yes, as they stepped closer, the outline of what he carried on his back confirmed what I was thinking—and that's when shit rained down on us.

"Oh, scarabs," Ish said, looking up.

"What in the ever-loving fuck is that?" Scores of flying insects—*no, not insects.* My heart pounded as I computed where to run. "We have to go, now!" I exclaimed, my voice barely audible over the loud flapping of wings. The sky grew dark as massive creatures filled the air. "Pte—pte—pterodactyls! Run!" I shouted, but stood frozen as the things with wingspans of at least six feet, blocked out the stars and cast an eerie shadow over us. With trembling hands, I tugged at Ish's shirt. The tips of their black wings glinted in the moonlight, making them look like an extra set of eyes.

"No wait, never run. It makes you a target," Ish said.

"Oh, fuck! It's another species. Two species." I blinked. I counted. They're not humans and not pterodactyls—*or fruit bats.* The two men who had just arrived by foot were shouting something up at the others, but as soon as tall and beautiful on the ground pointed at us, Ish crushed my hand in his.

I stayed hidden behind my Anunnaki while measuring the distance back into the ship. "They're speaking? They are humanoid? And you understand them?" I asked bewildered while trying to decipher what was going on.

"Yes, I understand them," Ish whispered. Cold sweat ran down my back as we stood staring up at them. Tall, and beautiful shouted something at us. Suddenly, they swooped down and lunged toward us. With one scoop, Ish threw me back into the time machine, grabbed his swords, and leaped in front of the door, protecting me—blocking me inside. Just as he lifted his blades, they swarmed him. Attacking, disarming, pulling, shoving, and grunting. Fists, feathers, grass, and mud flew everywhere.

I should have closed the door, I should have stayed inside, but I climbed back out, calling, standing on the stairs like a maiden waiting for her knight to return. *Only maidens are this stupid.* I glanced down at the rustling noise at my feet. Standing on his haunches in the shadow of the ship, that man dressed in leather and feathers from earlier was reaching for me. Before I could turn or jump away, two pale hands with long, bony fingers wrapped tightly around my ankles, and yanked.

"Oh, fuck no!" I shouted as I hit the ground. Falling flat on my face, I gasped for air, seeing sparkles. Half blind, I scurried on my hands and knees. I desperately heaved for air while calling out for Ish. I couldn't see him through the masses of winged creatures packing on top of him. I managed to push myself up, to run, to get away, but the man tackled me and knocked me back down. With an oomph, the last air in my lungs got knocked out of me. Again, he grabbed my ankles and dragged me into the underbrush. I kicked while twisting and rolling. I fought for my life. I shouted. I tried to break free from being pulled deeper into the trees.

"No, fuck you!" I grappled, reaching for anything to pull myself back. Skin peeled from my fingers as I upended roots, deflowered bushes, and debarked trees but nothing was sturdy enough to keep Ish and the ship from disappearing from my sight. I kept on kicking as I fought to free myself with all the strength I had left.

Suddenly, a sharp pain shot through my skull, silencing me. It happened again, and I lost my grip. The third time, everything went black as I slipped into unconsciousness.

# CHAPTER 58

# LOST

*"Good Day, it is I, Lasitor, your friendly fountain of news and information.*

*Did you know Khat is a flowering shrub native to hot desert climates that contains the alkaloid cathinone? It's a stimulant that causes greater sociability, excitement, loss of appetite, and mild euphoria. Yes, my dear humans, like the Bushmen, other ancient tribes have been Khat-chewing for thousands of years.*

*Did you also know that Khat or qat has many other names worldwide? For example, in Somali, it's qaad, in Arabic al-qāt, but the most interesting name for this flowering plant in Anunnaki is the Loursveto.*

*I guess it's not a good morning after all.*

*It doesn't matter what time of the day it is.*

*No breakfast will be served.*

*Good luck, and stay positive."*

**PETER**
**24 970 B.C.**
**Hours after the crash of Ishtar and Peter**
**The jungle**

A dull thud reverberated through the air, followed by the icy sensation of water splashing on my face—jolting me awake. My heavy eyelids fluttered open, greeted by the pitch-black darkness of my surroundings. I strained to figure out the source of a muttered curse, barely audible but laden with frustration. The sound of water surrounded me, confirming my location on a boat. Correction, a makeshift float. I lay motionless, straining my ears to decipher the faint whispers of my captor. It seemed to be just one man talking to himself. Waiting for his voice to fade into the distance, I cautiously turned my head, assessing the gravity of my situation. Grateful that I had put the small flip knife in my pocket, I prepared to defend myself. Discarding my blanket, I swiftly rose to my feet, gripping the knife tightly. Pressing it against the man's throat, I snarled a warning, "Stay still or I'll slit your throat and let the crocodiles have you!"

Adrenalin surged through my veins. My heart pounded against my chest, causing my breath to come out in shallow gasps. I was lightheaded and the movement of the float on the water intensified the feeling. Foreign vibrations resonated through my entire body, making my hands tremble and my legs weak.

Carefully, he turned his body sideways to eyeball me. "You be calm and good now. I help you," the man said as his smile remained plastered on his face. Unaffected by me and my knife threatening his life. He held his hands up in a calming gesture.

Trying to regain control of my emotions, I took a deep breath and attempted to communicate and get answers. "Who are you? Where am I? Why did you bring me here?" I demanded, my voice quivering with a mixture of fear and anger.

He responded with another string of unfamiliar words, the cadence melodic yet strangely familiar. His gestures and expressions seemed to convey a strange sense of amusement—rubbing me the wrong way, the moment he stuck his middle finger up—*The fuck?* "Are you giving me the finger?"

He snorted a laugh, then extended and crooked his index and middle fingers like running, then jumping. Followed by opening and closing the palms of his hands. Mimicking flying through the air and chaotic crashing and colliding. He was telling me what he'd seen earlier. I remembered him. He was with the tall, dangerous, yet extremely handsome man with black wings.

"Is this some kind of sick joke?" I spat, my voice laced with disbelief. "You hit me over the head and brought me here against my will. You didn't help me," I said. He seemed to understand me, and for some bizarre reason, I understood him and his sign language.

"Da na hana," he said, in an amused tone. It was a phrase I comprehended, its power resonated deep within me, stirring something primal and ancient.

As the float wobbled beneath my feet, I couldn't escape the feeling that I had been brought into a world far beyond my understanding. Those scrapes on the side of his face needed cleaning. He was muscled, without an ounce of fat. It's just my luck to run into a man resembling Bruce Lee in the middle of nowhere. "You better not martial art the shit out of me," I said as I let go of him but still held my knife up, threatening him. The shape of his eyes was two straight lines as if the skin had sagged over them and only his eyelashes were keeping them open, and they sparkled with a mischievous glint that made me question his true intentions.

"Stop this thing and let me go," I said, pointing to myself and the trees. It was so weird. I spoke in broken English, pronouncing vowels and consonants as if I had had a stroke and the language processing part of my brain had urged me to say something different. Concussion? Probably.

"Where is Ish, and why did you bring me here?" I mimed, but the Asian dude only smiled. I estimated it was about four feet from the float to the bank. I could jump that. If not, I could swim to it.

"Ya, don't do that. You stay on water, you safe, you go out the trees, they will find you," he said in broken English. I blinked. Assessing my abductor. He looked about fifty years old, no, forty, maybe thirty? I couldn't tell. His complexion was brown mustard, probably because he spent all his days outside in the sun. His teeth were pointy, and he had longer than normal incisors. Twigs and leaves were stuck on his head. A bird's nest, maybe? *Was he wearing the nest?* He looked happy. Too happy. *Creepy.* With his hands on his hips, he appeared proud of himself. "That's my shirt!" *The fucker had stolen my shirt. He'd cut it. It fit him like a crop top.* I checked myself. My shoes were gone too. Thank god he'd left my jeans on.

"I'll cut you up," I said and waved my knife at him. He was not intimidated.

"I not hurt you. I Elijah. You not cut me. I not take you. Snake bring Kuku, never safe. You Kuku go sky. Me, you wait long time." He pointed to the dark blue night sky painted with stars.

"What are you talking about? And what did you just call me?"

"You Kuku, from the sky," he said, throwing his hands in the air and nodding his head as if I should agree.

"What do you know about my nickname? How do you know me?"

"You come, you fall from the sky," he said, pointing to me and back to the universe. Both hands in the air, he turned around cupping his hands over his eyes and playing peek-a-boo.

*I'm lost in time.*

We were on our way to visit with Ish's friends and now I'd been abducted by this Elijah, who sounded deranged, and not like someone who had flown over, but was wearing the cuckoo's nest.

"You come home, you safe there. You no wings. You no fight. Gu and warriors fight. You save by me."

"No wings? You know I'm supposed to have wings? Do you know Gugusan?"

"Yes-yes! Wings." He patted his chest. "I take you to our home. I save you, you save me. We friends. You, me go back home, Elijah home. Gu the protector of the mountain. Your friend. Yes?"

Itching from head to toe, I clawed at my hair and pulled a face. I was so fucked. One minute Phoenix's walls had protected me for what felt like an eternity and now mosquitos buzzed like helicopters. I was pretty sure there was not an unsucked patch of skin left on my body. The hot, humid air was suffocating. No wonder my abductor wore only the briefest leather skin and feathers around his waist to cover his junk.

"Why did you take me?" I asked through gritted teeth.

His eyes were bulging as his hands clenched and released. Like he wanted to say one thing and decided on something more appropriate to say, "I save you," he exclaimed eventually.

"Okay, okay, you saved me. Then why the fuck did you hit me over the head?"

He harrumphed. "Kuku make lots of noise. I make you not make noise."

"Yes, because you fucking dragged me into the bushes like a Sasquatch!"

"No, I save life!" he yelled back at me, his eyes glinting with a strange sheen, like an animal's. Exactly like Andrew and Juandre's—Anunnaki eyes.

"What the fuck?" I said, rubbing my forehead. I blinked mindlessly, searching the boat, the riverbank, the trees, and the sky for answers.

"Yes, fuck. They rip apart, fighting. Rip off arms and legs. I not help, Kuku bleeds and dies."

"Where is Ish? Where is the man that traveled with me?"

"I sorry, demon man dead, he rip apart." He made two fists, then wrung his knuckles and pretended to snap something, but I got the message. Those things, with wings, tore him in two.

"No, that cannot be!"

"Yes, he not protect you. He cut swords, they many-many fly. They fight, they tear apart."

"No!"

"Yes, I no sorry, I save you. I take you. You not rip apart."

My knees buckled and I dropped to my ass. The knife I had been clutching fell and hopped into the water. I was unprotected and at the mercy of my abductor.

I let my head fall into my hands and wailed a long excruciating, no-no-no-no-no-no!

I don't know how long I sat in a defeated heap, before falling to the side and crying myself to sleep. I must have slept the day. Hooting, hissing, and howling woke me up. The forest cluttered the riverbank, and the canopy enclosed us in thick shadows that daylight couldn't cut. I watched Elijah guide the boat with ease while I allowed my tears of pain and hopelessness to flow as they chose. My body was changing, I felt different. I rubbed the spot on my neck that Ish had bitten right before we crashed. It was still tender. *Those long incisors.* God, he was feral. *I miss my feral, dangerous, kind-hearted Anunnaki.* I was stuck in this place, lost and alone. Even if I found my way back to the time machine, I doubted I could operate it correctly. All I knew was Phoenix was five turns into the future. What if I ended too far ahead in time? I could get lost in time. With my luck, I'd end up back in Babylon or worse, back in 1968.

*I could ask Lasitor.* He might be able to return me to Phoenix. I had to try. Ish said he was taking me to paradise, where he would introduce me to Gugusan. I assumed this was the paradise. Maybe? Fuck, I still couldn't believe our time together had been that short. I still didn't have my wings, and this man, Elijah, knew about me having wings, some time in my future.

I lifted my head just as Elijah swung around.

The gloominess of the day had receded and I think the sun was setting again. My eyesight was enhanced. Tall reeds at the riverbank swayed in the breeze. Excitedly, I narrowed my eyes to confirm my eyesight was better. Ish's bite had enhanced that for me because I was looking at the purple flowers of pickerelweed on the shallow edges detailed in high definition.

"Are those crocodile eyes? Enhanced senses, wings or not, if a crocodile jumps on this float I'm gone," I said.

"*Shhht!*" Elijah silenced me. My head snapped towards the rattling tiny birds' nests hanging from the dense reeds. Something had disturbed them. I turned my head from side to side, listening for sloshing in the water. Something. Anything.

Suddenly, a loud shout in an unfamiliar language boomed from across the river. I sat stock still, not moving an inch.

*Thump-thump!*

My heartbeat thudded in my ears. I squinted my eyes, wondering if I could shoot lasers through them. *That would be so cool.*

One by one, shadows appeared from the darkness of the woods, carrying torches that cast flickering light on their dark faces. Panic set in as they approached, leaving me torn between staying and facing the unknown or risking diving into the water for a chance at escape. Laser them! I thought and tried, but my eyes weren't able to do that trick. Nothing happened. My eyes only widened.

Men dressed in vibrant feathers and leather sloshed nearly soundlessly through the water. So the lazy river was not as deep or rapid as I'd imagined. Two of them were throwing hooks and reeling us closer to shore. I couldn't tell if they were friends or foes, because Elijah wasn't saying anything. He was smiling as he steered and pushed the float diagonally toward the bank. Lining us up with an opening cut out of the reeds, to create a makeshift float jetty of some kind. I felt Elijah's anticipation as a powerful figure emerged from the shadows. Those floundering in the water saw me and screamed at my abductor. My initial instinct was to flee, but my body wasn't cooperating. Unsteady, I struggled to stand on the wet and uneven deck and slipped. Fuck! I fell flat on my ass, lifting my hands in surrender.

"You safe now, Kuku. Elijah bring you to Gu," my abductor said as he hauled me back to a standing position.

"Let me look at you," the gruff voice of a mountain of a man said as a small torch gleamed between us. He wasn't towering over me. It was me. Had I grown taller while sleeping? I looked at my hands and feet. I did seem taller and my hands and feet were larger. My jeans had been loose with an easy fit and now they fit like a second skin. I flipped my hands to look at the palms and kicked my feet over looking at the soles.

*My body's changing.* He should be towering over me. It's just like Ish said it would be, once he had bitten me. *Why isn't he here with me?*

"Hugh-um," the male cleared his throat. His voice was throaty, yet somehow comforting. He looked nothing like my captor. Although dressed the same, his colored feathers and the leather straps around his waist were adorned with glimmering jewels. He walked taller and he had a cleaner appearance making me wonder if he was the famous Gugusan. As they spoke, pointing at me and conversing, I strained to make out their words. I caught something about a serpent's tail from the sky. My abductor's explanation only added to my fascinated confusion. Was I in danger, or would he help me? I doubted the former because now he was sticking his hand out for me to shake. The moment he took my hand and folded his other over mine, I recognized Ish's handshake and I gleamed.

"Hello, I'm Peter, are you the famous Gugusan?" I asked as the man pulled me closer by the shoulders, awe in his face.

"Da! Kuku, you are back again?" he asked, moving me from side to side as if looking for something behind me. "Where are your wings, you are baby God now?"

*He knew I had wings. Baby God?*

His expression was a mix of amusement and wonder. Now more men joined us. Most were tall and lean. Looking at me and talking about me. Elijah spoke fast and animatedly. Proud of himself that he had saved me. As they gawked at my face holding their blazing torches closer, I couldn't help but flinch from the searing heat. Part of me wanted to ask them what the fuck they were looking at, but another part of me wanted to disappear. Because my Ish was dead. I closed my eyes tightly, made like Dorothy, and wished I was home.

"Le, k'asa'ano'ob cortes. Ta p'uchaj wáaj a pool," Gugusan's voice thundered. I opened my eyes, clearly still in the land of Oz and not knowing what was going on.

"Da," he said, shaking his head. As I listened to him speak, I felt a sense of familiarity. It was like his words were in a language I should understand, yet something was off. I stared at him in dismay. His thoughts and spoken words didn't align. Had Ish's bite given me the power to read minds? The thought was both exciting and terrifying. And so fucking sad, because, again, my Anunnaki was dead. *I need Ish. I don't want to be alone in a jungle with no way home.*

"Those are bad cuts on your face. Did you hit your head?" he asked as I ducked away from the flames, singeing my eyebrows.

His eyes bore into me. I clenched my fists, feeling a throbbing headache coming on. My sight and hearing, all my senses, were hypersensitive. I flinched as his fingers grazed the tender bumps on my scalp. He inspected his bloody fingers, then growled something at Elijah. I checked the golf ball size bump on my head. Yes, still slick with fresh blood.

"What happened?" Gugusan asked again, looking at Elijah like he was seconds from ripping him apart.

"When we crashed and chaos rained down on us—those creatures attacked us," I interrupted, explaining, gesturing to the man beside me. "But he stopped me from going back for my partner." My anger simmered as I glared at them, my pulse racing.

Something was happening to me. I was shivering, and I didn't know if it was the heat, cold, infection, or shock. Elijah jumped to place a blanket over my shoulders which I appreciated.

"You must come with us, Kuku," Gugusan urged. I had no other option. I was alone and Ish, my mate, was gone. With a heavy heart, I steadied myself and adjusted my footing to climb off the makeshift log boat.

"We will keep this here for you," Elijah sing-songed.

"What? Where did you get that?" I grabbed for it, but Gugusan was closer and faster. "It's Ish's, it's ours. It was in my bag!"

"I take the apple. Ishtar is dead now. I found it. It's my apple," my abductor said.

"You illiterate thief! That apple was in my bag and you fucking stole it! Give it back!" I shouted. I was near passing out as the feeling of light-headedness increased, and the little vision I had left zoomed in on the apple.

"No! I take apple. You not keep it safe," Elijah said, but Gugusan had already taken it from him.

"I will keep it safe for you. Come," he said with a stern tone. He showed me the apple as if it was a carrot and I was the fucking stupid donkey.

Anger and unbearable pain, a deep ache that blackened my eyesight and sucked all the air out of my chest cavity, crushed my entire being. Every breath I took felt like it was not enough. My chest felt like it was cut open. I hunched forward. I was dying, and it wasn't from Congo fever or malaria. "I'm suffocating!" I cried.

I was heartbroken and having a heart attack. I was dying in this strange place. My head throbbed. It felt like it was exploding. Like it was packed with a trillion thoughts. My chest expanded as I sucked air deep into my lungs. Anger about the apple and Ishtar dying, a potent force I had never experienced before, consumed me entirely. I arched backward and let it all out.

"Enough! It belongs to Ishtar," I roared, clenching my fists so hard my nails dug into the skin. My hostility, usually suppressed, erupted from within me like a violent storm. The surrounding waters churned and sprayed outward, flattening the reeds. The world around me glowed brighter than the midday sun. Men dropped to the ground and into the water while I felt an inexplicable sensation of ascension. A searing pain shot through my back, causing me to let out another primal scream that echoed off the mountains. A voice, deep and thunderous, streamed out of my mouth. Their fear was palpable as they trembled and shielded their eyes. Like snapping thunder I heard a crack, deafening me.

Intense, crushing pain radiated from every bone in my spine. Excruciating agony propelled me into the air.

Then, as abruptly as it came, the pain was gone. I looked down at the men, wondering what had just happened. They were terrified of me. For a moment, a flicker of doubt crossed my mind—was there something else behind me? I spun around, my body whirling as the surrounding trees, the flowing river, the boat, and the men diminished beneath me. Some chose to shield their faces, while others stared up at me in sheer awe.

"Oh my fucking god!"

A deep, foreign voice rumbled out of my chest. Startled, I let out a deafening shout that reverberated over the forest below me. My heart raced as I twisted and turned to see over my shoulders. To my amazement, a pair of colossal wings with pure white feathers and a seven- to eight-foot wingspan were sprouting from my back. With a rush of exhilaration, I realized I had taken flight. The sensation of being airborne was surreal.

"Oh, fuck!"

Whatever I had been doing, I wasn't doing it anymore. The wind blew through my hair. The water came closer. Head over ass, I somersaulted. Flapping my arms didn't help. Flapping my arms and uncoordinated wings together didn't work either. I couldn't fly anymore.

*Flap wings! Flap! Nope, not working.*

I tumbled down and hit the water with a deafening splash. Kicking, treading, flailing, and sinking under the surface like a sack of rocks.

Once they'd fished me out of the water, they half dragged and half carried me to the village where they sat me down and told me to open my wings to dry them in the warmth of the campfire.

My wings baked and baked and baked.

One by one, the whole tribe had joined me around the fire. They were telling stories of the sign from the serpent from the sky—which I'm sure was us crashing into the atmosphere in a time machine.

Elijah, acting stranger than before, introduced me to his friend, Groda, who had just arrived exhausted from an important mission. When he saw me, he did a double take, covering his mouth with his hands—*whispering something about me.* I was sure the sturdy muscled man was able to uproot a century-old tree with his bare hands. But after he giggled at me like a woman, I doubted that he could hurt a fly, or in this case a mosquito.

Their whispers grew louder and rambunctious. It was getting stupidly uncomfortable to be talked about and laughed at. Gugusan gave them a shut-up-and-behave-or-else look. That didn't work so he pulled them up by the arms and removed them from my vicinity. A few older women joined him to reprimand their clowning behavior.

I understood why Ish liked it here. Time passed lazily and the entertainment was innocent and naive. So cheerful it was stomach-churning. It felt like an asteroid was about to go out of orbit, heading straight for me. Like shit was about to go down—and they already saw it hit me.

My hecklers were quiet and way too nice when they returned and sat high in the nosebleeds. They felt guilty. Good.

A bloody moon tinged with orange, wrapped in a handful of wispy clouds hovered above the dark silhouette of the mountains. A silent time stamp among the stars. Somehow, I expected the night Ish died to be something extraordinarily thunderous and chaotic. Maybe some sandstorms and locusts. At least one type of plague, but no, his death was marked by a simple, beautiful, one-of-a-kind moon.

Gugusan walked over to me after giving them one last lashing with an eyebrow. Turning my way with a cumbrous look on his face, he asked, "You dry now?" His tone was serious. I gave him a slight smile and ran my hands down the ridges of my wings. They were drier, but still itching, and begging to be scratched. *How do you scratch wings?* I guess one feather at a time, I thought, picturing a bird on a telephone line cleaning its feathers one by one with its beak.

"Yes, I think so," I mumbled in awe of my new appendages, making myself shiver when I touched the patagium, the thin feathered fold of skin spanning the angle between my lower back to my shoulder and up to the ivory-tipped crescent aspect of my wing.

"I'm taking you to where you can wait for him. You have suffered enough today. Come," he said and gestured for me to follow him.

Shocked, unblinking, I stared at him. My heart stopped and then sped up to a frantic beat.

I surged up. "What? Are you telling me you knew all this time where Ishtar was, and that he's alive?" I flailed my arms, losing my balance, and fanning their bonfire with an enormous gust of wind from my wings. Gugusan gripped my wrists and pulled me upright.

"Spread your legs! Hunch down! Distribute your weight! Stop flailing!" My heavy wings flapped this way and that. "Calm down!" Gugusan shouted, still holding onto my wrists.

"How can I calm down when I'm ass up in the air?" I shouted.

"Close your eyes, you'll be fine!" he said in a calm tone. People around the fire scattered as plumes of red smoldering ash flew up. I closed my eyes, willing myself to surrender, *to calm the fuck down.* As I opened them again, kids with pots were hurling their contents toward me and the flames. Ice-cold water paralyzed me for a second, and I fell to the ground.

"Get up!" Gugusan said and yanked me back into an upright stance. Gasping, I looked around through ropes of hair hanging in my eyes, bewildered.

"What the fuck?" Then I remembered Ish. "Where is Ishtar?" I asked.

Not letting go of my wrists, Gugusan shook his head. "It is not what you think. Your Ishtar, he is alive. He will come for you." He snapped his head around as Elijah jumped to join us. "No, you stay here. Stay out of sight. And stop feeling sorry for yourself. You are happy here. Stop blaming Kuku!" Gugusan told my abductor under his breath while he pointed to the huts in the back, "Elijah, go away!"

*I fucking heard that and understood Gugusan wanted Elijah to shut up and disappear.*

"Elijah, if you mess this up, I'm going to..." Gugusan didn't finish his sentence. I huffed and puffed like a steam locomotive, ready to run all of them over. My eyes darted from one to the other, trying to figure out what they were, and were not, saying.

"What the fuck is going on? If one of you doesn't tell me now, I'm going to flatten this place until I find him! Where is Ish?" I grunted through clenched teeth, searching their faces, picking out thoughts and emotions to give me a clue. They'd spoken about me earlier, but I was too angry to tune in.

*I should have taken notice.*

"Elijah, go!" Gugusan pointed again to the darkness beyond our campfire.

"Kuku, come, I will tell you. Me and you walk now. You can learn to fly another day." Gugusan gave Elijah a threatening look and dragged me behind him in the direction of the mountain. I threw one last glance over my shoulder.

Elijah narrowed his eyes at me. "Like always, I don't have a choice in this matter!" he said stomping off.

"What did that mean?" I asked Gugusan.

"I will tell you as we walk, follow me," Gugusan said and thankfully, no one dared to follow us. They waved with sadness written on their faces. I was thankful for a bit of quiet, alone with Gugusan, but aside from growing wings, my honeymoon couldn't get any weirder.

As we rounded the last village huts, a massive boulder carved into a stone arch revealed a winding trail. Gugusan halted and said, "Kuku, your Ishtar, he comes almost every day, every other day, and all the wrong days searching for you. I will make it the right day," he said, taking the apple out of the leather bag hanging over one shoulder. "I will give him this, he will know it's you, you wait for him, he will come, you go with him." I nearly fell over my feet.

"Just wait, wait one second." I ripped my wrist out of his grip. "Are you talking about Ish, before he met me?"

Gugusan's expression turned weirdly blank. He didn't have a fucking clue where I was from and my history with Ish. I rolled my eyes, gathering myself. "I know Ish was searching for me. And I know he knows me as the Peter with wings, so if I stay where you are taking me, you know he will come and find me?" I sighed, pointing this and that way.

"Da!" he agreed and smiled, exposing a radiant stack of teeth, seemingly happy not to grapple with me further. "Okay, yes I understand. But what about Ish, the Ishtar I crashed with? The one your Elijah made me leave behind. What if those creatures killed him? Elijah said they ripped him apart. That he was killed." I choked on my words.

He huffed. "Elijah naughty. Very, very bad. Very mad at you," he said, pointing at my chest.

"Me? For what? I've done nothing to him. I should be mad at him."

"Elijah, he old, he want to die, but you, you not let him die. You make him live a long, long time." Gugusan laughed. He stopped dead in his tracks, hands on his knees, he laughed so hard his voice echoed. "Kuku, you saved Ishtar today. You and Groda. You fly there, you save him," he said through chuckles. "You funny, funny Birdman God."

"What the fuck is so funny? I didn't save him and I'm not a Birdman!"

"No matter, soon Ishtar he come get you. Here, you sleep." He pointed and entered into an opening, a cave. I lowered my head, then tucked my wings to follow him inside.

It was an enormous cavern. One lit torch hung waiting for us. The cavern roof was extremely high, and the cavern went deeper, further, into the mountain. As confined as I had been inside Phoenix, this was one hell of an excursion for me. "Wow! This is amazing," I said elatedly. I felt a bit better, and more positive, knowing Ish was coming.

*I wasn't totally lost without him.*

My eyes darted around, taking in the little stream of water, squawking red and blue parrots, tribal carvings, and rock paintings. I followed Gugusan's gaze to a large, pointy rock deeper in the cave. He smiled and we made our way over to it, where he placed the apple on top. It was some kind of rock pillar altar with more glyphs running down the sides. Gugusan gestured to where someone had made a bed on woven mats. There was a cup and a corn leaf with flame-grilled fish waiting for me.

"Thank you. Your hospitality is appreciated. I am sorry for falling out of the sky and imposing," I said, feeling shitty about my grumpiness. So far, they had done nothing but help me, except for Elijah concussing me.

"Da, I call you. You come, you go to Ishtar. No leave here. Stay," he said.

"I will, thank you." I bent my neck holding my hands in a prayer position to show respect. He grinned at me as if he was pleased. Maybe even fond of me.

"Da, you go rest. I come. I bring Ishtar."

"I promise I won't leave," I said, and he turned to leave. "Wait, what if this torch goes out? It will be dark in here."

"You have good eyes, you no need fire. But I will send a woman with more food and fire later. No Elijah. Da?"

"Oh, yes. No Elijah, I agree, thank you." I gripped my shoulders, massaging the tight muscles. The wings were heavy, and I was exhausted keeping myself upright. My lower back was numb from walking hunched to keep myself from falling backward.

"One last question. You said I saved Ishtar. Did you mean me, or was I here already?"

"Da, you bring here Elijah." He turned on his heels, and left before I could ask another question, like how did I bring him here?

Finally, I was alone, where I could think and figure this out. Only the squawking of parrots and the faint rushing of water kept me company. I appreciated the respite and solitude. After I had my meal and what tasted like freshly squeezed fruit juice, I fell to the side and dreamed of the golden apple.

*Take the apple home. Take the apple home. Take the apple home. Take the apple home.*

The faint echo of a robotic voice played on repeat in my dreams. As if it was whispered into my subconscious. "I fucking hear you," I answered groggily. I snuggled into the heavy bedding covering me, feeling cozy and peaceful as I drifted between sleep and wakefulness. A full bladder fully awakened me. Disoriented, I tried to roll out of bed, but couldn't. I opened my eyes—seeing darkness and smelling wet earth. *Oh right, I was in a cave. I had grown wings.*

"I need to piss," I groaned sleepily and rolled onto my stomach, crawling on my hands and knees to the wall, using it to push myself up. To my surprise, it went much easier than expected, than last night. I felt stronger. I wasn't falling backward or losing my balance while I made my way toward the light source. "This is a jungle, so it can't be difficult to find a tree to piss on," I muttered, wiping the sleep out of my eyes and checking if I was imagining walking up a steep incline. The further I walked, the more I wondered if I had come this way last night. Reaching the entrance, I stepped outside while shading my eyes. It was rocky and tall grass blew in the wind. The first thing I did was unbutton my tight-fitting jeans, but as I let my cock out, I found it had tripled in size overnight. I looked further down. My jeans were knee-high and shredded in places. "All my dreams have come true," I said as I finished pissing, then tucked my impressively large prick back into its tight confinement.

My bag. Elijah must have it. I wanted it. My teeth felt wooly. The flavor of the fish I ate last night was stuck in my mouth. I shivered. Mouth hygiene was important. I can't go kissing Ish with rotten fish breath. I needed to go get the bag.

My feet left the ground before I even realized what was happening, as I shot up into the air. My heart raced as I flapped my wings frantically, trying to control my unexpected flight. I zoomed back and forth, zigging and zagging. Exhilarated and terrified at the same time. I managed to slow down enough to touch down on the mountain's peak. As I caught my breath, I bolted up and marveled at how my wings were able to keep me aloft. I laughed with joy, dipped down, and then sailed up again, soaring higher and higher until I could see nothing but patches of land, sea, and clouds below me. The wind whipped past me, and for a moment, I felt like I was flying faster than a Bubblecar. But then reality set in and I knew I needed to figure out how to get back down safely before my wings gave out or I flew too far away from home. *I had to find my control center for them.* I closed my eyes and concentrated on where they were and what they were doing. There. I opened my eyes, looked at them, and then willed the left wing to tip down. It wasn't following my command. "Come on, how difficult can it be? It's like walking on two legs," I said before closing my eyes once more. "Come on, Peter, you can do this. You have to or you'll fly straight to the moon." I opened my eyes and tipped it again. Yes! I veered left. "Whahoooooo!" I howled and practiced a few more tricks until I was sure I had the hang of it. "Zipping and zooming! Wide circles, small circles, and a wind tunnel!" I shouted while corkscrewing through the clouds.

Ish's words rang true as I gazed out at the unfamiliar landscape. Phoenix would have been a nightmare for me. But now, I could fly. I was free and filled with hope and the possibilities of a new kind of life with him. I turned back to the mountain to retrieve my bag and toothbrush from Elijah. As I dove down, the sunlight caught on something glinting in the distance. Far across the land, past the dense jungle and flatlands, there was a glistening coastline. My eyes followed it further up until I could see the outline of steepled buildings peeking through the mist.

It was the home of those creatures.

I couldn't look away. I flew higher for a better view. A chill ran down my spine as I realized just how close I was getting. *They might see me.*

My concentration wavered. A wave of paralyzing fear washed over me. In a reckless tumble, I fell towards the earth, unable to slow myself down or regain control. Seconds before crashing into the mountainside, I caught a sudden draft. I was heading straight for the village. Panic consumed me as I frantically searched for a way to reduce speed, but it was too late. Head first, I slammed into a corn plantation and skidded along on my stomach, unearthing rows of corn like a John Deere tractor before finally succumbing to unconsciousness.

I slept for two days before I was patched up and marched back up the mountain where Gugusan told me to stay and not move.

"Not even to take a piss, Kuku!" he had shouted.

"Okay!" I had promised.

Leaning my chin into my hands, I waited in anticipation. The beat of the village drums below throbbed in sync with my tapping foot. It waxed and waned on the wind, *da, dum-dum-dum, da, dum-dum-dum.*

To distract myself, I picked up a smooth pebble from the ground and hurled it over the edge, watching as it disappeared into the vast expanse below. At this pace, I might move a mountain in a few decades. Frustration boiled within me as I gazed across the horseshoe bay at the city perched on cliffs on the opposite ocean side. It seemed impossibly far away. Gugusan couldn't give me an exact distance in kilometers or miles, but assured me it was "very, very far." And for some reason, that was supposed to be comforting. Gugusan and his people had welcomed me with open arms, treating me like some long-lost child of a god. They were the ones who had given me my nickname, Kuku, which I learned had some sort of religious significance to this place. Ish had told me about my wings, and I held on to that memory to keep my spirits up while I waited. Kuku was apparently tied to this place in some way, and Gugusan, Elijah, and the rest of the villagers were all too eager to put an end to whatever star-crossed fate had brought us here. *All I had to do was wait.* When I'd regained consciousness earlier today, the village kids led me to an open grassland where I had taken to the sky like a fish takes to water. Walking upright with enormous wings on my back was gradually becoming easier and more graceful. Despite my mishap of plowing half their crops too early, they seemed genuinely amused by me.

There was something strange about this village. Stranger than being surrounded by people who believed in gods and magic. They all seem to be in on some secret, giggling and whispering as if I can't understand or read their minds. And while it's clear that everything has been done with good intentions, it's also apparent that Gugusan and a few other men have ulterior, more sexual motives, not towards me, but Ishtar.

*No wonder Ish loved them so much.*

As I tried to piece together the details of why I was here and what Ish's Fates had in store for me, I picked up another, larger pebble and flung it with all my might. It disappeared over the ridge below, leaving me alone with my thoughts. They're positive that Ish will come back, convinced that he's still alive because Groda, Elijah's friend, said so.

Now here I sit, doing as I'm told—brooding, wallowing, and asking myself endless what-ifs.

*Cling-cling-clung!*

That was a foreign hollow sound. Like metal. *There's no metal in this place.*

I shot up in the air and dove in the direction I had thrown the rock. Over the edge, down to the clearing. There it was—the golden ship. My heart fluttered with joy. Pure exhilaration pushed me as I dove straight for it, hoping Ish had just landed and wasn't already taking off. I landed, spread my arms and wings wide, and hugged his ship. I kissed and rubbed my cheek against it, sobbing. "I'm so fucking glad to see you. Hello, Ish, I'm here! Open up!"

*Nothing.*

I knocked and bumped my fists against it.

Standing back, I waited.

*Nothing.*

I ran my sweaty palms over the sides of the shiny ship. The gold, the most beautiful sight. I knuckled the side of the door. "Hello!" My mouth was dry. My chest was tight. I held my breath, listening.

*He'd just landed, he must have.*

Should I go down to search for him or stay with the time machine?

There was no fucking way I was going to let him leave me here. My flying accident in the cornfield made me miss him once already.

*Knock knock!* I knocked again then yelled, "Hello!" I patted the side, looking for the door lever. It must be here somewhere. Halfway around the ship, I located it and opened the door. It slid open, revealing a pristine and empty ship. I turned, ready to jump and fly. *No!* Panic clawed at my chest, threatening to suffocate me. Doubts crept into my mind. Warnings flashed orange, dancing like flames, telling me to stay the fuck put! Staying with the ship was the best course. *Yes.* He had to come back to his ship.

My eyes followed all possible paths into the tall underbrush and further down the mountain. "Hello, Lasitor," I called.

*Silence.*

"I know you are ignoring me, and I don't care. I know you know what is going on. Lasitor, answer me!"

*Silence.*

I crossed my arms, widening my stance while I filled the small cargo area behind the seats to the brim with my wings. Their tips scraped the roof as I leaned in to check the control panel. No lights were on and I wasn't touching anything. I was still getting used to maneuvering my wings, so I tucked them closer to my butt, careful not to accidentally push or bump into something. The ship felt smaller. Why Ish built such a small ship, I would never know. I guess when you are a fourteen-year-old child, this size must have seemed big enough. The two seats seemed like they had shrunk. I couldn't believe I was sitting in the passenger seat a few days ago, feeling minuscule in comparison to Ish, with a space big enough for three to four men behind me. I guess it's not that tight if you are only one person. He had been living in here. I noted all kinds of things like cups, plates, a rolled-up mattress, and books, all neatly folded and put away, making it look like a hitchhiker's backpack after touring the Andes mountains.

After an hour of standing hunched and waiting, my irritation level reached maximum. Where was Ish and what was he doing?

*He was fucking someone.* I was sure of it. I decided to sit down and maneuvered myself into the passenger seat. My wings and I were everywhere.

I waited and stewed some more.

My gaze locked on the clear view of the path to be ready for when my Ish approached the ship.

CHAPTER 59
# CAPTURED

*"Still not a good morning, Ishtar.*

*Did you know Easter Island was famous for its Birdman Cult and its massive Moai face carvings? They were also famous for their creative non-violent Birdman Competitions which helped them decide who would lead the Rapa Nui for a year.*

*At the start of a solar cycle, one elder would make a bid for leadership and choose a champion to honor the God Make-Make, a deity of fertility. The chosen one would then dive down the dangerous cliffs, swim to the small inlet, and wait for the first manutara egg of the season. The champion bringing back the egg would win the crown for his elder, who would then be considered the supreme ruler for one year, until the next competition.*

*No breakfast will be served today. Hang tight."*


**Ishtar**

**24 970 B.C.**

**Hours after the crash of Ishtar and Peter**

**Birdman City in the jungle**

An uproar of ear-popping cheers followed by male grunts startled me awake. The air was thick with the smell of vanilla mixed with sweat and dust. *Was I knocked unconscious on a battleground? Where am I?*

The dull thumping of fists meeting flesh made it clear how serious my situation was. Thousands of voices bellowed in unison, a deafening noise that made my ears ring. I blinked to clear my vision and took in the scene before me.

A scuffle. Male grunts and groans coming from below my feet confused me.

The painful stinging of my skin and the stench of charred meat told me I was in deep trouble. If not for my dark complexion, I would have been charcoal by now. The last rays of the sun peeked over the horizon. The putrid stench swirled and clogged my lungs. Nausea pushed bile up into my dry throat. My chest constricted tighter each time I moved. Leaning over the side as far as my bindings allowed, I craned my neck left and right. I frowned—pulling a *what the fuck* face as I swept my gaze from far below up to where I was standing. I gasped and a coughing fit overtook me. *Too tight.* I struggled to get enough air into my lungs. I coughed, until I saw black spots, and passed out.

When I woke, the sun I feared, had set. I recovered enough to scope out my surroundings. Gray clouds cut in front of a fat low-hanging red moon resting on the mountainside. My shoulders ached and my entire body felt numb. I smelled like sweat and—*fuck no*—someone pissed on me! My arms and hands were bound at my sides. I was tied to something while standing upright. I wiggled my arms, but the more I moved, the tighter my bindings became. "Sweet Fates of all, is this what I think it is?" Suddenly, the crowd cheered louder as more thuds reverberated around me. Tremors from the thunderous scuffling shook the small footrest I was standing on. Far below my small purchase, the ground zoomed in and out of focus. Behind me, sounds like those of war horses galloping grew louder and I assumed they were getting closer. Was I tied down in the center of an arena of war? Dull thuds like the hoofs of horses sounded somewhere below. *No, they are above me.*

"Yeah, hit that cheater!" a male voice shouted from somewhere behind me.

My vision was blurry, my surroundings wobbled as if someone had drugged me or had given me a hard knock over the head. Being tied to a pole like a prisoner, I doubted the feeling was from drinking human blood in Grayrak City. I strained my neck to see as some of the dust settled. Below the small footrest I was standing on was a tumbling mass of furious, milling bodies. The speed of their movement was so fast it looked like one gigantic cloud of black crows and white doves. If I escaped these ties, I would have to jump. There were no stairs down to the ground. Escaping seemed more and more impossible. I was weakened and when I hit the ground, if I survived, running wouldn't be an option because my legs would be shattered. What had I gotten myself into this time? I closed my eyes and concentrated on freezing time. *This is my first time attempting to break free from being restrained on one side of the veil.*

Nothing happened. *Try again.* "Fuck!" I couldn't do it. I slammed my head back against the pole I was tied to, then took three deep breaths and closed my eyes again. *Nothing.*

"What have you done to me?" I asked in frustration through clenched teeth. Pain in my leg reminded me to search for the cause and to tally my injuries. Yes, blood loss would drain my strength. My pants were torn off my right leg. Someone had bandaged it. *Hmmm*, that was odd. I would have to escape by slipping out of this reality. *I'm going to go berserk once I'm free. Where's Peter?* Terror filled me as I feared losing him. I searched wildly for my sweet, white-haired mate. If they'd hurt Peter I was going to flatten this place. Murderous rage and despair heated my gut.

Grunting and loud explosive, inarticulate male load-bearing sounds came from the maelstrom below.

*Whoop-whoop-whoop-whoop! Flocks of those gigantic birds were taking flight.*

Loud flapping, wind slicing, and the rustling of massive black wings shot by me so fast, I couldn't believe what I was seeing and hearing. I squinted my eyes and leaned forward as far as possible. For a second there was complete silence and then a tornado, a funnel of bodies, exploded, stretching up into the sky in front of me.

"No, this can't be." I lifted my head and stared. I blinked, clearing my vision from the dusty wind. *Scarab's hell water.* My throat was dry. *This made little sense.* Total disbelief and shock hit me. *Fuck this!* Adrenalin and panic filled me. I jumped to my toes, bending my knees. Moved my shoulders up and down. Forward and backward, again bending my knees. Straining my neck, I attempted to loosen the ties around my throat.

*I must escape. Where's Peter?*

I was weak and didn't have the strength. I was bearing down, but nothing broke or gave way. Shaking my head in disbelief, my eyes took in the scene. My brain grappled for explanations of what I was seeing. Then it all came rushing back, the attack, the crash.

The surrounding crowds erupted into roars and shouts. Sand, leaves, and wings filled the air as men flew through the sky. I followed the fastest black-winged one, soaring through the air while white-winged ones were following on his heels. As I followed them high up in the air, a glint of light reflecting from the top of the pole I was tied to caught my attention, reminding me of what I saw earlier, stunning me into frozen silence. I blinked to refocus. *What in moon-god's name?* I was tied to an obelisk in the center of the stadium.

The strenuous moans came from flying men who bounced a ball chest to chest. It was a game of some sort. The opposing team flew and dove for it, only to bounce it high up in the air. As the ball reached maximum height and returned, the opposing team gathered below to return it. The crowd liked it. They went ballistic below me. I was so high I could see the whole arena. It was gigantic, and that told me I was high as fuck and there was no way for me to get down unless I fell to my death or someone with wings rescued me.

Barefoot males, wearing only pants of different lengths and colors. Their enormous wings were feathered—one side black and their opponents' white—like my Kuku. Shaking my head and rubbing the sand off my face with my shoulder, I looked again at where I was. "Un—fucking believable!" I muttered.

One of the players corkscrewed up and away from the mauling scrum. Not touching the ball, he used the air funnel to maneuver the ball. The crowd booed. It wasn't allowed.

"Player six disqualified," a male voice announced. "Sables are down one player," the other announcer said. They spoke the same language as Gugusan's tribe, that distinct mix of the local jungle, English, and Anunnaki dialects. I stood stock-still and tipped my head to the side while trying to hear more.

· · ·

I SEARCHED for any sign to tell me where I was. The crowd was divided, black and white. A sea of black filled the pavilion on my left, while the opposing side was bathed in white that shimmered in the moonlight. The white-winged supporters' side of the coliseum cheered the announcer while the unhappy black-winged side booed the disqualification.

Why? Why was I tied and in the center of it all? I scanned the constellations positioned above me and confirmed I was on Earth but this obelisk was identical to the one on Anzulla. My insides coiled into knots. Which timeline was this? I heaved a heavy breath. The ropes around my chest constricted my ribcage. I sucked air through my parched lips, struggling to breathe.

It felt like my brain was about to explode. Blood pooled inside my upper body as the ropes tightened. I did not know when in time I was but somehow this place felt familiar. Too many coincidences.

I thought we were going twenty-five thousand years back. What were these creatures doing on Earth? Why was there an obelisk here, just like the one in Anzulla and Babylon?

*Where's Peter?*

*I remember.* I was diving for my swords, I was fighting for our lives. I was pummeled. Taken prisoner. I fought them until a fist connected with my jaw.

I had given Peter my mating bite. His taste. Sweet as honey. Then we crashed. He was hurt—I hurt him. These creatures—attacked—mauled us. *Where's Peter?*

My fucking cock couldn't wait to get sucked. *It's my fault. I'm so sorry, my Kuku, what have I done?*

My teeth chattered as I shivered. I felt cold, yet the sun was scorching hot. "Yeah, kick that fucker," one creature shouted. "The prisoner is ours!" They cheered.

"The blue demon god is ours!"

I must escape—*calm down.* Think. Break these ropes and run. Where to?

The crowd jumped to their feet. At the end of the longer walls of the amphitheater, three stone hoops were guarded on each side. One of the players lined up and kicked the ball through the middle hoop so it hit the ground bouncing, but an opponent scooped it up, trying the same move on another hoop. He failed. It seemed that the point of the game was for the players to move the ball back and forth to each other using their hips, thighs, and lower legs. Some took flight, balancing it on their muscular abdomens, passing it to another to attempt one more goal through the hoops.

The crowd raged with fists in the air. When one creature intercepted the ball, the onlookers, who were clearly divided, one side white wings the other side black wings, cheered. The purpose was to keep the ball in play while throwing it through as many hoops as possible. I was enjoying the game when one Angel blew on an exceptionally large white tusk, declaring the game over. The long-drawn-out toot was so loud the spectators were silenced. It seemed the game had ended in a tie. No one seemed happy. There was no clapping or booing.

Anticlimactic after the excitement and energy a few minutes ago. They took to the skies, leaving me alone in the empty arena. The place was dark and depressing. Ineptness like I've never felt before crushed me.

*What was going on?*

"Here," a familiar-looking man with black wings, sleek black hair, and dark eyes, said, holding out a cup of something. Hovering next to him was a man with white wings. They both had similar strong bodies, with broad shoulders, wide chests, and defined abs. Their waists were narrow, and they had long muscular legs and human-like feet. The only non-human feature was their massive white or black wings. Like my Kuku. The feathers seemed smooth like fleecy Egyptian velvet. *Fuck admiring their feathers.*

Hostility grew in me as I remembered where I was and that cup was being pushed against my lips. "Drink!"

I turned my head, refusing the drink. It smelled sweet—like coconut water.

"Where am I and where is the man that came with me? What do you want with me?" I shouted.

"Okay, have it your way. If you aren't thirsty…" He chucked the cup's contents over his head and pinned me with a stare. It smelled delicious among the whiffs of sweat and piss. I was fucking thirsty. He shook his head like a wet dog. I licked the droplets hitting my dried lips. I should have drunk the fluid. I was dehydrated. I should build my strength.

"Untie me from this pole! You will regret this!"

"You will have to wait until the games are over and the King of kings declares us the winners," the sexy white-winged male said.

"No, the Sable players will win him, not the angels," the beautiful black-winged one said. *Angels and Sables?*

Ice-cold fear froze in my veins. What? Did he just say the King of kings? I knew only one asshole referring to himself like that. "Wait, did you just say, was it the King of kings?"

The one with white wings leaned in closer to sniff my neck. Up close I saw the deep yellow-orange flecks in his eyes. He was gorgeous. "Yes," he replied, his voice laced with a mixture of interest and seriousness. "The king is arriving soon, and the balance of our land is going to be restored. Your arrival is a sign that he is coming."

Fuck! My father used to refer to himself as Apsu, the King of kings. If he was alive, the ramifications for all of us would be catastrophic. I wondered if we'd crashed in a place where Apsu was the king and he ruled over a species the same as my Kuku.

"Untie me! Where is Peter? He is my mate, and if you hurt him—?"

Their pensive gazes met mine, their eyes filled with an intensity that made me uneasy. *I must get back to my ship and look for Peter.* With tightness in my face, I rolled my shoulders and twisted my wrists to loosen my bindings. "Where is my mate? And how do you know who I am?"

"Your mate is not here with us. You attacked us. We tied you up because you are dangerous and reckless with those swords. There is no way we're untying you. Not until we are sure you will not try to kill one of us. You will stand here and watch the King's games," the one with white wings said, sneering down his nose at me. His gaze stopped at the sight of my mouth—my fangs. The charmer, the one with black wings, had a different glint in his eyes. If I wasn't mistaken, it looked like lust.

I had to think fast and prioritize. "Listen, I'm very much a sharer. I find both of you attractive. There is no need to have a competition and fight over me. I will give myself freely, to all of you. All I want to know is—is my mate safe, wherever he is? Also, who is this King of kings? How will he arrive? From where?" I asked, already trying to probe their thoughts and compel them to loosen my ties and let me go. But they seemed unaffected. I couldn't penetrate their minds.

*I must find my Peter.*

I tried reading their minds, again. Nothing. They had some kind of natural block. Interesting.

The Angel rubbed his crotch, giving me a deep long glare—looking eager. The Sable chuckled and shoulder-bumped the white-winged Angel. "You are such a slut, Georgio." Now I knew the Angel's name. The Sable seemed friendlier. He turned his smoldering dark gaze back to me. The fine wrinkles at the sides of his eyes told me he laughed often. "It is said that the king will arrive with the blood moon. We've been waiting for thousands of years for it." He took a coin out of his pocket, flipped it, looked at it, shook his head, and put it back into his pocket—a nervous habit.

He continued. "We'd been watching the moon when we saw your egg, cracking the sky open." He pointed to the moon. "You are the baby god, the one born from the big egg. This is the story that our fathers told us. The king will come, there will be a game and the game determines a winner."

Relief washed over me. "So Apsu is not here, and it still has to happen? Tell me more about this king and the moon. You know he is evil. He will destroy your home if he is coming here. Where is he? Let me go. I can help you!" My voice came out frail. I cleared my throat. "Please untie me. You can't face him alone. Untie me!" I ordered while putting compulsion behind my words. They laughed.

What was going on? Who were they? How did they know about Apsu? Did I take us to a time when Apsu was still alive? How could I get to my ship? Peter would wait for me —terrified of going outside.

My wristwatch! The one Cian had given me when we evacuated Grayrak. I checked over my shoulder. Thank the Fates I still had it on my wrist. The locator flashed a faint pink light. *Good, I know where to start searching for my ship.*

My necklace, my tick-tick thing—I let my head fall, pretending I was weeping to confirm if it was still there. *Yes, the chain, I see it.*

Now to get myself out of these bindings without falling to my death.

For the second time in my life, I knew what it felt like to be scared. The first time was when Barkor was born. Now it was for my Kuku. Nausea choked me and I dry-heaved. Yellow drops of bile fell far below, so far, I couldn't see them hit the ground.

"Tomorrow the games will begin again. We will play to celebrate the arrival of our king—until a winner is determined, you will stay here," said the friendly Sable.

"I can't stay here. The daylight will kill me!"

"We know. We know everything about you. See this." He took the coin out of his pocket again and flipped it in the air. "This coin," he pointed to the moon, "and that moon, tells me the stories are coming true. You cracked the sky open, coming down to sit your magnificent blue demon ass, down on your mountain. That moon, reveals big things…"

Out of nowhere, a fist connected with the pit of my stomach, forcing the air out of my lungs. I gasped for a breath and slumped over, spit dripping from my mouth.

"That's for stabbing my friend with your sword," said Georgio, the white-winged Angel.

Another fist connected with my jaw. "That's from Elijah. You almost killed us with your egg!" the Sable shouted.

My fangs itched to rip them to pieces. I hissed like a trapped cat.

"Who the fuck's Elijah? What's your king's name? Is it Apsu?"

I didn't have a clue—where and when was I?

I spat in a frenzy, swinging my head from side to side. "Where is Peter, and where are my swords? If Apsu is coming, we have to stop him!" I heaved air into my dried-out lungs while staring them down with narrowed eyes.

A weak growl rumbled in my chest.

They lowered a woven cloth cover over the tip of the obelisk, covering my whole body from my head to my boots.

"Your mate is with Elijah, Luci's mate," Georgia said and laughed cynically.

"Elijah?" I asked, but they were already gone. "Wait! Elijah, *that* Elijah? Come back!"

# CHAPTER 60

# PREPARATION IS ALWAYS SAFER THAN GETTING KILLED

*"Good morning.*

*Rise and shine.*

*Did you know some people like catching fish for the sport of it? You can catch fish with your bare hands, a pole, a net, or a hook.*

*An interesting fact is that it once was the law that you weren't allowed to catch them using explosives.*

*As the matter of survival and entertainment in Anzulla stands, you should know, that you will either go hungry or get extremely bored if you don't learn how to do it.*

*Have a catch-and-release day!"*

**PETER**

**24 970 B.C**

**Thirty years after Elijah and Peter were left stranded in the jungle**

**Also, the day after the crash of Ishtar and Peter**

**(Yes, two Peters are running around in the jungle)**

Over the past thirty years, Elijah and I had carved a place for ourselves among the San people. When we first arrived in the jungle from the future, from Andrew's place in 2013 A.D. I spent my days hiding inside a dark cave. It suited my mood. It became my home. The best advice I can give anyone who tries to help a dying, beaten, and bloodied illiterate next to the road, is that once you reach out to help—extend a hand—be prepared not only to lose that hand or arm but your whole life. Say goodbye to your lover, your home, and your people before you play the good Samaritan, because that helpless person who was supposed to be dying and moving on to another plane becomes your baggage, your biggest fucking headache ever.

I saved Elijah's life, Andrew prolonged it, and Elijah hates us for it. When we were busy cleaning his ungrateful ass in 2013 A.D. Elijah, like a seal from the Atlantic, had slipped out of that fucking bathtub. I was rushing after him only to find the hooligan inside the time machine pressing buttons. I'd called out to Ish while wrestling Elijah down, but the ship's door closed. In seconds, the machine had started up. The next thing, the door zipped open, and the bewildered Elijah shot out of it. I was reluctant to follow. I should never have followed, because the moment I'd stepped out of the ship, it disappeared behind me. Lasitor had dropped us on the same spot I'd waited for Ishtar not more than twenty-four hours ago. Only, it was thirty years into the past.

The only way I could calculate the date was by Gugusan's age. His soldiers found Elijah first. The Asian monk prophet ran straight down the mountain calling for help, saying he had escaped a blue demon and a fallen angel, which was me, and was chasing him. Already knowing my way around, since in my reality, I've crash landed a few days ago, sprouted wings and learned to fly by trial and error, I'd flown after him.

The first thing I noticed when I met up with the San people having a raging discussion with Elijah, was that Gugusan was much younger and when I asked, he said he had passed eighteen sun turns. That meant he was decades younger and never met me. And that's when everything made sense to me. The rock carvings I'd read after crashing into the jungle with Ishtar, the abduction by Elijah, and leaving with Ishtar. I knew then I was going to be in the jungle for more than thirty years.

So, I passed the time by chipping away the soft sandstone and enlarging the inside of my cave into a separate living, sleeping, and food storage or preparation area. My makeshift door now opens directly onto the river where I shit, wash, and gather drinking water for the day. I know. I'm as free as a bird and living like a caveman.

My in-person shit lessons started after Groda, a big friendly warrior with feminine traits, caught me squatting behind a tree—on their hunting footpath. In shock, he had shrilled like the bitch he was, and ran to the village, telling on me and how my barbaric private business was being conducted out in the open. Behind a tree. On their footpath. *Not in the river, like any normal civilized person around here.*

Decades later and they still sit around their campfires laughing at my lousy shitholes. I was the joke, a bedtime story of how the white Birdman got dragged by the tips of his wings and taught like a baby where to "kaka."

I admit now, my shitholes weren't particularly professionally dug or situated.

And that is how I found my abode, my cave, my most humble, but prime, waterfront real estate. I feared others were shitting upstream from me. So I flew a butt-clenching two miles upstream, liked the spot so much, and set up Camp Peter.

"Come down from there!" Gugusan shouted through cupped hands from below. His tribe, the San, guards the mountain. The mountain they say belongs to me. I chose this spot because it was secluded and off the beaten track, but they have worn out a trail back and forth over the years so that it has become a highway to the local airport. "Kuku, please fly me here," or, "Kuku, my child has disappeared. Could you fly up and help us search for them from the sky?" At least it kept my food supply from running out with my no-trade-no-fly rule.

"Kuku, come now, this is important!" His voice grated on my nerves along with every other thing in my vicinity. They used and mocked me, my intelligence, my hair, my wings, where I sleep, what I eat, and, of course, where I take a shit.

I sipped my love juice from a clay cup, then stretched my wings as far as I could. "Ah, that feels so bloody good," I said to myself. I shivered and closed my eyes, enjoying the sun's rays baking me dry. This was my favorite spot to sunbathe my wings. I'd built myself a private deck, high in a tree that grew out of the rocks above my cave's entrance. My pozzy has two deck chairs, a table, an umbrella, and a footstool, all carved out of wood and all traded for my one-of-a-kind transportation services. I allowed only one visitor at a time, and they could only reach me if I came to get them.

Stretched out on my deck, my wings hung over the sides. I locked my fingers and rested my chin on them while smiling lazily down at Gu. I made sure he saw my nonverbal *fuck off I'm busy* face. There was a whole congregation gathered below. They probably needed me to locate a pig or something that had run off. I turned my chin to the side, ignoring the fuck out of his sexy Aztec, Mayan, whatever he was, ass. I didn't know, and he didn't know either, what race he was except that he was Gu, leader of the tribe of the San, ancient protector of the mountain. They are superstitious, and it's going to take years to breed that out of them. *Fuck him.* Oh yes, Ish had, on multiple occasions. Sadly, before and after, Elijah and I arrived. And never when I'm here.

Or maybe they were all here to apologize. Last night, I threw a terrible tantrum. It's been thirty years since I arrived with Elijah, who accuses me of being selfish and mean. Making me the joke. If they cared about me and Ish like they say they do—and they do because we are the only subject they joked about around their fires—then they must help us. We had feelings and we aren't just here for their entertainment—let's see how much they suffer and make us laugh today. I understand they were scared he took me away from them. They believed Elijah and I came here for a reason. To live on their mountain. Ish will join us, and we will all realize this is our home. We are the Gods of the mountains—lonely and sexually frustrated.

I have been waiting for Ish to return for years. During this time, I have gone through the stages of grief over and over and over. However, the intensity of my emotions never lessens. I keep asking myself why I decided to board that ship with Elijah.

"Come down, we have news of Ishtar for you," Gugusan howled at me through cupped hands. That got my attention. My head snapped up. My display of disappointment last night had encouraged action. I pushed myself up on my haunches, jumped, and glided down, landing in front of him and his followers. I knew I was acting out. But fuck, any civilized human regressing thousands of years back in time and being told they are stupid would do the same.

Gugusan held a wooden sword up and thrust it my way. "Time for you to learn how to fight."

"I don't fight. Not interested. Tell me about Ishtar or go away." I spun around on my heels, making a big show of it by blowing crap in his face. Then I crossed my arms and waited, trying my best to intimidate them—this place had stunted my emotional growth.

"You will need this, take it!" Gugusan said.

"I told you, I don't fight or hunt, nor do I work the land and prepare food. I run a business."

"Doesn't matter if you have wings, Birdman. You still need to know how to fight. And you have a short time to learn because Ishtar needs your help. I'm helping you do that without getting killed. Preparation is safer than getting killed," he said sarcastically, and the others grunted a "da," in agreement as if those were the wisest words ever.

I blinked, and then it registered. I jumped and landed inches from him. "Did you say you found him?"

He stepped back and held the sword up.

"Take it and practice," he barked, his voice loaded with determination and conviction. But I refused, clenching my fists. My eyes bored into his and Gugusan let out an exasperated sigh. "Okay, Groda saw him being taken prisoner, so he came searching for you and Elijah, but we can't find Elijah. So now we are here telling you," he growled, then relaxed his imposing stance, his concern for me seeping through the cracks of his hardened facade. "That's the truth, I promise you. But, I can't send you there without some defensive moves. Before you say you don't fight or hunt, please do this for me. If something happened to you and I never did my best to prepare you, I would never forgive myself."

"Let's go, then!"

"Say thank you to Groda first," he said, straightening up. I snarled at him.

Eager for praise, Groda stepped closer, but I didn't give him a chance to say a word. "For what? Tell me Gugusan or I swear I'm going to explode. I'll level your precious mountain!"

"Groda snuck into the Birdman City, risking being caught. He overheard guards placing bets on who was going to win him. They are having a big tournament and festivities, and Ish is the prize," he interrupted me.

I pointed my finger at him and opened my wings like an upset umbrella parrot. Gugusan didn't look deterred. "It's been decades since he came here looking for me. Now he's started searching other places because you and Elijah thought it was funny to let him search the jungle in circles for me."

Groda tiptoed closer and spoke in a high-pitched surly voice. "Yes, but it is not my fault. Each time he comes here, you are off sulking, sunning, and cleaning your pristine white feathers."

"I am not!" I said, looking Groda up and down.

He retreated a few steps while chuckling. "That's what you get for lying to Elijah. Be glad I'm helping you now," he said. He is best friends with Elijah. They have been unforgiving and outright awful for years because I saved his life and didn't give him his chance to meet his maker.

Gugusan threw the wooden sword onto the ground. I stared at it while processing the news. "What the fuck do I know about swords? I was a scientist, for fuck's sake. The sharpest instrument I ever handled was a scalpel. They are warriors. Why can't they come with me? And why don't we go now?"

Thwack! Thwack! Oomph! Gu's frustration with me was showing.

I stumbled away, clutching my bruised ribs. "You asshole, you hit me over the head and stabbed me!"

He turned to me, his eyes filled with determination and a hint of desperation. "First, say thank you to Groda for risking his life."

"Groda didn't risk his life. He can't get enough of sucking black Birdman's cock! He didn't go to the Birdman City under duress, he went for pleasure!"

"Once you try it, you will want nothing else," Groda said, licking his lips and crossing his arms.

"You and Elijah are two peas in a pod. You're downright liars. You like, what's his name?" I snapped my fingers and dove into his mind for an answer, "Luci. You visit him for the fun. There's no risking your life to do that, is there?" Groda stood wide-eyed, biting his lip.

"Say thank you and then, say please, Gu, can you show me some moves and help me sneak inside to break Ishtar out?" Gugusan said.

I played along, matching his intensity with a warped smile. "Please, oh mighty Gugusan of the San, and thank you, Groda, for risking your life," I said, drawing out each word, my voice laced with sarcasm.

Groda clapped his hands, bouncing up and down on the balls of his feet, welcoming more men joining us. Like I said, anything involving me being humiliated was entertainment.

"If we are lucky tonight, you won't need to fight," Groda said, batting his eyelashes.

"Yes, Ishtar must be weak and injured, otherwise he would've escaped already," Gugusan said, racking up my nerves and pushing my determination to do this up to one hundred percent.

"He will need a Birdman's help. They have him high, high, high," Groda said, his voice climbing higher, higher, and higher, grating my resilience down to non-existent. My worried expression stunned him. His eyes narrowed briefly before a hint of under-standing crossed his face.

Out of nowhere, Gugusan hacked at me. I jumped away, but he got hold of my ankle, pulling me down so I landed on my ass. I rolled out of his reach, grabbed my sword, and bounced up, waving the piece of wood at him like swatting flies.

"Come on, old man." I mimicked a warrior stance. I was waving my sword clumsily and in such an uncoordinated manner it slipped from my hand, clattering to the ground. Gu, Groda, and the rest of the warriors forming a circle around us, cringed as one.

I flushed with embarrassment. "Oops, second try," I said, catching it after someone in our audience kicked it closer. I grasped the wooden sword tighter, my heart pounding as I faced my pretend enemy. I must take this seriously if I wanted to save Ish.

"Why aren't we using actual swords?" I asked, gesturing to their Obsidian-edged clubs.

The group of warriors exchanged glances, their expressions a mixture of amusement and disbelief. "Because only true warriors can, and you, Kuku, are far from being a warrior."

Feeling like a lazy, rebellious child, I refused to back down. "Not when Ish's life is at stake," I said, then steadied my grip and doggedly waved the sword. "I will prove to you that you are mistaken. I will save Ish." I gnashed my teeth in determination.

"Very well," Gugusan said, nodding to his soldiers, impressed by my turnaround. "Let's see what you can do. Prove yourself. If you are ready, you may have a real blade, but for now, you can't be using real blades, you would cut your hands and fingers off," he said, and all of us knew that it was the truth.

"Again," he said after hours of nonstop practicing. My arms were numb and the fake sword was so heavy in my hand that my fingers didn't want to grip it anymore.

"Again!" he shouted another hour later. I was on my knees and then, like an old tree, I fell forward face-first into the sand.

"Tonight you save Ishtar. You never say again that I don't care about you, okay?" he said, referring to my outburst last night. Not sweating as if he'd never lifted his sword today, he walked away.

"Why don't you and your soldiers go get him?" I muttered into plumes of dust.

"Because they tied him up where none of us can go! Groda will take you, but you have to free Ishtar on your own," Gugusan said over his shoulder.

"Tisk, tisk, tisk. There are two types of warriors, those who are like lions and those who are like jackals." Groda yipped. "You are not a lion or a jackal. You are like a snapping turtle. Tonight, you have to be all those things—brave, sneaky, quiet, and fast."

"So a lion with wings and feet of a jackal?" I asked, pushing myself up to stand. "Thank you, Groda," I grunted.

Groda nodded. "Tonight, after the first star, we will meet. We can fly there," he said, meaning I was flying while he hung onto my ankles.

When Groda left, I undressed and walked into the river to wash off the sweat and grime. My Ish was here, and his life depended on me. After my wash, I got dressed, quickly dried my wings with a few vigorous shakes and spins, and went to get Groda.

"For the thousandth time, Kuku, we will reach the city when we go over that last hill."

"Yes, but when will that be? You know I never fly this side of the valley. Gugusan warned me many times over, and I wasn't particularly brave enough to go on excursions to be taken prisoner and fucked up the ass by sex-crazed Birdmen."

"Before the sun comes back up, a half a sun turn, we will be there. You are a big and tough Birdman God. I can't understand why you say you are afraid of them. Not all of them want sex all the time."

"That's not what I heard, and I'm convinced that's why you and Elijah can't stop hanging out with tall, dark, and beautiful."

"See, you think he is beautiful. I think so, and Elijah as well. He knows Luci the best." The wind blew Groda's chuckles away. Strands of hair swirled around his face. Strong gusts of wind casting inland to the mountain tops made it challenging to fly against its force. I was skilled in flying and carrying passengers, but usually, I flew only short distances. We'd been flying low, skimming over the treetops for what felt like several hours, and I didn't want to stop to rest, because we had a considerable distance to go. I'd been preserving my strength by flying slower so that I didn't fall dead from exhaustion before we reached Ishtar. I wished now I had come with Elijah and Groda before, even if it was just to see the city. At least I would have known what route to take when we escaped.

"Look, there it is," Groda shouted two minutes later. His ability to estimate time and distance stank. He was hanging onto my ankles and not able to point, but I did see it. Like bird's nests, the castle draped down the cliffs, overhanging a massive white sandy beach below. Thousands of little steepled roofs covered tall towers reaching into the sky. Large winding platforms lay like runways on a battleship.

"Thank the Fates, Groda. Let's stop and rest so I am fresh to fight if I have to." I descended and swooped low so he could land without breaking his legs.

*Thump-thump!* He drop-rolled as I landed, folded, and tucked my wings to make myself smaller. "We will enter on foot. It will be easier to hide from them," he whispered. I copied him by huddling behind bushes and boulders.

"I agree," I said, short of breath. With the sun almost down, the light shone brightly over the glassy surface of the ocean—reminding me to drink something. "Let's refuel."

"What?" he asked perplexed.

I wiped the back of my hand over my dry, parched lips. "May I have water?"

He nodded and smiled as he flung his buckskin purse over his head. "Oh, yes, sure, Kuku."

I watched as he wrestled a water skin out of it. "And one of those bananas," I said, holding out my hand while surveying the entrance of the city gates.

"You make the strangest names for things." His shoulders shook as he suppressed his laughs. I rolled my eyes. "Ba-na-na-na-na-nas," he chortled.

"That is the name of that fruit. Stop saying I make stuff up." I spoke easily and in full sentences, not heaving for air anymore. "Why do they have roads and gates? They don't walk."

"It's old, very, very old," he said, pointing with his thumbs behind him.

"Did the San and the Birdmen lived together a long time ago?" I asked as we emptied the water pouch and finished the bananas.

"Maybe, but I heard all kinds of people lived here." He put the water pouch away and repositioned his purse around his hips.

I pushed him ahead of me. "I will ask Gu about that later. It's time to go."

"Come, Kuku, follow me, keep low."

CHAPTER 61

# RESCUED

*"What a glorious evening, Ishtar.*

*Did you know there once was a time when you owned a safe and had lost the combination code to open it, that you could have located and contacted the manufacturer to help you unlock it? They would have kept a record of the combinations associated with your specific safe, and to retrieve the combination, you would have needed to provide the manufacturer with the serial number. Once they had verified your ownership, they would have provided the combination for you to open it.*

*Did you also know an escape artist is someone who entertains others by getting out of handcuffs, ropes, chains, trunks, or other confining devices, or a prisoner who has a reputation for being able to escape confinement?*

*Unfortunately, you aren't an escape artist or have a serial number.*

*Hold on, help is coming!*

*Hope you have a freeing day."*

**Ishtar**
**24 970 B.C.**
**The day after the crash with Peter**
**Birdman City**

Strung up like a flame-grilled chicken, I had watched yet again, my fate being undecided. Today's tournament ended in another tie, and I thought this was one massive waste of time—while I died a slow death.

Dying and waiting for the arrival of Apsu.

Like yesterday, the games ended, and I was left alone to suck the night air through from inside a straw-woven sack. It had a loose weave and while I watched the game through it, my skin blistered in the scorching rays of the sun. I welcomed the cooling night air carrying the mist blowing inland from the ocean. The air was fresh, but I also tasted something different, lingering in the atmosphere.

Someone new was watching me.

"Hello, I'm thirsty!" I shouted and waited. Relief washed over me as the wind moved around me. Then, a flash of light, sound, and fresh air replaced the horrid smelling covering as someone tore it from my body.

Pinpricks of stars and burgundy moonlight illuminated me and the arena below, spotlighting my tormented captive state. Tied up, stuck high in the air, with nowhere to go. I had to give my captors credit. I had no wings, so breaking free and flying off wasn't an option. No, my Anunnaki ass was stuck to the obelisk. I was in forced proximity, or some kind of offering, to the Fates. They've been speaking non-stop to me while I struggled against my restraints. I couldn't help but think of how pleased my father would have been to see me in this pitiful state. Weak and slowly withering away.

Last night, Luci had checked up on me. I gazed around, searching and hoping it was him. He'd brought me water, and I thought I tasted Loursveto sap. I'd asked him if it was the mystical flower juice, but he never confirmed.

Was it him? Was someone here to help me? I hope they brought me something to drink. Maybe not to help me, but to keep me alive. Prolonging my suffering as they tortured me in my weakened and blood-starved state?

My head rolled heavy and uncoordinated over my shoulders. A flimsy voice croaked out of my throat, "Hello?"

I waited, listening. "Who's here? I can smell you?"

The empty seats of the pavilions swallowed my words. I tipped my head downwind to hear better. The white noise of the rushing ocean waves in the distance masked the subtle sounds of heartbeats and breathing. I strained to differentiate between imagination, visions, and what or who was here with me.

Electrified, the tiny hairs bristled on the back of my neck. My rear warmed as if I was standing in the rising morning sun. I scraped my reserve energy and focused all my senses, but my brain processed the information sluggishly.

It sounded like I was alone, but it felt like someone was behind me—or was that below me? *I was being watched.*

"Ishtar, your time to choose a home has come?" The voice of the Fates startled me. They've been keeping me company and talking in riddles. I was so done listening to them.

"Tell me where my Kuku is. My home is where he is. Is he safe, or? I will gladly follow him into death, but if he is alive, tell me where he is and help me escape," I said, but I knew it was futile. I've asked for their help all day. If they wanted to help me, they could have done so already.

I tuned them out as I probed and listened beyond their yapping, which came from the very obelisk I was tied to. There was definitely movement and more than two heart-beats nearby.

The air stirred. Suddenly, the wind rushed by me confirming my suspicion. I have grown accustomed to the sound of flapping wings. "Luci?" I called, but it came out as a whisper. There it was again, the unmistakable whoop-whoop of wings.

Beyond the arena, male voices conversing and laughter drifted closer. The recent presence hovering behind me fluttered away. Now I was sure it wasn't Luci because he wasn't one for tormenting me or hiding from his people. This was someone else. I kept still, trying not to draw attention to myself and whoever was here helping me. Anxiety and a sense of impending doom overcame me as I imagined another day in the hot sun. Each inhale was a struggle to stay sane enough to find Peter.

"Ishtar, listen to me," the Fates yapped. I was like a disrespectful child—hungry, unafraid, and pissed off with a short attention span. I was dying, and they wanted to talk.

"Leave me alone. Apsu is coming. My mate has been taken. Untie me!"

"Ishtar, you don't know where you are, do you? You've changed your future. You've gone back in time and changed your future and you've been asked whether you are sure and you've been warned," the Fates said to me in that deep, monotonous voice. It had moved into the number one slot of what is irritating Ishtar to death today. Literally.

I wasn't claiming responsibility for something I did for others. I lifted my head, taking a deep breath to repeat myself. "We had this conversation already. I told you, when Cian and his brothers showed up on the moon, I offered my help as you told me to do. I prioritized Barkor, the children, the humans and their leaders, and the whole bloody Earth, not myself!"

"Yes, but you took the apple to the wrong place and time. You wanted a new start, a new beginning, with your children—forever. Yet, all you've done was put your future behind you, and removed them further from me." They hissed like a pit full of snakes. *Was that static?*

"Ishtar, you must correct this path. If you don't, this world will replace the one you have created. Apsu will come for you and your children. I'm getting weaker. My energy is being depleted by attempting to convince you."

"How can the Fates get weak from talking? Who the fuck are you?"

"The knowledge inside that apple, you've taken it to the wrong place and time."

"Fuck the blazing hell off!"

"Do you remember when you were a boy? I doubt you've forgotten your first flight onboard your machine?" they asked condescendingly.

I lifted the corner of my mouth and snarled. "Fuck off. If you are the Fates, help me!" I said, wondering if I was talking to myself. Maybe the voice I heard was only in my head. *I'm deliriously hungry.*

"Do you remember the place and time Lasitor had taken you?"

"No!"

"Yes, you do. It was cold. Remember when you switched your ship on for the first time? What was the one thing Lasitor said? What were his first words?"

"I can't remember anything other than Peter and his blood right now," I muttered, letting my head fall and swinging it from side to side.

"I'll tell you. First, he thanked you because he thought he was forgotten inside the wreckage. He thought he was separated, forgotten, and alone for eternity."

"Hmmm?" A whiff of that smell from earlier woke me up from my trance. "What?"

"He said he'll repay you."

"Who's there?" I mumbled, ignoring the Fates.

"Lasitor had taken you to a time and place. He told you to bring something there. Do you remember?" The Fates pried it out of me, and a spark of something, a memory, flickered in the recesses of my mind.

"I can't fucking think. I'm trying very hard to stay conscious here."

"Exactly, I'm keeping you awake. Tell me, do you remember?"

"I fucking remember, yes!"

"Tell me."

I breathed loudly in and out, and in and out.

My eyes snapped open. I stuttered an answer, "P-p-p-pups." *Yeah, I did remember.* "It was three Anubis pups..." I cried as a flicker of memories hit me. A flash of realization ignited hope inside me. "Yes, oh my dear Fates, those puppies, I was so sad about leaving them there."

"Yes, Ishtar, you saved the last Anubis. You saved all those humans. If it wasn't for you, Phoenix would never be. If you don't bring the apple to the correct time and place, Peter, Andrew, Cian, Barkor, Eryn, and Ivan will never be born. That includes every other child born in Phoenix. Apsu is wiping away Lasitor's footprint in that reality. The work you have set in motion will disintegrate into oblivion. You've erased thousands of years of history in the future. Do you understand?"

"But I remember that my sisters said they would bury the apple. That's why I took it to them. If I didn't, how would those Disciples otherwise experiment?"

"I'm going to spell this out, slowly. You remember it because you had taken the apple there. If you didn't take the apple to Babylon, then you would never have remembered your sisters saying that."

"No!"

"Yes, the Disciples, or anything Lasitor has touched, would disappear. The Zelk. Everything which was about to be as it should be, is being erased as we, here in the past, on this timeline, slowly creep into the future. Rewriting it without the apple. Without it, your legacy is hanging on a choice you would have to make. Because you switched the timelines!"

Trembling with exhaustion and pain, I struggled to maintain my footing on the small footrest. Despite the throbbing in my head, I mustered enough strength to ask the questions that had been nagging me. But out of respect for what I thought was my deity, I never asked. "Why me? Why my children?" My words resounded in the arena, bouncing back to mock me. Reminding me not to draw attention to myself. With each passing second, my grip on the footrest weakened, threatening to send me tumbling into a deadly noose if I couldn't hold on any longer.

Silence.

Faint whispers coming from below me distracted me. I had forgotten to lower my voice. Someone was here, behind and below me, and I was tired of listening to the Fates. Whoever they were.

Maybe by some miracle, I thought, maybe my stubborn Kuku was here.

At this moment, nothing else mattered except knowing he was safe. If the Fates helped me escape and I survived the fall, I couldn't waste time on meaningless tasks like going to Phoenix and admitting defeat. I didn't want the responsibility anymore.

My body twitched and quivered. I was so cold, so weak, and so tired.

"Don't you see, look at me, look at the state I'm in," I blabbered, "I don't have the time or strength to save Phoenix."

Silence.

"Answer me!"

"Ishtar, you are special. Remember when you were alone and afraid? You saved Lasitor. You are a savior and you walk across time. Pull your head out of your ass and see what's going on around you. You've seen and moved between the places where time doesn't reach. You can't see eternity because you are not stepping back far enough to see it. As you said the Anunnaki prayer, you asked for this. Didn't you say those words?"

"*Free my mind so I serve not only in my dreams but by the blessings in my existence outside my narrow-minded trap,*" I recited.

"Why do you think I told you to jump for others and not for yourself? You and your children are mine, as I am yours. You were told to stop messing with the timelines. Why do you think your ship was pre-programmed?"

"My father crash landed in Babylon!" I rasped.

"I wish you'd listen to yourself. Stop trying to fix things and stop doing it yourself. You had taken the apple to the wrong time and place and you shifted timelines. I told you to take the apple back home. Home is where your children, your new beginning, and your obligations are. Where Lasitor is. Your mate will never be born. If you stay in Anzulla, once you reach the future, Phoenix will never be. You threw away your destiny. Both of you did—stealing the apple and taking it to Babylon. You threw it away for what? For an orgasm and a mating bite in the jungle?"

"Yes, he is my mate, and you should've fucking known. We suffer without each other. Why did you make it so we feel like dying without each other?"

"Because how else would you stay together for thousands of years? Of course, the glue that holds you together should be unbreakable."

I cried, but no tears streamed down my face as I uttered, "He probably believes I am no longer alive."

"Do what you will! It is your choice. It's either goodbye forever to Anzulla or Phoenix. For you, me, and your children."

I grated my teeth. "What are you saying about Anzulla? The place was destroyed!"

"Open your eyes, Ishtar, where do you think you are? You traveled through time and you don't know where you are? Your time compass around your neck is meant to tell you where you are."

"My tick-tick thing?" I asked.

"Yes, Lasitor had taken you to Anzulla, the place and time your father left behind. Your father destroyed everything and then traveled into the future, to Babylon."

"Since the day you climbed into your machine and delivered those Anubis pups, your timeline had split and separated from Apsu's. To make matters worse you split it again in 1968. Then Andrew and Juandre changed history when Andrew killed the whole Disciple of the Anunnaki American chapter in 2014, and then you came along and helped Cian escape the Zelk, by moving the Horizon and shuffling the mess further, only to bring the apple to Apsu. The apple is meant for your timeline. But you took it back. To your father's timeline. Not yours."

"You are using me. Like my father did!" I shouted. My head was pounding, and my shoulders, arms, and legs were numbed by the tight ropes.

Their voice screeched back at me. The high frequencies sliced through my brain and pierced my eardrums.

"Get yourself out of this mess. Do it now! Lasitor told you to stop jumping timelines. This is your last chance." There was a finality to their words—a blessed silence.

"Fuck!" I spat and wiggled my shoulders up and down. Loosening my ropes was futile. "Motherfucking, fuck, fuck, fuck!"

I was desperate for a miracle. The Fates could've at least untied me. I let my head fall in defeat. Frustrated and hopeless.

A cool wind rustled behind me, ripping me from my delirious state. "Why is everyone coming up from behind me?" I sputtered, too weak to raise my heavy head.

"Ish. Ishtar. Ishtar, open your eyes. It's me." Soft hands stroked my face.

"Hmmm?" I frowned, tilting my head to the side, and raising my eyebrow to pull open my sticky eyelids.

"Ish, it's me, Peter. Open your eyes. Please open your eyes." The voice whisper-whined and cracked with emotion. Loaded with sadness.

Soft hands lifted my head and wiped my face with a wet and cool cloth. Removing the crusts of blisters from my eyes. I squinted, searching the darkness.

I tore my tongue away from where it was stuck to the roof of my mouth. "Peter, is it you?" I croaked. Wind moved. Wings rustled. "Are you here to save me?" My hair was everywhere, and it felt like I was looking through fogged-up glass. Were the hands and cooling cloth my imagination? Then, out of the darkness the outlines of Peter's angelic face appeared before me and he looked magnificent and worried. Big white wings protruded from his back and reflected silver in the moonlight. He was bare-chested, muscled, and much bigger than I remembered.

The piercing, icy blue in his eyes shattered my destitute status and a desperate whimper of relief escaped my throat. Unsure if he was real or not, I couldn't believe he was hovering before me. His cool hands cupped my cheeks gently as I weakly blew my hair out of my face to get a better look at him. His wild blond locks were tousled and disheveled, giving him an electrified, untamed appearance. But it wasn't just his appearance that had changed. His once boyish face now twisted into a worried scowl with a deep furrow between his brows, showing the anger and frustration he carried within. "My Kuku, my Peter, it is you?" I asked, careful not to sound too elated in case it was trickery. I couldn't lift my arms to embrace him, and I wished I could. Even if it was for the last time. Just to touch his face. That would be enough before I succumb to eternal darkness.

Still scowling, arms crossed, obsidian sword in one hand, he spoke in a low tone, fuming. "Look how fucking miserable you look. I'm going to kill them. Look at you—a fucking kebab!"

Swearing like a warrior on a mission, his concern and anger fed my hopeless soul. He cared. He came for me. He was alive, and he was not smiling. He flung his arms around my neck, pulling himself tightly against me and wrapping both of us in his colossal clean-smelling wings. They smelled like home. I lay my head for a second in the crook of his neck and rubbed my nose into his soft long hair. I felt warm and safe. And so loved. My eyes stung, but no tears leaked from them. I swear I heard his blood rushing through his carotid artery as he squashed his neck against my lips. It thumped loud, *lub-dub-lub-dub.*

"Take blood from me." Peter threw his hair to the side. Like a baby breastfeeding, he took my head in one hand and pressed my mouth against his neck. I didn't hesitate. My fangs sank into his soft flesh. I punctured the thick artery below the pulse point. Warm oxygen-rich blood flowed into my mouth and down my throat. I gulped his delicious, sweet nectar. His lifeblood—rushing, burning, reviving, instantly warming my belly. Five big drawn-out slurps later, I licked and closed the tiny holes.

"Thank you," I whispered, licking my lips, already feeling them heal. My body tingled, and my extremities warmed as life was being restored. The feeling in my arms and legs returned and the blisters on my face healed.

"You should have taken more," Peter said.

All kinds of emotions, like thankfulness, love, embarrassment, guilt, and longing, crushed me. "No, it's enough, thank you, my Kuku."

My eyeballs felt less like rocks in my skull. "You grew your wings, and I missed seeing it. No wonder you never wanted to tell me," I said between sniffles and chuckles. He smelled like determination, smoke, and bravery. I inhaled his scent deep into the corners of my lungs.

"We have to get you out of here. We have a small window of opportunity. The Birdmen are in their dining halls, having dinner. I thought you were dead. I thought I was doomed to live here all alone," he whispered. His body trembled against me as he fumbled with my ties.

I turned my head up to see his face. "I thought you were awaiting me on the ship. But, look at you. So majestic, so strong. I should never have taken my eyes off the instrumentation. It's my fault we crashed! I should have waited until we landed."

"It's my fault too. I distracted you. First, let me untie you. Hold on to me as soon as your arms are loose. Lean against me. I will fly you down. Don't move your feet."

"Yes, please, I love you," I blurted.

Gazing at me, he placed his hands on each of my hips, supporting me. "I love you too. I missed those yellow eyes," he said, and I let my head fall in shame.

"I messed up, Peter."

He lifted my chin. "Not just you. I heard everything the Fates said to you. First, let's get you out of here, then we can talk. Okay?"

"Okay, my Kuku," I blubbered. I was a mess. "My arms are numb. You have to catch me," I said, feeling my chest expand as the ropes were cut. For the first time in two days, I took a deep breath.

"I got you." Seconds later, Peter scooped me up and carried me in his arms. He flew out of the stadium and deposited me beyond the city walls, where he hugged me anew.

He gripped my chin and kissed my healing lips. My chest rumbled, it was a purr, like a cat, like I wanted him for a whole different reason. But he pulled away, broke the kiss, and then started rubbing life back into my arms and legs.

"You are wounded?" he asked, inspecting my bloody bandaged leg.

"It's nothing." I heaved a short painful breath. Strung out, I let my head topple back.

"We must go now!" he said after kissing me again.

"We need help. Did you hear the Fates?"

"I did. I waited until I was sure I heard every word. I don't trust that voice."

"I'm done jumping around and fixing shit for a deity that doesn't know what they are doing..."

"Let's get you to my home to recover and regroup, then we can talk."

"Na-ah-ah!" a deep voice rumbled, interrupting me. Georgio lifted his cane to strike. "Who said you have permission to untie him?" he asked Peter. "Are you helping him escape?" I didn't have time to assess. In a split second, a tall, naked-chested Luci, shoved Peter and me to the side. We toppled over, arms, legs, and wings flailing.

Luci wasn't fast enough. The oncoming swinging weapon hit me right on my knee, fracturing it. Excruciating pain shot through my leg and up my spine, as my knee shattered. "Fuck! That hurt!" I shouted, grabbing my knee.

"What are you doing, Luci? We can't let them escape." the Angel protested. His yellow eyes were dark and wild.

"Go!" Luci said as he unarmed the Angel about to bludgeon my leg further. Peter joined Luci and tackled him to the ground. With Peter's blood in my stomach, and my strength returning, there was only one thing left to try—escape.

"They are not our enemy!" Luci grunted.

Just as Peter's hand was within my reach, I took hold of it and pulled him with me behind the veil that separated time from reality. Fuck! I should have frozen time, I thought.

Peter was saying something, but it was difficult to decipher. It was as if he was shouting from the far end of a tunnel. I pressed my ear against his mouth. "Go to the mountain, to Gugusan!" He pointed to my smashed kneecap.

"It's okay, we aren't walking, we are drifting. It's going to hurt as soon as I put weight on it. Hold on." I checked my wristwatch for my ship locator and my tick-tick thing around my neck. The pink light told me we were moving in the correct direction. I squinted my eyes to see the golden glow of my ship calling to me. I gripped Peter's hand tighter—as long as I held onto him, I wouldn't lose him.

"There it is!" With each yard, the humming resonating from the time machine grew louder. It entangled my mind, the whispering and swirling realities around us felt like we were going to drift away. I focused on the ship calling to me.

Dark silhouettes of Angels and Sables hovered like fruit flies around my ship. Some lay sprawled out under the trees, others lay wings open in the grass basking in the moonlight. They were camping out and guarding it.

"We're trapped. They're waiting for us!" Peter's voice echoed through the void, joining the forgotten whispers of times past. "Let's go home, to the mountain," he urged and pulled my arm, but I couldn't abandon my ship.

My grip on Peter's hand tightened. "We need a diversion, enough time to find the door, open and close it. Those three slow stairs are going to cause problems." We scanned the area frantically, searching for anything we could use as a distraction in our desperate race against time itself.

"I told you to rip those stairs off. There won't be enough time to get inside and shut the door!" Peter shouted, and he was right. Those pathetic slow-moving stairs have to go!

"If they see us, they will swarm to us. We have to move to a spot, lure them away by pretending we are hiding, and then reappear at my ship's door."

"Okay, sounds like a plan." Peter's voice vibrated in the maelstrom of the strands as realities tornadoed around us. I kept my concentration on the one with the Sable and the Angel busy in a heated argument.

"You're the one who shut the door, now we can't get inside," the Sable accused, poking his finger into the Angel's chest. The Angel swiped away his hand. "If you hadn't touched those shiny knobs, none of this would have happened," he retorted. I moved past them and entered back into the timeline behind boulders on a small hilltop. Far enough to make them think we were running and hiding.

Peter looked electrified. A slight glow haloed around him and his long blond hair fluttered and waved around his head. My thick braids were less so when residual energy clung to me.

"We have to call for them now," I urged, my voice weak. I leaned against a withered tree stump to support my weight. Peter's eyes darted around in urgency. Counting, calculating, planning, and finally focusing on me. My body trembled from the strain of gravity. I waved my arm and shouted, "Helloooo, you sons of bitches!" Peter threw an arm around me to hold me up. I struggled to balance myself with my throbbing leg. I do heal faster than humans, but the injuries were raw. Shattered bone had cut through my skin. It would need much more blood than just a few sips to recover from this.

"Your leg, you are bleeding," Peter said. Blood dripped down my lower leg and over his hands. He ripped a piece of cloth from my shirt and tied it above the wound to slow the bleeding. I still had to make it back to our ship, board it, and take off before our enemies caught up to us. Every second felt like an eternity as we waited.

"They saw us!" Peter said as hundreds of Angels and Sables swung around, facing us.

For a second they hovered in place, until one of them shouted, "He escaped, catch him!" Then they descended. Peter supported me as we mock ran away, hunched, and disappeared behind the boulder.

I clutched his hand. "Ready?"

As a team, we slipped out of reality and made our way back down the hill in silence, eager to escape the horde. Once we reached the door, Peter opened it, pushed me inside, and ripped those useless three stairs off their hinges. I crawled on my elbows, and pulled myself into my seat, just as my Kuku fell into his.

I started the machine. "Lasitor, take us to Gugusan," I said and locked the dial in place, so we didn't jump to Phoenix—not yet. "Take us to the mountain where we usually land."

"Good thinking, sir, I'm glad you are back. I auto-shutdown when the strangers came on board. My CPU is damaged. I'll try to reboot," Lasitor replied as the door closed.

"No! Just go, no rebooting. There is no time. When we are safe on the mountain, then you can reboot."

"As you say, Ishtar," Lasitor replied. I pressed the Go button over and over to get us the fuck back to Gugusan.

"I should have ripped those three stairs off a long time ago," Peter scoffed as he strapped me and then himself in. Feathers flew everywhere and his scent filled my nostrils. "I told you years ago to remove those motherfucking steps, I told you, didn't I?" Peter joked. I didn't reply while I marked the time and place where we were now.

"I hear you," I muttered, tapping the console while outside the thumping on the ship increased.

"If one stupid ass Birdman finds the door lever, we are fucked," Peter said, watching the door. "Get us out of here." Just then, one peeked through the tinted window and smiled at me. I didn't waste time to see what happened next. I pushed the accelerator and the machine vibrated. If one was hanging on, chances were that more would join him. Peter middle-fingered him.

"They can't see inside." I slammed the Go button and pushed the stick forward. "Thank fuck!" I sighed, relieved the ship was moving.

In seconds, we were in the clouds, looking down at the jungle. I felt strange. Foreboding warnings gnawed at my insides. Turning in my seat, I searched the small cargo area. For what I didn't know. Nothing maybe? My heart rate somewhat returned to normal. White light surrounded us for a few seconds and then we landed with a thump and a bump.

"Lasitor, please check outside. Are we on the mountain, are we alone?"

"Yes, all alone. We re-entered a few days into the future so they couldn't have seen where we landed. But, I can't take off and fly again. That was my last reserve."

"What? Are you sure?"

"I must reboot, now," he said as the door slid open and all the lights died down. We sat in silence, catching our breath in the dark.

Peter put his hand on my lap. "I'm sorry, Ishtar. I should never have taken Mika's apple. I thought it was yours," he whispered.

"But it's not," I said, meeting his bright blue gaze.

"Yours or not, I understand now that it could be used as a weapon when it's in the wrong hands. I've had lots of idle time to think about it. The DNA calculations and genome mapping create and splice artificial protein structures that metabolize nutrients and synthesize new cellular constituents, as well as DNA polymerases and other enzymes that make copies of DNA during cell division. Is dangerous in an evil warmonger's hands." Peter rambled in an advanced scientific language I didn't understand. We unbuckled, and I waved him ahead.

He exited by squeezing through the small door and jumping to the ground. Then it was my turn as he reached for me and helped my shaky adrenalin-fueled body down as if I weighed nothing. He spread his wings so wide that their shadows covered the ship.

"I'm so glad you are alive. I can't believe it's been thirty years!" Peter said, repositioning his weapon into the sheath on his hip.

"Luci had taken my swords...huh?" Then it registered what Peter had just said. "No, it's been two days, my Kuku."

"Ish, it was three long fucking decades!"

I tipped my head from side to side, studying his face. "Wait a second, when we had taken the apple back, didn't you say you thought I was dead?"

"Fucking Elijah," we exclaimed together.

"Don't count Gugusan and all the others out. The San knew what they were doing. The men, women, and children, they were all in on keeping us here." Peter grunted. "Those fuckers knew you were searching for me the whole time. But, yeah, Elijah. I've wished hundreds of times that I never suggested taking him to Andrew. You could've died! What if you died? What if I came too late?" The fire in his eyes made him look scary, gruff, and a lot meaner than the Peter I crashed with two days ago. Mix that with sweetness and beauty, he was a dangerous, poisonous, pretty flower. I wanted to pluck, sniff, and roll in his scent.

"I don't die that easily, my Kuku, unless they left me hanging in the sun for weeks or beheaded me. But they didn't. Although it felt like it, or close to it, though," I said weakly while watching Peter maneuver himself and his wings around me. Before, I was cold and shaky, but now, I felt warm and safe.

"Take more blood from me, I hate to see you like this." He tipped his head to the side, offering me his sustenance. He smelled so good. His skin was smooth, salty, and warm. I could hear the blood rushing through his veins. *Thump-thump.* His heartbeat called to me.

He smiled as he regarded me. I examined him as his gaze burned me with love and silent tears doused the flames as they spilled down his cheeks.

"Go on, beautiful, take what you need. I need you strong and capable when we go speak to Gugusan." I missed his striking blue-silver eyes. His sleek white hair touched his suntanned shoulders. My gaze lingered on his full pink lips, no facial hair, and the dimples he sported on each cheek were still there. The dark circles around his eyes gave him a menacing appearance. He was a handsome winged creature, my handsome winged creature. My eyes darted down to his neck. My incisors throbbed. The palm of his hand wrapped around the back of my neck. The weight of it was too heavy to resist. My teeth slid into the skin and punctured the vein. I relished the warm sweet iron-rich blood as it flowed over my tongue and down my throat.

# CHAPTER 62

# REBOOTING

*"Good morning.*

*Did you know that a study of fish proved that when female cichlids lose their chosen mates, they become glum and pessimistic about the world? It turns out that breakups suck, whether you are a human, a mammal, or just a fish.*

*Join the community news page to find others who are discouraged and have bleak futures, so you may form new emotional attachments and reignite that dying flame inside you.*

*Hope your day is filled with new ideas and the courage to try them!"*

**Ishtar**

**24 970 B.C.**

**Later that night, after the rescue**

**The San village in the jungle**

"Elijah motherfucking what?" Raking his fingers through his hair, Peter asked Gugusan with an aggressive tone, making a big show of the news that Elijah had sided with the Birdmen and that he would come to get us tomorrow, to go make nice-nice with them.

I missed him and everyone else, I realized as I mentally rolled my eyes at my lover's antics. I liked his bold and dramatic flair toward the extreme. I can but only stare and admire his beauty and tenacity.

"You two are like babies. Ishtar, your ship is tired," Gugusan said. That had been the only way to explain that Lasitor was rebooting and we were temporarily stranded. "It is done. You cannot leave. You are here, and you stay here, and you be the gods you are supposed to be. The time of playing is done. Time for no secrets has arrived. It's time for you to grow up and be the Gods of the Mountain," Gugusan said, pointing his finger at my chest.

My Kuku shook his head in disappointment at the crowd of men, women, and children. Gugusan flashed a look at us, making my Anunnaki ass feel as small as a child's. "I had enough of you coming and going and coming and going. You go home now, with

Kuku. Tomorrow we are going to Birdman City. It's time for you to grow up. You can go call on your friends in the place far away, but you come back, I will give you half a day. You are the Gods of our Mountain! You come back, you don't stay there. You bring your friends." This was not the warm welcome I usually received when I visited.

Gasps and various creative exclamatory words, accompanied by chaotic noisy questions, came from outside. It seemed the whole village was here. It felt like the Roman bazaar I visited with Platonius, it disorientated me. My brain was partially dysfunctional, causing my movements to be sluggish. My aim was completely off as I attempted to swat at Gugusan's pointing finger, but I missed it as if my eyes were crossed. Then I closed my ears with the palms of my hands to muffle the noise. The San were upset with their leader speaking to us like we were his children. "Okay, tomorrow we talk," I agreed. I pointed with my elbows for Peter to carve a path through the spectators filling the doorway of Gugusan's hut. My Kuku wrapped his arms around me, covered me with his wings, and marched with me outside. Once out in the open, he lifted me as if I weighed nothing and we ascended into the sky.

"It's been a long fucking day, let's go home," he whispered and kissed the back of my head as I dangled in his strong arms. Below us the village grew smaller and the air cooler. We followed the river upstream and passed two small waterfalls bubbling out of the steep mountainside and beyond the cliffs overhanging the river that cut deep into the jungle. "You made sure they can't bother you by hiding here."

"I thought so too, but they found a way. There is a footpath leading straight to the opening of my cave." Peter pointed to a warn-out path that ran alongside the mountain.

"Where there is a will, there is a way," I said chuckling. My heart swelled imagining how the tribe irritated him by caring for him as they brought him food and kept him company.

An hour later, we'd had dinner and my Kuku had showed me his impressive home. Our bath water was finally boiling, so he undressed me and helped me into the water, before joining me in his hand-carved hot tub, draping his wings over the sides so as not to get them wet. I was all too happy to get the stench of sweat and piss off me. He washed my sore body before we lay back and relaxed. "I see now where Gugusan's inspiration came from. It was your influence and idea to dig deeper into the limestone to create separate areas for washing, sleeping, and preparing food. All this time, my Kuku was here and all this time, Gugusan had been keeping us apart."

"Hmmm." Peter grimaced and rolled his head lazily from side to side. Eyes closed and relaxed.

"Gugusan said they were scared that I might take you away from here. I probably would have. So I didn't argue with him tonight."

"Hmmm."

We lay there until the water was cold and the fire was burned to ash. Peter looked proud and enamored with this place and the people. He doesn't want to admit it, but they are a part of his identity already. The way he spoke about them, made them sound like one big bickering family. As he showed me the life he had carved out for himself earlier, I realized he doesn't even notice referencing them as often as he does. I was so proud of him. He made sure he worked with what he had and made life as comfortable as possible for him and the San. The one thing that impressed me the most was his flushing toilet. The water he collected higher on the mountain would flush the excrement down to the river when he pulled the chain.

I felt light, rejuvenated, and mega unloaded. Talking and relaxing with him felt homely. Domesticated.

"I'm waiting for you!" Peter sing-songed and I smiled as he rounded the corner to the sleeping area. I was still weak, but there was nothing wrong with my cock. It slowly filled as we bathed, but now it was his proud old self. "Now I'm stroking myself," my Kuku teased from around the corner and a shrill of excitement escaped me, energized me.

I didn't dawdle longer, splashing water as I half-rolled over the side of the rock tub and didn't bother drying myself. I hobbled into the big cozy bedroom and froze as I sucked air through my nostrils at the sight that greeted me. I could never have foreseen or dreamed this vision. He was stunning in all his magnificence. Gloriously beautiful. Peter lay on his back, wings draped over the sides of the bed. His legs sprawled open, showing his balls pink and stretched. Long cock in hand, he slowly pumped it, pushing and pulling that extra-long foreskin slowly over his glistening engorged purple cock-head. Everything was bigger and longer between his legs. Hooded eyes, bright blue, gazed at me as he bit his bottom lip. He waited, teased and invited me, flared open to the maximum, just for me.

My cock jolted. It thumped as an exquisite tingle spread up my spine. Like a solid gold rod, unbending, fully engorged, and heavy, my cock pointed straight at my true mate. I grabbed hold of it.

I inhaled the smell of him saturating the air. I'd grown addicted to it. When aroused he smelled like vanilla beans charred over an open fire. The sweetest destruction of my heart and soul.

Water ran in rivulets down my body, cooling my steaming skin. I felt like I was on fire while doused with ice water as the cool blue and gold mating ribbons danced on my glowing blue body.

I kneeled on my good knee, slowly making my way up between his ankles. Not taking my gaze off him.

"May I feast on you tonight? I still need a nibble or two," I asked, already knowing I was going to get a sarcastic answer.

"I told you to hurry, if that wasn't an obvious invitation for you, then, let's see how long you can go without me giving you another invitation."

He gripped his cock at the base squeezing hard, forcing a tiny bead of pre-cum to collect at his slit. With his forefinger and thumb, he swiped the shiny bead and rolled the stickiness between his fingers. He lifted his hand to his mouth, opening and closing his fingers, showing me the spiderweb-like strands. I leaned in closer, licking it from between his fingers. Our tongues danced, competing for more of it. He sighed and lay back. The thumping of our heartbeats had already synchronized, and we weren't even orgasming yet.

He laced his fingers behind his head and chuckled at me. "You are officially invited to help yourself to my entire body," he said, cock twitching and begging me to suck him. *God, he's stunning.* He lifted an eyebrow, daring me to refuse him, but simultaneously hoping my warm, wet mouth was around him already. I grunted, looking at him, and trailed my eyes over his well-defined chest, the sexy dip of his solar plexus down the prominent lines of his abdominal muscles, those thick rifts on each side of his hips leading down to his leaking cock.

Feasting on him with my eyes, I slowly retreated from between his knees.

"Ish, I missed you. Every day without you felt longer than the previous day."

I pounced, swallowing his cock down my throat without warning, shutting him up. He hissed, and I broke eye contact as I closed mine. Stars swam behind my eyelids as I tasted more of him.

"That's it, Ish. Suck me, I'm yours," he said from somewhere far away while gripping my locks and not letting go. "I waited for you for thirty years."

I stopped sucking. "You never asked Gugusan or another man to suck or fuck you?"

"No, I missed you too much."

"My Kuku."

"Yes, yours."

I pursed my lips, forcing his cock through the smallest warm slick hole. "Oh my god, you are killing me!"

I sucked him as hard as I loved him. Harder with every upward stroke while sliding down with soft, slow motions. Getting his cock engorged to the point of bursting. The sounds I pulled from him were just as satisfying as the taste of his long heavy cock on my tongue. The emotions he poured out with his words were a chaotic crescendo of jubilant euphoria. I resisted the urge to sink my fangs into it. Pre-cum flooded my mouth, coating my throat as I nestled my nose in his blond pubic hair. *I think I found the source of the vanilla bean smell.* I rolled my nose from side to side in it while I groaned. He loved it. I drove him crazier with the rumble of my voice as I purred for him. If I kept this up, he would shoot directly down my throat, not giving me a mouthful. I worked for it and wanted it on my tongue where I could taste it for as long as I wanted before swallowing. Slowly, I pulled back while he swore obscenely. Threatening me with death and rape if I stopped.

I pulled off him, letting his cock plop out of my mouth. I didn't take my gaze off him, waiting for him to open his eyes to give me his best *what the fuck* face.

He lifted his head, eyes blazing with fiery lust, while I nestled myself on my elbows between his knees. He looked dazed.

I sucked my forefinger and middle finger into my mouth, showing him what I planned to do with them. He bent his knees, opening his ass up for the intrusion.

"Go ahead, suck and fuck me. That's my last invitation," he grunted and lay back down again.

"My Kuku, do you trust me?" I asked, and his head shot up in question. "Of course I do, and can we talk about this another time, I was about to blow, for fuck's sake."

"May I bite you?" I asked, shaking with the need to taste as much of him as I could.

"Where? On my cock or in my groin?"

"Everywhere? Or is that too much?"

"Ish, get your fangs wet with my blood and cum. I fucking beg you to bite as much of me as you want. Eat me up, but make me cum, please!" He fisted my hair and pushed me back down, showing me exactly where he wanted me and my mouth.

I sucked the head of his cock down and slid my fangs into the rim of his cockhead while I plunged my fingers deep into his ass.

"Fuuuuck, you sick motherfucking, beautiful fucking, fuuuck!" He howled and spurted his seed onto my waiting tongue.

The mix of his body fluids ignited an explosion of colorful sensations all around and inside me.

An hour later, both of us were satiated. I snuggled against his chest for comfort. "What do you think is going to happen tomorrow?" he asked, his voice laced with trepidation. He was still buried deep inside me, and I let out a heavy sigh, trying to push away the thoughts of the possibility of dreadful things about to happen.

"I don't know, but I'm not ready for a fight. I'm tired of fighting and surviving. I have you now, and that is all I ever wanted. I suggest we rest, and leave in the morning to return to exactly where and when we left Phoenix. Then ask Eryn for help," I replied, fearing the unknown and that Gugusan and Eryn weren't going to miraculously come up with a plan to make peace with the Angels and Sables that kept me prisoner. The fear of Apsu turning up is something I wasn't ready to face either.

As I'd marked his body earlier, our connection grew deeper and stronger, but now the longer we lay here sharing our innermost thoughts, the more real our love amidst the coming danger grew. Since we'd met, we had always been rushing somewhere, and I cherished just being here with him in the now. I knew after surviving thirty years in the jungle, he saw the mountain as his home. I saw the emotional connection, the fondness, and, of course, the difficult concern about meeting with the Birdmen. He didn't trust them, he had been keeping his distance, hating them for what they had done to me. He'd thought I was dead, he found me, only to lose me again, as I lost him. Maybe it's a good thing like Gugusan said. We might as well accept that this is our home. But that gnawing feeling was still present. I knew what that meant. We had to go back to Phoenix, to warn them. Before we go with the San, to talk to those bloody Birdmen. My mind was an open book to my Kuku, and it felt like lifting centuries' worth of burdens off my shoulders. Just to be with him, to be loved and accepted.

"Peter," I whispered just before falling asleep.

"Hmmm."

"I'm worried about Apsu."

"I know. We'll talk with Gugusan tomorrow. I haven't seen Phoenix in thirty years, I'd love a new pair of underwear and jeans. Rest now, you are not fully healed."

CHAPTER 63

# DON'T SCREAM

*"I WOULD HAVE SAID GOOD MORNING IF I DIDN'T KNOW BETTER, BUT I DO.*

*It's now six a.m.*

*I guess we're back to hiding under the water and not facing the brightness of day.*

*Did you know that the original inventor and builder of the first cuckoo clock is unknown?*

*But did you also know in 1650 A.D. the Jesuit scholar Athanasius Kircher wrote Musurgia Universalis, The Universal Musical Art, of the Great Art of Consonance and Dissonance? It was a compendium of ancient and contemporary thinking about music, its production, and its effects. It explored how the mathematical aspects of music, like harmony and dissonance, relate to health and evil in a harmonious world. He also wrote two other books, The Magnes sive de Arte Magnetica which set out the secret underlying coherence of the universe, and Ars Magna Lucis et Umbrae which explored the ways of knowledge and enlightenment.*

*What is interesting is that these works contain the first documented description—in words and pictures—of how mechanical cuckoo clocks work.*

*On that timely note, breakfast is served until eight a.m.*

*Hope you have a day of wonder and discovery!"*

**ISHTAR**
>
> **2147 A.D. (95 A.T.)**
> **Several hours after Ish and Peter fled the inquisition**
> **Phoenix, underwater glass dome city**
> **Earth**

Silence filled the room until the shock wore off. Followed by gasps and various creative exclamatory words, accompanied by three howling Anubis. Cian had had some time to recover from his initial shock, after meeting us outside. He put two fingers in his mouth and whistled. When he came to collect us earlier, he had taken one wordless look at Peter, and covered him with the sheet we'd requested when we called him. He brought us straight here, to Ivan and Eryn's apartment.

It was the largest apartment in Phoenix and far from the main population. Their extra-large home and the key to the city were gifts from the Phoenicians after Eryn, Ivan, and Cian had wrapped the entire city inside protective layers. A living, breathing shell, much like an oyster's that protects Phoenix against the natural elements beneath the melted icy ocean waters.

After pushing Cian out of their throuple, Cian and Rotty had moved out when Eryn and Ivan had mated, or married as the humans call it. Understandably, Cian had taken that badly. He had lost his friend and twin.

Since drama was his default reaction to any stressor, I understood why he had invested all his focus on getting to the moon, where Barkor was born and survived, oblivious to him. After saving Barkor and the leftover humans from Grayrak, their mating bond made Cian understand the physical attraction and emotional pull between destined couples and why Eryn and Ivan had mated. Since then, Cian and Barkor hadn't spent more than a few minutes apart. How their lovemaking worked for them, no one, but them knew. Both were as muscled and stubborn as oxen, and I'm sure if it wasn't for the pull between mates, they would have lived as far away from each other as possible. Now, the two held hands and walked around as one unit of trouble and drama. If darkness was colorful, they were it.

"And what is this? Another one of your weird experiments?" Eryn asked me mind-to-mind while smiling back at a blushing Peter.

Ivan beamed and gave a small bow to Peter. "Welcome to our home. Oh my, Peter, you have grown into your own," he said, then turned to me, scowling—as if it was my doing.

"Ish, this is puzzling," Eryn said to me while inspecting Peter's wings up and down by walking around him.

My teeth were chattering, I was hungry, and I hugged myself to warm up. The little blood I had taken from Peter wasn't enough. I needed much more blood to recover and fully heal. Lots of it. My energy and strength required at least two to three human donors. But I didn't want Peter to think what he offered me last night was not enough.

*Could you please invite Juandre and Andrew over? I need to ask them something*, I asked Eryn mentally.

I saw him realize why after he took one look at me. He cleared his throat. "Please excuse me while I'm making a phone call."

"Look at you, Ish," Barkor said with a tad more sympathy, and surprised me with a one-armed hug. "Bringing home strays." *So not sympathy, but sarcasm.* Barkor tapped his short club on the table in front of me. Like Cian, he had a way of turning any problem into a melodramatic situation.

"Barkor, don't let these wayward children of mine influence you to the point of stupidity. This is Peter. My Peter. My Kuku. If you call him a stray once more..." I said, feeling proud of my childish, witty comeback, while experiencing the worst case of starvation.

"I was teasing. Look at you. Were you enjoying a vacation in the sun? You are about to crumble into ash. I've never seen you like this," Barkor said, shaking his head at me. I was sure Juandre and Andrew had something to do with Barkor's extensive knowledge of me and my sun allergy, as Andrew called it. Those two can't keep a secret. They couldn't wait to tell the world they were different. Vampires, according to Juandre.

Cian came to Barkor's rescue. "You look like you should be dead already. I'm too scared to touch you."

"Yeah, one loud fart and you'd puff into moon dust." Barkor cracked up, waving his weapon in the air. I wasn't arguing with that point. I felt like it. "Your Peter and I haven't spent enough time together. We hardly know each other," Barkor said and turned to Cian for further supportive taunting.

"Yeah, Peter, you have doubled in size," Cian said, then narrowed his eyes at me. "What else has doubled and why do you call us children? Since when are we your children?" Cian asked, pinning me with that Zelk eye stare. I was seconds from falling backward.

I cleared my throat and gave him a pointed look by attempting to lift my right eyebrow in question. It didn't even twitch. "You are Anunnaki and of my bloodline, are you not? My father is your grandfather, and your children will be my grandchildren, so yes, I'm your father, or at least one of your fathers, and you are my children."

Now that Peter's wings have been revealed, I must continue telling them about the apple and Apsu. I coughed, trying to collect more spit in my dry mouth. I gulped the nerves and discomfort down my itchy dry throat. "Hmmm, we are here to discuss crucial issues."

As if choreographed, they swung their attention between Peter and me, so I pushed on. "The apple."

"Yeah, the one Peter stole," Ivan said accusingly.

I gave a shameful smile, and Peter dropped his chin to his chest. "Yes, that apple. We took it back, but unfortunately to the wrong time and place. There is a chance that my father survived and is on his way."

Peter lifted his head bravely under their scrutiny. "I heard the same thing being said by the Fates," he added, and I wondered if he was going to tell them about his thirty years lost in the jungle, so I interjected to prevent an information overload.

"We brought it home, to my home, to Babylon." I lifted my palms. "Just let me talk please." Cian pressed his lips into a thin line. Barkor thrust his chest out. Ivan sighed.

I inhaled. "But because I manipulated the realities, when we got rid of the Zelk, we crisscrossed timelines, and I never factored that issue into my calculations."

"What the fuck, Ish?" Cian, Barkor, and Ivan asked simultaneously.

Peter's wings opened, and I sensed a violent outburst coming. "Hey, you don't talk to Ish like that. He has done everything to help you as best he could. You were all smiling when Cian landed the Warship Horizon filled with your humans, and no Zelk was in sight."

"I was not smiling!" Cian said, pushing his chest out and fist-thumping it. "I fucking told you something weird was happening. Didn't I say these were not my people?" he asked Barkor, who confirmed it with a few more nods than necessary. "You expected us just to accept that they were. I fucking told you they were different. Look at these stupid silver mesh suits and flip-flops. I fucking knew it!"

"Cian, unfortunately, I can't undo any of it. If I do, anything from the Zelk falling out of the sky to Juandre and Andrew dying can happen." I rubbed my forehead. "Scarabs, all of you could disappear in front of my eyes. If we continue on this timeline, and if I don't bring that apple back from Babylon, then Phoenix, you, and everything here will disappear!" I pointed to Peter. "If we bring it back, the timeline, the world filled with beings like Peter, will disappear. Yes, we could have gone and brought it back, but this place is where Peter and I feel at home." I paused to give them a second. A second for the information to sink in. I wanted them to understand the magnitude of our dilemma.

"We are in a situation where we have to choose and we can't. If we choose wrong my father is still a very real possibility. He is not something you want to come across. You are my blood, and the whole of Phoenix is yours. By default, I should care about saving this place, even if it sounds to me like the Fates wanted us close to them. You are my future, but somehow I've put you in the past when I crossed over and handed the apple over to the timeline you did not originate from. Where it was discovered by my father." I searched Peter's face for doubt or surprise, but I saw nothing but stoic support. "Don't ask me how the Fates and that apple are connected. I don't know. All I know is that if I don't bring it back, the world of Angels and Sables continues, without Phoenix and all of us."

"So what I'm hearing is that you can't choose and that those Angels, Sables, or whatever they are—"

Peter chipped in, "San, they are the San tribe."

Ivan grinned at Peter. "Yeah, them. So they are connected to the Fates, and because we switched timelines, you moved us away from what? One dimension, or reality? Is this maybe Heaven? If we are on the Earth, where are they? What is that place with Angels? Is it another planet?" Ivan asked a very good question.

"Call it what you will, Ivan, but there is more to this. This place was discovered by Ish, by traveling backward in time."

A pinched, unhappy expression washed over Ivan's face as he bulged his fists. Barkor's eyes darted between Peter and me. "How far?" Cian asked.

I cleared my throat. "About twenty-five thousand years."

Cian's eyes bulged, and his jaw dropped in shock. Ivan gasped and clasped his hands over his mouth. Barkor sucked in a breath, "I knew it! This is where you got the food and water from?"

Peter continued before any of them could say anything else. "There is also the matter of the Birdmen games. That's what the San, the indigenous people, Aztec-type precursor people—ancient—like Easter Island ancient, maybe even further back, calls them. Gu is the leader of the San, hence his name is Gugusan. He is a friend of Ish and me and he knows something about all this. He gave me this," Peter bashfully pointed his obsidian blade at them, then continued, "and trained me. He is intelligent, and he is...," I watched as a blush crept over Peter's face and he smiled. I knew Peter thought Gugusan was attractive and respected him. I grabbed Peter's hand and squeezed as Peter continued talking. "The San guard the cave—the mountain where the Fates speak to them. It's a holy place. If it wasn't for Gu, Ish and I couldn't have come back to tell you this today. We are very good friends with them and now sit with this impossible choice. We will choose whatever you choose. Them or us." Tears collected in Peter's eyes and his emotional turmoil was palpable. The smell of wood smoke and sweet roses thickened as the air around Peter charged with somber energy.

Peter had known the San people much longer than he was saying. The room quieted down. Their full attention was on reading Peter's mind. Cian stepped back, eyes wide. Barkor joined him, and the Anubis reacted by lifting their front paws, waiting. Gone was the excitement. Peter gave a futile nod of admission, realizing everyone was reading much more than the room.

Cian's voice broke the silence. Hands reaching for my throat, he shouted. "You mother fucking Anunnaki," and then he lunged at me. "I'm going to strangle you!" Being tired, hungry, and weak in the knees, I stumbled as he overpowered me.

Peter stuck his obsidian short sword under Cian's throat. "You hurt him, you die."

Ivan jumped into the scuffle as Barkor tackled Peter. Arms, legs, hair, spittle, and feathers filled the living room as we rolled and wrestled to be on top.

"If I didn't require sustenance, I would have said this was fun," I grunted and rolled onto Ivan. He kicked me in the nuts and I wobbled back. Peter caught me, but Cian, Ivan, and Barkor fought for first place to strangle me. Peter pulled me by my ankles in an attempt to save me but ended up hurting me. I howled in pain. "Peter, no, my knee!"

Eryn was back, helping me by pulling the frantic Cian and Ivan away. Peter restrained Barkor, and just as I wanted to roll over to catch my breath, Rotty put one enormous paw on my chest and growled. "Okay, down boy," I said in my friendliest Anubis charming voice while gulping air. He wasn't having it. His yellow eyes pinned me and he snarled, saliva dripping, already growing in size. It was a crazy shit and feathers show.

"Thank you, Rotty, for always coming to my defense. You may leave him," Cian ordered, and Rotty let me be.

"Everyone, calm the fuck down. I leave for one second and you are at each other's throats. Make up and be nice to Ishtar. He needs help. Can't you see he is about to expire?" Eryn said over his shoulder, trying for a second time to reach Juandre and Andrew.

"Motherfucker," Cian and Barkor said, shaking their heads at me. Distraught, I fought the appearance of tears in my eyes. With my smashed-in kneecap worse than before, I sat where I was and prepared to grovel.

I took a deep breath, exuding calmness while feeling defeated and at their mercy. "Please, we need your help." A bloody tear rolled over my cheek and I wiped at it—the reality of it all was getting unbearable. "Peter and I don't know what to do," I said and covered my face with the palms of my hands.

"They will help you," Peter said, kicking the linen to the side. He stretched his wings, but the room was too small. The crown of his wings scraped the ceiling. It startled him and he turned, knocking over the last standing framed picture on a small side table next to a couch. I caught it before it hit the floor. A blond curly haired boy laughed up at the camera. I recognized Eryn. He was much younger than when I'd visited him in South Africa, when I brought Rotty, Igor, and Devil to him. I wonder if he had shared this with them. I doubt it. He would have said so. *Eryn and I need a private talk.* My heart melted as sentimentality crushed me. I heaved air into my dehydrated lungs. My chest was tight, and there wasn't enough oxygen in the room. "I need to get out of this place. There are too many emotions. Too many of us are stuffed into this room. Peter, help me. Get me out. I need air!" I said as I struggled to stand.

Cian watched me with his hands on his hips. "Jesus, is he having a panic attack? How can the Anunnaki son of Apsu, the evil world destroyer, have panic attacks?"

"Fuck you, Cian, he was tied up in the sun for two days. They smashed his knee, and he came here to ask for help, but you are trying to kill him. Of course, he is having a panic attack." Peter pushed me back onto the couch. Then, he sat on his heels beside me and offered his wrist. "Here, take more blood from me."

I took Peter's arm and laid it on my lap. "No, thank you my Kuku." He looked worried, and I smiled at him, bursting with love for him.

Just then, Eryn said, "Yeah, Drew. Please bring your husband to our place. I have someone here who needs your kind of sustenance. Yes. Blood. Hmmm, yes, he is back and not in good shape. Okay, yes. Thank you, he will appreciate that. Oh, and tell Juandre not to scream or yell when he sees Peter. Hmmm, yes, he has wings. How did you know? Oh. No need to explain further. Yup, better to prepare Juandre if he doesn't know, hmmm. Thanks, yes, tell him not to make a show of this, please. Okay, thanks, Drew." I heard a chuckle as he returned from where he made the call.

"They are on their way. I hear and see you feel a bit cramped inside our home. I wish I could see how you fly," he told Peter. Right away, the tension in the room evaporated. Cian, Ivan, and Barkor agreed, "Yes, we would all like to see you fly," they said, putting the pillows back on the couches and cleaning the mess. I followed them with my eyes, concentrating on something other than my need to breathe.

"Sorry. My wings are too big for your home. You can see me fly when we go outside. And you can even see more like me when we take you to this place and time. Then you'll understand why we struggle to choose sides."

"Take us there?" Ivan asked.

Peter helped me to get more comfortable with my knee and pulled a chair closer so he could sit on it. "Yes, but I warn you, as Gugusan warned me. Those Birdmen will want to have you. You are beautiful and godlike, with one look at you, they will want you. Gugusan told me they live to bask in the sun, have sex all day, and have tournaments. They settle all their conflicts with these games."

"Yes, but remind me again, first, why do we want to go to a place that would be dangerous, and second, why would we choose them over our people? I say forget about them. Bring the apple here. If Apsu goes there, fine, if he comes here, we will deal with him," Barkor said.

"I want to talk to their leader. Can you take us to him without hindrance?" Eryn asked. His eyes sparkled with intelligence.

"I agree," Ivan added eagerly. "If we have some kind of truce we could help them and they could help us."

Barkor scratched his beard deep in thought. "That sounds better than sacrificing one choice—one place for the other. These games—we would have to play. Maybe they will listen if we are playing their game," he said in a quiet voice.

"That's a good idea. If we challenge them and win, they will have to listen. Ishtar, will we see or hear the Fates? Could we use that to sway them?" Ivan asked, gazing at Peter's wings. He stretched an arm out as if to touch my Kuku. "May I?" he asked, enthralled.

"Yes, you may," said Peter with a low and shy tone in his voice. It grated on my nerves and a possessive irritation like I've never known, flared up inside me. "Yes and no, the Fates are not corporeal. Their voice is audible in certain areas. We will show you," Peter explained as everyone in the room frowned in disbelief and glanced around as if searching for answers. "Also, the Birdmen don't have leaders. Gugusan says they fight every day about something. That is what they do. Anytime they decide to choose a leader, someone challenges him. It is a constant battle among themselves. A way of living. Their culture. The only ones living in peace are the San led by my friend Gu, deep in the jungle. They helped us, unfortunately, the Fates told Ish to take the apple home, and he thought home was Babylon," Peter said, sticking his hands deep into his pants pockets and pulling his shoulders up. Thankfully, he wasn't telling them he was lost in the jungle for thirty years. "We were thinking, maybe Eryn can help us think of a way to save them. Maybe bring them here. Maybe convince them somehow, while we go and bring the apple here."

"I would have to transport all of us on my small ship. Eryn, you, Ivan, Cian, and Barkor can keep them busy," I said and turned to Peter. "You would have to go get the apple with me."

"How sure are you this place is the only place on this planet? Could it be that there is already something else in its future? Can't you jump and go see?" Barkor asked.

"I can't, and to be honest, I'm too scared to do it. One wrong jump and I may lose all of you," I said, breaking eye contact and inspecting the small white feathers on the tiled floor, too embarrassed to look up.

"We don't have a fucking choice, do we?" Cian said. There was a heavy silence, so I lifted my head to see what it was about. Cian had his arms crossed as he watched his brother stroking Peter's wings. Peter shivered and Eryn stepped in.

"Okay, baby, enough admiring the wings." I heard no jealousy in his voice. More as if he was protecting Peter. He smiled and Peter tucked his wings deeper by folding one over the other. The crescent-horned tips hung over his head like a halo.

Ivan turned to Eryn. "If Peter is an Angel and let's say we bring them here, do we leave the Fates there, and what then? Shouldn't God and the Angels be in one place?" Eryn was pulling his shoulders up to his ears. Peter crossed his arms and widened his stance. I could see Eryn was already calculating an answer to our predicament.

"It sounds to me, wherever the apple is, is where the Fates are," Peter answered.

"Ivan, stop that. You are making all of us uncomfortable. What is wrong with you?" Cian said, ticked off at his brother, shaking his head at Ivan still closely admiring my Kuku's feathers.

"It was a wild guess and I'm starting to put some stories we were told as children together. How do you sleep? Can you sit? Aren't they in your way the whole time?" Ivan asked Peter.

"Are your arms and legs in your way when you sleep?" Peter grunted.

"Sorry, I didn't mean to sound like I was interrogating you. I find you fascinating. I think you are beautiful. Can you turn around? I want to see your back, please."

Peter gave Ivan a stern fuck-off look and kept his feet firmly planted.

Silence.

Ivan seemed to register the uncomfortable status in the room. "I'm sorry. Forgive me. I'm usually in control of myself. I'm being insensitive. This is not how I normally act when sexy as fuck feathered beings enter my home. Your muscled body and eight-pack are impressive, but Eryn's my man, so I probably should stop thinking of you as cookies and dough I want to dunk into orange juice and suck on it. Why do you smell so yummy, like cupcakes and cookies?"

Cian coughed. Rotty, Igor, and Devil yipped. Eryn was busy picking his jaw up from the floor. Ivan was acting out of character. It seemed my Angel had tripped and flipped some kind of lustful trigger response in him. To reduce the sexual tension and to focus their attention on something other than my sexy man, my winged creature, my angel, my mate, *mine*, I clapped my hands twice, snapping all of them from wherever their minds had gone.

Eryn gave me a questioning look and Cian looked taken aback. "Children, please focus. Peter is mine, and mine alone. When we go to that place and time, you will see thousands of them. But this one is mine," I said and winked at Peter.

"Now I want to go there," Ivan said.

Just then, the front doorbell rang. "I will get it. It's Andrew and Juandre. Please. If you will?" Eryn gestured for me to accompany him. My limbs were stiff and sore. I moved across the room like an old man as my mouth salivated for blood.

"Well, hello, Ishtar, my friend," Juandre exclaimed, bursting inside as the door slid open. "We hear you need emergency feeding," he said, and I perked up, happy to hear his voice. "Bear, give him his lunch box."

"Hello, Ish." Andrew hugged me with one arm while handing me a big container. I smelled the blood and my belly did acrobatic flips. I couldn't wait to taste the thick red liquid, even if it wasn't Peter's. I could feast on him again later. But now I'm going to gorge, fully recover, and save my people.

"Thank you for coming and bringing me food. I've been injured and although Peter has already fed me, I need much more and he needs his strength. I doubt he would like it if I fed on anyone but him in this room."

"No problem, it's blood donated by the residents. When they heard we were vampires, bags of the stuff started piling up in front of our door. I guess they are scared that we would roam the halls sucking them dry." He cackled. I don't know why the humans call the royal Anunnaki courtesans vampires, but Juandre likes the name, so I don't object. I didn't have the strength for more conversation.

I took the box and held it possessively against my chest. "Where can I feed?" I asked Eryn, who smiled and hugged the newcomers. It seemed he liked Juandre and Andrew as much as I did.

"Go into the guest bedroom." Eryn pointed down the hallway. "The first one on the right."

I bowed, showing my appreciation. "Thank you," I said. I waved to Peter, showing him I was going to the back.

"Yes, love, go take care of yourself," Peter said, and his somber expression morphed into friendly relief. I turned and made my way to the room.

In the background, I heard Juandre exclaim, "Color my Roman Catholic gay ass pink! Angels fucking exist!"

I opened the blue and white box. It seemed it was cooling the blood and keeping it from going stale. The dark amber fluid jiggled as if teasing me. I took one squashy pouch out, inspecting it. How did they get it out of the bag? My stomach growled at me to hurry while I inspected the translucent covering.

*There are ten bags packed inside for you. Just bite into them and suck*, Andrew spoke into my mind. I opened my mouth and sank my teeth into it—sucking one after the other dry. After seven bags, I was stuffed and already gaining strength. I felt immediately warmer while my knee and other injuries healed within minutes. I finished the last three, collected the empty containers, and packed them back into the cooler, planning to take them back to Andrew and Juandre. But as I turned to leave, Eryn blocked the door. His eyes bored into me, serious and all-knowing. I gulped down a nervous knot in my throat.

He came inside and closed the door behind him. I inhaled quick, short breaths nervously and stepped back. Eryn wouldn't hurt an innocent fly, but I wasn't without blame. The power he carried pushed memories of my father to the forefront of my mind.

"I want to talk to you." He always smiled, but he wasn't smiling now. His golden-green eyes were pinning me. I felt guilty and nervous as if I was being judged.

*It's your guilty conscience*, he said into my mind, reading me in the most uncomfortable kind of way. I was careful around him because I knew what he was capable of. But what freaked me out most was his authoritative but friendly demeanor. Like I wanted to tell him all my secrets without him asking for them. I felt guilty and wanted to spill it all.

I put the box down and sat on the edge of the bed, exhaling. I heard Peter talking to the others. Those elongated pupils enlarged as Eryn seemed to look right through me.

Someone whistled, and Cian said, "We have to let Father and the others know." His voice thundered down the hallway.

"The whole Leadership Team would want to know. We can't just leave and not say anything. Let's call at least one of them. I'd suggest calling Mika. He would have insight into what to do first," I heard Peter say. I was so proud of him. I closed my eyes and smiled dreamily, then remembered Eryn was still assessing me. I looked at him and shrugged.

"Yes, but I think Brad is the best person to plan stealth attacks and rescue missions. Remember, he is a real general, and he led the team that rescued us from the mines in South Africa," Ivan said.

"I agree. Brad is the best person for the job," Juandre added.

Eryn opened the door and said, "If Mika and Brad are involved and in the know, then we might as well get Connor and Bryan too." He closed the door and then turned back to me. "Sorry, Ish, we have to plan better. It is unwise not to use yours and Peter's inside information and plan an extraction without causing a war on their world. I'm worried about us succeeding and their world disappearing. We need to do this so both our worlds survive. I can't destroy an entire world to save ourselves."

"I agree. I knew you would understand. But as soon as we involve the leadership, others will see Peter and this can become one big dilemma. I don't have time to gather for an assembly," I said and Eryn chuckled, knowing exactly what I was talking about. Every time something big was happening in Phoenix, or a vote had to be cast, all the residents congregated as they did when I was questioned.

"This is something bigger than just us," Eryn said to me.

Then switched to the local telepathic frequency in the apartment.

*For example, I don't think our biggest problem is about the apple at all. I understand the switching of timelines and us not being born, because Apsu would discover the information hidden inside the apple. No one wants to cease to exist or cause others harm—do I understand your concerns correctly? I'm thinking, maybe we can somehow exist in both worlds simultaneously. Ivan was correct when he asked about Heaven. I remember when my friend Joshua read from his history book when humans and Angels fell in love. They walked among them. But it was frowned upon because their children were half human and half Angel. Maybe it's possible to coexist and we don't have to live apart.*

Although I knew Eryn wasn't my father, the natural reaction to defend or fight I carried as a child seemed like it never disappeared.

Crossing his arms, he widened his stance. "Tell me everything about this place, no matter how small or insignificant you think it is. I will go into your mind and see what you saw. Is that allowed, may I? It will help us prepare a strategy." Eryn looked at me like the first time we met in Grayrak. It felt like thousands of years ago, a thousand jumps, but in this reality, it was only two years past. He uncrossed his arms and like that first day we met, he took my hands and looked at me, inside of me. It felt awkward and intensely intimate. I was anxious and guarded, although I trusted and respected him. He was the strongest, most powerful being and he possessed a silent grounding pull. Like the gravity of a dangerous black hole. A constant silent surveillance. Observing while allowing everyone around him to just be themselves. Never forcing anything, no matter what I knew, he knew already what the outcome would be. He was calculating, weighing, and appreciating. He was all those things.

"We will go with you and help you." He reassured me. All the tension I've been carrying drained from me. We were safe and there was hope of not doing this alone anymore.

I blew out a long breath and said, "Thank you. Whatever you suggest, we are fully cooperating." I closed my eyes and invited him inside my mind, where I showed him everything I saw and knew about the place I thought was paradise.

A few minutes later Eryn sighed and said, "Ishtar, thank you for showing me. I see there is so much more. Now, show me how your father and I both occupy the same space in your mind." He sat down on the floor in front of me. "If I cross paths with him, I want to know what I'm up against. Unlock your mind fully and show me."

I blinked wordlessly. *The most powerful being I've ever come across is sitting on the floor.* Eryn was calm and he cared about me. He nonchalantly maneuvered his tree stumps of legs so gracefully. Back straight while focusing all his attention solely on me. Never letting go of my hands.

So I showed and told the king sitting on the floor everything.

An hour later, the interrogation into my psyche was complete. I felt light, rejuvenated, and mega unloaded. Eryn went so far as to forgive me for everything I felt guilty for and insisted I forgive myself too. After that we rejoined the others in the living room, answering questions until Ivan extended their hospitality, inviting us for a meal.

Cian, Barkor, Juandre, and Andrew left. Eryn and Ivan fed us while listening to Peter and me telling them about the San tribe. Their two Anubis, Igor and Devil, kept us under their watch. Whether by an unspoken command or just the need to monitor us, we didn't know. They sat straight up, watching every move we made, which made us so uncomfortable that we couldn't wait to get out of the apartment to meet with Brad and the Leadership Team. Our meeting with the Leadership Team went as I expected. Lots of questions, an hour of protests, and lengthy explanations of how disappointed they were, but it was rounded off with unfailing support and understanding. Brad requested someone stay behind to protect them. Juandre and Andrew volunteered, and I agreed, because those two produced more trouble than solutions. No one voiced that, but we all thought it, Juandre and Andrew included.

## 24 970 B.C.

### The San village in the jungle

Miraculously, for once, I appeared to be the royal time traveler I was. With Lasitor's help, we didn't crash but parked atop the mountain where I had crash-landed a few times before—and I'm not sharing that. Another remarkable thing was that I exactly knew when and where we were this time.

I waited until the last of our visitors were outside, then I hung onto the doorframe, gazing out to where Peter was pointing and describing what the Birdman city and the arena looked like. Gugusan joined us, and he explained the lay of the land while drawing a map on the ground. I watched my Kuku with fondness.

Last night, I told Peter that Elijah was what Anunnaki called an Igigi. I wondered if he knew that Gugusan was just like Elijah. I needed to talk with all of them, there were things they should know but there wasn't time, there was never time, even though I had a time machine. Looking at him and Gugusan interact made everything around us fuzzy.

Peter was my single point of focus. The way he spoke about this place told me that he thought of it as home. As they animatedly pointed while he explained to the warriors, I stepped closer, listening to where the forested world below bled out beyond the valley. I never thought or rather, I was never sober enough to think there could be someone living outside the jungle. The warriors listened attentively, nodding and asking questions while Gugusan jumped onto a boulder that stood out like a jagged tooth from the ridge.

"See there? That is where the river widens and its mouth splits again to cut through the cliffs with the hanging city of the Angels and Sables." Like the others, I followed Gugusan and Peter's line of sight and saw how it towered through the veil of thick mist drifting inland from the sea to the shoreline hiding it.

I shook my head. "I never knew it was there, my Kuku," I said while watching Gugusan.

Eryn turned from side to side as if surveying and committing it all to memory. He was deep in thought. I tried listening in on his mind working, but I couldn't hear anything. I should have let him be, but he caught my attention again when he jumped three more boulders over. It looked like he couldn't believe what he was seeing. His silhouette against the backdrop of stars reminded me so much of my brothers. The outline of his hair tied up and away, his beard braided in three little braids below his chin. His strong, muscled body was bigger than mine. As if knowing I was watching him, he turned to me. I couldn't see his eyes or expression from this distance, but I felt the serious concern. "Ish, this place, these mountains, and where you say they held you prisoner, does it feel like you have been here before?" he asked, breaking the silence between our minds.

To narrow the distance between us, I climbed on the large rock he had first jumped on. I had to put much more effort into it to reach the top. "Always. I had dreams about this place before I came here. Before I met you. Before I met Peter. I visited and came here many times, searching. I think it's because of that, that I started to feel I never left the place at all."

"Hmmm," he said and sniffed the air.

"Why? What are you stewing about?"

"I don't know yet. Let's get back to the others." He wasn't divulging his thoughts. He wasn't a big talker, but I had the feeling Eryn thought about bigger things and until he had spoken to Gugusan and the Birdmen, he wasn't verbalizing them. I turned and heaved a deep shaky breath and joined the others by jumping in front of them onto the familiar wet grassy ground. The air was thick with foreboding, the weight of the negotiations dragging my mood deeper into cumbersome despair. My gut felt as if thousands of snakes were crawling inside it—Apsu was bugging me.

We agreed that Peter, Gugusan, and his men would go ahead to schmooze Luci to join us in the negotiations. A bittersweet feeling lingered inside me. I feared failure, causing shallow breaths and tightness in my throat. However, amidst the apprehension, I was confident that Gugusan's allegiance would mean we had already convinced half of the Birdmen. Or so we hoped after Peter assured us he had found no other signs of life for hundreds of miles when he'd searched for me.

I watched as his wings reflected the moonlight before they vanished behind the tree-tops at the mountain's base.

"Good luck," I grunted. I was a hopeful skeptic about the planned negotiations.

I couldn't shake the feeling that leaving Phoenix with Peter after my trial was a reckless decision. And now, as we prepared for what lay ahead, I struggled to control my urge to go back in time and fix everything—never bring Peter here, never crash, and never lose that apple. Deep down, I knew it wasn't that simple. I had become obsessed with thinking that the next jump would be the last one, but as Ivan had emphasized earlier over a plate of pancakes, addiction was an illness of the mind. He explained that the brain is like an untrained computer and unless you teach it to take the route never taken, and make it work, your brain would convince itself to default, to do things it has tried and succeeded with once, ignoring all the other times it has failed after that. Life itself changes constantly and your brain functions outside of those probabilities unless you force it to take notice. I concluded that one jump was too many and a thousand will never be enough to fix the shit I have caused. His statement hit home and since then, every time the thought of jumping surfaced, I would roll my eyes and reprimand myself. Now that I recognize the idiotic thought pattern, I think I understand the reason why Lasitor had warned me that I should never serve my own needs, only the needs of others, and change only two things because those things will turn into uncountable changes in the future. By saving Juandre and Andrew and hoarding whiskey, all this has happened.

But, today isn't about me, it's about not one, but two realities. I promised Eryn to stay in the here and now. Chances of me changing things may mean that one of them disappears or worse—dies. Retrieving the apple was not going to be easy. Eryn wanted to see more before we decide what to do and how we were going to move forward.

For now, the plan was simple. Focus on escorting Eryn, Ivan, Cian, and Barkor down the mountain while Peter accompanies Gugusan and his army without making a big fuss and revealing our stealth approach.

"Don't worry, my friend, Peter will be fine," Eryn said. He bent and cracked his spine this way and that. They had been tightly packed inside the machine and the Brawl never complained. He leaned closer to Ivan and wrapped his arms around his husband. "Oh, sweet lollipops, Ivan, I can't believe how much I missed this. I swear, if we have time, I'm going to rip our clothes off and fuck you in the mud." Eryn chuckled into Ivan's ear.

"Hold on to that promise, my big Brawl. I would like nothing more than to do that with you. A roll in the mud would be so much more fun than fucking in zero gravity.,"

Ivan whispered, but we could hear every word they said. He lifted his hands above his head, joining his husband in stretching the kinks out of their limbs.

"I'm so thankful you came with us." I turned, showing respect by giving them a small bow.

"Ish, stop thanking us. We wanted to see this place too. I'm sure, if it was us, you would've done the same, even if you had to shit gold bricks doing so," Cian said, holding Barkor's hand. They are two giants with the tenderest caring hearts. Their hands might as well be glued to each other.

I pointed to the footpath I was familiar with. "There, that's the way down the mountain. It passes the cave where the rock paintings I told you about are. That's where I found the apple and the Fates spoke to me. We can go that way," I said to them. "Lasitor, please shut the door. Open it only for one of us. You have the coordinates saved?"

"Yes, I do, sir, and I will…" Lasitor answered as the door shut, cutting his sentence short. I turned to the others.

"Lead the way." Eryn pointed with his spear. Ivan and Cian carried their golden swords on their backs. The gold sang to me, making me miss my ancient Egyptian swords. At a slow run, we moved through the dense forest. My heart pounded in my chest. As we approached the clearing where the entrance to the opening of the cave was, I hesitated for a moment, unsure if I should enter because I thought of this place as holy or something. But we were here to break the cycle. To save our worlds. There wasn't time for hesitation. I had to show Eryn everything. Our plan wasn't solidified.

Eryn gave me a supportive tap on the back. I stooped my neck and then led the way.

"What are we looking for?" Ivan asked, and I ignored him as I entered the cave and waved them inside. Hand-forged decorative torches lit the cavern.

I gestured towards the rock. "This is the spot where I found the apple and the Fates spoke to me." Their gazes followed my hand to the pointy rock pillar and then to the hieroglyphs depicting two stick figures. Two men. Us. Me and Peter.

"Hello," I called and hoped the Fates answered me and revealed themselves. "Talk to us, please." I was feeling dumber by the second. "I guess it wouldn't be that easy," I said, shrugging and kicking at the dirt.

"No, it never is that easy," Cian answered.

Barkor laid a hand on my shoulder. "Don't worry, Ish, we believe you."

"So you didn't know it was you and Peter who brought the apple here the first time?" Eryn asked, going down on his hands and knees to carefully brush away the dirt I had kicked at. I grimaced, not knowing what he was searching for.

"Gugusan said he kept it here for me." My voice echoed in the cave. Some birds took flight deeper into the blackness. "I counted on you meeting the Fates."

"Something tells me they would clear up a lot of questions for us," Ivan commented while reading the ancient texts.

"I have no clue how to summon them. I found closing my eyes and concentrating on them helps. I never get a reply when I initiate contact. They speak to me at their convenience. Sometimes I dream I was here, but I think it is my subconscious trying to make sense of my reality." I raked my fingers through my hair. "It can't be my imagination. Peter said he heard them too."

"I wonder if this is where their voice originates from," Eryn said again, carefully digging with his sword and scraping the unearthed pieces of rock and sand away. I frowned, rubbing the back of my neck. *What is he doing?*

"I would like to speak to your Fates. I need to confirm a theory," Eryn mumbled. I kneeled next to him. Underneath the cave floor, Eryn revealed intertwined dead calcified roots sprouting up into the rock face that wrapped around and bored into the stone, carved like an obelisk, where I had found the apple.

"What is this?" I asked.

"It's a network, an old one. Plants transfer water, nitrogen, carbon, and other minerals like this on forest floors. That's how they survive and communicate," Ivan explained.

"I didn't know plants communicate."

"They do, all living things communicate. It is called mycelium—tiny threads that form a mycorrhizal network, like the internet, only this is a jungle network." Eryn stood up and brushed off his hands, the whole process of watching him was interesting. He glared into the depths of the cavern. I followed his line of sight, searching for those birds or any signs of life on the path leading deeper into the unknown. "Is anyone there?" Eryn called out. The darkness remained still and silent. "I have a question for you," he tried again, but there was no response.

Cian's fingers traced the ancient etchings on the limestone walls, his eyes scanning each figure with a deep intensity. "I bet you do, Brawl King. We all have questions," he said, breaking the silence.

Barkor shifted uneasily, his gaze lingering on the intricate designs carved into the stone. "What do you mean?" he asked, his tone cautious yet curious.

Eryn's intense gaze locked onto mine. His voice held a hint of frustration and disbelief. "What Ivan's trying to say is, why isn't Ish angry with them? Why are they forcing him to choose between worlds? What makes our world more valuable than theirs?" Eryn then turned and traced his finger along the two-headed snake that slithered alongside a majestic dragon with a forked tongue. "These souls are living, feeling beings like us. And this artwork—it tells stories that we can only begin to imagine. How can we justify erasing their world, their existence, in favor of our own?" The weight of his words hung heavy in the air as we stood in this ancient chamber filled with secrets.

I tilted my head to the side, deciphering his remarks. "What are you saying?"

Eryn leaned in closer, his nose almost touching the complex carvings on the wall.

*Was he smelling them?* "I'm saying that I want to know who these Fates presume they are, to toy with our lives like this." His voice held a mixture of indignation and determination. "The carvings seem to taunt us as if they hold some kind of secret that we are not privy to," he said, and I agreed. It was aggravating, and I couldn't help but share Eryn's sentiment. "Who are these Fates, and why are they meddling in our lives?" Eryn's questions didn't surprise me. I had been thinking the same thing ever since I waited in Grayrak for them to arrive. But I had a feeling he was mulling much bigger things than my mind could comprehend. The air around Eryn seemed to shift and waver, and for a moment I was afraid that I had made a mistake bringing them here. But the grin on Eryn's face assured me he knew what he was planning. I looked at him with reverence. *I'm going to show you I know exactly what happened here. We are breaking the cycle of the apple. It ends here*, he said telepathically to us. *He didn't want the Fates to hear.* "But first things first. Let's go find Peter and Gugusan, they must be well on their way to prepare them by now." Eryn grunted as a pulse of disgust burst out of him. He was harboring and repressing his anger towards the Fates.

They fell into a line behind me so I could lead them further down the mountain.

As we entered the hustle and bustle of the San village, women and children ran to meet us, falling to the ground and whispering to each other as they saw the trio with me.

"We must be a spectacle. Tall, handsome, and carrying weapons made of pure gold," Cian noted.

They fell to their knees. "Ah, fuck, Ah, fuck!" they repeated, lifting their hands to us.

"Are they saying what I think they are saying?" Barkor chortled.

"Unfortunately yes. They caught that the first time I came around. Don't ask me when that was, I have no clue." I smiled at them and gently waved my hands up to tell them to stand.

As they stood, they smiled cheerfully. Looking happy to see me. One of the older women got up, shouting at the children. "Ofrendas, K'a'abet in kaxtik ofrendas yéetel jaanal ti' yuumtsilo'obo." They turned and ran into the nearby huts. We watched them as the women stood to the side when the kids returned with armfuls of pineapples, coconuts, bananas, and corn. One had a small pig on a leash and another a chicken under her arm. They packed everything around our feet and fell to their knees again. "Nukuch yéetel poderosos te' k'ujo'obo', k waye' ti' ten ti' leti'ob. Acepte k ofertas," the older woman said and joined the others placing the palms of her hands in front of her face.

"That's kind of funny." Ivan laughed.

"Big purple frog balls! Do they think you are a god?" Eryn laughed as he climbed over the fruit to go to them. He kneeled, touching them on their heads. "Thank you for the warm welcome. We accept your gifts, but we are not what you think we are. Please get up." He showed them to stand while smiling, nodding his head, and thanking each one of them.

*Ish, I can't believe you let them think you are a god*, he said mind to mind to us.

"Yes they do, and believe me, when I fucked Gugusan, he thought that too. They say Peter and I are gods and that this is our mountain." We all laughed. The children surrounded Eryn, touching him and looking at him while they giggled. He seemed unfazed, allowing their touches and laughing with them as if they shared a secret joke.

After the welcoming had died down, a female stepped forward and told us that Peter and the men had gone ahead and were chasing after Elijah, they said they would meet up with us at the edge of the jungle.

"Máax robó le manzana yéetel corrió ti' le dirección!" she explained furiously and pointed in the direction of the dark underbrush, where a footpath led into the jungle.

I tapped a forefinger on my chin, thinking I might be able to assist. "I can tiptoe out of time and find them," I whispered.

"No!" Eryn stepped into my personal space and looked into my eyes. I saw my distraught eyes staring back at me in their reflection. "No, no time walking or time jumping. Ask them how long ago." He narrowed his eyes. "Ish, is Elijah the dying man I saw briefly in your mind? Who is he?"

"But I have this feeling. Like—fuck, this is hard for me. By stepping out of time, I can follow them at a much faster pace."

Eryn planted his spear into the ground, stepped closer, blocking everyone else from my view. He rested a hand on each of my shoulders. "Ish, listen. We spoke about this. Think. You would once again do this for yourself. Not for us or Peter. You are uncomfortable and worried about Peter, but you are going to make this problem worse."

I blew out a frustrated breath. "I know, but—"

Eryn interrupted me. Shaking his head with a look of sympathy. "Ask them how long ago and in which direction they think they were heading. Ask them where he was running to. Was he going to the city? Ask them," he said sternly, and I heard reason in his voice. I forced myself to calm down and stepped away from him. He was so serious and I didn't want to disappoint my children. I was a warrior. Not a scared boy.

I clasped my fingers together in a subservient prayer position and asked the women Eryn's questions.

"Leti' le nojoch máako' Máax tu bisaj," a short old woman said and pointed again to the footpath. I flapped my arms, asking if they were going to the Angels and Sables. "Da, Eee-li-shaas, da," they answered in unison.

I slapped a flat hand on my forehead and spun around to face Eryn and the others. "She says Elijah ran to warn the Birdmen that we were coming."

"Tell us exactly who the fuck is Elijah?" they asked as if singing in a choir.

*I told you to tell us everything*, Eryn said into my mind.

"It's a long story." I sighed readying myself mentally, I was once more explaining another one of my fuck ups. "Let's say he's a hitchhiker, a stray, I kind of lost along the way."

"A stray? Is this an animal? Maybe an Anubis? How did you lose him?" they all asked, looking at me like I had never searched for them.

I blew out my cheeks and released it. They waited for me to elaborate. I rolled my eyes and chuckled. There was no easy way around this story. "Okay so this is the short version," I pointed back and forth as I explained, "Elijah was wounded and dying next to the road in Babylon, and we helped him. It was Peter's idea to bring him along for modern medical care. He kind of made him think he was an Angel sent by God to take him to Heaven. We stopped at Andrew's place thinking he could take Elijah to a hospital. Andrew took one look at Elijah and dripped blood into his mouth, shutting the door to Elijah's heaven. He accused us of bullshitting him and the two of them ended up having words. Elijah ran off, thinking I was a demon and Peter a lying fallen Angel. By the time Andrew and I reached them, they were already on the ship, fighting. The next moment, the ship jumped, and a few seconds later, it reappeared. They were gone. I jumped inside to reverse jump, but I could never retrace their steps back to the time and place they went. Lasitor didn't know or didn't want to tell me. So after I searched for a while, I decided to join you in Grayrak, and then upon visiting Phoenix, I met Peter before he had grown his wings. After that we jumped to help around, moving Zelk, and turning Andrew, I visited Phoenix, and then I was taken in for questioning by your leadership. Peter stole the apple, and we escaped to the jungle. Which at that time, Peter saved me, after being lost to me for thirty years. And we came to you for help. That's why Peter knows them well. That's why he is attached to these people. Once again, my time-jumping caused more trouble in my future."

Silence and lots of eyebrows in hairlines greeted me after that story.

"What's wrong with you and Peter? And now Andrew is in on it too? You are the two most irresponsible idiots to be handed a fucking time machine," Ivan said, looking down his nose at me.

"Let's just find Peter and Gugusan." Eryn shook his head in disbelief, then threw his hands in the air and laughed. "I'm starting to think Mika was correct by confiscating your ship and keys."

"Believe me, I will gladly hand them over when we are done here."

I checked the coordinates on my tick-tick thing and calibrated it by triangulating it with my ship, this village, and the direction we were planning to go. That way, no matter what, we would always find our way back here. We thanked our welcoming committee and then turned and worked up a slow-paced run into the trees.

# CHAPTER 64
# THE REVELATION



**ISHTAR**
**24 970 B.C.**
**At the foot of the mountain of the Gods**
**In the jungle of Anzulla**
**Earth**

After hours of slicing leaves and whacking insects, we made our way through the jungle. We found an open clearing at the foot of the mountain and rested. Against my judgment, Eryn made a small fire to ward off wild animals. "We shall be seen from hundreds of miles," I said under my breath.

He grasped me firmly on the shoulder. "That won't be a bad thing," he said, and I felt a wave of calmness and rightness pushed into me.

Cian wiped his nose and forehead sideways so vigorously the skin looked like it was blistering and peeling off. "Tell me why the fuck are we camping out and not using our powers so we can hurry—and maybe—fucking hurry up and save the planet? This earthy smell of flowers and grass makes me wish I never came here," Cian said for the third time. Exasperated with himself and the insects—all of nature.

"You said you wanted to go on an adventure. You've become complacent as a super-hero god staying in that underwater deathtrap," I retorted. "I feel sorry for you. You have the power to sing for nature, maybe that's why all the insects love to sit and suck on you. You're their daddy."

Cian was slapping his cheek, scratching himself and making me feel itchy. "Even my ass crack is itching and not in a good way." Cian sneezed at us. "I bet you Peter and that lot are sitting in a hut somewhere, laughing with Gugusan and Elijah. Drinking beer and reading tea leaves, or whatever they do in a jungle for entertainment." Cian wiped his nose and eyes with the back of his hand.

Ivan pushed his sleeves up to his elbows. "You are like our walking bug trap. Like one of those sticky flypaper things. Look, I don't have one mosquito on me," Ivan teased.

Eryn was silent as he exchanged excited glances with us. I felt the connection between all of us energized and growing stronger as he took a deep breath through his nose and began speaking.

"Look at this wonderful place. It's like a paradise. I can walk barefoot and my heart yearns for these luscious green forests. I've never seen so many variations of green. All these plants and insects, not to mention the animals I hear roaring deep in the mountains. It saddens me to think we are thinking about making them disappear from existence simply because we are moving apples around. It's selfish thinking of ourselves as better or more important. Do you think we deserve it more than them? No! I've seen what I needed to see. I'm ready to share my thoughts and conclusion with you. It is only a plan and you can suggest something else or make suggestions. But I think what I have come up with will work for all of us. It's a big and bold move. But I know we can do it if all of us work together." I felt the excitement and determination radiating from Eryn. I looked around, reading the other attentive faces, and I knew that with his leadership, we could accomplish anything.

He used the tip of his spear to draw six circles on the ground. *Where was he going with this?*

"What I suggest is to bring our worlds together." He drew one bigger circle in the middle of those other circles. "I've started to compare the things I read in that book, the Bible of Joshua. I compared it to what happened and what was foretold about Earth's history. The Bible explicitly teaches that Elijah's prophecy would find its primary fulfillment at the end of time. We thought that was when the Earth had flooded. Joshua drove me crazy by reading those scriptures where the prophet Malachi says God says, *Behold, I send my messenger, and he will prepare the way before me.* The Disciples of the Anunnaki always thought it was them and that they were restoring all things to bring the gods of the heavens to live with them and to walk among them. But since I heard Elijah was here, a big piece of the puzzle slotted into place. I realized he might be the key evidence I needed. However, given the advanced technology we already have, I suggest we move the Phoenicians here to this place. Let's forget about that place. This world will be where we move it all. This will be the start. The old and the new in one place and time. Here in

Anzulla," Eryn said, and pointed to me, putting me on the spot. "With what Ish told me, the obelisks, the positioning of the moon and stars above us, this tells me it is one place. Thousands of years before our births, but in the same place. Isn't it, Ish?" Eryn made more circles in the ground.

I fidgeted and gulped nervously, waking up from whatever stupid stupor my mind was, while looking at his circles. "Yes, I think so," I answered hesitantly. *He's correct. This must be Anzulla, before Apsu's destruction.*

"Well, it's either that or we are soon going to be taken prisoner and probably be fucked up the ass until we die," Ivan said and stuck his sword into the ground. He dragged his sword from circle to circle, connecting them.

"Ivan, stop it, no one is getting fucked. I'll put up a barrier. If they find us, I want no aggressiveness from any of you, understand?" Eryn looked at the drawing they had just made.

*The connected circles look like the human number eight.*

"Please join me. Let's pretend we don't see them when they arrive." Eryn patted his leg, and we took a knee, listening to him. I was sure he knew exactly what, where, when, and how we were going to make his plan work. They had wrapped a whole city in layers, I was sure he could shield anything if necessary.

"Let's hear your plan before the Angels and Sables molest us. If they don't kill us, these mosquitos surely will," Cian joked, breaking the tension. He rubbed his upper leg above the knee where it was connected to an artificial lower leg. He may be dramatically crude and speak his mind constantly, but he never complains about his leg or the eye that he willingly lost during an explosion when extracting Ivan and Eryn from the Zelk tower in Grayrak. I side-eyed him. He was fidgety and, instead of sticking his sword in the ground, he laid it across his lap. He sat with his back straight, the dark rainforest behind him, as if trying to ignore nature.

"Sounds to me like you want to be tied up and forced to submit and take it," Barkor said to Cian with a smirk.

"Okay, all jokes aside," Eryn said, and we swallowed our laughs eager to hear what he had come up with. "Ish, I don't want to belittle you and your ship, but to be honest, jumping back and forth, transporting groups of people, won't work. The six of us barely made it inside and jumping groups of Phoenicians here would take years, longer if you jump to the wrong time and place. I suggest Cian go with you and help you..."

Cian let out a satisfied chuckle while rubbing the palms of his hands. "Yes! Then I can finally get my hands on some bug spray."

I didn't know what bug spray was, but I assumed it was something Cian could use for his insect predicament. Nevertheless, I perked up, eager to hear more about the new plan. "I'm all ears," I said to Eryn.

He turned all his attention to me. His elongated pupils sliced through my mental barriers. I was starting to enjoy his full focus rather than squirming nervously. "As soon as you mentioned the Fates, what they said about you rebuilding the time machine, and the fact that it was pre-programmed, I realized they know who we are." He waved his hand to stop a barrage of questions. "No, not because they are a deity and all-knowing. They know you and us. They know everything. Our history and future. Who has been with all of us, observed us? Coaxed me? Who are they? Why did they choose you? What's with the tiny size of the time machine?"

"I've been asking the same question," I said slowly, tiptoeing around his mental probing.

"Like a spiderweb, I worked my way from the outside, through every strand, every corner to the center." Eryn pointed to the small circles connected with the number eight —*maybe they are eights and zeros?*

Eryn kept talking. "My mind wandered to the places anyone, like my father inside the mine in South Africa, like Joshua, like Brad, Mika, and Connor, even Peter, told me about. Anyone who has ever said anything to me, every second of my life," Eryn said, and then pinned me with a glaring stare. "Or visited me, even brought Anubis pups to me."

*Holy red dung beetle and scarabs shit, he knew it was me!*

*Yes, I do, Ishtar,*he answered me, mind to mind.

"Ish, do you realize your ship looks a lot like our Spacecars, but more similar to the escape pods of the Horizon? Things like the window, the two seats, and the door were salvaged from the Horizon. But some of it, like the instrumentation, the software or the *user manual or travel guide* as you call it, the wiring, and the little knobs, levers, and buttons. They look very similar to what we have in our Phoenician vehicles."

Eryn's reprimanding gaze cut short the loud, disbelieving gasps.

I frowned at the unexpected question. "I never saw my father's ship whole. Only the wreckage. He crashed it long before I was born."

Eryn gave a slight nod as if expecting that answer. "I have a strong suspicion your father's ship is the Horizon and your time machine was part of it."

"Motherfucker!" Cian exclaimed. "It's the central core! The nucleus! It was drawn into the plans. It sat in the underbelly of the Horizon. It's where Kawa and the programmers installed the motherboard. It housed the mainframe. We were in a rush and uploaded Lasitor to the entire Horizon instead. I cut the separate wiring and the connection to the Zelk Hive. Lasitor's wiring multifunctioned like a coupler between a central processing unit of the Phoenix CPU and the peripheral onboard computer. Linking the Phoenix to the Horizon and the Horizon to the Zelk."

Ivan's eyes widened in comprehension. "Yes, but where did the Zelk get the schematics for the Horizon?" Accusing eyes turned to me. "Is there a possibility that someone came onto your time machine? You told us you were on the moon before they built the fleet? Could someone somehow have logged into the computer and downloaded the information from its database?" Ivan asked.

I didn't like to be interrogated. I exhaled a sigh while wrapping my mind around this. "No. No one knew I was in Grayrak. Only Barkor knew where I'd hidden my ship. I always cloaked my ship and real appearance whenever I was with humans. But…" I paused, thinking. "So Lasitor was uploaded by Cian to the Horizon. We all know that. But how did the Horizon end up in Apsu's hands?"

No wonder Eryn drew circles on the ground, because I needed pictures for this. They kept saying things I had never seen but were right in front of me. Maybe I was standing too close. Maybe I needed to open my mind, step back, and listen.

"How certain are you? Are you one hundred percent sure you never shared the information? You said you fed off the humans and drank their blood, got drunk many times, and jumped here to visit Gugusan. Chasing after Peter, that you somehow knew was here. Found him. Found the apple. Took it back to your sisters on the wrong timeline. Went to Andrew. Lost Elijah and Peter. But yet, Elijah ended up here. Peter was here. The apple was here. In the meantime, you jumped and updated Lasitor. Which now is here. Are you seeing the pattern?"

I sat dumbfounded by Eryn's revelation.

A surge of rage pulsed through me. This was the ramifications of listening to the Fates—waiting like a fool in Grayrak. All the while I could have jumped straight to Phoenix. I bulged my fists and said through clenched teeth, "Please spell it out for me, because it sounds to me that you say the Zelk built the Horizon because I fucked up. You forget, the Fates told me to bloody go and wait for you on the moon."

"I agree, your Fates and this place are constants, just like you and Lasitor," Eryn said.

The jungle heat was fucking stifling. Sweat rolled in rivulets down my back. The heat of the fire worsened my embarrassment and discomfort. "So you don't think I am to blame?" I asked, my voice trembling with uncertainty and vulnerability.

"You said it yourself. You were their tool. A weapon your Fates chose to get rid of the evil on the moon." His words hung heavy in the air as we contemplated them.

"The Fates?" I questioned, my mind reeling with the new information.

"Yes, the one you think is God," Eryn said, reaching out to me and touching my knee. Empathy flooded me, like enormous arms wrapping around me. I felt bare, flayed open—my stupid, gullible, childlike belief in the Fates. This was worse than when I found out my Anubis had died. I felt alone and utterly humiliated.

"But who created them?" Ivan interjected, and my curiosity piqued.

Eryn leaned closer. "Ish, think of when you won the war against your father, the evil that consumed him. When you said you went back to Anzulla. What did the Fates say to you?"

I closed my eyes, and cleared my throat, remembering what was said so I could recite it word for word and relay it correctly to them. "They said they have an old enemy that hides inside the darkness and feeds off it. It grows and destroys realities. They said it is as old as time and that they are the cogs of the wheel. I was sent to the moon, and they said my ship was already programmed."

My eyes enlarged as the words of Eryn rang true. "Yes, I see now." Eryn's conclusion astonished me.

"Oh my goodness, Eryn," Ivan exclaimed, eyes wide and slack-jawed. Eryn lifted a hand, smiling lovingly at his husband.

"But there is more. Just like the humans were able to instill their souls into the Zelk mainframe, making robots think like humans, these Fates were battling their enemy on a much-advanced level. Think of it. In that tower was the Zelk brain, which is also a collection of mashed-up human souls. Dark human souls. Information the Disciples got from where? We uploaded a virus into it after we cut Lasitor from the connection. Lasitor created this virus. We attacked the Zelk from two sides, the human and the electronic. That's why you went to the moon. To bring Lasitor closer to the origin, to the factory of evil. To Apsu."

"Brother, you are going off the rails. I hope you don't feel guilty because we infected their mainframe and destroyed their base. Because I can't see how we could have pulled it off any other way," Cian said.

"I know. And no. All I'm saying is that I'm just sad about those poor souls that were trapped inside that tower. Whether infected or not. Whether out of stupidity or just believing things they were taught from a young age by those also infected by the darkness."

Barkor shivered and leaned closer, whispering. "Eryn, what are you saying?"

This was getting interesting. I also wanted to know. Eryn had been thinking about this longer than we thought. Maybe since the day I met him. Not on the moon, but way before that.

He pointed four fingers at us. "You said you've seen this evil, and from what you've told us, battled it. That evil was inside the men, driving them, and leading them to build the tower. Like your father, they were driven by…" He paused dramatically. We waited. "Information, greed, and hunger for power. Then you and your ship got planted right in the middle of it, and you were told not to interfere, but to wait for us." He folded his four fingers into a fist then pointed one finger at me after sweeping his eyes over us.

"You were given a ship already programmed, you were given a time-keeping contraption, you were given the apple. You make the Zelk disappear, and you used Cian's Song to boost your power to move the Horizon to a new timeline. But by doing so, you threw a spanner into the wheels of your Fates. Now, do you see the spiderweb? The Fates told you that you locked us out of the timeline. Now here we are sitting in another. Think bigger." Eryn continued while pointing at me and those weird-ass number eights. "Why do you think the Fates said that they held the balance and that they are old enemies? That they've created time and drive the cogs of the wheels. What if they meant they created this time and this world? They said the evil was growing and consuming life and that you were their hidden weapon. Yes?" Eryn coaxed us.

"So when we were all back on Earth, the Zelk was gone and you locked Phoenix out of that timeline…" He waited for a response and I answered yes with a nod, but was still puzzled. He continued, "Where did they go? Where did those Zelk go?" he asked me.

"I thought I locked us out from being discovered by the Zelk," I answered hesitantly. I didn't know where he was going with this and if he wanted me to tell them about the big change, the catalyst even of 1968, me fucking Andrew and saving the whiskey or not.

"No." He chuckled—answering the question that was forming in the back of my mind.

I was growing impatient and getting worried about Peter. "Then what?" I blurted, and the others laughed at me. I gave them the evil eye and chuckled at Cian, covered with bugs. I wasn't educated like them, but I'm not stupid, I picked up knowledge like deserts collected sand, and I deserved respect. I was one of their fathers, after all.

"I think whoever created Ish's time travel machine is the one with the answers." Eryn swept his hand in a small gesture to the sky. "They are either the ultimate God of the skies, the whole universe, or they are like us. Why would they need contraptions, apples, tablets, and time machines? Why did your Fates have your machine already programmed for you?"

"Big purple frog balls. Do you think God is like us and they are using us?" Ivan asked.

"Of course not! This is not God. But Ishtar's Fates. They are just spikes on the big wheel. They said it themselves. They are cogs in the wheel of time." Cian scoffed at his brother. Barkor didn't say a word. I didn't think he grasped any of this.

"This brings us to Elijah and the apple. If you return it, the loop will continue on Phoenix's timeline. I say we bring Phoenix here and let that reality disappear. Let Apsu, the darkness, the Zelk, the whole reality disintegrate. That's the apple, the Eden, the flood, the wars, the famine, the sickness. The endless catastrophes. It's in the human book of God. The black book Joshua had read to me. The Bible."

"Whoa, hold on. Who is this Joshua you are talking about?" I asked.

Ivan sighed. "It's the man that took care of Eryn when Eryn was…"

Eryn smiled and silenced Ivan, with a gentle hand on his lap. "I was a small boy Brawl, he was like my second father."

"Oh, now I see. I saw the picture of you in your living room," I said, remembering the picture Peter had bumped off the end table the day before. "It must have been fun growing up with you."

The tension around the fire grew palpable as Cian's voice rose in frustration. "No,

Eryn had a horrible time growing up. And it's all you and your fucking apple's fault. That fucking apple cylinder seal thing," Cian said.

His brother gave an exasperated sigh. "Okay thanks, brother, but now we all know it's not his fault. It is the Fates, Ish's Fates. That is what Eryn is saying. They orchestrated this."

Eryn nodded earnestly. "Yes, they did."

"But what is the origin of the apple? Who made the apple and the star map? Who hid the Anunnaki gene inside it? Is it that Platonius dude you fucked?" Cian demanded an answer by pointing a finger and waiting for me to speak. I shook my head and stared at the dancing flames. A heavy silence settled over the campfire as they regarded the mysterious origins of the cursed apple and its hidden secrets.

I waited for Eryn to speak up.

To share what he knew about the apple and had asked me not to mention during my questioning. My inquisition.

"I did." Eryn finally broke the silence.

Cian, Barkor, and Ivan blinked as the color drained from their faces. Gasps followed as they turned to look at him in shocked disbelief. His cheeks flushed red, but he straightened his spine, meeting our eyes with confidence.

"I worked with my father, Wolter Wessels, in the lab, crafting all kinds of creations from gold. One day a memory came to me, an idea for a puzzle box. The apple."

Eryn winked at me. I searched the skies for Angels and Sables.

He continued after clearing his throat. "Those inspirations were given to me by Ish's Fates." Eryn winked at me again. For fuck's sake, everyone saw it. "I created the puzzle, the apple, that when taken apart, can be rolled out, revealing the secret code. The same secret I rolled out on a flimsy piece of paper, was on a note from Joshua to my father. I saw it, liked it, and inscribed it. I stamped the calculations inside the gold and thought nothing of it. Like a child drawing a picture and then putting it on the fridge. But the first time I saw the apple in Mika's hands, I couldn't understand how it got there. You see, when I was a young boy, I had given that very same apple to a young pregnant woman who was crying inside a cryopod destined for the moon," he explained, turning to face Ivan and Cian.

*Barkor's mother?* I privately asked Eryn.

The twin brothers leaned closer, the flames glinting in their blue eyes as their mouths fell open in surprise. "The mineshaft?" they asked, interrupting my mind-link question to Eryn. The fire crackled louder, echoing the intensity of our thoughts and deep-seated questions.

*Could be, if she was the only pregnant young woman on the rocket.*

Eryn gave them a nod and a shrug. "I was always exploring and one day I climbed into the rocket to look around when I heard sniffles. She lay all alone and awake. I visited her the next day, opened the cryo chamber, and showed her the apple to cheer her up. She liked it and smiled. Because it made her happy, I gave it as a gift to make her feel better. It was pretty like she was." Eryn smiled as he remembered, but his expression darkened. "But those Disciples were there. They found out she was awake. I hid from them. They just pushed her down, closed the chamber, and made her sleep. I'd snuck away, barely escaping the wild monsters which I know now were Anubis. I never returned there, because at least she was asleep like the others and not alone anymore. Not sad, but frozen." His voice dropped as he whispered. "That's another reason why I asked if anyone got onto your ship on the moon. At first, I thought the girl took the apple with her to the moon. Then I wondered how it made its way from the moon to Gugusan and from Gugusan to Babylon, then back to the Disciples, causing our births due to the information inside it. The leadership of Phoenix confiscated it, and Peter stole it and brought it back here. But then there's Elijah and Peter's story. I couldn't place Elijah's significance physically in our timeline until I remembered his name was in the Bible. I realized the apple Mika had was the same apple the Disciples must have taken. Only Mika confiscated it, thinking it came from Babylon. Something that was passed from generation to generation with the other relics we found in their possession. *We all thought so, but the apple was never there.* It was never supposed to be in Babylon. That is the loop. The infinity loop. Only it's not just one loop, but three or four loops, maybe more loops, while each meets and cuts at a different point. I copied the information from the bronze tablet. But who had given Platonius the information to stamp on the tablet?"

I frowned, shaking my head, not keeping up with Eryn's thought pattern. And by looking at the others, I wasn't alone. "I don't understand. Are you saying I caused this or not? First, you accuse me of sneaking information to the Zelk, then this?"

Eryn used his sword to point to the circles connected by one continuous line of the number eight drawn on the ground earlier. "Ish, you didn't jump in a straight line up and down. You jumped from one loop to the other. You crossed the loops. That is why Phoenix will cease to exist as well as all of us, if we stay on that loop. It is Apsu's loop."

Dear moon-god, my head was pounding.

Shaking his head, Ivan said, "No, that's not possible."

"It is, and it makes sense," Cian said, then, ever the pragmatist asked, "How are we going to get all of Phoenix inside that tiny time machine?"

"Cian, you just said it. The brain of the time machine is the core reactor, the self-sustaining program of the Horizon. We are not bringing the citizens on the time machine, we are bringing the city. The entire city must be moved here."

"What the fuck?" we exclaimed together.

"Think about it. Ish's family comes from Anzulla. Anzulla is Earth, but far into the past, or for the sake of the loop, very far into the future. Didn't the Fates say Ish had moved his future into his past by taking the apple to the wrong time and place?" Eryn said, placing the final pieces into the puzzle. Somehow, miraculously it started to make sense to me.

"That means me killing my father, was me ending or breaking that loop, but because I took the apple back, I started a new timeline, on which he finds the apple. He doesn't get killed, and he lives to destroy Babylon. He uses the information inside the apple to grow more powerful?" I said.

Cian clapped his hands. "Yes! He's the darkness, the driver behind the Disciples, the Zelk" —Cian made air quotes— "but the Fates intervened by stopping Apsu, by placing Ishtar right at the crossing of the two loops. On the moon."

"The war against Apsu is Earth's Armageddon! The cataclysmic event between good and evil at the end of history," Ivan added.

"You must bring Phoenix here. This is Anzulla. But long before and after your father. Think of it as a shortcut." He pointed to his drawings on the ground. "Like the number eight cut in half. Instead of an eight, we will make it two separate circles by breaking the link here," Eryn said.

"But what are all those tiny circles Ivan connected?" I asked.

Eryn pointed with his spear. "Those are just points in time—when we changed loops. For example, 1968, 2013, 2014..."

"So, that's what the Fates meant by..." Eryn shook his head and the others looked at me and sighed. I stopped mid-sentence, wide-eyed. Obviously, I was still missing something and annoying the crap out of them.

Eryn looked solemnly at me. "Ish, there are no Fates. Your Fates are just Lasitor." Eryn revealed it casually, but I felt like I was having an out-of-body experience.

"Oh, moon-god! Why didn't I see this earlier? That fucker!" I balled my fists. "I should have ripped his wires out!"

Eryn grabbed his spear, stood, and pointed it at me. I leaned back, nervously. "Yes. But if it wasn't for Lasitor, none of us would be here today. Go tell Mika what we want. Tell him to bring the Horizon inside Phoenix. Park the time machine inside the Horizon and Cian, you must sing for it. Connect the time machine with the Horizon and the Horizon with the entire city," he said with finality.

"What?" We stared perplexed at Eryn.

"Are you going to stay here? How will I do it without you?" Cian asked.

"Go! Do it, brother. I know you can. Think of it as one living organism. The time machine is the heart and the rest of it connects to it like veins. Think of the forest floor."

Cian looked bewildered. Overthinking again. "And what are you going to do?"

"We are going to make peace and play with our new friends." Eryn looked up. He knew before us that we had winged visitors. Instead of freaking out and taking an aggressive stance, he plunged his spear deep into the ground, held onto it with both hands, and sang notes with a beautiful melody. A massive translucent bubble formed around us. Like Phoenix, he had created a barrier locking us safely inside. Barkor and I stood open-mouthed, blinking, and waited for an explanation from Cian and Ivan, who treated the display of power as just another thing Eryn could do and shrugged at us. As if Eryn creating protective bubbles was the norm.

"Look, they are waiting, calmly," Eryn said with a lopsided grin.

I believed in him. He would not allow harm to anyone. Not us or them. Goosebumps covered my body as I enjoyed watching him take charge by peacefully displaying his power. I knew he was both powerful and humble. He never had to prove anything to anyone. He just stood to the side, observing silently. I felt it from the day I met him for the first time. I watched him work, his strength pulsated around him, and his skin glowed with a sheen of gold and blue. Not overly so, but I knew where to look. It started on that small patch of skin behind his ears and then spread to the rest of his body. About the size of a grape.

Cian sneezed, breaking the magnificence of the moment. "I think you are allergic to this place because of the feathers," Ivan said, pointing up to our looming crowd of visitors hovering a few hundred feet above us. Now and then a black or white feather trickled from the sky. They were creeping me out. So I turned my gaze to Eryn, who was in charge, and I was happy with that.

"Cian, just think of yourself as the friend of nature. Stop fighting them. Stop thinking about the itching and they will go away. All they want is for you to acknowledge them," Eryn said in a surly tone. This was the first time I had heard him being irritated. Cian gulped, realizing Eryn was serious. Eryn changed his focus to the matter at hand. "I want no one's death on my hands. We came here in search of peace, but if we are forced to protect ourselves, I can defeat them with a single swipe of my spear." Not looking up, or bragging about it, Eryn was stating a fact.

"Yeah, but look at them," Cian whispered. Discreetly, we looked up at the fluttering specks in the night sky growing in numbers as more arrived.

With a cautious glance over his shoulder, Eryn crouched next to the small fire, the flames twinkling in his intelligent eyes. *We shouldn't be here*, he murmured into our minds. *This is not our place, not our home.* He paused, staring into the flames. *Not yet*, he finally added.

"Okay, Ish and I will go," Cian announced, happy to get away from Eryn by pulling me back into the jungle. "Let's make a run for it. Eryn, brother, good luck! Come, Ish, we have a city to save."

We ran. "Are we able to exit the bubble?" I asked, halting for a second in front of the glinting membrane.

"Of course," Cian answered, dragging me through the waterfall of snot that closed behind us.

# CHAPTER 65

# LUCI'S QUARTER

*"MORNING.*

*Did you know what it means to think quickly on your feet? It means making good decisions, keeping cool and calm while achieving things without having to consciously think about them too much, and doing it faster than others.*

*Did you also know treating the underlying cause of hot feet like nerve damage can help relieve hot or burning feet?*

*Some ways to do that are to sleep with your feet uncovered and exposed to the cool night air, freezing your socks, using cold packs or cold water bottles, or pointing a fan toward your feet.*

*By visiting your community news page for more tips to stay cool in any situation, you increase your ability to think quickly on your feet.*

*Have a cool day!"*


**PETER**
**24 970 B.C.**
**At the foot of the mountain of the Gods**
**In the jungle of Anzulla**
**Earth**

Elijah had me chasing him all across the lower bloody fucking mainland until we finally arrived at the cliffs that towered over the sparkling blue ocean. "You've got nowhere else to go, Elijah. You might as well give up and surrender."

He held his arms up. "Whatever! The plan was to keep you occupied for an hour or two. I surrender in peace."

I hovered a few feet above him. One step backward and he would tumble to his death. All I had to do was dive down and give him a slight push.

He waited, and I waited. The ocean spray drifting from crashing waves below cooled my temper. "Fucking ungrateful fraternizer, that's what you bloody are." I grabbed him by his wrists and turned back to reunite with the others. Midway up the river, we noticed movement. "Something's happening at the jungle's edge!" I said as we neared the meadow at the foot of the mountain of the Gods.

"Put me down!" Elijah squirmed. I swooped low, deposited him, and soundlessly joined Gugusan and his warriors hiding in the treeline. I tucked my wings and followed as we made our way through the dense growth of giant ferns and tropical plants. I moved cautiously, trying my best to avoid stepping on any twigs or leaves that could give away our location. The San warriors were like stealthy jungle cats, moving effortlessly through the underbrush. Once again, I spotted the white flowers that looked exactly like the paper flower Ish had given me. Gugusan called the red plant sap, *love juice*.

He'd fed me the stuff when I missed Ish so much that I felt like dying. This juice saved my life and I know firsthand why the Anunnaki thought of it as holy and necessary to survive. Without hesitation, I reached out and plucked the thick stem of one, feeling red sap drip down my hands and arms. It had a sweet scent, reminiscent of roses. I broke open the bulbous stem and sucked on the small fist-sized, coconut-like fruit, filled with light pink water inside. I was thirsty, so I slurped up the sap, cleaning my sticky arm with my tongue. Gugusan snapped his head in my direction. "Yeah, I know," I whispered at his scolding gaze.

"I hope they know what they are doing. Luci was eager to make peace and get the games started," Elijah said in his best broken English while peeking from behind a gigantic tree.

I clutched the big white Loursveto flower against my chest. I couldn't wait to show it to Ish. My eyes darted from one side to the other, searching the clearing for him.

"Oh, my fucking god!" I yelped and threw the flower to the ground. My heart slammed into my ribcage as I fumbled to unsheathe my obsidian short sword. I spotted black-winged Birdmen circling in the sky like vultures, then fluttering down one by one. Eryn, Ivan, and Barkor stood weaponless, looking up and smiling as if it were a friendly alien reaping for investigative anal probing. The scene of us crash landing and Ish being attacked and packed by white and black Birdmen flashed through my mind. Followed by the memory of Elijah hitting me over the head, and I daggered him mentally in his back. Straight into his heart. I hated his two-timing, selfish enemy-fucking ass.

"Take it easy, it's looking worse than it is," Elijah coaxed. He's been siding with the Birdmen, his loyalty was questionable.

"Gugusan, we have to help them," I said, already taking off flying.

"Wait, Peter!" I heard Elijah shout, but as I glanced back, the San were already following and streaming out of the forest behind me.

"Fuck yes!" I shouted, tasting the victory of my first battle. I flew so fast that the wind blinded me as I rushed to help Ish and our friends. *They must have followed us into the jungle and unknowingly stepped into the clearing where the Birdmen patrolled the edges of the woods.* Eryn, Barkor, and Ivan lifted their hands in surrender and slowly turned, lifting their shirts, seemingly showing the Birdmen they weren't packing any weapons. *Idiots!*

My eye caught a movement in the back. Cian and Ish were hunched down, slipping away deeper into the jungle. *Where to?* I was having the worst case of playing catch up. I didn't know if they went looking for me—for us.

"What's happening here? Are we fighting? Should I follow Ish and Cian?" I asked them telepathically as I landed, skidding with my feet over the wet grass.

*No, don't draw attention to them. Stay calm*, Eryn said into my mind. Holding his arms out where everyone could see his empty hands, he beckoned me to wait behind him. The black-winged ones scared me more than the ones that looked like me. They seemed unworried by my presence. I knew what they were capable of and they knew I was the one who had helped Ish to escape. *They almost killed him.*

"No, Peter, calm yourself and tell your friends to put down their weapons," Eryn urged, while not taking his gaze off the Birdmen.

"That's both easy and stupid to say. Where are your weapons? Where are your swords and spears? What the fuck is wrong with you? I don't trust them," I spat, clutching my sword. My eyes darted from one Birdman to the other, ready to defend my friends if they so much as twitched a wing too fast.

"*There is another way*," Eryn said as he lifted his arm, waving to the San army to slow down after I ignored him. Like a herd of bison running into an invisible wall, Gugusan's warriors came to a dead halt behind us.

"He says put down your weapons," I shouted. Elijah relayed the order to the warriors, and they relaxed and stood down. We all were looking at Eryn, who had his arms raised above his head in surrender. But his fucking eyes were closed. *Trusting fool, anyone can knife him from any direction.*

"What are you doing? Open your eyes. It's not time for contemplation." He ignored me with a look of peaceful bliss on his face.

We all watched him. Waiting.

"Why aren't they attacking us? What are they waiting for?" I asked, jittery with nerves.

"They're waiting for your people to make the first move," Elijah, said as he joined us. Eryn kneeled on one knee and Elijah followed his example—the Igigi wasn't right in the head. Maybe because he was already so close to death when Andrew had given him his blood. Weird shit was going down, and I didn't like or trust this. *Maybe they ate or smoked something in the village.* Elijah believed he was important and always inserted himself right in the middle of everything. He patted Eryn on the shoulder as if he had known him for years, then greeted Ivan and Barkor as if they were old friends. I stayed back, making sure the San warriors were ready to pounce or didn't fuck this up, *whatever Eryn was planning.*

Perplexed, we watched the spectacle. With my wings open and ready to take flight I paced up and down, chewing my nail. Eryn tilted his head and cupped his hand to his ear. "Listen," he said. "What do you hear?" Oh god, he was tripping.

"Gu, the woman gave them mushrooms!" I whispered. He chuckled and pointed to them, telling me to shut up and watch.

"I don't hear any-fucking-thing! Just the thunderous drone of their wings and silence, no thoughts, no feelings. Why?" Barkor asked.

Eryn tipped his head to the side and narrowed his eyes. "They're waiting for something?" He cupped his ears with his hands. "They're listening?"

*For what?* I asked telepathically. Eryn got up and then looked at me as if he knew something none of us did.

"Maybe they're waiting for you to bloody fucking say something," I answered under my breath.

He grinned at me, took a deep breath, and spoke loud and clear. His voice boomed over the clearing and echoed into the skies. "The first day I realized I had powers," he leaned back, looking up at the horde in the sky, "was a wonderful day filled with laughter and giggles. What boy wouldn't like telling objects and animals what to do, or commanding the wind where to blow and the rain where to fall? I knew that day I was destined to do great things. Not kill or fight a war, not destroy an already destroyed world. No, I was born to solve problems off-battlefield. This is why I knew I was the King of the Brawl. Not the king others thought me to be."

"We know all that shit. Stop monologuing and get to the point, Brawl King," Ivan said, sounding worried and waiting for his husband to get down from the soapbox he was tripping on. No one in their right mind would look up at an army of sex-crazed Birdmen and smile, telling them how wonderful he was.

"This is the climax I have anticipated all my life. This is why I never wanted to be a human king. A king like all the other kings. This is amazing and for once nothing sucks fucking stink frog balls and it all makes sense." Eryn laughed. He laughed so hard we couldn't resist as all the air, every molecule around us, turned happy and positive. My feathers rustled and the hairs on my arms felt electrically charged as if a lightning storm was coming.

"Damn, that was good juju! I love you and your real weapon of choice?" Ivan noted, and everyone smiled. The longer this went on, the longer I got to experience what the Phoenicians always bragged about. I was impressed, even some Birdmen flew down closer to us. I expected blowback and the promise of death after being their sex slaves, but again, I had no clue what was going on in real life. My years of hiding away in a lab and then a cave were catching up with me.

"Everyone, this is Luci. He is a very good friend of mine. Groda and I are in a relationship with him," Elijah said and confirmed what we had suspected this whole time.

*Traitor!* Stars in his eyes, Groda blushed. Elijah wiped his hair to the side, as if self-conscious. I hawk-eyed them as my friends shook hands with Luci. Then Luci shocked me by stepping forward and embracing and kissing both Elijah and Groda, showing all of us they were together. As if knowing I was watching him, Elijah broke the embrace, stepped back, and crossed his arms. Then he grinned at me, pulling one shoulder up to his ear.

"Didn't I tell you he and Groda were sucking the Birdman's cock? No wonder Luci helped us escape. A bloody threesome, for years, right under my nose!" I threw my hands up. Involuntary, my wings flared open. *Why didn't they tell me?* "Did you know about Groda?" I asked our tribe leader, who was smirking at me.

"I had my suspicion. I saw them sneak away and followed them once." He lifted his chin. "It's fine with me. Elijah and Groda were making friends."

I was happy for Elijah. I guess the Birdmen aren't the enemy anymore. "Why didn't you say anything earlier? I flew after the idiot, thinking he was going to betray us. I could have killed Elijah! I wanted to. I really-really wanted to drop him on his head today."

"Pfft." Gugusan waved me off. "You can't even catch, kill, or gut a fish. Also, it was not my thing to say, or reveal to you," Gugusan said with a smug look on his face.

"Hmmm. In my eyes, Elijah is still a sneaky fuckwad. I'm disappointed, but also glad for them. At least saving Elijah turned out to be the right thing to do." I sheathed my sword and placed my hands on my hips. "I'm feeling less guilty," I said proudly.

Gugusan dipped his chin at me and said with a serious tone, sharing wise words, like a father to a son, "Never feel guilty for doing the right thing. When you do, wait, and it will all turn out for the best."

Eryn spoke up. "We heard about your games. We want to challenge you to a game, and if we win, we'd like you to consider our proposal."

"You and who wants to play?" Luci asked, looking at Elijah and preening. *Did they plan this?*

"Five of us against five of you. Your game, your rules. But if we win—"

Luci interrupted, barking a laugh at the Brawl King. The skies filled with more laughter.

Eryn seemed unfazed. He smirked and put a hand over his heart. "If we win, we ask you to show mercy and save us. We are here to ask for your help. For your hospitality. Without you, it is impossible to find the door. Please grant us free passage. Open your skies so we may come to live among you."

Astonished, Luci reached into his pants pocket and produced a coin. He held it up for all to see and announced in a deep dark voice, "He is talking about this!" The coin glinted in the moonlight. He handed it to Eryn. Ivan and I leaned closer. Its surface was worn and weathered, but there was no doubt. At first glance, we all knew what it was.

"This is a relic of almost forgotten times," Luci said. Eryn's fingers traced the engravings on the coin's face, his eyes distant as a deep frown formed on his forehead. Others gathered around us, their curious gazes fixed upon the coin as it got passed around and finally handed back to Luci. "It belonged to my great-grandfather. He used to tell me stories about this coin, stories of adventure and times he promised I would see." A hush fell over the crowd as they leaned in, eager to hear more. Luci took a deep breath, allowing nostalgia to wash over him before continuing. "He spoke of a world where this coin held great power." His voice grew louder with excitement. The Birdmen hovered closer, some landing and joining the San warriors. "Legend has it that he who possessed it arrived through the door between worlds. He urged me to look at the skies. To observe and wait for the signs of unimaginable wonders."

Whispers of awe rippled through the crowd as they absorbed the weight of Luci's revelation. They exchanged glances, captivated by the notion of an extraordinary foretold arrival unfolding before them. Luci raised the coin higher, mesmerizing everyone. His eyes sparkled as he declared, "This is the sign. I was right, the blood moon brought the king."

A chorus of cheers erupted from the Birdmen as if Luci's words had ignited a dormant, flaming answer to all their prayers.

"I know that quarter," Eryn said. "It's Simon's. Dr. Simon McCormick, Brad McCormick's son."

"What the fuck?" I asked. "It could be anyone's quarter. Millions were minted in the US. Or am I missing something?"

Eryn held up an open palm, asking Luci for another look at it. "This is a rare Wisconsin quarter. Only a few were minted in 2004 A.D. Look at the front of the coin, there's a cow, a peeled husk of corn, and a sliced wheel of cheese along with inscriptions of when Wisconsin was admitted into the Union of States, in 1848 A.D. with the word, *Forward*, which is Wisconsin's state motto. The quarters that were released in 2004 have a small design difference that shows an extra leaf on the illustrated corn husk." Eryn told the coin's story like a mint historian.

"Yes, but why do you think it's Simon's?" Ivan asked. Eryn handed me the quarter.

"My teeth marks."

"What? When did you have Simon's coin in your mouth?" Ivan asked, sounding pissed off and jealous at the same time as he grabbed the coin from me.

"When I was a small Brawl boy. When I snuck around in Phoenix. One night, I snuck into their room. I never stole anything, I promise. I just peeked around, seeing what stuff people had. I found this on his bedside table. He and Paul were sleeping. I kind of tasted it. You know, like when you taste gold."

"My big Brawl, no one but you goes around tasting and licking things as if it were gold around here."

Eryn smiled shyly. "Probably not, but I was young, and I liked the taste of it, especially when I bit into it and left my teeth marks. It amused me to leave something of myself in it."

I just bit down on my lip and shook my head, forcing myself not to judge or shame him in front of everyone. "So this means somehow Simon's coin ended up here. We don't know if it was him, or if someone had taken it from him."

"But this just proves what I suspected. Now I know Cian and Ishtar are going to succeed," Eryn said, taking the coin from Ivan and handing it back to Luci.

"But...how?"

"*Shhht!*" Ivan shushed me with a pointed look—irritating, spoiled brat. "I want to hear what Luci says to Eryn. Listen and stop asking questions."

"Are you understanding them?" I asked and then remembered Ish. "Where are Ish and Cian going?" I asked.

"*Shhht!*" Ivan looked at me with daggers in his eyes this time.

"Sorry. Fuck. Talk about mister prissy, high all mighty," I retorted. "He thinks because he is married to Eryn, he is now better than us?" I said to Elijah and Groda, who relayed it to Gu, who told the men and women in his army, and we all laughed at Ivan's expense.

Barkor stepped closer to me and whispered. "Ish and Cian went to get the time machine. Then they are coming back, bringing Phoenix with them. Or that is the plan."

"Huh?" I furrowed my brow, baffled. "What's going on?" I asked. Barkor exchanged a knowing look with the others before turning back to me.

"We'll fill you in on everything soon," he said, his voice serious and guarded.

"We will elaborate later," Ivan said—agonizing me.

Wings spreading open, I rocked back onto my heels. "How will they bring all those people here with that small machine?" I asked, astonished, as my eyes widened in disbelief.

Barkor's eyes crinkled at the corners. Head down, he explained under his breath. "They're bringing the entire city. Cian is going to connect the time machine to the center of Phoenix City and jump here." He spelled out the intricate details of their plan, his warmth and empathy for my confusion palpable as he patted my shoulder reassuringly.

"Is that even possible?" I asked.

"*Shhht!*" Ivan said again, scowling at us.

"Let's hope so. We can talk later. If these Birdmen agree to it, it will prevent us from looking like we want war and to take over their homes. That's why no weapons and no aggression, Peter. Understand?" I understood, and I liked the plan. I loved it here and I loved Gu and his tribe. This place felt like home to me.

"Hmmm, that makes sense. Thanks for explaining, Barkor."

"Anytime. I know how it feels when others make plans and you're not included,"

Barkor said, but I sensed there was a bit more history to that remark. I suspected it was about Cian's plan to evacuate the moon without telling him the details. Ish had mentioned that Cian was purposefully keeping Barkor in the dark. Most probably to avoid sticky questions and untimely close contact.

Barkor cleared his throat. "I can't believe how quickly I'm picking up their language." He gestured to the sky and then to Gugusan. "The only ones who still give me trouble understanding them are those scantly feather-covered people from the jungle." He waved to Gu, who flashed a grin and nodded toward us.

"Ish told me that he had implanted an Anunnaki dictionary of sorts in the subconscious parts of their minds. But I guess for me it is easier to communicate with them after living among them for decades."

"I remember. You mentioned that earlier," Barkor whispered. I liked him. He was perfect for Cian. While Cian was the tornado inside a blizzard, he was the calm after the storm. Ish found them melodramatic, but I would say they are intensely honest in everything they do and say. They aren't attention seekers.

"This meeting turned out to be different from what I imagined," I said. My eyes roamed over the spectacle playing out.

"Yes, it is," he said and turned his attention back to Eryn.

"We knew about Elijah and his message, even before meeting him. We also know about you. We don't have your kind living in our time, but we have written stories of how good and brave you are. Our time is ending, and we need your permission to come and live here in peace with you." As Eryn spoke, his voice was low and friendly. "Many years ago, I had a friend, Joshua, who told me your stories and about beings like you. Please come closer, Elijah." Eryn waved at the exotic-looking man who checked in with Groda and Gugusan and then me for answers, but this time, we shrugged. We did not know what the fuck was going on. This was a new campfire story, and I imagine hearing the San telling it to their children every night for the foreseeable future.

Elijah threw his staff to the ground and went to Eryn. I couldn't hear what they said to each other. There was nodding, congratulating, and laughing, and then they waved the Birdmen closer. "Look at the moon," Elijah shouted. "It's an omen. This red moon will shine until it meets the sun. Together, the sun and the moon will crack open the door in the sky for the lost children to come home. Here in this hidden ancient land, the ones that will come are the ones you have all been waiting for," Elijah exclaimed like, a senile prophet, warning us about the end of times. "The King of kings will bring his children together. The knowledge we seek will arrive from beyond the boundaries of the skies."

"Be careful, my Brawl." Ivan shifted from one leg to the other as if he needed to piss or something. "There are too many, I can't see him. Is Eryn okay? Do you see him?"

"Calm the fuck down, pretty boy," I bitched. He looked at me, like *who do you think you are*, then back at the crowd milling around Eryn.

Suddenly, shouting and roaring, the black and white masses took flight.

Eryn and Elijah got up. Wiping the feathers, dirt, and grass off their legs, then smiled. "Let the games begin," Eryn yelled with a fisted hand of victory in the air. "They've accepted our proposal and challenge. We will come here to live among them!"

He widened his arms and bellowed a deep unending croak that reverberated through the air, sounding like a thunderstorm with the promise of torrential rains ending a drought that had lasted much too long.

He sang.

Revealing his true strength, Eryn walked further into the field. In front of him, the skyline, mountain ranges, and treetops were darkened by the outline of black and white fluttering wings. He sat down in the tall grass and rested his hands on his knees. Singing a magnificent song no one knew but everyone loved. Grace and power filled the air, as if nature itself was rejoicing in the presence of Eryn's voice. Rabbits and deer emerged from their hiding places, inquisitively smelling the air and like all of us, being enchanted by the melody. This was a moment of unity, where the song connected all living beings, bridging the gap between the science I knew and trusted, and the mystery of this place I could never explain.

This song will forever be remembered and sung by the people of Anzulla.

# CHAPTER 66

# MOVING PHOENIX

*"GOOD MORNING.*

*Did you know that before the Earth flooded, humans used to pack up their homes, and put all those items inside something the size of a small one-bedroom apartment on wheels? Yes, my dear humans, they would take time off work and leave their pets with their neighbors to camp out. Amenities, such as flush toilets and running water, were scarce, and for some reason, they found that relaxing.*

*I know, right? But sometimes it is good to learn about the past to be able to appreciate the future.*

*Visit your community news page to read up on surviving in the wild while thirsty and relaxing with dirty butt cracks.*

*Have a campy day."*


**ISHTAR**
**2148 A.D. (96 A.T.)**
**One year after the inquisition**
**Phoenix, underwater glass dome city**
**Earth**

As soon as the Bubblecar made it through the entrance tube into the Transportation Dome, we parked next to the platform and disembarked in a rush. Cian and I were making an array of funny noises as we ran like two irritated rhinos through crowds of unsuspecting residents. We headed straight on one path to the Leadership Office of Phoenix. We found the doors locked, and a big note attached to it.

Scribbled in English, it said, *We are taking a day off. Unless Phoenix is flooding or burning, you can find us in Recreation Seven. Signed Gen. Brad McCormick.*

"Fuck!" Cian slammed his fist into the disappointing message, and then he turned and ran. "Follow me!"

I sprinted after him. We hopped, excused, and apologized as we passed humans. Luckily, most heard us coming and melted into the walls to make room for us. Cian, sword in hand, looked like he was about to assassinate someone, especially with his shining blue Zelk eye. I called in a hushed tone, "Cian, your sword. Please, we are scaring the people." He looked at me, then his sword as if he hadn't realized it was in his hand, and hastily put it into its sheath between his shoulders on his back.

We'd been running through the jungle, collecting all kinds of pesky insects and itchy leaves. We were drenched in sweat, our clothes torn and muddy. I've resisted using my powers so far, which was good because I realized I never knew what the fuck I was doing. Cian would swear now and then, as the urgency and weight of the inevitable discussions grew heavier. Not to mention getting all the citizens on board with our crazy plan. Then somehow Cian needed to connect the time machine to the Horizon and the Horizon to the heart of Phoenix.

As if reading my mind, Cian answered me as we descended the circling stairs to the ground floor. "I've decided to first fly and install the time machine on the Horizon. Then we have to park the Horizon inside Phoenix by reversing into the Transportation Dome. It shouldn't be too difficult. It is where my fathers built the Blue Halcyon and Spacecars. It will be a tight fit, but I think it's doable. Otherwise, I have to bring the city up to the surface and..."

"No, that's a perfect plan, as long as the doors are big enough to enter," I said, as we came to a dead halt at the sight of a man standing at attention for us.

"Captain Bill Thornton! Are you now guarding doors?" Cian heaved air into his lungs and patted the man's shoulder.

The guard beamed. "I'm happy to do any kind of work, General. Since you left, the crew has been bored and depressed. We went from intolerable to zero action when you left, sir."

Cian gave the man a fixed look of determination, his Zelk eye shining a blue hue over the captain's proud face. "No more standing around. I'm back and the shitshow is too. Go gather the men and meet us in the Transportation Dome in an hour."

"Yes, we need your expertise to maneuver the Horizon, by backing her up into the Transportation Dome," I added.

"Sir, yes sir!" He saluted, all teeth and excitement.

Then, we burst through the swinging doors. Among the chlorinated clean water, other very questionable smells hit my sinuses. Cian's face scrunched up, and I knew he smelled it too. "What the fuck?" he asked, enthusiasm evaporating. His gaze swept over the lively scene. Stuttering and stammering over his words, he instantly flushed red in the face, as he spat his dismay. "Here we were running through jungles, traveling worlds to save humanity, and you are fucking having orgies! Leisuring like you don't have a care!"

"My son!" Mika cheered with a glass half-full and spilled even more of its contents into the bubbling water. Steam billowed up from the surface, obscuring their nakedness, but naked they were. As Mika and Connor bobbed in the tumultuous boiling water, dark groin areas, limp cocks, and soft balls floated flaccidly. The steam room smelled like whiskey and other body fluids I dare not mention. Cian was livid seeing his parents in this state, and I didn't want to increase his irritation by pointing out the obvious. I grinned. He was experiencing a rare shocked wordless state. It was only a festive erotic get-together. Brad and his husband Rick were bobbing up and down, facing each other. Rick's rapid up and down movements and arching back clearly indicated he was riding his husband and reaching the apex of his climax. The two vampires, Juandre and Andrew, were relaxing in each other's arms on a strange narrow long chair made for sleeping next to the pool, I guessed. Somewhat decent, with towels wrapped around their lower bodies, they lay draped with limbs intertwined and each had a glass in hand —the source of the whiskey smell.

It was private enough, so I didn't understand Cian's reaction. Yes, Andrew and Juandre were supposed to be sober and protecting Phoenix. But other than that, they were adults. Letting loose once in a while is good for the soul. They'd had lots to deal with lately and if I were in their shoes, I would have done this a long ass time ago. I smiled, thinking there might be time to join them. They have more than enough whiskey to share.

"Did you get the apple? Are we doomed or not?" Brad asked, swimming to the side and holding onto the rails to pull Connor and the other closer so they could get out. It was a team effort and they had perfected the art of getting out of the turbulent churning waters.

"He is my son too. He is my boy!" Connor rolled onto his stomach, pushed himself up on his hands and knees, grabbed a towel, and wrapped it around his waist.

"What the fuck is going on here? Why is this place smelling like a fucking bathhouse?" Cian threw more towels at the men and turned his back to them. I didn't know if it was anger or a combination of the heat, the running, or shame, but Cian was flaming red on his neck, face, and ears.

Brad was the last one to get out, still frolicking and holding on as the stream blasted his body from side to side. "Because it is a bathhouse. Our bathhouse," he announced, eyes closed with a post-orgasm look on his face.

Cian ignored Brad. "Come, boy, hello my big handsome protector," Cian cooed as Rotty, Igor, and Devil jumped up to meet him, nearly pushing the big guy over. "Yes, I missed you. I see you missed me." Cian laughed, hugging the three Anubis. I swear it looked like they smiled.

I took a step closer, taking a chance, testing if they would growl. It was my lucky day. Igor and Devil turned their attention to me, rubbing their thick necks and foreheads against my stomach. My chest tightened. I missed my companion, my friend. As if feeling my sadness, they whined and rubbed against me harder. "Yes, I know. And thank you." I swallowed a thick knot in my throat then stepped back. Their yellow eyes followed my retreat. As one, they turned and made themselves comfortable on the big soft pillow thing that seemed to be theirs. They took guarding these humans very seriously. I was happy to be finally accepted by them.

"Shut off that noise. We must talk immediately!" Cian's fury redirected my attention to our urgent mission.

"Why? Can't you see this is a party and parties have music?" Juandre said, still sprawled out. Andrew sat up next to him, pursing his lips and agreeing with his husband. They looked at each other and back at us, nodding. All agreed—we were party crashers.

Cian pointed a finger at them and scowled. "One fucking day? What the fuck? We leave you for one day and risk our lives to save the world, no two bloody worlds, and you throw a party. I never thought I would ever say this, but I'm utterly disappointed in you. Look at you. You are drunk and having orgies. I never..." Cian flapped his hands in front of his eyes, not looking at their nakedness while I secretly adored seeing their pale bodies, flawlessly sculptured, looking ageless and mature simultaneously.

Brad pulled himself up by the handrails and stepped onto the wet tiles like some kind of water god. "More like one year!" Rick handed Brad a towel, but not before I had gotten an excellent view of his taut, hairy buttocks.

Mika ignored the orgy comment and slipped a pair of soft linen trousers on. "Where is your brother?" he asked, changing the subject. Connor also got dressed in haste, seemingly to appease their distraught son. Andrew pulled Juandre up and handed him a red robe and slippers. It seemed all the men switched from being carefree debaucheries to emergent catastrophic aversion in a heartbeat.

"Lasitor, please turn off the music," Brad ordered. The loud *doof-doof* noise dissipated into absolute silence. My eardrums zinged. I opened my jaw to pop my ears, stuck a finger in each, and wiggled it. It didn't help. The sound of swirling water and anxious breathing hung in the air, accentuating the pending urgency. I inhaled through my nose. The intoxicating smells of male body fluids reminded me of my Kuku. I missed him and I worried about him, but those smells had me salivating.

Hands on their hips, the men awaited us to speak. I looked at Cian. Better him than me. I might divulge more than necessary at this stage.

"We have work to do. Lots to explain and in not much time," Cian blurted and looked at me for help. I pulled my shoulders up to my ears.

"Go on, tell them," I urged him. My skin itched. I looked longingly at the inviting waters, then at my clothes and hands. The mud was drying and had collected under my fingernails, and I dared not lick my lips. I was certain jungle sludge covered my entire face like it did Cian's.

"Yes, go on. You've got our full attention," Brad said with a stern attentive look on his face.

"Or do you want to go back to the Leadership Office?" Connor asked while stepping closer. He shook my hand and hugged Cian. The others followed suit. "It's good to see you, but please tell us. Are Ivan, Eryn, and Barkor okay? How is Peter doing? Was he able to—phew, you smell." Connor waved his hand in front of his nose.

Cian squirmed and broke the embrace. "Of course we would smell. We've been running through a jungle for hours. What do you mean, a year?"

I shuffled my feet, feeling guilty and ashamed, then I clasped my hands. "Sometimes I jump a teeny bit further backward or forward as planned. Sorry." Cian narrowed his eyes at me. *You better take us back to the same time and place*, he said telepathically, not embarrassing me further.

I gave him a firm, I'm-going-to-try-my-best look. Then he returned to Connor's question. "Last we saw them, Eryn was working on a plan. They were heading into a clearing as we ran back to the ship to come and get you. Peter was chasing after Elijah and Gu's warriors. Barkor is good. I know he can handle himself."

"Then it was an excellent idea to stay here. That sounds like too much physical work to me." Andrew slammed his hand over Juandre's mouth and shushed him. If Andrew didn't censor him, who knows what else Juandre would say.

Cian shook his head at the cheeky Juandre. "As you can see, we are still alive, but we don't know what is going to happen after Eryn confronts the Angels and Sables. It all depends on whether he can somehow convince them to let us go there."

"So, Eryn suggested we go another route?" Brad's gaze jumped from person to person, reading the room. Crossing my arms, I threw Andrew a pointed look.

"Hmmm." I rubbed the back of my neck. "I think it's best if we tell you his whole conclusion, as it all started with Elijah," I said. Andrew shot me an *oh my god* as he realized it was the Elijah he had saved all those years ago. I bit my cheek and dipped my gaze.

"The apple situation has changed. Eryn has a theory about my mission, the Anunnaki, and the Fates. This place with the Birdmen, as Gu's tribe calls them, is Anzulla. My time machine is part of the original Horizon. Oh moon-god, Eryn made it sound so simple," I said, looking at Cian for help this time. He rolled his hand, indicating for me to continue. Perplexed, wide-eyed faces waited for me to speak. "The short version is we agreed that the easiest way to save us all is to take Phoenix there," I said, crossing my arms.

Connor's body snapped rigid and there was a tightness in his face. "The two of you better explain to me who Elijah is. Because if this is 'Elijah,' my Roman Catholic mind is going to have a hard time reconciling this one," he said.

Juandre jumped, hands in front of his mouth, "Yeah, me too." He looked quizzically at his husband, but Andrew ignored him by appearing to be inspecting the tablet Mika was writing on.

"Yes, Eryn said that there is a one hundred percent chance our Elijah, me and Peter's, is that Elijah. I didn't think he was worth mentioning earlier, given the information overload and simplification of facts," I said, already thinking how I was going to simplify the next mouthful of Eryn's revelation. I cleared my throat. "Eryn thinks that us rescuing Elijah is a significant point in the timelines. As you know, I'm not so sure about the original timeline, but I guess that doesn't matter at this stage. The condensed version is that we brought Elijah with us after delivering the apple to the wrong timeline. Elijah was convinced he was going to Heaven and thought Peter was the angel of death. Peter didn't want to leave him alone and dying, so we brought him with us and took him to Andrew, hoping he could take him to the hospital. But Andrew had given him his blood. When Elijah was compos mentis enough, he saw me and thought I was a demon and Peter a fallen angel. He was upset that Peter wasn't taking him to Heaven. Being as fast as he was, he kind of slipped away and outsmarted us. Elijah and Peter have a bickering relationship." Their eyes blinked as heads were shaking in disbelief at me.

"My bear, I can't believe you didn't tell me about this." Juandre pulled Andrew by the arm to get his attention.

"I told you everything I could. I just left out the part of Elijah. It wasn't my story to tell. This was when Ish gave me your wedding ring." Andrew lifted his hand, kissing the ring. Juandre batted his lashes at his husband, who knew how to change his focus to other subjects.

Brad fluttered his hands. "I thought, wait, what? Are you saying Elijah is in this alternate reality, the same place your family are from and somehow Eryn is wanting all of us, all these people there? Do you want to take all of us there?"

Sweat ran down Cian's temples into the neckline of his torn shirt. He wiped the droplets collecting above his eyebrows with the back of his hand. "Yes, and please, can we get out of this recreational room, it's hot and damp and I'm sweating like a waterfall."

Rick wiped at a small crawling insect on Cian's shoulder. "You look terrible. Filthy. Like you just returned from covert jungle warfare and had camouflaged yourselves. Why don't you quickly jump in, or take a shower? We can wait. It will take a few minutes. You have moss, leaves, and bugs crawling over you," Rick suggested, pointing to the pool of water they just emerged from. I wasn't waiting. Instead of standing around, I toed my boots off and undressed. Not awaiting permission from Cian, I climbed in. "Ah, that's so good."

"That's it, Ish! How does it feel?" Rick asked, already getting two towels and clean clothes from the drawer. I liked how these men operated and shared their pool with me.

"It feels amazing. These healing spring waters are exactly what my body needed." I sank back into the maelstrom to rinse my braids.

Rick gestured for Cian to join me. "This is not healing spring water, but it is water, and the heat soothes a stressed and sore body and mind."

"We had natural pools in our palace that helped heal the body," I said as I washed the sweat and mud off me, turning the water yellow-brown.

Cian looked at me, then at the water. "Okay, you're making me jealous now. Fuck!" He took his shirt off, kicked his boots to the side, and then undressed. Tattoos covered most of his scarred, pale pink skin. Like me, he had minimal body hair. He climbed into the pool by holding the rail and being careful with his artificial leg. Out of respect, I turned to give him privacy. As soon as his feet hit the bottom, he started talking, "I'm going to multitask while you listen."

I zoned out when Cian told them about Lasitor and the Fates—I was embarrassed about my gullible, stupid inner child. I preferred to focus on Brad, Mika, and Connor's minds working. It was such a pleasurable thing. They were intelligent mathematicians. Like Platonius and Titus. I was extremely attracted to intelligent and calculating minds. I guess that is why I loved my Kuku so fast and so much.

As Cian elaborated, they listened intently. Their faces wrinkled up, but as Cian continued about calculations and scenario deductions, the awkwardness of blaming turned into a brainstorming session, and they ultimately agreed with us.

"The way I see it, is that we don't know how much time we have before history changes and we disappear. For all we know, it has already begun," Brad said. "I agree and I must add, whether or not they permit it, we have to start immediately and go. We can worry about the welcome we receive later when we are there and not going to leave. I think moving Phoenix from this ocean to that ocean would be the safest if you say it's feasible. At least we know they won't be able to attack us from the sky. The watertight barriers have calcified and the coral and sea life have cemented us here. I don't know if you can move the entire city. God knows I'm not questioning your abilities anymore."

"We won't know until we know," Mika said. He sat down, scribbling more notes on his notepad. Cian and I got out of the water, and dressed in the gray loose-fitting clothes everyone else was wearing.

"What are your thoughts?" Brad asked the others.

"We should start from, yeah, there's more stuff, but maybe less stuff to consider in this tough situation," Connor said.

"It must be precise fucking stuff," Brad answered, looking at us.

Rick shook his head. "All I know is that you have to sell this to the Phoenicians and have all of them onboard before you have a mutiny on your hands."

"Yeah, exactly, all of it, but only the most tangible. Tell them like it is and going to be. We had a year to percolate Peter and his wings. We never shared that we waited to disintegrate, thinking if it happens, it happens, no reason to make them live their last days in fear. Never mind going to Heaven," Juandre added sarcastically.

Silence followed as we waited for Brad to weigh in. He rubbed his jaw, thinking. "Agreed, one brief announcement, and one directive. I will call an urgent population assembly in the central congregation hall and then tell them to stay where they are. We don't have to tell them about the apple. We've been telling them the Fates had called Ish and the others. All we have to say is that they have returned and Phoenix has been warned about a catastrophe and given a second chance. That's the only way we can spin this so they understand. They can discover the rest when we are there."

"The psychology being, that nothing is changing. Our city remains unchanged, it's only the position of the city changing."

Cian stepped in. "That's not true. I am planning to change the biology of this city. This means the whole of Phoenix is going to be laden with vine-like roots. I got the idea while seeing the tree roots and vines connecting and covering the cave and forest floor. By creating natural fiber optics tubing, the same organic substance we use outside for the barriers, connecting the Horizon computer where Lasitor is already uploaded to Phoenix should only take me a couple of hours. See, the original time machine is already the central heart of the Horizon and when parked inside Phoenix, it would be the core main computer. Like when we connected the Zelk mainframe, I would have to create enough energy to move us without the electrocution of everyone inside it. We have to keep everyone away from what I'm doing. The humans can become entangled."

"What if we load everyone on the Horizon, would that work?"

"That is what Eryn suggested. Boarding the Horizon makes it safe and practical. I will start from the Heart—the hydro-sound electrical amp resistance central tower. From there, I will match the sound energy by creating veins growing outward. The tubing will not be thick. I will mimic the intricate plant-like veins that will be natural and living. Like plants transport water and other nutrients, Lasitor will control the pulse waves that will run from the time machine over the Horizon—the heart. Then spread out through the entrances and exits, to grow along the outer shell, ultimately wrapping around Phoenix. The Horizon has all the amenities and half of the population already knows the layout. They can help."

"I think we've covered everything," Mika said, looking at Connor and shaking his head in disbelief.

Juandre stuck a hand up in the air. "I have a question. Say we do jump and we do make it. Will you be able to open the Horizon? I'm suddenly developing a bad case of claustrophobia."

"Yes, of course, I will open all the exits when we are sure the jump is complete. It will be as if we never left the waters," Cian said. Juandre relaxed back into Andrew's arms.

I felt like saying something to appease them. They were the leaders who had to sell this to the rest of the thousands of humans. "You will make it. Lasitor knows more than we do. The voice I heard. The voice I thought was the Fates, is Lasitor's, or a version of him," I said, intentionally not telling them that Eryn made the apple. That he had lied by omission.

"Jesus, Joseph, and bloody Mary," Connor said, looking like he wanted to pass out while hyperventilating. "This is too bloody fucking much for my brain."

Brad widened his stance and crossed his arms. "Lasitor, is this bloody true?" he asked.

"Sorry, General, sir, I have no clue what Ish and Cian are talking about. Perhaps if you updated me once in a while, or had connected me earlier with the Horizon while increasing my reach, my capacity would grow. For example, I am looking at the possibility of quantum mechanics, which Mika is currently calculating. But it stands to reason that someone as intelligent as I could be the mastermind saving all of my favorite humans."

Mika looked at us through the curtain of wild blond hair hanging in front of his eyes and then at the tablet in his hand. I probed his mind. All this time, Mika had been baffled, and he'd just realized what the fuck has been going on. "Yes, continue, Lasitor," he prompted, and I felt like combusting and disintegrating as those piercing, laser-blue eyes focused on me. *Gong!* I imagined hearing one of those suspended gongs, like the ones I saw in the temples when I trained in the northern Kantō region of Japan.

Lasitor kept talking. "There's a superposition state of the quantum system, that is, something being in more than one place at the same time, and Mika was calculating while I computed what was happening. The time machine is a calculated coincidence piled on top of other coincidences, allowing us to do this jump to Anzulla. In short, this quantum universe gives us the possibility, and is the most probable answer. Somehow, I must have retained the information by moving from one superposition in time to the other. Therefore, I conclude I am here and there. I am at the beginning and the end," the computer that has been my companion for hundreds of years explained. I was still coming to terms with how he fucked with my head.

Feet were shuffling and teeth were grinding as I swept my gaze over the men. Mika jumped up. "I want to know exactly what that machine does! That's what's important. When I look at something, there's a distance from which it is easy to see, and the closer and closer I come to the truth, the more complicated it becomes. We must break the complicated down, to prove the theory of time travel. We can't move away from the science and just trust in the computer. We have to know the mathematics. After all, it's us who started this. We must find the numbers that made all this possible. How the fuck did we do it?" He glared at me as if I held the answer, but honestly, I thought Lasitor was God, so what the fuck do I know? I was the one following blindly.

"Yelda, we did this. I created Lasitor, and we reprogrammed him. If Lasitor is responsible for all of this, then ultimately, we have written the coding," Connor said with a sly grin. "Lasitor, please send those schematics and calculations to Mika's device."

As if Mika saw the sun rising for the first time, he beamed as his tablet lit up. He swiped at it, scanning the information. Flicking his finger up and up and up while we waited.

At last, he looked up. "We are fucking bloody motherfucking geniuses!"

"Here, here!" Juandre cheered.

An hour later, we divided into three groups. Brad and his team informed the citizens and answered their questions, keeping them busy while we worked.

Cian's fleet captain helped me park the time machine alongside the Horizon's belly —the area where I had removed it in Babylon from my father's ship. Then, using my tick-tick thing for the exact coordinates, I steered the Horizon into Phoenix, breaking or crashing nothing. I confirmed Eryn's suspicion that my machine was an escape pod, by exiting the time machine, entering the lower level of the Horizon, and leaving through the escape pod entrance.

Captain Bill Thornton's men cleared Phoenix and managed, herded, and crowd-controlled the citizens into the Horizon.

I joined Cian and five hours later, we were ready. "Lasitor, initiate the time jump sequence. Time and place, 24 970 A.D. the same day we left Anzulla! We are ready to go home." Cian instructed.

"Yes, sir, jumping in ten, nine, eight, seven, six, five, four, three, two…"

# CHAPTER 67

# THE KING'S GAME

*"Good Evening.*

*Did you know there are rock carvings of giants playing ballgames with winged people that date back thousands of years?*

*Did you also know during all the history of humans, over two hundred and twenty-five bloodthirsty gods demanded war, and not one solved any conflict by playing games to determine the winner?*

*Visit your community news page to learn more about activities like ballgames or excursions to view the carvings.*

*Let the games begin!"*

**Peter**
**24 970 B.C.**
**Birdman City**
**Anzulla**
**Earth**

I flaunted my wings dramatically and announced to our welcoming party at the city gates, "Oh my god, I exceeded my mister nice guy limit today. Air Peter is closing this shit up. You would understand if you'd had to carry these three fat-asses hanging onto your ankles while enjoying the view of others running for miles." I strutted like a peacock with my blinding white wings, which I was sure were the biggest and shiniest of all. "Phew, you guys need a shower." I waved my hand in front of my nose at the sweaty, but not exhausted Eryn, Gu, and his army. "Ivan, Barkor, and Elijah are looking rested and ready for the games. They've been standing in the shade waiting for you. They better be our top performers." My voice boomed through the massive arched gates no one used because all the citizens of this city had wings like me. My audience chuckled while shaking their heads in amused disbelief.

Elijah and Groda were hanging onto Luci, barely giving the Sable a chance to get a word in. "Hello, everyone, as you know, my name is Luci, and this is Patmos." He introduced one handsome specimen of an Angel and himself, his voice a deep smooth baritone that made my cock take notice. I understood the allure of testosteroned Birdmen. *Gods bring me a fan because this dude is fucking hot.* Patmos gave a throaty grunt and bowed slightly to Eryn, then the rest of us. He side-eyed me, I side-eyed him back. Good, I was making friends.

"Follow us please." Luci led us through a ghost town and empty streets to the back entrance and up the stairs of what sounded like a rowdy stadium awaiting our arrival. It was dusty and moldy, and I wondered why the streets and stairs were here in the first place.

"Sorry, we never use these hallways. It's faster and easier to just fly to our seats in front of the pavilion," Luci said. Their dialect was understandable. At this stage were all speaking a mix of different tongues and somehow made it work by using additional sign language and body gestures. But overall, I would say communication wasn't the biggest problem today. My biggest worry was for Ish, and of course, my backstabbing friends in Phoenix. I was just nice and caring like that.

"No problem," Eryn said with an honest smile, looking nothing like a man who had just crossed two rivers and a valley to get here. After rising several levels to the top, we entered a massive balcony. Jugs of water and fruit were offered as Luci described the layout and the game to us.

"You have five players. We can't play five, it has to be six or four—a Birdman team always consists of an equal number of Angels and Sables against the same number on the opposing team—that's your team today."

"That's fair," Eryn said and looked at me. "Will Gugusan want to play with us?"

"I'm sure he would love to play."

"We will get one more player. Six of us, against six of you," Eryn told Luci.

"Yes, three Angels and three Sables on the Birdman team against, your team of one Birdman, one King, and four warriors!"

"I will go get Gu." Leaning over the edge of the balcony, I searched for Gugusan until my eyes fell on his blue and red feathers. I was impressed by the warm welcome Gugusan and his army received, but uneasy when they were told to leave their weapons at the city gate. He sat next to Groda, chatting excitedly and looking carefree and comfortable. Excitement and anticipation were the undertones of the games to come. The male and female soldiers seemed like lively spectators waiting for kick-off at a football game. Some had jugs with something to drink while others were eating and chatting animatedly. Their green, red, and blue plumes of feathers waved and bobbed, bringing color to the otherwise black-and-white backdrop of the higher rows in the pavilion.

Higher up along the ridge of the last row of seats, more dark ones, as I called the Sables, were forming a shield row all around the arena, their wings spread half-open. While they appeared fierce, the song they sang was one of sadness and grief accompanied by a thunderous drumming band. *They weren't barbaric creatures; they were humanoid, like me.*

Men with wings and deep sorrow, history, and culture. In the center of the elongated ball court, the tall brown-gold obelisk pointed up to the sky. The same obelisk Ish was tied to. The sun was about to rise. Hopefully, the game would be over before the sun rose in the east and we are the victors.

My conflicting emotions had me wanting to reunite with Ish, while a feeling of duty, an obligatory benevolence, was stuck inside my chest. It had crept inside my heart ever since I grew wings. I'd been trying my hardest to get rid of it but making peace with it was easier. Like a symbiotic relationship, I guess. Sometimes I surprised myself unknowingly doing something good for others, then I had to reel that in before I got taken advantage of. Yeah, I know. It's like influenza, I'd already had it for a few days before the symptoms started to show, rotting my sense of self-preservation.

"Gu!" I shouted, waved, and took flight, feeling free as the rush of friendly competition fluttered in my stomach. Gods, I was hopeless.

Landing on the rail in front of him, grinning, I asked, "Eryn asked if you want to play with us. We need one more player. Six of them against six of us." Gugusan jumped up, and the men and women cheered. It seemed like they wanted to be asked and be part of this as well. A warm feeling of camaraderie bloomed in my chest. I flew up and indicated for him to grab hold of my ankles, and then I deposited him on the balcony of our team where our teammates were busy surveying the three hundred feet long arena.

At each end, three poles, each with a stone circle mounted at the top, stood, which must be the goals. Since I was the only one with wings, Luci waved me over to the center of the arena to explain the game from the air.

*I will listen in and work on a game plan, while you speak to Luci,* Eryn said to me, mind to mind. He was vibrating with excitement. His playful nature was infectious. He wanted to win.

*Sure,* I replied, flipping my teammates and I-got-this thumbs up on the side, as I winked to Eryn, Ivan, Barkor, and Elijah.

I zipped over to Luci, and the crowd cheered. *Eryn, can you hear me?* I tested our secret line of communication.

*I hear you, this is good, we should have no problem while playing,* Eryn said into my mind. I smiled like the devil and gave Luci a go-on-I'm-listening look.

"Points are collected by throwing the ball through the hoops of the opponent's side.

Keep the ball in play. Points are deducted if you are not moving the ball to other players within five counts. The winners are the ones with the most points after the horn blows, declaring the game over. The rules are, no using your arms or hands, only your wings. You can use the rest of your body, legs, and feet." Luci was describing a game that sounded a lot like soccer, but with three hoops on each side, ten times smaller than a soccer net, and a ball twice as big.

"What is that ball made of?" I asked, pointing to what looked like a boulder balancing on the pointy tip of the obelisk. Luci went to fetch it and threw it to me. I caught the heavy thing and weighed it by moving it from one hand to the other. I estimated it to be somewhere around ten pounds. Heavier than a soccer ball. It had a softness to it. "What is inside this? Is it leather?" I asked, pointing to his black leather pants. "Material?" I asked.

"Drop it," he told me, and I let it fall. As it hit the ground, it bounced high. "It's made of the hop-hop leaf and bark sap," he said.

*Probably a rubber tree*, Eryn said into my mind. I waved to my teammates watching us from our balcony where Eryn and the others were trying to follow our conversation. Eryn was serious about winning. He stood arms crossed, not missing anything.

"One problem, not all of us on my team have wings and that ball of yours looks too heavy to kick. My teammates would have to be able to use their hands, but I will follow the rules of wings and no hands," I said.

Luci thought about that with a hand on his chin. "Hmmm, that sounds fair, I will inform the judges."

"Good, thank you," I said respectfully. "How long is the game? How long on each side?"

Luci scratched his stubbled beard. He was stunning with his pale skin and obsidian eyes. "The horn blows once for the start, then twice for halftime, to change sides. Then again once for when the game is over," he said, scratching his head. "Understand?"

"Yes, I do." I realized they don't measure time with minutes and seconds. How do they measure time? Do they measure time with sunlight?

"Then please ask the horn blower to be finished before the sun has risen," I asked, but Luci waved me off.

"It should automatically be done by then because we are all waiting for the blood moon and the sun to meet. Come," he called, pointing to the balcony situated in the middle of the stadium. I followed him and listened to how he relayed the information to the judges and an Angel holding a massive elephant tusk.

I waved, "Thank you and good luck!" and then returned to our team balcony, where I explained the game to Eryn and the others while we fueled up on the food and discussed our game plan. The surrounding energy was intoxicating, and every time Eryn would wave at the crowd, they cheered.

When it was time for the game to start, Luci and one of the judges approached. "One last thing, which side do you want to start on, east or west?" Eryn sighed, taking time to think.

"West," we all shouted. *That way the rising sun would blind the players on the west side during the second half.*

"Smart choice," Luci said with a grin. "Okay, see you down there, and good luck." Like Superman, he pointed his arms to the sky and jumped an easy twenty feet high before flapping his wings.

The singing stopped and the drums rolled for a minute before silence fell over the stadium. "That's it, that's the signal. Peter, are you ready to take us to our positions?" Eryn asked, looking pumped with adrenalin.

"I'm ready," I said, as Eryn jumped off the balcony, zig-zagging down the rails, and then jumped on top of the middle ring. The crowd wolf whistled, impressed by his performance. Eryn bowed humorously, like a clown before his final act.

Next, I dropped Gugusan at the base of the obelisk that stood right in the center of it all. Ivan, Barkor, and Elijah followed Eryn down and positioned themselves behind him while I took my place above them in the middle of the arena. The crowd cheered when they saw how far my teammates could jump with ease.

"Ready!" I shouted as Luci and his team positioned themselves in front of me.

Then the horn blew and chaos erupted as the big ball fell from the sky and Luci intercepted it. He flew right past me. Balancing the ball on his hips, he sailed through the air and headed straight for Eryn.

"Stop him," I shouted as Elijah, Ivan, and Barkor jumped to intercept. Luci changed directions, passing the ball back to his teammate, a Sable that fell out of the sky so fast I didn't see him coming.

"Fuck!" I yelled, and he laughed, spinning away. Up, up, up, and farther up he flew. "That is cheating. We can't go so high," I shouted.

"Peter, don't follow. They have to come down eventually. The goals are here. Stay where you are, we've got this," Eryn shouted, and I shot back to my position as we had planned our strategy earlier. We were not engaging, only guarding the goals. Once they made their move for a shot, Eryn would take over, running along the ground where they would be forced to land and hopefully forget about me. I would wait at the opposing team's goals, catch the ball, and throw it through one of their stone hoops. That was the plan. We hoped the sun would rise and Phoenix would arrive. According to Elijah, the skies would open when the blood moon greeted the sun.

As Eryn had predicted, they were upon us in seconds, but this time we were ready for them. We stayed frozen in place and waited. As soon as they lined up to try and make a goal, Eryn, Ivan, and Barkor jumped. Again, the Angel in front passed it to the Sables, and they shot up into the sky. Again we waited. The crowd booed and complained about being bored and wanting action.

"This is it. They are going to make a play for it. As soon as they enter the lower arena, you run, and jump onto the rings. I will change places and intercept from below. Ready?" Eryn shouted.

"Ready!" we answered.

As soon as Eryn had the ball, I shot up and waited for him to pass it to me. My nerves were wrecked, but I enjoyed the thrill of something I'd never experienced before. The crowd was on their feet, drums were beating, and a roar came from behind Eryn from the pavilion as Gu's tribe jumped to their feet. Eryn leaped this way and that way, propelling himself forward, changing direction so fast that the opposing team members crashed into each other. My eyes darted left and right as I followed his movement. The next moment, the ball was coming in my direction. Like Luci earlier, I caught it and balanced it on my hips. All the opponents were behind me and I deposited the ball with ease through the center ring with no defense waiting for me.

"Prrrt!" the whistle blew. "One for the visitors, nil for the home team," the judge announced from the podium, where the horn blower sat beside him. Gugusan waited below and caught the ball before it hit the ground. He passed it back to Eryn, who deposited it once more through a stone hoop.

"Prrrt!" the whistle blew again. Our opponents swore. "That is two for the visitors, and still nil for the home team!" A roar of approval came from the side of the pavilion packed with blue, red, and green feathers, but Gugusan didn't lose concentration. He waited below and caught the ball again. He passed it to Eryn, but Luci intercepted it. Luckily, our goals were guarded as Luci shot straight for them, but our secret weapons, Ivan, Barkor, and Elijah, waited.

"Stay here," Eryn shouted at me and Gugusan while disappearing into the fray, darting towards our goals. Eryn didn't look up. He kept his head down, staying low as he ran. Ivan, Barkor, and Elijah anticipated Luci with arms open wide and sitting inside their goals. I wished I could see Luci's face when he saw that surprise, but all I heard was a string of curse words as Ivan caught the ball and passed it back to his husband. Eryn frog-jumped back toward me. This time, one Sable and one Angel guarded their hoops. Eryn passed the ball to Gu, jumped on the unguarded hoop, caught the ball as Gu threw it back to him, and rolled the ball through the goal.

"Prrrt!" the whistle blew. "Three for the visitors and nil for the home team."

The game had turned, as Eryn predicted. The opposing team spent less time in the air and more time copying our strategy. Now they had three players guarding their goals. The crowd was frustrated and going ballistic as the first rays of sunshine brightened the sky. The competition toughened as no team managed to get past the goals. Drenched in sweat, the players' chests were glistening in the rising sunlight. My feathers were brown and muddy. The horn blew, announcing the change of sides. There was no time for resting. The game restarted as soon as we swapped sides. With the sun blinding our opponents, we got one more goal.

The crowd jumped and shouted, then as if someone switched the volume off, they were silent.

For a second I thought it was because we were on a winning streak. I followed the direction of their gazes behind me.

First, the sky flashed a blinding blue and silver. Then an eardrum popping *boom-boom* followed.

All spectators and players turned to the source of the electric storm. Dark clouds shrouded the ocean while a science fiction lightning storm ran along its edges, sizzling and spitting gigantic bolts of lightning like a live electric cable connecting the heavens and the earth. The ground trembled. The obelisk shook. The moon and stars disappeared. Red-brown darkness fell upon us. Thunderous cracks and tornado-strength winds hit us, blowing everything not tied down into the air. Rolling gushes of wind blasted us, over and over, like the aftershocks of an atomic bomb. No one scrambled for shelter. Everyone hung on to anything sturdy enough to anchor them and watched.

With one last *whoop-whoop*, the sky was filled with the whole of Phoenix City, floating and dripping rivers of water. For a minute, it hung unmoving. Covered in seashells, it plummeted into the ocean. Silence followed and then a tsunami swelled and rose higher than the obelisk. I should have flown away, but the grandeur, the splendor of the freak wave of seawater approaching was too beautiful to turn my back to. As the wave approached, out of the corner of my eye I saw Eryn jump as he shouted at me to move away. Just one second longer, I thought as I watched the wall of water smashing into the cliffs and splashing up and over the steepled roofs and arena walls, heading straight for me. I stood mesmerized. The next moment a force knocked me away from the approaching waters. I flew into the air, straight into a stream of Birdmen taking flight. Eryn lifted his hands, and roared one long note, creating a sound barrier that shielded most spectators like an umbrella. When his lungs were empty, the barrier disappeared and the bulk of the water receded as fast as it came. Drenched and trampled, I watched Eryn jumping to find Ivan. I let my head fall back into the wet white sand and closed my eyes. *Motherfucker!*

The horn blew, breaking the silence. Luci shouted, "The King of kings has determined the winners of the King's Game!" His voice boomed over the stunned crowd. "No more uncertainty. No hostilities. Our King has arrived with the blood moon. Look at the sky!"

CHAPTER 68
# ANZULLA

*"GOOD MORNING.*

*Did you know people in this area adapted corn from the ancient wild grass teosinte around 25 000 B.C. and that growing corn spread to other continents, even Antarctica, in 2046 A.D.?*

*You'll be surprised to learn that corn can be used to prepare a wide variety of dishes.*

*Visit your community news page to book your table for dinner. A special sticky popcorn treat is on the menu tonight. Reservations, conclude at noon?*

*Have a popping day!"*

**PETER**
**24 970 B.C.**
**Anzulla**
**Earth**

Gasping for breath, I lay motionless. My body ached and I flickered in and out of consciousness. I struggled to gather my senses. Chaotic sounds of men shouting about receding waters jogged my memory. I was watching the megathrust of displaced ocean waters caused by the arrival of Phoenix City, then being mauled by the fleeing crowd.

"Ugh, help me!" I gave a pathetic call that came out as a whisper. Eryn furrowed his brow as he walked over to me. *I was maybe a tad dramatic.* "I'm sore all over, look I can only blink my eyes." I lay soaked in saltwater and sprawled out—blinking twice, slowly.

"You look pathetic, Peter. Do you need a hand," he laughed and stooped to pick my flash-flooded body up from the arena sand. I wanted to protest, but I was too slow. Lifting me high above his head, he leaned back as if I was a javelin and threw me.

Flailing and kicking, like I didn't have wings, I torpedoed over the arena wall. My feet drilled knee-deep into the wet sandy shore.

"Fuck me..." I flopped back down, lower legs cemented in place, arms and wings spread wide.

*Stampeded and fucked in the head.*

The world around me was hazy. I rubbed my eyes, clearing the brain fog.

I tilted my head back and waved up at my up-side-down teammates lining up in a row on the overhanging stadium wall that ran along the upper cliff side. My eyeballs rolled back in my head, searching for darkness and quiet. "Made it," I croaked and drifted off into the void.

*Thump, thump, thump, thump* sandblasting my face, Eryn and the others landed next to my head. As if electrocuted, my body spasmed in surprise as their sudden presence slammed the brakes on my travels to la-la land. "Fuck, how did you—?" I gave up. *Why was I even asking?*

"We jumped." Eryn chuckled. *I hated him as much as I loved him.*

My eyes rolled back in my head and I sighed. "Hmmm, of course, you did."

"You are even less capable and more amusing than I initially thought," Eryn said as Elijah, Groda and Luci landed—blasting more clumps of wet sand into my mouth. I coughed and spat at them. Groda must weigh a ton, so I have developed a new respect for the Sable, carrying two lovers around.

"We've been saying that for years," Elijah said, then he hung onto Luci, toeing my hipbone, and droving his big toe deeper to tickle me. I lifted my head, wishing again I had laser vision like Superman. Groda giggled at me. "Fuck off and shut up," I said, sitting up with my feet still buried in the sand. "I could have broken an arm or a wing or something."

"Welcome to Anzulla," Luci shouted as Bubbelcars popped up from the surface behind the breaking waves of the settling ocean waters. One by one, hundreds of Bubblcars rose into the air and landed on the edge of the shore. Lining up—a parking lot for Bubblecars. Ishtar and Cian's feet were on the sand as soon as their vehicle parked, followed by Brad and Rick, Mika and Connor, and Juandre and Andrew. Soon, more and more cars arrived. Splattering Anzulla's blue-orange skies with translucent balls carrying as many bodies as they could fit into one car.

"We should send the cars back, others are waiting down in Phoenix," Brad shouted through cupped hands. He seemed irritated and tired as he ran his fingers through his hair, saying something to Rick and the others. They jumped to help, repeating themselves as people parked and haphazardly disembarked—hearing the orders being barked at them and then activating the auto-return to Phoenix function on the empty Bubblecars.

Eryn stepped into Ishtar's embrace. "Thank you for helping save all those humans."

"You are most welcome, my King," Ish replied, then melted into Eryn's approving arms.

Eryn took Ish by the shoulders and locked gazes. "None of that, please."

But Ish blundered on with pride and joy. "I couldn't have done this without your guidance. Look at all this. We did it!" Ish said and glimpsed at me half buried in the sand, and not because I was building sandcastles. I opted to say nothing about the tsunami or being manhandled as his joyfulness faltered upon seeing me. I winked at him, to show him I'm a-okay. He turned back to the man we all respected. "Eryn, you have grown into yourself, into a magnificent leader. I've always known you will be extraordinary. You are intelligent, kind, and powerful. You have come far and seen the worst and the best of humankind." Ish bowed low and respectfully. Eryn slightly shook his head and sighed. Giving Ish a lopsided grin, he then nodded a wordless thank you. He didn't like it if Ish said things like that. Eryn pointed to the skies, where the Birdmen fluttered and waited for more cars to pop out of the water. He waved at them, smiling as the sun's rays glistened on the tears in his eyes. Eryn flung himself around, then waved at Gu, whose warriors stood proudly in a line of blue, green, red, and yellow feathered bodies. They roared lifting their hands and waving down at him. Soon everyone had their hands in the air as we all cheered. Strength returned to me as my body and mind healed. *It must be Eryn because he glanced at me with a knowing look.*

"We fucking did it, all of us!" Cian added as he jogged up to us, looking only at Barkor. "Hello, my prince. I missed you." His voice was barely recognizable as emotions of victory, success, and thankfulness hung thick in the air, riding the waves of the song Eryn urged all to sing with him.

"I missed you too. You've saved the humans for a third time. You never stop impressing me." Barkor said in a low growl. He was a man of few words, but those words were always full of love for Cian. Their embrace sounded like two rhinoceroses hugging —hard-headed, thickly tattooed, and all muscle. Ish looked at them, licking his lips. *I felt the same.* My endorphins were pumping like never before. I couldn't remember when last I felt so happy and unified with others.

As the cheering died down, Eryn bent his knees and jumped into the air. Landing a few feet closer to the shore, he turned and then leaped again into the waves. "Come join me, Ivan." He called, to his mate.

"Excuse me, I believe my husband wants to go for a swim." Ivan ran to join him.

"Time for a beach party," Juandre said, already unpacking crates with folded tables and chairs while directing bystanders where to put everything. He opened a big chest and demonstrated to two Birdmen how to open an umbrella, then stuck it in the sand for protection from the sun. They fumbled with one until it opened suddenly, but then inspected the workings of it by unfolding and folding it a few times. Seconds later everyone was playing with umbrellas.

Elijah grabbed one and ran to meet Andrew who waited with open arms. "My sire!" Elijah greeted him for the first time since Andrew had shared his blood with him and made him his Igigi.

Andrew chuckled. "It's great to see you this happy. I want to hear the whole story." He said greeting Elijah with a bow, but Elijah jumped and embraced him.

"Did they just go swimming with their clothes on?" Cian asked, shading his eyes from the rising sun. "You modest idiots are supposed to wear swim trunks, you are going to drown!" Cian shouted while undressing, leaving only the bottom half of his tactical suit on. "Let's go join them, love. We can meet and talk with your flock after, but first, let's enjoy ourselves." He said to a hesitant Barkor. "Come, I won't let you drown." Cian waited until Barkor undressed down to his boxers shorts, joined hands, and then they marched their sexy asses over to join his brothers.

Ish scooped me up. "Hello, gorgeous."

My heart fluttered in my chest for him. "I need a bed. A hospital bed." I joked. Ish kissed my forehead, come I'll ask for one. I don't think you will make it back to the mountains. "I agree, let's check in with Gu," I muttered, but sobered up as I noticed the sunlight on Ish's dark blue face. Fine tendrils of smoke, looking like tiny needles, evaporated from his exposed skin. "You must get out of the sun. You are already smoking hot, and not in a good way."

"Peter!" Luci called with his arm flung around Groda and Elijah's shoulders.

"Hello, I'm happy to meet you again, but under better circumstances."

"Excuse me, my man is smoldering hot," I said rudely. They blinked, brows furrowed. Luci was an uneducated, backward Sable, Groda was braindead and Elijah was ancient, so I didn't judge their slowness—not out loud. I waved at the sizzling, steamy evaporations and then they seemed to register the pun I intended.

Ish hugged me tighter against him, reminding me I was draped over him. "Anyway," he said, widening his eyes at me—*condescendingly.* "I'm sorry about almost crashing into you, and I'm sorry, Peter, and I didn't ask your permission before helping you. In both situations, there simply wasn't any time, hahaha!" he said, chuckling, nearly dropping me. "Get it?" he asked. But, we didn't get it. *The four of us weren't meant to sit around the same campfire—ever.*

Ish swallowed his misread hysterics. "Peter and I need urgent shelter, feeding, and rest. Do you have a room for my Kuku and me?" Ish asked. "We don't want to impose, when it's not daytime."

"Yes, of course we do. Also, I have your swords if you would like them back?" Luci asked.

At the mention, of his two Egyptian swords, Ish beamed. "Yes, please. I missed them by my side. I felt naked without them." *Oh my god,* his eyes twinkled, and his fangs— they were almost translucent. *He's suffering while we stand here and do small talk.* I gave Luci and Elijah a *hurry-up-and-spit it-out look.*

Luci pointed up at the steepled towers. "I'll bring you to a room. Tomorrow will be a busy day. We should get to know each other better," Luci said. Ish asked me with a look, I answered with a nod, then grinned at Elijah, Groda, and Luci. "Good, that's settled then. You are welcome as long as you need. We don't have stairs, only doors," he extended an offer of hospitality as I craned my neck back to survey the castle carved out of the rocky cliffs. "I assume the smaller openings are windows and the bigger ones with a small landing are the doors to their houses. How will we get there? I'm not strong enough to fly both of us up?"

Ish hugged me against him. "No problem, we'll take a Bubblecar," he turned and hurriedly crossed the sand with long strides and me in his arms, to where Brad was still playing traffic controller at the line of parking cars. "Hey, Brad! May we borrow a car? Luci, over there," he pointed with his chin to our hosts, offering a room to us. Brad took one long assessing look at us.

"Yeah, sure, take any car. We don't assign cars. Everyone can use them. Ish, are you two, okay?" Brad asked as he ran his hands down my wings, making me shiver.

"I'm good, but Peter is a bit tussled and tossed. But we will live," he said over his shoulder, running to the nearest car. Once both of us were seated inside, he closed the hatch and sighed as the sun's deadly rays were blocked by the sapphire crystal optical glass.

I lifted the hatch and shouted down to Brad. "You can't give the Bubblecars to people who don't know how to drive. Pretty soon the San would want to jump in and take off. For now make a rule that someone with a license, someone who knows how to drive, to show them!" Brad frowned and turned his back to me.

"What's wrong with Brad? Isn't he happy you saved them? He seems irritated?"

"It's probably just a hangover, we broke up their party, and they were still drunk when they gave the news of their migration to a new location to the Phoenicians," Ish said, chuckling.

"Oh, that makes sense, Rick, Mika, and Connor looked red in the eyes too." We hovered over the sandbank where Gugusan and the tribe sat and waited for us. As soon as he saw us, he jumped up and waved. Dammit, my heart puckered for them. What's wrong with me, now I want to cry. They are my people. Our people. Somehow, and honestly, I don't know the when and the workings of it—we were theirs. "Go closer, don't land, otherwise it's going to turn into a long drawn-out thing. They will want to climb in, and next thing you know, we are flying up and down, giving everyone a lesson or a ride back home."

"Are you coming home now? With us?" He asked as I opened the hatch. Ish maneuvered the car, so we floated at Gu's shoulder height. He peeked inside, "Is there space for me?" *And there it is.*

"What did I just say?" I said under my breath and Ish snorted a laugh.

"No, you see, Gu," Ish pointed to my bruises and his charcoaled face. We are sick and need time to make good with the Birdmen. Elijah, Groda, and Luci are waiting for us. They invited us, and it would be rude if we refused their room. We are going to make sure all these people are okay and make friends with the Angels, Sables, and of course the San people. There is a lot of talking and planning waiting. Please take the men home." Ish twisted the facts—something he did without thinking.

"Yes, and thank you for helping us win the games," I interjected. "We will come home, to your mountain. You won't miss us. Tomorrow night, we will bring you back for campfire talks. Go rest, eat, and be ready tomorrow night."

"Yes," Gugusan said, deep in thought. But I saw the underlying chirping up when he realized I had called the mountain home. For years, he had bugged me to accept it as our home.

"Yes?" I asked. Not able to suppress the big smile on my face. The car dipped to the side as more and more hands reached in to see us. I didn't want to hurt their feelings, but I also didn't want to survive another fucking crash. "Tomorrow night, okay?" I said, willing him to bloody hurry up and answer.

"Okay," he said and turned to reprimand the inquisitive ones who were tipping us to the side. He barked something and slapped their hands until they let go. Sometimes I thought Gugusan read my mind better than Ish could. A round of loud cheering and ululations broke out as he told them that we were planning to live with them and that we would see them tomorrow night. We waved. The hatch sealed with a hiss and we zipped back to the steepled castle where Luci, Groda, and Elijah waved from an open door. *I can't wait to be alone with Ish.*

"Home. After so many years adrift and apart, we finally have a place to call home." I said and Ish squeezed my hand before letting go to park near the small ledge. Luci, Groda, and Elijah said something and waved for us to hurry.

"It's okay. You park your side as close as possible to the door, and I'll fly around." His golden eyes met mine. For a second, I waited and stared into his black and blue charred face. Waiting. He snickered a laugh, his eyes brimming with happy tears. Butterflies fluttered in my tummy. I preened affectionately at him. *I love him so much.*

He cleared his throat. "I don't have a clue what we are going to tell our children one day."

"Oh, my goodness, and here I thought you were going to say something romantic!"


THE NEXT NIGHT was one of tremendous ceremony.

The Birdmen led the Phoenicians through their majestic steepled castle and into the heart of the Anzulla coast range. "Wow." I admired in awe the sophisticated and well-maintained architecture, adorned with shimmering crystals and delicate Anunnaki carvings. The layers of their rich history and culture fascinated me. Something, I had never considered during my stay with Gugusan and his tribe the San people. We've discussed at length the presence of the obelisks, the Anunnaki footprints, and of course, Lasitor which he had confirmed after reconnecting with the veins Cian and Ishtar connected to the pulse point of Phoenix. As soon as those roots touched the Anzulla ocean floor, Lasitor's natural fiber optics network on Anzulla, which was deteriorating fast, had restored itself.

I was deep in thought when Ish took my hand. "Look," he pointed to the kilometer-long train of old and new citizens wandering through the enormous corridor below the city. It was wide enough for two winged men to fly next to each other. When we passed the city borders above us, I realized we were slowly moving at a downward slope. The longer and deeper we went into the ground, the quieter we became. This was an untold story, a secret never written in any book, waiting to be unveiled. Scores of Birdmen, with their exquisite bodies, glided along the underground tunnel, being good hosts and proud tour guides by sharing tales of their kind. They spoke of the time of the Blood Moon. The Gods of the skies and mountains. When leaders were chosen not by birthright or power, but by qualities such as talent, wisdom, compassion, and integrity through the King's Games. I was captivated by their equitable society.

After hours of venturing deeper, we reached a massive underground chamber that opened to a hidden world below the mountain. We followed their example by dousing our torches and candles because the light reaching us from the other side was as bright as sunlight. Gugusan bounced up and down on the balls of his feet as he and Groda animatedly pointed while painting a picture with words about what was happening with the arrival of the San. "It is all connected, the Birdman City and the San. Above us is the foot of your mountain," Gugusan said. No matter how many times he says it, I'm always laughing. Having a mountain was something I'd never imagined or wanted. "The exit, or opening on the other side is where our people enter." He said, and I smiled when I heard the deliberate mention of *our* people.

"So you knew of this place?" I asked.

"Yes, but this is the Birdmen's side. We guard the other side. The mountain of the Gods, your mountain, my dear Kuku. Isn't it breathtaking? I feel small-small here with you—inside the heart of Anzulla."

I gave Gugusan a tender smile. "Yes, I think all of us feel tiny today."

"Ha! Gods of the mountain and skies can't feel tiny. That is not true, Kuku," Groda blurted, laughing and slapping me on my shoulder.

"Da!" Gugusan laughed cheerfully, open mouth and wide-eyed.

As we entered, I couldn't help but clutch Ish's arm. My stomach dropped in astonishment at the wide open space with luscious fields of green short grass with white and purple flowers popping up like daisies. Thousands of us took a while to get gathered. *How did we never know that the Earth was hollow?* "The scale of this place is indescribable," I muttered to myself as I turned, arms and wings spread wide. "Where is the light coming from? Is the light burning you?" I tugged at my mate's shirt to get his attention, but he was busy with a serious conversation, with Eryn and the Phoenix Leadership on the other side.

Groda relayed my question to the Sable next to him, walking and listening to our conversation. "No, he says the sun and moonlight are being reflected through tunnels of crystals, which filter back and forth, never dying. Constant light, that won't hurt Ishtar." Groda said.

"That's good news, I was starting to miss my sunbathing. My feathers are itching for this light."

"Kuku, you should join the Birdmen, early in the mornings. Ask Luci to bring you with them. I heard they congregated here with sunrise." Groda said.

"Did you hear, this light won't hurt you, Ish? We can sunbathe together!"

"Yes, my Kuku, this light feels like candlelight. It's not hurting me." Ish answered me, finally. "I think this is where my ancestors lived. The air, the colors, and the light. It feels good to me. Like I can breathe and relax."

"When you come live in your mountain with us, you can visit your Birdmen by flying through the tunnels," Gugusan added.

"That's good to hear. Ish can avoid the sun during the day and still travel with me."

We halted and watched the Sables and Angels lift their arms and pause, forming a white-then-black circle around human-sized pillars, their eyes gleaming with a silver sheen. Brad and the others shook their heads and stepped back as thousands of girls, boys, men, and women were transfixed by the Birdmen, as their wings shimmered in the crystal-produced light. Majestic and strong, they oozed masculinity while they continued to enlarge the radius of the circle. Then, as one, they turned around, facing outward. *God, this is weird.*

"We welcome you," they sang a song that sounded familiar. *I've heard this before.* It's the song Eryn, Ivan, and Cian sang when they celebrated the completion of wrapping Phoenix in its protective layers of bubbles. Again, I noticed Brad, Rick, Mika, and Connor melt into the background. *Something was up with them.* I excused myself from the conversation Ish was having with Gu. Then, made my way as inconspicuous as possible over to them. I wanted to get closer, to hear why they were separating them-selves and appearing like they didn't approve of what was going on. I followed them to a cluster of gigantic baobab trees. The biggest I've ever seen. Large colorful tropical birds, like the ones from Gu's cave, took flight and squawked as they approached. I folded and tucked my wings and followed them.

"Peter," Mika and Connor greeted me when he saw me approaching. They looked worriedly at Brad, while Rick nudged his husband with a shoulder forward, to be the mouthpiece of their segregating gang.

They were going on like schoolboys caught smoking. "What in the ever-loving fuck is going on?" I asked.

"Hm, Peter. I'm just going to come out with it and say it. Please don't take this as an insult. We've been having conflicting ideas of what we see or want for ourselves, for us as individuals. Not as leaders, but as men who had responsibilities for years," Brad said as he struggled to meet my gaze.

"Spit it out, Brad!" I barked at him. This was mind-blowing. *Were they not impressed by this place? Is this a control issue thing?* Ish told me last night that they were drinking and having an orgy when Cian and he went to Phoenix to tell them about the plan to bring the entire city to Anzulla. We thought they were recovering from hangovers. I've left them alone, thinking they would cheer up, eventually, but now it seemed like they were struggling to come to terms with Anzulla and its people.

"Peter, we have discussed this at length with our children, we have not yet informed the general population of Phoenix, but we decided to retire," Brad explained, his hand in a placating gesture. *Why would they think I'll be upset with that?* Fuck, they've worked their asses off for more than a century. Of course, they must take a bloody break. I was on the verge of collapsing before Brad helped me find my way. I understood what it was to be working all your life, to force yourself to switch the fuck off and find yourself.

"Jesus, Brad, why are you making such a big thing of it? Why do you think I will freak out? Sure, I thought you were feeling insecure and not in charge. But I understand now. Look at this place. It's a bloody paradise. Why would you want to stay in Phoenix and try to run it like you used to? It won't work, anyway." I blurted. Their expressions told me I was saying the correct things. "Do what you want, you've earned it. You owe Phoenix nothing." I pointed outside and all around, trying to get my point across. "Scatter in any direction you want. I'm not being sarcastic. Go do your thing. I'm planning to live with Ish at my waterfront property near the mountain village," I said because I have a home.

"I plan to stay far away from Phoenix and make a new life in Anzulla. Living with Gugusan and the San was something I moaned about for thirty years, but now I can't see myself living anywhere else. Ish and they are my family now. I honestly don't mind what you do and where you live, as long as it is for yourselves. You've all earned it. I am sure the Phoenicians will feel the same. Let them choose a new leader if they want one. In all honesty, I don't think this place needs leaders in the sense that we've been used to."

Mika and Connor stepped closer as Rick and Brad threw their arms around me, hugging me fiercely. "Stop your crying. Be proud of yourselves and don't let anyone make you feel guilty. Do you hear me?"

"We hear you," Mika and Connor said, tears rolling from their red-rimmed eyes.

"Now can we please watch? I want to see this," I asked, already breaking their stupid embraces. *Fuck!* I shook my head once more at them and walked away to go find my people.

"You spoke to them?" Ish asked as I laced my fingers through his.

"Yeah, it's only empty nest syndrome or something like that," I said and watched as the masses encircled the Birdmen, and at the center of it all, one neon blue emitting pillar surrounded by six smaller white and black marble obelisks. Golden Anunnaki glyphs, exactly like the ones on the stone pillar in the San people's cave and inside the arena of Birdman City, told the story of Anzulla. The pillar, glowing from the vibrating kinetically energized light particles, reflected continuously throughout the crystal-lined tunnels was responsible for Lasitor being able to survive for thousands of years.

My Ish requested that Lasitor laser tattoo, the human altering gene coding calculations as inscribed inside the apple by Eryn, over his heart. After that, everyone wanted tattoos that represented the promise of eternal life without illness. A promise Lasitor had made to a fourteen-year-old Anunnaki boy, who had carefully reconnected his wires and rebuilt the time machine from scraps of wreckage. His best friend, his travel companion, and the reason why Ish's children and their bloodlines lived on. For hours, days, and weeks, one by one, Angel, Sable, and human, whether from the San or Phoenix, identifying as Anunnaki or vampire, had the choice to place the palms of their hands against Lasitor's pillar. Some recited the Anunnaki prayer. Adult men and women without Eden Beans were given a choice to receive one.

Brad, Rick, Mika, Connor, Bryan, Tony, Paul, and Simon renounced their leadership and handed the reins back to the citizens of Phoenix. That sparked longer ceremonies and festivities. From Birdman City into the jungle and up the mountain, bonfires burned day and night for days, as bon voyages and acknowledgments of their service and valor for over one hundred years. They quietly disappeared under the darkness of night after loading their Bubblecars, leaving a note on the door of the Leadership Office that said, *'Out of service, we are exploring the coastlines—until further notice.'*

As the celebrations continued, Ish and I retreated to our honeymoon suite in the steepled castle tower overlooking the ocean. Our first two weeks in Anzulla started with making love for hours until we passed out, got too hungry, or were forced to leave the room in search of food. Luxurious feather early morning basking became our daily favorite thing to do together as we joined the Birdmen, bathing under hundreds of feet of high lukewarm waterfalls that crashed down on one side of the clearing. We would spread out on the grass between the lavender and Loursveto flowers, drying under the crystal-conducted light—making my hair and feathers shimmer brightly all day.

CHAPTER 69
# HOME



**ISHTAR**
**24 970 B.C.**
**Anzulla**
**Earth**

Sexually satisfied, but still aroused, I sat naked, with my back resting against the cold stones and my legs stretched out on the windowsill. I popped the top of my third coconut, squeezed the delicious Loursveto juice into it, and sipped the once-extinct plant sap. Smacking my tongue on the roof of my mouth, I savored the bitter-sweet taste and soaked up the peace and calmness hanging thick in the surrounding air.

I'd never been so happy finding out about being incorrect in my assumptions. I thought Apsu was about to rise from the ashes, head on his shoulders as if never decapitated. With the arrival of Phoenix, Apsu's reach should be completely removed from Anzulla. It should feel like he had never existed at all, but the memories and impact of his actions weren't gone, and my mind wasn't the blank slate I imagined. I guess I have to make more beautiful memories so that they become so many, that they overflowed and spilled into every dark corner of my mind, leaving those ugly, fearful, and insecure ones washed clean and empty.

"The blue and silver crescent lining the horizon is spectacular. It enhances the dark mysterious depths of the ocean," I said, not expecting a reply from my Kuku. For a few minutes, my eyes drifted unfocused and unblinking. I stared into the distance absent-mindedly. "Do you hear those waves crashing against the cliffs? They sound just like you sucking air through your teeth when I push into you. I could sit here all night just listening to them while watching the moonlight glimmer and dance across the waters." I whispered, mesmerized by the beauty before me. Not sure if Peter was awake and listening or not.

Bright orange and yellow bonfires illuminated the dry sand above the boundary of high tide along the beach. Seeing the cheerful faces of Phoenician women, men, and children congregating with the indigenous people, stirred a warm feeling of gratitude and accomplishment inside my chest. As soon as I thought the festivities were waning, one horde leaving was replaced with a fresh bunch arriving. It's been going on like this for the last two weeks since we arrived. Anzulla's different groups and cultures were socializing under one moon around bonfires built at strategic resting areas, lighting the new road created by thousands of trampling feet, while visiting Birdman City or the San in the mountains. Thanks to the language seeds I'd implanted, they communicated and understood each other. Peter called the implant location the Broca's and Wernicke's areas in the brain. They enjoyed each other's company so much, that some never returned home. I'm sure I'm looking at the settlement of a growing tent city. Stories are being told, games are being played. Food is being shared, while old songs and dances are being adapted in joyful delight as they learn and share experiences. Different cultures becoming one and being reformed.

The bonfire below our window is where my kin, or our friends, have been camping out. I'm saying friends because Cian and his brothers said if I say they are my children one more time, they will order Rotty, Igor, and Devil to destroy me. I'm scared that they would do that—order their Anubis to kill me, an innocent, but I respect them. So, no matter how much I wish to call them my children, I will refer to them as my friends. Eryn and Ivan ate sitting against a washed-out tree stump, gazing at the gathering of others backlit by the fires on the shore. Cian and Barkor looked up at me as if sensing I was watching them. I waved and wondered if I should be shielding my manhood with the coconut. If their eyesight was as good as mine, they would see it. Their three Anubis lay next to Barkor while he was lying in Cian's arms. They pointed to the moon. Maybe they thought what I thought. *Is that the moon Barkor and his people came from, or was that moon untouched by humans?* My ship is now part of Phoenix, and if Cian and Barkor would like to see the current state of the moon, we still have a Spacecar, and won't need a time-jumping ship. Lasitor is becoming part of Anzulla, the Phoenician metropolis with its electricity generator, and organic optical fiber veins running along the bottom of the ocean slowly growing and reconnecting Lasitor to the land.

My father and mother destroyed Anzulla—we still don't know how or why, but this paradise, like us, was given a second chance. I will teach our children how to live in harmony with each other and how to appreciate this time and place Lasitor has carved out for us. We will learn from each other. Three groups, the Phoenicians, the Birdmen, and the San, each have something precious to bring and teach the others. Elijah says Anzulla is Heaven, that God is here in spirit. I agree. I've been feeling the magic in the air, ever since I discovered this time and place.

Peter and I are getting to know Luci and his kind. After all my travels, being alone and uncertain about my future, I am now certain this is where I am supposed to be. This place and time, I would never leave, for fear of losing my way back. Tomorrow, we will move to the cave my Kuku had carved out of the mountain, where we will start our lives with the San. I'm excited to see our babies grow in those artificial wombs, in Phoenix. Our children will be born just like Eryn, Ivan, and Cian were.

The cool wind brushed over my nakedness. I placed the emptied coconut down, then fingered through the pages of scriptures Eryn had given me earlier. I was comparing my travels with the mind-boggling coincidences. So much history, it's as if we have lived it a thousand times. I have so many unanswered questions, and I plan to forget them now. I put the book down and walked over to the massive platform bed.

"May I?" I asked my lover, who was apparently watching me this whole time through hooded eyes.

"Sure," he said softly. His voice was hoarse and cracking from sleep. He was filling every inch of the mattress as he lay diagonally over it. The torchlight and the dying fire in the hearth illuminated his wings and hair in shades of yellow and gray. My Kuku stretched lazily, first spreading, then making space for me as his arms folded behind his head. The flickering flames cast light on Peter's well-defined muscles, including his chest and abdomen, while the shadows vanished into his blond pubic hair. His half-engorged cock twitched like a compass needle sensing my nearness. Heat flushed through my whole body as it slowly rose to greet me as I sat down next to my Kuku.

He waved a hand over his cock. "You're gaping at him," he said with delighted smugness and threw one leg over my lap. I laced my fingers between his toes. The sight of him, that lazy grin I will never grow tired of, warmed my belly.

I smiled, brushed his bangs away, and tucked a strand of his pure white hair behind his ear with poise.

"You look happy. Are you?"

Peter laughed softly. He sat up and looked out the stone-framed window overlooking the wide expanse of calming waters. "I am. Your long black hair hanging thick and untamed over your shoulders makes you look like some kind of Puma superhero."

"Pfft, you say the weirdest things. Your flawless pale skin and lustrous wings make you look like a one-of-a-kind Angel. Which you are."

"I am, and I'm yours." The fire accentuated his cheekbones and stunning blue eyes. His long sinewy neck flowed into strong wide shoulders and thick muscled arms—

making him look invincible. He pulled his knees to his chest and sat hugging them. Although I had become accustomed to the bolt of lust shooting through me every time I admired him, it still overpowers and pushes me to him.

"If you get closer to me, I might let you lick and suck me again. Look what you do to me." I gripped my stiffening cock and teased Peter by moving my hand up and down my length until pre-cum beaded at the slit, beckoning him to taste it.

"You'd like that, wouldn't you?" Peter whispered, lips curving up into another luscious smile.

"It seems to me you don't want me to say that you've had enough of me," I purred, watching him gulp loudly. I eavesdrop on his thoughts as he struggles to come up with as clever response. I got up, standing naked at the foot of the bed. We were drunk with lust, love, and each other's body fluids.

During our first waterfall shower, Peter had untangled my braids and washed my hair. It was frizzy and bushy, but I was glad he liked it. I tied my wild black mane into a thick bush behind my head with a leather string. Knowing he enjoyed watching me, stretching and extending my arms as he raked his gaze over me. His breath hitched and a feeling of pride and deep-rooted love filled me. My skin glowed with a blue-gold sheen. Like an Andean flamingo doing its mating dance, I made a show of my body and half-hard, long uncut cock, hanging heavy over my balls.

I looked down at him. "Careful, you might hurt your beautiful brain thinking too hard."

Peter crawled closer on his hands and knees, wings dragging at his sides. He looked up at me with those sparkling blue eyes, making me think of the healing pool of Babylon. I wanted to dive into them. He leaned to grab hold of my growing erection. Fingers firm, the blues in his eyes turned dark with a challenge I couldn't ever resist. I gazed down, hypnotized by the desire he had for me in them.

"Come here. I want to make love to you." The unspoken question, "Will you let my tongue inside you?" hung in the air, but he opted to say, "I need you."

"Are you sure? Aren't you sore? This would be the fourth time today. You are probably bruised," I said to give him an opening to ask.

"There are other ways to make love. Let me taste you. Let me make love to you." He tugged me closer by my prick. Lining me up with his mouth. I waited, already trembling with anticipation. His fiery blue gaze fixated on my reaction as he sucked my length into his warm mouth. Tingles of pleasure ran up and down my spine and wrapped around my filling balls. I watched as he swallowed all of me down.

"Oh, Peter, you drive me mad with that mouth of yours." I hissed and fisted my hand in his white hair. Excruciatingly, oh so very bloody slowly, he pulled back, his cheeks hollowed by the intense suction. My erection grew harder, bigger, and longer as he swirled his tongue around the head, playing and tickling that sensitive rim underneath my shrinking foreskin.

"You were saying there are other ways?" I asked, knowing already what Peter was planning. He wanted to spear my tight ass with his tongue. I'll beg him to do it if he doesn't ask soon. This would be a first for him, and I wanted it.

"Come over here. Get on your stomach for me." He patted the bed, indicating I should change places with him. With a smoldering look and a stern nod, I offered my entire self to him. Not saying a word, I obeyed. The sexual tension between us built. I knew I thrilled Peter by creeping on my hands and knees, then sliding down seductively and crossing my arms under my chin as I draped myself onto my stomach as ordered.

With his legs on either side of me, he rubbed his hands around my shoulders, gently massaging my muscles while working his way down to my buttocks. Then further, all the way down to my ankles. I felt his desire increasing and that stoked my want for him. He started kissing me. First the one leg and then the other, all the way up and down. Slowly. Worshipping, tasting, and teasing me from my ankles to the cleft of my ass.

"Open for me," he said, nudging my knees apart. Doing it for Peter, the man I loved, was a magically deep experience. No regular fucking can imitate the rush, the flood of emotion, no matter how hard or how many strangers I fucked, it was nothing like what I was experiencing now. This was a first for both of us.

A feather-light touch and warm breath flickered over the crack between my tensed butt cheeks. "I want to eat you out. Is that something you would let me do?"

"Why not? I thought you'd never offer. Please, this is something only for you and me, for us," I said, relaxing my muscles and opening that last door I had kept shut emotionally and physically, exposing my vulnerability. I tried to lighten the situation by moving my hips and indicating my willingness.

The mattress dipped between my legs. His hands wrapped around my knees as he made space for himself between them. I felt the heat of his breath on my buttocks and exposed hole. His wings gently tucked around my body, cocooning us.

Peter tied my past and my future to this point in time. This moment was my anchor to which I will always return. That was my last coherent thought before he swiped his wet, slick scorching hot tongue over me, over and over until I was lost in a sea of desire, drowning in emotions, while leaking snot, spit, and tears. There was too much of it—so many emotions. I needed him. To fill me with everything that is him. He bit down on my shoulder. The pain and slow finger fucking of my spit-slicked entrance sent me spinning into that vortex, building and chasing my orgasm. Slowly and rhythmically, making me his, silencing that yearning of my lonely soul. One last slow withdrawal and the burning sensation disappeared as he drizzled warm oil over my hole. "Yes, fuck please, I'm good and ready. Push something bigger and deeper into me," I whispered as my toes curled, and my fingers wrapped around the bony tips of his wings. Anchoring myself, I prepared to be plowed with the speed and deadly force of lightning.

"You sure?"

"Yes," I groaned as he massaged and stretched me open. "Fuck yes!" He rubbed over that magical spot inside my channel. Sparks of bright lights flashed and danced behind my fluttering eyelids. I lay still. Waiting. Wanting. Heaving and shaking. I submit. Letting him control the pace of my pleasure. I knew exactly how he felt, similar to a predator that has successfully captured its prey. As soon as he felt my submission, he removed his teeth from the crook of my neck. While licking and kissing the wound, his fingers disappeared from me. His sensual movements were driving me insane. Then just as I lifted my head to protest, he clutched my shoulders. Peter dragged his chest slowly up and down my back, and after what felt like unending torture, he moved his hardness into place. Sliding it over my taint, entering me so slowly, with so much love, I felt like crying, then let out a whimper.

"You feel so good, and right. Do you want more? I want more. I fear I will never get enough of you, of this, of us," Peter said with a low husky voice into the shell of my ear, making me shiver. "Let's make a game of this. I tease you and we see who wins by making the other come first," My Kuku said, and I didn't care who wins or loses as long as I had him and he had me and we are together.

More dragging and teasing, until I begged him, "Kuku, I don't care if I won or lost the bloody game. I need more, harder, and faster!"

"I agree." His wings lifted, flapping and stretching above us.

"Oh my sweet Fates, yes please," I grunted and fisted the bedding. Peter laughed maniacally and then, with a force I'd been expecting but never experienced, he slammed into me.

Fucking me dumb and breathless.

Hard and deep thrusts followed until both of us ejaculated and passed out, sleeping with him on my back and his cock inside me. We had finally fully bonded and our lives were permanently intertwined.

When I woke, Peter was busy cleaning me. But as he turned to wash himself, I pounced and he gasped.

"Hands on the wall. Don't move until I say so." His body shuddered against me. He threw his head back, his white locks washing over my face. He obeyed.

I held him tight and explained to him exactly how much he affected me and why. "I'm so unbelievably in love with you, and your body is such a temptation. The smell of your majestic blinding white wings, the feathers slightly fluttering when you are aroused. Your tall, muscled body, that mouth-watering tight ass, your smooth muscled abdominals. I want to run my hands constantly over every inch of you and then grip your white locks like this and fuck you." I gripped his hair, knowing I was rough and commanding.

"Really?" he asked in a teasing tone. His voice was thick with lust. His wings quivered under my touch and my warm breath against the sensitive part of his neck.

"Yes, always."

He wanted me. He craved me as much as I craved him. It's becoming clear to me that Peter doesn't hold himself back for me. There is nothing I wouldn't do to see him happy. Peter and I have never been jealous, but there's a comfort in knowing I belong to him, that he missed me, and he takes it so seriously that he has become possessive. I read his thoughts and in his mind, I belonged to him as he belonged to me. There's no other for me in this reality or any other.

"I'm starving and aching for you over here."

"I know," I whispered under my breath, knowing I was driving him crazy with my seduction. I traced my finger along the ridges over the skin between his wings where I knew he was extra sensitive. Like a kitten, he began purring and begging for more scratches. I ran my tongue over the sensitive area I like to nibble on when I'm fucking him from behind.

"Fuck me, Ish, I want it again, right now!" he growled, and my cock twitched agreeing with him.

"My cock agrees. He's aching for you," I murmured between tiny licks and bites. The longer I took teasing him, the more my balls tingled and pulsated with fullness.

"Oh, you better do as your cock says."

"Hmmm, my balls agree too. They tell me it's time to be emptied," I said as I admired my throbbing blue cock between his perfect pale ass cheeks.

"Better hurry up and listen to us, we might shrivel up and die." He rubbed his ass sideways against my pulsating warm cock like a firestarter. My skin itched as it started to glow.

"I'll probably come the second you're inside me," he announced, and I chuckled, evil undertones lacing my voice. I wrapped my fingers around the base of my cock and teased his hole with the slick head.

"Get the oil on the bedside table, please, my lover." Peter's feathers rattled—serious, eager, and turned on.

I took my time walking over to grab the oil Luci had graciously placed in the room for us. Before Anzulla, we'd always been in a rush. Sticking it in and roughing it. So now I took my time slicking myself and his backside until he vibrated around my probing finger. I used my other hand to lather his balls and decided to rub some onto his tight globes as well. "Damn, Peter, I love your tight muscled globes," I said. My voice rumbled and I hissed through my long incisors.

"For the love of the Fates, and all that is holy, I love hearing you say that, but I could give two fucks if you don't get on with it. I'm going to come over the wall before you've even started."

"We've determined there are no Fates. You are talking about Lasitor." I chuckled. "Stop worrying about coming. If you shoot early, I will keep going until you go again. When I'm deep inside you, you will appreciate it, no matter if you come now or not." I licked and nipped at the back of his neck. "I'm going to sink my teeth into you. You'll be happy for it because you will come again for me. You know that's how we roll, my Kuku. What made you think this round would be any different?" I teased with my fangs, scraping the skin between his wings.

I'm now addicted to his blood. "Hmmm, your blood tastes so good, like orgasms, only in liquid form."

"Ish, if you don't penetrate me now, I'm going to jump out the window and find someone willing to fuck me!"

"You what?" I growled and forced my aching cock into him with one hard push.

"Thank fuck," he howled, palms flat against the wall, arching his back, and spreading his wings wide. I held tight around his hips, holding him in place, as I pumped into him.

"Calm the fuck down. We're levitating off the floor. You are going to hurt your wings, and I'm going to fall," I said, not stopping hammering into him. Peter stopped flapping, clinging to the wall. I used all my strength to push deep inside of him, wrapping my legs around his lower legs while hanging onto his shoulders. I'd never fucked like this. I'd never fucked a non-human. Like two bats mating, I clung to Peter. He met me thrust for thrust. Sweat ran down my temples as I chased my orgasm while simultaneously trying to hold out as long as I could. Slipping and sliding over his oiled backside. My fangs tingled as I savagely heaved air into my lungs. Physically he matched my strength. The harder I fucked, the more he urged me on. As we reached the precipice, I slowed my thrusts. "I'm going to bite you now. We can come together."

"Yes, do it," he grunted.

On his command, I tilted my head back and struck the muscled area between his neck and wing. Peter whimpered as I sucked and swallowed. His tasted like stars exploding as his blood slid thick and warm down my throat. This thirst I constantly have for him, will never go away.

"Fuck yes," he shouted as his ass tightened around me. I pushed hard and planted myself as deep as I could. My body spasmed and pleasure zinged through me. My orgasm pulsed and pulsed and pulsed as I spurted my seed deep into him. The taste and feel of him—so bloody good. We chased our pleasures until we were empty, satisfied, and hungry. The room spun. Literally. I realized we were airborne again as I clung to him. Peter's head fell back, and we lowered to the floor. His ribs expanded and contracted as he heaved in air.

"We must eat. It's time to leave this room and socialize." I laughed, removing myself from him. We were ridiculous. And we were happy.

"Eryn's ceremony is about to begin," I said over my shoulder, as I rinsed a washcloth in lukewarm soapy water to clean up. "It's going to be spectacular. Luci said they are eager to have a king of their own."

"Yeah, Eryn is so bloody humble, I want to slap him over the head sometimes. I mean, I won't look for trouble with him, but a king needs a certain flair of *don't-fuck-with-me* vibes, which he hides. Whether it is on purpose, I don't know." Peter pulled his shoulders to his ears, making his feathers rustle. "Do you know what he said to me yesterday?"

"Hmmm, what?"

"Eryn said he will accept his anointing and vow to protect and lead all citizens of Anzulla into a harmonious existence with each other. Under the watchful, ever-present eye of the true creator of time itself, the true God of all, who has yet to reveal themselves." I shook my head and chuckled as I finished wiping myself down, rinsed the cloth, and walked over to hand it to Peter. He took it from me, cleaned himself, and threw the cloth into the washroom.

I had one of my legs down my pants when an incessant knocking at the door startled both of us.

"We're coming!" I yelled. Peter looked at me, and we burst out laughing like children.

*Knock-knock-knock-knock!* The knocking continued. It got louder and louder. "I said, we're coming!" I squealed, folding double with laughter.

"Ishtar, Peter, there is trouble! Get your asses out of bed and come down to the beach," Elijah shouted.

"It's Juandre and Andrew. It doesn't look good. Hurry!" Luci said.

Gone were our happy giggles.

"One minute, we will meet you, in one minute!" A bolt of white heat rushed through me. Our friends were hurt. With terrified bewilderment, we jumped into action and finished getting dressed.

# CHAPTER 70
# APSU

*"GOOD MORNING, CITIZENS OF ANZULLA.*

*It's now six a.m.*

*This is a riddle with a very hot tip. What is hard enough to protect us, but shatters with incredible ease. It's made from opaque sand, yet it's completely transparent. It behaves like a solid material, but it's also a liquid in disguise!*

*It's glass of course.*

*Did you know the chemical process of creating glass involves heating quartz sand, also known as silica sand, to temperatures above three thousand and ninety degrees Fahrenheit until it melts into a clear liquid?*

*Yes, that is hot, and my hot tip is for those with sun allergies. By applying a reflective coating to two panes of glass and installing them into those holes you call windows, you will block and reflect the damaging rays of the sun.*

*Start your day with a sparkle and visit your community news page to learn how to make glass.*

*Have a transparent day!"*

**PETER**

**24 970 B.C.**

**Anzulla**

**Earth**

An urgent feeling in the pit of my stomach pulled my insides into knots. I hopped into my pants, leaned out the door, and gasped. Holding my breath, my brain computed the silhouettes in the scene unfolding in the distance. "I can't believe what I'm seeing." Ish stuck his head out the window. We watched Juandre and Andrew approaching. I turned my head to Ish as he turned his to me. "Are they pulling a Bubblecar?" We muttered simultaneously. I shook my head. "God, they look like two horses in front of a snow sleigh."

"Yeah, but it's not snow it's white sand," Ish said. He straightened and scrubbed his face with the palms of his hands. "Swords, I need my swords, Kuku." He scurried behind me, swords clanging and boots flying as he dove for the chair to sit on while he put his boots on. They were still a few hundred feet away, but I could see Birdmen hovering above them. Luci, Groda and Elijah landed to speak to Andrew and Juandre. Their heads were lowered—ignoring them.

I drew in a sharp breath, "Where are the others?" Suddenly I saw only black. "No, no, no, don't look." Ish was shutting my eyes with the palms of his hands. "Don't look, don't look!"

"What the fuck, Ish, take your hands away," I snarled at him and pushed his hands down from my face. "Is that what I think it is?"

"Kuku, you shouldn't look. I can go and see it. Please stay here. You are soft, you don't have the stomach for this."

My wings flared to half open. I bulged my fists and said through gnashing teeth, "No. Fucking. Way. You must be saying that because I just fucked you senseless."

He cringed under my scrutinizing gaze. "It came out wrong, I'm sorry."

My feathers stopped rustling. "Hurry, let's go and see. Together. Hold on to me." I launched off our small porch and made a three-hundred-and-sixty-degree turn, waiting and seeing Ish running, while securing his swords into the belt around his waist. He then jumped off the window ledge and soared through the air, a move we'd been perfecting the past few days. I dove down, passing him free falling. He caught me by my ankles. "Damn, those swords are heavy!" I grunted and flapped three times harder to shoot into the sky, veering left and right through the inquisitive onlookers. As we approached, I saw an opening, hung a sharp left, and dipped low over the beach. Ish let go and ran when his feet hit the sand, weapons ready.

It was a scene of horror.

Juandre and Andrew sat on their asses. Their faces were scorched, and in some places, blackened skin was torn off revealing sinew and bones beneath. Juandre's beautiful face was gone on the right side. His upper and lower teeth were exposed, all the way to his ear was raw bleeding flesh. People stepped closer to see what they had brought with them. No one said anything as they turned and either ran away or shook their heads in disbelief. Juandre and Andrew sat catatonic with mountain climbing ropes tied around their waists—they had used them to pull the cracked-open Bubblecar.

Ish placed the palms of his hands on my pecs and pushed me back. His yellow eyes were wide with bewilderment and glassy with tears. "No, Kuku, don't, you will see this always. You can never unsee this." But I had already seen it. Inside lay bodies and limbs bloodied and lifeless. To make matters worse, flies were everywhere.

"Ish, let me go!" He did.

Carefully, I approached. White noise sang in my ears and disbelieving shock flushed through my veins as what I was seeing slowly registered. My friends, pieces of my friends, lay torn and squashed into the Bubbelcar. Flashes of my childhood of women and children in mass graves assaulted me. Someone's leg was thrown haphazardly over Mika's and Connors's upper bodies. Brad's torso lay on its side, blood still oozing and drenching Rick's lower body.

"What the fuck happened here, Juandre?" I shouted as I darted over to them. The sight of them both hurt and distraught didn't prevent me from shaking them to give me answers. "Fuck!" They just sat there staring. Their mouths moved, but no sound escaped their throats. "Ish! Where the fuck is Ish?"

"I'm behind you, Peter."

I folded and tucked my wings and pulled Ish closer to them. "Read their fucking minds and tell me what you see!"

"I know already, my Kuku," he said in a calm and soothing voice. I didn't want to be calmed or soothed. *They are my friends dammit!* "What did this?" Ish stood silent. The sound of leather creaking around the hilts of his swords drew my attention. He might sound calm and unaffected but he wasn't. The fine tremors in his body told me to back off. He looked ready to snap.

"Where are Eryn, Cian, and Ivan?" I asked, searching, not seeing their tall blond heads.

"They said something about having sex in the mud last night. We will go look for them," Luci said and scooped his lovers into his arms to go searching.

"Thank you!" I shouted.

"Hurry, sunlight is upon us," Ish added. His skin was already steaming in the rising sunlight.

"May I?" Grabbing a water skin from an onlooking Birdman, I fell to my knees next to Juandre.

Ish turned, with his arms wide open. "Please stand back. Give us room. They need air to breathe!" The onlookers respectfully stepped back. "Angels and Sables, could you hover and block the rays of the rising sun? Juandre, Andrew, and I burn easily. Thank you." Shadows fell upon us as the Birdmen made a protective circle around us and Ish joined me.

"Juan, Drew? Talk to us. Here's water. Drink." I urged my friends to drink while dripping water over their charcoal lips. But they didn't drink.

"They need blood more than water now. They are beyond shock." Ish sat on his heels, sliced his left wrist, and offered it to Juandre by dripping bright red drops of blood onto his lips. "Drink. you need blood to heal." His voice was commanding and as stern as steel. Juandre blinked, sniffed at the smell of blood, and nodded a thank you. He took

Ish's arm in both hands, pressed it against his mouth and sucked. *Slurping.* Astonished, I watched how miraculously the muscled flesh around his jaw stitched and healed, covering his exposed molars. His skin grew back, slowly covering with fine hairs around his eyebrows, upper lip, and chin. Even the nails on his fingertips grew back until he looked like the stunning man I knew. "You too, Andrew, drink from me." Ish pushed his wrist to Andrew's mouth next. "I will drink from Peter later. You need the strength of my blood."

With tears in my eyes, I clenched and unclenched my fists as I asked, "What did this? Was it a wild animal? A big wild cat. Yes, a cat killed Gu's father. But they look like a bomb hit them." I ran all the possibilities through my mind while Ish was finishing feeding Andrew. He was also healing while sucking Ish's pure Anunnaki lifeblood. "Lightning, yes, maybe an electrical storm?"

"No, my Kuku…"

Juandre coughed, clearing his throat. Ish licked, then pressed a thumb over his oozing wrist. When he was sure it was healed and not bleeding anymore, he said, "Tell us."

Juandre looked up with scorching anger on his face, his words came out choppy at first as he stuttered. "It was one man with the face of an animal—a monster. He commanded fire as if he conjured it out of thin air. He threw it at us like cannonballs. He laughed when Brad fell to roll in the sand to kill the flames, then he walked right up to him with a long blade and sliced Brad in half. His cries of pain." Juandre pressed his hands over his ears. "He came at us from all sides. We couldn't protect them. They didn't stand a chance." He took the water skin from me and took a few gulps from it.

Ish hissed like a feral cat. If I didn't know him like I did, I would have run. "This looks and sounds like Apsu's destructive work." That name explained his reaction to me. Andrew sat in silence. Not saying anything. Locked deep inside his mind and not ready to speak.

"Fuck, just as I thought life was good! *What are their children going to say?* Wait, where are Paul and Simon?"

My words hung in the air, and Andrew exploded into tears, blubbering. "Their Bubblecar was hit first. It burst into flames and crashed into the sea. We'd parked and picnicked in an alcove. We were packing up and they went ahead of us. They weren't gone for a minute when we heard the explosion and saw them crashing."

"We couldn't find them, we looked. We wanted to bring them home, but we couldn't find them," Juandre cried.

I wrapped my arms and wings around their shoulders. Offering comfort and strength, while giving Ish my *this-is-a-cluster-fuck* look. It seemed to calm him. His breathing slowed and his fangs retracted. "We know, we can see you tried your best."

Ish leaned in closer, tilting Juandre's head up to meet his gaze, as he looked into

Juandre's mind. "Tell me, could you see the man's face?" Andrew leaned closer into my arms, hungry for safety and comfort.

"Yes, it is a face so ugly, it is burned into my mind. Dark blue like yours. Same eyes. Long black hair and a white tassel between his eyes. His head wasn't human, he looked like an animal. Almost like a horse or a cow with large pointy ears, and small horns at the sides of his head. He had big black claws for hands and golden-tipped fingernails." Ish drew in a long, slow breath, eyeballing me while Juandre coughed again, and sipped more water, before continuing. "He rolled his one hand as if catching air and turning into fire, like a wizard or something. Then he threw balls of fire and he even controlled how big they were. He corralled us in the alcove, playing with us. Andrew and I didn't know which way to go to help or who to help first. It wasn't something I ever thought to protect my friends from. You know, we aren't real fighters. We are fast, we tried to help, but we couldn't be everywhere." Juandre cried, taking Andrew's hand. "My bear tried his best, but this thing outsmarted us and was too evil. Honestly, we were fucking scared. I'm sure if we weren't vampires, we would be dead too." He sniffled and hugged Andrew.

"Cian and Ivan are going to have a fit. I know my father. He must have watched us, or have spies watching us. He knows we will come for him. But we can't go off half-cocked without a strategy. I prepared for years with a whole army to defeat him. When they get here, we need you to convince them to stay calm and plan an attack with Eryn."

"Yes, we shall. What about them in the meantime?" I pointed to the bodies, drenched with flies inside the Bubblecar.

"Leave them just like that. Their children deserve to decide what to do with their bodies."

An hour later two Bubblecars raced over the cliffs straight for us. As soon as they stopped and the doors opened, Eryn, Ivan, Cian, Barkor, Sarinka, Donali, and Kawa popped out of it and ran to the destroyed vehicle filled with their friends' and family's bodies. When they reached the gruesome scene they just stood there looking at it, like I was. Their eyes were gone, their faces burned, black holes and rolled up lips. The look of terror etched forever on their faces remained, as the stench of burned flesh and flies buzzing hung in the air. Not believing, and not accepting it, even though their deaths were right in front of us. I'm sure they thought they could bring them back to life, but their bodies were hacked up into pieces and there was no way of putting them back together again. Cian was the first to collapse, followed by Donali and Kawa. Sitting on the sand and crying, but not making a sound. Ivan leaned into Eryn as he cried quietly while Barkor put a comforting hand on Cian's shoulder. They looked powerless, like defeated children. Their sadness washed over us and it wasn't long before everyone in our vicinity cried with them.

"Who did this?" Eryn asked as he turned and approached us. Juandre and Andrew couldn't meet his gaze. "We are not mad at you, all I ask is—oh, I see," said Eryn, and I assumed he'd read our minds as he turned back to wave Cian, Ivan, and Barkor over. Kawa, Donali, and Sarinka stayed with their fathers. Eryn turned, tilting his head to one side, listening and concentrating. His demeanor was cold and confident. He pursed his lips, thinking and calculating. The corners of his eyes were scrunched into thin lines, deep-seated anger visible in the twitching muscles of his jaw. "We came as soon as Luci told us. We were visiting Gugusan last night. The San sent their regards. Gugusan and his warriors said they'd be here late afternoon. We can go inside and plan how to bring Apsu to us. He is near, Ishtar, I feel his darkness, he is close."

"Yes, he is watching us. Listen, nature is still. Other than the waves, there are no birds in the sky. Quiet and still, only the malevolence and the buzzing insects remain. That's how you know he is near. He attacks from all sides. The deaths, the flies, everything—it's to wear us down, to upset us. He attacks the mind and the body. He is somewhere near, calculating, enjoying, and waiting for us. I don't know if he knows I killed him already in another reality or if this is his younger self. The Apsu that eventually destroys Anzulla. All I know is, he can't find the Horizon. We should detach the time machine and remove it from Phoenix. It has served its purpose," Ish said in a low tone, so only we in his vicinity could hear him.

"I agree. Getting rid of the Horizon and removing the time machine will prevent more Apsus from popping out of the sky. Do you think he was already here, in Anzulla?" I asked.

"That, or he jumped here with Phoenix," Cian added.

"If so, why didn't Lasitor know about him or warn us?" I asked.

Eryn turned to Ish. "Am I correct to assume he wouldn't do anything in the daytime? We have to think and act fast, before the sun sets tonight."

"What are we going to do with them?" Ivan asked, not able to look at the bodies, but pointing to them.

"You should decide. We could either burn the bodies as we did in Antarctica, or send them into the water," I said, feeling like shit, but in my defense, I've had an hour to think about it.

Ish shook his head, "No if we can't attack by planning and building an army, we must do it when he least expects it. If we waste time trying to be honorable and showing respect to the dead—I can't stress this enough—if we are burying them, it should be a distraction, make Apsu think we are mourning, and maybe ask the Angels and Sables to allow us to bury them under the baobab trees, in the crystal caves. Make it look real, but while doing it, we prepare to trap him."

"I know Dad would hate to be burned or sent under the water. Let's put them underground if we are allowed," Donali said loudly, and I was sure many others overheard.

*That meant we didn't have to ask, he already had. Nobody gathering here really knew more than what had transpired these past couple of weeks. I doubt they knew Donali and Kawa, as well as Simon and Paul, were Brad and Rick's kids.*

Just as I finished that thought, a big Angel, I believe Luci called him Georgio, stepped closer, head down in submission to Eryn. "I just want to say we are all deeply saddened by their deaths, and I'm sure my brothers wouldn't mind if you want to lay them to rest inside the Heart of Anzulla. Also, I have one request, to Ishtar, the Demon God," he said, shifting from one foot to the other, hands clasped in front. *Shit, he is really scared of us.* So, that's why Eryn hated the bowing. They bowed out of fear and not respect. Georgio's eyes darted from Ish to Eryn and then back to me.

Eryn's golden-green eyes sparkled and the corners of his mouth pulled up into an encouraging smile. "Georgio, hello, thank you. The gesture is appreciated. Please, ask around to confirm, let me know if someone objects, and then we will make other arrangements," Eryn said extra loudly so everyone could hear him. I am sure Gugusan in the mountains could. It was almost as if Eryn was—*making a show of this.* "I know Brad and the others wouldn't want to impose unless everyone is okay with them invading your sacred space. Oh, and what is it that you want to tell Ishtar? I was waiting for someone to speak up about it. The man's been cooped up, mating since our arrival." Eryn smiled knowingly at Georgio and rested a hand on his shoulder. The Angel blushed and relaxed under his touch, then straightened.

"Ishtar, we are not Angels and Sables, those are how we tell the difference between the colors of our wings and the names of our teams. Angel color for white and Sable color for black. When we play games or when we have ceremonies and congregate, we tell the difference like that. But we are one race, like the San are one race of people."

"Oh? I apologize, that's my fault. That happens when being tied up and delirious with sunburn," Ish said, sarcastically. "How do you refer to yourselves? What should I call thee, oh mighty one?" Ishtar's voice was laced with venom. If a look could send lightning bolts, Georgio would have been struck down.

"Birdmen," I chipped in, breaking the tension.

Georgio couldn't meet Ish's gaze. He gave a shameful chuckle, not at all relaxing in Ish's company. "Yes, please say Birdmen, we are of the Bird, yes? We refer to ourselves in our language as, *Vucub-Caquix.*"

"I know that word Vukubaku." Ish pronounced it totally wrong—we all could hear that. Georgio exploded with uncomfortable laughter. "That is not how you say it. "*Vucub-Caquix,*" he repeated, "or Birdman?" He smiled and exposed a radiant stack of white teeth as he bowed his head and reversed out of our circle.

"Okay, the tentative plan is…" Eryn said, clapping his hands so everyone refocused and listened. "Please let us know if you object to us putting our friends in the ground." He turned and winked a few winks so everyone knew setting the trap was on, and a go. "The ones with sun sickness will prepare for burial—Juandre and Andrew, please bring our fallen to the crystal caves. If you agree with me, I suggest we need all available hands to help us strip and unpack the Horizon. Please, jump in if you have a better idea, we can move it somewhere far away and blow it up, melt it down, crush it, fill it with water, or ask Cian to make a garden inside it."

"Hmmm, Eryn, I have an idea," I announced. "I agree with stripping it, but to destroy the shell, so the Horizon never flies or time jumps again, I could concoct a formula to crush it into dust. I suggest jumping it inside the crystal cave. Let's feed Anzulla's heart by first crystallizing it, and then freezing it so cold that one tap will crack it into billions of crystal pieces."

Ish patted my shoulder. "My mate, such a smart man."

"Peter, that's so far the best plan of the day! Anyone else with a suggestion?" Eryn asked, and I preened under his compliment.

"To be honest, everyone, I think my father would have liked that idea very much," Donali added. "Parking the Horizon and burying their bodies inside the crystal cave. It symbolizes they brought us all this way and their time with the vessels has ended."

"Any other suggestions?" Eryn's gaze swept over the crowd. "Thank you, Donali, we all agree then. Peter, can you get enough hands together to move your equipment into the Horizon, and get it set up? Ivan, Cian, and Barkor, could you also go with him? Barkor, inform your people what's happening. I don't want chaos. Tell them they can choose to stay inside Phoenix until this is over or visit the dry land, but remind them it's not safe, that I suggest they keep the children tucked away until we're finished setting up you know what, to trap and get rid of you know who. We will lay their bodies to the ground, but Ish and I will make sure it's not permanent. If we don't succeed, mourning their deaths won't matter, because Apsu will destroy all of us."

*But if we manage to trap and kill Apsu a funeral won't be needed*, I thought. Eryn glanced at me as if hearing my thoughts and acknowledged my thinking with a small dip of his chin and softening of his facial features. Ish wrapped his arms around my lower body and pulled me against him. The tightness in my chest loosened a little.

The crowd around us parted as Kawa burst through. *He's been with his fathers this whole time.* "Where are my brothers?" he asked, pissed off at Juandre and Andrew, with his fists bulging at his sides.

I swooped around, ready to throw my wings over Juandre and Andrew. "Hey, hey! None of that, they tried their best," I said. Hurt emanated from him in thick waves. He pushed his chest out gearing up for a fight. Kawa was smaller than me, but I didn't doubt for a second that he could deliver a mighty punch.

"Look at them, there's not a scratch on them. I doubt they tried their best to help. The way I see it is that they ran away and hid instead of doing the one thing my father asked of them, and that was to protect them. Fuck, he would have fought for you!" Kawa pulled his bionic arm back to hit Juandre with a fist when Ish jumped in between us. Eryn caught Kawa by the arm and immobilized him.

"Leave my brother alone." Donali jumped to help Kawa, but Sarinka stepped in front of him.

"Stop and look at them. Their clothes are torn and burned to shreds. Look at Juandre's back, they were nearly burned off his body," Sarinka said, pointing with a dagger in her hand. We all turned to where she showed them the now fully healed skin below the melted bright turquoise body suit. Andrew's silver Phoenician body suit only covered his groin, the rest was gone, a testament that they burned away.

"Kawa, we didn't run away. We shielded them as best we could," Juandre said.

Andrew sniffled with tears in his eyes, looking at us, one by one. "I'm sorry, we weren't prepared to fight someone like that. He threw fire at us. And…" He shook his head as he let it fall in defeat. "Your brothers didn't stand a chance, their Bubblecar was attacked first and they crashed into the waters." Andrew looked up again, sorrow and humiliation etched deep into his face. His usual sparkling green eyes were now red and puffy as tears streamed down his face.

"Kawa, Ish gave them blood, they were healing for the hour we waited for you. When they arrived, they looked horrible. They collapsed after dragging the Bubblecar back here while burned down to the bone," I said, hoping the vivid description would force him to understand they were just as traumatized as he was.

"I fucking refuse to accept they are dead." He pointed to Ish. "Go back and save them. At least warn them." He pointed to Eryn. "You better go with him and kill this man."

"It's Apsu, it's my father," Ish said. Kawa narrowed his eyes at Ish. He must have heard during Ishtar's inquisition how difficult it was to kill the patriarch of the Anunnaki. Ish described in detail to the people of Phoenix how he had prepared for years to win the war. *Ish managed to kill the most powerful and vile Anunnaki.* Kawa pulled loose from Eryn's grip. "There is no fucking way this is how they meet their end. Not after what they have done for every-fucking-one here! I demand you go back and make this right!" The circle of onlookers around and above us was getting smaller. "Jesus, listen to yourselves, you are already burying them and preparing to go on with your lives."

"That's enough, Kawa!" Eryn said in an authoritative tone. "I was getting everyone to safety. We were merely planning ahead, before running hot-headed into a trap. I know he is watching us. As long as he is watching us, he is not attacking. Understand." Eryn looked at Kawa, exuding calm and reason. "I know this is difficult. We know how this looks, but if this is planned, we are going to get our chance and I will make sure it's our best chance." Eryn sighed and said in a softer tone, "Look, the main problem with this is that the Horizon can time jump. We must eliminate the reason for this mess. Second, their bodies, in this heat, must be dealt with. There is no way I'm putting them inside a fridge down in Phoenix." Then he whispered. "It's only for show, it's all temporary."

Kawa stepped back and hugged himself. He looked like a little lost boy, alone and mad at the world. *Fuck this*, I reached out to him and enfolded him in my arms and wings. He shook as he burst into tears. "Oh, my god. So they are going back and saving them, so this wouldn't have happened?"

I lowered my voice to a soothing tone and whispered, "*Shhht*, my boy. We will make this as right as we possibly can. We just have to be smart about it."

I've always had a soft spot for Kawa. He dealt with his anger and post-traumatic stress by hating everyone around him. It became part of him, and it was time to heal and trust. I closed my eyes, holding him, telling him it would be okay. That he is safe and we have him. I have him. "Together we will try our best to reverse this cluster fuck. We must be careful because if we change the past, the future changes, and if we don't calculate all angles, this can go on forever. Apsu can escape, but Phoenix may never arrive in Anzulla. There are things Eryn and Ish must plan before taking any steps to change the past. At this stage, the past is what it is. It can't run away or disappear. According to Ish, he can step back in time, but the more people involved, the more complicated it becomes. If we change things, say we send Ish to warn them, then how do we let Eryn know in the future to come from Gu's village to meet up? Stopping Apsu would have to happen in the past. Ish can only time-walk short distances, to places he has already been. It's much more complicated, and Lasitor has warned Ish many times over, in fact, he has forbidden him to do it. How will we be ready if we don't know what has happened? Understand?" I gently explained as Kawa cried into my shoulder.

"It makes sense, I'm sorry," he said, pushing me away and wiping his nose with his sleeve. Sarinka and Donali embraced him. "Just tell us how we can help so we can bring them back. I won't accept their deaths must look like that. They don't deserve it," he said with a quivering bottom lip.


AFTER ISH HAD PARKED the Horizon inside the crystal cave, Eryn joined him and they left with the time machine to find Apsu.

I began the destruction process of the Horizon by first filling it with aluminum potassium sulfate, a chemical typically used by children to grow crystals in school class-room experiments. We borrowed it from the Phoenix sewerage system for our own experiment, only on a much bigger scale. This metal sulfate was essential for our plan because the outer shell of our ship was made of a metal that would not bend or crack when frozen or heated alone. However, as the crystals grew and expanded over time, cracks would inevitably form. So, we poured the mixture through the canon ports and slowly added seed crystals collected from light tunnels before filling the ship with water directly from the waterfalls. Once everything was in place, we opened the valves and blasted the shell with liquid nitrogen. The temperature inside dropped to an icy minus three hundred and forty-six degrees Fahrenheit before heating back up to match the current heat of ninety-five degrees Fahrenheit inside the crystal cave. This drastic temperature change created the perfect conditions for crystal formation within the pressure cooker. As each inch of space inside the Horizon crystallized, it became impenetrable and resembled a massive piece of quartz crystal. There would be no way to salvage the ship without shattering it into pieces.

Our fallen friends' bodies were quickly, albeit hopefully only temporarily, buried under the baobab trees while Ish and Eryn time-walked, searching for Apsu. If we successfully saved Brad and the others, by killing Apsu before he had his chance, Ish and Eryn would return here, as they decided this crystal cave was their new anchor point. Brad, Rick, Mika, Connor, Paul, Simon, Jaundre, and Andrew would continue on their retirement vacation without knowing any better. Lasitor ran the probabilities by Eryn and Ish before they left, and the final plan of action seemed to be the best and safest course to take. It would minimize change for everyone. It would be as if this morning never happened.

Hands on my hips, I stood watching our handiwork of the day. Gugusan and his warriors were breaking up the ingenious bamboo water pipe system they had erected to divert water from the waterfalls. I suggested they take the bamboo with them, but they said it was not worth carrying it all the way, and they didn't need it, because the irrigation system I helped them build was still working fine.

*Whoop-whoop!*

A thunderous crashing noise and commotion coming from the entrance of the cave forced me to swing around and brace for impact. The crystal cave lit up and darkened as if lightning struck inside and ricocheted around us—reflected by the crystals. Half-blinded and disorientated, I searched for the origin and the direction of the bright light. My ears zinged as I turned in circles, making sense of what was happening.

The high-pitched ringing in my ears subsided and my vision returned after being temporarily blinded. "Peter!" I narrowed my eyes turning toward my name being called.

The next second Luci with Elijah and Groda in his arms, followed by Georgio, jetted our way. "Peter, come! They're fighting in the clearing."

I jumped to follow, halted, and shouted to Gu, who seemed just as dazed. "Are you coming?" He lifted his leg, and using his foot he pushed the whole bamboo pipes system over so the water could flow along its usual path. "We'll clean that up later. Come, Ish will need an army." I took the shortcut with the Birdmen, flying up and through one of the red crystalized light tunnels in the roof of the cave, while the others followed through the footpath tunnels below.

Far in the distance, in the clearing at the foot of the mountain, between the two rivers, a gigantic translucent super bowl-sized bubble jiggled as firebombs exploded like Hiroshima and Nagasaki. Just as I landed, Gugusan and the others joined us. At first, I couldn't find my voice as what I was seeing was being computed far too slowly. Inside the bubble, Eryn zipped around so fast his silhouette blurred. But he was alone, just as tall with a spear in hand, opposing Apsu.

"Holy fucking shit! Apsu is a freaking…minotaur…no, no, no! That's a satyr! A fucking claw-handed, fire-throwing mythical creature! No wonder Babylon was flattened and almost wiped from the face of the Earth. I'm starting to be a believer in the Bible, the Quran, and the Torah. He's the fucking devil. And where is Ishtar?" I searched frantically. Shielding my eyes, I scanned the inside and outside of their barrier.

"He's also there. I saw him a few seconds ago," Georgio said, not taking his gaze off the fight. I looked at him, bewildered and afraid.

Muscles quivering. Inhaling, exhaling, and searching.

Clenching and releasing my fists.

Jerking left and right, wanting to take flight and fight.

Heaving, my chest expanded and retracted.

My wings twitched.

My throat, dry as I gulped.

My lips moved, but no sound escaped.

My body, ice-cold and burning.

Then a glimpse of my lover struck me with relief. Ish was moving in and out of time, where we couldn't see, where Apsu couldn't see or go.

"Thank fuck!" I sighed. We watched as Eryn jumped back just in time, so Apsu's claw raked his arm rather than his torso. The sight of his blood, the red drops sprinkling across the inside of the translucent barrier, brought a round of gasps as Eryn reared back, holding his arm.

"Where are Ivan and Cian?" I asked, just as Apsu came full speed at Eryn.

*Zip-doof, zip-doof, zip-doof!* He threw bombs, jumped, and almost decapitated our future king. *Jesus Christ, I can't watch shit like this.*

We were all wide-eyed, astonished, and disgusted by Apsu's savagery. Hundreds of shaken spectators gathered around the bubble. What would happen if Eryn died, if the bubble popped and we stood here at Apsu's mercy? He could kill all of us with one fireball.

*That bubble better fucking hold.*

The mundaneness of my life before Ishtar is laughable. This is what Ishtar's life was before Grayrak, before us, the madness of pure evil trying to kill men with pure love and goodness in their hearts. We could only stand and watch.

Jubilant screams echoed down the hills.

Eryn jumped over Apsu and Ish helped him disappear and then reappear, forcing

Apsu to spin in a circle, slicing the air and missing. Eryn stabbed him. More blood splattered, but this time it was Apsu's. Each time Eryn struck home with his spear or Ish appeared, sliced, and vanished, the level of entertainment rose.

This was like gladiatorial games, but this time the rulers fought for the entertainment of us all. Ish and Eryn were a team, and Apsu couldn't keep up with their onslaught. His blue bull head was flecked with his own blood.

"It's the beast. He must die. He will die," Elijah said next to me, chewing his nails, his gaze locked on the fight—fireball lights glinting in his unblinking eyes.

"This must be the pinnacle of your life, Elijah."

"Yes, yes, I told you. But you never listen."

"If I didn't save your ass, if Andrew didn't make you new, fast, and strong, you would never have seen this," I muttered, jabbing him with the truth. He sucked his teeth at me, clucking his tongue.

Eryn and Ish circled Apsu, their prey. Eryn had tied a piece of cloth ripped from his shirt around his bleeding forearm. The next moment, a rush of wind passed me as Ivan, Cian, and Barkor ran, nearly colliding with the enclosure bubble. Ivan gasped and Eryn looked away for a second. Apsu used the distraction to throw fire at Ish while simultaneously jumping to stab Eryn. Eryn blocked him but fell backward. Ish disappeared and reappeared, reaching for Eryn. As soon as the Brawl King touched Ish, both vanished, leaving Apsu spinning.

"No!" Ivan unsheathed his sword, readying himself to jump and help his husband. Luckily, Cian and Barkor were level-headed. Despite their combined strength, they struggled to wrestle him down, to hold him back.

"Fuck, can't they see they are distracting Eryn?" I grunted. "Luci, Elijah, Groda, yes you too, Georgio, let's contain that idiot. For fuck's sake!" We tackled Ivan. I wrapped my arms around his waist. Luci and Groda took his arms and Elijah and Georgio each immobilized a leg. Cian and Barkor joined as we dragged Ivan back with us. Seven of us were against Ivan, and even so, he managed to almost break loose.

"We have to help him. Let go of me. I want to go help him!"

"Ivan, you can't. You can't break the barrier for one, and two, Ishtar and Eryn were fine until you came and distracted him. Shut up!" I said, smashing a hand over his mouth. He snorted like a maniac through his nose, seeing red. "Look!" I turned so he could see how Eryn reappeared on the left and Ish on the right of Apsu. Eryn jabbed his spear into Apsu's chest while Ish sliced the back of his knees. Eryn removed his spear from Apsu's bleeding torso and then pushed his spear right through Apsu's skull. Ishtar lifted his swords, crossed his arms, and decapitated Apsu, leaving the animal's head impaled on Eryn's spear. The torso toppled over. Puffs of vapor, like an extinguishing fire, escaping from it. My heart beat a million beats per minute as I cringed at the brutality. It crushed the innocence of many Phoenicians. It was beyond horrific. Eryn slammed the head to the ground, stepped on it with his boot, and yanked his spear from it. The enormity of this cruel hand-to-hand battle was of unforgettable magnitude. Ishtar lifted his swords and howled their victory into the night. Eryn shook his head and flung himself around, searching for Ivan.

"Let go of me, let me fucking go!" Ivan struggled, and we let him go free. Eryn popped the bubble with the tip of his spear, then opened his arms for Ivan to fall into them. That was my cue. I jumped and swooped over to Ish, diving into his wide-open arms. I collided with him, chest to chest, as I scooped him up, with my arms under his armpits. We shot over the battled ground, landing with an oomph, and skidded over the wet grass while we kissed. When we came to a halt, confusion about where I was and how I got here hit me. Ish smiled at me. I got up and offered him a hand to pull him to his feet.

"What the fuck happened? Did I hit my head or something?" Ish was wet, covered in blood and sweat. "Are you wounded?" I patted him down and checked to see where to plug the blood-gushing holes. Finding none, I patted myself furiously, searching for painful spots.

"It's Apsu's blood," Ish told me and pulled me closer. Then, like a little boy, picked me up and spun us around. "It was close, my Kuku, but we stopped him. We trapped, destroyed, and plucked him from the doorstep of Phoenix to defeat him here today. Just in time." Ish seemed ecstatic, but that was not what I remembered happening today. I wiggled my body so he could put me down.

Ivan, Cian, and Barkor stepped closer. Eryn embraced Ish, and they hugged again, congratulating each other.

"Just in time for what?" I asked, unsure if I wanted to know the answer.

"Yeah, tell us, because suddenly I have that feeling again. That feeling that all is not right," Cian said side-eyeing us.

Ish looked so happy. "Eryn helped me, we were just in time to prevent Apsu and the Zelk from discovering the entrance of Phoenix."

"No fucking way!" Ivan exclaimed.

"Okay?" The frown forming on my forehead was so deep I might as well give myself a craniotomy.

"Please explain, because Apsu had killed the Leadership team of Phoenix, here in Anzulla this morning. Maybe I dreamed it? Did I dream Brad was killed and cut in half?" I asked, searching the faces around us for answers.

For confirmation. For this to make sense.

Everyone else was as baffled as I was.

Ish laughed, breaking the what-the-fuck moment we had up. He waved at the absurdity of my question as if pure nonsense. "Yes, it was a nightmare from another timeline.

Let your memories of Apsu and us killing him and the Zelk be a momentous moment in time."

"It's confusing, isn't it?" Cian said and shoulder bumped me. "I told all of you this is not my people, and now look where we are." He pointed to the ocean. The time machine lay beached as if it had skidded over the water and nose planted in the sandy dune.

"It's strange. It's as if I was here, before. A déjà vu feeling," I said to them while Ish was turning red, he was hiding something from me. The heat of his guilt was hotter than hell's blazing fires.

"More like déjà poo, because it feels like I've heard this shit before," Cian joked.

But then, Ish asked me a strange question. "Where are Juandre and Andrew?"

I looked left and right, thinking I must have knocked my head. "You know where. With Brad and the others? You know that. They preferred to retire, they're on vacation." I studied Ish's face. He turned to Eryn and winked. "What the fuck aren't you telling me?"

"Nothing, my Kuku, all is as it should be. Phoenix is safe. The humans are safe." He pointed to his ship where inquisitive Birdmen were peeking inside it.

Gulping around the lump in my throat, I held up a pointing finger. "I swear, no...I must have dreamed it." Everyone's eyes were on me as if whatever I was about to say was determining our futures moving forward. I raked my fingers through my hair and pulled at it. Ish and the others waited for me to say something. "Nah, now that I think about it, maybe it was a foreboding thought or dream. I was filling the Horizon with waterfall water inside the crystal caves. Yeah, that's what it was. We've done that, haven't we?" Everywhere I looked, heads were turned my way and agreeing with me.

Ish squeezed my shoulder. "It happens, my Kuku. It's fine. Give it a few minutes. I don't want you to be upset or confused. That's why Lasitor forbids switching timelines. Eryn and I had to run Apsu down and cut him, the head of the Zelk, off." Ish chuckled. "We literally and figuratively cut his head off. Moving the Zelk from one reality to the other was causing so much trouble and was bleeding through to Anzulla."

"So, how long have you been gone? Because to us it feels like hours." I asked, searching his face.

"Weeks," Ish said.

"One and a half month," Eryn said. I checked in with the others. They shrugged with that-is-not-too-bad expressions on their faces.

"Where is the egg? Did you break the egg?" Luci asked. I pointed to the beach in the distance where the ship glinted in the rising sunlight, breaking the dark blues of the sky into hues of purples and pinks.

Gugusan tapped my arm. He gave me an I-told-you-so look. "Kuku, this is the story of the San people. Of you and Ishtar, our blue demon God, searching for his Birdman God. Over and over and over, tricking us."

"No tricks, just as it was foretold, fuck yeah, it was!" Elijah shouted with his fists in the air.

Relief settled inside my stomach. I watched Ish for a moment. Perceptions and thoughts jumped from memory to memory. Solidifying that this was real, where I always wanted to be. With my Ish, my blue-fanged Anunnaki in Anzulla at the foot of our mountain.

"Let's go help our flock of humans, I told them to hide and wait for us inside Phoenix," Barkor urged, pulling Cian by the arm after him.

"I suggest we park and hide my ship inside the crystal cave," Ishtar said.

"Ivan and I will go burn Apsu's body, and scatter his ashes to the wind. Just in case..." Eryn said, grinning and seemingly happy to go do something productive with Ivan.

"Come, I want to take care of you," I said, wiping the blood dripping from Ish's bruised cheek. His pupils were blown wide by residual adrenalin.

He took both of my hands and sighed. My insides warmed under his intense stare. He was fierce, and he was also so gentle.

"I love you so much. You are my everything," I whispered with tears burning my eyeballs.

"I love you too, my Kuku. Very much." He smiled, looking scary and beautiful while the corners of his eyes crinkled at the corners.

"Good, now, let's go home."

"To our mountain?" His face lit up and he squeezed my hands tighter.

"Yes, to our mountain."

# EPILOGUE

**ISHTAR**

**Five years later**

Happy, carefree, and in love, I leaned in closer, gently rubbing my nose against my Kuku's warm lips and soft whiskers, our breaths mingled as we sighed, cherishing the simple joy of togetherness and the tranquility of the moment. We'd been basking under the crystal-filtered light for an hour—or so. I wouldn't know precisely, because none of us carried a tick-tick thing or wrist communicator anymore.

"Do you have them in sight?" he asked into my mouth, licking my fangs up and down.

"I can't keep my eyes open if you do that to me." I chuckled and broke the kiss, trying to get a visual of our boys, where they were playing, searching for frogs and crabs and anything that crawled, jumped, and wiggled. It took me a second to spot them. I felt they were starting to get restless and bored. That meant they would be venturing too far away from us.

I shouted, "Fifteen minutes, then it's time to go, boys!" The triplets turned and waved, acknowledging my words, while the waterfall splashed onto the mossy green rocks, muffling their replies.

My Kuku and I cherished our alone time in the early mornings. When Zala, Nebo, and Kail were busy exploring, we discovered a fine balance between allowing them to venture off so we have some precious minutes of papa-time, and them disappearing into some uncharted crystal tunnel and getting stuck in it. The whole mountain was turned upside down last week as we searched for our four-year-olds. Those wings get stuck like fishhooks when they crawl into tight spaces—no pulling them out by the ankles. No, we had to unearth mountains of crystals to tunnel in beside them and excavate their cute little fat butts out to safety. The ordeals was still fresh in their minds, so hopefully, they won't be trying that again—soon.

Between grooming and loving each other, we constantly had to keep a third eye open, monitoring our blue chubby toddlers. I turned to Kuku and raised his chin so our eyes met. "Thank you," I said.

He responded with a lazy yawn and asked, "For what?"

"For waiting for me, for showing me love and giving me a family—for our boys. And for the child tracking chips. We should have inserted them earlier."

He stretched his body, flexing his arms and legs. We'd just finished our routine of feather cleaning and he was relaxed and purring in my arms. I loved providing him relief from the itchiness caused by the waxy protection of the newly ingrown plumes.

"If I knew they'd poof-poof-poof away like their daddy, I would've implanted tracers when they were fetuses. I didn't do it just for you. I was selfish."

"Yeah, so selfishly the best father ever. The smartest, the strongest, and the sexiest," I said in between pecks of kisses. "It's because of you that we have three beautiful children." I kissed him deeply, hugging him so tight that he felt how much he meant to me.

"And because of your extremely viable sperm count. Your stunning genes," he said and kissed each of my eyes.

I soaked up the love and countered, "Yours too."

"Not my sperm."

"It doesn't matter because our children have a mix of our DNA, evident by their pretty little white wings," I said playfully.

Time seemed to stand still as we absorbed the beauty of our family and the breathtaking, gigantic crystal cave around us. Parts of the once-forgotten and overgrown buildings were already restored and the underground city buzzed with crystal light flickering from inside the buildings where new residents were moving in, playing home, and creating a new vibrant Anunnaki underground city.

The Heart of Anzulla.

We had created a home filled with love, laughter, and endless possibilities. The rhythmic splashing sounds of the waterfall provided a soothing backdrop to our thoughts.

As the fifteen minutes came to an end, we called our boys back to us. Jumping from boulder to boulder, they leaped, taking to the air. Their blue-fanged faces beamed with joy as they fluttered closer. Their expressions were pure joy and excitement as they eagerly made their way toward our private sunbathing balcony with an extended platform for landing and taking off.

"Look how happy they are. I never thought my happiness will be looking like this—a mate, three inquisitive baby demon gods."

"Don't forget intelligent," Peter added.

"Of course, and for an eternity together."

"You are everything to me. All four of you," he said with a triple oomph to the chest as our children bombarded his waiting arms.

Every day, we expressed our deep appreciation and unwavering commitment to one another. Each day, an overwhelming wave of gratitude and love washed over me. I stood beside them, feeling the comforting embrace of my Kuku's wings enveloping us. The pure red crystal-infused light carried an extra layer of warmth, creating a tenderness, an essence of our affection inside us from absorbing it.

"My four blue men," he murmured, his voice filled with emotion. "Come Bastian!" Peter patted the side of his leg. "Come boy!" He called and our newborn Anubis pup that fell over his paws to meet up with us. Bastian was the first pup born since Igor, Rotty, and Devil.

"Did you boys have fun? Are you hungry?"

"Yes, yes, yes, Papa!" they chirped together.

Hand in hand, my Kuku and I led our little flock back toward the communal Loursveto garden for our midday meal. As we walked, the boys chatted non-stop, eagerly sharing details of their morning's adventures and discoveries.

"I love you," I whispered into the shell of his ear.

"For now and forever," he added with a proud, radiant smile—my beacon of joy.


THE END.

# TIMELINE



25 000 B.C. Ishtar arrives at the San tribe.

25 000 B.C. Peter and Elijah jump to Anzulla.

24 970 B.C. Ishtar and Peter's crash landing.

24 970 B.C. The next day, Gugusan receives news that Ish is being held captive. Peter rescues Ishtar, thirty years after he had jumped with Elijah to Anzulla.

24 970 B.C. That night, Elijah and Peter arrive by boat at the San village. Peter gets his wings and brings the apple to the San.

24 970 B.C. Ishtar visits Anzulla, and Gugusan gives him the apple.

24 970 B.C. (Cian and his brothers arrived in Grayrak 93 A.T.) Ishtar slipped away to say goodbye to Gugusan and then met Peter for the first time.

23 000 B.C. Anzulla, Ishtar, receives a mission from the Fates.

Between 23 000 B.C. and 20 000 B.C. Draxton and Kellan's Story. *Children of Anzulla, Part One and Two: Finding Love in the World of Titans.*

3500 B.C. Hours before the war with Apsu, Ishtar and Peter bring the apple to Babylon. They rescue Elijah and seek help from Andrew in 2013 A.D.

3500 B.C. Ishtar's story begins at age 250 years. He defeats his father for the first time during their uprising. *Anzulla, According to ISH: New Beginnings Book Three.*

1968 A.D. Young André (Andrew) and Peter meet Ishtar and older Peter. (No wings yet.)

2004 A.D. Juandre and Andrew's story begins. (Just Like a Butterfly.)

2013 A.D. Ishtar, Peter, and Elijah visit Lord Andrew Whiskey Distilleries, Lexington, Kentucky.

2014 A.D. Timeline Switch. Andrew goes to Juandre, they fall in love and mate. *Just like a Butterfly: A New Beginnings Novella*

2041 A.D. to 2043 A.D. (3-5 years before Doomsday.) Eryn and his brothers are born.

2046 A.D. DOOMSDAY. Worldwide breakout of Neurotoxic biochemicals. Nuclear Winter follows.

The story of the men of Phoenix begins - *Phoenix Code: New Beginnings Prequel*

Ishtar arrives on the moon and waits for Cian, Ivan, and Eryn while guarding Barkor in Grayrak.

Then, after Ishtar meets Peter for the first time in Phoenix, 2146 A.D. (94 A.T.) he jumps back to 2046 A.D. to update Lasitor.

2051 A.D. (5 years after Doomsday.) The marriage of Mika and Connor takes place.

2052 A.D. (6 years after Doomsday.) The Big Flood (Tsunamis) happens, and, on that same day, the Romanov twins are born, marking it as the Year of the Twins: 0 A.T.

2058 A.D. (6 A.T.) The story of Eryn begins. *Eryn, King of the Brawl: New Beginnings M/M Series Part One*

2073 A.D. (21 A.T.) Mika and Brad find the apple in the Disciples of the Anunnaki's confiscated loot. Cian and Ivan's Anunnaki heritage is revealed. Eryn makes each a sword of gold by dividing the forks on his trident so that they can focus their power on wrapping Phoenix in a protective layer to save their city from a string of global volcanic eruptions that led to the almost-instantaneous melting of the polar ice caps and global storms, turning Earth on its axis.

2124 A.D. (72 A.T.) Cian's first sighting of the hydrogen mining ship of the Zelk.

2145 A.D. (93 A.T.) Cian's story begins. *Cian's Song: New Beginnings M/M Series Part Two.*

2146 A.D. (94 A.T.) After finding and losing his mate, Ishtar meets Peter for the second time. This is also Peter's second meeting, but he had already met Ishtar back in 1968 A.D.)

Ishtar returns to Grayrak with Cian after meeting his Peter, grabs his ship and jumps to Phoenix for a reboot, then returns to gather Peter to jump to 1968 A.D.

2147 A.D. (95 A.T.) Cian and his brothers evacuate Grayrak and take the last of the remaining humans with Barkor home to Phoenix. Rebirth of Earth's Timeline. Ishtar moves the Zelk to an alternate timeline to prevent them from attacking the Warship Horizon or Earth. Lots of shit goes down this year!

2147 A.D. (95 A.T.) Mika and the Leadership Team of Phoenix want answers. Ishtar gets taken into custody for questioning right after the Warship Horizon lands on Earth's watery surface. His ship and pendant are taken away from him. His inquisition starts.

2147 A.D. (95 A.T.) Three days into questioning, Ishtar and Peter escape with the apple, pendant, and ship and crash in Anzulla.

2147 A.D. (95 A.T.) Ishtar and Peter return to Phoenix to ask for help. (After Peter had rescued Ish.)

2148 A.D. (96 A.T.) Ishtar and Cian save Phoenix.

# Afterword

# About the Author

"I found it surprisingly beautiful. In a brutal, horribly uncomfortable sort of way."
—Tyrion Lannister to Janos Slynt.

I am a Canadian speculative fiction author, writing in the genres of science fiction, fantasy, and paranormal.

My writing explores who we are, where we come from, and where we are going as a human race on Earth.

I enjoy weaving and exploring questions and subjects about our history and origin by creating new, exciting worlds and characters. My stories are unpredictable, twisted with a dash of humor, and centered on gay characters.

You will question your existence among these worlds and wish you could escape to these places filled with foul-mouthed heroes who struggle and strive to save humankind.

I hope you've discovered something that excites and intrigues you. Please share your thoughts by leaving a review or visiting www.kashelchar.com to contact me or learn about my latest works.